Playing the Cards You've Been Dealt

(A Trilogy)

Peter C. BonSey

ISBN: 978-1-4958-1928-5 paperback
eISBN: 978-1-4958-1927-8 eBook

Published September 2022

INFINITY PUBLISHING
1094 New DeHaven Street, Suite 100
West Conshohocken, PA 19428-2713
Toll-free (877) BUY BOOK
Local Phone (610) 941-9999
Fax (610) 941-9959
Info@buybooksontheweb.com
www.buybooksontheweb.com

Playing the Cards You've Been Dealt Trilogy

Three of a Kind
The Cane Family's Hand

An eleven year old son of an Essex country village working class family changes the destiny of the Cane family. The family's mantra of playing the cards you've been dealt never loses its influence on him. Rural wits are pitted against street smarts. The world becomes the stage upon which good and bad events unfold, only to be outridden, not always above board.

A Royal Flush
The St-John-Brown Family's Hand

This family has built its status on dubious origins. While wealth and Royal family connections appear to come with un-written and perceived privileges, they are often abused, and are displayed with belligerence and arrogance towards the lesser recipients. The St-John-browns have a mixture of decency which tends to color their true character.

Now! Who's the Joker?
Julian Fetter's Hand

One family is influenced by strong opportunistic women, while the other by strong moralistic men. It takes 150 years for a collision of their bloodline values in the mid-twentieth century to culminate with a shockingly ironic result. Murder is the act that changes an intense sibling rivalry into a spirited alliance. What some view as greed others, view as survival.

Three of a Kind
'The Cane Family's Hand'
Playing The Cards You've Been Dealt Trilogy
by Peter C. BonSey

My name is Jim the Carters lad, a jolly chap am I
I always am contented be the weather wet or dry.
I snaps me fingers at the snow whistles at the rain
I weathers storms for many a year and will as go again

Crack crack goes me whip I whistle and I sing
As I sits on me wagon I'm as happy as a King
me 'orse is always willing and I am never sad
There's none can lead a jollier life than Jim the carters Lad

Me father was a carter many years ago
Up and off to market on a Thursday he would go.
Sometimes he took me with him, 'atic'alar in the spring
I loved to sit upon his cart and listen to 'im sing.

Crack crack goes me whip I whistle and I sing
I sits on me wagon I'm as happy as a King
The 'orse is always willing and I am never sad
There's none can lead a jollier life than Jim the carters Lad

The girls they always smile at me as I go trotting past
Me 'orse is such a beauty and trots along real fast
We cover many a weary mile an 'appy times we had
There's none can lead a jollier life than Jim the carters Lad

Crack crack goes me whip I whistle and I sing
As I sits on me wagon I'm as happy as a King
The 'orse is always willing and I am never sad
There's none can lead a jollier life than Jim the carters Lad

(Old English folk song circa

ENGLAND - MUCKING & DOCKLAND

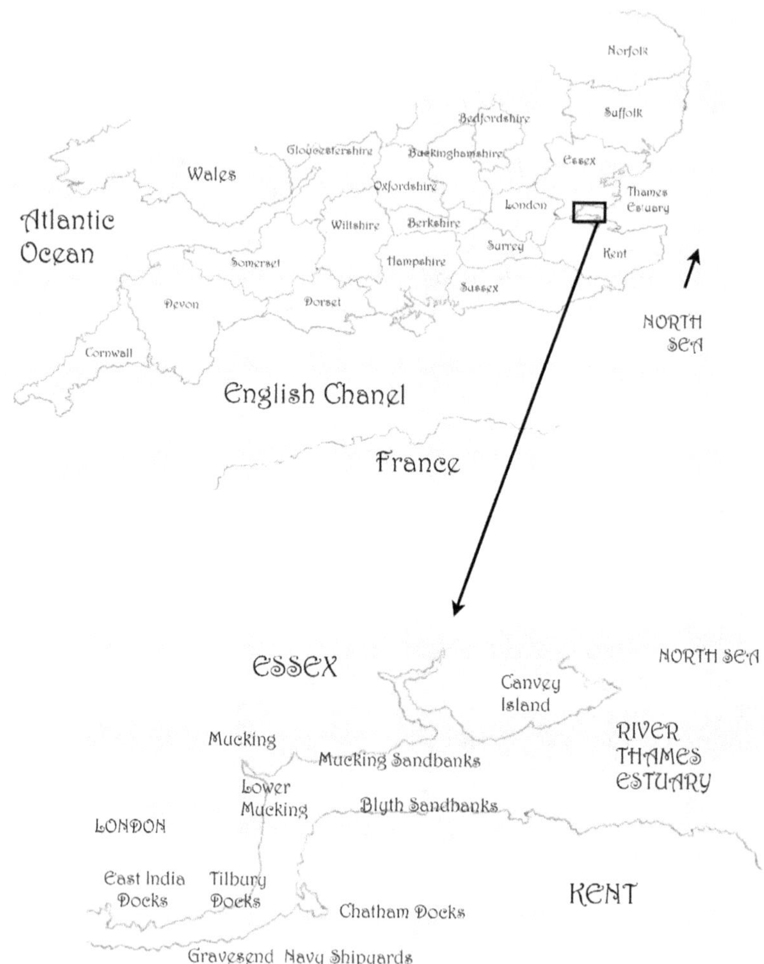

Chapter 1

Davey Blacksmith was fourteen, and Judd saw him as an older brother, a mentor. As Davey would often say, "I can learn you things, me boy, you can only dream of." One windy May night, Davey Blacksmith told Judd, "I's a rekonin' that Jim and his dad, you and me, could just be a-going out this night figurin' there might be a beauty going down on the Gravesend Sands. Likely as not weem be gonna take us some good catchings." That night, the winds roared in off the North Sea with such force that tree limbs blew across the village green A number of mighty oaks and elms cracked like gunshots as they split and fell. The whole village was battened down for the onslaught.

Judd lay on his bed, torn between the thrill of potentially going out with Jim and his dad and the fear of the howling wind and thunderous noise. His mind raced with pictures of sea foam, blowing debris, and possibility of getting some booty.

He eventually fell asleep, only to be awakened by Davey calling out his name. As he hastily threw on his cloak and opened the door, Judd was shocked. Farm carts lay on their sides. Boxes, barrels, crates, and tree limbs thicker than a man's leg lay strewn about. In Judd's eleven-year-old mind, if it was this big, strong, and frightening, and you didn't know what it was, it must be God. This looked to him as if God's hand had brushed through the village in a fit of anger. As he left the cottage the night sky was tinged with the eerie glow of approaching dawn. Everything was calm, quiet and still.

Jim the carter was across the village green upon his cart and beckoned the boys to be quick. "We's got to be the first on the shore, boys," he said. "Them as what gots anything left will be too busy a-cleaning and picking up to bother us."

The flotsam on the shore was a sight to behold. The *Arcadia*, a thirty-two-gun behemoth of a galleon, lay forlornly on its side, cargo strewn as far as Judd could see. All three masts were snapped just above the deck line. The magnificent ship had been built around 1750, and even with all her oceanic rendezvous, nautical miles and weather-beaten hull, she still was a thing of incredible beauty to Judd. It was as if a great creature of the sea had died, and its carcass washed ashore. The main mast looked as if Neptune had picked it up in fury and rammed it into the sand. The rigging and tattered sails hung on the upside-down mast in the stillness like a sad laundry line.

The quartet of scavengers were alone on the beach, and they stacked the cart so high in such a short time that it was almost comedic. Judd found, and greatly admired, a small lady's writing desk that had come ashore undamaged. Jim said "Some'at that genteel would be out o place in the village, but he relented when Judd spoke so highly of it to allow him to have it. The wagon was loaded so high with spoils that Judd and Jim's son lay spread-eagled atop the load, hanging on for dear life to prevent things from falling off the bouncing of the wagon as it slipped and slid in and out of deep muddy ruts. Nothing could throw them.

At the end of particularly grueling Herculean effort that night after Jim set Judd down at the cottage Jim the carter made a gift of the lady's desk to Judd. Judd scurried away with the desk, and set it up in the cowshed beside the house before anyone from inside saw him. He removed the large, tattered piece of sail that he had used to protect the desk as well it could from the rain.

After setting some sacks on the dirt floor of the cowshed and lighting some oil lamps to better inspect his treasure, Judd sat on an upturned crate and simply gazed at its beauty. Away from all other distractions, the desk had an air of elegance that captured his imagination. He inspected the long, gracefully curved legs, so thin they reminded him of a swan's neck looking up to the sky. The four legs stood about two and a half feet high, about up to Judd's waist. They shimmered a burning red-gold color, just like Mary Washerman's hair. Strange, that this inanimate piece of furniture would remind him of her. He'd never admitted to himself that she had so much of his attention before. Connecting the two front legs was a drawer that bowed out slightly in the center, with a deep curve on the underside that with the curve of the legs, gave the impression of a heart. Across the curving front of the drawer was the most delicate inlaid design of leaves and vines and flowers, centered on a brass-edged keyhole. The inlay was of the most delicately hued rosewood and ivory. The bouquet commanded Judd to gently draw his fingers across. There were no indents or raised surfaces. Judd marveled at how finely the tiny pieces of wood and ivory fitted into the surface, as if they had grown there.

The area in the center was inlaid with dark green, almost black leather. This was still wet. Judd knew it would change color as it dried. In one front corner, a tiny section had started to lift. Judd searched the barn floor for something to hold it down while it dried. He was worried about staining it. He eventually settled on a cobblestone of quartz, which he put gently in place. He thought it looked so clumsy, sitting on the front corner above such a fine leg.

On the rear corners of the desk surface were two small boxes each housing a drawer. Judd moved a lantern to see them better, discovering a circular stain on the leather inlay. He deduced that these were stains from candelabra's hot wax. He imagined some fine lady had sat at the desk and done her correspondence. The fretwork in the brass connecting the back of the two drawers was so intricate Judd could not imagine tools small enough to do the work. He was used to seeing the blacksmiths' great, thumping iron mallets and anvils, but this was of another world. It was unbelievable that something so fragile-looking had withstood the ravages that nature had put it through in the last few hours.

Judd ran his hands over the silky, smooth surfaces until he could keep his eyes open no longer. He crept up to his room and slid into an exhausted slumber.

Not long after he awoke, the family gathered in the small parlor set aside for special occasions, and Judd made a grand gesture of presenting this treasure to his mother. He could see that she was concerned about where he got, but said nothing

Judd's father often spoke of the great gales of 1824 that wrecked three mighty ships at one time the *Caravalho*, the *Colville*, and the *Leonora*. Judd never connected the fate of those ships with the shipwrecks he had witnessed. After all, they were in Dorset, the other end of the country. They might as well have been in another world. But Judd was to learn later in life that "that other world" was just around the corner.

Chapter 2

Eighteen twenty-six was one of those years of great innovation in England. Up and down the length of the British Isles, new inventions were appearing every day. With King George IV on the throne of England, the industrial age was well underway. The year before, the world's first public railway, the Stockton-Darlington line, had opened. Bigger and faster ships were being built as the empire expanded its grip on the world and the demand grew for products from abroad. Factories, springing up in the north of England, chewed up the raw materials and spit out gadgets and gizmos for everyone, even for the common man.

Slavery was not to be abolished for another eight years, but industrialists were constantly on the lookout for cheaper labor, and in child labor, they found a solution. Poverty was quite common in the cities, and often, children were forced into labor by families unable to feed them. Children, as young as five and six, performed simple tasks in factories, enabling the wealthy owners to keep costs down.

But to those who lived off the land, who were cautious country folk, the rumors of children vanishing in the night were city problems and couldn't happen to them. It was beyond their comprehension, that anyone would take a country child. Some villagers believed these were tales dreamt up by the travelers to frighten the many illiterate local people, but these stories lingered on in their minds. Even with all the changes, many villages, which lay great distances from the cities, were still accessible only by muddy roads and tracks. Many still operated on a system of self-governance, as they had for over two hundred years. They clung onto the rules and methods they had always administered to themselves as needed.

To them, there were two worlds: those that had and those that didn't have. Some villages were happy to operate as they always had. One such village was Mucking.

***

The village of Mucking, not to be mistaken with Mucking Down, stood across the river from Gravesend and Chatham which were great naval ports. Mucking lay one mile inland from where the River Thames flowed into the North Sea. Whereas Mucking Down hung precariously to the banks on lower-laying stretches of mud flats and survived off sea and river-fishing. Mucking was a farming community with both seafaring connections and commercial enterprises. Both villages had great stretches of water on one side and miles of rolling hills and farmland in the distance on the other. Mucking's access to Tilbury and the great docklands of the East India company, made it superior to Mucking Down, which was often cut off from the rest of the area by the periodic swelling of the river. Also, just north of Mucking was the great London Road that ran from the port of Harwich, on the North Sea coast, to London. This road carried much trade from the North Sea ports and fishing villages directly into London, and many small businesses sprung up to capitalize on the passing traffic.

Mucking had four families that were looked upon as the core of village life. The Blacksmith family. As their family name indicated, they actually were blacksmiths. Nobody could recall a time when the village was without a blacksmith by trade or a Blacksmith by name. David and Tilley Blacksmith were parents to a boy, David, and two girls, Joanna and Priscilla.

Then there were the Carters. The moving of objects large or small, short or long distances, was their domain Naturally they had horses, oxen, and two strongly built drays capable of carrying large loads. As well as assisting the local farmers at harvest time, Jim the carter had regular runs to London. Though the Carters were considered one of the better-off families, this carried little weight in the village. Jim and his wife Elizabeth, had three daughters, Jane, Hermoine, and Eliza, and two boys, Ben and Jim. Jim was named after his father.

The third family was the Canes, Will and Mary. While the patriarch of the Canes laid no claim to a trade or profession, he was noted for his work ethic and ability to turn his hand to any task. He would leave the house at dawn, and could always be seen scurrying from one place to another carrying out some job or other. More often than not, he could be found at the country manor of the Earl of Essex. There was always work to be done in the gardens and on the buildings, for which the Earl preferred to pay for as used. While the Earl spent most of his time in London, Cane maintained the country home for the him, and always liked it to be well kept. Many an evening would see Will Cane drag his weary body home into his kitchen, where there was always a hot meal on the hob and a jug of ale. He would eat as if starving, fill his tankard with ale, sit in front of the fire, and fall asleep.

His wife admired his work ethic and appreciated his ability to provide for the family. She was always proud that the local people turned to her husband when they needed help. In times of hardship, it never hurt to have plenty of work from local villagers who wanted to stay on her husband's good side. Their only child was a son named Judd. It was assumed that the boy would follow in his father's footsteps. Mary Cane was obsessed with giving her son every opportunity that she could. Using newspapers and anything she could find she taught Judd to read and write at an early age. She drummed into his head that if you understood numbers they would always tell you a story that could not be hidden by clever words. She would point out numbers everywhere around them from the number of spokes in a wheel to counting the birds flying south for the winter.

The final of the four families was Mildred and Michael Washerman, the most industrious of all. Both husband and wife would leave their house in the wee hours of the morning and visit three adjacent farms, where they would take a team of young girls from the village and oversee the milking of the cows. They would repeat this process in the evening. The girls would be paid with milk, cheese, and an annual share of beef when slaughtering took place. Mrs. Washerman also gave the girls a silver sixpenny piece at the end of each week, which they kept for themselves. These girls were from poor families, and the milk and cheese they took home was quite often the only food their families had.

Each farm paid the Washerman's one steer a year and twenty-five percent of the daily milk. From this milk, the Washerman's made cheese, which they would sell on the weekly market day.

The Washerman's were blessed with a daughter, Mary, who was four years older than young Judd Cane. Mary could read and write and from ten years old she had been responsible for the record keeping of the family business. Her industrious nature tended to keep her aloof from the other village children.

Mucking had twenty-one cottages, as well as a blacksmith's forge that reaped the benefits of the new age of industry and mechanization, although much of the smithy's work came from the docks. David Blacksmith's oldest memories were of his father's forge belching smoke and spitting fiery plumes of sparks into the air as the burly forge men fashioned the great iron hoops that were to strengthen new ships masts or repair old ones.

A small bakery woke the villagers with the pungent smell of breads and fresh baked delights early every morning. In the late morning, the baker's window was filled with fresh pastries and cakes yearned after by every child in the village. In the afternoons, village folk would gather around the bakery to buy a baked potato, the fashionable, inexpensive alternative to the common pea soup or hot eels that were to be had for a quick snack. Slowly, as word of mouth spread, the bakery had gained notoriety among the travelers' passing by the village. The hot potatoes not only raised the income of the village baker, but also tempted the travelers on the great London Road to stop at Mucking more frequently rather than passing it by. The fresh country air and river breezes mixed with the hunger-tugging aroma of potatoes, pea soups, hot eels, oysters, fried fish, pies, trotters, puddings, whelks, and hot green peas were often enjoyed in the warmth that emanated from the smithy's three large forges next door. Gradually, the forge became the center of activity, and a village green and square evolved from common land across the road from the forge. On one side of the common was the village pub, 'The Weary Traveler.' The pub was tiny but managed to boast a public bar, a snug bar and a private. The 'private' bar was most commonly used by passing merchants and business people. The 'snug' was used by the genteel folk, and women of the village, who would rather stay apart from the boisterous public bar. The public bar, a noisy place, was where men would meet after a day's work to relax and socialize and often brawl.

The volume of people passing by generated opportunity, and soon, a haberdashery was established. This business served all the smaller villages, and supplied the local folk with yarns, wools, boots, and all manner of millinery, including bolts of cloth from the great mills up north. Much of the inventory of the haberdashery was bought from passing traders, while more esoteric merchandise was obtained from the East India Docks nearby. Not all of it was obtained above-board.

There was a one-room hall that stood alone to one side of the village green, as if keeping watch over the village. It was used by the local folk to settle disputes and manage the common affairs of the surrounding villages. Most of the meetings were held amid noisy chatter and smoke-filled air from clay pipes of the menfolk, accompanied by laughter and jeering. In 1829, in London, a group of order-keepers was formed by Sir Robert Peel. It was the English version of the Royal Irish Constabulary that had proved so successful. It wouldn't be until 1839 that the hall was taken over and used by a local constabulary.

Small English towns and villages in the Essex countryside offered little real excitement for an eleven-year-old boy like Judd Cane and his friends. But at harvest time in July under the full summer sun, when the threshers and all the village-folk came together to gather in the harvest, there was fun to be had. All the youngsters were brought together in a ritual bond by the thrill of chasing the rabbits running from combines and threshers and clubbing them with sticks. It left the girls out of breath, easy victims for youthful boyish pranks. The boys would chase the younger girls, whirling dead rabbits over their heads to scare them. Judd would rub his hands in the fresh warm, bloody carcass of a rabbit mangled by the combine and try to daub the girl's faces with the blood. Mary Washerman, being the oldest child in the village would be allowed to ride atop the combine where she would sit out of harm's way and ward off any attempts to involve her in what she considered the childish goings on. Certainly, everyone ate well through the summer, and life was easier, but there was real fun to be had at harvest time with David, or Davey Blacksmith, the smithy's son, and Jim, the carter's lad.

***

It was after one such fun filled, exciting day that Judd asked his father, "What's a rent man pa?"

"A rent man tis the man who collects the rent for the house every week. Why does you ask?"

"Some of the boys were teasing me because we have a rent man and they don't. Why doesn't everyone have a rent man?"

"Acause some people haves the good fortune to own the house wot they lives in. Not everyone be that blessed."

"But, pa, why don't we own our house?" Will Cane thought for a minute and instructed Judd to fetch the playing cards from the kitchen and bring them to the parlor table. He then shuffled the cards and dealt four cards face down to himself and four to Judd. "Now tell I your four favorite cards."

"The king, the queen the jack and the ace. What are yours, pa?" replied Judd.

"I don't got me any favorites." Judd's father then turned each of Judd's cards over revealing a four, a two, a ten and a jack. Judd was disappointed at each turn except for the Jack, at which he jumped up with delight. His father then said, "watch I carefully". He turned each of his cards stopping to study each one. There were no picture cards.

"I won, I won," said Judd.

"No, you didn't. You had three disappointments and one success. I had no disappointments."

"But pa I got one card I wanted."

"Think about this my boy. Life, tis like a game of cards. If you goes into it expecting reward, you might get a reward every now and then, BUT, you are going to get a lot of disappointment. If you go through life your way, expecting a lot of good things, it will not go your way. If you go through life my way, you will deal with what happens to you more easily, acause there is no disappointment. Do you understand?"

"I think so pa. It is nice to win though."

"Yes, it is, but it is much nicer to live with less disappointment. I calls that 'Play the cards you've been dealt, not the cards you want."

"Ok pa, can I go outside now?"

***

The English countryside was different from the big cities when it came to highly spirited boys, who carried an air of rebellion. They were given the title of being a "lad." While rural village-folk were laid back, they faced the same issues with their youngsters.

As far back as he could remember, Judd Cane's best friend was Jim, the carter's lad. Upon reflection, it was Jim who pulled Judd into the more questionable, adventuresome activities that made him a "lad" as well. Often, they could be found being the ringleaders, instigating a game of 'Knock Down Ginger'. In this game, children would knock on an unsuspecting villager's door and run and hide to witness the confused dweller searching for the nonexistent visitor. 'Scrumping' was a popular activity in which the boys would allow the braver girls to join in. A lookout would be placed in the vicinity of a fully laden apple, pear or plum tree while the more agile children would climb the tree and throw fruit down to the other children. An alarm from the lookout would send the scrumpers scrambling for cover or run away laughing and giggling, while gloating over their haul. Often the boys would pick the most beguiling girl and have her knock on the front door to ask the time of day if the door was answered, while, the scrumpers would be hiding on the side of the house ready to rush the targeted tree as the lookout child would keep the homeowner's attention away from them.

After one such raid, Judd was confronted by Mary Washerman. Standing with her hands on her hips she delivered a tirade at him. "Judd Cane, you are nothing but a common thief."

Throwing a large red apple towards her Judd replied, "I might be that, but who has the apples, me or you?" As the apple hit the ground, Mary made no attempt to pick it up.

"You, Judd Cane should be ashamed. Your ma would whip your arse if she knew."

"Oh yes, and who is going to tell her, you? You might think you're the prettiest girl in the village, and, you might think you are grown up, but little miss prim doesn't have as much fun as the rest of us. So, go and tell my mummy, see if I care," said Judd in a sing song voice.

Mary waited for Judd to disappear before picking up the apple and taking a big bite. As the juice ran down her face, she was content and smug in her sense of superiority.

Later that afternoon as Judd laid out his bounty of apples and plums before his mother on the kitchen table he was greeted with, "Judd if you aren't a chip off the old block. Your pa would be proud of this little lot, but if you ever get caught it won't be pride, he will be showing you. No sir, young man, it will be his belt on your rear end."

"But ma, I am just trying to help. Has Mary been telling you tales again?"

"No, she has not and if this is the way you want to help, instead of working alongside your pa at the mansion, there will be a price to pay."

"Ma, I don't want to work alongside pa. Those big ships that come up the river to London, they, well I, oh ma will pa make me work with him?" The pleading voice softened his mother's scolding tone. "Young man, there is plenty of time for you to find your direction. Your pa just wants you to make something of yourself".

"Being a servant to someone like the Earl is not exactly being something. I want to be someone, not something."

His mother raised her voice in anger. "Don't you ever talk that way about your pa. He works hard. He is honest and everyone in the village respects him and it will bode you well to do the same."

As Judd ran out the door he shouted back over his shoulder, "Not honest enough to refuse the apple pie you will make." The banging door ended the conversation. Walking round the corner of the house to go through the rear garden Judd saw Mary sitting on the swing under a huge oak tree at the end of the garden. She smiled and waved to him, still eating the apple he had thrown to her. Judd felt a flutter inside as he waved back at her and reversed his direction and backed out of sight behind the house. "You think you are a princess! Ever since you heard that Queen Victoria is being crowned your head is full of things grand." He called out over his shoulder, more in a whisper than aloud. Will I ever be able to just talk to her and be friends with her? When she looks at me with those big blue eyes, it's like she is mocking me. He avoided close contact with Mary because she made him nervous and he felt he would never find the words to 'talk' with her.

Chapter 3

In 1837, King William IV died and Queen Victoria ascended to the throne of England. The coupling of mourning and celebration around the country was tumultuous, but to many children confusing. Queen Victoria was the first queen in the House of Hanover, and it appeared that a time of great political and social change had arrived. In recent memory, the great sea battles of Trafalgar (1805) and Waterloo (1815) had clearly defined England as a dominant seafaring nation and a colonizing force to be reckoned with. The massive trading ships that plied the great oceans of the world were a regular sight in English waters and docklands. The English Navy enjoyed respect and glory around the world, their control being tenuous at best, as Spain, Portugal, France and Holland's navys were quickly developing and challenging the British Empire's grip around the globe.

Naval life was a risky business for the lower-deck sailors and was fraught with corruption and brutality and death. The underbelly of this great war beast was infected with fear, distrust, and dissent, creating a hierarchy of rank and entitlement often based on social and economic ability over seafaring skills. Many ships' officers' held positions which bore no relationship to their nautical prowess or lack thereof.

***

At the age of eleven, Judd Cane had been on many middle-of-the-night forays, helping Jim and his dad move crates and boxes and all manner of objects from one farm barn to another, even plundering shipwrecks. It was a thrill to hear Jim banging on his window in the dead of the night, urging Judd to help. Quietly, Judd would creep past his snoring father, asleep in front of the fire's dying embers, sometimes with his pewter tankard still dangling from his hand. On many occasions, in driving rain and screaming winds, Jim's dad would head for the great yawning mouth of the River Thames, where it spewed London's effluent and detritus into the powerful North Sea. He had word that a ship was about to go around on the Gravesend sands, and he had to be there first to pick through whatever came ashore.

It wasn't until much later that Judd realized the implications of someone knowing a ship was going to wreck before even the sailors did. At his young age, the thrill of scurrying around the beach with salty spray dousing him was enough. To see the huge vessels flounder, roll, and buck and jump as if a wild horse was telling them what to do, was hypnotic. The huge masts would give resounding cracks like cannons being fired as they snapped and crashed into the foam. The screaming of the wind in the rigging and ripping tattered sails ignited Judd's adrenaline. General flotsam and jetsam, along with crates, bales, bundles, and even loose objects, would wash ashore before the ship finally faltered on the sand bars and rocks.

In Judd's eyes, Jim and his dad were omniscient. They always seemed to be first on the beach, just waiting to fill their cart and leave. Nobody ever seemed to bother them. Any survivors of the wreck would often lie, too exhausted from their ordeal to offer any objection. It was a tiring adventure, but it never failed to leave Judd full of wonder at the fury of the sea—and yet, at the same time, also full of wonder at the variety of treasure that washed ashore.

The spoils of shipwrecks usually took more time to deliver than to collect. Jim's father always gave the boys a few big copper pennies that just barely fit into their fists, and a hock of ham or big, fat, lean pork leg, and sometimes even a jug of brandy for Judd's father and big round cheese for his family as rewards for their efforts. Occasionally, there was even a trinket for his mother. Judd never thought about getting into trouble with his parents for his nocturnal activities until one night he found ma sitting by dying embers in fire grate. Still fully dressed and asleep with her head lolling to one side, Judd saw her jerky reaction to him opening the kitchen door. "Sit down young man," was her command. "Take off your wet clothes first and wrap up in a blanket. We need to talk."

He presented his bounty of food, and his mother coolly praised his efforts. She gave him a crushing hug in her ample bosom and let him know, as only mothers can, that she cared for him as she pulled a warm woolen blanket around him. As she was placing some coals on the fire Judd knew he was about to get lectured. "You do know Judd, that what you are about with Jim and his dad is wrong. It is stealing. I hope you know if the constables find you, pa and I cannot help you, you know that don't you?"

"Ma, Jim says that the stuff we pick up belongs to nobody. The dead in the ship have no use for the stuff."

"Judd, you're not a fool. Everything in the world belongs to someone. Just because you don't know who owns it or the owner is not around doesn't mean you can take it. It is not yours."

"But ma, Jim's dad says that if we don't take it someone else will or the tides will destroy it."

In an exasperated tone his mother calmly and pointedly explained again. "Judd, you do not own these things. They are not yours. It is no business of yours who owns them. I know you think it a waste to just leave those things there to face destruction by nature, but your pa and I have raised you to be honest. You talk about those big ships that interest you. Do you realize that some of them take men, women and children to Australia? Transport them, for stealing. Doesn't that scare you, just a little bit?"

"But I don't steal ma."

"What do you call it when you take something that isn't yours?"

"Oh ma, that's just evening things out. Spreading things around. You have to be out there in the wind and the rain. Hearing the screaming of rigging in the wind and to see those huge ships like dead whales, you don't think of anything else. I really do have fun." Both Judd and his mother turned to see his father, Will, coming down the stairs with his nightcap sitting askance his head and a weary confused look on his face.

"What the heck is going here?" he asked. Mother spoke first. "I am talking to Judd about these so called, adventures of his."

"What about them?" demanded Will.

"There's talk around the village that the constables think the plundering of ship-wrecks is coming from this village, and I am worried about Judd."

"Woman, there is always talk around this village. Sometimes I think all the constables do is start rumors. They are only trying to find out things." Turning to Judd he said, "You are old enough to know what you are doing. Your ma's right enough about the risks. If them is the cards you play, then you live with the conse-quences. I ain't saying it's right. I ain't saying its wrong. That's for you to decide. One thing I will tell you boy, when you does something, right or wrong you never tells anyone. Never admit, never deny. If you want to do bad things you better do them alone because, you, are the only one you can trust." Turning to his wife he continued, "If you are now concerned about what he's doing, I think it's a bit late to start. Thanks to his efforts we have had some mighty fine rewards. Bit late, tis what I say. I'll tell you one thing, if I see a gold sovereign lying on the road and I know it isn't mine, I'll be strange in the head to leave it there for some other lucky sod to pick up, just because it isn't mine."

"You mean you do not care what he does?" she fired back.

"I do care, but, if he is too high and mighty, or to proud, to learn from me, and work the way I do, to provide for us, that's his choice. The Earl has been good to us and can be good to him. If Judd wants to travel another road, he is a willing lad and I have faith in him." Sitting across from Judd he went on. "Tis sure I know that you are aware of the love I have for your ma. I chose my road for your mother's peace of mind. We live in an upside down world, and your ma's way has given you the ability to read and write and with that you are blessed. Not many young un's in the village can do that. You know your numbers real good, nobody can take that away from you. Right now, you live your life for your way. Be warned that one day you will be willing to live your life for someone else, and that is good." He paused to watch the effect his words may have had on his son. "What do you think Mary would say if she knew what you do?"

"Pa, all the village children know, and what's so special about Mary?"

"You only think they know. Most of them are just far too busy with their own lives to worry themselves with you. Now Mary, there's a smart lass. You are never going to tell me you don't care about what she thinks. Ma and I see the way you to behave when she is around."

"No pa, I don't care about what Mary thinks."

"Don't care was made to care my boy. Now, Let's us all be off to bed, and Judd, keep your life private. Them whats know, can be them what tells. That's all I got to add. Come to bed Mary, the boy's good un. We got enough to worry about with the house. I'll talk to the Earl in the morning about that.

"What's wrong with the house?" asked Judd.

"Oh, nothing to worry your head about," said his mother. Turning to her husband she continued, "You can't keep your mouth quiet for one moment can you. The boy doesn't need to know."

Know about what ma, know about what pa?" Judd anxiously asked. His father turned around and sat on the stairs and proceeded to explain. "Your ma and I have been in this house since we was married. Paid our rent on time every week. Kept the house and yard clean and repaired. Now the rentman has decided that he wants his son to have the house and we have got to move. Don't know where. Don't know how, but move we must."

"But this is our house pa!" Judd cried.

"Well, no, t'ain't, tis our home, but not our ouse. You see son, it's the rich people what owns the land and the poor folk what rents the houses. Don't worry yourself. I think the Earl will help us out. There is an empty carriage house that he don't use no more. I can fix it up good if he lets me. We will talk in the morrow. Now… off to bed".

"But pa, does that mean the rent man can make us leave?"

"I said off to bed with you."

***

At breakfast the next morning Judd asked his father, "Pa, are we going to move today?"

"Now don't you worry your head about such things. This is grownups business," said his mother.

Will continued, "'tis what keeps the world goin' round. When you own some fing, you can do with it what you will. Aint nobody can tell you wot to to do with it. Same goes with land and ouses and shops. I, owns me own skills and when I do fings for the Earl, he pays me wot I asks. He can't make me use me skills and I can't make 'im give me money. We trade, wot I got, skills, for wot he's got, money. That's business. Do you git it now?" Will watched his sons face and could see him digesting what had been said. He got up from the table and with a smile, ruffed up his son's hair and said, "I's off to do some business wiv the Earl." And he left.

***

Judd and Jim, the Carter's lad, sat on grassy slope on a hillside looking out over the hamlet of Lower Mucking that was between them and the river. The hamlet was small compared to Mucking but was on the river's edge. On the edge of the great sands lay the destroyed wreck they had been at the night before. Its shattered hull lay on one side with its bow torn off. The rigging and masts were a tangled mess and all was calm. The site struck Judd as odd against the background of great sailing ships making their way in and out of London. The Thames was so wide that two and three ships would pass each other as if racing to be the first to get to the North Sea. With the sun on their faces and stiff breeze the boys seemed hypnotic.

13

The silence was broken by Jim as he said, "You are fascinated by these ships ain't you Judd?"

"The ships, as they sail off to other lands, seem so strong and indestructible. They are, I don't know, it's like they know something we don't."

"What the heck are you talking about?" retorted Jim.

"I would think that it must be exciting to work on a ship and see places we only read about and to see foreign lands. I'm not saying I want to do it, but it sure makes me think."

Jim asked, "Would you want to go to sea?"

"Oh, I don't know. Me ma would never hear of it, so it's no good even dreaming about it."

"Dream about it! Are you doo lally? They say men die at sea. To bloody scary for me."

Judd thought for a moment and turned to Jim and asked, "Seriously, Jim, want to go the docks, the East India Docks tonight and look at the ships? Maybe we can get on one to have a look."

"Sounds good to me, but me dad an' me is going to do a carting job tonight and we will be staying in Harwich. How about tomorrow?"

I'll see," replied Judd.

Chapter 4

Some two months later, as Judd lay in the sweltering summer heat of his room and listened to the sounds of the young village girls, the Blacksmith girls, the three Carter girls, and Davey Blacksmith's two sisters screeching and giggling, he longed for his own excitement. If only Jim's dad would send Jim for him.

As the dusky evening folded around, the sound of reveling villagers on the green in front of the tavern drifted across the night air. Chirping crickets combined with the flapping sound of bats wings as they chased the night insects invaded Judd's ears, crowding out his own thoughts. Judd suddenly decided go to Tilbury docks across from Gravesend. As he crept from the house, he calculated the journey would take him about half an hour. If he was nimble, he would have time to see some of the big ships intact and up close, and be back in bed before anyone awoke. Judd moved quickly and quietly, slipping out of the door, keeping his eye on his father, who snored loudly by the black, sooty, empty fireplace.

Tilbury, home to the East India dockside, was a swarming hive of activities. Merchant ships of all shapes and sizes came up the Thames Estuary to dock and off-load their cargo from China, Africa, and India before turning back out to sea. As Judd drew nearer, the names of these faraway places bounced around in his head, only to be interrupted by the flashing lighthouse out on the head of the Thames Estuary. Often, he had seen frigates and gunboats from the Royal Navy coming upriver to Gravesend, where the Queen's navel men and the merchantmen sailors would mix.

There was a sinister reason behind the surface camaraderie between the sailors. Judd would only come to learn of this later. It wasn't long before Judd was winding in and out of the cargo sheds, smelling, seeing, and drinking in the world that was so far from his rural life. There were people that his young mind could only imagine. Yellow men with long, wispy beards and little eyes that frightened Judd, squinting at him and speaking in a strange language, big, ugly men, like bears, with drawings all over their arms and heads, and some with long beards and greased, platted hair. The pipe tobacco smoke, liquor smells, and other exotic aromas that wafted through this place overloaded his senses. Something about this cataclysmic aura enveloped him.

Two boys who appeared to be about Judd's age played a card game on an upturned tea chest. As Judd watched them, a crowd gathered, reminding him of the end of market day in the village, when all the farmers and traders would pack up their wagons and sit around drinking and laughing. Somehow, he still felt safe.

The smell of an old barque with three masts holding up yardarms with tightly furled sails stimulated his senses and set his imagination spinning. He had read in the penny newspapers that these were the smaller, fast ships that pirates liked to use. The caravels were only a little bigger than the barques, and they were preferred by explorers. The square riged masts and larger sails enabled them to go greater distances and faster. Seeing the great array of ships stretched out in front of him brought his readings to life. Today, there were not one, but two galleons. To Judd these ships were huge. The cargo coming off these decks looked as if it was almost enough to sink the ship. Judd wondered why pirates would attack galleons like these. When he saw the huge canons ,these ships carried for defense, he began to think how brave the pirates must have to be to face this foe.

Judd saw two smaller square-rigged ships that were moored alongside each other. They were narrow-stern ships that sat low in the water. Judd approached two sailors standing on the dockside. "Excuse me sir, would it be possible to come aboard? I have never been on a ship before".

"That aint no ship," said one of the sailors, pointing to a huge ship tied alongside the freighter. "The HMS Vanguard, now, that's a ship, a battleship no less, and if you was, to be quick about it and run across the deck of this ere Soldado said he naming the small ship that was tied up between the warship and the dock. We will show you a real warship." The men gathered around roared with laughter at his comments. They hoisted Judd over the gunwale onto the Soldado's deck and quickly crossed the deck. With a flourish, they lifted him over the gunales of both ships, and hoisted him onto the deck of the HMS Vanguard.

Looking over his shoulder, Judd noticed the sailors on the Soldado appeared less organized and more casual in their demeanor than the sailors on the Vanguard. Even though a group of sailors sat around the deck, laughing and joking, there was an air of seriousness about this ship, with the cannons tied down to the decks, the ropes coiled, and the brass shining. Some sailors spliced ropes. Some coiled and stowed supplies. The ship was cleaner than Judd had ever expected. The sense of purpose stirred something in him. This ship smelled, as did all the ships berthed here, but this smell along with the cannons lined along the decks left no doubt this really was a warship.

"Why are the guns tied up?" Judd asked more to the air around him than anyone specific.

"Them's cannons, boy, cannons aint no guns. You don't want them rolling around all over the place at sea. Could take yer leg off," was the reply from someone.

"Is that mast one tree trunk?"

"Tis indeed. The best English Oak, best in the world if you ask me."

"This is the biggest ship, warship - I have ever seen," Judd said full of awe.

"Tis the newest, biggest, fastest and most powerful warship of Her Majesties Navy. Ain't nuffin like it. We is bigger than anything the Frenchies, the Spaniards or anyone else is got."

Judd slowly turned around full circle taking in everything that lay before him. A sailor pushed an upturned crate and invited Judd to sit.

"Ow old is you boy?" the sailor asked.

"I'm not a boy. My name is Judd, Judd Cane and I am eleven years old, nearly twelve." Judd relaxed as the men around him laughed.

"Then you is old enough to be a sailor," commented another sailor. Another elbowed the one that had spoken and hissed, "Shut yer gob. The bosun'll ave yer." Judd did not hear this exchange.

One of the sailors, who frightened Judd with his leathery face and blackened teeth, offered Judd his tankard as he said "The Master at Arms seed fit to let the boy see our ship, so that's good enough for me. Where you from young master Judd?"

"Mucking sir, Mucking that is, not Lower Mucking."

"Well Judd, Welcome aboard. Join us in a toast to her Majesty. This, is a real man's drink. The king's best rum."

Another laughed and said, "This is not yer kings. 'E's dead and gone. We be got a queen now, Victoria. Drink to 'er, me boyo, if you can."

Bravado swelled in Judd's chest. He had tasted rum once before, on a cold night out with Jim and his dad. This tankard felt heavy in his hand even though there was only a small amount of liquid in it. Lifting the tankard to his lips he took a sip and recognized the sweet pungent odor and flavor. Taking another sip, he heard the sailors chant 'God save the Queen.' As he drained the last drop, a gold sovereign tumbled onto his lips. He quickly grabbed it before it fell to the ground. This alone, he knew, was worth many of those big copper pennies Judd had earned from Jim, but still he asked, innocently, "What is this?"

A huge barrel of a man, the sailor who looked to be in charge, stood up, looked at Judd, and said, "That's the queen's sovereign, boy. Do you know what it means?"

Judd smiled and said, "I guess it means I'm rich."

The reply was firm, cold, and authoritarian in its delivery, "No, laddy. You just took the queen's golden sovereign. That means you are now the queen's man. Welcome to the Royal Navy." Judd suddenly felt two huge hands grab his arms and lift him clear of the deck. "Take him below bosun. Put him in the brig 'til we sail."

"Hey! Put me down! What are doing? You can have the sovereign," Judd yelled.

The man who gave the order smiled and said, "Keep it, young man, you is going to earn it, and you may need it. Give it to any of these scum and it won't see the light o' day ag'in. Alright boys there's no need to be so rough, you're both bigger than him. We have him. Take him below."

"What are you doing, where am I going? Please let me go."

One of the sailors taking him below deck told him in a quiet calm voice, "You is now a pressed man Mr. Judd. That means you are now a sailor for Her Majesty Queen Victoria and will serve her on this or any ship she pleases."

"I don't even know the Queen Sir. Why would she do this?"

"It's just the way things is done in the navy nowadays," was the answer as Judd writhed and wriggled trying to escape their grip. As he was taken below decks it became darker and more ominous to Judd's young mind. One of the sailors spoke with a firm and threating tone. "Now look ere boy, quit the hollering. Aint no one going to come to yer aid. This ain't 'ell, it's just seems like it. If'n the bosun thinks you is going to give trouble, he will give you trouble pretty quick to slow you down."

As Judd went quiet to listen, the other sailor said, "Many of us was pressed men. We was all scared, like what you is now. If you' aves any sense in that young 'ed of yours you will be quiet and calm down. 'twill be better for you."

Judd had no time to understand what was happening before he saw a large, solid door, as wide as a stable's, slam behind him. He sat in darkness and started to cry, not to himself but out loud and mournfully, like an animal in a cage, which, of course, is what he was. After a long period of shouting and banging on the door Judd became tired. He lay on his back and pounded his feet on the heavy door, gradually settling down to rhythmic thump. As the ominous silence and darkness and exhaustion overwhelmed him, he fell asleep.

The fast-growing British Empire was ever in need of more men at sea. Even the implementation of Samuel Pepys's modern and inventive changes did little to attract the large numbers needed to staff the great new warships, but Judd didn't know that.

Sometime later the movement of the deck beneath his feet and unfamiliar sounds woke Judd up. All Judd knew was that just a short time ago he was in the village, smelling the fragrances of the new harvest drifting through his window and tasting the sweet sickly rabbit's blood on his fingers. He recalled the idle chatter of the children playing outside his window. He wished he could be back there. How would his parents know what had happened? Who would tell them? Could they help him?

The big ship's steady, rolling movement did little to allay his terror. Examining his surroundings assisted by chinks of light coming through the brig's walls where the large thick planks met, Judd realized 'the brig' was like the etchings he had seen of prison dungeons. This one was wood, had a low ceiling, and was very small. There were manacles fixed around the wall. Some were up high and some were close to the ground. The floor showed that it had been scrubbed many times as it was softer than the walls and smooth to his touch. He saw a small iron barred grate above his head in the door. Reaching up to grip the bars, he pulled himself high enough to push his face between them. There were voices, and men scurrying about, all were paying no mind to his shouts for help. A sailor approached the door and told Judd to back away so that he could come inside.

"Why did you put me in here? What I have I done to you? Are you letting me go free?" demanded Judd without waiting for an answer.

The sailor towered over Judd as he backed him into a corner. Judd sank to the floor and pulled his knees up to try and protect himself.

"You had better keep yer mouth shut and speak only when you is spoken to. Twernt me what put 'ere. Twas the bosun and what he says, goes. As I sees it, yer got two choices, one, do as you is told or, two, spend the next six years in this 'ole." Makes yer choice, right now." The man backed away to allow Judd to stand. Turning and leaving the brig he held the door open and with a mock bow and wave of the arms he said, "So w'ats your choice, Master Cane, one or two?"

Judd moved cautiously from his corner and slinked past the sailor. Quickly looking around him, he saw no way of escape. The sailor knew what he was doing and approached him with both hands held up, palm outwards. In a gesture of peace, he spoke in a less boisterous tone.

"Look 'ere Cane, I know things is lookin' pretty bleak right now. You aint the first pressing I've seen, an' I'm sure you won't be the last. But the truth is you aint gonna get nowhere fighting. The navy is bigger than you and me, and all these men put together. We is 'ere and we is going to be 'ere together for a long time. Now, I gots me own problems, and you, you gots your own problems. Sure, don't make no sense for us to 'ave problems wiv each uver."

"My ma and pa don't know where I am. I want to go home. What am I going to do?" pleaded Judd. "You stole me, that's what you did, you stole me from my family."

"I didn't do nothing of the sort. You took the Queens sovereign. No man made you take it. Them's the rules."

"I was tricked. I didn't know that's what it meant." Judd was now gaining a little courage.

"Life is gonna trick you a lot more afore your done young fellow. Right now, you is gonna just do as you is told. You is gonna look and listen. You is gonna try and keep on the good side of everyone you meets. Soon you will meet some of the cabin boys and deck boys, they is young uns like you. Believe me, things will get better. You can get one of the older seamen to write a letter for you to your mum and dad."

"I can read and write myself," prompted Judd.

"Well, there you are then, one step up on some of the others already. See, aint so bad is it? Follow me and let's get you some breakfast." He strode away ahead of Judd towards a group of sailors sitting around trestles set up on barrels with their heads bent focusing on their food. Waving his arm and demanding silence of the men seated around eating, the sailor spoke. "This 'ere is our new pressed man. Cane is 'is name and 'es about as scared as most of you 'ave been at one time or anuver. Feed 'im. Show 'im the ropes. Give 'im trouble and you'll 'ave me to deal wiv." A full platter of food was slid across the trestle towards him.

As he thought he was a prisoner, he was surprised to find no hostility or violence around him, just an earnest feeding frenzy. The sailors paid more attention to their food than to him. In a short time, the sailors were clearing away the trestles and the deck was being swabbed. Judd stood to one side not knowing what to do.

A heavily tattooed sailor approached him and spoke. "Just stay there lad. They will send someone down for you soon. Me name's Conker, and you is?"

"I'm Judd Cane sir."

"I aint no sir, I's just a plain old sail maker, ordinary seaman that is. If this shit hole gets yer down jus come over to the sail locker. We be a friendly bunch over there." The man turned and shouted something unintelligible to whoever was listening, then he turned and exited the lower deck taking three rungs at a time up the ladder to disappear above Judd's head.

***

Still, afraid to move in any direction that might be wrong, Judd stood silently waiting. As sailors passed some of them would give a gesture acknowledging his presence. Some spoke but Judd's mind did not allow him to absorb what was being said. Soon, a man he recognized as the bosun led him up toward the deck. As he emerged from the hatch, shielding his eyes from the glare of the early morning sun, he saw the main mast as a huge cloud of sails. For Judd, it was a truly awe-inspiring sight, as he had only seen sails from the shore, and then it was only from a great distance. At first, he thought the clouds were moving back and forth in the sky, slowly from left to right and back again, but when he saw the shore in the near distance on both sides of the ship, he knew the clouds were not moving, but rather the ship was gently rolling from side to side in the swell created by the swift river Thames current meeting the deep North Sea tides.

As Judd stood looking skyward, absorbing the spectacle unfolding before him, Gibson, the bosun, approached him. Judd saw the man and spoke, "Sir, I do not understand what is happening. Why have I been taken away like this? I do not want to be in the navy. My parents do not know where I have gone. They didn't even know that I was in Tilbury."

Holding his hand up to silence Judd, Gibson put a fatherly arm around Judd's shoulder and said "This'll be your 'ome for the next two years, an' maybe longer if'n you does good, so you had better accept it. I was told that you can write and read. Soon you will have time to write to your parents and tell them all."

"Two years! Why two years? Can I do something about it?" was Judd's plea.

"Two years if we come back to England in that time, and, if you have not done anything to make them keep you longer, or you could go another navy ship. None as good as thisun thought. Do you understand?"

"No, I do not. How do I know what is right and what is wrong? I have never been on a ship before. But this is worse than the workhouse the poor get put in."

"You can make something of yourself in the Navy, you can't in the workhouse. You will learn the ways of sea life as you go. In the early days they will cut you some slack, but don't count on that for long."

"I am not happy and my pa always said happy people work the best."

"No need to be lippy. A bit of lip aint healthy for you. 'Appiness will come and go as it does ashore. The big difference at sea is everybody 'as to obey orders, no exceptions. There are going to be times that our lives depend on the man or boy next to us doing duty. Now I think you should find out more about your new home.

***

"This 'ere ship is the HMS Vanguard, my boyo. She is one of Her Majesty's newest, finest, and fastest ships. She's has only 'be commissioned for two months. Takes yersell off, and get to know her quick me boyo, as there's work to be done. We be sailin' down the English Channel to protect some of them merchantmen 'round the coast of Spain to the Mediterranean. Us is like an escort you don't mess about with. You can work hard, listen, learn, and become a part of this crew, or you can do things the 'ard way. Many of these sailors take the 'ard way. That bain't the way for me, an' if you be a-listenin', it won't be the way for you. I know that you are frightened. That's healthy. Everyman jack aboard this ship has fear. Fear is nothing but a signal from your brain telling you to be careful. Be proud of your fear and pay attention to it. It could, save your life. Now be off with you, look around and don't bovver anyone, and be back at this spot by two bells. Don't be thinking of going over the side, 'cause it'll be the worse for you if we haves to stop and git you."

"Go over the side, what do you mean"?

"Swimming for the shore to escape. You are now in the Navy and the local constables will catch you and return you. They haves no choice. You are the Queen's man now. As big as the Vanguard is, we can turn it round and get to you before you get to shore."

"What's two bells?" Judd asked.

"To you, my boyo, when you talks to me, it's 'bosun, sir!'" said Gibson. "Two bells is a clanging of the bell two times. You'll hear it loud and clear. We rings the bell on every arf hour 'til we's done it eight times. Then we starts again. So if you knows what watch is on duty, then you counts the bells and knows the time o' day, or night."

"Yes, bosun," Judd replied, He hadn't understood what he had heard, but he didn't want to show it.

"It's 'bosun, sir!'" the bosun bellowed. "And you better make it loud and clear, so's I can hear your respect."

"Yes, bosun, sir!" shouted Judd as his attempt at a marching gait quickly turned into a run.

Judd had thought adventure was only what young boys read about in the newspapers and the penny dreadfuls that found their way to Mucking, but here he was faced with it and it was real, his own adventure. He was a seaman in Her Majesty's Royal Navy. He was not sure if it was going to be as exciting as he had imagined. In fact, it looked a lot more threatening to him.

As he worked his way around the ship, Judd could see that there was so much to know. Crewmen were scrubbing decks, coiling ropes, and attending the rigging of the ship's three massive, sky-hugging masts. He approached those who seemed the friendliest looking and least intimidating. He learned from one sailor that these men were proud of their Vanguard. The ship, he discovered, had been laid down (the keel set as the initial building step) in 1835. Completion wasn't until her launching in 1837 and she was commissioned into the Royal Navy just two months ago. The entire crew was new, just like Judd. The ship had taken sixty men four months to lay the keel and ribs, and one hundred eighty-six man-years to build. She took 3,560 tons of the best English oak. The enthusiasm of this man towards his ship engaged Judd's interest.

Suddenly, with a loud clatter, a long metal object hit the bulkhead behind Judd, bounced off the wooden wall, ricocheted off the huge mast that passed through the deck above Judd's head, hit the floor, and rolled right toward him. Judd's fear kicking in had him covering his head with his arms and dropping to the floor.

A tall, thin man with a pigtail and hands covered in tar reached down to help Judd up. "Der you thinks I was after killing e, boy?" he asked, laughing.

"No, sir . . . well, yes, sir . . . what was that you threw at me?" Judd asked.

"Speak up, boy. No one kills no one, on Her Majesty's ships. We only kills them what is doing wrong on the high seas."

"But . . . but, this thing," Judd said, picking up the large metal object that looked about the size of his mother's rolling pin, with one handle cut off and the stump sharpened to a fine point. It was heavy, and made of iron. "It just missed my head."

"That's a belaying pin. You sees them around the ship's gunnels," said the man. "We ties the sheets—them is sails—to them to hold the sails in place. When we cast off from Tilbury last night, it got damaged, and I's a splicin' a new end on it. We forces the sharp bit down atween the ropes sections and twists it open. Then we forces bits o' the rope back through it. It's like the darnin socks' your mamma does, only a lot bigger."

"Then why throw it at me?" asked Judd.

"When them big ropes get forced open, they's a-tryin' to close up, an' if'n you ain't got 'old of the belaying pin proper, the rope can close up and spit the pin out, close 'round your bloody finger, and Bob's your uncle this is wot 'appens," he said, laughing and holding up a hand with half a finger missing.

Judd quickly got up and ran off, the sailor's taunting laughter trailed off behind him. Now, not sure if what had just happened was mocking him or was serious, he cautiously looked over his shoulder and peered around corners before going round them, as he continued his tour of the ship.

The HMS Vanguard was a Symondite warship meaning she had a "V" shaped hull, and not the traditional "U" hull. Her high beam allowed her to carry nearly twice the amount of sail as older ships. She was built for speed. On both her gun deck and upper gun deck, she was armed with twenty-six thirty-two-pound cannons and two sixty-eight-pound carronades. On her quarterdeck, she had fourteen thirty-two pounder cannons. Her forecastles had two thirty-two pounders and four thirty-two-pound carronades. Finally, her poop deck held four eighteen-pound carronades.

Judd investigated the stores of cannonballs and powder, and more—in fact, the stores were like great warehouses filled with everything imaginable. There were sacks and barrels, and dried meats hung out in the open, heavily wrapped in sacking with salt rubbed into the surfaces. Judd recognized some of the great iron hoops he had seen Davey Blacksmith's father making in the forge while he and Davey pumped the giant bellows that kept the coals red hot and glowing to heat the iron ready to be bent.

All of a sudden, he missed Davey, Jim, and some of the other village larrikins. He felt alone in this strange place. He was fascinated by the sights, sounds and smells of this 'alive' ship but he could not help but be taken back by his memories of the 'dead' shipwrecks on the mucking sands. Those memories were flooded by images of his friends and other village folk and frustration and confusion welled up to overtake him. This opened the door to allow his fears to surface.

Judd slumped on a sack and started to cry. When he wiped his eyes, he found, sitting across from him on another sack, a big, pot-bellied man with a kindly face. He was puffing on a clay pipe, which he offered to Judd. Judd declined.

"Look e 'ere, my boy. Wot's yer name?"

"Judd . . . sir."

"I knows you is a-feelin' pretty bad right now. An' I knows acause I was pressed into service some twenty year ago. Bain't goin' to 'elp yer non by cryin'."

"What did you do when they pressed you?" asked Judd, wiping his eyes with the piece of cloth the man offered him.

"Pretty much what e be doing right now. Felt real sorry for myself did I."

"You look happy enough now. Why?"

"Well, to tell e the truth I used the only thing knew ow, food. This 'ere belly came from burying me sorrow in food. Me father was a baker so I got to cooking. Sorta takes yer mind off things." The man rubbed his large stomach and chuckled as he spoke. "You must be good at something."

Judd responded with the first thing to come into his head. "I can read and write and I know my numbers real well."

"Well, there you go. I guess lot more than arf the crew don't do neither. When you sees the letters come aboard let the crew know you are willing to read for them and even write letter for them to send ome.

"Why would they get letters if they can't read?"

"Everyone knows someone that can read. In the villages there are teachers and tradesmen that can. 'Ere at sea, aint so many. We all haves a skill wot we can turn our 'ands to. Use yours. I will tell e one thing. When I gits to go 'ome, and I sees wots going on wiv the lads I grew up wiv in my village, I know I's in the right place. The Queen's, or back athen as it was, the King's Navy saved my life. I gets home every now an' then. Me wifes 'got a nice little 'ouse, the kids is all going to school. Did you go to school?"

"No, sir," said Judd. "My mother taught me to read and write and do sums."

"So, this could be good thing for you, my boyo," said the man. "I is a-guessin' that yer parents don't know where you are. When you gits settled, you gottta ask the quartermaster about yer pay, and tell 'im to send some as you like to yer parents. It 'elps 'em, and lets 'em know you're all right."

"Pay? I get pay?" Judd asked excitedly.

"Yes sir, you do. Regalar as clockwork you gets paid. They keeps most of it in a big old ledger and you just asks for some and they give it to you."

This exchange started Judd on the road to adjusting to his new environment. It provided a light at the end of the tunnel.

"An I'll tells you wot. If any of these weevil-eating scum give you trouble, tell 'em they can deal with me. I'm the cook, and I knows just 'ow to get back at 'em. If'n you needs it, boyo I will be yer dad while we be a-sailin'. Me name's Trott, an I's called Lezza by the lads—Lezza, 'cause I's like a leezard – cool, calm, and smooth. Now, be off wiv yer—and cheer up."

Judd was beginning to feel a little more at ease. He knew that if Lezza was a good person, there had to more like him on this ship. Two bells rang out. The hour had passed so very quickly, and Judd knew where he was supposed to be. It was just a matter of finding the quarterdeck again.

Chapter 5

The quarterdeck held the most intrigue for Judd, as it was from here, he could see the whole ship spread out before him. The sailors could be seen scurrying about their tasks as the bow pitched and heaved. It appeared to Judd that the quarterdeck was the command center of ship, with the ship's wheel the focal point and officers standing by, some quietly giving orders and others barking out commands. While standing at the gangway up to the quarterdeck, where he was to meet the man who he recognized as the bosun. A man in uniform asked Judd what he thought of what he had seen to that point. Judd studied the man carefully before speaking. "This ship is so big. I am not sure if I will ever know my way around all of it."

"Believe me, a few days at sea and everything will fall into place. It is like if you never left your home village you would know every inch of it, and so you will of this ship."

"The noises confuse me. It sounds like the ship is about to break into pieces."

The man laughed as he replied. "Very quickly you get to know each sound and what causes it. The ship is made to flex with the huge pressure put on it by the winds and currents of the oceans. The wicking, that's the black tar stuff you see between the deck planks keeps the water out but allows the movements. Every sound tells a story. You might say that is the language of the sea. Some sailors claim that when they gets ashore they cannot sleep without those sounds."

"Sounds scary to me sir." Judd like the way this man spoke in a calm, confident way. He was not as intimidating as many he had met.

The man told Judd that he had seen him asking questions of some men and not others. Judd said, "Some men you can learn from and others you can't."

"Good man, Cane," he said. "I am First Lieutenant Walker. The captain of this ship is Sir Thomas Fellows. Mr. Miller is our sail master. It would heed you well to observe these men and learn how to behave in their presence. It is the role of new recruits to do what they are told when they are told, without question. While we do not condone flogging, it will be carried out if necessary, and we have other ways of maintaining discipline. Is that clear?"

"Yes, sir, Bosun, sir," said Judd.

"I am not the bosun, I am Lieutenant Walker, sir, to you."

"Yes, sir, Lieutenant Walker, sir," Judd said.

"Do you read? Write? Do sums?" asked the lieutenant.

"Yes, sir, Lieutenant Walker, sir. I maintained my father's work records, and I helped the local surveyors when I could. I am very interested in why and how things are done."

"If what you say is correct Cane, we can add to those skills you already have and make you a valuable addition to The Vanguard. Dishonor this trust in you and you will find we will come down very hard on you. If you think you know fear, the wrath I am capable of is far worse. My men on this ship expect me to be dependable and reliable, I will not let you tarnish my record by your deeds. Is that clearly understood?"

"Yes, sir, Lieutenant Walker, sir." Judd observed the precise manner with which the men on the quarterdeck were speaking to each other. They used titles, and it appeared almost as if they were acting in a play. Judd had seen plays at the village hall performed by traveling players and had always thought them to be exaggerated in their speech and mannerisms. But this really was the way some people talked. He sensed an air of respect and he liked it.

The lieutenant instructed Judd to follow him up onto the quarterdeck and then walked over to another man. "This is Quartermaster Henson, and he is the right-hand man of First Officer Ben Tillet, our navigator," he said. "It is normal to have new recruits such as you start below deck and learn their basic seaman skills." He turned to the quartermaster. "Ordinary Seaman Cane here appears to be a gifted young man. He can read and write. I think he should be at the side of the First Officer. I think that we can make something out of him. I want to see him at the wheel before week's end. If he steps out of line once, just once, put him in the brig, and then he can start from the bottom." Turning to Judd he emphasized, "Six months deck-wicking if you put one foot wrong. Do you hear, Cane?"

"Yes, sir, Lieutenant Walker, sir."

Henson saluted the lieutenant as he turned to walk away. He then turned and summoned over a sailor, who took the helm. "Hold her steady on 270 degrees" he said as he guided Judd away.

"Let's go below and get you a kit and show you where you'll be bedding down," said Henson. "Any officer that approaches you and speaks, you salute him and listen. When he leaves, you salute him. I don't know how old you are, Cane, and I don't really care, but right now, you are mine. Boys usually start in the service at age eleven. That's a good age for us to get them. We don't take them if they are sixteen because they think they know it all."

"I'm twelve," said Judd, thinking he would impress Henson, who just grunted and led the way.

As the two of them came down from the quarterdeck, Judd looked toward the bow of the ship to see a steady heave upwards and a dip down as the HMS Vanguard headed for the open sea. Judd knew this was the North Sea, and an upward glance showed him three masts with sails full of wind, looking like giant laundry sheets on the washing line.

For the rest of the first day of Judd Cane's life as a sailor, he was exposed to the routines, the dos and don'ts of shipboard life. He was going to be taught how to read charts, navigate the seas, and aid the ship's officers in carrying out their duties. "Keep your nose clean, my boy, and you could be a midshipman before the year's out," said Henson. "Many men are at sea for a lot of years before they reach that station. Many of the ruffians below deck will never see it. It is the first step on the road to being an officer."

"What are all those men in soldier's uniforms here for?" asked Judd.

"They are marines my boy. They are like soldiers but they belong to the navy. They do most of the fighting. This lets the sailors get on with the business of sailing. I mean we all fight but they are the professionals. They do help with ship board duties but they are, what I call, sea soldiers."

There was an eerie quiet as the wind filled the sails. The Vanguard slowly arced south as it entered the great North Sea tides, and before long, it turned westerly to meet the English Channel's swift-moving Atlantic Ocean currents. These currents tried constantly to push the Vanguard toward the English coast, and so sails were furled, unfurled, and trimmed constantly to keep the mighty warship in the open waters.

Chapter 6

At eleven years, or as he thought, nearly twelve, young Judd did not fully comprehend what lay ahead, and in many ways was too innocent to be aware of what his future may hold. He did know he would not be playing with his friends in the village for a long time. Henson told him that, although he was to learn navigation, his first duty was to the safety of the ship.

"That means, my boy, when the damn French, Spaniards, Dutch, or any other ship with bloody piracy or plunder do come near, we got us a fight on our hands. If you hear 'man the guns, all hands, on deck', you go to the powder room and keep the two thirty-pounders supplied until you are told to stop. Do you get it?" he asked, pointing to the two on the aft port side of the quarterdeck.

"Yes, Mr. Henson, sir . . . quartermaster, sir." The answer was as bold as he could make it sound, but it was at this point, hearing about cannons, gun powder, and fighting other ships he had the realization that his life really had just changed forever.

"The next time you hear 'battle stations', go to the powder room. You will be shown what to do. From there find the fastest way to your battle station," Henson said. "Get it fixed firmly in your head."

***

HMS Vanguard was an escort ship for the great merchantmen leaving England bound for the Mediterranean. These ships were filled with products of the great industrial area north of England, to be traded in Italy, Greece, and North Africa. The route was a perilous one, as the north coast of France was on their port side the entire time until they reached Spain. Then it was the Spanish coast until Portugal, then the Spaniards again, and then the French again, until the convoy was comfortably in the Mediterranean. These nations had been a thorn in England's side since time began. The opportunity to plunder these merchant ships was always a temptation for the French, as well as for the many pirate ships that lay waiting on the North African coast and in the many inlets along the Mediterranean.

Quartermaster Henson decided the first thing for Judd to learn was his place. It was mid-afternoon, and he sent one of the cabin boys to find Judd and bring him to the foxstle. The cabin boy found Judd poking around the stores. It appeared that all new recruits seemed to head for the food.

"Oi. You. Boy. The quartermaster wants you on the foxsil on the double," said the cabin boy. I ain't got a clue wot yer game is, but you ain't as good as you finks you are. An' why they got you arfway up the bleeding ladder instead of a-startin' at the bottom, I doan know. You better watch your arse, 'cause there's a few of us wan's ta kick it." With this, he took off running up the gangways three decks up and toward the front of the ship.

Before he managed to emerge from the third gangway Judd was upon him. Grabbing his ankle, he pulled the boy back down and confronted him. "If you want to kick my arse, don't wait for your mates. Do it now. But you had better know if you do, I suggest that you don't go to sleep tonight."

The boy backed right up and held his hands up to ward Judd off. "Blimmey mate, bit bloody touchy aint we."

"I'm not your mate. Mates don't treat each other that way."

"I can get yer anuver time." The boy jeered at him.

"Go for it. You will only do it once. From then on you will have to keep one eye open - even when you sleep. Bet you can't do that."

The cabin boy softened his tone as turned and continued up the gangway. As he ran, with Judd following, he shouted over his shoulder, "What's they call you, boy?"

"Cane," Judd said.

"I know it's Cane. Ain't you got a first name?" said the cabin boy.

"Yes . . . yes, my name is Judd, and I'm from Mucking!" Judd shouted back.

"It's from Mucking you are? Now, that's bleedin' funny, 'cause it's the muck you'll be in before much longer ifn me an' my mates have anyfing to do wiv it."

As they approached the forecastle they slowed to walking pace and Judd whispered to the boy, "Shall I just call you one eye from now on? 'Cause you are gonna get bloody tired keeping the other one on me."

"Alright, truce it is Judd, for now. That's the quartermaster over there." With that the boy turned and was gone.

***

"Sit your arse on the capstan here, Cane," said Henson. Judd climbed onto a chain as thick as a tree trunk that wound around the capstan and passed through a large opening to the side of the bowsprit, where it was attached to a huge iron anchor. "We have a few things to go over," said Henson. "This is Her Majesty's Royal Navy. We are a big ship. To run any ship, we need discipline. What do you know about the Navy?"

"Well, sir, I know about some of the big sea battles our ships have won. I know about the Battle of Trafalgar with Lord Nelson. He's the one with one eye," Judd said proudly.

"He had two eyes, boy, only one was useless. Got shot in it in a battle." Then, the quartermaster's tone softened a little. "As a country boy, you don't know much about how things work in the Navy. Now listen, and listen close, because, you have been given a leg up the ladder, by Lieutenant Walker. I don't know or much care why, but it will help you on the one hand and hurt you on the other."

"I've been given a leg up?" said Judd. "I've been stolen away from my family. My mum doesn't know where I am and my dad needs my help. They'll worry. I don't know where I'm going. I don't know how long I'm going to be on this ship. How is that giving me leg up?" Judd spat out.

"They might worry for a bit," said Henson. "Their life will go on. Many boys your age end up in worse situations. Just think how happy they're going to be when you go home a man, as one of Her Majesty's tars. I'm thinking they will be mighty proud. Now, who's to say you'll even want to go home?"

"Why wouldn't I want to go home?"

"Well, lots of sailors find their little villages or even big city pasts no longer offer them anything. That's why most become lifers at sea. It becomes their home. As for as how long . . . well, pressed men usually do about six years. The way things are going these days, you may well be able to become an enlisted man." Henson appeared to be taking a friendlier tone. It helped Judd relax.

"We have until six bells before I has to go the chart room, so I'm going to give you a little education. I'm only going to do this once. You are going to learn about the HMS Vanguard and its crew from top to bottom. Have you ever been on a ship afore this?"

Judd wasn't sure whether he should reveal his shipwreck plundering, but he took a chance. "I've been over plenty of shipwrecks, sir, some of the cargo galleons that flounder on the Gravesend Sandbanks. But I don't understand some of the things I see, sir."

"Let's do it his way, then," said Henson. "We shall work our way round the ship as I explain some of the things we see."

He began his explanation: "The Vanguard has 720 men and officers, and they are from everywhere. There's good, there's bad, there's lazy and hard workers. There's thieves and honorable men. There's those you can trust and those as soon as cut your throat. You just got to be careful who you trust and who you stay away from."

Quartermaster Henson took a deep breath and shifted his weight from the edge of the capstan. He put his heel into one of the large spa sockets in which the men placed the spars, to enable them to get good enough leverage to turn the capstan. This would turn and haul the anchor chain from the muddy ocean bottom up through the hawser pipes.

He gave a quick turn now, to be seated atop the capstan, where he crossed his legs underneath himself. Placing his hand in his tunic, he pulled out a soft leather pouch with a thong drawstring. As the pouch opened, a pungent, sweet-smelling aroma wafted into Judd's nostrils, burning a little. Henson removed a clay pipe stained with tobacco's oils and smoke. Taking a pinch of tobacco in-between his thumb and finger, he proffered it to Judd. Judd backed away with a grimace on his face. "I don't smoke, sir," he said. "I never had money to do it, and the only time I tried it, I nearly threw up, and my eyes watered for a week."

Henson laughed. "The baccy that you had where you come from was rubbish. We get the best stuff, us who goes to where they grow it always gets the pick. Smell it, boy," he ordered, placing a wad in Judd's hand.

Judd turned it over. It was warm from lying against the quartermaster's body, but it was not dry, not wet. It felt just like one of the tiny field mice Judd would catch at Mucking's harvest time, except it didn't move. Judd sniffed the wad more closely. He recognized the smells of cinnamon and nutmeg that he remembered from the bakery in Mucking, and also that of the dark rum Jim the carter sometimes gave him to take home to his father. It flashed through his mind as quickly as it left: *Will I ever see Mucking again?*

The quartermaster struck a flint, and his pipe exhausted a puff of smoke that wasn't white and wasn't pale blue, but was rather a combination of warmth, color, and calm. There was something mysteriously aloof about the way he puffed as he spoke, almost as if he was a different person. Judd let out a deep sigh. This man, despite his rough exterior, reminded him of his father, Will. His feelings of safety around this man were clouded with the warning voices about who to be careful of.

Henson motioned for Judd to sit beside him on the capstan. "Let's us get down to your learning, my boy," he said.

He learned about who to obey and who to be careful of, "Some don't have any mercy for anyone in their way," said Henson. "So, the order of the day is for you to be as afraid of them as you are of your daddy. No—be more afraid, 'cause they can get you flogged."

"Flogged? Flogged?" said Judd. "I heard Lieutenant Walker talk about flogging. I thought flogging wasn't allowed! I read it in the paper!"

"And who, young man, is going to stop them when they are on the bleedin' high seas? Those gentlemen, is what keeps this whole crew in place, and if a bit of the old cat-o'-nine-tails is what it takes, man or boy, you will get it."

Henson sighed, then, he spoke quickly. "About half of this lot will die before we get back to England. That could be two or three years. Those men on the quarterdeck have to answer to the Queen for every man jack of us. Let the bloody lot below deck think they can do as they please and we've got a mutiny on our hands. I lived through one of those. Throats cut while you're sleeping. Jacks throwing those they don't trust over the side in the dead of night. Not good, my boy. I'd rather take my chances with the officers. The captain may be king while we're at sea, but he sure answers to the Queen when we get home." Henson drove home his point with a great exhaust of breath and a softly spoken, "I hope you get that one, boy."

Judd was beginning to understand what was expected of him. He learned about the pusser, who clothed and fed them, and he followed Henson below deck to find his mess table, lowered down as needed for eating and off-duty activities.

"You are the powder boy for the cannon on either side of your mess table," said Henson. Judd was confused as he had been told his battle station was the canons on the quarterdeck. He decided not bring it up at this time. Henson carried on, "Each mess table sits eight crewmen. This is your group. The seaman in charge of that mess is a leading seaman. Then there are two able seamen, four ordinary seamen, and you. When the Captain decided that you were to learn navigation and you aren't with the navigator, this is where you spend your time." Judd was to keep the area swabbed and clean. Every sailor in his mess was his boss.

"All the new recruits are either a volunteer that chooses to be here or a pressed man," Henson said. "You are pressed. That's the lowest of low. Pressed men spend up to three years on this ship afore you are able to leave the ship and go to another or leave the Navy. All pressed men usually get the dirty work and get a tough deal. You can go along with it or buck it. Bucking it isn't going to get you friends or comfort. If you have a rough time with one of the lads, don't tell me, tell him."

Soon, Judd had visited the pusser, a large, official-looking man, retrieving a hammock, all manner of clothing, including trousers and shirts, and, finally, a wooden chest in which to put his things. He pulled the stack in front him neatly into his chest, slung the hammock over it, and, dragging the chest behind him, started off on his journey to find a suitable location in which to sleep. Standing at the top of a gangway, he peered down into the dark, forbidding deck below. Then he turned and looked skyward. Four decks up, he could see the powder-blue, pristine sky, as if it were a picture painted on the ceiling. He turned and looked again into the darkness below him, trying to decide which direction to take.

That's when a small hand grabbed his shoulder and turned him around.

Chapter 7

"Allo. Me name's Dickey, Dickey Lemon to me mates. Follow me." It was the cabin boy who had taken him to the quarterdeck. "Forgit about the punch up you was offerin' earlier. Aint no sense in us fightin' atween ourselves. I allays comes of strong. I fink that if they's a bit scared of you they leaves you alone."

"You started that fight, not me," Judd replied tersely.

"Right little bleedin bulldog, you is mate."

"Why are you telling me this?" questioned Judd.

"Anyhow, we all needs us a friend. Summat tells me we is going to git along just fine," said Dickey. "We 'as to stick togever to be safe. I'm 'appy to look out fer ya, as long as you does asame for me. I heared them talking about where they was going to put you. You aint goin' to be no officer, but you is gonna be where you can know fings."

"What sort of things?"

"Just what theys finkin and what they is gonna do. You is a nuffink to them, an they forgit you is even aroun sometimes. It appens to me a lot."

"I still don't understand what you are telling me." Judd's voice was getting louder with is confusion.

"Information is power. Information kept quiet to be used later could mean safety," said Dickie touching the side of his nose in a secretive gesture. I'ves git almost a year in the Navy, and I'm figuring, by the time I's twenty, I'll 'ave enough know'ow to go it on my own." He smiled. "'Er Majesty's Navy ain't a bad life, an' I know what I don't know. There's nuffink to stop us living off the fat of the world. Forgit your fat o'the land. The world is bigger than England, and there's plenty for everyone to 'ave some. Woder yer fink?"

"Well, I don't know what to think. Everything is happening to quickly for me," said Judd as he glanced up through the decks again."

"I fink I makes a better friend than a enemy." Dickie shot back.

"It ain't no good a-lookin' up there," Dickie said, pointing to the upper decks. "The more experienced seamen sleeps there. They gits to sling their 'ammocks atween the guns, an' they gets the breezes on 'ot nights. I fink it ain't werf it, though, acause you also gets the bloody cold wins when they's blowin'. Now, you don't want to go deep in the belly of ship. Too much trouble 'appens down there. I 'angs me stuff as close as I can to the cooks. They stay about the galley, an' there's always decent little scraps to be 'ad. 'ere. Follow me," he said, taking off ahead of Judd and down a gangway. Judd noticed that the bulkheads above were low enough for him to touch. All the older seamen were constantly ducking to avoid hitting their heads on the low beams that ran from side to side.

As they reached the next deck, they headed toward the ship's stern, Dickey, darting around all manner of bundles, packages, and crates and Judd lagging behind trying to drag his chest.

The two boys found a corner between the rear wall of the galley and dry storage area, and that's where they hung Judd's hammock. Dickey told him if you hung it crosswise, you slept better. "The ship rolls more than it pitches," he said, "so your 'ammock only swings when the ship goes up 'n' down."

The spot they had settled on was above the waterline, and Judd thought if things ever went really bad, he had a better chance of getting out. He spoke with Dickey for almost an hour, and Judd agreed that they would keep their friendship a secret, although he did not understand why. Dickey said it might be better this way—they would be able to find out more of what was happening around the ship. Two sources of information were better than one. "The Vanguard is too bloody big for one little fella like me to stay on top of evryfing," Dickie explained. But in Judd's mind, it was only the village girls who had secrets, and they seemed to spend their lives giggling about them. As quickly as that thought left his head he recalled the night trips to wreckages and realized that he too had secrets.

"I've bin on me own since I was five. Livin on the streets of London weren't no fun," Dickey seemed to be reminiscing.

Judd interrupted "So, you were pressed like I was?"

"Nah. Not really the same. One night it was bleedin cold and I couldn't find nowhere warm to kip down for the night. I was in the Queen's Warf basin area and I snuck onto a ship, found a corner, and dossed down. When I woke in the morning the sailors fed me. After telling them how I was living, one of them told me about the Royal Navy. Three meals a day, and a job with pay sounded too good to be true. He took me to 'The Mariner's Wife', a pub, and toll me to go wiv this uver fella that turned out to be a Pressman wot runs press gangs. The pressman gave the sailor that took me a gold soverign, so to tell you the trufe, I fink I was sold to 'im. Never the mind anyway. I was ten years ol and fings worked out fine. I as like be dead by now if I stayed on the streets, twer a bloody sight rougher life than this."

Judd listened with shock. For one person to sell another was a strange concept to him. "Are you happy living like this? Didn't you mind being sold?" he asked.

"I was not hungry, for once. I'm not sure I was aware of wot was 'appening. Appy? I ain't miserable anymore. That's good enough for me. I tries to be as onest as bess as I can, but a, we gotta do wot we gotta do. Little bit o larceny never 'urt no one."

Judd was intrigued by Dickey's persona. "What about your ma and pa, didn't they worry about you?"

"Nah, I tol' you. I was livin' off the streets. Me dad, I never knew 'im. Me ma, she done 'er best, but she 'ad six of us nippers an'a new fella every time I turned roun. She was a right bottle basher, alays had a flask on her, or a mug in 'er fist. I'm better off 'ere.

Something about Dickey reminded Judd of Jim the carter's lad, who was always so confident and sure of himself. He said to Dickey, "The quartermaster said he'd send some of my pay home to my family. Will that really happen? Will they know where it comes from?"

"Oh, yes," said Dickey. "This is 'Er Majesty's Navy. They do things proper 'ere."

Suddenly, Judd heard a shrill whistling sound. It was jerky and erratic.

"Bosun's call," said Dickey. "Means we gotta go." As they ran across open deck and up gangways, Dickey explained that the bosun had a silver pipe. Many tasks had their own sound, or call, and this sound was the cabin boy's call.

As they came into sunlight, the bosun stood towering above them. "I was wanting you to get Cane for me," he said to Dickey, "but I see you read minds. Cane, take yourself off to Officer Tillet. He's in the chartroom," he said as he pointed to the quarterdeck. "Lemon, at ease. Dismiss."

Judd stood there for a moment digesting the strange, one-sided conversation. Then, he took off to the chart room, located on the aft end of the quarterdeck.

When he arrived on the quarterdeck, Judd was stunned by the vision he beheld. Never had he seen so many ships at once. There were ships as far as he could see— maybe twenty, or even forty. It was clear to see which ships were Royal Navy, as they flew the Union Jack flag topmast and a colorful array of flags on the other halyards. Judd didn't know at this time that these were the method of communication between the ships. The sight was spectacular and had an overwhelming effect on Judd. Little did he know how these colorful flags would impact his life. He would see them put to use during confrontations with other ships. There was one flag for each letter of the alphabet to be used in sending messages between ships. The ships were in formation. Two Navy ships led the convoy and two brought up the rear, while four others, two on either side of the convoy, floated on the broadsides of the fleet. By now, the French coast on the port side and the English coast on the starboard were moving further and further away. The ships looked like the great groups of frogs Judd saw in the spring, swimming across the large village pond in search of safe spawning grounds. The ships' bow waves were hypnotic. Each ship appeared to be dipping to push its way through the waves, only to rise out the other side and shove past the next wave. The lack of noise seemed incongruent. Something this big multiplied so many times should make more of a sound than just the soft whistling of the wind through the rigging.

HMS Vanguard was the point ship on the portside, and its view of the Atlantic Ocean ahead was unobstructed. To the starboard side of the convoy were the two Navy ships, and behind them was the first of the merchantmen. It appeared a few of the merchantmen had cannons, but they didn't need many with the Royal Navy for protection.

***

Judd's entry into the chartroom was like nothing he could imagine. In the middle of the room was a large, heavy wooden table, not unlike his mother's kitchen table, except that it was finely crafted with a slight slope and a fine polished top. In fact, it's finish was reminiscent of the desk Judd had given his mother.

On the underside of the table was a row of four drawers, each as wide as the table but only half a palm in height, with big brass handles. The top drawer was open. In it lie some large charts.

Atop the table was a chart with heavy brass weights holding down each corner. The bulkhead opposite the door Judd had entered held a row of leaded glass windows, through which Judd could see the convoy as far as his eyes were able. He knew he was directly underneath the quarterdeck. Along one wall was what looked like small square cubby holes, each housed a rolled-up chart. Beneath this was a section of larger cubby holes, some of which held an array of rolled-up signal flags and other flags. Judd noticed that some slots had letters of the alphabet at the top edge and others had more detailed labeling.

Along the final wall was a magnificent desk of cherry wood, polished so highly he could see his reflection. Behind the desk was a bookshelf full of volumes of every shape and size imaginable. Books were something Judd had always wanted to experience more of. On the desk was a large, leather-bound journal, and beside it, quills, inks, and various other writing implements. The room made Judd think of things he had read about school. The opportunity had never been available for him.

Officer Tillet entered the chartroom without being heard by Judd. He stood silently, watching Judd's reaction. It appeared that Judd was not like many of the young lads he had encountered in the navy. He could tell, by the look of curiosity, and wonder, on the boy's face that he was really concentrating on what he was looking at. Tillet felt relieved. This could be a kinder burden on him than his past subordinates.

"So," a voice said. Startled, Judd spun around. "Tell me, Cane. What do you see in front of you? What do you feel about what has happened to you?" He paused. "You can stand at ease. That means you can relax, you stand at attention only when you are told to, or you are addressing an officer."

"Sir, well, sir, I do not quite know what I'm looking at. I am very happy to be able to read the books. That is, sir, if I am allowed to read them. I think there is much to learn, and I believe this to be a great opportunity . . . I am a little scared of the dangers that could happen to me, and, I don't want to die, sir."

"I can tell your brain works well, but why do you think you might die?" asked Tillet.

"I hear the men talking and dying seems to be in everyone's mind."

"You're right to be scared. There's not many a man in this crew that is not a little bit scared. They just don't name it. The truth is, Her Majesty's Navy or, indeed, sea life, is dangerous. There is much we don't know about this world of ours. God's fury is rent upon us all at sea, with no mind to good or evil. All we can do is be good Christian men, and do our duty to queen, country, and each other." He paused. "I will not labor you with God, other than to beseech you to be a good Christian to your fellow man. This, I believe, will make our burden here on earth a little easier to bear. If my daily praying offends you, be sure I intend no offense. I will respect your beliefs, but I require the same respect."

This sent Judd's mind bouncing like a shuttlecock on the afternoon breeze. "Sir," Judd said, "I don't know much about God. If you want to teach me other things, then I will learn." Inwardly, Judd was proud of the way he was able to respond. He felt as if he were on the bulkhead, watching himself. "I hear the talk of death, and how many men do not return from these voyages. I would think the discipline and order would keep everyone safe."

"If that what you see before you does not make sense, I agree," said Tillet. "One of the principles of survival is to make some sense that you can live with. Many of the deaths that occur at sea could be avoided. But in the last one hundred years, our English seafaring ways have changed for the better. I digress, young man. Let me show you an example."

Ben Tillet pulled three rolled charts from the cubby holes. "The world is round," he said. "Anything that is round can be cut into sections like an orange. For the purposes of navigation, the world is cut into 360 sections from top to bottom. We call those latitudes. There are 360 sections from side to side, and we call those longitudes. So, starting at any point, when you have crossed 360 sections, you are back where you started. We call each of those sections, degrees. If you know which latitude and which longitude you are on, then you know where you are. More importantly, so does anyone else. You can send another ship to where you have been and they will find it. Do you understand so far?"

"Yes, sir."

"Now, we are bound for Gibraltar, which is on the tip of Spain." Tillet unfurled a chart and spread it on the large chart table. After holding it down with brass weights in the shape of miniature ships, he pointed out England, France, and Spain. Just below, he pointed to Africa and three small islands off its Western coast. Showing Judd the lines that crossed them he said, "If the person who made this chart is to be believed, what do you see is the latitude and longitude of the Gran Canarias?" He ran his finger along the horizontal line, then the vertical line.

Judd read out the coordinates: "36°07′33″N 05°20′35″W", as the navigator wrote them down. He furled the chart, returned it to the wall storage, and then repeated the exercise with the second and third charts. Each revealed a different set of coordinates. Judd was confused.

"What you have just seen is the result of sloppy navigation, or dishonest chart-keeping," said Tillet. "Either way, we in Her Majesty's Navy do things one way—the right way. While we will use old charts, when we find errors, we keep detailed records so we can advise the Admiralty's chart-makers to produce corrected ones."

He then went to the bookshelf and removed a new, unused leather-bound journal. He opened it, sat at his desk, and, in a carefully controlled hand, inscribed the inside cover: "To Judd Cane. May God go with you." He signed it, turned to Judd, and said. "All officers are required to keep journals. The Admiralty has the right to inspect and keep them. This, Cane, is your private journal to keep and do with what you will. I hope you receive it with the warmth that I offer it and that you do well by it. Remember, what is written is not forgotten. What is not forgotten is valuable."

"Thank you kindly, sir," Judd said.

Tillet continued, "As a midshipman in training, you get paid two shillings a week. You are going to earn that, and honestly so."

Quickly Judd did the math. "That's five pounds, four shillings a year!" he blurted out.

"Can be more, with bounties and spoils. We'll just have to wait and see. There was a time when a sailor under a fair captain did well for himself. Don't know what tomorrow brings, but I do think Captain Fellows could bode well for your pocket."

***

Judd was to have his whole perception of life, the world, and people change. As HMS Vanguard escorted convoys of traders around the tip of Portugal and Spain and through the Mediterranean he slowly become skilled at map reading. The art of reading the night skies was proving difficult for him. One balmy evening while the ship lay at anchor of the port of Algiers, Judd, with a rolled chart under his arm, approached Dickie and a group of cabin boys leaning on the ships rail. "Hey, Dickie I want to tell you something."

"Oi, oi, Ben Tillet's special little friend wants to talk to Dickie, everyone be quiet," was the sneering comment Judd heard.

"Shut yer gob," demanded Dickie to the tallest boy.

"Make me," the boy said squaring up as he raised his fists. As the boy faced Dickie his attention was off Judd, who dropped the chart and dived headlong into the boy's side, banging his head into the boy's ribs and knocking him off his feet.

"Take the piss out of me and I'll knock it out of you," he growled. As the boy rose, a gash appeared on his forehead where he had hit the ship's rail.

"Whoa Judd,' said Dickie pulling him off the boy. "You don't have to kill him." Turning to the group he continued, "I've bin tellin you lot, Judd is one of us. It aint is fault they gived him the job they did. If any of you want a piece of im you'll 'ave to have a go through me."

"I don't need your protection, thanks," Judd said.

"No, you don't. You don't need to go in the brig niever. Use yer 'ead! You might win the fight wiv any one of these, and your reward, if an officer sees it, is to lose your cushy little job. Be smart."

Judd stood and absorbed what had happened. The injured cabin boy slunk away from the group with his tail between his legs. Judd addressed the group. "I was going to tell Dickie that we are allowed to send letters home from this port and they have to be ready by 4 bells in the forenoon watch. I was about to offer to write for Dickie, but I suppose if any of you need it, I can help anyone that want's to." The group erupted into a gaggle of chatter.

"No point in me sending a letter, me ma and pa don't read, an if they could I wouldn't be able to read a reply, if they sent one." Billy Lyons owned the defeated comment. To which Dickie responded, "Sometimes you lot is fick. Do I 'ave to tell you everyfing? Your ma and pa aint too stupid to ask someone to read or write for them. Judd has offered to write for you, an, if you is proper polite 'e might even read your letters you get back." Smiling at Judd he added. "Bleeding fick as two short planks, they is." With this event Judd entered an era of respect and appreciation from all the cabin boys. In a conciliatory move Billy Lyons offered to stand the next watch for Judd in return for help with his letters.

Out of the shadows of the deck Leeza came over, grabbed Judd by the collar and hissed,"Get yer arse down to the galley now!" He let go of Judd and stormed off in the direction of the galley. He was leaning against the huge butcher's block that had a slab of brined pork on it, with his arms crossed, as Judd entered.

"What's wrong?" was Judd's bewildered expression.

"What's wrong, what's bloody well wrong? I'll tell you what's wrong. What you just did, attacking that lad, could put you in the brig. It could lose you your rank and even git you a flogging if the master sees fit. You is a midshipman, and fighting aint tolerated between the ranks, let alone an upper deckie attacking a lower deckie."

"But I wasn't attacking him. I was defending myself."

"I saw it all. That un said somefin to you and you went for 'im. Good shot, and great to get your enemy before 'e git's you, but Judd, you know better than to do it in broad daylight. Right out in the open. Bloody foolish Judd! Bloody foolish! Take yersell off and calm down. Stay in control of that temper. Do you hear me?"

"But Leeza I didn't lose my temper. I just saw the opportunity to put a stop to the snide comments and make an example."

"You ain't never goin' to stop no comments. Wot do you care wot they say. You is bigger than that. Their yap aint gonna git them in trouble but it can sure cost you a lot. If you must git even, pick the time and place that suits you. Yer git it? Now be off wiv yer."

Chapter 8

Almost six months had passed before Judd received a letter from home. The Harbor Master at Naples had brought the letters aboard and the bulk of it was either official or for the older crewmen and officers. As the Quartermaster passed out the letters, he stopped calling out names and stared at the remaining letter he held. "Lyons getting mail, didn't know you could read. Cane, I'm not surprised, but you, Lyons." As he held out the letters, Billy approached with a big wide grin on his face, to accept the offering.

Judd stepped forward to collect his letter and spoke. "I am helping Lyons sir." His attempt at reducing the sneering tone of the quartermaster was met with, "Should be more careful who you help around here sunshine! Diss-miss."

The excitement in Billy as he rushed over to Judd was evident on his face. Billy was anxious to find out what had been written to him. Judd did not have the heart to make him wait. All the while he was reading Billy's letter his own heart was pounding inside him with anticipation of his reading his own. When he finished, he sent Billy off and sought out a place to read his own letter. As he walked toward the chartroom, he lifted the envelope to his face and smelled it. His hopes of gaining the slightest smell of Mucking, of home, of mother, failed. This was a plain envelope. A little heavier than those his friends had received, but nothing out of the ordinary. He closed the door behind him and was alone at last. Sitting in the navigator's chair he pulled out his pocket knife and slit the envelope open. Two folded letters dropped out onto the desk. He took a deep breath to try and gain control of his emotions that were welling up from deep within. Emotions he had spent what seemed like a lifetime learning to control. Unfolding the first letter he proceeded to read

Dearest Judd, my son,

Where in the world are you? Your pa and I learned that you had been taken some four months ago when we received money from the Navy. We get the money every month. We were so worried. We thought you had run away. We still don't know if you ran away or were forced into the Navy. What matters is that you are safe and well. You should keep the money for yourself, we can manage without it, although we do appreciate your thoughtfulness. Pa went to the Admiralty and demanded to know how you got into the Navy. All they would tell us is that you were in the navy and that you were on HMS Vanguard. They did say that you had been paid a sovereign to join. Pa and I do not understand that. Why so little amount of money? Were you so unhappy at home? Your pa is very proud of you being on England's biggest warship. He is a celebrity down at the 'The Weary Traveler'. Me, I am afraid for you. The very sound of the word 'warship' scares me. You are the talk of the village. I am proud and frightened for you. I was so happy that the Admiralty will forward our letters to you. We look forward to getting news from you. Tell us what you do, where you are and if are you happy. What happened when you joined up? So many questions! Davey and Jim ask about you all the time and we do not have much to tell them. Pa is doing so much work for the Earl these days he hardly has time for anything else. Mary comes over to our house when she wants to get away from her house for a while. I let her sit at my special desk to write her letters. I hope you don't mind that I let her send a letter to you with mine. She so often seems to be lonely, being the oldest child in the village. Although you have been gone four months ,I still expect to see you come out of your room. I sometimes sit on your bed to be closer to you and I shed a tear. It's a ma thing you know. Are they feeding you well? Do you need anything? When will they let you come home? I do hope it's soon. Sorry for so many questions and no answers yet. I have to close now as pa is taking your letter to the Admiralty this afternoon to send to you. They do this without us having to pay any postage, so I suppose that is good. Pa sends his love and wants me to tell you to be careful and look after yourself. Me, I send all the love I can muster. Please write soon.

 Love ma.

Judd leaned back in the chair and tried to absorb what he read. He felt a tear run down his cheek, which he quickly wiped away. His life had been so full of new experiences. That he had managed to suppress thoughts of home, in an effort to keep control of himself, surprised him. After carefully folding his mother's letter and placing it in his journal he contemplated the other letter. So, he thought, a letter from Mary. He opened it, flattening it out, he started to read.

 Hello Judd,

Your ma said I could send you a letter, so here I am. All the kids in the village were surprised when you disappeared. Your ma was beside herself with worry. It was like you went to bed and the room sucked you away. Nobody guessed you joined the Navy. I have to admit that was very brave of you. The big thing is that you never told anyone you were going to do it, not even Davey. Were you scared? I was scared for you when I found out. I blame Jim's dad for getting you involved with those shipwrecks and all his wild adventures. He must have filled your head with big ideas. Jim says that the world is bigger than Mucking, and you will do well. I hope so. Davey says that he feels like he has lost his brother. At first both Davey and Jim got into trouble with the constable because they kept pestering him to find you. They wanted a search party until the constable told them if they could tell him where to search and he would think about it. At first your dad was very sad and got into trouble a few times at the pub. They threw him out more than once. I think the landlord knew he was having a hard time. It was like he was trying to drown his sorrows. But don't worry he is good now, quite proud in fact.

Every now and then my ma lets me sleep over at your house to keep your ma company. I hope you don't mind me sleeping in your bed, as it does seem to help your ma.

They say all the nice girls love a sailor. Judd Cane, the sailor. Sounds like a pirate's name. Have you met any nice girls? You are still too young to think about girls anyway. If you want to write to me .I would love to hear from you and am happy to write back. Take special care of yourself.

Your friend, Mary Washerman

While Judd was folding Mary's letter and placing it alongside his mother's in the journal, he heard the shrill whistle of the bosun's call summoning the crew to muster on the main deck. The Captain stood at the rail of the quarterdeck with his arms folded across his barrel chest waiting for the crew to muster.

The bosun shouted "Attention!" The crew quickly stood erect and silent, waiting.

The Captain spoke in a loud commanding voice. "Lads, there are reports of pirate activity on the coast of North East Africa. Merchantmen are being attacked. It is our duty to respond. We shall weigh anchor and head west. All of you must remain alert and ready for action, should it be needed. I expect that every man shall do his duty. God save the Queen." With this he turned and spoke to the bosun, who then gave orders to prepare for sailing and dismissed the men. Ben Tillet was waiting in the chartroom when Judd arrived. He stood upright and with an official tone in his voice he said, "Now is the time Mr. Cane for you to put into practice some of the things you have learned. Pull the appropriate charts, and plot our course to the North East African coast. Let's say, head for Algiers. I am going topside to take charge of clearing Naples bay."

"What do I do then, Sir?"

"What do you mean do what do you? You do what you have seen me do many times. After plotting our course, you stand to the side of the helmsman and instruct him of the course he is to steer. You check his course from time to time and instruct for corrections or course changes. You know that. Now get to it." With that he left Judd to his own devices.

Running into the galley with great speed Judd crashed into Leeza. "Wot the 'ell is going on?" demanded Leeza.

"Well, you will never believe this, I have just been given sole responsibility to chart the course for our next port. Officer Tillet said not to ask him to check it. What if I get it wrong?"

"Just relax Judd. You aint gonna git it wrong. You do wot theys teached you and then you go ask ask im to check it."

"But he said not to ask him."

"He is an officer Judd. Full o is own piss and importance. E might grumble but e sure will check an eiver praise you or correct you. Can't do nuffin to you for asking. I learned a long time ago ask an officer anyfing he will puff is chest out and then tell yer. They likes to feel superior to us. Now git out of ere an let me cook." Judd ran off shouting over his shoulder, "Thanks Leeza."

Upon returning to the chartroom and taking out his sextant Judd went onto the quarterdeck and took readings from the sun, making adjustments to the instrument. He knew that if his sextant was incorrectly, set he would not be able to get accurate readings. Being satisfied, he returned to work on the charts. This was the first time he had set a task that carried with it such great responsibility. He checked and double checked his calculations. Taking the chart in hand he approached officer Tillet. "I have our course charted sir and would appreciate your opinion."

"Believe in yourself Cane. I'll only check your work this once. From here on in you better be damn well sure you do your job properly." Looking at the chart he asked Judd to explain his reasons for certain routes that had been selected and was satisfied with the answers. "What must you keep foremost in your mind while standing watch over the helmsman?"

"The winds sir, and, to regularly check our bearings," Judd proudly said.

"Exactly. You are relieving me. I shall be in the wardroom should you need me." He turned to the helmsman and stated, "Midshipman Cane will be navigating for the balance of this watch." He then left.

The helmsman acknowledged Judd with a smile and proceeded to say, "Clark is my name sir. Well done on your promotion Sir. Some of us below wish you well. You may be a young'un, but you got spirit. We heard tell of your run in with Billy Lyons. We was all waiting for one of you juniors to pull him up. Didn't think it would be you."

"What's our course helmsman?"

"Due south sir, at 185 degrees," answered the helmsman.

"245 degrees West by south west, and hold her steady," commanded Judd.

"Aye, aye sir, 245 wes be sou wes it is Mr. Cane, sir." Judd watch the huge sails billow out as they filled with the wind and the bow slowly pulled to starboard. Moving closer to the helmsman he spoke in hushed tones. "Why is it taking so long to turn? Get a move on man."

"We are one mighty big ship sir. The sheer weight and length of us takes a while to respond to the wheels' direction. Would you like to get the feel of her power?" He looked enquiringly at Judd for a response. Judd's expression told the man he was uncertain of what he should do. "You are the officer of the watch sir. By rights you should be steering but you 'ave other important things to do and that is why you have an assigned helmsman. Not all seamen are capable of holding her steady, it takes practice. You have the right to take the wheel whenever you choose, or to appoint whoever you choose to be helmsman. There are ten of us aboard who are designated helmsmen."

Judd took the place of the helmsman as the bow, continuing to turn, moved the ships compass to 265 degrees. Judd spun the wheel to port to correct the course. Holding the wheel down tightly until the compass read 245 degrees, he turned the wheel back but the ship kept turning and leaning heavily to port. The helmsman, pointing over the ships' stern, spoke to Judd. "See the big old snake shape of the ships wake. That shows you how the man at the wheel, has to be more gentle, feel the movement of the bow and compensate in time to stop what you just saw happening. Here, let me take the wheel back before anyone notices."

Judd stood back and watched as the helmsman skillfully corrected the ships course. He concentration was broken by Ben Tillet's thundering voice. "What the hell is going on helmsman? Are you trying to turn us over?"

"No sir, I was showing Mr. Cane how the ship reacts to erratic movements of the wheel, sir."

"I'll thank you to leave the education of Mr. Cane to myself if you please. Step aside," he ordered. The helmsman took two steps backwards, saluted the navigator and stood at attention awaiting his next order. Turning to Judd the navigator took hold of the wheel and spoke in a milder manner. "You will notice how my hands are placed, both on the wheel at all times. My feet are spread apart to enable me to feel the movement of the ship in response to the wheel. It takes experience to understand how such a smooth turning small thing like the ships wheel can move such an immense object; but it can, and does very effectively. Helmsman Clark here is one of our best at the wheel. When you give an order and bearing you wait for the helmsman to complete the turn. He will tell you when the ship is on the corrected course." Turning to Clark, the navigator signaled for him to return to the wheel. Looking at Judd, he smiled and said, "You need more than your eyes about you when you command a ship. Well done lad for trying. Be aware of who you expose your weaknesses to. Dilutes respect! Not with Clarke, but could be with many. Carry on."

With that the navigator left the quarterdeck. Shortly after the helmsman called out "245 wes be sou wes it is Mr. Cane." Judd continued to read his sextant and charts and soon gave the order, "270 degrees due west helmsman."

"270 degrees due west it is sir," came the reply.

The midday sun beat down on the Vanguard as it sailed west in search of the reported pirate ship or ships. Judd had settled into a more relaxed manner. In between checking his map and bearings the talk between the two men moved to more personal information. Periodically the helmsman would not answer a question as his attention focused on correcting the ships course, or which tides would push the ship one way or the other. The Medditeranean Sea was calm and the winds were steady.

Suddenly a voice from high atop the foremast crow's nest broke to calm. "Ship ahoy. Dead ahead. Ship ahoy. Dead ahead." rang out with watchman's Welsh accent seeming magnified in Judd's mind. A scurry of activity broke out. The navigator, captain and duty officer all appeared on the quarterdeck. The crow's nest watchman was unable to identify the ship and asked for a stronger spyglass, which was hoisted, by rope, up to him. "Tis a merchant man. Looks like a fast rigging, sir. No colors flying." The conversations were being relayed from the crow's nest to the deck and along to the quarterdeck, before reaching the officers.

"Pull our colors, until we know what she is," the Captain ordered the quartermaster. As quickly as the order was given flags came running down the halyards to be removed. The captain turned to the officers and said, "if we don't know who she is, she can't know who we are. Head on she is. There is no way she can know of our power. We will not give that away until we are within range. She could be a Frenchy or Hollander. Let' stay vigilant gentlemen. Pirates don't bother me but a fully armed Frenchy could spell trouble."

From the crow's nest came, "She's holding course and we are gaining on her." That phrase was repeated until it reached the captain.

"She must know we are behind her. If she is not turning about, I guess she wants to remain unknown to us. I can only think of one reason. Call battle stations quartermaster. I sense trouble."

From the crow's nest came the announcement, "Her name is covered. And she is furling her sails." It was repeated. "Her name is covered. And she is furling her sails. She is close to range." The statement echoed along the decks as the Vanguard erupted into a flurry of activity. The order was given to drop the wheels off the port side cannons to allow greater distance and to charge the guns. Ben Tillet arrived at the wheel and told Judd to go to his battle station and that he would take over for now.

Taking off for the powder room and then the main gun deck Judd saw the HMS Vanguard take on a new identity. The whole atmosphere went from being a ship to being a warship. Judd's battle station was at the two 32 pounder cannons on the aft side of the quarterdeck. There was a powder room three decks below where Judd was expected to go and keep the two cannons supplied with gunpowder. When Judd arrived, the gun crew had removed the wheels and were in the process of tying the two great cannons to the bulk head. This would prevent them from recoiling and injuring anyone in their way. When He returned from the powder room to his station there was a silent calm among the crew. Expectancy was in the air.

From the crow's nest the watchman bellowed, "She's turning to port, turning to port and she is armed. She's turning to port and she is armed."

Captain Bellows gave the command, "Hard aport, hard aport. Hold your fire."

The smaller ship was able to turn quickly and as she gave a broadside to the Vanguard, she fired off four cannons. Judd had never experienced what happened next. He saw four large puffs of smoke leave the side of the ship and flashes of flame. A split second, latter the roar of the cannons explosive sound reached his ears. Another split second passed before four huge plumes of water rose out of the sea a short distance from the Vanguards port side. All this was happening as the huge bulk of the Vanguard slowly swung round.

The captain held his spyglass up and shouted, "Run up the colors! She has seen what we are and she is running for it." As he said this the fast rigged ship ahead of them turned away. With only her stern showing Judd could see her sails being set as she took off. Captain Bellows gave the instruction for the gun crews to give a full broadside salvo. They were not to aim at the pirate ship, but either side of her and to make sure some landed ahead of her. Upon being questioned he said, "If we blow her rear end off, she's done for, gone, and probably no one will know about it. If we show her our power it will be talked out in the circle those scum mix in. Pirates will know that Her Royal Majesty's Navy is in the area and means business. I'm sure there is talk on the high seas of our presence. I want there to be talk of our power."

As he went quiet the gun decks of the Vanguard spat out a terrifying, thunderous roar. Pale blue smoke enveloped the decks. Judd's ears rang and felt like they were echoing the sound of gunfire. His eyes watered and he coughed. The shouts of excitement gradually entered his deafness. As he looked about, for the first time since being at sea, he saw the bond among these men. He felt the excitement but was not aware of what it was. His reverie was interrupted by calls for the ship's surgeon. The navigator told Judd to go with the surgeon and assist in whatever way he could. Three decks below the surgeon pushed his way through the crowd of sailors surrounding an injured man. The man lay in the arms of a crewman who spoke to the surgeon. "Tis the bloody gun. It broke the port side rope and spun round backards. Took arf 'is leg orf. Tis over there. Got me belt round his leg to stop the bleeding, but it aint workin." The surgeon cut back the remnants of the man's pants to reveal crushed bone, splinters and strings of muscle and tendons. The man was sobbing, and saying that it wasn't him that improperly tied his side of the gun.

The surgeon stood and gave out orders. "You, you, and you, get this man to the sick bay. Cane, fetch the foot, wrap it in an ensign, and throw it overboard quickly, then come to the sick bay. You and you swab the deck down." With this he turned and left, barking orders out to the men.

Judd stood and looked at the mangled remains of the leg, as if paralyzed, until he was garnered into action by someone saying, "Judd…Judd…git the bloody leg an take it quick." Another voice, "It's to chewed up. He just wants it out of our way so we don't git scared." A different voice added, "Who cares why, just do it Cane, you pick it up." Judd, in a state of numbness picked up the limb and took off running. The acrid smell of burnt gunpowder, compounded by the low bulkhead and lack of breeze, clung to his nostrils as he clambered up the gangway to the ships side. Standing at the ships rail with the tattered remnants of the man's leg in his hands, Judd was immobilized. He heard a voice, "Throw it over man." Judd turned and shouted at no one in particular, "this belongs to a human being, a man, a sailor. I can't do it." Equally fast the reply came back. "Obey your orders, or pay the price." Judd turned back to the rail and with trepidation he dropped the limb over the side, into ships frothy wake. Without looking to see the results he turned to leave for the sick bay when he heard the watchman shout from the crow's-nest, "LEG OVERBOARD!" followed by laughter. Shocked by what he heard Judd stopped dead in his tracks, not knowing what to say or do. A chorus of raucous laughter came from the deckhands. Judd grinned as he thought how base and cruel a seaman's humor was.

When he arrived at the sick bay, he saw the surgeon holding a surgical saw in his hand. The surgeon looked up as Judd entered the sickbay. "We are about to remove the shattered parts of the bone and make a clean cut to allow removal of any foreign matter and clean up the wound. Will make a better end for the stump. Brave man this one. Do you wish to participate?" The crewmen that were holding the injured seaman down with leather straps all looked up at Judd.

"No, thank you Sir." Judd saluted, turned and fled, stopping at the ships rail to vomit over the side. Leeza Trott came up behind him and put his arm around Judd's shoulder. "Ain't no shame in that my boy. Blood just don't sit well with some men.

Those seamen you seed 'elpin' the surgeon, they does that all the time. Just strong stomachs, tis all. Stop by the galley an' I'll git you a mugga of 'ot tea. That will settle yer down."

The day's activities had raised the crew's spirits to a level of excitement Judd had not witnessed. Small groups were busy at work replacing the wheels to the cannon carriages. Others were swabbing decks and returning the ship to its pre-battle stations order. Judd could hear some men singing a sea shanty as they toiled. There was an air of unity and purpose.

Below decks when the evening meal was served the men relived the day's efforts and enjoyed the power of victory. The quartermaster entered the mess deck and shouted out, "The captain congratulates you all for a job well done and he said, 'splice the main brace for all hands." A roar of appreciation went up from the men. An extra issue of grog was an accepted sign of respect from the captain to the lower deck crew.

***

Later that evening Judd was invited to sit in on the officer's evaluation of the days' action. He listened intently to the discussion that seemed to focus on piracy. There was an overwhelming distaste for pirates and the havoc they wrought. He heard the term 'thieves' and 'stealing' frequently. After the meeting was over and he was returning to the chartroom he asked Ben Tillet, "I can see the wrongs of piracy, but what of shipwrecks?"

"What do you mean of shipwrecks. What do you know about shipwrecks?"

"Well, where I lived there are a lot of sandbanks and I've seen some pretty big cargo ships wrecked."

"If you touch the ships contents that's, technically, stealing. However, if you do it the right way, by that I mean salvage, then it's not stealing."

"I am not sure I know the difference."

"If you take the cargo into safekeeping to prevent any further loss you can be paid salvage fees. Sometimes that is paid by allowing you keep some of the salvaged cargo."

"So. Is it stealing?"

"The simple answer is, if nobody knows you took it, it's stealing. If someone does know, you could claim it's salvage. It's a very fine line."

"I have seen people, poor folk, go out after ship wrecks and take things they need. It didn't seem bad."

"Morals my boy, morals. Some folk have been known to set up lights on cliff tops to lure ships onto the rocks. They then pillage the wreck. Does that sound right to you?" Judd could feel the reaction he was getting was becoming hostile.

"I don't think stealing in any form is right sir." With that Judd took off to his quarters. He lay in his hammock and tried weighing up the difference between legal stealing and illegal stealing, moral and immoral, right and wrong. He came to the conclusion that the deciding point lay in discovery and secrecy. He felt a little better about his past life.

Chapter 9

The HMS Vanguard spent the entire summer of 1841 patrolling the Mediterranean and had been ordered to return to Portsmouth. Judd's training in the art of navigation was extensively utilized by Ben Tillet. Judd found himself standing many watches in the navigator's stead. His confidence had become stronger as he developed working relations with the many crewmen he was exposed to. When not on duty he would spend time below decks, often with Dickey Lemon and some of the cabin boys. He got know more about Dickey and understood the bravado the boy displayed was his protective shield. Dickey was well liked among the older seamen who often shared their tobacco and sometimes grog with him. It was evident to Judd that some of the men look on Dickey in a fatherly fashion. Judd saw just how street wise Dickey was when he broached the subject. "You know Dickie a few of the gunners and sail men treat you like a son."

"I aint nobody's son! If thems want to fink I am, and do good by me, I ain't gonna stop em."

"I didn't say you were. It's just a good thing to have someone care about you and want to guide you."

"Bleedin' 'ell. Do you fink I need guidin'? Most people wot cares about yer wants somfink in return."

"And just what do you think I want from you Dickey, bloody Lemon?"

"Nah. I don't mean you. You knows wot I mean. You can't trust everyone just cause they is kind." Dickey was trying to undo the offense he thought he had given Judd.

"No, you can't distrust them either. There are some good men around us. True friendships are important."

"Yeah, well I ain't used to real friends. Least I weren't till I met you." With that being said Dickey got up and left the group and Judd knew he had found Dickey's soft spot.

Judd went off to the main deck to get some night air before bedding down for the night when he heard the watchman call out from the crow's nest. "Land ho on the port bow." Judd went to the ships port side rail, and looking ahead, could see a tiny conical peak of land. He knew from his charts that this was Gibraltar. He went to the quarterdeck to find out if they would be stopping there. Ben Tillet spoke as approached, "let me guess, you want to know if we are going alongside in Gibraltar, right?" he asked.

Judd replied with, "Not exactly sir. I was thinking that we might be staying on course out of the Bay of Biscay and round Gibraltar before heading to a Spanish port."

"Well done Cane. I'm glad to see you thinking ahead. The Captain has not yet given any orders to that effect, but I do expect him to. I'll bid you goodnight Mr. Cane"

Judd had been summarily dismissed. It seemed like he had only been in his hammock a short while when he heard the ships anchor being freed as it dropped to the oceans bottom. Judd did not make a move to get up. He laid silently absorbing the sounds and movements and interpreting their meaning. The creaking of the ships timbers and the gentle movement of the ship with the swell of the ocean closed the day on his awareness.

***

At dawn, and voices of seamen that awoke him. Stepping out onto the deck, with the brilliant Spanish sun beating down on his head, he saw the Little Cherub, a three masted schooner, at anchor, close to the Vanguard. Far off on the horizon Judd saw Gibraltar, a tiny lone speck of land. He joined the crew gathered around the ships rail but could see nothing. Quickly, he ran up onto the quarterdeck for a better view. As a midshipman he was one of the few crew allowed access to this deck without having to be invited.

Another ship was anchored close by the Vanguard. The two ships lay in close proximity to each other in the bay of the small Spanish town of Algeiras, where the Vanguard could take on supplies. The Vanguard lowered a lifeboat that contained six burly rowers, two marines and a coxswain. They rowed over to the Little Cherub, whose captain, Jacob Ashley, demanded to be taken to the HMS Vanguard. As the lifeboat returned alongside the Vanguard, Sir Thomas Fellows stood at the opening in the ship's side and demanded an explanation, "What is your business Sir?"

The man, holding a large folio above his head, said, "Captain Ashley here sir. I am commanded to deliver this Admiralty commission to Sir Thomas Fellows. Is that you, sir?"

"It is, sir. The coxswain can bring it to me after returning you to your ship," said Fellows.

"I am bound by my duty to hand it to no other man, sir."

"Then come aboard, Captain," said Captain Fellows curtly. He turned to the duty officer and spoke in hushed tones, "Bring the pompous little man to my cabin, if you please." He retreated to his quarters.

With much bustle and pretense, Captain Ashley was ushered into the private quarters of Captain Fellows. He was visibly interested in the spartan, but substantial accouterments in which his counterpart lived. "The Navy sees you well, Captain," he said. "Perhaps I should change from private sailoring to serving Her Majesty."

"How come you by an Admiralty dispatch?" said Fellows.

"The harbormaster delayed my permission to sail from Plymouth, as your last sighting had you off the coast of North Africa," said Ashley. "The Admiralty knew we should pass in the forenoon watch today. I was to approach you and deliver the dispatch. That is all I was told."

"I thank you kindly for your service to Her Highness and wish you safe journeys," said Fellows. "Could I offer you a simple meal, and perhaps a glass of fine port?"

"Sir, I am more intrigued with what so urgent a commission could be, that I was called to serve it with such folderol," said Ashley with a smile.

"Intrigued you can stay. It is Admiralty business, Sir! As such it has no significance to you. I thank you for your service. Now, if you will excuse me," he said. Turning to his cabin boy, he said, "Show the Captain to the lifeboat and return." Captain Ashley had been summarily dismissed.

With that, he stood, turned, and walked to the rear of his quarters, gazing out the rear windows to where the Little Cherub rode the gentle swell. Unaccustomed to the common and ungentlemanly prying of Captain Ashley, he was noticeably offended.

***

Dickey Lemon stood at attention inside the captain's cabin door. Captain Fellows bade him to come sit with him.

"We have been at high seas now nigh on three years Lemon," he said. "We have lost no men. We have served and protected, and for that you should be proud. But I fear this dispatch brings news the likes of which some will not be happy with. You have been a trustworthy and, dare I say, likable young man. I may be surrounded with a good crew and fine officers, but a captain must keep counsel close to his chest. Do you swear upon your mother's life not to impart what we are about learn?"

"Aye aye, sir, Captain, sir," said Dickey nervously. Rarely did a cabin boy gain the confidence of senior officers, let alone the captain. For all of Dickey's bravado, he was conflicted between his desire to go home and, excitement of what was about to happen. He could sense the same feelings in his captain.

The captain broke the great seal of the Admiralty. He pulled charts out of the folio and placed it on his table. Silently, he read the dispatch. His face showed no expression. He muttered the word 'Australia,' closed his eyes, and held his hands over his face. Slowly, his hands dropped to his lap. He picked up the dispatch again, leaned forward on his elbows, and said, "Lemon, I wish I could share this with you. But as a fair man, it would not be just of me to burden you with this alone. I will share it with the entire ship's company at the same time." He slipped the charts back into the dispatch case, handed them to the cabin boy, and instructed him, "Take these to Navigator Tillet and require he place them under lock and key without perusing them. Then, advise Lieutenant Walker to muster all hands on the poop deck at once. Now be with you."

Dickey ran out of the cabin, ducked around some bulkheads, and sat in a dark corner. He opened the folio and looked at the labels on the charts. While he could not read, he knew the shapes of some countries. Quickly, he closed the folio, jumped up, and ran to the navigator, delivering the instructions as he was told. He then ran, jumping over open deck hatches and bundles of supplies waiting to be lowered into the ships hold, until he found Judd.

"Follow me, don't ask, just do it quick," he said. "Fings is goin' to get pretty 'ectic in about five minutes."

Judd followed obediently until they stopped in a dark corner behind the rope locker. Dickey gasped, out of breath. "We . . . we are going places, Judd. I fink we is going to Australia." As he spat out the information, the bosun's call began to sound all hands on deck.

"No, wait," said Dickey, stopping Judd from leaving. "I'm a-tellin' you, Judd, this is good news. I know we ain't goin' home yet, but this is somfing big. Let's go."

***

The two boys stood among the throng of sailors on the poop deck. Even though Judd had been on the Vanguard for nearly two years, there were still some faces he rarely saw. Crew men were aloft on the rigging, standing in every conceivable spot. Next to Judd was the cook, Lezza Trott, the quiet, calm man who Judd could always turn to. Over the last two years, they had spoken often of home and life around them. Judd often would see Lezza in the background as if he was keeping an eye on him. As Lezza once promised, he had become Judd's father at sea.

"Wot's this all about, Judd?" said Lezza. "Have you caught wind of anything? Why they wants all o' us?"

"Shh . . . the captain's about to speak," said Judd.

Captain Fellows walked to the railings on the front of the quarterdeck. Regaled in his full dress uniform, with medals, ruffs and gold trim shining in the midday sun, he looked every part a gentleman and a captain. He looked out over the crew as if acknowledging each man. Gradually, the entire world seemed to stop, as if the wind and waves bowed to the captain's presence.

"At ease, all," he said in a booming voice few had ever heard from him. "Today, I received a dispatch from the Admiralty. Any interruptions will find you in the brig. Is that clear?" The response was mild. He bellowed, *"Is—that—clear?!"* A thunderous roar emerged and just as quickly ended, as if some unseen conductor had sliced the air with his baton.

"We are commanded to turnabout," said Fellows. "We will continue to resupply for our journey. We will be here in Algeciras for two days. You will be divided into two watches doing twelve-hour shifts. You will be allowed ashore for one of your twelve-hour off-duty watches. We will depart in two days. Anyone left behind will face charges of mutiny. As you all know, the Spaniards have no more time for mutineers than does the Royal Navy. I will now read the dispatch." He cleared his throat and took another prolonged gaze around his crew.

"The HMS Vanguard is to proceed to Botany Bay, Australia, stopping at Grand Canarias, Saint Helena, Table Bay, South America, Madagascar, Socotra." The

51

captain went silent and watched the reactions of his men. He held his hand high for silence the murmers and carried on.

"The Queen intends to increase transportation of the criminal classes to the Antipodes while simultaneously increasing efforts to encourage settlers to Australia." The captain looked up. "It is expected that your voyage shall take two years." The crew's expressions had not changed much since he had last looked. "Her Majesty has authorized me to pay a bounty of fifty pounds to every crew member upon his return safely to England," he said. "To the family of any unfortunate souls who do not survive this historic voyage, a payment of the entire voyage pay plus two hundred and fifty pounds, plus lifetime privileges at the Royal Naval Hospital in Greenwich."

To the captain's surprise, the crew erupted in a cheer. It was a new thing to be paid for their services and their risks alike. But this provided little reassurance to Fellows. He knew many did not like what was about to happen. Indeed, his experience told him there would many chances for them to display their displeasure. The southern hemisphere would bring temptation, danger, disease, and death. Each situation would build and fester in their minds. He would need the utmost support and backing of his officers, and it wouldn't hurt to have an ear below deck.

"Man your battle stations for inspection," said the captain. "Any dissension can mean time in the brig. Not many have survived a long stay in the brig, and none—I repeat, none—will. Is that understood?" he bellowed in a staccato manner. The reply was less than overwhelming, but still clear enough for the captain to be satisfied. "Dismissed," he said as he turned to Navigator Tillet.

"Chartroom. On the double, sir. Have Cane with you." He turned and went to his quarters. Tillet summoned Dickey Lemon and sent him to fetch Judd, warning him not to waste time with idle chat. As Dickey ran toward the forecastle, he spotted Judd with Lezza Trott. They were both huddled in secretive conversation, which abruptly ended upon his approach. Lezza glanced at Dickey and whispered to Judd, "The way I see's it, that's the one wot'll get yer arse in the brig. Don't say yers ain't been told." He stood erect, glared at Dickey, and strode away. The two boys ran off. Dickey pulled Judd behind the capstan and dragged him to the deck, out of view. He told Judd to get to the chartroom. "Just shut yer gob, listen and say 'aye aye'," said Dickey in a high-speed chatter. "By the time yer gits back to England, you'll be a man. I don' care what the captain says: We be gonna fightin'. We's big enough to win an' we will. But as everyone aroun' us is fightin', me an' you, Judd, we's goin' be learnin'.

"I haven't got a clue what you are talking about." Judd answered.

***

Judd could not believe what Dickey had just said, and yet there was a determination and fire in Dickey's eyes and voice that excited Judd. He stood up, straightened his uniform, and took off for the navigator's chart room. On the way, as he jumped coils of rope and dodged around seaman scurrying to their inspection stations, his heart was beating fast. He knew the speech the captain delivered and what Dickey said didn't quite match up, but the battle-station directive given by the captain suggested more than a peaceful mission.

Reaching the chartroom, Judd stood just inside the door at attention and saluted. "Seaman Cane, sir," he said, his hand snapping to his side.

"At ease, Cane. Come in closer. Walls have ears, as, indeed, do bulkheads," said the captain. Judd stepped inside. "If you ask me, pressed men are usually more trouble than they're worth," said Fellows. "That is why Her Majesty pays her sailors, and damned well if you ask me. You are a fortunate young man to have Mr. Tillet take you under his wing. He tells me you have done well by the stars and the tides. Your choice of companions could be improved, but that is your business. Upon the advice of Mr. Tillet, I am hereby making your promotion to midshipman formal. You are no longer a lower deck man. You are not to disclose this promotion to anyone. It is my job to announce that. Do you understand?"

"Aye aye, sir, Thank you, sir. I will not let you down, sir" Judd replied.

"Good. By the time this trip is over, you will have amassed a tidy sum to return home with to your family. If this voyage serves Her Majesty as commanded, you will have recommendations from the entire ship's company of officers for entry into the rank of officer. My connections at the Admiralty can guarantee that."

"Aye aye, sir," Judd said rather hesitantly, as he was not sure what he was getting in to.

"I will leave you, Mr. Tillet, to brief Midshipman Cane of our plans," said the captain. The navigator came to attention and saluted the captain, who turned and left the chartroom.

"Relax, Cane, just relax. That seems like a lot to take in, I know," said the navigator with a grin. "He was correct, though. You have learned everything that you been asked to. I'm sometimes quite surprised at how quickly you grasp the complexities of navigation, but you have, and you deserve this promotion."

"Why the secrecy?" asked Judd. The navigator smiled. He leaned back in his chair and proceeded to fill, light, tamp, and relight his pipe, then create a cloud of pale blue mist that hung below the upper deck beams and above the deck. This slow, deliberate act calmed Judd. He had seen the navigator do this many times, and he knew from this experience that things were going to be fine.

"It is not secrecy Mr. Cane. The order of things is that the Captain makes the announcements, not the crew. By the time we return to England, God willing, you will be a man. I do not need to tell you that many of the arguments and brawls below decks, and I am sure you have seen more than I, are fueled by rage, disappointment, and often jealousy. There is jealousy about the amount of food or assignments, or someone getting the prettier girl while ashore. Those resentments are brought back on board, and they fester until they explode. I'm sure you can name those cabin boys and, indeed, some ordinary seamen who resent the progress you have made. The captain, in his wisdom, wishes to keep any potential conflict to a minimum. Captain Fellows, myself, and you are to go ashore after he has finished his inspection to make arrangements for provisions. A new skill for you to master." Eight bells sounded off in the distance.

"Afternoon watch is coming on duty," said the navigator. "Go and eat. Keep close counsel with yourself, and be back here at two bells. We have a lot of planning to do." He waved Judd out of the room. Judd stood to attention, saluted, and left. Two bells into the next watch found the captain, navigator and Judd being rowed ashore to commence seeking provisions.

The captain said, "Mr Tillet, I am going to arrange for the letters of credit while you and Cane seek out fresh meat and vegetables. We should make the most of fresh, while we can."

"Aye, aye sir. Where shall we meet?"

"Meet. Meat, very funny I must say said the captain. The local ship chandlers, shall we say about noon, then?"

"What are letters of credit?" Judd asked Ben Tillet.

The captain spoke first, "We cannot roam around the world at the Admiralty's will with our pockets full of gold coins and pound notes. No sir. The Captain of all her Majesty's ships has the authority to buy whatever they need and the crown pays for it. Instead of money we use a letter of credit giving us that authorization. Understand?"

"No sir, that isn't the same as money," responded Judd.

"Actually, young Cane it is the same. Her Majesty's Government is respected all over the world and when surrendered for repayment that letter of credit is as good as money in the bank."

"How does that work, Sir?"

"Ben Tillet explained, "The local merchant takes that letter to his bank or to the British Consul, or Governor, whoever it is in their country, and they are given local money in return. It's a respected method of trading."

"Can anyone use a letter of credit?" ask Judd.

"If they have the authority and they are trusted by the people they are dealing with, yes they can."

"Can I make my own?"

The Captain laughed and said, "I have no doubt young man, that one day you will be substantial enough to do just that." The rest of that afternoon Judd was to learn the intricacies of bartering, and trading without the use of actual money. He was fascinated and intrigued by the opportunities this could provide. He sat quietly in the rowboat as it returned to the Vanguard while the Captain and Navigator were deep in conversation. He was processing all that he had seen and heard that day.

***

Later, when Judd returned to the mess deck, his mind swam. Should he tell Dickey? Should he tell anyone? He was still processing everything he had learned. His mind was cluttered. These men had stolen, no, kidnapped him from his family. Wrenched away his way of life, and surplanted it with their own. When these men spoke of 'pirates' with such disdain, he felt they were no better themselves. They pirated his life. Shouldn't they be responsible for something? His thoughts were interrupted as he noticed that inspection had been completed. Much had to be corrected. It appeared every seaman had the rest of the day filled with work—work that appeared to be preparatory rather than maintenance. There was an air of expectancy and urgency that struck Judd as exciting. As Judd passed two seamen he had become friendly with, one called out, "So, young Judd, are coming ashore with us tonight?"

"I would like to but I haven't been given my watch yet. I'll seek you out when I know."

"No ale to be had here, but the wine and women are pretty good. We will be in the rope locker for the rest of the day. Come and see us later." The expectancy of going ashore had galvanized the men into an upbeat mode.

As the daytime's warm sun gave way to the dusky evening skies Judd found Nobby Clark and Dobbin Lay, the two seamen he had spoken to earlier, waiting for him at the ships rail. Both men were seasoned sailors and despite their huge size and tough appearances were simple, kind men, surviving in a harsh environment. While being rowed ashore Nobby asked, "What is it we want to do tonight boys?" Dobbin spoke up, "What I want is some good home cooking, a bottle of chianti and a good woman, well not a good woman but a gooood woman." The man roared with laughter at his own humor.

"And you Judd?" he said turning to Judd.

"I would like to look around the town and maybe find a little trinket for my ma. I guess the sound of a good home cooked meal does tickle my fancy though."

"What about a lass? Do you need a lass?" Nobby asked innocently.

"I don't think he has ever had one. Looks at his fine pink cheeks. The Spanish ladies are going to be all over him," laughed Dobbin. Judd remained quiet through the discourse. Nobby leaned over and spoke in hushed tones, "Pay him no mind, everyone has to have a first time, aint no shame in that. I know a few ladies in Algeciras, you just let me know." The lifeboat came alongside the wharf and the off duty seamen tumble ashore scattering off in all directions. Nobby, Dobbin and Judd walked off in the direction of the brightly lit bars and restaurants. They settled on a sidewalk restaurant the two men knew and ordered food. Throughout their eating they were frequently approached by women of the night, offering their services, which were pleasantly declined. Judd devoured his meal with a ravenous speed. He had forgotten what unsalted food tasted like. The smell coming from the kitchen was intoxicating. He wasted no time finishing his plate and readily agreed to second helpings, which he washed down with the sweet red wine, local to the area. Having finished eating he leaned back on his chair with his arms folded over what he felt was a full and protruding belly.

With his satiated belly and comfortable glow, he attempted to take control of his tongue. He spoke slowly and deliberately, "I'll shay - you two fellows sure know where to eat. This was good. Sho what did we do, do we did, do we, now?" His shipmates laughed at his speech. Dobbin signaled and three females appeared, suggesting they go somewhere more comfortable. The small group went through the rear of the restaurant to a private area. Dobbin quickly disappeared with one woman as Nobby said to another, "Young Judd here, is new at this. First time, you know. Be gentle with him."

The youngest girl, an olive skinned, thin rail of a girl, approached Judd and took his hand in hers. Her black hair in curls, framed her face, and lay over her shoulders. Judd thought how her eyes sparkled in the dim light. Her lips were full and the softness of her hands holding his appealed to him. He wanted to touch her face as they entered a small bedroom. She stood a little taller than him as she put her arms round him and held him close and said, "Relax, tell me what do dey call ju?"

"Judd, what is your name?"

"In jour country my name would be Victoria." She moved to the bed, pulling Judd towards her. Judd sat rigid and looking up at her he asked, "can I have a glass of wine, please?" The girl knew he was uncomfortable and left the room to get his wine. When she returned, he was stretched out on the bed with his eyes closed. Putting down the glass she sat beside him, and gently touched his moving chest. As she moved her hand down, she started to unbuckled his pants. She felt that he was limp and unresponsive. Quickly she undressed him and disrobing herself, lay alongside him.

A short while later he woke to find the naked girl asleep, cuddled into him, her hand firmly holding his crotch. Her small pert breasts were topped with large dark nipples, which he touched with his fingers. He explored her breasts in his hand and felt their emanating warmth. As he ran his hand down her firm tummy. He found her bushy pubic hair. He jerked his hand away quickly in surprise. He did not know that girls had hair down there. She moved as if she were awaking from sleep, and whispered, "Oh my, jou were so good. jou didn't even wait to have jour wine. I must excite you so good." She moved her hand from his crotch, and kissed him on his cheek.

"Did I finish too quickly?" He asked as he blushed. He was relieved that in the dim light she would not see his flushed cheeks.

"There is no such thing as too quickly with a joung stallion like ju."

"Did I do 'it' right, is there a right way to do it?"

"There are many ways you to do it." She kissed him on the nose and continued, "Sailors always make big about the sex. It is only important that jou make a lady she happy."

"And did I make you happy?" She turned and straddled him placing her hands on his chest as she looked down on him and said,

"I liked for sure to do again." From his reaction she knew not push the issue. She handed him the glass of wine. He felt her warm hands against his crotch and wondered what the fuss about sex was all about.

"No thank you, not that I didn't like it. You are very beautiful."

"And jou sir, I think, are a leettle drunk. But thank jou anyway. You are a handsom young man. I hope that jou will come back and see me tomorrow? We must go now. Jour friends are wait for ju." He turned his back on her as he dressed, embarrassed to see her watching him.

Entering the bar area his friends sat grinning at him and applauded. Not knowing what to say, he took a mock bow. The three men left the establishment, arms around each other's shoulders, singing a sea shanty, as they made their way back to the quay. Climbing the gangway Dobbin turned to Judd, grinned and said, "You aint no virgin any more Judd Cane."

"What's a virgin, exactly?" Judd asked. The men left him guessing as they went to their quarters.

Judd was not to get to return to his maiden. He went in search of Leeza. He had questions. Leeza was standing at his butcher block work surface with a mug of steaming tea in his hand. "Well, well, look what the cat dragged in. Are you drunk?"

"I don't think so. I am a bit foggy in the head, without you taking the piss, can I talk to you about something private?"

"You can always talk to me, you know that. I spect someone got their first taste of sex tonight. Is I right?"

"How did you know that? Does it show?"

"No, the two you went ashore with gave it away."

"Why, how, what did they say?"

"They didn't have to say nuffin. I know them, I know you. It had to 'appen one day. I's a finking you is not too sure wot you just did. Don't say nuffin. If you don't remember much, then, maybe that's good. The women, cause they aint no ladies, do the sex fing wiv anyone wot pays. That's their business. Now as for you young Judd, they sometimes will give you sex for no money, special like if its your first time. You might even get a bonus."

"Bonus, like what?"

"The pox, that's like wot. Bleeding orrible, if you git's the pox. Cain't always be cured. Probably aint never seen the pox in Mucking, but there sure is a lot of it going around sailors. I fink it's best if you keep your willy in your pants till yer finds the right girl for yerself. Now, let me get you a cuppa tea and yer can tell me all about it."

"Thanks, I'd like some tea. Right now, I'm not sure that I want to discuss this any further. How do I know if I got the pox?"

"Just relax. It will take a while to come out. Your willy will itch and it will hurt to piss. Yer sure will know right enough. Don't go worrying yerself. Yer might be lucky this time. I 'ope so for your sake." The two sat in silence as they drank. Leeza could feel Judd's discomfort and kept quiet.

***

After the two days had passed HMS Vanguard heaved anchor, pulled out of Algeciras Bay, and caught the early morning breezes as she headed south for Grand Canarias.

Judd ate his morning meal, then went to the forecastle and leaned over the bowsprit, watching the sea cleft apart by the huge wooden bow as it disappeared below the water to become the keel. The Atlantic Ocean stretched out in front as far as the eye could see. As he watched what lay before him his thoughts wandered to his night of passion in Algeciras. He regretted that he could not remember much about it other than his pounding headache the next morning. His discussion with Leeza did little to ease his mind. He couldn't even remember the sex act itself, although he was able to recall the naked girl, her breasts, her tawny skin and her sweet smell. Both Dobbin and Nobby spent the next day jibbing him about his prowess. No matter what they said, he just did not remember much other than the meal and Victoria. The forward thrust of the ship propelled by the huge sails, puffed out to capacity, created a breeze.

In his attempt to sort out his thoughts, his father's voice echoed in his head: "Play the cards you're dealt, not the ones you want." Which cards he had been dealt wasn't quite clear to him. But he felt a little better having talked with Leeza. He was giving serious thought to saving the sex thing for the right girl, or at least until he knew more about it.

***

Later, as the sun bounced on the starboard side, a glowing fireball in the darkening blue horizon slowly sinking where the sea meets the sky, the few clouds became iridescent before they dropped from sight. Judd knew they were now on a heading of 180 degrees, on a southerly course. He had spent the afternoon and early part of the evening watch plotting the stars and charting the Vanguard's course. It would not be long before Africa—the dark and hidden continent—would be on their port side. Unfortunately, it wouldn't be until morning that Judd would be able to see the coast.

Judd's watch being over, he went in search of Dickey Lemon, all the while turning over in his mind what and how much he should share. He eventually found Dickey in the cable locker, where the mighty anchor cable's links lay in total darkness in a mountain of iron. Dickey sat atop the heap, an oil-burning lantern hanging from an overhead beam. The shadows made eerie and strange shapes, and made Dickey appear almost ominous as he peered down at Judd.

"It took me one hell of time to find you," Judd said.

Dickey whispered. "My mind's all over the place, 'cause something big is goin' down, an' they aint tellin' us true."

"That's what has me confused," said Judd. "I'm going to tell you some stuff they're telling me, and you have to promise you'll keep it to yourself. It could cause me a heap of trouble, and even get us flogged."

"That's a 'eap of cow shit. They bain't so quick to flog anyone these days. They be tryin' to scare you," said Dickey. "Look 'ere. Let me tell you wot I knows. Then you tell me wot you knows. Then, we work out us plans." He paused. "There lots o' talk atween the old sea dogs. They's sayin' big trouble ahead. The Dutch has made a treaty with us over Sumatra and the Spice Islands. The Germans, the Spanish, an' the Portuguese is not happy. The old hands is saying we's headin' right into trouble. Many of them think it's an invitation to pirates. They uses confusion and uncertainty to do some good for themselves. We is a warship. Why is the Admiralty using a warship to chart navigation routes and all that cow shit? I might add, Judd, the finest of Her Majesty's warships—the newest, the biggest, the most powerful. Why? I'll tell why: trouble. They expect a lot of trouble. Now. Before you say anything . . ." Dickey stopped and gasped for air. Judd could see Dickey was excited and fired up, but he didn't quite understand. Dickey went on: "The big fing 'ere, Judd, is we baint be staying in this line of work forever."

"What do you mean?" asked Judd.

"Being a sailor for the Royal Navy never made no man rich, and more often than not got 'im killed. Learn somefing and usin' it to better yoursel'—now that is bein' smart. Are you gonna be smart, Judd?"

"Yes, I want to be smart, and I don't want to get killed. If you're right, how can we be smart?" said Judd.

There's a few of the older sea dogs who ain't past bein' pirates themselves." Dickey stopped and watched Judd's jaw drop open, and then continued. "I ain't, we ain't, saying nothing bad is goin' a 'appen on this ship, but we can learn a lot to use later on. None of us is goin' a get as good a sightin'. Now you keep your own log. Nuffin' to do with anyone else. Record everyfin' you see. Pays a mind to 'ow them other ships sail, change direction, uses the wind, the night, the weather. When our time is up in this navy, maybe, just maybe . . . well, who knows? Make yersel' notes on what 'appens on the quarterdeck here. Wot do our officers say, wot do they do, how do they plan? Do you see where this is leadin' us Judd?"

"Yes. I think you want us to become pirates," said Judd in a sarcastic tone.

"I ain't sayin' that. If we knows how the pirates work and how the Navy works, then wotever we do later on in our sea life, we knows both sides. I doan know about you, but I loves the sea. I'm just not sure about Her Majesty bein' my boss for the rest of my life. If'n I'm going to take the risk of life at sea, then I wants to take the rewards. That's all I've got to say. Now it's your turn." Dickey folded his arms and watched Judd intently.

Judd was silent as he weighed in his mind what to say. He knew that he understood things way beyond his years. He realized now that Jim the carter's skill at finding shipwrecks was no accident. He was aware that the weather was often predictable, and it was not only the domain of sailors. While a cart had its wheels on the ground, a ship never had a stable point from which to recover from nature's actions. The only thing mariners had, were, land-based points of reference, such as lights—lights placed by men, and not necessarily trustworthy men.

It was at this point Judd realized his opinion of himself was not accurate. His view of the nights spent on adventures, fighting the elements to scavenge from shipwrecks, was nothing more than thievery. His self-inflated view of Midshipman Cane was somewhat comical in its shady past. He felt that if he wanted Dickey's trust, he had to tell Dickey the truth about of his past.

When he finished, Dickey slapped him on the back and said, "W'en you tol' me about playin' the cards you 'ave been dealt, well, that's wot you've been doin' all your life. That doan make you bad. It doan make you good neever. It just means you're one of us wot does wot we 'aves to to survive. All I'm tellin' you is that me an' some of the lads reckon that, if this voyage turns bad, we got to be ready to make the best of it."

"Dickey, I was just a common thief. If you think about it I was part of a gang of thieves. I didn't have to do it to survive. I did it for the thrill."

"So wot, you was an appy feef. Some 'ow I fink there is lot more feeving in our futures."

***

As the HMS Vanguard carried out its duties, sometimes the battle stations fired their cannons, either one or both sides or all at once. Careful record was made of the effect these firings had on the ship's handling. Measurements were made and recorded. When all the cannons on one side were fired, the warship would roll, and it would take a long time for the ship to steady enough for the next salvo to be fired. The gunners' ears would ring.

Judd had acquired a deep, rich, golden glow and a confident swagger, partly from learning to walk on a rolling and pitching ship and partly from the sheer joy of sea life.

When the Vanguard sailed into Tenerife on the Grand Canarias it tied up behind a merchantman, The Duke of Kent. As was customary the two captains met and exchanged information, social gossip, and nautical news. The Duke of Kent had left England bound for India and was expecting to meet up with the Vanguard somewhere off the African coast. They had mail sacks for the Vanguard. This news was greeted with joy from all aboard the Vanguard. Judd had not expected to get mail for a long time due to sudden change in Admiralty orders. He expected news from the oustide world to be slow in catching up. His letter from his mother also contained a letter from Mary. Mother's letter went into length about how his letters had become a village event. She now not only shared them with the Blacksmith and Carter families but with anyone who was interested. The admiralty had notified them of his promotion. Other village gossip and chat filled the pages.

Mary's letter evoked deeper thoughts. As he read it, he thought of how the Spanish girl had been about the same height as Mary. As best he could remember the body shape was about the same. Beyond those thoughts, try as hard as he could, his picture of Mary was blurred, but still, the letter meant something. He was not sure what it was. He was happy, here at sea surrounded by excitement, activity and new things every day, and yet, there was a little bit of loneliness buried deep within him. He felt a tear welling up from deep inside which he did not understand. He escaped the emotions by turning his attention to what was happening around him.

Many of the rules of the "new" Navy that bothered the older hands were, in Judd's mind, just the way things were. He had not known the 'old navy'. Judd matured through experience and exposure to foreign cultures. While the officers dealt with the local natives in a condescending manner, Judd detailed in his private journal the wonders and beauty of these lands. Judd saw wealth in the weather, the beaches with white sands, so different from Lower mucking's muddy beach. The food was an ever-changing kaleidoscope of experience. At every opportunity, the crew would use their shore leave for drinking and womanizing; Judd, meanwhile,

60

watched and wrote. He did not see beauty in the dark-skinned savages, as the officers called them. In fact, his fear of the pox prevented him from doing what sailors were expected to do. He recalled the black livery boys, pageboys and houseboys the wealthy London society employed and he found it difficult to equate the two. The abject poverty he saw in black cultures and the deprivation around the world seemed to keep them different from their London counterparts.

During this time, he often saw huge, fully rigged ships. Some were known to the crew, but the thing that surprised Judd was how many were not. In one of Judd and Dickey's secret meetings, during which they would keep each other appraised of goings-on above and below deck, they discussed all the huge, anonymous fleets. Often, a ship would appear on the horizon and approach the HMS Vanguard, only to turn away unexpectedly. It was only when a ship would turn away that the crew would stand down from their battle stations. These could have been pirates, French, Dutch or any other nations' ships that did not want to confront or be identified. The reasons for avoidance were always based on assumptions on the part of the Vanguard. These actions confirmed to both the boys that there was almost no control on the open seas. It was easy to see why one had to be cautious.

Judd and Dickey soon learned of another cause for caution. While sailing the Indian Ocean off the coast of Australia in late September, as the spring season approached, Dickey came upon Judd coming off the end of his forenoon watch. They chose an open deck area in full view to meet.

"Billy Lyons is mouthing off," said Dickey. Billy Lyons was the first officer's cabin boy. They never let Billy in on their discussions.

"He's been drinking rum rations from somewhere, and he's threatenin' to expose a few of the older seamen as pirates. It's a lot o' cow shit. But if the officers 'ear the word *pirate*, they'll fink mutiny. We gotta stop 'im."

"If we expose him, we could still face the same concerns from the captain," said Judd, concerned, "we need to scare him. Put the fear of God into him so he settles down. Do you think we could talk to him?"

"Nah . . . he's too drunk. Two of the gunners 'ave 'im down by the brig. We gotta move quick as like. We should drag 'im up on deck and expose 'im before anyone else does."

Judd thought for a moment. "If we do that, he may talk too much and plant ideas in the minds of the officers. We need to discover him and discredit him at the same time."

"'Ows about, you, git the duty officers into the chartroom right at the start of your midnight watch," said Dickey. "I'll get two o' our men, one on each side of the main deck. On my signal, the forard group by the capstan will make a lot of commotion, a just-havin'-fun sort of fing. T'other group will throw Billy Lyons overboard."

"Whoa! He'll drown!" said Judd.

"No way! One of the seamen will go over right after 'im and save 'im. We looks, good 'cause we saved 'im. You can say he been talking about being a pirate, an' I'll say he shouted 'Hoist the Jolly Roger!' as 'e jumped."

They both laughed as they agreed to this.

On the appointed hour, everything went to plan. While all duty officers were in the chatroom below the quarterdeck, Billy took his fated launching. One of the other cabin boys even shouted, "Hoist the Jolly Roger!" As soon as Billy was hauled back on board, soaking wet and protesting loudly, the quartermaster had him thrown in the brig to sober up. The officers sought to find out the cause for the commotion. Judd explained relaying the plan worked out by Dickie.

Judd suggested to Officer Tillet a mock trial, one that Billy would think was real, to teach him a lesson. The idea was greeted with approval. Captain Fellows agreed to the plan on the condition that only himself, the navigator, and Midshipman Cane were to know of the ruse.

The master-at-arms attended the miserable, weeping, Billy Lyons and told him that Captain Fellows had ordered a flogging to take place at eight bells of the morning watch. He talked overtop the babbling protestations of Billy's innocence and sternly advised Billy to take his punishment. After all, it could have included being draw and quartered.

The next morning as Billy lay whimpering, spread out between the deck's teak grating like some giant starfish drying in the sun, the master-at-arms charged him with creating a disturbance with the intention of inciting piracy.

As planned, Judd stood and requested a hearing on behalf of the accused. "Excuse me Captain, Sir. May I speak on behalf of seaman Lyons?"

The Captain responded, "seamen charged with piracy were not entitled to a hearing, you may speak on behalf of the accused in my cabin." Judd followed the captain to his quarters. Here he was surprised.

"My leniency," the captain said, is conditional upon you keeping an ear below decks for any further rumblings. You are to report directly to me." Stunned, Judd agreed.

When they returned to the crew, chattering died instantly. The captain announced that he would cancel the flogging. "Billy Lyons you are indebted to Midshipman Cane. You will serve seven days in the brig and no rum rations for thirty days." He also added, "You should all take note that, although flogging is no longer practiced in Her Majesty's Navy, as your captain and protector of your lives and souls, I will not hesitate to use flogging as means to keep this ship in order. Is that clear? Restore the rum rations to the crew and not the prisoner," he instructed the quartermaster.

It was not clear if the roar from the crew came from support of the statement or happiness that their rum rations were not being suspended. Judd retired to the chartroom reviewing in his mind how the recent scenario had passed. He had had an important lesson. It was that Lords, Ladies and common folk shared a common thread and it was that most were willing, for a price, to be less than honest. But it was apparent they all fought vigorously to appear other than what they really were. He was no different.

Chapter 10

HMS Vanguard, was caught in the doldrums off the tip of South America. As Judd sat quietly in the chartroom, reviewing the old dispatch, he recalled Captain Fellows reading that same document.

Abruptly, the door was thrust open, and Ben Tillet, the navigator, stood as a dark shadow blindingly backlit by the sun's vibrant glare. As he closed the door, taking shape, he walked over to his large desk, muttering something about Lloyd's register of ships. Judd picked up the thick, well-worn book and handed it to the navigator, whose mind appeared to be somewhere else.

Suddenly, the loud boom of a signal mug, that was used to invite inspection from one ship to another or a harbormaster to come aboard, broke the oppressive air. The navigator began to flip through the book, telling Judd he was looking for a ship known as the Governor Ready. They found the entry. The Governor Ready was a 512-ton merchantman, sheathed in copper, about twenty years old, owned by Welford and Company. The Lloyd's register showed that in 1830 she was a slave transport between the Caribbean Islands and the east coast of Africa. She was now London-based, and a regular on the New South Wales-to-London route. Ben Tillet muttered to himself that she was an American-built ship—well, Prince Edward Island anyway.

"Topside now, Cane," said Tillet. "We have an interesting situation. The Governor Ready is approaching, and she appears to be in some sort of trouble."

The Vanguard's battle-stations alarm sounded, and the decks burst into well-trained action. Cannons were brought to bear. The marines manned every open space on the upper deck of the Vanguard, small arms at the ready. An eerie silence hung in the air.

Judd saw clearly that seamen lined the gunwales of the Governor Ready, with hands held high in the air. It was the strangest thing he had ever seen. Huge fender beams were lowered over the side of the Vanguard to prevent the approaching ship from getting close enough for their crew to jump the divide.

Captain Fellows hailed from the quarterdeck. "Ahoy there," he said. "Have your captain present himself."

"No officers on board, sir," a voice replied.

"No officers? Who is in charge?" Fellows said.

"No officers. We only have senior crewmen. We need assistance," said the spokesman.

Captain Fellows ordered the rigging of a sling to bring the apparent spokesperson aboard the Vanguard. He instructed his marines to stay vigilant. He turned and strode away, informing the duty officer that he would receive the spokesperson in his dayroom.

While the man was being hoisted from the Governor Ready to the Vanguard, order slipped into chatter, seamen on the lower decks calling through gun ports to seaman on the Governor. Very quickly, news spread through the lower decks of the Vanguard and up onto the main deck, where marines were still at the ready with arms drawn. The word was that the officers of the Governor Ready were all experienced officers, and that the ship had been a slave trader until a few years ago. Captain Ian McKellar, a Scotsman, and his officers had ruled the ship's crew with ruthless dominance, with lashes commonplace and food abysmal. Pay and leave were almost unheard of. But no person claimed to know about the disappearance of the entire officer contingent.

When Captain Fellows spoke with the Governor Ready's quartermaster, the picture became no clearer. Every man in position above quartermaster and bosun had disappeared between sundown and sunup. There were no signs of hostility from the quartermaster, though he did suggest the Governor was better off without the officers.

"If this should be a mutiny, my man, the penalty is clear," said Captain Fellows. "What was the duty watch doing during the night?"

"Sir, there is no mutiny here. The watch was alight one as we were in port." said the quartermaster. "We have not taken control of the ship. If that was the case, sir, we would not have turned to Her Majesty's ship for aid. Four days ago, we left Easter Island, where we stopped for fresh water. It was to be our last port of call before heading for the Americas. The locals wanted to host a festival in our honor sir. The Captain allowed only the officers to attend the festivities ashore, for fear of desertion. When they returned, sir, we were told to raise the anchor and set a nor east course til morning. They were all quite drunk sir. They bedded down and about midnight that's when things started to get bad.

"The ship's surgeon was the first to go, sir. He came up to the quarterdeck during the morning watch. Three bells, sir. He stood on the rail and jumped overboard. By the time we organized a rescue crew and lowered the lifeboat, it was too late, so we furled sails and decided to wait 'til the morning light."

"The other officers, man. Where were they?"

"The duty officer, First Officer McClean, was dead on the chartroom floor. The bosun and I quickly searched and found every officer to be dead or at death's door. There was a strange stench about their bodies, and some were foaming through the mouth and nose. Between us, we suspected the black fellows on Easter Island had poisoned them. All but the captain was dead, and he was delirious. It took us, the bosun and myself, until seven bells to wrap and bury the bodies at sea. You will find this in the log, sir."

"Quartermaster, you are aware that it is not your place to record anything in the ship's log. By your own words, your captain was still alive, and he, being the senior officer, had that duty," said Captain Fellows.

"Sir, by this time, the captain had died, and we quickly buried him. We swore the helmsman and a few trustworthy seamen to secrecy to give us time to work out what to do next. Without a navigator, we decided to head for land. That's what we were doing when we sighted you on the horizon."

"Land, Mr. Quartermaster, was due east of you. To find us, you have been sailing sou sou east."

"That's my point, sir. We have no navigator," said the quartermaster. "I place the Governor Ready under your command, sir, as is the correct procedure in these unusual circumstances." The quartermaster took one pace backwards, stood erect and saluted the captain.

"Ex-Royal Navy, I presume," said the captain.

"Yes, sir. Ten years behind the mast. Paid off ten year ago."

The captain told the man to return to his ship. "Have your entire ship's complement muster on the main deck and await my instructions. Obtain your manifest, your ship's log, and your current charts from the chartroom. You are to maintain order at all costs. Do you require any marines to assist in this control?"

"I don't think I will need the marines, but it could be a wise move. Am I to tell the crew about our situation?" he asked.

"No. Tell the crew that they will be considered men in the Royal Navy, and will be treated as such pending the resolution of this situation. I am sending a party of marines and our surgeon, Doctor Miller, to inspect your ship and report back. If my inspection party finds any crewmen not in muster, I will treat that as disobedience and deal with it severely."

The quartermaster was returned to the Governor Ready, along with fifty marines and the Vanguard's surgeon. Then, Captain Fellows ordered all officers to the ward room. There, they discussed how the situation was to be handled.

Navigator Ben Tillet suggested they transfer Midshipman Judd Cane to the *Governor Ready* as its navigator as he is competent enough to get her back to England. The captain agreed and laid out the other transfers to be—First Lieutenant Walker to captain the Governor Ready and cook Lezza Trott to oversee the situation and cook for the transferred men. "What about the Governor Ready's own cook?" enquired the Captain.

"We are not sure where the poisoning came from so I don't want our men at risk. Trott is a good man. I will make it clear he is in charge," answered the navigator.

If it turned out the quartermaster and bosun were to be trusted they were to remain in those positions. Fifty marines, two sergeants-at-arms, five corporals, and three midshipmen were to assist in control and discipline.

The Governor Ready would return immediately to Portsmouth, England, and return to its owners. The Royal Navy sailors would then receive their reassignments at the Admiralty's will.

The captain dismissed the officers and summoned Midshipman Cane to the wardroom.

When Captain Fellows told him the news—the transfer, the promotion, the raise in pay—Judd stood in silence, not knowing what to say.

"Well, Cane, what say you?" asked Fellows.

"Aye aye, sir," said Judd, "and thank you for your belief in me. May I ask at this time which officers are going with me?"

"Cocky young sod you are, Cane. No, you may not ask." Turning to First Lieutenant Walker he asked, "Is there anyone in particular you wish to join you?"

"Yes, sir. Do you remember a few years back, the incident involving cabin boy Lyons? Billy Lyons, sir. It was your cabin boy, Dickey Lemon, who kept us informed of the below-deck rumblings. If he was to be the cabin boy it may well assist the flow of information, sir."

"Rough diamond, but a good lad. Take him, he's yours." Judd had to take control of himself, not to reveal his excitement at Dickey going with him.

"Damn poor show to lose him myself, but good deeds need to be rewarded. If that is your choice, then so be it," said the captain. He warned Judd not to tell anyone until the official transfer announcements were given.

Judd saluted the captain and left the wardroom in as casual a manner as he could muster. As the door closed behind him, he took off like a cannonball. As he ran past Dickey Lemon, he beckoned him to follow as he continued to the cable locker. Dickey soon joined him, eager to know all the scuttlebutt. Judd fired off the information without stopping to take a breath, and told Dickey to go collect their hidden notes and logs and stow them in his chest.

Dickey punched Judd in the shoulder and, with a hoarse, noisy whisper, said, "Yes, yes. This is it, Judd! I toll you fings would 'appen for us! I heard from one of the seamen across on the Governor that full-scale offensives are taking place in South Africa and the Boers, and Afrikaans are getting it on big time. The Vanguard will be stuck down there, and we're going 'ome."

After leaving Dickey, Judd took off for the chartroom. While collecting his journal and personal effects, he heard the bosun's shrill pipe whistling them all to stations. Running at top speed, he found his chest and stowed what he had collected, then went to his station beside the navigator on the quarterdeck.

The full HMS Vanguard crew gathered on the main deck. The four hundred marines lined up on one side, the regular seamen on the other. The captain ordered the men at ease and stood with hands firmly planted on the quarterdeck rail. He informed the crew that the Governor Ready had been cleared as safe. Soon, bodies were running to their quarters to prepare for the transfer.

Chapter 11

The Governor Ready's giant rope ties to the Vanguard broke like an umbilical cord, and the two ships gradually parted as the Atlantic Ocean currents wormed their way between them. The two crews waved and saluted each other. First Lieutenant Walker, now Captain Walker, ordered the quartermaster to muster the entire crew on the main deck, with the exception of the helmsman and Navigator Cane. He instructed Cane to plot a course North, for the Canary Islands and await further instructions.

He then directed his attention to the crew. His directive to the body of men was brief and to the point: "Gentlemen, I shall inspect your ship right away. Be warned that, at this time, the Governor Ready is under the command of Her Majesty's Royal Navy and will be run according to her rules. I will spend the rest of the afternoon watch learning how your ship functions, and I expect to receive your advice when I meet with you individually. I do not require salutes, standing to attention, or other military actions, but I do expect and give respect. You will all muster here at eight bells. Our cook will work with your cook to improve your rations, and it is my aim to run a happy and efficient ship."

***

Upon completion of his inspection, Captain Walker and his officers met in the captain's quarters to plan their trek. There had been little, if any, resistance to the takeover. If anything, the crew seemed subdued and hesitant to become involved. All they wanted was to be fed properly, not beaten or whipped, and to get back to England and away from the Governor Ready as soon as possible.

Judd sought out the bosun one evening when all was calm. In the early evening breeze, as the sun slowly sunk behind the horizon on the ships port bow, he struck up a conversation with the man. "So, bosun, you seem to have a strong, united crew beneath you. Why do you think that is?"

"Simple sir, we have been through a lot together. That makes a sailor's bond with his shipmates very strong." The man exuded a rough confident air about him as he spoke to the younger navigator. "Most of us have been on the Ready since her maiden voyage. She was a slave trader til about 1840. 'Twas about then the Americans turned to eliminating slavery altogether. The Ready's owners, or the captain, stopped their involvement in the trade and we never went back to England. We traded between America, Canada, and the new Australian colonies of South Australia and Western Australia - spices, silks, and the luxuries of the Orient."

Judd interrupted the bosun, "I don't understand. Didn't anybody ask what was going on? Wasn't the new plan explained to the crew?"

"No Sir, you didn't question the captain. He was on the violent side. Soon as throw a sick slave over the side as tend him. We knew that he had to rule us with an iron fist when we had slaves onboard, for our own safety. It just never changed. I guess we just accepted it."

Thinking out loud, Judd said, "The poisoning of the officers looked pretty much like a stroke of fortune for you all, if you don't mind me saying."

"spose you could say that. Circumstances saved us from doing something we had never given thought to. Mind you, it could have come to that," was the cautious reply.

The two men continued to question each other about their backgrounds long into the night. Judd bid the bosun a good evening and returned to the quarterdeck to resume his watch.

At eight bells in the morning watch, the captain summoned all crew to the poop deck where he stood them at ease. The sea was calm and there was little breeze. In a clear voice he started to speak. "I am hearing many stories about your recent experiences, all of them second hand. I would like to get an accurate picture of life aboard this ship up until the recent tragic deaths." There was an undercurrent of voices. Pointing to one man he said, "You. Name and rank! Talk to me."

The man spoke with a booming voice, "able seaman Crouch, Sir. We used to be slave traders. 'T is like we have all become slaves ourselves. Since we stopped slave trading fifteen crew members have jumped ship in various ports rather than submit themselves to further harsh treatment. Four of them were apprehended in their attempts. Two were flogged at sea and died of the injuries inflicted, and the other two, we were told, had escaped from the brig and disappeared at sea."

The comments opened a pandora's box of sailors willing to tell stories of their life under Captain McKellar. Captain Walker believed that these actions had resulted in fear and a mistrust of authority. They had also created a compliant crew. He knew from experience that forced compliancy was one step away from rebellion or mutiny. After much thought he felt the need to show these men some act of faith as this was not a Naval ship so much as a private ship.

He decided that to appoint temporary officer status to the crew members who appeared to be leaders. They would create enough watch divisions to run the ship efficiently. The marines would then be divided into seven groups, one group for each watch, each group watching for any signs of discontent.

***

The captain instructed Judd to meet with him in his cabin. As the men settled down across from each other, Judd broke the silence. "Most of the crew appeared to be good men, sir. What do you think about continuing with the ship's planned course? Disposing of the cargo in America would allow us to be sure the men get paid what is their due."

The captain stared at Judd without speaking for a moment. He smiled, and said, "You have the soul and heart of a good man Cane. It is not my place to change orders of The Admiralty."

Judd interrupted, "Sir, our orders are not from the Admiralty, they are from Captain Fellows. Now that you command the Governor Ready, is it not for you to decide what is best for her?"

"Best for the ship or best for the men?" was the response.

"Isn't one the same as the other sir?"

"Cane, you are playing word games with me, but I do understand where you are coming from. Let me think about it. I guess that a little kindness, tempered with profit never hurt anyone, particularly if all are to profit."

Judd stood to leave the captain's cabin as the captain spoke, "We will stop at Tenerife in the Canary Islands for supplies. In the meantime, consider your course for the coast of Gran Canaria."

"Yes, sir, thank you sir." Judd saluted and departed.

***

Under the guidance of its new navigator, the Governor Ready continued to sail north as the sun slowly set on the port side. The course having been set. Judd started to organize his new chartroom. It was the rich mahogany that decorated the room and the day bed, far better than anything he had slept in over the last three year that made him decide that it would also be his cabin. Organizing the room in the fashion taught him by Ben Tillet, everything had to be in its place. The chart table, desk, and the chair were of fine quality. He recalled his father would often use the phrase 'fit for a captain'. It now meant something to him. This chartroom had a warmth and comfort that was lacking in its naval equivalent. He found a myriad of documents that had no place being in a chartroom. The records of cargo and victual receipts and all manner of paperwork belonged in the care of a purser. These documents, Judd bundled and tucked into a locker. One document looked like an ancient map of an island. On it were listed previous owners, with the last name being Captain McKellar. Attached was what looked like a legal document. Judd had seen maps of the islands in the River Thames and could see that this island was rather large. The document was obviously important as it had a number of embossed seals and was on high quality parchment. Something urged Judd to put it away safely, so that he may try to understand it more clearly later.

Leaning back in his chair he pondered what had just transpired with the captain.

It was evident the captain was considering selling the cargo. This meant he was open to less than scrupulous activities. With his hands behind his head, he looked up at the burnished, smokestained ships woodwork and silently congratulated himself on where his life was going. In a rash moment a thought entered his head and left it just as quickly: 'Why steal the cargo when you could steal the whole bloody ship!' He suddenly sat bolt upright, shocked at his thought. He smiled as he turned his attention to the huge chart of the Atlantic Ocean and his current course.

***

Three days later the Canary Islands came into view on the ships starboard side. Crewmen gathered on the ships rail to observe the approaching islands. There was talk of shore leave and what might or might not happen. The crew's spirits were high. While Judd was giving the helmsman directions for the approach to the largest of the islands, Grand Canaria, the Captain signaled for him to approach.

"Mr. Cane, while I am still of the mind, we shall be in port just as long as it takes to take on provisions and water. No longer than the morrow. I want us underway on the first morning tide, north by north east, or thereabouts."

"Thereabouts, it will be sir."

"Do not share our plans until I say it shall be so."

As the Governor Ready entered the shelter of Tenerife Harbor Judd saw a large merchantman tied up alongside the quay. His musings about what he saw was interrupted by Captain Walker.

"As soon as we go alongside, I shall pay a visit to the merchantman and see what information they may have that may or may not be of use to us."

"Should I come to see if they have any more recent charts than what we found on the Ready sir?"

"Capital, capital. Let's make this trip a short one, shall we."

The visit turned out to be quite fortuitous. It appeared that the merchantman had stopped in at Gibraltar and had been given some mailbags destined for the HMS Vanguard. The harbormaster believed that the merchantman would eventually connect with the naval ship.

After the situation had been explained, the sack was opened and mail destined for some of the marines, Leeza Trott, and Judd taken out. The nautical charts were the same as the Governor Ready had and after a brief social visit the two men returned to the Governor.

The recipients of mail were surprised and happy to receive their unexpected news. Dickey pestered Judd to read his letter to him as he did not get one. The reaction to the letter was somewhat indifferent, which surprised Judd. Judd's envelope contained a letter from his mother and one from Mary. Mother's news detailed all the work his father had done on the cottage at the manor. Its' content brought to mind that his mother had never told him that they had been evicted but, his assumption had been correct. Mary's comments were full of village gossip and a multitude of questions for him. While he was putting the letters back into the envelope, he noticed a fragrant smell. Careful examination told him that Mary's letter had been sprayed with a floral odor. He didn't know what it was but he liked it.

The balance of the day was spent with readying the ship for the trans-Atlantic journey. Dawn's first light saw sailors straggling back to the ship after a night of carousing. A quick roll call set the tone for the ship to ready itself for departure.

Hawsers left the dockside and splashed into the water as sails were set. Soon the Governor Ready was heading out of the harbor. Even in the early morning the sun beat down on Judd's neck as he stood on the quarterdeck issuing course instructions. Clearing the harbor entrance, the order was given, "East no'r east, 280 degrees and hold her steady."

"Aye aye sir, East no'r east, 280 it is sir."

***

It would take a fortnight for the Governor Ready to reach the easternmost tip of Brazil, where the course would be changed to north by northeast, heading toward America. During those eight days, shipboard life was calm. The general feeling of Captain Walker and his officers was that the seamen on the Governor were good, hardworking sailors, all of whom had chosen life at sea. They painted a picture of a tyrant captain and officers who ran amok and ruled by fear.

Unexpectedly on the fourth day at sea, as the ship was in the middle of the Atlantic Ocean, a southwesterly storm from Antarctica hit the boat with ferocious strength. Without warning, the full sails pushed the ship along at breakneck speed, the gale swinging from west-northwest to a full westerly, in a few moments making the sails sag empty and flap with great strength. The ship rolled precariously to its port side.

The riggers worked as a team to tighten the slack halyard only to have the wind revert back to its original direction, forcing them to set the sails again. This went on for over eight hours, and the crew stayed at their posts without changing watch. As the wind finally subsided to a steady, manageable strength, there was a joyous revelry among the men at having stood steadfast to overcome nature's fury without a damaged sail or a lost man. Walking among the men the captain could see how these men, totally exhausted, were determined to carry out their duty. The captain ordered the main brace be sliced for every man jack of the crew. He stopped to chat with the crew members that had suffered rope burns from flailing lines, and cuts and bruises dished out by the weather. One older seaman had a large gash on his shin where the force of the storm had pushed him under the edge of the capstan. The captain had to order the dismantling of the capstan head, to free the man's leg, before anyone would do it. It appeared that the crew were not used to these types of considerations, as they profusely thanked him.

One of the younger crewmen approached the captain, and a marine quickly stepped up to protect him, but the captain signaled for him to stand down. "Under Royal Navy regulations, sailor," said Captain Walker to the crewman, "you do not approach an officer without being called. If you wish to address me in the future, you go to your able seaman or leading seaman."

"Humble apologies, sir, Captain, sir," said the young boy. "It's just that we ain't never been respected like that. We know 'ow to sail this 'ere ship, and we was once proud an''appy men, an' you is givin' us that back. We is behind you, sir, one unerd percent." The boy smiled broadly, attempted a salute, and turned and ran away.

The captain turned to Judd Cane and said, "Like we need his approval. He's behind us because we say so, but it gives a man a great feeling of strength and courage to hear it said out loud. Cane, if men say they will follow you, you have one of life's unique gifts. It is our responsibility to use it well."

Judd smiled inwardly as he recognized that the young seaman was, in a round-about way, boasting of the crew's skills, but the Captain only saw his own authority. Without realizing it, the captain was starting to give away more about his person than he was aware of.

The wind calmed down to a steady twenty knots. The ship sailed into the night and all was well. As the Governor settled down, Judd calculated that they should see North America in about ten days. He knew from his charts that, in five to six days, they should see the islands of the Caribbean. He wondered how different these would be from those around Madagascar and around the tip of India, and the many other islands he had visited in the Malaysian and Indonesian seas. The tales he had heard from the marines and sailors aboard the Vanguard had seemed heavily influenced by the state of drunkenness and revelry of the storytellers while visiting these places. To a great extent, Judd had enjoyed the islands he'd visited, but they had not lived up to their what he had been told. He'd found many of the native people to be dirty, smelly, and untrustworthy. Although many lived in apparent poverty, Judd's only reference was his hometown, and even the poorest of people in Essex washed. It was perplexing to him.

The day-to-day calmness aboard ship allowed Judd to ponder his future. He was not required to keep a duty watch, as he was the only navigator, and he had to be on call when needed to check their bearings and correct any off-course wanderings. His mind wandered back to Mucking, and the letters he had received. There would not be any more for a while due to the unexpected turn of events. His mother's letters made him emotional for where he wasn't, but his pa's pride in what he was doing was evident, and made him happy. He suddenly realized that today was his birthday. So much had happened to him. Thoughts flashed through his mind. 'Would ma and pa be thinking of me today. Where would he be? What would he be doing? Maybe working on the Earl's estate with pa…what if… Her news would flood him with warm memories of his boyhood. There was news that his old friend David Blacksmith had married Jane Carter, Jim's sister, last year in the warm and prosperous times of harvest.

Jim the carter's lad—what a friend. Just how sweet the memories of their escapades together were. It was hard for Judd to fully to grasp that the flaming red-haired little sister who used to beg to go along with him and Jim was getting married.

Judd lay in the dim light thrown out by his cabin lantern, which he watched as it swung slowly to port, suspending still for a brief second before swinging to starboard. The huge ship's timbers creaked and groaned in unison with the lantern's sway. There was a different groan for each direction, and another sound for the pitch. It was as if the ship had a personality of its own. Even the smells were different from those of the HMS Vanguard. The Vanguard had a masculine, strong, defiant military odor. The Governor Ready had more mysterious, lingering odors of spices, rum, coconut, hemp, and other cargo, all neatly tied together with the sea's salty tang. This, the Governor Ready's signature, would be forever planted in Judd's brain. This unexpected turn in his life's road had come so unplanned and yet was turning out for the better. He knew that those around him, the helmsman, the crew and even Captain Walker, saw him as the job he was doing, not as the boy that he sometimes felt himself to be. He felt that the act of giving orders to the helmsmen, men much older than he, was why he was becoming more and more sure of himself. It amused him how the captain would periodically ask him, in a paternalistic tone, "How are you handling everything young man?" Then the man would switch to his officer voice as if he was uncomfortable letting his guard down.

***

As the days passed and the ship sailed on, Judd, in a quiet moment decided to pull out the ancient map he had tucked away and try to understand it. To his surprise, he could see from the coordinates that the island was St. Eustatius, part of a group of islands that included some English, some French, and some Dutch, and was near his current course. He would be passing right by it. Closer study of the map indicated it was an addendum to the legal document, which he studied so intently the ambient sounds of creaking timber, the wind whistling through the rigging and distant voices disappeared. It was a contract for the sale of a plantation on St. Eustatius, as well as the property deeds. It appeared that the dead captain of the Governor General had purchased the plantation from a Colonel Jemson of the British Army. The sum paid made no impression on Judd, as he had nothing against which to reference it, but he did know that the Earl of Essex, on whose estate his father frequently worked, was said to have interests in a plantation in the West Indies and the South Pacific, and he was very wealthy. The contract was a simple document with few clauses, but two struck Judd. First, the plantation was sold as it stands, with all servants, slaves, structures, furniture and equipment, and the second was that the contract could not be cancelled.

There were official stamps and a seal on the contract, the deed, and the map. A second look at the map showed the location of the plantation being close to Gallows Bay on the southwest coast. It was quite near the capital, Oranjestad. One question stood out. Now that Captain McKellar was dead, who owned the plantation? He had to find out more. He knew from his father that owning land was something very important. Rich and powerful people owned land. His family never had owned any. If the Captain was dead and had owned the land for a while there was a great chance nobody knew that he owned the land. While sitting quietly, thinking about the document in his hand, the ship gave a bigger then usual roll to the port side. Slapping his hand on the chart table to prevent it's contents sliding off, he missed one item. A letter from his mother dropped to the deck. Picking up the letter he noticed something that had slipped his attention before, an embossed seal on the back of the envelope. The seal contained the coat of arms of The Earl of Essex. It was this that made Judd read the return address, written in his mother's hand.

'Caretaker's Cottage. Earl of Essex Estate, Stanford LeHope. Essex.' It was then he fully understood, that his parents had indeed been thrown out of their family home. He wondered if there was something he could do about it. He became angry at what had been done to his parents and his thoughts turned back to the deed in his hand.

"Damn it, I am going to own this piece of land," he said to himself almost aloud. Putting the land deed back in its hiding place, he resumed his duties. Judd left the chartroom perfunctorily, stopping to check the ship's bearing and leave his navigation instructions with the helmsman. He then set off to find Dickey to discuss his thoughts.

Two decks below the main deck, he found Dickey playing cards with three marines and two deckhands. He stood quietly, watching the raucous play and the way the players distracted each other while trying to keep their own cards hidden. He could clearly see that they weren't really fooling each other. It was the ritual of camaraderie that had evolved. A marine won the hand, and as nobody made a move to pick up the cards and shuffle them, Judd saw his opportunity. "Have any of you men been to St. Eustatius?" he asked, holding his breath.

"The Governor Ready should make that 'er home port," said the more boisterous of the two deckhands. "For the past four years, we been tradin' atween Africa and St. Eustatius. We calls it Statius. In the ol' days, we'd sell the slaves there, pick up cargo, and head to Australia. Then, as like, we go up to India, back to Africa to sell wot we got in India and pick up more slaves, and back to Statius."

The quieter deckhand said, "Statius used to be a big plantation then, but, things changed to trading. I swear, sometimes it was busier than the East India Docks in London. We sometimes 'ad to wait to git 'longside 'til someone left."

"What happened to the plantations?' asked Judd.

"Well, most of 'em just wivered away. But then there's Gallows Bay Plantation, only now it's just called the Plantation. They turned the big ol' sugar sheds into ware'ouses an' storage places and fings like that. Nearly all the fings wot goes into Statius pass through the Plantation. Lots of ships stop there"

"Who owns the Plantation?" asked Judd.

"That," said the raucous deckhand, "ain't nobody knows. "There be a foreman. He got a few slaves, although no one admits they is slaves. Then there's a few white folks. I think they's lowlanders. Some say Welford and Company owns it. I ain't so sure. We ain't bin back to England in over four years and I, or no one else for that matter, has heard or seen any of the company's representatives. It's a-like, since we stopped tradin' in slaves, Welford doan own us no more."

Silence dropped over the small group, and Judd could see the thoughts running through the crewmen's minds. He told Dickey that Captain Walker wanted him topside on the quarterdeck. Dickey followed him up the gangway. Once on the main deck, Dickey said, "All right, Judd. Wot's yer up to now? All these bloody questions. You doan know nuffin about no bleedin' useless Statias."

"St. Eustatius," said Judd. "We need to stop for water and fresh fruits, and I wanted to take a look. I thought you wanted to help me choose where we stop." Judd was thinking on his feet. He didn't want to reveal to Dickey what he was thinking until he had worked out what to do. As his pa said, 'keep your cards close to your chest.'

"Fort you said we was stopping at Euslasias," Dickey said.

"St Eustasias," corrected Judd. "Just come with me. I want to show you something."

They went to the chartroom, where Judd removed a chart of islands between the northeast coast of South America and Puerto Rico. Judd knew the Captain would leave the decision to him to choose where to stop, and something told him that the last place he should have the Governor Ready stop, was where it might be known. Somebody may ask questions about Captain McKellar. He realized he was being less frank with Dickey than he felt he should be. The choice was made to stop at Barbados because it would buy time for him to devise a plan. He decided to tell Dickey of his idea for the Governor Ready.

As Dickey turned to leave, Judd cleared his throat. Dickey stopped and turned, inquisitively. Judd signaled for Dickey to sit.

"Dickey, you once told me you didn't want to spend your whole life in the Royal Navy. Over the last ten days or so, I've been paying careful attention to what's going on around me. I'm not sure if I can trust anyone. I've stopped recording anything in my journal."

"You sure as anyfing can truss me. Why you stop doin yer journal?" said Dickey.

"If you just shut up and listen you will find out," snapped Judd. "What I'm about to tell you can't be told to anyone—not your marine friends, not your deckhand friends. No one."

"You got me nervous, Judd."

"If you tell anyone, we could get flogged, or worse, and I'm serious." Judd took a deep breath and looked Dickey in the eye. "This ship is owned by a company that has not been in touch with it in over four years. The entire crew of this ship are capable of sailing her without officers, and they did, even though they were going the wrong way. This ship is full of valuable cargo, and it's a young, tested, seaworthy craft. This ship is named the Governor Ready—but, with a clever bit of carving by the carpenter, it could become the Governor Read, or something else. I think I have a plan."

Dickey Lemon's face broke into a grin. He jumped up, slapped Judd on the back three times and said, "Judd, you is bloody marvelous! We gonna steal the ship! How the 'ell are we gonna pull this off?"

"I'm not really sure yet, but here's what we need to know: Has the Governor Ready ever been to Barbados? Does Welford and Company have an agent in Barbaodos? Let's start with these two things. Put the word out below decks that the captain is thinking of stopping in Barbados. Don't write anything down. Oh, I forgot—you can't write, you little twit." They laughed.

"You got it, Judd," said Dickey. "I knew you an' me was goin' be somefin one day."

Looking Dickey straight in the eye Judd said, "Dickey, we are in this together. It is serious and probably dangerous. I am trusting you. When you ask questions of the sailors, as soon as one asks you a question, you change the subject. Got it?"

***

Sleep would not come to Judd that night. He had put something into motion, but he knew deep down that he didn't even have much of a plan. He reviewed the map and the contract again. The contract, which was indeed in the name of Captain McKellar, had been executed four years earlier, so it was safe to assume that whoever was running Gallows Bay Plantation could continue to do so unaffected by his death. He reasoned that, at this point, Gallows Bay was one issue that he would keep to himself. As for the Governor Ready, a plan was taking shape in his head.

Chapter 12

As the night passed, many thoughts were going through his head. What was wrong with Naval life? Would the crew go along with his idea? Just how would owning a ship improve his life? Why should he bother to take risks to get a ship? For each question he found an answer. Life on board the Governor Ready was more relaxed and less rigid. The sailors appeared to be less confrontational and better paid. He reasoned to himself that if he offered them a better deal than the one they had before they would follow him. As for how owning a ship would improve his life, he decided to talk to Lezza about this point. He believed there were benefits, but wasn't quite sure of what they were. The issue of risk didn't bother him. He rationalized it by virtue of how well he had survived being press ganged and if he not only survived that, but made great strides forward, then it was worth it. He promised himself that everyman who followed would be well rewarded and treated with respect.

An idea slowly revealed itself to Judd. There was a simple way to take over the ship without any bloodshed. If he could convince Captain Walker to order the ship into a port never used by the Governor Ready, he could reduce the risk of being discovered. His concern moved to thinking about who he would involve in his ambitious plot.

What about Lezza Trott? Was he to involve Lezza, who had befriended him on HMS Vanguard and protected and advised him from the start, and risk everything? Early the next morning, after carefully checking the ships course and bearings, Judd headed off to the galley. Leeza was leaning against the big butcher block with a mug of steaming tea in his fist as was usual "Bit early for breakfast, aint you young man?"

Judd took the mug from Leez'a hand and took a mouthful of the hot tea. "Leeza, tell me something. Do you see much difference here on the Governor Ready from the Vanguard?"

"Oh, sure I do. Ain't the assle. There don't seem to be the bovver among the men. Foods good. Still, I gotta say that, don't I? Why do you ask?"

"If you could choose between the Royal Navy and the merchantmen, which life at sea would you rather?"

"I 'spose I could do more by my family cause they get much better pay 'ere an' they git's bounty. But ain't no choice for me cause I signed up fer the Navy, so mighter make the bess of it. What's chewin your pants boy?"

"Nothing, thanks Lezza, I was just curiuos that's all," Judd responded over his shoulder.

Leeza put his mug down and put his arm around Judd's shoulder and in a quiet voice he said, "I's bin aroun a long time. You is up to somefing an you int quite sure about it. Talk to me."

"If I did something really wrong, and really big, would you support me?"

"Depens ow big an ow bad. Wot is it? I spose as long it doan git us killed. Sure I'd support you."

"Then just trust me for now and very soon I will explain everything as soon as I have it clearly worked out." With that Judd turned and left the galley.

***

During the morning watch the next day, Judd convinced the captain to stop for water and fresh provisions at Barbados, an English colony from which they were less than one day away. They would stop at the main port of Bridgetown.

Land was sighted the following afternoon, as the morning watch was changing. The stiff breeze had aired out the lower decks, the crew had taken care of their laundry, and the ship was spic and span. Every hand not working crowded around the ship's side to view the approaching island. By now, word had gone around that they would be heaving to in Bridgetown's harbor before sunset.

Captain Walker had the bosun call the men to "fall in," and they gathered around the base of the quarterdeck. As the captain stood there, looking down on the crew with the sails full, he felt an orderly air and a sense of peace.

After announcing shore leave for all, a tumultuous roar emerged from below. When the crew calmed down, he explained that every crewman, marine, and person aboard would get a twentyfour hour pass. "The existing crew will take the first leave and the marines and Vanguard crew will take the second leave. Go ashore," he said. "Take care of your urges to drink and whatever you desire. But if one of you step aboard this ship in a drunken state, all further leave passes will be cancelled and no man will go ashore from that point on. There will be military consequences for any infractions."

Dickey Lemon went to the chartroom and found Judd standing over a chart. Judd put his hands on his head and ran them down over his eyes, holding them over his face. Then, looking Dickey straight in the eye, he said, "It's just about to start. We need to be very careful. You and I cannot go ashore. From the moment we fire the signal pot, I'll watch the shoreline, and you stay close to the carpenter."

"'Ave you decided what to do about Lezza Trott? Are you gonna tell me how we's doin it?" asked Dickey.

"I am going to get together with him right before he goes ashore. I think I can offer him an honorable direction that will not affect his Naval career. Just trust me, if my plan works nobody is going to get hurt and we will be on our way to being rich."

"Good enuff for me," said Dickey with a wide grin.

***

On the fateful morning the Bridgetown harbormaster and local surgeon inspected the ship and gave the health clearance. Judd kept a low profile as Captain Walker set about organizing fresh water and supplies.

The captain summoned Judd and instructed him, "Go ashore with the harbormaster and obtain the most up-to-date charts you can." Just before leaving Judd quickly told Dickey Lemon what was happening and to and keep a low profile. This turned out to be a fortuitous move, as Judd had not considered the implications of the suspect charts in the ship's possession. This was an opportunity to get the most recent, accurate ones available.

Judd ignored the sights and sounds, and the enticing smells of the food on the streets. He was panicked about what might go wrong while he was away. As the returning harbormasters boat approached the Governor Ready, bile rose in his throat. It appeared that everyone on the ship was on the main deck, just milling around.

Passing his many new charts up to the deck, he climbed the ladder and, as he saw the crew already stowing fresh water to the hold, let out a noticeable sigh of relief.

"Is it really that bad ashore, Mr. Cane?" The captain's comment surprised Judd.

"No, sir. It's just that—just that I had not considered how incorrect the old charts might have been." He sighed a breath of relief as the captain said, "The day you think you can't make a mistake, could be your last day."

"Also, sir, the Governor sends his compliments and requests the pleasure of your company, along with the senior officers, at his residence for a gala celebration. Unfortunately, his invitation is for the night we planned leave."

"No need to be concerned. Leave that decision to me." The captain turned to walk away. Judd could not see his face. "We shall accept the invitation, you, our three midshipmen, and myself." I shall take the marines with me as a guard of honour to show our respects to the Governor.

Judd wondered where was Dickey? Had something been noticed?

Judd collected the charts off the deck and went to the chartroom. Dickey Lemon sat at the chart table, a big grin on his face. He had decided the best way to keep out of trouble was to keep out of everything, and this he had done by hiding away in the chartroom when not performing his daily duties.

At eight bells in the afternoon watch, the lifeboats were lowered, and the first wave of shore-leave sailors left. Excitement was evident in the raucous jocularity emanating across the still waters of the harbor. It took five runs of all the lifeboats to get the entire original crew ashore.

The next day was spent finishing resupplying the ship. Lockers were cleaned and decks swabbed. The cargo was checked for condition and stowage safety. Stories of the last shore leave were told, and the entire ship was calm. Many of the shore-leave sailors fell asleep in the boats that brought them back. Some looked the worse for wear. One boat had two women that members of the crew were trying unsuccessfully to smuggle aboard. Many of the seamen had objects purchased from local traders, like tropical fruit, bottles of rum, and bolts of brilliant cloth. There was a celebratory air. The pending return home was on everyone's mind.

The morning of the third day passed quietly until eight bells, at which time the final shore-leave crew assembled on the main deck. The marines were rigged out in full dress uniform and the transferred officers fully attired in their ceremonial uniforms, prepared for dinner with the Colonial Governor. Dickey Lemon hid below deck, hoping that his absence would go unnoticed. As the last man climbed into the lifeboat for the journey to shore Judd approached the captain.

"Captain Walker sir, I have a few, last minute details to take care of in the chartroom. If it is alright with you sir, Trott and myself will come in the next lifeboat." Judd had earlier spoken with Lezza Trott, requesting that he go ashore on the last lifeboat with him.

The captain offered a mock salute and said, "s you wish Mr. Cane."

As the last crew left the ships side for their leave, Judd called the crew to the ships' quarterdeck. It seemed to Judd as if everything had happened at an accelerated speed.

"I have a plan to share with you all. You will notice that the only people on board at this time are you, the original crew of the Governor Ready, Leeza Trott, Dickey Lemon and myself. We can set sail under the dark of night, tonight, and proceed to the nearest port and sell our cargo. We then sail off and, while at sea, change the name of the ship. We can return to Southampton at high speed, at which time you will all be able to leave, should you desire. If our trip has been a success, we can then become our own masters of our future and repeat the exercise. You will all share in the profits of the trip." Judd watched the crew break into chatter. He waited for a voice.

One seaman called out, "What if some of us don't want to do this. What will you do to us?"

"As soon as we pull up anchor here you will be allowed to leave us in a ship's lifeboat. There will be one set of oars and you will be set adrift at the head of the bay to allow the tide to take you back into port. There will be no hard feelings from the rest of the crew."

Another shouted, "How do we know we can trust you?"

"I am but one man, with Dickey Lemon and Leeza. You are many. I want to make a better life for myself, and any who want are free to join me."

"Won't they come after us?" shouted another.

"They will have to find us first. We will move quickly. Take one half an hour to decide your own wishes, after that we move. Men! I am proud of you all and have no doubt that we will make a solid crew."

While the crew broke into small groups, discussing the plan, Judd was witnessing the earnest concern, but there appeared to be no hostility. Judd approached the stunned Lezza. "Leeza I have the greatest respect for you and will understand if you do not want to be part of this. We can lock you in the brig during our departure, and then set you free in England. When we leave England could report that you had been drugged and held hostage. When you came round you found yourself in a local park with no idea what day it was or where you had been. We will pay you your share of the profits, and you can return to the Royal Navy with an untarnished record, or, if you preferred, you can join us in new adventures."

"Young Judd Cane, I now know why you were asking the questions you did yesterday. Got balls, you have. I aint gonna make a decision about something this big just like that. Hows about you ask everyone to go along with your plan for now, then, one day before we land you give any man that wants the opportunity to go ashore as a hostage or rejoin. Same wot you gives me."

"Your idea is smarter than mine," said Judd. Calling for attention to the crew Judd laid out the suggested offer that Leeza had formulated. Every man chose to go along with the new plan—including Lezza.

For the next hour, all boats were turned away from the ship. Through his spyglass, Judd could see the officers arriving at the governor's brightly lit mansion on a bluff overlooking the bay. The crew bustled about, preparing to sail, and the secretive mood was eerie. Once the tide swung the ship around on its anchor hawser, the rising anchor would not be visible from land. Judd's order was whispered nervously from one crewman to the next: to hold still until the final order was given.

As Judd saw the tall wooden doors close at the governor's residence closing the night in on the festivities, the word went out. The anchor broke through the calm bay waters, under the exerted muscle-power of twice the normal amount of crew. The capstan had been greased for quietness. The dark silhouette of the Governor Ready drifted out of the harbor.

Upon reaching the open sea, sails were hoisted, fully rigged amid cheers of excitement from the crew of the Governor Ready, making their voyage into oblivion. The voice the crow's nest watchman, rang out in the night air, his joyous lilt amplified by the silent night air. "Land aft side an disappearin fast."

Judd smiled to himself as he closed the chart room door.

Chapter 13

In the warm Caribbean sun and gentle breeze, the Governor Ready-made course for Martinique. There was a knock, on Judd's cabin door, Leeza entered and sat opposite him.

Leeza broke the silence, speaking in a clear determined tone, "I know wot you just, we just, pulled off, but, I gotta say my piece."

"I hope you will always feel able to talk your mind with me."

"Fine! I doan know ow you got everyone to go along wiv you an' I do know you aint quite big enuff to control this lot for long. They is seasoned men and sure gonna be one or more of them will see the opportunity to turn on you."

"What do you mean?" asked Judd is a bewildered tone.

"See, you didn't fink that far ahead. I 'ear fings below deck, an, I've seen mutinies go down. Look at you. You is only, wot, nineteen, tweny maybe and you aint very big. If'n you want me to stay wiv you, I got me own terms." The man sat and watched Judd as he was processing what had been said. "Yer' as a plan on ow to divide up the profits, an I spose you gits the biggest share. There aint nuffin wrong wiv that, but I sees it a bit different. Ifn yer takes your share and my share, puts em togever and we splits them even, we is even partners." Leeza leaned back in his chair and crossed his arms over his large belly and studied Judd's face. "Yer doan afta decide now, but yer better do it quick. As soon as I put word out that anyone that bovers wiv you as gotta go froe me, I fink we can relax a bit better."

Judd's shoulders gave away his position on the proposal.

"You is shit scared down inside, aint yer?" Lezza asked.

"Mr. Trott, you sly old dog, I'm not shit scared, but I am very nervous about what might happen. I am happy to go along with your deal but I want it kept between us. I don't want any jealousy or grievances to be caused by it. Do you want a contract or something?"

"Doan need no contract. You is a man of your word, young Judd. 'Ere's wot I bin finking. Yer can't truss everyone, so some fings you have to keep close to yer own ches'. We should sell the cargo in Martinique. Tell the men they will be paid off in full and signed off their contracts wiv The Governor Ready. Those wot want, can re-sign on, but not on the Governor Ready. You 'aves the new sign on log ready wivout no name of the ship. When we sails away, we changes the ship's name and there aint nobody ashore wot will know what the new name is. Then we just puts the new name atop the sign on log."

"I can see you are going to be a really good partner." Judd said with a smile.

"Yes, well that may be the case, but, wot you an me discuss is only atween us. An' I mean you doan tell no one, not even Dickey. E's a good un but if we is to be partners, an we stand back to back, there aint no one can git us from behind, if yer knows wot I mean."

Judd spoke, "I agree. You have raised some good points that I hadn't thought about."

"That's wot partners do for each other." Leeza interjected.

"Sure, but, the thing that is on my mind is what to do about the crew we left behind in Bridgetown. Is there a way we can tell someone without causing ourselves any harm, and, maybe look good should we need it?"

"Just before we leave, I could go ashore and send a telegraph to the Admiralty wivout my name on it telling them."

"Oh. Captain Fellows has probably already sent one." Judd said.

"All the more reason to git in and out of Martinique quickly. I fink we should leave Martinique wivout any cargo. That will speed us up. We can stop somewhere else for a new cargo under the new name."

With the new partnership in place The Governor Ready sailed into Martinique and went about her business. Leeza was the first ashore and he told Judd that the telegraph was sent without any questions being asked. He had, in fact asked about any news the telegraph office had seen that might be of interest from around the world. His question was met with a disinterested "nothing much happens around here."

The decision was quickly made to sieze the opportunity and purchase a new cargo. This was done with much haste, through the port's ship chandlers. Most of the crew members had expressed a wish to remain, and the others had been paid off handsomely.

Later that afternoon The Governor Ready rode low in the water, full of cargo as she caught the tide and headed north.

***

The first of the next two days of sailing northwest, the ship's carpenter and his assistants were lowered over the bow and stern, where they removed the great carvings bearing the ship's name. They carefully separated each letter and endeavored to reassemble them until they came up with a new name. The carpenter suggested "GIDEON ROVER," but they did not have an 'I'. Dickey Lemon, not being able to read, asked Judd what an 'I' looks like. Judd drew it with a wet finger on the warm deck, and Dickey, without hesitation, suggested removing the bulbous front and leg from the letter 'R' so it could be made it into 'I'. At that, the Gideon Rover was born.

Judd held many meetings with the crew. When the weather permitted, they would gather under the billowing sails on the main deck. One such meeting was to be the turning point for most of the seamen. Judd had their attention as he explained his plan. "The whole exercise of being at sea, to is earn a good living. You have to forget what has been done to you in the past. To this point our coffers are well lined with cash."

A voice came out of the crowd. "Wot's appenin to the money we got for the cargo?"

"Some of the proceeds from the last cargo have been spent on our new, and more valuable cargo. There will be a cash payout of about two hundred pounds per man, depending on your position on board, when we set into the English Channel." The crew broke into a tumultuous bout of cheering and shouting. Holding his arms high above his head, Judd shouted, "But boys, you have earned more than that." Judd stopped and let the excitement die down. The cargo we carry will be turned over to a chandler for sale. The proceeds would be cashed. A portion of the money will be used to purchase a new cargo for us to take to the orient. Then the crew will receive their due, on board the Gideon Rover two weeks after docking."

Judd went on to make it clear that they were pirates—in fact, worse, as they had stolen a ship—so secrecy was paramount. "Any man that wants to sail again, the terms of payment will be set prior to leaving. I am sure you will all fare better under my command." Pausing for breath Judd made the offer that he had promised in the harbor of Martinique. "We are close to docking in Southampton. As promised, those of you who do not wish to continue will be set ashore on one of the Channel Islands with your pay. The money due to you for the sale of our cargo will be sent your families. We trust that your silence will be kept, and, you will be welcome to rejoin the crew at any time. Those of you who wish to accept this offer should come to my cabin in the forenoon watch today."

During the afternoon watch four crewmen came to the captain's cabin. They came as a group. Their common concern was where they stood legally. Judge pointed out that, to the letter, they were outside the law. This is why they would be doing a very fast turnaround and leaving port. He felt the only risk is what the Royal Navy Officers, that they left in Barbados could do. Or had done. "We will have a good idea where we stand within hours of docking in Southampton." He said, "I have a good feeling that we shall be safe this time, but from here on I don't know what the future holds."

The men agreed to bide their time and give Judd their final decision in Southampton. As they left the cabin a large fist caught the door from closing. It was Leeza Trott. The man entered the cabin and sat across from Judd. Wiping the sweat from his brow he said, "Young Judd Cane, who would have known. What are you now going on twenty?"

"Just about," Judd replied.

"I like you Judd, you know that. I am sort of proud of how you have handled yourself. I'm just not sure about what is going to happen. I got me own kids you know."

"Yes, I know Lezza. You have been a good friend to me. I was a soft little snot that was scared of nothing and terrified of everything, and you, stood by and supported me. That's why we are partners. I would like for you to continue to be part of my life, but that's a decision for you to make. Is there something you want me to do?"

"You can convince my wife, that the damn fool thing I am about to do, is ok by her."

"I am going home to Mucking and if you want me to, I will stop on my way back and visit you and your wife. Give me a week."

Leeza stood up and approached Judd. He put his arms around Judd's shoulders and spoke quietly to him, "The next few days are going to be very scary. If we survive them, nothing can stop us." With that said he turned and left.

***

Docking in Southampton, the Gideon Rover met with no untoward conflict. They were berthed at the quay of Duggan Ship Chandlers. Judd went ashore as most of the crew hurriedly melted into the chaos, leaving for their homes with full pockets of cash, and to many, full of hope. Upon entering the offices Judd was met by a tall statuesque lady.

"Madge Duggan at your service. How may I help you?"

"Cane, maam, Judd Cane of the Gideon Rover, and this is Mr Trott, my partner. I presume you offer security, cargo unloading and all manner of chandler services."

"Gideon Rover, I have never heard of her, from where does she hail?"

"Tilbury, Essex, ma'am. Look her up in your Lloyds Register."

"A lot of good that will do, they burned down last year. No record of anything. Utter chaos if you ask me."

Being street wise Leeza quickly spoke up. "You mean The Gideon Rover aint in no registers anymore? Wot the 'eck do we do bout that?"

Madge replied, "They are trying to rebuild the register. It is going to take a long time. Most ships in England were able to do it quickly. Now they are trying to re-register the ships as they return to England."

Judd interrupted, "We've been gone a while longer than that. As we don't intend to stay very long do you have any suggestions as to how we may go about taking care of this?"

Madge responded with, "That's a lawyer thing. Let me see if we can set this in motion for you while you are away. My Lawyers, Pettigrew & Lumley, may be able to help you."

"Thank you, ma'am. I would appreciate that. Now to other business, I wish to dispose of my cargo, what services do you offer?"

"Everything sir. We can buy your cargo in full, unload and sell your cargo, supply your ship for your next voyage, fill your holds with all types of tradable goods for export. You name it. We, sir are the chandlers of choice for The Royal Shipping line, perhaps you know them."

"Royal Shipping Line, can't say I do, where is their home port?"

"Right here sir. The St-John-Brown Family of Bath have offices in Bath, Bristol and London. Sir William St-John Brown is the Member of Parliament for Somerset. House of Lords, you know. Rather large privately held family company sir, sizeable fleet of merchantmen. We have at least one of their ships alongside almost every week. Sir William's a likeable gentleman of high integrity. Perhaps I can affect an introduction the next time you are in port."

"I have never heard of Saint John Brown or The Royal Shipping Line" said Judd.

"Oh my, they get really upset if you say their name wrong. They pronounce it "Sinjon Brown.""

"Sounds a bit toffee nose to me," remark Leeza.

"I guess you could call them that. If you would like to follow me gentlemen, we can take care of all the details in my office." Madge led the way.

Some two hours later Judd and Leeza shook hands with Madge Duggan and departed. The two men boarded a carriage to take them to the train station, bound for London. In the quiet of the firstclass carriage, they reviewed the arrangements made with Duggans. It had gone much smoother than they had ever imagined. The Duggans would take care of so many business activities about which they knew little. According to their calculations each of the crew men would end up with money equal to three years' pay working under other masters. The plan was to make one or two voyages a year, and this would prove lucrative to those who stayed and were loyal. In two weeks, the Gideon Rover would be emptied, filled with new cargo and revictualled ready to sail. He felt that although he would not be getting the best prices, right now the ability to turn around, and leave before the abandoned crew of the HMS Vanguard surfaced, would be a priority.

***

This was the first time that Judd had been on a train and the clackity clack of the carriage on the steels rails and strange sounds lulled him into a weary sleep. It was only a few hours before Judd was awakened by the shrill whistle of the locomotive as it pulled into the huge London terminal of Waterloo Station. Judd alighted from the carriage and bid farewell to Leeza, promising to meet with him within the week. Leeza turned away and strode off with a purposeful gait. Judd was surrounded by people rushing to and fro with bags, trunks, and all sorts of parcels. The high domed glass covering of the station seemed to fill with the din of hissing steam engines and porters, shouting. This was a far cry from the comparative quiet of sea life. His attempts to get assistance were met with hurried, rushing bustle of people, hell bent on their own focus. Finally, he pulled out a silver half crown and held it out in front of him, suddenly he was surrounded by willing people. He chose one and asked how he should get to Essex, Mucking, to be exact.

The small boy he selected explained. "Well sir, you can git a 'orse an carriage, but that's gonna take a long time. As likely, you might ave to change a couple a times. Most Londoners aint willin' to go that far. You could git a train to Tilbury, that's by the East India Docks, then go by orse from there."

"Help me get to the right place for the Tilbury train and you can earn another half crown."

"You souns as if you ain't never bin on a train," the boy said with a laugh.

Chapter 14

Sitting in the privacy of the Tilbury bound carriage, Judd thought about the St Eustasius and the contracts. His aura of contentment and his ego were fed by the incredible feat he had pulled off—no, masterminded. It took less than two hours before he found himself leaving the platform of the rural Tilbury train station and hiring a horse and carriage to take him Mucking.

The village green was quiet, as the late summer sun crept lazily over the horizon. The heavy dew sparkled on the well-kept grass. The damp morning air held down the pale blue wisps of smoke emanating from the bakery's wood-burning ovens, carrying with them fragrances burned in his memory. These wisps lay in layers, as if waiting for the sun to dry the air and set them free to escape up into the skies.

Everything felt somehow less imposing than he remembered it. The smithy wall was now made of a handsome red brick, and an imposing carved wooden sign announced ***David and David, Custom Blacksmiths***. Judd peered through the small glass windows and saw an office, something Davey's dad had no time for once upon a time.

The familiar sounds and smells began to open the memories he had kept so tightly closed all these years, only to be occasionally unlocked by the letters he received. The fresh-bread ovens were the smell country folk set their clocks by. The small shop from which they sold pies and cakes had become so big, and Judd could not imagine how they could do so much business. The village was grander—there were new shops now. The old church had been completely rebuilt, and even had a parsonage. There was a building he did not know. His curiosity was piqued.

Suddenly, the sound of cowbells woke him out of his reverie as they clanked their way into view across the village green. Milking was usually completed before dawn, and now the cows would be taken out to fresh pastures. Judd had forgotten the sound of cowbells, the look of cows, the smell of morning dew, and the sound of a blacksmith. All this had been locked away. He stood in awe, aware of what he was: a villager from Mucking, and, what he had become, a man of the world.

Now he knew why sailors spoke with a rapturous wonder of their homes. He put his head in his hands and inwardly nostalgia overwhelmed him.

A young woman appeared, driving the cows. As she walked past Judd, she gaily greeted him. "Mornin', sir. 'Tis a beau'iful mornin'," she said, looking Judd up and down. "'Tis not many a mornin' I sees a fine-looking gentleman out of his bed so soon after the sun rises." She smiled a radiant, fresh-scrubbed beam of contentment at Judd. His French-style goatee and drooping mustache gave him a gallant air, and his sea- and sun-tanned skin projected worldliness. Judd's fair hair had also thinned out and it shone like spun silk in the early morning sun's rays.

She stopped, looked, and then suddenly threw herself at him. Jumping up, she threw her arms around his neck, bursting into tears on his shoulders. "Judd Cane, Judd Cane, Judd Cane!" she cried. Her grip was so tight, he had to free himself. Judd felt his heart pounding, and his head was light.

All these years, he had remembered Mary Washerman. She had not changed in his mind, but she had, she was different. She had changed into a beautiful country girl, more exciting and vibrant than he could ever have invented. Without thinking he said, "Twentyfour and now such a pretty sight. Letting go of Judd, Mary did a mock curtsey and replied, "why thank you kind sir."

"Will you walk with me, if you don't mind, while I put these beasts in Farmer Loring's field? Oh my, I feared that I would never see you again. Your ma is going to be so happy. Oh my, you must tell me everything," she said. He walked alongside her wanting to hold one of her hands, but not having the courage to do so. She used a willow switch to keep the cows ambling along at their pastoral speed. Closing the gate behind them, she flipped the iron bar across the stile, turned, and sat on its step. "Judd, I have been thinking of you so often," she said. "Your ma read me your letters. What were it like when they stole you away? Did they hurt you? What brings you home? Are you still in the Navy, on the great big warship? Did you get my letters?" She did not wait for answers to her questions.

Judd held a finger to his lips signaling he wanted to speak. "I got your letters for a while and then nothing. I thought you might have found a young admirer for yourself. Maybe you decided you didn't like me anymore"

"Oh no Judd, I still like you. I think you are more likeable now than you were before you left. There's no fellow in the village that appeals to me. Not that I wouldn't consider changing my mind if I found someone. I never stopped writing. I wondered what happened to the letters. Do you think the Navy lost them?"

Suddenly, Judd understood what had happened. Of course, he didn't get the letters, they were going to the Navy and he had stolen the Governor Ready. He knew he couldn't tell her what he had done, so, on the spur of the moment he brushed it off with, "Oh, now I know. The Navy transferred me to another ship. I bet the letters are roaming around the world trying to catch up with me. Oh well, let's not worry about it, I am here now.

As Judd listened, he just kept staring at her. She was more beautiful than he could imagine. She had just left the milking sheds, and yet she was more feminine and radiant and alluring than any of the wenches he had seen in his travels.

He grasped her hands and lifted her to a standing position, touched her cheek, and quietly whispered, "Mary, dear Mary, dear dear Mary, May I visit with you while I am home?" They stood in a tight embrace and clung together. Mary said yes over and over again, until a large, wet, drooling pink snout of a cow leaned across the fence and rested on her shoulder, letting out a long, deep moo.

"I guess your cows approve," Judd said. To that they both laughed.

"How long are you going to be home for?"

"I have to rejoin my ship in about a week," he answered.

"So soon. Why? Is the navy that strict on you?"

Mocking her acent he replied, "Tis that they are. But I ain't in the Navy no more."

Mary stopped and pulled Judd to a halt. "If'n you are not in the navy....I'm mighty confused. What are you doing then?"

"I am captain of a merchantman, The Gideon Rover. She is in Southampton and we sail again in a fortnight."

"Captain Cane. Oh my. Judd. I like the sound of that."

As they walked across the village toward Judd's home, Mary told Judd of all the changes in the village. There was now an inn. There was a stagecoach station. There was even talk of a post office. When Mary talked of the Earl of Essex and how he had been performing the duties of magistrate while in residence, but was soon to give it up to a permanent local man, Judd stopped walking. He suddenly realized that he had been going to where his parents used to live in Mucking. They now lived on the Earls estate. Judd's father had been provided more work from the Earl, and had been at the mansion more frequently. As they reached the old Cane house, Judd could see that no one had been the one taking care of it. It was in need of some maintenance and appeared vacant. Judd's heart started to race, as he told Mary he had to go and see his parents at the estate and that he would come for her in the evening.

Turning away from Mary he vowed to himself that he would get the family home back for his parents. They were an integral part of life around the village green. It was wrong that they were not there. Observing the people that he passed he realized how much he must have changed because the people that greeted him did not recognize who he was.

A trap was trotting up behind him and Judd called out to the driver, "Sir, could I ask that you take me to the Earl of Essex Estate for a fee?"

The man looked at him and said with a smile, "Judd Cane, I'll gladly take there for the price of lunch. You don't recognize me, do you?"

"Can't say that I do, but I know your face for sure."

"Allan Shore, that's me. As for you, boy, have you grown up. Your ma tells me you're in the navy. Fact is she tells everyone about you."

Judd jumped up on the trap beside Allan and said, "Not anymore, merchant seaman now." The two recalled childhood memories and Allan spoke of the mystery of Judd's disappearance and everything going on around the village. When they arrived at the gatehouse of the mansion estate they stopped and sat, continuing to talk.

Hearing voices, Judd's mother opened a door that now had glass set into it and stepped outside. She shrieked, and Judd's father came running out to see what was going on. Through her tears of joy, his mother heard Judd say, "I'm sorry ma, I'm sorry pa. I didn't know what could happen that night I went to the docks. How could I have known? I never wanted to cause you pain."

As the two of them gained composure, his father with a slow deliberate voice said, "Tis many things on this earth a man don't know. Many things can appen to e. But e might remember, your ma and I told e to play them cards what e got and not them what e wants. Looks to I like you done that real and proper like. Twernt what you did to us, twas what you did to yersel. Looks alike e did pretty good to me." Turning to his wife Will said, "Mary, looks like we got us fine young man, indeed it does. Knew as like 'e'd be 'ome one day. The money wot you sent us 'as been put away, son. Did stop coming a while back. Don't know why. It's yours, and we's been a-keepin' it for you." We needs to talk more. How long is the navy letting you home for?"

"Pa. I'm not in the Royal Navy any more. I am captain of a merchantman, the Gideon Rover." I am home for a week. I want to get together with Mary tonight and tomorrow we can talk when I have got things figured out in my head. To change the subject pa, who owned our house in the village that told you to move out?"

"The Sainties - Mr. Martin if I got it right. But theys relatives ain't alivin there no more."

"Then why don't you and ma move back in?"

"Taint that easy, son. We would like to move us back in, but for why, so they can turn us out again. No. We loved our house there on the village green, but the truth is, we be safer here with the Earl, sides it closer to my work."

***

With the greetings and reconnections over Judd went back into the Village to see Mary. When he found her, they walked hand in hand across the village green and sat in the late afternoon sun in the forecourt of The Weary Traveler. They talked about what had happened in the village and Mary explained all the changes. The gossip and reminiscing soon gave way to long spaces of silence during which they just looked at each other. Mary timidly asked, "Do you have a beau, somewhere?"

"It isn't really easy to have a relationship when you are on the move like sailors are," was his non-committal reply.

"No but you must meet some beautiful, exotic women."

"See them, but meet them? No not really."

"Not really, what does that mean?"

"Mary, I don't know what it means. Has any girl caught my eye? Perhaps. Do I want a beau? I don't think so." Seeing Mary's expression falter, he quickly added, "I have thought of you often, but so much has happened in my life. I'm not sure I would know how to be a beau to anyone. You are my friend, although I'm not sure I knew that when I left, and, you are a girl, so, I guess you could be my girl-friend."

Mary stared at Judd without speaking for a moment and then quietly said, "My pa says I should be married at my age or I will be a spinster, so I think being a girl-friend is not going to work, but, thank you."

"Thank you? Have I just been politely rejected?"

Quickly Mary reached across the table and held Judd's hand. "I could never reject you Judd Cane, never, never."

"Then what do you propose we do?"

"We, what do we do? I have not a notion."

"Perhaps we should marry." Judd said without stopping to think of the consequences of his statement.

Mary sat in silence and stared at Judd before she spoke. "Do you love me Judd Cane, for I know not if I love you?"

"I do not know if I love you, for I am not sure if I know what love is, but I do know this, you have been the image in my brain that is constant through good and bad times. I know that the very thought of you causes my heart to skip a beat. If that is love, then I do. If that isn't love, then I know not what is."

"How long do you plan to stay at the seafaring life?" Mary asked as if changing the subject.

"Until such times as being apart from you is more than I can bear," he remarked with a nonchalant, cavalier flourish."

"Then if you are asking me to marry you, Captain Cane, I will think on it, but, first you must ask my ma and pa. Walk me home then and we shall talk to our parents in the morning if we are of the same mind."

As Judd walked Mary to her parent's home he asked, "Who are the Saintees, that owned my ma and pa's old home?"

"They live behind the forge. They have fallen on hard times. Mr. Saintee now works for the Blacksmiths, why do you ask?"

"There's something I need to take care of."

Standing in the doorway of her parent's home Judd and Mary held each other close, as if communicating through osmosis. They bid each other farewell and set to meet in the morning. Nary a kiss passed their lips.

***

Judd stopped in at the forge on his way back through the village. Opening the huge wooden door to the forge room David and his father, each had tongs in one hand and pounding hammer in the other. The two looked up to see who entered and simultaneously shouted a greeting. The younger David put down his tools, threw off his leather apron and went to shake hands with Judd. "What a sight for sore eyes," he said as Judd gave him a bear hug. "Judd Cane, home from the sea. Took you long enough to come home. So, what are you now, sailor, pirate, man of the world?"

Judd held up his hand to stop David as he looked over to David the elder and said, "Hello, Mr. Blacksmith. It's good to see you looking so well."

The man replied, "Mr! you can call me David. Judd Cane, it is good to see you. Your ma and pa will be really happy that you are home. Are you here for long?"

"No sir. A week at the most."

"Still in the Navy, working for the Queen, eh."

"Not exactly sir, but still at sea. Let's get together and catch up this evening. I stopped by to see if you know anything about the Saintees, that own the house we used to live in."

Mr. Blacksmith spoke in a low voice. "Martin and his wife had some rough times. Sad to see, but Martin has got his self back on the road and, actually he works here in the office for us."

Judd said, "I want to buy the house, and I seem to recall he owned the piece of land next to the house."

"Boy, you will give him some hope. There are some in the village that never forgave him for turning your parents out just as you went missing. Never the mind, your ma and pa seem real happy at the estate. They come into the village every Saturday for the market and we have lunch together either here with Priscilla or over at the Weary. Let me call him."

Shouting at the top of his lungs he called out, "Martin, Martin get yer arse in here, someone to see you. A small man with pince nez glasses perched on the end of nose came out of the office and stood staring at Judd.

David broke the silence with, "Relax Martin, young Judd aint going to do you no harm. Fact is he wants to buy the old Cane house and the bit of land next to it."

In an attempt to calm the obviously agitated man Judd sat on an anvil and said, "Mr. Martin, name your price. I want my parents to return to the house they were so happy in."

Martin spoke, "I'm so sorry, for what I did. My son…" The man stopped talking, took out a handkerchief and dabbed his eyes.

David spoke up. "Martin's son and daughter-in -aw were killed in a train crash, some five years ago. He aint never been near the house since. His wife couldn't handle the loss and took her own…"

Judd interrupted, "No need to explain, I understand."

David said, "why don't you both use the office to sort out your affairs."

Martin and Judd went into the office and closed the door. Some twenty minutes later, Judd returned to the furnace room wearing a big smile. "Got the house back, and the piece of land. Ma and pa will be happy."

David said to Judd, "Hope you didn't give him so much money that he isn't going to work for us anymore. Your ma and pa has been settled in a long while up at the estate. Don't be surprised if they want to stay there."

"Thanks for the advice, but I'm sure it will please them. Changing the subject, I am going to have a get together at the Weary Traveler. I'll let you know more. Gotta run for now." With that, he hugged the father and son and left.

Returning to his parent's home on the Earl's estate Judd sat in the warm glow of the gas lit kitchen, across from his ma and pa and started to talk. "Ma, I think that I asked Mary to marry me this evening."

His father spoke quickly, "you did or you didn't. Aint nothing to think about I says.

Judd's mother jumped up and hugged him, saying, "Oh my, such a nice girl. Judd, did she accept?"

"I don't know ma. We are going to talk in the morning."

"Do you love her?"

"I think so."

Pa spoke up. "You do or you don't. Ifn you don't, you should know."

"Pa, I think Mary would make a good wife."

"You think you love her. You think she will make a good wife. Bout time you started knowin fings boy, and stopped finking."

His mother interrupted, "Be quite you old fool. The boy's trying to work things out for hiself."

"It feels right, ma."

"How does she feel about you being at sea?"

"That's what we need to talk about tomorrow. I have to ask her pa's permission yet. Do you approve?" he asked them both.

His mother reached across the table and held both of Judd's hands in her own and said quietly, "We approve, Judd, pa and I, both approve."

"There, you aves it," said his father. "Here endeth the lesson, her ladyship has spoken."

Mary picked up a wooden spoon, threw it at Will, and all three laughed. She studied Judd's face before she spoke. "Something else is on your mind young man. Out with it."

"Are you and pa happy, living up here away from the village and your friends?"

His father took a deep breath and answered. "Like I was allays telling e. Yer plays the cards yer bin dealt. I's got regelar work. We got a roof over our 'eads and the Earl is real good to us. I's pretty much 'is 'andy man, 'is game keeper and I even drives 'is automobile sometimes. He lets us take it to market on a Saturday. We's like real toffs then. So, we is good. Why you askin?"

"I bought the old house and piece of land for you today."

"Saintee sold it to you?" his mother asked.

"Yes ma, it is sad what happened to his life. It seems he has moved on."

His father said, "Well, ifn you and Mary is, gonna git married there's yer ome. Tell yer wot. For a wedding present me and ma will do all fixin needed on the ouse and make it good and cozy for Mary."

"For Mary and me, you mean."

"Thought you was a bloody sailor. You got yer ship, she got the ouse, till such times as you've 'ad enough of yer wondering ways."

Judd told his parents that they were no longer poor. He gave his mother two hundred pounds in large white five pound notes the size of tea towels. When his parents said that they didn't need the money, Judd refused to discuss it any further. "Pa, I'm going to meet Davey and Jim for an ale at the Weary Traveler. I shall be back later."

"Your dad would enjoy an ale or two," his ma said.

"Just me and the lads for now, we have plenty of time together pa. I am going to need your advice on a few things. With that Judd, left the Estate and returned to Mucking.

Chapter 15

Judd set about evaluating how the people he remembered had changed. He also needed to find someone he could trust to help place the plantation deed in his name. He did not want to involve his or Mary's family. The less they knew how things had evolved, the less they could judge him by. That left Jim Carter and Davey Blacksmith. He was giving careful consideration to the value of keeping the ownership of the Gideon Rover and the plantation on St. Eustasius as private matters at this point.

Upon entering the forge, he studied Davey more carefully. Davey, now twenty-three, bore no resemblance to the boy Judd remembered. He was over six feet tall, his leather apron stretched tightly across a huge belly. His hair was thinning, and his ruddy complexion made him look as if he had been toasted by the redhot coals, of his forge fire.

But within minutes of seeing each other, it was as if no time had passed.

"Back so soon? I thought we were getting together tomorrow," questioned Davey.

"Me too, but I need some advice on the quiet," Judd answered.

Davey called for Jane, his wife and Jim's sister, and she emerged out of the office, full of child and glowing. Her pregnancy gave her a rich, healthy color that she radiated. She took one look at Judd, flung her arms around his neck, and wept tears of joy. She told him Mary had become so quiet since Judd's disappearance and that the only time she seemed happy, was when Judd's mother gathered her, Davey, Mary and Jim around the huge anvil in the smithy and read them one of Judd's letters.

Judd told them that he and Mary were talking about getting married. There was joy and congratulations all around. After chatting for while Judd leaned over to Davey and said, "Can you get Jim and meet me over the Weary Traveler in about half an hour?"

"Sounds like a mystery to me, but sure. Don't mind if I go over the pub with this rapscallion, do you dear?" Davey enquired of Jane.

***

The Weary Traveler was the rebuilt village alehouse. Sitting at a large rustic table on the stone slab forecourt of the alehouse with Jim and Davey, Judd laid out his dilemma. Davey was very quick with a solution. "My pa, when he needs some document, gets the Earl's secretary to help him out," he said. "He's a queer old coot. He won't take no money. Says it makes him feel crooked. Mind you, he ain't above an 'ansome gift as like."

Judd asked about the risk involved in having someone so close to the Earl know what was happening.

"'He ain't close to the earl. He works for him, just like your pa does. He can copy anything perfect-like, so you wouldn't know the difference. The best thing is, because he works for the Earl, he can get the new contract signed, sealed, and officiated by the Earl himself - stamp and all. Tell you what. Your ma showed that desk to him that we got from one of our night escapades. He loved it. Tell him you'll get a good one on your travels. That'll pay him good. An' he likes your pa, 'cause he is always getting the villagers' documents for him to do. Your pa doesn't take nuffin' for doing it, so they gets on fine together."

Judd thought for moment and said, "I have a great captain's desk on the Gideon Rover. I can have it sent to him straight away. A pretty impressive captain's desk it is, too."

"What's the Gideon?" asked Jim.

"The Gideon Rover is the ship I work on. She's in Southampton right now."

"Who would have thought that the three of us would be sitting here in front of the pub, drinking beer, for all the world to see?" said Jim.

Davey replied, "I don't think many people in the village would believe some of the things we used to get up to."

Jim and Davey peppered Judd with questions about his life at sea late into the night. After bidding each other goodnight Judd set out to walk the three miles to the Earl's estate. Country lanes came and went lit by the brilliant moon above. It struck Judd how different the moon was when viewed from land. It threw shadows which were not seen at sea. His mind was filled with the different country smells and sounds and the richness they provided. Before he knew it, he was at his parents' cottage and quietly let himself in the door. As he turned to close the door, he was surprised to hear his mother speak, "You will never know young man, how many times I have wanted to sit up late at night, just to hear you come in the door."

"Oh ma. I'm sorry."

"Don't be sorry. I had begun to believe that I would never hear that sound again. You have just given it back to me. Now let me show where you will sleep, and off to bed I shall go, a happy mother." And, so it came to pass. The documents were prepared within two days. Judd met with the Earl and swore an oath to the correctness of the transaction. The trusting Earl did not even notice the document was not dated. The secretary quickly added earlier dates supplied by Judd, and he became the owner of the Plantation.

***

The following morning Judd walked back to the village and to the Washerman house and dairy. Michael and Mildred Washerman welcomed him with open arms and Michael said, "Mary rarely walks the cows in the morning these days. She was helping as one of the dairymaids is sick. She might never have run into you."

Judd replied, "There is no way I would come back to Mucking without seeing Mary. I have this picture of her in my head that has never left. She is nearly as lovely as you Mrs. Washerman." His grin gave away his attempt at humor.

"You might have one heart in this family young Judd, but it better not be Mrs. Washerman's," Michael Washerman laughed. "Your ma has been so good at keeping us all informed of what has been happening to you. Mind you she was beside herself when you just up and went."

"I didn't just up and went. I guess you could say that I was wented."

The laughter died down when Mary entered the parlor and scolded, "Wented, Judd Cane, what sort of language is that?"

Mary's mother rebuked her daughter. "Mary, get off your high horse. You have carried a candle for Judd Cane for as long as I can remember. Make the boy comfortable, get a pot of tea and let's catch up. We all loved your ma reading us the letters you sent. Whenever we saw her come into the village on a Satday we knew she had a letter. You're a good boy Judd."

"A cup of tea would fine. With milk and sugar if I may. Fine fresh milk has become a luxury to me. At sea we don't see such a thing." There was a long pause before Judd spoke again. "Mr. and Mrs. Washerman, the life I now lead robs me of the time I would like to take to do certain things. I propose -----"

"You propose!" interjected Mary.

"Be quite woman and let the boy speak," demanded Mary's mother.

"Then I suggest…" Mary's faced dropped at the change in Judd's voice.

"I suggest that the conversation Mary and I had yesterday could be considered hasty. I could propose that, maybe, I should slow down. I am to be sailing again in two weeks and I do not want to spend my next voyage thinking that my hesitance could cause me to lose your daughter to someone else. Come sit with us Mary," Judd said as Mary came from the kitchen with a tray of steaming tea.

"What did I miss?" asked Mary.

"Nothing, Judd was telling us about all the beautiful women he meets at sea," said her father.

"Mermaids, the like," snorted Mary.

Judd continued, "Mary and I spoke about marriage yesterday. Mary asked if I loved her, and to tell you the truth, I have not had much time to think about love. I am not sure that I know what love is. But what I do know is there is something about Mary that warms my heart. There is gladness when I see her. I think these are strong foundations upon which we can build, if she is willing. I promise to provide for and support her."

"What do you say to that Mary?" asked her mother.

"Weirdest proposal of marriage I could ever imagine," was her reply. "But, still the best one I have had so far. I like the idea. See, pa, I will not end up a spinster." Amid the laughter Michael and Mildred welcomed Judd into the family.

The wedding was set for Saturday week after Judd explained he had to go to London on business and would be back for the weekend to marry and must leave no later than the following Tuesday.

Judd returned to his parents to announce that his marriage offer had been accepted and what his plans were. The following day Judd left for London to keep his promise to Leeza Trott.

Chapter 16

Judd caught the early morning train from Tilbury to Waterloo Station and was in London by noon. Garnet Street, Wapping was off High Street, by the Shadwell Basin. As Judd stepped down from his carriage on High Street, which stood alongside the River Thames, he was shocked by what he saw. As far as the eye could see, looking at Tower Bridge and then turning around to look at Canary Wharf, there was nothing but dockside buildings side by side on each side of the river. Ships of every shape and size were either anchored in the middle of the fast-moving river or alongside, loading or unloading cargo. Streets were strewn with refuse, and the smell was heavy and unpleasant.

Judd had never stopped to think about London. It had always been the big city upriver. He had read newspaper reports of the city, and had been warned of the dangers. To see the writhing, crawling, noisy mass of humanity made him long for the order and predictability of shipboard life at sea. He was buffeted and shoved and shouted at as he made his way to Garnet Street, where carts, drays, and hand-pushed barrows fought with each other either to get to the river or to get away from it. The river at his back and the sun on the right side of his face told him he was going north on his journey. Lezza had told him that his home was about a half mile on the right-hand side.

The heat increased the unpleasantness of the fetid smells. He crossed the street, shaded now by the tall warehouse buildings, between which he could see what he assumed to be the basin. In the basin were a myriad of small, shore-hugging ships and river craft, going on about their business. The big buildings shading him opened out onto the dockside of the basin. The clatter of iron-hooped wheels on the cobblestones and shouting was all so alien to him. He did not understand why Lezza spoke so fondly of this area.

Within a few minutes, the road curved right, revealing rows of brick-built houses, closely packed. They were a single room wide, squashed tightly together with an alley between each block. Each block had six front doors and six bay windows. He found the home he was looking for was at the end of a block.

Rapping on the front door provided no response, so he walked down the side alley to the rear. As he turned at the far end of the alley, he found that each house had a long, narrow garden no wider than the house and about as long. Each yard had a small, square brick outhouse. Sitting on an upturned barrel, leaning back against the wall of the house with his eyes closed and face angled up to the sun, was Lezza Trott, asleep. The woman standing next to him saw Judd and whispered to her husband. Lezza jumped up and ambled down the plot to greet Judd. His wife never moved, she just stared.

As the two men approached, she said to Judd, "You doan look old 'inuff or big 'inuff to be God, like 'e finks you is."

"Woman, get yersell into the 'ouse and make us some tea," said Lezza. He turned to Judd. She ain't too sure about wot we be a-doin', Judd. As they entered the tiny kitchen area Lezza asked. "Wot you lookin at?".

"All these 'Mother's Fine Foods' biscuits, tea, sugar. Where have I seen this before?"

"That's the Co-Op. That woman in Soufhampton - Duggan somefing. She has signs for The Co-Op and muvvers. Must own it or sumfing," Leeza told him.

Judd stored that tit bit of information Leeza just gave him in his head for future reference then said, "I'm not sure about what we are doing, either. But one thing is for sure. I now own the ship, and since Lloyd's register burned seven or eight years ago, there isn't any way of checking us out. So, I tell you, Lezza, we can go about business all legal. The telegraph you sent about the crew left behind doesn't seem to have caused any stir at this point. So, I think the sooner we sail out of here this time the better. So, if you want in..."

"I wants in. The missus says we should have an unerstanding afore we does anyfing. Let's go inside." Lezza led the way into a room that housed a cast-iron wood-burning fireplace. In one corner of the room was a copper kettle set into a brick surround with an open fire grate underneath. This was for laundry. Past the table and chairs was a door into another room.

Peering through the open door, Judd saw a rug in the center of the room and an open fireplace against one wall. The opposite wall had a narrow set of stairs to the upper floor, and between them were the bay window and front door.

It was obvious why Lezza was nervous about changing the status quo, but the lure of more money was overwhelming. The children were well fed and educated. They all had shoes. Their home was better than many, and all this at the simple cost of their pa sailing away at sea. His wife kept a good home for him.

As she poured the tea, she wiped invisible crumbs off the table. Lezza looked at her with a warm, affectionate smile and said, "Tell the captain 'ere wot we's decided, my love."

The idea was simple: The captain should take one quarter of the voyage's profit with another quarter divided between any persons in charge, such as the navigator, quartermaster, bosun, carpenter, sailmaster, and, of course, chief cook. The last half would be divided evenly among the crew. Lezza's wife explained what her eldest boy had calculated—that if they took three trips every two years and each voyage was successful, each crewman could expect up to five years' pay every two years, as long as the Gideon Rover was willing to share profits, something no other merchantman was doing. If Judd was willing to promise Lezza this arrangement, she said, she would support everything.

"You do know the Navy will come looking for him sooner or later, right?" she said.

Leeza responded with, "Woman I aves me uver papers, same wot I use in me capers when I aint at sea. So, you see, there is two of me, each wiv a different name."

Judd took a few moments to ask some questions and mull over their proposition. He then said, "So we are going to add my share and your share then divide it equally between us."

Leeza looked at his wife and said, with a grin, "See. I told you 'e was a right gentleman, that's our Judd."

After a short time, Judd stood, and shaking Leeza's hand agreed to their terms, complimenting them on how thoroughly they had thought everything through. Judd took his leave after telling them of his pending marriage and arranging for them to meet at in Southampton Tuesday week at the Gideon Rover

Chapter 17

Judd took the next train to Tilbury, arriving in the early evening. The rest of the week passed at breakneck speed, with the wedding preparations. Judd was happy to let his, and Mary's parents take control of the plans for the wedding. The afternoon before the wedding Judd took Mary for a walk. They went to the rolling hills that overlooked the wide mouth of the Thames. Judd pointed out the different ships and told of places they might be going and cargo's they might be carrying. Mary noticed a warmth in his voice as he talked of the sea.

"Do you think that you will always be at sea?" she asked in a quiet voice.

"Oh, my lord, no. It's a means to an end. Let me show you what I mean." He pulled a package out and untied the ribbon around it. Unfolding the first paper, he explained, "This is a bill of sale for the house my ma and pa used to live in, by the village green. It also includes the piece of land next to it."

"What does it mean?" asked Mary.

"It means that we own them. I have paid for them and the Earl's secretary will transfer them to our name. My pa said that he will do any repairs to make the home comfortable for you. I have given him the money. If you want to build a new home on the piece of land and knock down the old one, or rent it out, you decide."

"Our own home, no rent to pay, no one can evict us? Oh Judd!"

"Hold on, there's more." Judd unfolded a sheath of papers, pulling out the map of St. Eustasius. Placing a stone on each end to keep it flat he pointed out The Plantation. "That's our's as well."

"Plantation? I am having nothing to do with slaves and plantations Judd Cane. It offends me that you would."

"It used to be a plantation many years ago, they tell me. Now it is trading place for the big clippers that come from the orient. It is more efficient for them to sell their cargo in the Caribbean and return to the Orient than it is for them to come all the way to England. The lower price they get for it is more than made up for by a speedy repeat of their trips."

"So how is it that you own it?"

"The owner was sea captain that wanted to be rid of it before he left the sea, and I offered to buy it."

"Where did you get the money?"

"Questions, questions. Read the deed transfer and you will see it is all in order. I owe no money on it and it is earning us money while we are somewhere else."

"So, what exactly does this mean to us?"

"It means that Mary Cane, or the person who will be Mary Cane tomorrow, must look after these papers very carefully. Because, her husband, that will be me, intends to seek out enough properties to promise us a comfortable and worry free life together."

"How long do you think that will take?" Mary asked with trepidation.

"I have no way of knowing. So much has been gained is a short time, but I don't expect it to be repeated anywhere near as quickly. Oh yes, one more thing, I own the Gideon Rover. We, own the Gideon Rover."

"Judd Cane, you are spinning me a yarn," said Mary as she pushed his shoulder, sending him rolling across the grassy slope.

"No.....I have been blessed by circumstance and followed my pa's advice."

"Which was?"

"Play the cards that you have been dealt, not the cards you wish for. Mary, I have been dealt some pretty incredible cards. You are the Queen of Hearts in my hand."

"Let's go and tell my ma and pa," said Mary as she stood up to leave. Judd took hold of both her hands and pulled her to face him. With a stern yet gentle manner he said, "Mary, you don't need to speak of the house in the village, for people will see that we own it. St Eustasius and the Gideon Rover are our private business. I won't say I forbid you speak with others of them, because something tells me that I have no need to. Let's not ignite jealousy, envy, or any start of negative thoughts around us." Mary agreed.

Walking back across the hills into the village Judd listened to Mary explaining her work at the dairy and how it had expanded.

"I keep the books for ma and pa and write all the correspondence they need. I also keep books for five of the farmers, whose cows we tend. Would you believe so many people in the village have got to know about what I do, that I am often asked to read and explain documents and letters that the villagers get? So much so that pa has set up a small office in our house for that purpose." She noticed Judd was listening very intently to what she was saying, frequently interjecting with questions.

When she finished, he looked at her with serious expression and said, "Our new home in the village that pa is going to fix is perfect. The cow shed on the side of the house can be turned into a real, proper, office with its own entrance."

Mary clapped her hands together in excitement and said, "I think I might be very happy to marry you tomorrow Mr. Cane."

***

As weddings go, the Cane-Washerman wedding was the event of the decade in the village. Everyone was welcomed. An array of colorful home-made and professional tents was set up on the green. The evening before, Davey Blacksmith set about building a large cooking pit over which a whole steer was to be roasted. This endeavor was started in the middle of the night to be ready for the festivities. Everybody in the village contributed to the preparations and the festive air started long before the ceremony. At around noon on Saturday the party started. Lower Mucking had sent over their championship Morris Dancers who whipped the crowd into excitement as they practiced. The excitement was pushed up a notch as the Stanton Hope Morris Dances were sent along to help celebrate, by the Earl. The friendly competition between the two teams was enjoyed by everyone Their 'hoodening' style of 'Morris' dance was the local favorite. The air of country gaiety was enjoyed by all, as was the two huge trestle tables set outside the Weary Traveler pub. The tables held three huge kegs of ale and small oaken casks of pussers rum, in honor of Judd.

At four o'clock a large brass band ensemble from Tilbury commanded attention with the booming bass tuba resonating sound. The village vicar stood on a raised platform where the ceremony was to take place. Standing beside him was Judd, looking through the crowd to see if he could spot Mary. Grown men had small children hoisted on their shoulders. Groups of children had climbed trees where they hung precariously, like over gown fruit ready to fall. Every house and building around the green had people sitting on the roofs to get a better view. Judd was overcome with emotion at the common goodwill he saw and felt. The band swept into the tune of 'Here comes the bride, just as Judd saw Mary on her father's arm. The crowd parted to allow the procession to approach the stage.

The band fell silent as Michael assisted Mary in mounting the steps to face Judd. The crowd roared and whistled endlessly, until the vicar held his hands high in the air, seeking quiet. He started to speak, "Dearly beloved." The crowd broke out with another round of whistling and calling out. The vicar tried again, "Dearly beloved." The crowd started again, as the vicar looked to Judd, who said, "Let them enjoy themselves, Vicar, just go ahead, they will quiet down. The crowd quickly did just that, each one straining to hear the ceremony.

As the couple exchanged their vows, an occasional voice could be heard calling for them to speak louder. The hush was pierced by Judd's voice, loudly proclaiming, "I do." The proud parents turned and shook hands with each other, not a dry eye among them. The crowd started to chant in unison, "kiss the bride, kiss the bride, kiss the bride". Judd responded by turning toward Mary and taking her face gently between his palms, he kissed her upturned face tenderly on her lips. Then, taking hold of Mary, he pivoted and dipped Mary in a theatrical way and kissed her in an exaggerated style. The crowd roared their approval. Out of the corner of his eye he saw their mothers hug each other and wipe away tears of joy.

Bringing Mary back to her feet, he grinned at her and she playfully smacked his shoulder. "That's right Mary, keep him in his place," shouted someone.

"Keep him in your place, is more like it," said another.

The jocular comments started to fly fast and furious as the crowd parted to allow them to leave the stage. They led a procession to where tables of food had been set out and the festivities settled in to last long into the night.

Throughout the evening well-wishers stopped by their table to deliver personal thoughts and well wishes to the happy couple. Seated at their table were both sets of parents, the Blacksmiths, and the Carters. Reminiscing went on throughout the evening. The merriment was periodically interrupted by the giving of gifts and small tokens of well wishes. Long after the sun set the black night sky sent tired, weary, and often drunk partyers off to their beds. As the night wore on, only Judd and Mary were left with their parents, and a few sleeping celebrants with their heads on a table of food left overs and upturned beer mugs. They were surrounded by a sea of party debris.

Things soon took a more sober tone, with Judd speaking first. "Look at this mess. Who is going to take care of it?"

His father answered, "didn't your mother always pick up after e.?"

His mother replied, "This time, husband of mine, it would be a pleasure, but David's father said he would organize that for us. Where will you two bed down for the night?" she enquired of Mary. Mary replied, "The pub landlord is giving us his best room for the night, with breakfast in bed. But nobody has been told." "He has made it special for us," she quickly added."

"What makes you think a secret can be kept in this village?" asked Mary's mother Mildred.

Judd looked at her and said quietly, "I have put the word out that we are going to be staying with my parents tonight, because I don't trust the lads not to pull any pranks on us. As you know, I must leave in the morning for my ship and my wife and I want to be alone." He turned to Mary, "My wife. That sounds really nice. Mary Cane, my wife." They all joined in the laughter that followed.

Judd's mother spoke up when quiet had returned, "I don't like you leaving us, especially Mary, so soon. Do you have to go?"

"Ma, pa, Mister and Mrs. Washerman, I suppose you are ma and pa as well. Mary and I have spoken at length about this and we are united in the road we shall travel."

His father spoke up, "Tis better that e should travel that road together, for 'tis sure to be a rough road sometimes."

"Pa, we have a plan. I'll not be at sea forever. This will build a better life for us."

"And what is wrong with the life we ave ere?" his pa countered.

"Nothing pa. It's just that we are choosing a slightly different way. Mary is happy with our decision, aren't you my dear?"

Mary was quiet for a moment before she answered, "Ma, pa, Mr. and Mrs. Cane, I have every faith in Judd, and, while I am a little apprehensive about the future, I am sure that I am no different from every other bride."

Judd's mother stood up, walked round the table and embraced Mary. "He will not let you down my dear." With a playful slap on the back of Judd's head she said, "or he will have me to deal with." Soon afterwards the group drifted over to The Weary Traveler where blessings, wishes, goodnights and farewells were exchanged.

***

Sitting on the edge of the large puffy bed, with her hands folded in her lap, Mary looked at Judd and solemnly said, "I have never done anything like this before."

"What, you have never been married?" joked Judd.

"Married, yes, but never been to bed with a man," Mary teased back.

"Oh, so, you have been to bed with a boy."

Before she could answer, Judd pushed her back on the bed and straddled her. Holding her hands out on either side of her head in a mass of down bedding he spoke, quietly, "neither have I." He kissed her to stop her reply. All the while her eyes were closed. She timidly returned his kiss. Rolling over on his side, Judd pulled her on top of his body. As she placed her hands on his chest, he pulled at the ribbon holding her dress modestly closed over her breasts. Leaning down she kissed him gently on the lips and rolled beside him. She ran her hand over the bulge in his trousers and quickly withdrew her hand, as if in shock. He kissed her neck and between her breasts. She nuzzled in closely as he ran his hand over her clothes, stopping briefly at her breasts and then feeling her mound between her legs.

"I am nervous, are you?" Mary asked.

"Very much. May I undress you, slowly? I want to place an image of you into my mind so deeply, that I will just have to close my eyes to see you when I am away."

"Please, Judd. Let's not talk." Mary turned to lie on her back and mockingly said, "have your way with me, my handsome pirate. All the nice girls love a sailor, but you, Judd Cane, are mine."

While removing her shoes Judd watched her as she closed her eyes. She took a deep breath and exhaled as if at peace. He lifted her dress to just above her knees and rolled her stockings down her legs and over her feet. Then, he pulled the ribbons that held her dress together and rolled her onto her tummy. Sitting astride her he slowly undid the long row of buttons down the back of the dress, kissing her bare back for every button undone. He undid the back of her corset and it fell to her sides. She sat up to allow him to lift the dress up over her head. She held her corset in place. Then she opened her eyes and let her breasts fall free. "Do you think I am pretty Judd?"

"Are you daft? You are more than pretty, more than beautiful, more than any man could hope for."

Mary rolled over and pulled the covers over her, still keeping her knickers on. She pulled a sheet up tight under her chin and studying her husband she said, "I want to watch you undress for me." Judd stood, turned away and quickly disrobed. "No, face me please. I want to see. Judd turned to display his swollen erection. Her gaze was fixed on his manhood and he was uncomfortable. Quickly he climbed in beside her. Silently they explored each other.

As if time had sped everything up amid the flurry of discovery, Mary suddenly felt Judd slide into her. She looked up and saw Judd smiling as he said, "My darling, I don't know where I end and you begin."

"I like it." She whispered, "I thought it would hurt."

"The only hurt I feel is the thought of leaving tomorrow." Judd replied.

Mary felt Judd shudder, and a warmth deep inside herself. "I really am your wife now," was all she could say. To quietly whispered, "I love you's", the pair fell into a blissful sleep.

***

Emotional farewells were had the next morning as, not being fond of parting emotions, Judd tried to slip away quietly. But Mary and their parents insisted on going with Judd to Tilbury to see him off. Mary appeared to be in high spirits about her new life, which pleased Judd a great deal, but, despite this, she sobbed uncontrollably. Judd felt a turmoil that was new to him. It was a combination of guilt for leaving Mary so soon and excitement that his life had now taken on a new purpose.

His mother ushered him off saying, "Go, just go. We will take care of her. The longer you take to leave the harder it is going to be. Make sure you write often. Do you hear me Judd Cane?"

The train's whistle shrieked, steam hissed, and the train started to move away mercifully putting a close to the difficult situation.

Sitting quietly by himself, his thoughts turned quickly to thinking about what he would and wouldn't reveal to Leeza and Dickie. One thing he was firmly decided upon was to make a priority of visiting the property on St. Eustasius. He promised himself he would acquire as much property as he could during his travels oversees, as he had become aware of how much property increased in value over time.

Meeting up with Leeza in London, they took the same train to Southampton. "You look real pleased wiv yerself," comment Leeza.

"I am. I most certainly am. Mary and I got married on yesterday and I feel that I have a purpose," replied Judd.

"Well, it doan make no difference wever you feels you got purpose. The truth is you do got a reason to ave purpose, an only you can decide wot to do about it," was the sage advice given. "I can tell yer got somfin else on yer mind. Spit it out lad, spit it out."

Judd sat silently for a moment before answering. "I noticed, when we were in Duggan's warehouse and office, that lots of things had labels from St. Eustasius. I poked around a bit and was told, more than once, that a lot of trading is done there. I know some of the men told us that, but it seems to be far bigger than anyone realized."

"So, wots yer sayin'?" asked Leeza.

"I think we should take a closer look for ourselves."

"Yer mean we should fink about using Eustasius as a base?"

"Yes. We can do three or four voyages to the orient a year before returning to England. It would be very profitable. Plus, the bother, if any arises, about the crew we left in Barbados, will die down somewhat."

Leeza smiled and said, "We is partners, but you, is the captain. Tis on yer shoulders."

Within the week, the Gideon Rover had been victualed, her hold filled to the brim with cloth from the great mills of the north and all types of new inventions and tradable goods from the factories that had sprung up during the great industrial revolution. Most of the crew had accepted the terms offered them, and the atmosphere on board was one of excited anticipation. Leeza and Judd had met with Madge Duggan's lawyers and set in motion the registration of the Gideon Rover at Lloyds of London Shipping Registry.

It was a bright, sunny day that saw a stiff westerly breeze push them out into the English Channel - destination St. Eustasius.

Chapter18

CARRIBEAN SEA - ST.EUSTASIUS

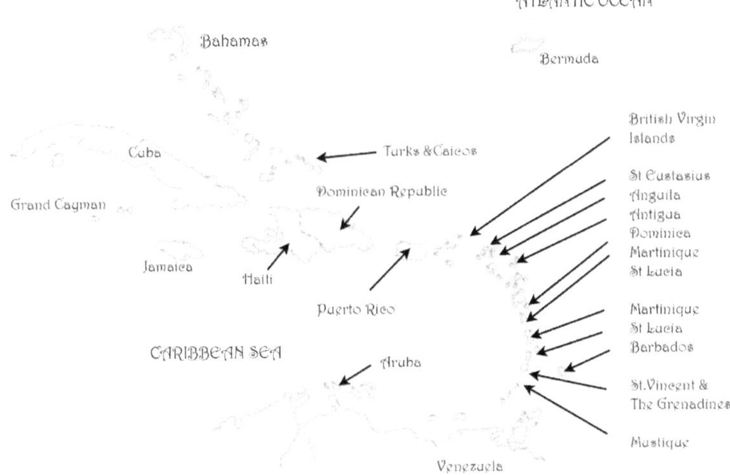

It was during this first visit to the Plantation that he revealed his ownership to the manager. Having set the crew about the task of securing the ships moorings alongside the quay and leaving them instructions to await his return, he left for the offices of the plantation. A dignified looking black man introduced himself as the manager. "Greetings Captain, I am Black Jack Tillotson, sir, and I oversee the business of the plantation. How may I assist you?"

Judd presented the man with a sworn affidavit from his Southampton lawyers that declared himself to be the new owner of The Plantation. He allowed the man to read it before speaking. "Mr. Tillotson, Captain McKellar passed away and I have come into possession of this property. I would like you to acquaint me with how the place is operated and run on a daily basis."

"I was wondering why I had not had any instructions with regards to transferring the profits to London for two years now. Captain McKellar was pretty regular with that. So, what should I do with those funds now captain?"

"Where are the funds now?"

"I have them put away safely, but I am nervous as the sum grows quite large."

"I will take funds now and will arrange for you make regular deposits to my bank in London. But, first, my tour of the place."

The two men spent the morning discussing how the plantation ran and Judd received his first real lesson in international commerce. Black Jack Tillotson was a wealth of knowledge and carried himself with a professional air - one that he probably acquired from his previous boss. While inspecting the books and being shown around the complex Judd learned that Jack was one of thousands of freed slaves living and working on what was left of the dying sugar plantations. Many of the bigger merchantmen found it more lucrative to sell their cargoes from the South Pacific and China seas here, and then return to trade again, rather than keep returning to England.

Jack was one of the few who could not only read and write, but had been given a fair education by his first owner. Much of his speech was closer to the English manner. Judd felt that the man had great potential.

Sitting alone in the office of the plantation, Judd started to think about what he should do. His thoughts were interrupted by Jack entering the room, followed by two young boys struggling with a medium side brass bound chest. They placed the chest at Judd's feet and were dismissed. Jack took a key from his desk and inserted it into the keyhole of the chest as Judd put his hand on the top to hold it close. He said, "I don't need to see the contents Mr. Tillotson. Captain McKellar spoke highly of you. Your report will be enough for me."

"Captain Cane, there is twelve thousand English pounds made up of English, Dutch, German and French bank notes. I maintain, on hand, about one third of that amount to enable the purchase of cargo from traders and the running of 'The Plantation'. This is the largest excess of cash I have ever held, and frankly it makes me a bit nervous."

"So, it should Jack, so it should. We must turn to local banking on a much more regular basis. Produce a letter of authority for me to sign enabling you to do that before we leave." Judd continued, "I'm curious. Why 'Black Jack,' and not just Jack Tillotson?"

"When I was child, my first master was here was a Mr Jack Tillotson, he had a slave called Jack, and that's how people knew the difference, between the two Jacks as the slave was known as black Jack although we never referred to the boss man as white Jack, he said with a chuckle. Black Jack was my father and he named me Jack as well. I think it was to create a little confusion. They called me Black Jack Tillotson junior until my father died. Tillotson" said Black Jack "has just stuck.

Judd said, "But you are not a slave now, so why do you not revert to your own family name?"

"I was born here on the island sir, of parents born on the island. In the old days most of us had only one name. Mr. Tillotson gave us his name of which we have become quite proud."

"You seem to have done a fine job with the business here," said Judd. "If you wish it, I want you to arrange to change your name to something you can be proud of for yourself. To me, you are a free man and—"

"How does Jack Freeman sound?" said Jack.

"Mr. Freeman. I like it," said Judd. "My first instruction, Mr. Freeman, is to have you arrange for documents to be prepared for the transfer of your residence from the Plantation's name into your own, along with one acre of land. When I return, if all is as I find it this time, I will sign those documents. I want you to be proud of what and who you are and to see some substantial rewards for your efforts. Do we have an understanding, Mr. Freeman?"

The other man's reaction was its own answer. His eyes welled up and a large tear slid down his cheek. Wiping away the tear he stood up, and said, "My own identity, Jack Freeman. My wife and I both wish many good blessings on you sir, Captain Cane Sir. He repeated as if to himself. Jack Freeman." His face split into a wide grin as he repeated his new name.

"You should be training someone to replace yourself as you move up in life, because I feel that you will," said Judd.

At Jack Freeman's recommendation, Judd decided to keep the ships present cargo and go south to trade it. The newly acquired cargo would be brought back to The Plantation and exchanged for a repeat trading trip. Jack also suggested going into town and exchanging the chest of cash for a letter of credit, as it would be easier and safer to transport. This was done and Judd returned to his ship. Seated in his cabin Judd had overwhelming surges of excitement about the huge sum of money that he had just been given. This was the catalyst, in his mind, that set him to thinking about what he should divulge to Leeza, and what he should keep private. After all, he thought, the deed has nothing to do with anyone else. He believed that this was really the corner stone of his and Mary's future security. Judd arose and went out onto the quarter deck. Here he found Leeza and Dickey sunning themselves. Sitting on the ships wide mahogany rail Judd spoke to both of them. "I've had a good look at The Plantation and like what I see."

"Don't look like no bleedin plantation to me cap'n," said Dickey.

"It used to be a sugar plantation and when the business failed, they freed the slaves and changed the place to a trading post." Judd went on to explain how it worked. After a lengthy clarification he said "I believe that we can do a number of runs to the Orient from here. Sell them our cargo and buy a cargo to go back to the Orient. When we are ready, we go from the Orient to England. Then from England, full of English cargo, we repeat the exercise."

Leeza asked, "So how does the men gets paid?

"We keep records of the transactions. The Plantation gives us letters of credit to use in the Orient. We have money to advance the men some of their pay. Each time we get to England they will have accumulated a tidy sum to take home."

"From where?" asked Dickey.

"You bleedin fool. We gives them some pay when they wants it. They doan git all they pay. The bit's o pay they didn't git all adds up for them to git when we goes ome," Leeza said with exasperation. Looking at Judd he added, "'e aint got a clue, but, I likes yer plan Captain."

Judd stood and gave the orders to prepare the Gideon Rover for sailing.

***

Within the year The Gideon Rover had carried out two successful trading voyages and the decision was made to make a return trip to England.

Workers were busy clearing the dockside to allow the Gideon Rover to cast off as Jack Freeman came running to the dockside waving his arm in the air holding a letter, which was addressed to Judd. One of the crewmen was lowered over the side on a Jacob's ladder to collect it. Upon being given the letter Judd retired to his cabin and saw it was from his mother. When he finished reading it, he sent for Lezza to join him. Handing the letter to Leeza, he said, "read this and tell me what you think."

Leeza started to read to himself, periodically stopping and looking up at Judd, who was studying Leeza's face intently.

My dearest son,

I am writing to you hoping that you can clear up a mystery. Late yesterday a man came to the village from the Admiralty asking after you. Fortunately, Davey Blacksmith sent him out to the Earl's where pa and I talked with him. We are both confused. The man said that a ship called the Governor Ready had disappeared with you and its' crew. Nobody has seen it since. The Navy has been looking for the ship for the last two years or so. He told us some marines and officers from HMS Vanguard were left on an island and have made it back to England. They were unable to help the Navy with their enquiries.

He wanted to know if we knew where you were or what had happened. Pa asked him if the Navy thought someone had taken the ship and its' crew hostage. He was told that the Admiralty did not know. As you and some other people were Royal Navy Sailors, they were doing their best to find you, he said 'for your safety'. We did not tell him about you and Mary getting married as we did not want to have the man frighten her. The Admiralty man said that everyone was baffled by the situation. Pa promised to let him know if we heard from you.

It was strange because the Admiralty man did not look like he was really concerned. Pa asked him who the other men were that were gone and he said that he wasn't allowed to tell us. Pa offered to take the man to the train station, and he did. It didn't look like they were trying very hard to find anything else out in the village. You must be careful when you come home. Please write and let us know what is happening. When do you think you will be coming home? Mary misses you, we all miss you. I don't know if you got our last letter, telling about your daughter. Mary gave birth to a beautiful baby girl, six pounds seven ounces of joy. Mary had her christened a fortnight ago. Her name is Agatha. She is so pretty. You will be proud of her. You two didn't waste much time getting your family going. We were surprised. Pa and I spend a lot of time with her and the baby.

Try and send us a telegram if you can. Oh yes, your pa says to tell you that he spoke with Mrs. Trott and nobody from the Admiralty has been to her house. I don't know if that means anything.

Lots of love. Ma and Pa

Leeza handed the letter back to Judd and heaved a great sigh before he spoke. "Congratulations daddy Cane! Did you know that you were to be a daddy?""No. I didn't. A letter must have got lost somewhere, but thanks anyway. Wow! Me a father. I am at a loss for words. Is there something…I don't know what I should be doing. Is there something I should do Leeza?" "No, babies is women's work. . She is with family. That's important."

"Leeza, you are a father, how did you know what to do, what is expected of you?"

"You don't know! No-one tells you nuffink. There aint no book. You is gonna make mistakes, but, wot's important is you is gonna luv the little bugger and do everyfing in your power to protect 'im, or 'er."

"But weren't you scared?"

"Let me tell yer some fing. I was scared when mine was born, acause I was at sea and couldn't 'elp. I was scared every time some fing went wrong acause I was away. You are gonna spend a lot of time being scared for your young uns. That's wot being a daddy is all about. I can't tell you not to worry acause every fing will work out fine. Allays does."

"I am excited Leeza! Wow, I'm a pa. Me a pa, now aint that grand."

Judd took a moment to catch his breath and compose himself, and asked "what do you think the Admiralty stuff is going to mean to us?"

"I needs to ponder this un. I sees sum good fings. One, it doan seem like they is to bovered about us. Two, they doan 'ave a clue where the Governor Ready is and aint worked out its name 'as bin changed. I do fink we should fink about muddying the water a little bit more."

"What do you mean, muddy the water?"

"Frow in somefing else to keep them confused. If'n they aint bin to my 'ouse an' we know Dickey aint got no 'ome fer them to go to, we should keep them finking about the ship, an' not you.me and Dickie."

"Alright, how?" asked Judd.

"Well, we can't change how it looks. If we makes this trip to England the last for the Gideon Rover and base 'er some uver place the Navy aint gonna be able to keep theys eyes all over the world."

"That sounds very complicated to me. Plus, you have to think about the men. They are going to want to go home from time to time."

"Wot if we go to New York or to St Johns in Canada? They makes a lot of good ships there. We could maybe sell the 'Rover' and buy us a new ship. Clean as a whistle, no trace, nuffing to connect the two ships or crew."

Judd leaned back in his chair and with a smile he replied, "Leeza Trott, you are a bloody genius. Sometimes I think you are wasted being a cook."

"'ang on a minit. I is a cook, *and*, I is your partner."

"I wouldn't have it any other way." Both men laughed together as they left the cabin to resume their duties.

***

Late in 1849, after five days of sailing in pleasant weather, north from St. Eustasies, the crew of the Gideon Rover had been lulled into a false sense of security. The skies suddenly grew dark and stiff winds blew in from the east. The shrill whistle of the wind through rigging quickly changed to a shriek. Hatches were battened down. All manner of moveable items were securely lashed to the deck and ships railings. Life at sea can be hectic, and it was about to get very hectic now. Judd, after discussing the situation with the helmsman and more experienced sailors decided to take shelter off the coast of America. The charts showed the ship to be off the coast of Georgia. A further examination revealed a sizeable island that divided a large river into two and therefore presented a possible shelter in which to wait out the storm. It took the whole day, even with the tremendous tail winds, for them to reach the shelter of the Columbia River. After securing a safe anchor Judd instructed the quartermaster, "Stand the men down for the night. Splice the main brace for all men and keep a skeleton crew on standby watch." With a grin he added, "And I don't mean the skinny buggers, make the fat one earn their keep."

The quartermaster laughed as he replied, "Aye, aye captain. They have all earned a rest. The men have done well this night."

The Gideon Rover had stayed at anchor for four days, weathering out the fierce storm. The winds were so strong that they even drove a tidal wave up into St. Christopher's Shelter where the ship was anchored. When the storm finally broke the crew took the opportunity to resupply the ship from Brunswick's large selection of merchants that ferried supplies to the island. There was one trading post on the island that provided many supplies and arranged for others to be brought down river to the Gideon Rover. Josiah Mielman, who ran this trading post, a diminutive little man, unkempt and obsequious, appeared to have his hand on the pulse of business in the area. Judd observed the man's skill in hovering among his customers while taking in everything happening around him. Josiah made no secret of his Jewish faith. Many people, in Judd's experience, felt trepidation in doing business with the Jews, but not Judd. He held the Jewish London bankers and business people in high regard and did not allow their ritualistic style of trading to deflect his watchful eye.

With this in mind, he gravitated towards Josiah, and the two men wove around each other in a thrust and parry, one giving information and then seeking the same. Neither appeared overly interested or anxious in parting with too much without receiving something of value first. It was when Judd accepted Josiah's invitation to dine with him that evening, and Josiah inquired about the *Gideon Rover's* cargo, that Judd knew the old man had a purpose.

At dinner that evening Judd learned that much trade bypassed Jakeskill Island's facilities, as most ships were destined for Columbus up the river and never stopped. Josiah's proposal was a simple one: In return for Judd's promise to bring one cargo a year for the next five years to him on the island, he would arrange an interview that could change Judd's life and wealth. He detailed the huge rift developing between the Northern and Southern States over the issue of slavery. The *Wanderer*, a slave trader, had earlier this year put ashore a cargo of 409 slaves. Many believed this was the last time this would happen in America. Many felt the slavery issue could tear the country apart.

"Sir," said Judd, "there are many thoughts regarding slavery. We could discuss them all evening. If you have, other knowledge from which we both benefit, please tell me."

"There is a so called, gentleman landowner who owns more than twelve square miles of this island. He is a notoriously brutal master to his slaves," said Josiah. "He has expressed concerns about what may happen if the States go to war. I believe that he fears his own slaves may turn on him. Should it come to war, he has not the courage to fight for what he believes against an enemy at least his equal. He calls himself 'General,' but I can't work out what he was ever a General of. Truth is, the dress uniform he wears is a mixture of an English Indian Regiment and a South African Rifles regiment."

Judd prompted Josiah to go on.

"The man I speak of seeks to distance himself from what may happen and return to England. I believe that you can be a man of discretion and come to his aid. What say you, sir?"

"Mr. Mielman, while I know of my integrity, you can only surmise it," said Judd. "A man who takes promises from a man on a ship for something to happen over the next five years is a man who lacks caution."

"With respect to your observations, Captain, my typical level of caution would have you sign for your promises in your own blood, but alas, circumstances do not allow it. I work within the limits placed upon me." Judd could see that Josiah was uncomfortable with his position.

"Do I understand correctly that you have been asked to aid in the disposal of this man's property?"

"You understand correctly, Captain."

"Here is my proposal to you, sir," said Judd. "I will return at noon tomorrow, at which time you and the General will provide me with evidence of the value of the property. You will have him, the owner, with you, and he shall bring the property deeds with him. If we agree upon a satisfactory deal, I will transport him to England on the Gideon Rover, where our transaction will be completed in legal terms. In return for affecting these transactions, from the day the Gideon Rover sails from Jakeskill, you will assume full rights to manage the property. You will have all the rights you require to transact on my behalf, and we will share the profits evenly. I do not plan to return and fully exercise my rights of ownership for two full years. If this meets with your agreement, we will meet again tomorrow."

The following morning Josiah met with Judd and provided him with evidence of suggested value of the property. He said to Judd he said "The general will present himself on the Gideon Rover tomorrow morning with the deeds and be ready to leave. I would be wary of this man and his integrity, as I believe he has little or indeed, none."

Judd replied, "You have done well Mr. Mielman. I look forward to a long and mutually rewarding relations

They met the next day on the Gideon Rover. The 'General' appeared to be a man full of himself, who carried a pompous air. "Show me to my quarters Captain if you please," he demanded. Judd beckoned the man to follow him into his own cabin. The "General" spoke, "this will do adequately for now captain."

"Sir, this is my personal accommodation. I have yet to decide if there will be need for accommodations for you."

"What do you mean? The little Jew, Mielman, told me that we had a deal."

"You may have a deal with "*Mr.*" Josiah Mielman sir, but at this time you do not have one with me." Judd placed great emphasis on the Josiah's name. There was a knock on the cabin door, and Leeza poked his head around the opening. "Captain, Sir, Mr. Lemon and me is right outside the door, should you need us. Judd stood, legs firmly planted apart, arms folded and spoke in a deliberate tone. "It is my understanding, sir, that I am to pay you twenty thousand pounds and give you passage to England, in return for which you will transfer ownership of The Palisades, plantation or whatever you call it, to me. Is that your understanding?"

"It is Captain. All the details shall be taken care of when we arrive in England."

"Please sit at my desk and put pen to paper. You do not leave this island without your written commitment to honor our agreement, and, consider this, if I catch as much as a hint of skullduggery, you will not reach England. Do I make myself clear? Your reputation precedes you sir, and I will have no hesitation in meting out my threat. A lot can go wrong on the high seas between here and England."

***

Within the month the Governor Ready sailed into Southampton and berthed alongside Duggan Ship Chandlers. The General had spent little time outside of the ships' brig. That area had been set up as the General's accommodation. Most of his meals he took in the brig. Once a day he would come on deck to take fresh air but otherwise he kept to himself. It appeared to Judd that the man was sulking or scared, neither of which caused Judd any undue concern. Making several attempts at conversation, only to be rebuffed, Judd left the man alone.

Having made sure the ship was secure, Judd came down the gangway to be greeted by Madge Duggan. "Tis a long time you have been away captain," was her greetings.

"Yes ma'am, we have been trading in the South Pacific and Caribbean, and I have a special cargo which you will have no trouble selling."

"When are you looking to sail again, and, shall we restock your holds again this time?"

"Always straight to business ma'am. You are looking well and I trust business is good."

"It is sir. Thanks to your patronage and that of your fellow captains, we do well." As they were talking the General came down the gangway and interrupted with a haughty air.

"I will thank you to give me my money captain and I will be out of your hair once and for all."

Madge glanced at the man and turned to Judd saying, "What is his problem?"

"You don't want to know. I need to go over to Pettigrew & Lumley to have this fellow sign some papers."

The general in a belligerent tone said, "I am the General if you don't mind sir." Turning to Madge Duggan, he continued, "I am the General, madam, at your service."

Ignoring the man, Madge looked at Judd and said, "We will work with your crew Captain and start unloading. Will four days be sufficient for your turn around?"

"Yes ma'am, I will stop in to see you when I have taken care of this business."

***

Martin Lumley, the managing partner of Pettigrew Lumley saw Judd approaching his office and went to greet him. The two men shook hands and Judd started to introduce the General only to be interrupted by him. "Get on with it man. I have things to do."

Lumley looked in disbelief and asked, "General, what, who?"

"That's my business sir," was the retort.

Lumley raised his eyebrows and bid the men enter his chambers. They got down to business in a strained atmosphere. After the situation had been explained and Judd set out his requirements, the General demanded twenty-thousand pounds more than had been agreed upon for the transaction to be finalized. He had already received his passage as promised and felt that he now had the upper hand. The lawyer, after being told the history and background of the deal, told Judd to let him handle the matter. The General and Judd sat listening to the lawyer, who asked for the deeds. The General gave them to him under protest, demanding the contract be signed first. Judd was directed to sign the papers and then the General was told the same. The General went to grasp the contract and the lawyer held it saying that he wished to be sure the deed was in order. He took a prolonged study of the document, and requested the letter of credit paying for the land. The lawyer spread the documents out on his desk. He handed the letter of credit for the original amount agreed upon to the "General" at which time the General became hostile. The lawyer told the man to calm down or the local constable would be called. He then handed the General an invoice for the transporting him to England. It was for the sum of twenty thousand pounds with the notation, "Paid in full". The General went purple with rage. The lawyer handed Judd the deeds and stated, "Gentlemen your business is concluded." The General was getting out of hand when the lawyer handed him a sworn statement, that he prepared earlier at Judd's instruction. It laid out the murders that had taken place on Jakeskill Island. He then dismissed the man saying, "I have original statements and I will not hesitate to take action on them if anything should happen of which I disapprove. The General stormed out as Lumley said to Judd, "General indeed."

Arrangements were made for the deeds to be registered and ready for Judd to pick up within a couple of days. Upon returning to the Gideon Rover, details were set out and the men given permission to take leave and return for sailing five days hence. Judd and Leeza travelled together by train to London and then Judd went on to Mucking. Leeza promised to try and find out as much as he could about the Navy's interest in Judd and the Governor Ready. Gossip was rife in the docklands and he felt it would be an easy task.

***

The Tilbury train arrived in the early afternoon and Judd went by horse and carriage to the village green. He was surprised at how his father had renovated the old family home and converted the cowshed into a neat business office. He approached close to the house before Mary saw him. She got up from the chair, where she had been sitting in the afternoon sun, and placed a child into the small basket at her feet. She walked over to the picket fence, opened the gate and burst into tears. "I never imagined how hard it would be just being apart."

Judd enveloped her in his arms and held her head close to his chest. "Feel how hard my heart beats," he said. Holding her at arms-length, he looked into her eyes, then, holding her face in his open hands he gently kissed her lips and then her forehead. "I understand that we have created something special."

"Come see Agatha. I hope you don't mind that I've called her Agatha." She proudly lifted the baby out of the basket and placed her in Judd's apprehensive arms. She ran into the house and returned with a chair and they both sat in the warmth of the sun, reconnecting.

After a while Judd said that he should go and see his parents and was she able to leave the business and go with him. "I have a young girl working with me. She can take care of things for a while. We have quite a good little business developing here," she said. On the way over to his parents Judd told her of the land he had purchased on Jakeskill Island and that he would have a courier bring the deeds to her in a few days. He spoke of the letters of credit and what she should do with them. She was amazed at the amount of money and didn't fully understand how Judd had acquired it, but questioning it at this time seemed unimportant.

Typical of village life, word had reached Judd's parents that he was in town before he got to their home at the Earl's estate. They were standing in their small flower garden watching the road for his arrival. When they got there, Judd's mother held her arms out to take the baby as she greeted him. "Young man, what have you been doing with yourself? Has the navy found you yet?"

"Have they been back looking for me?" Judd asked.

"No, but I'm sure they will."

"I don't think so ma. They are as confused as everyone else. It looks like one of those mysteries you read about."

Mary, with a quizzical expression, said, "What are you talking about? Judd, you told me that you aren't in the Navy anymore."

"That's correct, my dear. I'm not sure if they know it yet, but I am a merchant sailor these days. Let me talk to pa while you and ma catch up."

Father and son walked into the house and found a private spot where Judd told his father the whole story of the Governor Ready and Gideon Rover. He went on to say, "We are sailing in five days to America where we are going to sell the Rover and buy a new ship. Then we will all be legal, apart from the Navy thing, and I will worry about that at the appropriate time."

"Tis a rogue you be, I thinks, it is best you let me tell Mary when you are gone. Tis no sense in having a row while you is here so short a time. I thinks, a lookin at the navy thing, they aint got a clue wot to do, cause they don't know wot appened. Twas a proper smart thing, you sending that cable tellin where them officers was. Cause if theys own officers can't tell 'em they might as well be blind. How did you keeps all the sailors quiet?"

"Money pa, those that wanted nothing to do with it, got paid off handsomely, and those that came along have never been paid so well. Pa, I have been doing very well and can see that maybe in a few more years I will be able to give up the sea and never have to work hard again."

"Good finking my boy. Look after those around you. Me and ma will take care of Mary and the baby till you comes ome for good."

Chapter 19

AMERICA - JAKESKILL ISLAND

The Gideon Rover had stayed at anchor for four days, weathering out the fierce storm. The winds were so strong that they even drove a tidal wave up into St. Christopher's Shelter where the ship was anchored. When the storm finally broke the crew took the opportunity to resupply the ship from Brunswick's large selection of merchants that ferried supplies to the island. There was one trading post on the island that provided many supplies and arranged for others to be brought down to the Gideon Rover. Josiah Mielman, who ran this trading post, a diminutive little man, unkempt and obsequious, appeared to have his hand on the pulse of business in the area. Judd observed the man's skill in hovering among his customers while taking in everything happening around him. Josiah made no secret of his Jewish faith. Many people, in Judd's experience, felt trepidation in doing business with the Jews, but not Judd. He held the Jewish London bankers and business people in high regard and did not allow their ritualistic style of trading to deflect his watchful eye.

With this in mind, he gravitated towards Josiah, and the two men wove around each other in a thrust and parry, one giving information and then seeking the same. Neither appeared overly interested or anxious in parting with too much without receiving something of value first. It was when Judd accepted Josiah's invitation to dine with him that evening, and Josiah inquired about the *Gideon Rover's* cargo, that Judd knew the old man had a purpose.

At dinner that evening Judd learned that much trade bypassed Jakeskill Island's facilities, as most ships were destined for Columbus up the river and never stopped. Josiah's proposal was a simple one: In return for Judd's promise to bring one cargo a year for the next five years to him on the island, he would arrange an interview that could change Judd's life and wealth. He detailed the huge rift developing between the Northern and Southern States over the issue of slavery. The *Wanderer*, a slave trader, had earlier this year put ashore a cargo of 409 slaves. Many believed this was the last time this would happen in America. Many felt the slavery issue could tear the country apart.

"Sir," said Judd, "there are many thoughts regarding slavery. We could discuss them all evening. If you have, other knowledge from which we both benefit, please tell me."

"There is a so called, gentleman landowner who owns more than twelve square miles of this island. He is a notoriously brutal master to his slaves," said Josiah. "He has expressed concerns about what may happen if the States go to war. I believe that he fears his own slaves may turn on him. Should it come to war, he has not the courage to fight for what he believes against an enemy at least his equal. He calls himself 'General,' but I can't work out what he was ever a General of. Truth is, the dress uniform he wears is a mixture of an English Indian Regiment and a South African Rifles regiment."

Judd prompted Josiah to go on.

"The man I speak of seeks to distance himself from what may happen and return to England. I believe that you can be a man of discretion and come to his aid. What say you, sir?"

"Mr. Mielman, while I know of my integrity, you can only surmise it," said Judd. "A man who takes promises from a man on a ship for something to happen over the next five years is a man who lacks caution."

"With respect to your observations, Captain, my typical level of caution would have you sign for your promises in your own blood, but alas, circumstances do not allow it. I work within the limits placed upon me." Judd could see that Josiah was uncomfortable with his position.

"Do I understand correctly that you have been asked to aid in the disposal of this man's property?"

"You understand correctly, Captain."

"Here is my proposal to you, sir," said Judd. "I will return at noon tomorrow, at which time you and the General will provide me with evidence of the value of the property. You will have him, the owner, with you, and he shall bring the property deeds with him. If we agree upon a satisfactory deal, I will transport him to England on the Gideon Rover, where our transaction will be completed in legal terms. In return for affecting these transactions, from the day the Gideon Rover sails from Jakeskill, you will assume full rights to manage the property. You will have all the rights you require to transact on my behalf, and we will share the profits evenly. I do not plan to return and fully exercise my rights of ownership for two full years. If this meets with your agreement, we will meet again tomorrow."

The following morning Josiah met with Judd and provided him with evidence of suggested value of the property. He said to Judd he said "The general will present himself on the Gideon Rover tomorrow morning with the deeds and be ready to leave. I would be wary of this man and his integrity, as I believe he has little or indeed, none."

Judd replied, "You have done well Mr. Mielman. I look forward to a long and mutually rewarding relations

They met the next day on the Gideon Rover. The 'General' appeared to be a man full of himself, who carried a pompous air. "Show me to my quarters Captain if you please," he demanded. Judd beckoned the man to follow him into his own cabin. The "General" spoke, "this will do adequately for now captain."

"Sir, this is my personal accommodation. I have yet to decide if there will be need for accommodations for you."

"What do you mean? The little Jew, Mielman, told me that we had a deal."

"You may have a deal with "**Mr.**" Josiah Mielman sir, but at this time you do not have one with me." Judd placed great emphasis on the Josiah's name. There was a knock on the cabin door, and Leeza poked his head around the opening. "Captain, Sir, Mr. Lemon and me is right outside the door, should you need us. Judd stood, legs firmly planted apart, arms folded and spoke in a deliberate tone. "It is my understanding, sir, that I am to pay you twenty thousand pounds and give you passage to England, in return for which you will transfer ownership of The Palisades, plantation or whatever you call it, to me. Is that your understanding?"

"It is Captain. All the details shall be taken care of when we arrive in England."

"Please sit at my desk and put pen to paper. You do not leave this island without your written commitment to honor our agreement, and, consider this, if I catch as much as a hint of skullduggery, you will not reach England. Do I make myself clear? Your reputation precedes you sir, and I will have no hesitation in meting out my threat. A lot can go wrong on the high seas between here and England."

***

Within the month the Governor Ready sailed into Southampton and berthed alongside Duggan Ship Chandlers. The General had spent little time outside of the ships' brig. That area had been set up as the General's accommodation. Most of his meals he took in the brig. Once a day he would come on deck to take fresh air but otherwise he kept to himself. It appeared to Judd that the man was sulking or scared, neither of which caused Judd any undue concern. Making several attempts at conversation, only to be rebuffed, Judd left the man alone.

Having made sure the ship was secure, Judd came down the gangway to be greeted by Madge Duggan. "Tis a long time you have been away captain," was her greetings.

"Yes ma'am, we have been trading in the South Pacific and Caribbean, and I have a special cargo which you will have no trouble selling."

"When are you looking to sail again, and, shall we restock your holds again this time?"

"Always straight to business ma'am. You are looking well and I trust business is good."

"It is sir. Thanks to your patronage and that of your fellow captains, we do well." As they were talking the General came down the gangway and interrupted with a haughty air.

"I will thank you to give me my money captain and I will be out of your hair once and for all."

Madge glanced at the man and turned to Judd saying, "What is his problem?"

"You don't want to know. I need to go over to Pettigrew & Lumley to have this fellow sign some papers."

The general in a belligerent tone said, "I am the General if you don't mind sir." Turning to Madge Duggan, he continued, "I am the General, madam, at your service."

Ignoring the man, Madge looked at Judd and said, "We will work with your crew Captain and start unloading. Will four days be sufficient for your turn around?"

"Yes ma'am, I will stop in to see you when I have taken care of this business."

***

Martin Lumley, the managing partner of Pettigrew Lumley saw Judd approaching his office and went to greet him. The two men shook hands and Judd started to introduce the General only to be interrupted by him. "Get on with it man. I have things to do."

Lumley looked in disbelief and asked, "General, what, who?"

"That's my business sir," was the retort.

Lumley raised his eyebrows and bid the men enter his chambers. They got down to business in a strained atmosphere. After the situation had been explained and Judd set out his requirements, the General demanded twenty-thousand pounds more than had been agreed upon for the transaction to be finalized. He had already received his passage as promised and felt that he now had the upper hand. The lawyer, after being told the history and background of the deal, told Judd to let him handle the matter. The General and Judd sat listening to the lawyer, who asked for the deeds. The General gave them to him under protest, demanding the contract be signed first. Judd was directed to sign the papers and then the General was told the same. The General went to grasp the contract and the lawyer held it saying that he wished to be sure the deed was in order. He took a prolonged study of the document, and requested the letter of credit paying for the land. The lawyer spread the documents out on his desk. He handed the letter of credit for the original amount agreed upon to the "General" at which time the General became hostile. The lawyer told the man to calm down or the local constable would be called. He then handed the General an invoice for the transporting him to England. It was for the sum of twenty thousand pounds with the notation, "Paid in full". The General went purple with rage. The lawyer handed Judd the deeds and stated, "Gentlemen your business is concluded." The General was getting out of hand when the lawyer handed him a sworn statement, that he prepared earlier at Judd's instruction. It laid out the murders that had taken place on Jakeskill Island. He then dismissed the man saying, "I have original statements and I will not hesitate to take action on them if anything should happen of which I disapprove. The General stormed out as Lumley said to Judd, "General indeed."

Arrangements were made for the deeds to be registered and ready for Judd to pick up within a couple of days. Upon returning to the Gideon Rover, details were set out and the men given permission to take leave and return for sailing five days hence. Judd and Leeza travelled together by train to London and then Judd went on to Mucking. Leeza promised to try and find out as much as he could about the Navy's interest in Judd and the Governor Ready. Gossip was rife in the docklands and he felt it would be an easy task.

***

The Tilbury train arrived in the early afternoon and Judd went by horse and carriage to the village green. He was surprised at how his father had renovated the old family home and converted the cowshed into a neat business office. He approached close to the house before Mary saw him. She got up from the chair, where she had been sitting in the afternoon sun, and placed a child into the small basket at her feet. She walked over to the picket fence, opened the gate and burst into tears. "I never imagined how hard it would be just being apart."

Judd enveloped her in his arms and held her head close to his chest. "Feel how hard my heart beats," he said. Holding her at arms-length, he looked into her eyes, then, holding her face in his open hands he gently kissed her lips and then her forehead. "I understand that we have created something special."

"Come see Agatha. I hope you don't mind that I've called her Agatha." She proudly lifted the baby out of the basket and placed her in Judd's apprehensive arms. She ran into the house and returned with a chair and they both sat in the warmth of the sun, reconnecting.

After a while Judd said that he should go and see his parents and was she able to leave the business and go with him. "I have a young girl working with me. She can take care of things for a while. We have quite a good little business developing here," she said. On the way over to his parents Judd told her of the land he had purchased on Jakeskill Island and that he would have a courier bring the deeds to her in a few days. He spoke of the letters of credit and what she should do with them. She was amazed at the amount of money and didn't fully understand how Judd had acquired it, but questioning it at this time seemed unimportant.

Typical of village life, word had reached Judd's parents that he was in town before he got to their home at the Earl's estate. They were standing in their small flower garden watching the road for his arrival. When they got there, Judd's mother held her arms out to take the baby as she greeted him. "Young man, what have you been doing with yourself? Has the navy found you yet?"

"Have they been back looking for me?" Judd asked.

"No, but I'm sure they will."

"I don't think so ma. They are as confused as everyone else. It looks like one of those mysteries you read about."

Mary, with a quizzical expression, said, "What are you talking about? Judd, you told me that you aren't in the Navy anymore."

"That's correct, my dear. I'm not sure if they know it yet, but I am a merchant sailor these days. Let me talk to pa while you and ma catch up."

Father and son walked into the house and found a private spot where Judd told his father the whole story of the Governor Ready and Gideon Rover. He went on to say, "We are sailing in five days to America where we are going to sell the Rover and buy a new ship. Then we will all be legal, apart from the Navy thing, and I will worry about that at the appropriate time."

"Tis a rogue you be, I thinks, it is best you let me tell Mary when you are gone. Tis no sense in having a row while you is here so short a time. I thinks, a lookin at the navy thing, they aint got a clue wot to do, cause they don't know wot appened. Twas a proper smart thing, you sending that cable tellin where them officers was. Cause if theys own officers can't tell 'em they might as well be blind. How did you keeps all the sailors quiet?"

"Money pa, those that wanted nothing to do with it, got paid off handsomely, and those that came along have never been paid so well. Pa, I have been doing very well and can see that maybe in a few more years I will be able to give up the sea and never have to work hard again."

"Good finking my boy. Look after those around you. Me and ma will take care of Mary and the baby till you comes ome for good."

Chapter 20

It was in the summer of Judd's 22nd year, that he decided this voyage would be the one where they would dispose of The Gideon Rover. Dickey Lemon was shocked by Judd's plan. It was beyond his scope of understanding at this point that The Gideon Rover could be sold. It didn't take long for Judd to show how the new ship was in effect wiping their past slate clean. Leeza had spent his leave time hanging around the Admiralty, the London docks and pubs frequented by Royal Navy sailors. The only thing he uncovered was the story of the mysterious disappearance of the Governor Ready and the officers being left on an island. There was much humor had at the officers' expense. Nobody really knew if the tale was truth or fiction. So, the new ship appeared to be a strategic move with good points to be had.

The choice was made to use the port of Saint John in New Brunswick, Canada. This port had developed a stellar reputation for the ships being build there. The sale of the Gideon Rover in Saint John was a swift and lucrative deal as there were more people seeking ships than could built quickly enough. The Gideon's crew was housed in local establishments while a replacement ship was located and purchased. The Sovereign of the Seas was a 1,227-tonner built of pitch pine, tamara, and birch, sheathed in felt and yellow metal and bolted. Judd felt that when he left the sea, he would be leaving his crew with one of the finest, most seaworthy ships available.

As the new ship was nearing completion, Judd learned that it would take another two months for her to be fitted out for sea. He found another identical ship on the next dry dock, completed and already fitted out for sea. Judd offered a handsome premium to the shipbuilder to name the ship that was his and it was complete. The Sovereign of the Seas, could be sold to him and named the *Mary Jane* in honor of Judd's and Davey Blacksmith's wifes. A pair of twining poppies, the county flower of Essex, decorated both sides of the name. The captain of The Sovereign of the Seas, Captain Cruickshank, was not due to arrive to pick up his ship for two more months, and would never know the switch had taken place.

The *Mary Jane* was out of the shipyards within the week. It anchored in the Bay of Fundy, where the crew was familiarized with the ship, and they sailed for St. Eustatius within the fortnight. Much to Judd's pleasure, during that week he had managed to procure a cargo of hides and skins for the return voyage to St. Eustatius. Things were off to a good start.

***

Looking back Judd knew that his time as a midshipman had taught him that a happy, respected, and well-fed and paid crew was easy to control. The crew of the Gideon Rover enjoyed a quality of sea life almost unheard of. The pay promised them on that memorable first trip was far exceeded. Some of the older crew members retired, and their places were easily filled.

Now the *Mary Jane* had settled into a lucrative trading pattern of two years between the orient and St. Eustatius, as well trips from Asia to St. Eustatius. The return trips to England were welcomed for their dependability and lucrative rewards.

Six years passed and Judd started to give serious thought to retiring from the sea. The Plantation at St. Eustatius continued to pour money into his bank accounts and showed no signs of slowing down.

Lezza Trott and Dickey Lemon supported everything Judd attempted and their personal wealth grew. Dickey, having outgrown his youthful bravado, had learned to read and write and became indispensable to Judd. They both could see that the ways of the sea were changing. Ships made of iron were now more common. The steam packet, *Sirius*, had crossed the Atlantic in record time. Although England always seemed to be at war with some country or other, Judd at twenty-eight knew changes were coming and that his artful dodging was limited. While Dickey Lemon and most of his crew enjoyed the dusky women, paid or seduced, Judd's heart was tied firmly to Mary and Agatha.

Life at sea can be very profitable for one who can see and grab opportunities as they appear. Judd was just such a seaman. Since becoming the father of a daughter, Agatha Sunrise Cane, now eleven years old, had spurred his drive on relentlessly. His taste for land growing quickly, Judd acquired more properties throughout the Caribbean. He now owned properties in Dominica, the Turks and Caicos Islands, Mustique, and part of Jakeskill island off the coast of Georgia, in America.

In early May, as the *Mary Jane* caught a stiff southerly wind, Judd stood on the quarterdeck and took in everything that lay before him. Some years later at thirty-one, he had almost twenty years at sea. The afternoon sun warmed his face and memories flooded into his consciousness. He saw the sailors, spread out on the yardarms, sunning themselves with the wind in their faces as they leaned forward, arms outstretched, as if they were flying. Others trimmed the sails and leaned into the wind as it whipped their hair around. They were little specks against a backdrop of brilliant blue sky. It was at this moment that Judd decided it was time to leave the sea.

Dickey Lemon, tanned and well over six feet tall, had turned into a man, and Judd had never seen it happening as, indeed, he had not seen himself change. Dickey was deep in conversation with Lezza Trott when Judd signaled him to join him on the quarterdeck.

"Dickey, tell the helmsman, thirty-one degrees, one hour, sixteen minutes north; eighty-one degrees, twenty-four hours, four minutes west. Let's go and take a look at Jakeskill Island,"

"Bin a while since we bin there. Wot's we goin' for?" Dickey enquired.

Judd was about to answer when he remembered that neither Dickey nor Leeza knew that he owned property on the island. "Just to see what is happening there. The place intrigued me the last time. At least this time we are going by choice and not storm driven."

During the afternoon watch of the next day, the American coastline came up on the horizon, quickly transforming from a hazy dotted line into a rich, verdant spectacle. Rounding the southern tip of the island into Jakeskill Sound, the *Mary Jane* turned northward to run up the Jakeskill River. A looming wooden bridge connected the island to the mainland of Georgia. The calm of the river was a relief from the huge Atlantic waves that continually pounded the weather side of the island. After dropping anchor Judd went ashore is search of Josiah Mielman. The meeting was cordial and definitive. Josiah had been amply rewarded during the previous years of business. He had retained the best of the freed slaves as caretakers. All the buildings were now to be closed and shuttered, except for those essential dwellings needed. Josiah was to oversee the security of the property, which was fenced off from the balance of the island.

The island was approximately twelve miles long and three miles wide. It was divided in half by the road that met the bridge and connected the island to the mainland. The northern part of the island was a mixture of dwellings, businesses, and small farms, and was considered less desirable.

Josiah started to relate the history of the Palisades to Judd. "The southern portion was known as the Palisades, a network of grand plantations previously owned by the General. Each plantation was run by an overseer and had its own slave settlement, run brutally with no consideration for the slaves. The main estate drew its labor and lifestyle from the various plantations. The flatness of the island made control over its inhabitants an easy task. The ocean on the western side was intimidating, and the river on the eastern side, had been constantly patrolled by the General's men. The hefty hundred-dollar reward paid for a slave's return along with the public flogging of returned slaves and their families kept escapes to a minimum. It was rumored that, initially, escaped slaves would kill themselves if caught to save their families from retribution. But the General had carried out that retribution anyway as a further deterrent." The old man stopped speaking for a moment, gathering his will to continue with the story.

"The opulence and grandeur of the main house contradicted the other half of the island, which was fifty per cent swamp and mangrove. The General spared no expense in living in his isolated fiefdom. Conveniences and inventions were the most modern available, but did little to hide the seething undercurrent of discontent and pent-up hostility."

In the shadowy light of the trading store Judd noticed Josiah was looking tired and weary, and Judd asked what was bothering him.

Josiah turned and called out, "OJ, come. OJ, come to Jo Jo." A door in the dingy rear of the building slowly opened, and a little black boy poked his head around the door jamb, his eyes darting around the room. "Ojukwae, it is safe. Come here." The little boy relaxed and drew close. Josiah gave the boy a sweetmeat and pointed to the floor, where the boy sat obediently. Josiah explained that his faith required him to keep the children of the Lord safe, but the very existence of this child, at an earlier time, had put him and his family at risk. Judd demanded an explanation. Josiah sat down, took a deep breath, and told the story.

A new shipment of slaves was due to be brought ashore the year before Judd had brought the Palisades. There was a huge storm, and a great number of slaves drowned or disappeared. When calm had been restored, the General and a group of his slave masters scoured the island for four missing young boys, two sets of twins one year apart. He was so convinced he was the victim of deceit that he launched a reign of terror against his slaves. He started by murdering the father of the boys. Then, every night for two weeks, he murdered a slave that had come with the shipment, believing them part of the same family. The murders were carried out in a vicious spectacle. Only when he was convinced, he would be unable to discover the location of the boys did he stop the "daily" spectacle of murders. He merely committed one every month. The more the public outcry against him increased, the more he believed the boys were being held on the island. The problem was that he was partially right.

By the time Josiah realized the four little naked bodies he had found in his wood-shed that first morning after the storm were those the General was seeking, it was too late to hand them over. He knew the boys, five and six years old, had been put in the shed, because it was locked from the outside. Three of the boys were dead, of what he did not know. He clothed the surviving child, and to calm him, took him into his small, private place of prayer, keeping the boy close.

"Together, we buried the other brothers in my small flowerbed by the back door," said Josiah. "I had kept the boy in my store by day, and by night, he sleeps in my office. He's learned some English. As a Jew, alone in a strange land, my isolation makes me vulnerable. I feared sometimes that I could have become the vent for the General's rage. It's easy for the strong to destroy the weak in order to make themselves feel stronger. Can you imagine what this child of God must have gone through?" He stopped to gasp for breath. "I beg of you, take him to a better place. He has spent too much time in shadow. The child has no real family. I want for him to share in the goodness of life. The goodness that I see in you."

If anyone knew how an opportunity could change one's life, Judd did. If anyone knew how it felt when a child's world was suddenly flipped into an adult's world, Judd did. The boy was moved from the small trading post to the captain's cabin. The separation of Josiah and the boy tore at Judd's heart, and the three of them embraced, which Judd hoped would show the boy that he was safe.

What it actually did was confirm to Judd his need to leave the sea to be close to his daughter.

***

Ojukwae as the boy was called, was warmly accepted by many of the crew. Between Lezza Trott's fatherly protectiveness and the sailors, many, themselves fathers of boys, he was protected from those who saw him only as a heathen blacky. During the voyage, Ojukwae became a surrogate son to many.

One day as the morning watch took over Judd heard a cabin boy say to Ojukwae, "Hey sambo, you got some tar on your face." As the boy finished speaking, he looked up to see Judd towering over him and cowered away.

"Tell me what you mean by that," Judd demanded.

In a meek voice the boy replied "well captain, he is black like the tar in the deck joints, so I couldn't tell if he had some on him."

In an act of anger Judd turned, grabbed a deck swabbing bucket of water and threw its contents over the cabin boy. He picked the boy up by the scruff of the neck and seat of his pants and held him over the ships rail.

The boy shouted "Sorry, sorry," as Jud bellowed, "You look just like a fish, shall I throw you in the water because you look like a drowned fish?" He pulled the boy back and dropped him unceremoniously on the deck, and stormed off calling for Ojukwae to follow him.

***

The English Ojukwae had learned while living with Josiah and during his time on the *Mary Jane* was such a mixture of accents and dialects that it would be impossible for anyone to guess his origins. His delight at everything and the huge smile that cut his face clean in half was overshadowed only by his deep, booming belly laugh. Whenever Ojukwae laughed, anyone around him would break into a smile.

As September drew to a close, the *Mary Jane* trimmed her sails and changed direction from north by northeast to east to enter the English Channel. Sailors for centuries had named the first night entering the English Channel after a voyage "Channel Night". Spirits were high, old reminiscences were shared, and an era was coming to its end.

Standing at the ship's rail, Ojukwae joined in the revelry of returning home. Judd's heart was full as he watched the young boy. He knew that he had brought this child to a better place. Judd Cane was not one to readily, or unquestioningly accept the existence of God. There seemed to be no one who could answer his questions without shaking the Bible at him. But with the actions of the old Jew, Josiah, those of Lezza Trott in watching over the boy, and the way so many experienced, tough, sea-hardened men trusted him, there had to be something more to life. But what was the next step for the boy? Was Judd himself supposed to do more? Where was he to look for an answer?

Dropping anchor offshore at Poole in Dorset, the signal pot was fired to invite the port's surgeon for health clearance. As they rolled and bobbed on the mild surf, Judd had Dickey Lemon and Leeza Trott meet him in the ward room with the senior crew. Judd looked around the room taking in the faces that had become such a large part of his life before he spoke. "The time has come for me to step aside as your captain and return to shore life." There was an outburst of comments of disbelief. Judd waited for the room to settle down before starting again. "There is no reason for this way of life to end for you all. I am proposing that a new captain be appointed from among you." There was silence. "I have some men in mind, but I want this to be a happy transition for you all.

A huge, muscular, mountain of a man, Jumbo Barnes, the bosun, who picked up the duties of quartermaster, carpenter, and sail master, stepped forward and spoke. "I would like to put myself forward sir. Most of our men are married, to a wife. As you all know, I am married to the sea, or more specifically to this ship, and all you ugly mob." The room broke into laughter and cheers. It appeared that the heavy task had been easily dealt with by the crew themselves.

Judd spoke, "Is it your wish that Mr. Barnes becomes your new Captain?" Again, the room erupted in a cheer of support, with some men stepping forward to congratulate Jumbo.

Barnes shouted out, "It ain't Jumbo no more. It's Captain Barnes, and I thank you all for your support." The raucous cheer of approval told Judd immediately that the right choice had been made.

Responding to the signal pot, a tilley soon pulled alongside and began the inspection. Judd paid one of the tilley's oarsmen to send a telegram for him upon his return to shore. The harbormaster tried to encourage the captain to have the *Mary Jane* discharge her cargo in Poole's dockside. "Those six ships you see alongside belong to the Royal Shipping Line. This is their home port," he said. "If Poole is good enough for them, you should give it a try. Sir William St. John-Brown will be here this evening Captain. I am certain he would like to make your acquaintance. The company has great connections to the Queen. Could be good for business you know." The man tried his best but still, the *Mary Jane* left for Southampton on the evening watch.

Chapter 21

The late September sun slowly dipped below the horizon, sending billowing puffs of red, gold and yellow high into the clouds that reflected upon Mucking's trees, a palette of colors. Mary Cane sat in her office, gazing out through her hand-blown glass windowpanes at the dying embers of fading light. A tall, military-looking figure of the telegraph delivery man occupied her view as he entered the office. The brass bell rattled on its spring to announce his presence. He stood rigid at attention. His blue serge coat, with its highly polished buttons, and the thick, brown, shiny leather belt across his shoulder cut a figure of authority. The girls scattered around the office, busy at various ledgers and papers, giggling into their handkerchiefs.

"Ben Carter. Behave yourself. You're just delivering something. Give me the letter and be off with you," said Mary. Her rebuke brought about a round of laughter. "Girls! Back to your work."

"Miss Mary. I mean, Mrs. Cane. I have a telegram for you." He stepped forward. "From—"

"It is nobody's business who I get telegrams from," said Mary, speaking in her best professional business voice, "I will thank you to still your tongue." After taking a deep bow and saluting the office girls, Ben Carter handed her the telegram and turned on his heel. A shriek of laughter followed him out the door, and the jangling bell brought order back to the office.

Mary retired to her private office at the back of the main room and sat in the twilight, the unopened telegram on her desk. As word had spread of her skills in keeping the books for her parents at the dairy, she had taken on local businesspeople as clients. Since her marriage to Judd and the birth of Agatha, she saw the world in a different light. Judd had been busy at sea, acquiring land in far-off places. During their brief times together, they pledged to each other to give their daughter more opportunities than had been available to them. Judd worked for their future and Mary for their daughter's education.

"Agatha! Agatha! Come into Mama's office, please," she called from the office. The door opened, and framed by the outer office lights stood a small blonde child. Her hair was pulled back, held in place by a silk scarf. She wore calf-high boots, laced up the front, and the ruffles of her long dress stuck out from under her linen smock.

"Mama, the girls say you have a telegram," she said. "Is it from Papa?"

With a trembling hand, Mary held up the telegram. "I don't know, my dear. Why don't you open it and practice your reading by reading it to me?

Elevenyear old Agatha stood at the edge of her mother's desk and, with a flourish of importance, she slid the point of the ivory-handled letter opener into the corner of the envelope and slit it open. Silently, she read its contents and burst into tears. "It's Papa!"

Mary stood and leaned over the desk to take the telegram. Her heart pounded in her chest. Before she could read it, Agatha, through her tears, said, "Mama, Papa is coming home forever."

"Let's hope it is so," replied Mary as she pulled Agatha to bosom and held her close. She thought to herself, 'about bloody time'. It was 1860 and Judd was 34.

***

Agatha could clearly hear the whistle as the train left Tilbury station. Climbing the old copper beech tree in the garden, she watched the train in the distance fade from view. Would this be the one Papa was on? It had been over a week since the telegraph had been delivered, and Mama hadn't stopped cleaning, polishing, and tidying, even though her housemaid had done the same thing. When she asked her mother about Papa being home for good, her mother would simply say, "Well, he won't be home for bad, will he?" This did little to calm Agatha down. "Will Papa call me Agi?" she asked. All her friends in the village did.

"No, he will not, and don't let me catch any of the local children calling you that, either. Everyone is given a name for a reason, and you are A-G-A-T-H-A, Agatha. It will do you well to remember that."

Agatha climbed down from the huge beech tree at end of the back garden where she could see the road that came into the village, as she did every morning. Here she would climb and shout into the air to whoever could hear her, "Papa, where are you?" Then she turned and ran around to the front of the house to see a stack of trunks, sea chests, and canvas-wrapped bundles. Two large wooden crates stood alone, with a robustly built black child sitting on top of one. Her father stood with open arms and a huge smile, tears streaming down his face. She pushed his head back so that she could look at his eyes and wiped away his tears. "Don't cry, Papa," she said. "Today is a happy day." Then, she shrieked with all her might, "Mama, Mama! Papa is home! Mama, Mama come quickly! Papa is crying!"

Mary stood in the door and smiled. "Papa always makes me cry when he comes home," she said. "This time, it's his turn."

Judd looked at his wife and knew that his decision to stay had been the right one. His need to put down roots surfaced into his consciousness. "Yes Mary. I am home for good, and very excited about it. You are going to have to learn to live with me." Judd looked at the converted cow shed that was Mary's business office and saw that the signs were gone and it appeared unused. "What happened to the business?" he asked.

"Just hang on a minute, you haven't been home but a few moments and you are asking questions. There is plenty of time to explain about the business. We have new offices. We can get to that later." Mary glanced at the small but robust black child atop one of two very large crates. Judd lifted the boy down from the crate and said, "let me introduce you both to my friend, Ojukwae."

There was a quiet that dropped over the group only to be broken by Mary. "You cannot bring a slave boy into this house," said Mary. "I will not permit it. It's wrong, Judd Cane, and you know it. Is this how you've been living at sea?"

"Oh my, am I to have a slave?" asked Agatha.

"I am surprised at you, Mary, making such a judgment before you know the facts," said Judd. As for you Agatha, I thought that you were going to be my slave when I came home."

"Pa, slaves are black not white."

Mary burst out, "Agatha, how dare you speak that way in front of a guest."

Judd raised his hand to quiet them both and said, "Mary, Agatha, Ojukwae is not going to be a guest in our house. He is going to live with us as part of our family."

"Pa! I will be the laughing stock at school. People will think that I have a black brother. You can't do this to me pa."

Mary asked, "Do I not get a say in the matter?"

Judd suggested that they all sit down to a cup of tea so he could tell them everything.

As Mary was brewing the tea, she asked Judd, "What is in those two huge crates? Everything you ever saw while you were away?" Time will tell was the only answer she was going to get. "Why didn't you write or cable me about the boy?"

"Because I did not know what was going to happen with him and I only made the decision on the train from London. I just couldn't let him loose in a place like London, or anywhere else for that matter. He just seems to have attached himself to me."

When the table was set and tea served, Judd told the story of Ojukwae. It was then decided that Ojukwae would take the name of the old man on Jakeskill island that had saved him, Josiah Mielman. Oj will be Ojukwae Mielman. Mary told Agatha to take the boy into the village and show him around. If anyone asked, she was to introduce him as her new friend. The two of them left the house, and through the window, Mary saw Agatha walking ahead of Oj without looking over her shoulder at him. She sensed that this might be a hard road as Agatha was now eleven and Ojukwae was about the same age. The boy had spent most of the last year with Judd and Agatha had seen nothing of her father in a very long time.

Mary held her husband in a tight embrace. What he was trying to do, proved him to be the generous, kind, caring man she'd fallen in love with, even before she ever knew it. She then pulled away and asked what were the boy's traits, good and bad? What did Judd have in mind for him?

The questions would have kept coming but Judd held up his hand. "When I was just a little older than he is now, I found myself in the darkest part of a ship, a victim of the Royal Navy. After a while I chose to make the best of what I found myself in. And look where we are now. If it wasn't for this bad thing, our life might not be this good. Ojukwae has had his bad thing. I watched the boy carefully as he lived on the ocean with me, among some of the toughest men I have ever met. I have spent more time with the boy, probably longer than I have with Agatha. With our love and guidance, I think the boy will know how to make the right choices for himself. Now, woman, tell me about your new offices."

"They can wait; we have many other things to talk about. Judd Cane…I love you. Welcome, welcome home." Tears welled up in her eyes as she kissed him, a warm and loving, all absorbing kiss.

***

On returning to the Cane household, Oj was a babbling ball of energy and excitement. Agatha went to her room without speaking to anyone, and closed the door behind her. Judd took Ojukwae over to the village green where they sat. Judd watched the boy running his hands through the grass and said, "So tell me what you have seen and what you like." "Well, captain…"

"You can call me Judd. We aren't at sea anymore, and I'm not a captain round here.

"I think everything is so green. It is all so new. I like the school. Will I go to school?"

"Yes, you will. While the sailors have taught you many new things there is much more to know. I want you learn to read like Agatha."

"I don't think Miss Agatha likes me," Ojukwae said without any hint of concern.

"I wouldn't worry about that right now. She will learn to like you. When you first came on the *Mary Jane* some of the sailors seemed like they didn't like you. Tell me the truth, there were some sailors that you didn't like, but, as you got to know each other things changed, didn't they?"

"Do you really think Miss Agatha will learn to like me? I am a nice fellow." Ojukwae laid back on the grass looking at the sky and laughed. "That place with the fire indoors. I think Miss Agatha said it was a fork. I liked that lots."

"First Ojukwae, you can call her Agatha. That place you liked is a forge, not a fork. We eat with forks. The forge is where they make things out of iron and steel. They need the big fire to make the iron hot."

"Big strong men there, Mr. Judd. Big men. Except for Jumbo Barnes, I never see men that big before."

"They got big because of the heavy tools and hard work they do. My friend owns the forge. Later we will take a visit and I will have him show you some things. He might even let you work the big bellows."

"What is bellows?"

"Just wait and see."

"The trees are so big and green. There are so many people, all busy making things ship shape. I really like the smells from the bread shop. Make my tummy rumble Mr. Judd. Too many things to see all in one time." Judd decided to introduce Oj to David Blacksmith's son, Nathaniel, who was twelve years old. He remembered the escapades he and David had gotten into and smiled to himself.

***

Later that evening, Mary showed Oj to a small room off the warm kitchen, where she had made up a small cot with a chest of drawers standing against the wall. In the middle of the floor was Oj's sea chest. Mary told him that this was to be his room and that he could unpack his chest, and when he finished, he could put the chest at the foot of the bed. "The cot is for you. If you are cold tonight, you must ask me for another cover."

"I sleep on deck. Cot is for men. I am cabin boy. I sleep on deck. I like my cabin, Mrs. Mary, do I share it with other people?" said Ojukwae.

Mary put her arms around him and quietly whispered, "No. This is your room or cabin, and the bed—cot—is for you. Tell me, what is in the big crate Captain Judd bought home with him?"

"Cap'n say I no tell," Oj said with a big grin.

"Well now I am the Captain's wife, you can tell me."

"Cap'n say I no tell," he repeated.

Mary grudgingly accepted his answer, and she corrected the boys English. He spoke with a mixed accent, as he had been exposed to a wide range of dialects on the *Mary Jane* and had innately blurred them into one.

This day had been such a whirlwind of experience and emotion. It was hard for her to believe she was about to live her life with her husband by her side all the time. The family was complete, and even had a new member. Mary gave the boy a hug as only mothers know how to do.

"Why you cry, Mrs. Mary?"

"Because you and the captain…er…Mr. Judd, have brought me much happiness today."

The scullery door banged as Judd entered the house, calling for Mary and Oj. They left the bedroom and met Judd in the kitchen. He told Mary of his plan to take Oj to meet with David's son. Leaving Agatha in her room to sulk, they set off across the village green, and Ojukwae quickly saw where they were heading and took off running. By the time Judd and Mary reached the forge, Oj was entranced, watching David teaching his son to pound the red-hot iron bar across the giant anvil. He was beginning to make a horseshoe.

"I see you have met Oj," he said to Davey.

"Yes, I have. Agatha didn't seem very happy about him. So, what's the story with the boy? You certainly know how to spring a surprise."

Judd replied, "it's a long story. I'll tell you over a beer later. As for Agatha, she will get used to Ojukwae."

"Ojukwae, no wonder you call him OJ. Is Mary alright with this?"

"I have to admit that I sort of surprised myself when I decided to keep the boy. Mary's a good soul I think she will do fine with him. She has started to correct his speech already."

"That's Mary for you. Everything has to be done properly." Davey laughed, as he untied his apron, he turned to his son. "Nathaniel come over here and meet Mr. Cane. He is the 'Judd' you hear mother and I talk about." Nathaniel shook hands with Judd and asked his father permission to go outside and play with OJ. Both boys took off into the afternoon sun. Davey sat on the huge anvil and spoke, "you are looking real well Judd. The sea life must be treating you well. Let's go inside and catch up. Jane will be pleased to see you. Oh! Did Mary tell you about Jim Carter? He got caught by a rip tide, down on the Mucking sand flats. They didn't find his body for four days, right mess that was. That was two year ago and Jane still hasn't got over losing her brother."

"Mary wrote to me about it. Strange, how that happened. Nobody ever got caught on the flats as far as I can remember. "Least said, soonest mended, I guess. That must have been very hard on Jim's dad, the two Jim's were inseparable. He had plans for his boy to take over the carting business," was Judd's reply as they went into the kitchen. Mary followed behind allowing the two men their time together.

Judd, Mary, Davey, and his wife, Jim's sister Jane—sat around the kitchen table, sharing a pot of steaming tea and catching up on each other's lives while Oj and Nathaniel got to know each other. Davey and Jane were elated at the news that Judd was home to stay. When the chatter came to Ojukwae, they sat spellbound as Judd related what the boy had been through. He went on to explain that his goal was to build a better future for the boy, starting with an education. Oj had learned some reading and writing but he was behind where he should be for his age, "We are going to send him to the village penny school to acquire the basics of education. I do hope that he will settle in with the other children."

Jane said, "Why would he not? The school is small and he will have Agatha there for him."

Mary quickly responded, "Oh I'm not sure. We have seen black people from to time passing through Mucking, but, one living here, that's a different kettle of fish. As for Agatha, she can be moody and I think she is a little put out about the possibility of Ojukwae taking time away from her father that she thinks is hers."

"Really? How do you feel about that Judd?" asked Davey.

"They will have to work it out between themselves because Oj is going nowhere."

"The child is called Ojkwae and I will have him called that, if you please," Mary demanded. She continued, "If Judd saw fit to give the child an opportunity in life then who am I to say otherwise?" Judd glanced over at Mary to see if he could read what was behind what she had just said, but to no avail. After a while they planned to get together soon and Mary, Judd and Ojukwae returned to their home, with Ojukwae chattering away excitedly about his new friend. Judd's first day home had exhausted him and their cottage soon slipped into a silent scene of sleep.

***

Judd spent the next morning with his parents, repeating everything he had told Mary. His mother suggested it might be a good idea to find some way to create some form of legal identity for the boy now, rather than later, when something important could arise. His father said, "A birth certificate. That's the way to go my lad. The Earl's secretary and I are on very good terms. Let me talk to him in the morning."

"Spare no cost, and here's twenty guineas to get you started," Judd said.

His father replied, "best investment yer ever made was giving the captain's desk to the Earl's clerk. You is famous thanks to that desk. 'e shows it off to everyone. It's like he has a baby. He's 'as proud that it is you who gived it to 'im as he is of the desk itself. e's going to be at the Weary Traveler this afternoon, notarizing documents for the village folk wot needs it. On second thought, I think you should be a askin 'im yourself."

***

In the afternoon, while Mary worked at Cane Services, Judd opened the huge crate, carefully removed an old captain's chair, and polished it to a high sheen. The heavy brass castings, holding small wheels on its thick, mahogany-splayed feet, bore intricate designs. This was without a doubt a man's chair. He closed up the crate and headed across the village green to the Weary Traveler, where he spied the secretary's brig hitched to a rail. He hoisted the chair into the back of the brig then drew up a canvas rain canopy to hide it.

Judd entered the public house and spotted the secretary, who sat in the private bar enjoying his midday meal. A sheath of papers, quill and ink well gave Judd the hint of which man would be the secretary. He approached the man with cap in hand and said, "Excuse me, sir. I do not wish to interrupt your dinner, but I wish to speak of a private matter, if it pleases you. We have never met. I am Judd Cane."

Slapping his hand against the table, the secretary exclaimed, "Be damned, man! Well, I never thought I'd ever get to meet the man of whom I know so much about, and yet have never seen. Sit down, Mr. Cane. Join me for a bite." He clung to Judd's hand as if he would lose something if he let go. "Landlord! Landlord, fetch Mr. Cane a platter and ale."

Judd could not refuse, so he sat. He allowed the secretary to exhaust his appreciation until finally, he got to asking what he could do for him. Between bites of plump country sausage, cheese, and crunchy farmer's bread, and sips of the dark brown, bitter ale of which he had almost forgotten the taste, he went on to relate Ojukwae's story. Then he passed across the table a slip of paper, on which he had written, "Father: Josiah Mielman, merchant trader. Son, Ojukwae, born April 1, 1849."

"The boy needs an official identity, a birth certificate," said Judd. "The mother's name, place of birth, you can make up."

"Are you sure this is what you want? You will also require foster or adoption papers if you wish to give this child fully recognizable legal status in this country"

"Please, sir, whatever papers you feel will allow the boy the greatest opportunity in life."

"I have heard of your exploits from your father and Jim the carter. I see their admiration is well founded. Not many men would take on another's child, let alone a blackie. Are you to be among us for long this time, Mr. Cane?"

Judd stood, downed the last of his ale, and placed two guineas on the table. "I am home for good, sir. It is my pleasure to buy your lunch. And I found something in my travels you might enjoy. I've put it in your brig. Good day to you, sir." With that, he turned and left the private bar.

Two days later a messenger delivered a package containing a birth certificate and a set of adoption and foster papers. A brief accompanying note said: Use either the adoption or foster papers and destroy the other. You will see they have been signed under the authority of the Earl. You must learn their contents, should you ever be questioned. I am your humble and most respectful servant. The note was signed, and a notation by the signature read, "Signed while seated at the most magnificent captain's desk, in my new captain's chair. All is perfect. Thank you." Everything is now in order.

***

When Agatha and Oj came home from the penny school, wandering across the green, carelessly chatting and giggling, they spotted Judd and ran toward him. Agatha calling out, "me first pa, me first pa." Ojukwae held back allowing Agatha to reach her father first. Judd held Agatha by her shoulder until Ojukwae reached them, and then scooped one up in each arm and spun them round and round, until at last, he put them down, and neither could stand up. They giggled, enjoying the dizziness, then fell down and lay on the sweet-smelling grass, watching the clouds spinning until they stopped.

After the children changed their school clothes, Agatha came out of her room and stood solemnly in front of Judd saying, "Pa, I am your daughter and I should be first. Oj is just adopted, he should be second."

Using a stern tone, he rebuked her. "As far as that goes, young lady, your mother and I consider that you are both our children and are equal. You, are my favorite girl and Ojukwae is my favorite boy."

"Pa, you only have one girl and one boy."

"That's right and you might do well to remember that your ma and I look on you as both being equal. Is that clear?"

"Pa, we are not equal. I am white and he is black."

"And just you tell me young lady, what difference does that make?" As Judd finished speaking Ojukwae came into the room. As if a switch had been flipped, Agatha turned to Ojukwae and said, "let's go over to the fields." Judd shook his head in disbelief and followed them outside. The three of them took off across the fields, Judd showing them the places of his past.

"This is where I asked your mother to marry me," he said.

"This is where I used to catch rabbits."

"This is where I went fishing with Davey Blacksmith."

"This where we used to knock on the cottage door and run away before getting caught. We called that 'knock down ginger."

"This orchard is where we used go scrumping."

"What's scrumping pa?" both children said in unison.

"We would take apples from peoples' trees when nobody was looking."

"But, pa, isn't that stealing?" ask Agatha.

Judd answered, "Well, sort of," as he quickly changed the subject. The list went on.

They arrived at the top of a hill and sat in the shade of a huge, outspread oak tree. As far as the eye could see, field after field spread out in front of them, the huge River Thames slicing through them like a huge brown ribbon waving in the wind. In the distance, the small village of Mucking Down clung to the banks of the river, its cottages growing further apart as they spread into the countryside.

Judd pointed out the wide mouth of the river as it yawned to greet the North Sea. In the other direction lay the tiny spires of the churches in Tilbury on one side of the river, and those of Gravesend on the other side. He drew Agatha and Ojukwae's attention to ships of every shape and size journeying the river. There were warships clustered around Gravesend and sloops, galleons, and all manner of merchantmen plying their trade.

"Pa, tell me about your ships," said Agatha, putting emphasis on your. Pointing out some ships Judd talked about the HMS Vanguard, at which time Ojukwae asked if he could see the Vanguard one day. Judd promised, and inwardly hoped that day would never come. He went on to speak about The Gideon Rover and then The Mary Jane. At the mention of The Mary Jane, Ojukwae laughed from deep within and said, "that's when Captain Judd come to be my pa." Agatha frowned as she looked at Judd. Judd spoke quickly, "Not exactly. That's when we met. When we came back to England and you came to Mucking, that'd be when I became your pa." To break Agatha's sullen silence Judd asked, "Would you like to go down to the sands and see if there are any shipwrecks?" Both children jumped up and started to run down the hill. Calling them back, Judd, promised to take them down and show them some wrecks on the weekend. Judd thought to himself, as he walked back home with the children, that he could get used to life like this.

***

For three days the large crates sitting outside the cottage had been driving Mary wild with curiosity. Judd felt it was time to release Mary from her hours of speculation about their contents.

Sitting in the cool summer evening darkness on the forecourt of the Weary Traveler Pub, Judd handed the keys to his wife's business to Davey and instructed him how, under the cloak of darkness, he wanted a special favor carried out. He described the contents of the huge crate, how they were to be taken into the offices of Cane Services, and where they were to be set in place. The crate was then to be closed up as if it had never been opened.

After that, the two men spent two hours relaxing and enjoying their childhood memories. Judd listened carefully as most of David's memories were of the time before his own press ganging. When Judd asked about what happened after he was gone, Davey seemed to brush things off. It was clear to Judd that Davey did not want to discuss that time. Changing the subject, Davey said, "this crate malarkey you've got me doing is as if we are just on another escapade. This was one of the few times in Judd's life he had ever had so much to drink, as to feel giddy, and a little out of control.

Davey said, "You would not believe how upset Jim the Carter, was when you were press-ganged. He'd believed he held some of the blame, what with taking you on all those night trips to plunder shipwrecks."

Judd brushed the idea away with, "He didn't make me go to The East India Docks that night. To tell you the truth, I'm not even sure why I did it. It wasn't like I had been thinking about it. I wonder if I wasn't destined to go to sea, one way or another."

As their conversation wandered through childhood and marriage and careers, Davey showed his passion for the forge. He recalled that, as a young boy, the tasks his father assigned him, to interest him in the forge, seemed more punishment than motivation. When the Weary Traveler was built, he'd jumped at the opportunity to become the cellar boy, just to escape the forge. It was when he graduated to barman, then to running the bar when the landlord was absent, that his attitude changed. As he watched the hardworking men and women unwinding after a tough day's labor, he realized that the country life had a calmness to it, and after seeing it shattered by drunken brawls that often ended with the involvement of the village constable, he understood what the forge could offer him.

It was within his first year working full time with his father that he married Jane, and his name was soon added to the business. "When I saw the sparkle of excitement in Oj's eyes when he came into the forge," he said, "I understand what my father had hoped for."

"Do you see it in Nathaniel's eyes?" said Judd.

"Not really. His interest seems to lie in bigger things. Ever since the steam-powered ship, *Sirius*, crossed the Atlantic, Nate has talked of nothing else but building a ship out of iron. Just this spring, they launched the HMS *Warrior*—a full iron ship. I had to take him to see the launching. All I have to do is to convince him that the forge is where he should start learning about iron."

Judd suggested encouraging Nathaniel and his new friend Oj to make small objects out of iron in the forge after school or on weekends. "It might keep them away from shipwrecks down on the sandbanks," Judd laughed.

"Now," said Judd, "what is going on with these new offices that Mary is being so secretive about?"

Pointing across the green Davey said, "That red brick building, modern and all that, is what Mary has been building for the past year. She moved her business in there about three months ago. It's her pride and joy. Smart lady, that one of yours. She has such a good business head, that she outgrew the cowshed office, excuse the expression. I did all the steel work for her." He stopped to take a drink from his tankard before carrying on. "Has quite a few girls working there for her. It's my guess she wants the excitement of you coming home to die down before she shows you. You mustn't let on that I told you anything. I'm sworn to secrecy."

"Won't she get a shock when she shows me and my surprise is already in place!"

"Happy to oblige. I have to go now. There's a team of draught horses coming for shoeing at 5:00 am tomorrow. I'd better get started on the shoes." Davey left and Judd sat in the darkness drinking in the changes around the village green.

The following morning, as Oj and Agatha prepared for school, Judd asked if it would be in order for him to start frequenting the office, as he wanted to get their properties arranged in his mind.

Mary said, "I think it is now time I showed you our new offices."

Judd feigned surprise at the statement. "New offices, where, why?"

"Let me gather up the deeds from your exploits and we can go there together. All will be revealed." The children left for school, but only after Agatha had instructed Oj to fetch her satchel and school shoes and wait for her in the scullery. In his desire to please anyone he came into contact with, Oj jumped at every request, order, and bossy demand that Agatha made of him.

Judd asked Ojukwae to wait outside for Agatha as he wanted to speak with her privately. "You, young lady, had better stop talking down to Ojukwae. If you want him to do something, you can ask him nicely. Do not order him around. Do you understand?"

"Pa, he likes helping me. The teacher tells him to do things, so, why can't I?"

"I think the teacher might ask him. You should listen more carefully. Any way it doesn't matter what others do. You concern yourself with the way you treat Ojukwae. I hope I make myself clear.now? Off to school with you."

Sharply at 8 a.m., Mary returned to the kitchen, a bundle under her arm wrapped in canvas and tied securely with a red ribbon. She handed the bundle to Judd, then stood on her tiptoes and kissed him. "Husband of mine, this bundle is the result of your life up 'til now. When we open it in the office, it will become our future."

"It's the result of what you have allowed me to do by being supportive of my absence and long time away from you, wife of mine," he said. Hand in hand, they crossed the village to the offices, a spring in their step and joy in their hearts.

The red-brick, two-story office building was the newest in the village, modern compared to the others. There were displays in large glass windows on either side of the door. The one on the right was a mock study, centered on the ornate desk Judd had given his mother all those years ago. There was a fireplace in the corner and shelves of books. A coat rack stood to one side, holding a cloak, hat, and umbrella. An ornate sign in the foreground stated, in bold blue lettering with a gold-leaf edge:

LET THIS BE YOUR OFFICE.
ALL MANNER OF PAPERWORK AND DOCUMENTATION
PROFESSIONALLY EXECUTED FOR YOU.

The lower two lines were blood red. The sign captured the patriotic red, white, and blue of the Union Jack. The window on the other side of the door had cardboard boxes stacked chaotically and piles and piles of papers. Mary had used discarded runs of print jobs from a big print shop in Tilbury. The sign in this window read:

LET US MAKE SENSE OF CONFUSING PAPERWORK.
FORMS EXPLAINED AND FILLED OUT. BOOK-KEEPING AND OTHER
SERVICES.
The ornate, hand-carved oak doors with leaded glass panes bore the legend:
CANE SERVICES
Proprietor, Mrs. Mary Cane

Judd was impressed. The stairs from the ground to the first floor featured wrought-iron railings and banisters, heavily adorned with cast iron floral and fruit groupings alternating with exquisitely handcrafted twists, curls and adornments. The rails were the height of fashion in London and Mary had left no detail out. They were both practical and attractive. Judd noticed the wrought-iron work had been carried out by David and David Blacksmiths. As they entered, Mary noticed some straw on one step and stooped to pick it up. She was not alarmed. The senior girl who opens the office at 7:30 a.m. was already at work.

When Mary unlocked her office door, she was mesmerized by what she saw. Her desk had been moved to one side wall, along with all her heavy oak file cabinets. Centered on the rear wall was a seven-foot-tall oak and maple armoire. An ornately carved center panel ran from top to bottom. Each of the two solid panel doors featured carvings that swept from the center to either side in a French style, and the panels created by the divisions had a lower relief design of leaves, berries, branches, and swirls. The whole piece had been made from one tree, with a soft change in hue as the wood grain traveled its length. The armoire had a bowed front and scalloped base decoration. Its immense weight was evident. Judd chuckled to himself, imagining what a struggle Davey must have had getting these out of the chests and up the stairs.

On either side of the armoire stood identical writing desks. They were German in origin, richly decorated with brass feet and trim. There were three feet wide, slim drawers, and a luxurious dark brown leather inlay. Each leg was fluted and tapered with a brass flair where it met the desk's upper structure. They were neither feminine nor masculine, but rather a substantial working surface that dictated their practicality. His and hers. Now Mary understood where the straw on the stairs had come from. Turning to Judd with tears in her eyes she said, "They are so beautiful. Where did they come from? How did you know about the new office? They look as if they belong."

"I didn't know about the office. I had been thinking about where we would put them, even considering building a new house for us. Then last night Davey pointed out the new building by the village green, your building, so I had him take care of moving it in."

"Judd Cane, you know how to keep things to yourself. I love them…thank you."

Judd had her pick which one she wanted, and he took the other. It was at this point Mary really believed that Judd was home to stay.

Judd sat at the desk that Mary said was to be his, and untied the red ribbon around the canvas package. He felt the canvas between his fingers and smelled it. Mary told him it was from the remains of the sail in which he had wrapped the desk he gave his mother before the Navy stole him away.

Judd closed his eyes, and he wasn't sure if it was his imagination or if he could really smell the sea air and cordite from cannons. He turned to Mary and said, "We should get a small chest and put things in it that we would like to share with our grandchildren, whenever they come—little things that will tell them where they come from." Mary liked the idea. She was sure they would be visiting London in the future, and there they should pick something special.

Judd took the piece of canvas and tucked it way back in a drawer with the ribbon. He spent the rest of the day and late into the night reviewing his portfolio of properties, and was pleasantly warmed to discover just how financially stable his position was. Mary and Judd could build a small empire. The task that lay ahead of them was to decide their next step. Agatha was set to become a very wealthy woman on his and Mary's passing, but Judd knew there was no need to wait for his death to take the family to the next level.

Mary looked over to see Judd wiping a tear from his eyes. She jumped from her chair and put her arms around him from behind, "What is wrong, Judd, what ails you?"

"Just happy tears. I am coming over all unnecessary. I think of all the things that I have been through, and quite a few of them scared the living daylights out of me. Then, I think of how you have soldiered on, here, alone, building all this for us, probably being just as frightened, in your own way. We make quite a couple Mary Cane. All these thoughts come to mind and a feeling wells up from deep down inside and, and, it makes me feel all the love I have for you overwhelms me."

***

Mary sorted through the papers on her old desk, as she moved them over to her new desk she found a telegraph seeking information about Jakeskill Island. The telegram came almost a year ago and got misplaced and forgotten. She called one of the girls who came up the stairs and asked her to bring a pot of tea, fresh milk and sugar up to her. Mary took Judd over to the wrought iron railing along the edge of the upper floor that allowed her to look down over the desks and girls working below. She pointed out that this gave her the ability to keep an eye on things without being obtrusive, but more importantly, it forced the girls to practice self-discipline as they never knew when she was watching.

The office was starting to come alive with morning activities. Some of the illiterate country folk came to have papers read to them and to have responses to them prepared. Each customer was shown into one of the private smaller side offices to make them more comfortable. Mary explained that these types of transactions completely covered her overhead. She had to explain what she meant by the term overhead and Judd quickly related it to his own experiences. The record keeping and book keeping were maintained for the village bakery, forge, The Weary Traveler, all of the village businesses with the exception of the hardware/millinery store. She also had business from surrounding villages turning to her for help. Judd was very impressed. He told Mary that he was going to spend the next few weeks organizing their property assets before deciding what he was going to concentrate on.

When afternoon tea was served, they each sat at their own desks and turned to face each other while they chatted. Mary asked, "why are you not paying much attention to the lost and forgotten telegraph that I found, about Jakeskill Island?"

"I need to think a lot more about all the properties before making a decision about any one of them. If the telegram has been misplaced for any length of time it won't hurt to make it wait a bit longer." He revealed that beside providing for the family he had been given the opportunity to open an account at the merchant banking company Browne, Shipley and Company in Liverpool. This company was about to branch out into the City of London's banking business. He had worked with the bank to channel most of his earnings from cargo and the use of Letters of Credit into a safer position. He detailed how the letters had enabled him to use the minimum of cash in his business dealings thereby reducing risk of loss. He felt no need at this time to reveal the huge sum he had accumulated since leaving the Royal Navy.

***

Over the next few days Judd proceeded to carefully study the deeds and documentation that he held on his properties. He entered all information he possessed on each property into a leatherbound log. He took his time and his neat handwriting soon filled in the pages. His descriptions were a combination of memory, fact, and other useful notes, meticulously recorded in his own neat handwriting. There were six properties in all, the results of twenty-three years at sea, and Judd was still a young man. He felt he needed to lay out the financial position to Mary and between them devise a plan of what they were going to do from this point on. The combination of money in the bank, properties around the world and Mary's business gave them a substantial foundation upon which to move forward

His notes on the properties were detailed as follows.

"The Plantation", Gallows Bay St.Eustasius

This property is approximately two hundred acres that had been developed into a productive plantation in the late seventeenhundreds. By the end of the century the main source of trade had changed to trading with the vast array of ships that plied the area going to and from America and the southern hemisphere. The Plantation had made significant changes to move with the times, and large tracts of the land had been developed with cavernous warehouses and storage buildings. It is about a half mile from the capital, Oranjestad. It has about one mile of ocean front on the South western side and is bordered by a road on the north eastern side. The long strip of the island from Gallow's Bay to Kay Bay is ideally situated for future development and is returning more than twenty thousand pounds a year paid with regularity and promptness due to the tireless and faithful efforts of Jack Freeman, my manager of the property. Each year a report arrived in England and Mary attached it to the deed, unopened. The initial transfer of money had given me one hundred and ten thousand pounds which was deposited with Browne, Shipley and Company in Liverpool. The island is a Dutch colony and was the first to recognize America's independence from England. (I have decided to regularly write to Jack Freeman and inform him of any plans that I might make.)

Berekua Fields, Dominca

This property is comprised of two parcels of land of seventy-five acres each. They are strips of adjacent land that ran from the ocean front up towards Watt Mountain. Both are fairly steep and have sea frontage of nine hundred feet. I had accepted them as payment for passage for an extended French family of twelve people from Dominca to France. The Gideon Rover took them to Southampton where I had paid their passage to Paris. The land has been cleared and farmed with declining success. The family had seen the value of the land as their chance for repatriation. I believe the combination of its low cost in conjunctions with its views of, and close location to Martinque, give it some potential for future development.

Mustique, St Vincent and the Grenadine

The tiny island had been a successful sugar producer until sugar beet was discovered in Europe. The island was gradually overtaken by scrub. I purchased it for one thousand pounds from a connection made at Dugan's Ship Chandlers in Southampton. The man was a disgruntled farmer who had delusions of grandeur when he purchased the island, only to fail. Mrs. Duggan had secretly told me that she thought this man could fail at using the air God gave him. It was at a time when I was flush with the idea of owning land and the previous owner described it as a God forsaken patch of uselessness. At the time I acquired it I felt it was just another notch in my belt. Reviewing the deed and an old sea chart I feel that only good can eventually come from owning the island. There seems to be some potential here.

East Caicos, The Turks and Caicos Islands

This tiny island of 34 square miles had gradually declined from having a thriving salt industry, to plantations under English Loyalists fleeing the American War of Independence, to the production of sisal. Its tiny settlement of Jacksonville was sparsely populated, with Flamingo Hill being the highest point of all the islands. As far as I know, there are few if any people dwelling there now. This island when I last sailed by was a tiny jewel in the necklace of islands strung from Cuba all the way down to Trinidad and Tobago. Less than twenty years ago, in 1841, the Trouvadore, a Spanish ship engaged in the slave trade, wrecked off the coast of East Caicos putting nearly two hundred slaves ashore. They had been granted freedom and put through various apprenticeship programs for future employment, enabling them to be self-sufficient. Where they went from there no one seemed to know. I paid seven hundred pounds for the island.

Cinnamon Reef, Little Harbour. Anguila.

This long slender island was part of the British protectorate of Nevis-St.Kitts. It is mainly a nation of freed African slaves who are peasant farmers, seafarers and fishermen. The stark beauty of the island caught my attention when I was resupplying The Gideon Rover in the French port of Marigot, on the island of St Maarten. The local people brushed off any interest in the island with disparaging remarks. My curiosity was peaked. Upon leaving Marigot we sailed around the islands noting that the island appeared attractive and decided to go ashore at Crocus Bay. My enquires found there was plenty of land with spectacular locations and views. One of two older families, who it appeared wielded the power on the island, brokered most decisions for the island. A white haired, aboriginal man offered to sell me one half of a bay protected by a reef. His family had owned it for eighty years. The bay is known as Little Harbour, not for its size, because it is huge, but because only small boats and ships can traverse the reef to enjoy the lagoon. Standing on the bluff at the high side of the bay one can look out to see the huge ocean breakers spewing foam surf at the reef and inside the reef a calm tranquil bay is sheltered. I fell in love with it instantly. Old Man Lambs said to me, "We call this Cinnamon Reef." I agreed to purchase the property. The price demanded was a shopping list to be fulfilled in England and delivered within six months. The tools, furniture, cloth, a steam engine and numerous items had cost me about two thousand pounds. Although the island has a small cotton industry and a lack luster economy, it's potential appealed to me. This is the property closest to my heart.

The Palisades Plantation, Jakeskill Island, Georgia. America

This property is by far the largest of my properties, at over eight thousand acres. To some extent I am troubled by its history, but my angst is tempered with the existence of Ojukwae. So many unnecessary deaths, such brutality. My thoughts go to Josiah and to the self-appointed executioner, who called himself 'The General'. I thought, more than once, of just tossing the sorry excuse of a man overboard, but we had a deal and the one thing foremost in my mind was always my own integrity. America had challenged England's might and won. This country of which I know so little can only get bigger and stronger. This, I feel is the jewel in my crown.

Chapter 22

Looking back over the past ten years, it was difficult to recall the small, robust black boy who had become the magnificent specimen of youthful energy, vim, and vigor that Ojukwae was now. The rippling muscles developed at the forge had turned his closest friend, Nathaniel, into an amiable competitor. This work ethic yielded only positive results. Nathaniel at twentytwo had long left home to take up a position in the Millwall shipbuilding dry docks. His father Davey frequently expressed his gratitude to Judd for how things had worked out. Judd dismissed any credit. It was just a matter of having put the boys in the right place.

But Judd was bothered by the number of times he had to intervene between Oj and Agatha, who would ferociously defended Oj against anyone foolish enough to bully her "little black brother." She would bat her eyes at her father and plead kindness and love for Oj. "My little black brother," she said, was just her nickname for him. Oj would defend her, saying that he didn't mind. Once, Judd pointed out to Oj that the color of skin was not a good reason for a nickname. When asked how he thought Agatha would like to be called Little Miss Whitey, Oj laughed his deep belly laugh and told Judd, "She is white. I don't need to tell anyone what they can see for themselves. As for me, I am black, and as Jojo once told me, I should be proud, and I am." Judd asked him if it bothered him when he heard comments about his color and the way his sister sometimes spoke to him. "Pa, I know who I am. God knows who I am. I only have to glare at those that bother me and show them these," he lifted his arm to show his muscles, developed from swinging the heavy hammers at the forge and working the bellows. "Believe me pa, they are all talk. Agatha, she just talks big. She is much like ma, she has a kind heart, and, after all, she is my sister."

Judd grudgingly dropped his pursuit once again. He felt he could hear derogatory undertones in Agatha's voice, but he understood that Oj didn't want that battle.

Nathaniel would go up to London and work through the week at a large ship building yard, living in rented rooms and returning for the weekend. He and Oj would carouse the village on Saturday nights after working side by side in the forge on Saturday mornings. They often tried to encourage Agatha to go with them, which she only did once. Judd could never work out who was the odd man out. Did Nathaniel come between Agatha and her brother? Did Oj come between Agatha and Nathaniel, or did she come between the boys?

One Friday night, Nathaniel announced that there was an opening for a riveting job in the shipyard, which could lead to great jobs down the line. He had put Oj's name forward, and was told that, if Oj was as skilled and well-trained as he, the job was his. Nathaniel told Oj that he had said Oj was *nearly* as good as him.

They took off to the Weary Traveler jovially punching and shoving each other. Within the week, Oj had secured the job and some lodgings in Bethnal Green. He returned to Mucking for a few weekends, but gradually, the visits became less frequent. Judd was subdued. Oj was his tangible human connection to his own previous life. When he overheard Agatha telling a friend that the "nigger" was gone, so she could use that room, Judd's anger was so unlike him that Mary had to step in and hold him back.

In a tone of voice Judd had never witnessed, Mary said to Agatha, "Sometimes, young lady, you are no lady. Your mouth will drive away anyone with sensibilities. You should be so lucky to become the lady that rivals the man Ojukwae has become."

Turning to Judd, she softened her tone. "Ojukwae was loaned to us," she said. "We enjoyed what we had of him. Now, you must let him go so that he may become the person you have helped him to become, his own person. Be satisfied that he chooses to come home some weekends and not stay somewhere else. You made your imprint on the boy. Be grateful for that."

Nathaniel frequently met Judd in the Weary Traveler on Saturday at lunchtime, where Judd would sit alone, nursing an ale, hoping to see Oj walk in the door. In a knowing way, Nathaniel would put his arm on Judd's shoulder and tell him that he was a good father. It would lift Judd's spirit to hear Nathaniel say, "Oj said to tell dad" this or that. After a while, Agatha would join him in the pub. After some story swapping, Judd would leave the youngsters in the pub and go sit alone on a hilltop, staring out at the winding river and its never-ending relay of ships and fishing boats. He would hand pick his choice of fish to bring back home, more often than not just to smell their briny odor. The taste and smell of salt water was hypnotic to him. On one such trip when he returned with fish Mary asked, "Why don't you get a job on one of those fishing boats? You are always off in another world when you come back from there."

"One of my small pleasures. I really understand why some sailors feel married to the sea." was the only reply he would give.

***

One rainy autumn afternoon he thought about how long it had been since the discovery of the lost telegraph requesting the purchase of Jakeskill Island. He had been through the files many times and moved the desks and retraced steps, all to no avail. Income from the *Mary Jane* and St Eustatius steadily increased each year. Judd was undecided as to whether he should take a trip to review what was happening with the other properties. The advent of the typing telegraph, he reasoned, meant that he could have other people inspect the properties. The annual four-page letter he received from Jack Freeman at the plantation allayed any concerns he might have about that property.

Often, Mary and Judd would take a carriage and go across the moors to the great North Sea, where Judd would reconnect with salt water. Mary would watch as he put his hand into the cold brine and sipped a little water off his palm. She felt his love for the sea and would often, on their way back to Mucking, let him know that if he wanted to go back, she would not stop him. He once told her, "A man should never go backwards, for you cannot repeat an experience. It is better to keep good memories as just that, good memories."

Once a year, when the *Mary Jane* arrived, they would journey to Southampton and climb aboard. Mary wept inside when she saw and felt how strong the bond was between the men and her husband. He had chosen this beautiful ship to carry her and Jane's name proudly for all the world to see. Some of the crew had changed, all had grown older, and the smell of the ship Judd had so accurately described to her many times came alive as she stepped off the gangway onto the burnished deck. She would stand in the background so as not to intrude, and would marvel at her husband's connection to Dickey Lemon. She found him to be a common, foul mouthed, cockney, but there was no disputing his remarkable respect and affection for Judd. The man was so different to the silver haired, rotund Leeza Trott, who was also a cockney. The difference was night and day. Leeza was so polite, quiet, respectful and calm. Dickey seemed like he bounced off the walls, what the Londoner's would call a wide boy. A wide boy usually denoted a man who thought more of himself than he was his due. Yet, these three men had managed to find something in each other that bound them together. She did not understand it or want to be part of it other than to accept it was part of who Judd was.

One time, when Judd once again looked for the telegraph, Mary asked why he kept looking. His reply was simply that he thought of the place often and wondered, what if? Mary once told him that he would never sell that place—it was the culmination of his sea life. "It brought you the son you never had," she said. "It allowed you to be a good, honorable man. You are tied to it. Judd would never reply.

Laid out on his desk was a survey of each property for the purposes of comparison. On the wall behind his desk, to the side of the armoire, was a world map with a small flag on each property. He knew not what he was looking for, if indeed he was looking for anything. It all came to him on a hot Friday afternoon, July 22, at about four o'clock.

***

Agatha walked into her mother and father's office, apparently searching for someone. "So, who's missing?" asked Mary.

"Oh. Nobody. So, what's happening? Have you heard from Oj or Nathaniel?"

"Depends on which one you're looking for," said Judd.

"Young lady, you've been working the main floor all afternoon," said Mary. "You have seen everyone who has come in and out of this office. So why don't you tell us what this is about?"

Just as Agatha was about to try to talk her way out of it, the heavy oak doors below crashed open and a flushed, breathless Nathaniel rushed up the stairs. Hurrying to

Agatha's side, he grasped her hand and kissed her cheek. Mary glanced at Judd's stoic expression.

"Sorry, there was a lot of trouble on the Great London Road. I had to take some side villages to get around the jam. Did you say anything?" he asked Agatha.

"No!" she said.

Looking at Judd directly, Nathaniel said, "Agatha wants to get married."

Agatha looked at him with fury in her eyes. "Agatha wants to get married? Agatha? Agatha wants to get married! What the bloody hell does Nathaniel want?" Her voice raised a pitch as she pulled her dress hems up to her knees and ran full-pelt down the stairs, crashing into Oj as he came in through the door. The office girls giggled. Oj turned and watched Agatha run across the green to her house, as she vehemently shouted over her shoulder, "Work your bloody black magic on that one if you can!"

Nathaniel leaned over the balcony. "Come on up, pal!" he called to Oj.

"Does anyone want to tell me what is going on?" said Mary.

"Shall I?" said Oj to Nathaniel.

"Go ahead," said Nathaniel.

Oj explained that he and Nathaniel had found enjoyment in the shipyard, sharing a common passion for the iron ships, but where they differed was that Ojukwae saw a career opening up before him and was content. Nathaniel was looking for what came next.

"Mrs. Cane," said Nathaniel, "Mr. Cane knew where he was going when you got married. You allowed him to complete his journey. I've only just started mine, and I'm not sure where it's going to take me. I spoke out of order when I said that Agatha wants to get married. So, do I -- get married to her that is. But how can I be what I want to be to her, when I haven't yet proved anything to myself? She is strong-willed—just like you, Mr. Cane."

"When did this happen?" both Judd and Mary stated together.

"I know it looks like Agi and I, sorry, Mrs. Cane, Agatha and I are at each other all the time, but that's just our way. She wants to improve me and I see that. I want to "prove" me. Prove myself to me, that is. You know what I mean."

"I understand," said Judd, studying the boy closely. "Agatha can be a little strong-willed and demanding. I hope she is not with child."

"Oh, no, sir! Certainly not. I was supposed to come here today and ask for her hand, but, I guessed I messed that one up."

Mary spoke, "Do you love Agatha, I mean really love her?"

"How could I not, Mrs. Cane? How could I not? She is the only proper lady I see round here, oops, sorry Mrs. Cane, besides you that is. I think any man would be proud to have her as his wife."

"So, do I take it that you are asking our permission to marry our daughter?" Judd was seeking clarity.

"Oh yes sir, please sir, Mr. Cane, sir, but not yet. We aren't even engaged yet."

Judd spoke to Mary, "Mary, you can sort Agatha out, while Nathaniel and I go and talk this out over an ale at the Traveler's."

Mary left the office and walked slowly across the green, working out how she would handle Agatha. When she entered the house, Agatha was sitting at the kitchen table, sobbing. It didn't influence Mary.

"You see black and it influences everything you say," Mary said, referring to the way Agatha had spoken to Oj. "I see Ojukwae, a young man who has had the good fortune to be exposed to the kindness and good in your papa. If he doesn't owe your papa anything, he certainly doesn't owe you anything."

Agatha kept sobbing. Mary kept going.

"What did Nathaniel say that was so wrong? You want to marry. If you'd waited a second longer, he would have said he wants to marry you as well. But no, you had to interrupt. You're too impatient. Your temper needs to be reined in. If you want to mend fences, you had better change your attitude."

"Mama, 'mend fences, mend fences,' you sound so country."

"I am country, young lady, and so are you."

"So, what do I do now?" said Agatha.

"Wait until your papa comes home. Then we'll talk. You should be proud that the man wants you, wants to be worthy of you. You will only ever receive as much of a man as he is willing and able to give."

"Here endeth, the lesson," said Agatha.

"Quite." Mary said.

Meanwhile, at The Weary Traveler, Judd exited the pub with a tray containing three tankards of ale. "Best bitter, for this occasion," he said. Sitting opposite Ojukwae was Nathaniel with each waiting for the other to break the silence. The boys supped ale with Judd while a peaceful calm overcame them. Oj spoke first, "Pa, Nathaniel had always respected and looked up to you. He was fully aware of the plan with you and his pa to get him involved in the Blacksmithing. He went along with it out of respect and indeed got a lot of contentment out of it. If anyone should know, pa, you should, all men are different and Nathaniel is no exception. Pa, do you really need to ask if Nathaniel loves Agatha?"

"Well, actually yes I do. Until this afternoon I thought that they were good friends from childhood. Nathaniel, do you know what love is?" Judd's tone caused Nathaniel to think before answering.

"I believe that love is there when you find it impossible to imagine that anyone could love the one you love, more than you do. Mr. Cane, Agatha might have a bit of hard tongue. But she is the most caring, pretty, and kind girl I know. She is a good worker. She is respectful. She knows her manners."

"Alright, alright, I get the message. Very articulate, but love is when you are able to place the one that you love before yourself in everything you do. That is not a thing many men can do without feeling that they are giving in, or being weak. Or, even less than a man. So, what do you think of her outburst this afternoon? What about how rude she was to Ojukwae?"

Ojukwae comented "Come on, pa. Agatha is not rude to me. She is just Agatha to me. I don't mind."

"Not the point Oj. Nathaniel just pointed out that she is respectful. I am pointing out that she isn't always respectful."

"So, love is blind, what can I tell you Mr. Cane?" Nathaniel responded. He thought for a moment before continuing. "The difference between Oj and me is that he sees a ship that we are building as an end product, and I respect that. I, on the other hand, wonder where is the ship going to go. What is it going to experience? There is so much that I don't know. I want to give Agatha a husband like you. A man who is educated about life, and I don't mean schooled, but lived."

"Quite the flatterer, aren't we?" Judd joked.

"No sir, I am serious. I need to know that I am the man that I think I am. I want to be confident that I can be the man I think Agatha deserves."

Ojukwae spoke, "Pa, you have got to help Nathaniel find his way. He doesn't want to lose Agatha any more than he doesn't want to be pushed into anything he cannot live up to.

Judd thought for few minutes before going inside to refresh the ales. Upon his return he delivered his thoughts.

"My life thrust opportunity upon me, the only credit I take was for what I have done with it. I am the result of my life's experiences and it sounds to me like you want some experiences under your belt before marrying. I guess what you need Nathaniel, is some thrusting in a similar direction. Let me give it some thought."

Chapter 23

As dawn broke Sunday morning, Judd walked over to Cane Services. Arriving at his desk, he looked at the surveys lying in front of him and stared. Deep in thought he spent almost an hour drifting through his memories. He was searching for what? he didn't know. Each memory seemed to go back to his being pressed into the Navy. While he had no choice then, it was the point at which he would soon begin to make his own choices. He credited his upbringing with equipping him to make the right decisions. Given a similar situation, he felt that Nathaniel would be capable of making the right choices. So, he formulated a plan that would challenge the boy and hopefully placate Agatha.

He found Nathaniel and asked him to fetch Agatha and meet him in Mary's offices. When they arrived, Judd got right into what he had come up with. "Agatha, you are aware that your mother and I own some properties in the Caribbean. I want you to choose one and I will tell you what I have in mind."

"How can we choose?" said Agatha. "We do not know anything about those places." Nathaniel looked a little confused and apprehensive.

"I am proposing that Nathaniel be given a budget and the opportunity to make something of himself. If you want me to believe you have not looked at the surveys that have been into my desk in the past two years," said Judd, "then, young lady, you severely underestimate me. Not once, when you've looked through them, have you have never put them back in the correct order."

Blushing, Agatha said, "Well, all right. I like the Plantation on St Eustatius." Nathaniel looked from Judd to Agatha and said, "Mr. Cane, I do not know much about your properties, in fact very little other than you own them. On what basis do I ... we choose one?"

"Well, I think that my daughter has studied them quite carefully. Agatha, tell us why you choose St. Eustasius."

"There seems to be some form of a business there. Also, there appears to be quite a few people. It seems that many ships go there, including The Mary Jane." She paused to consider if she should keep going, then added "I don't know why I lean towards that place. I just have a feeling."

Judd turned to Nathaniel, who said, "If Agatha likes it and you approve Mr. Cane, then it's fine by me."

"You have chosen St. Eustatius, one of the finest of the properties," said Judd, "So here are your mother's and my conditions. Only in three years from now can you marry. Agatha, you will set yourself the goal of learning all you can of your mother's business and business administration. If we need for you to go further afield to learn more, we shall arrange it. Nathaniel, you have six months to prepare for your journey. You will stop work at the shipyard at once and work for me. I will help you prepare and pay you the wages you would have earned at the shipyard. There are no discussions to be had."

"What is it that you expect, or want me to do in St. Eustasius?" asked Nathaniel.

"That's for you to decide for yourself," said Judd, "Once you are familiar with your surroundings, let the cards fall where they may. Let what lies in front of you motivate you, and keep an open mind. I'm sure you will rise to anything you may be confronted with." He added, "my man there, Jack Freeman, is good fellow and you will be able to fall back on him should you need. Somehow I don't think you will."

"Pa, don't I get a say in this? Am I to be left here waiting for Nathaniel to do whatever he is going to do?" Agatha pouted and added "for three years!"

"No, you don't get a say, and no you don't have to merely wait. You should be very busy keeping your end of the bargain."

"But pa, three years?"

"Your ma waited longer than that for me and I damn glad she did. Now get out of here you two and give me your decision by this evening, no second chances."

***

Some two weeks later, while Judd and Mary were making plans with Nathaniel and Agatha, two finely dressed gentlemen presented themselves at the offices of Cane International, formerly known as Cane Services. They were shown to the first floor waiting area.

Judd, looking over the wrought iron railings, saw the men below and knew instantly they were of high degree by the quality and cut of their clothes. The heavier-set of the two removed his hat and gave them a slight nod of a bow as he called up to them, "I bring you warm wishes with a genuine desire to find you both in good health from a Mr. Josiah Mielman."

"Josiah! my God, is he here? Is something wrong with him? Does he need my help?" Judd then called out to one of the offices girls, "Please show these gentle-men up to our office."

"Mr. Mielman is well," said the other man. "Let me introduce my business associate, the honorable Sir Michael St. John-Brown, one of the principles of the Royal Shipping Line. I, sir, am Ronald Surtees of Commercial and Industrial Consultants."

Judd studied the business cards of both men as he spoke, without looking up. "I am familiar with The Royal Shipping Line and indeed with your chandlers, Duggan's. My ship trades through them and we have taken many of your products, Mother's Fine Foods, to the colonies."

Mary invited the men to be seated and called for refreshments.

"How did you make the acquaintance of Josiah, may I ask?" said Judd.

Sir Michael spoke, "I was visiting the area and had the good fortune to be directed to the place. Your man, Josiah, gave us a tour of The Palisades, on Jakeskill Island. My company has an interest in purchasing the property if it is for sale."

Judd replied, "With all due respect Sir Michael, there is another party interested in purchasing the property. We are currently in discussion of the terms of sale."

Both men glanced at each other. "I am in a position to make an offer to you today if you are in a position to commit," said Michael.

Playing her unspoken role, as if on cue, Mary smiled and said to Judd, "We did say that we are in no hurry to sell."

"Yes, we did, and indeed, we are not. But these gentlemen have traveled a long way. Either from Bath or London," said Judd. "I believe we should show them the courtesy of hearing them out."

"Yes, dear," said Mary.

Sir Michael pointed out that America was still suffering from the aftermath of the Civil War, and that there was still a lot of dissension in the South over the slavery issue. Jakeskill Island was off the beaten track, Michael argued, and he was willing to take a long-term gamble on its future possibilities.

Judd parlayed with his own observation of the beauty and location, pointing out that the fast advances made with iron ships made the island even more accessible. Besides, the two of them were not the only people interested. Sensing the men already had plans for the Palisades, he said, "If you are ready to make an offer, we will compare it with the other before making a decision."

"One hundred thousand pounds today, by letter of credit." Michael watched Judd's face for any sign he could interpret. There was none. "As a deposit," he quickly added.

Judd told Sir Michael they owned numerous properties throughout the Caribbean and were fully aware of the value of property overseas. The Palisades was by far the finest of his properties, and he would be willing to start negotiations at one million pounds. To his surprise, neither man showed any reaction.

The four of them sat in silence, each waiting for the other to speak first. At last, Michael broke the silence. "As I said, Mr. Cane, one hundred thousand pounds today, by letter of credit, as a deposit. And further, one hundred thousand pounds by letter of credit on the first day of each month for the next six months."

Again, there was no reaction from Judd.

"Gentlemen," said Mary, "while we respect your offer, our other offer claims to be able to complete a contract within two months. Should you, not be willing or able to complete a contract, we could find ourselves tied up in the courts, a situation to be avoided."

Sir Michael noticeably relaxed. "Mr. Cane, I have benefited from the counsel of a wise woman—Mr. Surtees's wife—many times, and I respect your wife's foresight," he said. "Can we shake hands on my offer if I agree to forfeit any monies paid if the contract is not completed within the six months?" Turning to Mary, he said, "I shall require the time to form a corporation and move monies from some of my other business interests to fund my plans."

Mary said to Judd, "If, for some reason the sale is not completed, we will have gained a minimum of one hundred thousand pounds, plus any other monthly payments Sir Michael may have paid. With the interest there is in the property, I am happy to wait for either outcome."

"Sounds fair to me." Judd replied as he stood and shook hands with Sir Michael.

The sale of the Palisades was agreed upon and, unexpectedly, finalized within five months. Mary noted that they would now have six hundred thousand pounds in the bank from that sale alone, not bad for a dairymaid and a sailor.

The proceeds of the sale of the Palisades were placed in an account at Campbell & Coutts, the same bank that the St. John-Brown..

Chapter 24

February was a cold and wet month in the South East of England. Minds were turning to the upcoming spring and there was restlessness created by the long winter and being shut indoors. The cold North Sea winds would sweep in from the wide mouth of the River Thames and batter the slopes of Mucking and Lower Mucking. It was during one of these times that Judd Cane pondered his situation. In quiet moments, while savoring his increased wealth, thoughts of the Royal Navy would jar him into reality. He did not understand why the Navy had pursued him and then appeared to have stopped. He decided to take the bull by the horns and try to resolve the situation. Wrapping himself up against the foul weather, Judd left for Stanfor LeHope, the Earl of Essex's country seat.

The Earl's secretary opened the door to Judd's knock. Both men were surprised at each other's presence. The Earl apparently was in London and his staff had been reduced for the winter. Judd was shown into the drawing room where he sat with the secretary exchanging pleasantries. "So, tell me, Mr. Cane, did you come to see me or the Earl?"

"I'm not sure. I need some advice of quite a sensitive nature, and I don't quite know who to talk to."

"I am sure that by now you know that I am a man of silence, so why don't you tell me the situation and we shall see what we can do."

Judd sat silently thinking of how to relay his story. Then he spoke slowly and deliberately. "As you probably know, way back in 1837, I was pressed into The Royal Navy. Everyone believed that practice has long been abandoned. Believe me, it hadn't. I spent a number of years at sea."

"Wait a minute. I thought you were a merchant seaman," interrupted the secretary.

"I became a merchant seaman. How the change came about is what I wanted to talk to you about. You see, I was fortunate in that I could read and write. I was taught to be, and eventually became a navigator." Judd talked long into the morning in great detail, about how the Gideon Rover was taken over and eventually sold. During the commentary the secretary took Judd into the great manor house kitchen where they found food and ate. The secretary was spellbound by the whole story. Judd made no mention of Dickey Lemon, Lezza Trott, or any of the properties he had acquired. While the secretary knew about the Plantation on St. Eustasius, he knew nothing of the other properties and they were not raised by Judd.

When Judd had finished his story, the secretary said, "Mr. Cane, what an exciting life you have led. But what is it I can be assistance to you with?"

"A few years ago, The Admiralty sent some men to my parent's house looking for me. They came only once and I have no idea what is happening. I don't know if it is right or proper to seek the aid of the Earl. I know that he has connections on the Board of Governors at the Admiralty."

"Indeed, he does. Many gentlemen from that board come to the estate grousing, or whatever it is they can shoot. I think the first thing to do is to find out what the Admiralty has done or plans to do about it. It is rather strange that there has been no public outcry. What happened to the officers and men from the Vanguard where you left them?"

"I had a cable sent to the Admiralty when I was safely away telling them where the men were and what had happened - in sketchy details of course."

"Damned embarrassing for the Navy to lose a ship and marines I would say. That might be an ace up your sleeve." I am to meet the Earl at the Admiralty sometime this week, and, I have few connections in the bowels of the building. Where the records are, you know. I shall make some discreet enquiries, anonymously of course. When I return we shall see what I have discovered. I would imagine that this is going to be quite a costly matter, as most fine gentleman seem to desire to have their palm crossed with silver, or should I say gold in this matter."

"The cost should not be an obstacle. I just need to put this thing to rest."

"I think that I will enjoy helping you in this matter. Quite intriguing, if I might say so, quite intriguing." The secretary walked Judd to the door, shook his hand, and bid him good afternoon.

While Judd rode a trap back to the village his thoughts were of his trust in the Earl's secretary. Was it the right thing to do? He knew the man's name was Archibald Sadler, from his father, but, the use of his name had never taken place. Judd made a note to bring the subject up the next time they met. There was a nagging, worried tug at the back of his mind. At this point the secretary knew more about Judd, than Judd knew about him. This was not a normal situation for Judd, as he had always been one step ahead of the people he dealt with – not the other way around.

Chapter 25

While awaiting the return of the Mary Jane, Nathaniel was busy with Judd's preparations for his voyage to St. Eustatius. He worked for a local home builder, for a brief period. He carried a hod, and learned the craft of bricklaying. When he had mastered the ability to read construction plans, he moved on to work for an industrial and commercial builder in London, improving his knowledge of construction. The winter saw him toil through the rigors of farming. When spring came, he worked in a small furniture factory and a machine shop in West Tilbury. A brief stint in Mucking village bakery was followed by laboring in the windswept coastal town of Herne Bay, where he learned the art of selecting the most useful rocks and boulders that could be used easily in construction.

Judd had him sleep outside in rain and cold. All these experiences were designed to open the young man's mind to anything thrown at him. Judd was to arrange Nathaniel's passage to St. Eustatius on the *Mary Jane* upon her return. Judd felt there was nothing left but to let the boy loose. As the time drew near for his departure, Judd took Nathaniel and Agatha to the Weary Traveler tavern, where they sat in the warm May twilight.

"The *Mary Jane* will be leaving in one week. You should both be spending as much time together as you can. This is going to be a hard road to travel and you will need each other's support, even though it will be from afar."

Agatha burst into tear as she said, "Pa, why can't I go with Nathaniel? We could do this together and be by each other's side."

"Because, Nathaniel wouldn't be proving anything to himself. Remember that is what this is all about. I am sure that when he is ready, Nathaniel will send for you."

"Will you send for me, Nate? I mean, really, will you send for me?" Agatha adopted her pleading tone that always worked with her father.

Judd quickly stepped in by saying, "never ask a man a question if you are not prepared to accept his answer."

"Pa, are you saying he won't send for me? How could you?"

"That's not what I said. Give Nathaniel a chance. He has no idea what he is going to face or do. He may just turn round and come home. You must let his decision be his, and not yours."

"Then there is no point in me being here for this meeting." With that, Agatha rose and walked across the green to her mother.

"This was not a meeting, just family getting together. Well, there you have it Nathaniel. Women…I suppose you should go after her, or not. It's little things like this that set the tone for the rest of your relationship together." Having said his piece, Judd sat silently watching Nathaniel as he struggled with what to do.

Suddenly, Nathaniel rose and spoke, "Let me refill our mugs Mr. Cane, and you can tell me everything you know about St. Eustasius. To tell you the truth sir, I'm ready to leave tonight - I'm that excited about things." Nathaniel returned with the mugs brimming over and splashing their suds onto the wooden table. The two men sat in silence listening to the awakening spring chorus of nature's sounds. It seemed early for the crickets to be chirping relentlessly, on and on. The occasional bat flew, swooping in front of them, searching for any unaware insect morsel. Out in the darkness dogs barked, cattle lowed. Children would suddenly appear, chasing each other across the village green, giggling and calling to each other before calm would return. Looking across the village green the huge barn doors of the smithy were open and the forge fire glowed brilliantly orange, illuminating anything in its path. Nathaniel could hear his father's rhythmic pounding of hammer against red, hot steel as he shaped it. Judd broke the silence. "Just as you can look around you, seeing and hearing things, take this picture with you, in your mind. See how rich the whole thing is. It is the sum of many things. When you get to Eustasius, do the same thing. Look at, and listen to, everything individually and then, build your own, new picture. I guarantee that an opportunity will offer itself."

"Can I ask you a personal question, Mr. Cane?"

"You can ask. I'm not going to promise that I can answer. After all some things are better kept to yourself."

"Were you ever afraid of what was happening to you?"

"Only a fool doesn't know fear. Those that deny fear are braggarts or fools. Acknowledging that you are afraid is the first step in conquering it. I have found that caution about the unknown is often mistaken for fear. When we know something is going to happen then we can decide what to do about it. That eliminates or reduces fear. Backing away and taking time to think about what you're faced with gives you time to gain control. Always remember there is often more than one solution to most problems. If you can relax, take a deep breath and consider alternative ways to resolve your fear, then it has become a challenge."

"That makes fine sense, I think," said Nathaniel.

"Good, because I thought it sounded pretty good myself," replied Judd, and both laughed heartily. Judd continued, "Take your time and really get to know the Plantation and its people. Work with Jack Freeman for a month in the plantation, while you find your feet. Jack Freeman is a solid, experienced man who can be trusted, and funds have been provided for your use, but try to be independent as quickly as you can. That way you are beholden to no man. I expect nothing of you other than the best you can do," said Judd. "Opportunity is everywhere in front of you. Look and see. Wait and think, and then, arse up, head down, nose to the grindstone, and don't let anything stop you. Things may slow you down or change your direction, but the only thing that can stop you, is you. Make yourself proud."

"What exactly is the plantation sir?"

Judd laughed as he spoke, "it used to be a slave plantation. As things started to become non-profitable the old owners saw the opportunity to turn it into a trading post for the huge lumbering merchantmen who plied their trade from England to the Orient and South Pacific. Those ships found it more profitable to sell their cargoes to the planation for a smaller profit and return to trading, than to keep coming back to England. Other ships make their money doing shorter runs from St. Eustasius to England and back. So, huge voyages have ended up being split into two smaller ones."

"So, why is it still called the planation?"

"Because, it was a plantation for a great many years. The property is deeded as a plantation, and everyone that has been there for the past one hundred years or so knows it as the plantation. It's just that its purpose has changed."

Judd saw Nathaniel yawning and suggested that they call it a night and as he stood to leave Nathaniel embraced him said quietly, "Thank you sir for what you are doing for Agatha and me. I will not let you down, I promise."

Judd smiled and nodded his appreciation and left.

Chapter 26

Judd awoke to the sound of voices in the parlor below his bedroom. Quickly getting dressed, he descended the stairs to see Archibald Saddler talking to Mary. The man turned to Judd as he spoke. "Good morning Mr. Cane, I apologize for disturbing you at such an early time, but I am off to London and needed to speak with you before I leave."

"Mary, could you make some fresh tea for Mr. Sadler and me? We will take it in the parlor. I will meet you in the office when we have finished." Mary understood the dismissal and left for the kitchen.

"I thought it wiser to come to your home, as this is a private matter." The man removed his coat and made himself comfortable. "I believe that I have some good news for you." The man handed Judd a large manila envelope closed with a wax seal.

"Should I open this now?" Judd turned the envelope over, as the man responded. "I suggest that you look at it in private, as you may wish to destroy the contents." There were no markings of any kind. Judd studied the seal to see that it bore the imprint the Admiralty. His heartbeat quickened. "What does this mean?"

"Through great efforts on my part, and, without involving the Earl, I have been able to access the reports produce by the Admiralty's investigation."

"Are these copies of those reports?"

"No sir, they are the original and only copy of the reports. As you will see there was a lot more investigating that went on than was apparent. It appears that Captain Walker went to great lengths to imply your lack of culpability in the act. I think it was a case of him trying to hide his embarrassment. He claimed to think that you were a victim of unscrupulous men. Most of the Admiralty's efforts have been centered around trying to find the Governor Ready, without success I might add."

"I don't understand. Does this mean the whole incident just went away?"

"Not exactly. No man, naval or otherwise, that returned had anything bad to say about you, publicly that is. It appears that Walker spoke negatively of you in in private to anyone who lend an ear. My sources tell me that he was never the same after that, took to drink. I'm not sure if he left the Navy of his own choice or was encouraged to do so. It looks as if your accomplices were not even mentioned in the reports. It is as if it never happened."

"But, why would that be possible? It wasn't exactly a small feat."

"I spoke with some trusted contacts of mine and was met with some red faces and serious advice to drop my enquiries. Just as I predicted, damned embarrassing for some people at the top. Mind you, I don't think it would have been the same if the Governor Ready was a Royal ship, no sir."

"So where do I stand now?"

"A very lucky gentleman, I would say. Somewhat in debt, but still very lucky."

Judd quickly understood the man's implications. "Does anyone know that you have, I have, these documents?"

"Oh, no sir. In fact, nobody even knows that I was able to view them." Judd leaned forward and put the large envelope on the floor beside his chair. He leaned forward placing his elbows on his knees, he clasped his hands together and spoke quietly to the man. "Mr. Sadler, Archie, if I may, I am very grateful to you for your endeavors. I am happy to reward you well, but I don't know where to start."

"I, too, have given this some thought. I have laid out some degree of money to gain the accesses that I needed. I feel one hundred pounds would more than cover those out of pocket, expenses. As for my own compensation, I leave that up to you. I believe that you are a fair and relatively honest man." He said with a chuckle.

"Let me make it easy for you." Judd leaned back in his armchair and asked, "There must be something that would make you a happy man. Name it, it will be yours."

"Money is not something a man in my position could suddenly acquire without raising eyebrows and gossip, but,"

Judd interjected. "But…there you are, name your but."

"Would it offend you if I suggested land? Ownership of that, can be obscured quite well."

"Do we speak of land here or abroad?"

"You read me well Mr. Cane. My wife and I have lived a frugal life under the auspices of the Earl and have a nice nest egg set aside. I believe that in a few years that will serve us better in a place less costly than England is becoming."

Thinking carefully about his properties Judd said, "How would you like to own your own island in the Caribbean Sea?" He was thinking about Mustique, in St. Vincent and the Grenadines. It had only cost him one thousand pounds. That would be a reasonable sum for the burden Archie Saddler had lifted off his shoulders.

"This place would be called?"

"Mustique, it is part of St. Vincent and the Grenadines. It is well located and I am sure it is going to be quite valuable as the development of the great iron ships moves forward. I have the deeds in our office. Would you like time to consider that or some other place?"

Archie stood up and offered his hand to Judd. "Mr. Cane, Judd, I, I did not expect such generosity. But if ever a man's silence could be guaranteed, you have just done it." The men shook hands and made arrangements for the deed to change hands the next day. Parting at the front door of Judd's home Archie turned and said, "You may want to just burn those papers. There are some quite rough things said about the men who pulled of the stealing of the Governor Ready." With that said Archie mounted his horse and took off.

Archie's last comment peeked Judd's curiosity and he returned to the parlor and broke the seal on the envelope. He felt a degree of suspicion about being advised to burn the envelope unopened. This was soon dispelled as he read. He discovered that at the time, The Earl of Essex, being a member of The Admiralty

Board of Governors, was quite vitriolic about what should be done, in his words, 'to these vicious, dangerous pirate types. They should be found, captured and publicly hanged, even drawn and quartered.' The man was unaware of who 'these' people were, fortunately for Judd. Upon further review, he saw that Captain Walker was the brother of another member of the board of governors and had purchased his commission on HMS Vanguard. This was usually considered to be a sign of less than perfect qualifications for the job. Judd could now see why there were attempts made to silence the investigation. It turned out that the man overseeing the investigation was a nephew of Captain Walker on his mother's side. The connection was never revealed. At this point Judd stopped reading and started a small fire in the parlor fire grate and meticulously burned every piece of paper ending with the envelope.

Saturday evening on the village green at Mucking saw a festive celebration to see Nathaniel off. All were invited. Two giant tents were erected for shelter, should it be needed, and beer kegs were tapped. Whole pigs were roasted, and the village baker provided bread, cakes, and pastries, while the Weary Traveler supplied trestles, chairs and mugs. The Cane and Blacksmith families were admired and respected by the villagers, and many wanted to contribute to the festivities. The village brass band, made up of old and young alike, played with great gusto. When the band rested, the Morris dancers entertained as the children danced around the edge to carefully choreographed historic rituals handed down through the generations.

The Canes basked in the joy that sharing their good fortune with the villagers provided. Periodically, Mary would see Agatha and Nathaniel embraced in a moment of fear, pain, and, at the same time, joy. She knew what the separation would feel like for her daughter. She had experienced those same feelings as Judd set out to the sea. She wanted to protect Agatha from the pain, but she knew she couldn't and shouldn't.

As the dark night bore down upon them, Judd, Mary, Agatha, and Nathaniel sat together at a trestle table, oblivious of the debris strewn around them. Davey and Jane joined them. They spoke of the past, and the memories brought tears and laughter. There was joy and sadness in the air. David held a mug high and proposed a toast to Mary and Judd for all that they were doing for the young couple. Nathaniel proposed a toast to the family. Agatha burst into tears, rose from the table, and stormed of across the green. Nathaniel chased after her and caught up with her sobbing by the ancient oak that stood at the far edge of the green.

"What is the matter?" he pleaded.

"None of you understand. There you all are being merry and gay, what about me?"

"This is all about you. You, me and our future."

"Yes, but I am seeing our paths following my pa's - him gone all the time and ma alone. I want more than that, for myself."

"This is not forever, not even for a long time. There is a whole world out there, and we can stake our claim to part of it. Aren't you excited about that?"

"Yes, I am excited, but I'm also scared. What if something goes wrong?"

"If it does, by then I shall have proved to myself, and to you, that I am capable of picking myself up and starting again. I am trying to be as sure as possible of being able to be worthy of you."

At this, Agatha flung her arms round his neck and whispered, "I will try to be strong. I love you so much, I am just plain scared."

"Then share that with your ma. She can help you get past that. She knows what you will be going through and you must agree, your ma is a wonderful caring person. Who else would you want to turn to?"

"Your right. I will pray for strength."

"You don't need to pray. You have it. I know you do. Now, take my hand and let's join the family." They rejoined the group and Agatha behaved as if nothing had happened. Judd thought to himself, 'I wonder if she is always going to be this fickle. I guess that's Nathaniel's problem, not mine anymore.'

The next morning, Davey and Judd took Nathaniel to the railway station, from which he was due to leave for Southampton and the Mary Jane. Davey handed him a handmade coat and said, "Your mother is so concerned about your welfare she has sewn five hundred pounds in five-pound notes into the lining. So treat it with care. You never know when you may need it." The three of them shook hands and parted.

***

That afternoon, Nathaniel stood outside Duggan Ship Chandlers, watching with apprehension as the *Mary Jane* prepared to cast of. Dickey Lemon shouted above the hustle and bustle that Nathaniel Blacksmith had better hurry if they wanted to catch the one o'clock tide.

Captain Jumbo Barnes greeted Nathaniel. "Welcome aboard master Blacksmith. Captain Cane has told me of your endeavors. Let me show you to your accommodation. Make yourself at home, 'tis going to be your home for the few weeks. I have to take care of getting out of this god forsaken harbor. We can talk later."

***

The voyage to St. Eustasius saw two weeks of picture-book calm, sunny days. Nathaniel was expecting at least a small period of stormy, violent weather and seemed disappointed when he spoke with Dickey Lemon. "I have heard so much about how rough the oceans can be. Why is it so calm?"

"bout this time of year we always tries to make this crossing. Summer in the'Lantic Ocean is the most peaceful time. Off the coast of Africa, that's' where we cross to the tip of America. Straight line it is. Aint never seen it this bloody calm. First time on a ship then? Wot you goin to St Useless for?"

"Yes, my first time on a ship. This one, The Mary Jane, is named after my mother and Mrs. Cane."

Captain Cane's missus, she is Mary, so your ma must be Jane."

"Jane Blacksmith, yes. I am engaged to Mr. er, Captain Cane's daughter. I am going to St. Eust…use, what did you call it?"

"I calls it St. Useless cause it always pissed off Judd, Captain Cane. 'e finks I doan know 'ow to say it proper like. We was boys togever a long time ago. I was a cabin boy when he was ganged." Quickly Dickey realizes that he could be speaking out of turn and redirected his conversation. "Judd learned me to read and write 'e did. Judd and I grew up, so to speak, at sea. Me best friend 'e is. Did'n wan 'im to leave and go ashore. Good man. I 'ope 'is girl is as good as 'e is for your sake."

"I hope so too. I am going to see what opportunities there may be on St. Useless so Agatha, Judd's daughter, and I can start a new life together." Both men laughed at Nathaniel's use of the islands name.

On the predicted day the island came from out of nowhere to reveal a busy seaport fringed by lush green tropical vegetation. Beneath the intense heat of the sun, it was a vision the likes of which Nathaniel had never imagined. Between this and the voyage, he understood why Judd had put him through such different experiences in just six months.

The firing of the signal pot broke into his consciousness. Quickly, the ship was cleared by the authorities and edged its way alongside the dock. Captain Barnes introduced Nathaniel to Jack Freeman, the manager, a rotund, jolly man, and then bid Nathaniel farewell and success in his endeavors. The *Mary Jane* was a hive of activity. Men poured on board, hatches were opened, and cargo was soon swinging over the side and onto the docks. As Jack gave orders to the workers, he assisted Nathaniel in gathering his belongings and took him ashore.

Jack took Nathaniel to his home, where the fence around his acre of land sliced through the native vegetation, cutting it off from the order and calm of his garden. Clustered around the perimeter of the fence surrounding Jack's home were fifteen small cottages, where the permanent plantation workers lived with their families. Jack invited Nathaniel to stay and dine with his family, but first, Jack had to return to oversee the unloading of the *Mary Jane* and the loading of new cargo. He handed Nathaniel a map of Gallows Bay and the Plantation and told him go off and acquaint himself with the area.

Nathaniel sat in the shade of the house and looked down toward the harbor. There were ships at anchor with tillies going to and from the shore, and ships in full sail disappearing into the horizon. Looking at the map, Nathaniel could see that, off to his right, encompassing the face of the hill from the brow down to the sea's edge, lay the Plantation. Jack Freeman's home was on the southern edge of the property, and on the other side was the bustling township. From his vantage point, Nathaniel could see how much more organized and well-kept the docks were on the Plantation than in the town. A little intimidated by what lay before him, Nathaniel decided to walk the seafront portion of the Plantation. He was anxious to separate himself from people for a brief time as his thoughts of Agatha, Mary, Judd, and his parents all fought for space in his mind. He was in an emotional turmoil. Soon the *Mary Jane* would sail away, taking with it his umbilical cord of emotional security.

Arriving at the dockside, he met with Dickey Lemon and Jumbo Barnes sitting on bales of hemp. They greeted him and, laughing, Dickey shouted over his shoulder, "Hey boys! Look who is seeking passage back to England!"

"No way! I just wanted one more look at all your ugly faces before you leave," Nathaniel retorted.

"So, you gonna miss us or somefing?"

"Probably the 'or something'. Seriously for a minute though, I just wanted to spend the last bit of time with you all before you leave. You have all been great fun to be around and I have enjoyed the trip. I have learned something from all of you, except Dickey, the bloody twit. Who could learn anything from him?"

"You'd be surprise wot you could learn from Dickey, an it aint all good," said Captain Barnes.

The three spent an hour chatting before Nathaniel took his leave after watching the *Mary Jane* untie from the dockside and allow the ocean currents to drift her out to sea.

Turning to look at the plantation from the water's edge he was overwhelmed. Judd had advised him to focus, so he decided he would simply enjoy this first afternoon.

***

The cool water was hypnotic, lapping up sand as soft and clean as anything he could imagine. Each piece of driftwood and each large, elaborate shell captured his attention. In some places, the brush grass came to the water's edge, and in others, the vast expanse of pristine sand lay unmarked by human or animal intrusion. He would frequently stop with his back to the sea and look up to the top of the hill, absorbing the view.

Being alone in this place did not seem to concern him. It was as if nature had erased all the pressures of life. The soft, sloshing sound of the waves as they broke on the sandy beach, were hypnotic. The sounds of the local birds and the wind rustling in the tall palms were like a soothing emotional massage.

The short brush was full of bougainvillea and wild birds of paradise as spectacular as any he had seen as a child at the great exhibition in London. Sago palms lined the top of the hill like a crown of green, surrounding and claiming their territory. He lay in the shade of a large, leathery-leafed tree whose branches stretched from the grassy scrub to almost touch the water's edge. Big leaves that had dropped from the tree curled up into hard, brown, crunchy tubes that had become caves where hermit crabs had scurried as he'd approached.

He lay back, relaxed, and drifted into another place.

***

With the inner emotional turmoil of being alone, missing Agatha, and being among strangers, on his first night he chose to sleep under the stars, only to be eaten alive by insects. The next few days had been spent adjusting his body to the strange new climate. But almost everyone he met dealt with him with kindness and warmth. There were some local people who found it strange that the plantation owner's kin had to sleep outside, away from everyone. They treated him with suspicion. The friendlier people showed him which plants could ease discomfort and which to avoid, how to choose the right location when sleeping outside at night, and what plants were edible.

On the third day, he was awakened by Jack Freeman with "Good morning young Mr. Nathaniel. We have been expecting you at the house and down at the docks. I trust everything is alright with you."

"Mr. Cane has kindly allowed me to be at the planation. I am to be independent and see what St Eustasius offers me in the way of opportunity," Nathaniel explained.

"It is my understanding that I am to offer you whatever assistance it is that you may need to do whatever it is you decide to do. I am to keep books on what you use from the plantation and to credit you in those books with whatever you add to the plantation." Jack sat down on the sand bank that Nathaniel had been asleep on and continued, "I am sure that you were not expected to sleep under the stars, although many do here. I have a bed for you in a private area of one of the sheds at the docks, should you wish to use it. Please join me for breakfast in the office of the main shed at the docks. Let's say half an hour." With that Jack got up and walked down the slope towards the docks.

Much to his chagrin Nathaniel was embarrassed that he had assumed he needed to sleep out under the night sky. Still, he felt much more relaxed as he wandered down to the dockside to meet Jack for breakfast. While they ate, Jack explained how the plantation ran, how the ships would frequent this island out of convenience. The man imparted much useful information and many good tips.

When Nathaniel finished his tea he said to Jack, "I have been a bit overwhelmed by everything and you have motivated me into action. What action, I'm not sure, but I shall start investigating and see what appeals to me. I want to try and start right from the bottom, but I will surely turn to you if I need to. I thank you kindly for your offer of the bed. Later today you can show me where it is. Thank you for a fine meal. Now I must get busy."

***

Standing with his back to the main shed Nathaniel studied what lay in front of him with a sense of direction. The Plantation was dotted with small- and medium-sized huts and abandoned dwellings left over from the slave days. Most were in dilapidated condition, as bits and pieces had been removed to be used elsewhere. It took Nathaniel a week to realize that the locations of these structures, which originally housed slaves, were dictated by their purpose. A few wrong choices quickly taught him what to look for when selecting a site upon which he would build his new dwelling. Some of the structures had wind-blown sand mounds banked up the sides, others had rotted timber, that appeared to be caused by ground water. Some structures had large burrows going under them. He rationalized that if things were wrong with those places there must be a reason. He kept up his search. Finally, he chose one for its views and ability to capitalize on the sea breezes while at the same time being protected from the occasional heavy Atlantic winds that would pound the weather side of the island, rolling over the top and swirling down the lea side like a wave returning to the sea.

While he was considering using Judd's gift of a leather-bound journal as a diary, Nathaniel quickly learned that personal notes would not be as valuable as records of fact and observation. One evening, as the sun set, he asked Jack Freeman, a jolly man who always wore a smile and a battered old English cloth cap that had seen better days, if the post had any leather bound, journals, so he could separate his personal notes from his work records, and, did Jack have any suggestions of what sort of things would be important.

Jack exuded a calm, content aura as he sat with Nathaniel and lit his pipe. Through the blue haze of pungent, sweet tobacco, he raised his hand and removed his cap to release a shock of tight, curly hair that fell and framed his face. "This old hat sees two things," he said. "On the inside, it sees what used to be an angry slave, wanting to fight the world for the injustices done him. It sees a man who felt broken, until that man understood the world is too busy to pay him any mind. It sees a man who, not by skill or brilliance of mind but by circumstance, manages the very property in which he had been enslaved, and is now at peace with the Lord and himself.

"Now, the outside of the cap has seen people admiring it, as it sat in some grand haberdashery window in far-off England. It saw rich and poor folk, grownups and children, and all on the same street. I think it saw orders given and taken. It saw fair and unfair. At some time, it saw country and then the sea, and then the sun. Like a lost soul, it was washed up on the beach here on Statius. When I picked it out of the tide pushing it back and forth, it saw me. For many a long day now, it has seen life go on around me. It has protected this old head from the sun and rain and the prying eyes that want to know what the inside has seen. This cap and I can share the inside knowledge, but only with special people.

"When I saw you come ashore and look up at this island in front of you, it was as if I stood in your shoes. It would be good if you could know what both the inside and outside of this cap knew. It could make your life easier." Pondering his next statement, Jack relit his pipe and continued. "I would keep one journal. In that journal I would record all things that seem important and that I think I might need to look back on. Then, I would record my thoughts and feelings on that point, if I thought it relevant. Then, on second thoughts, keep a private journal. One that you would only share with special people, like your children. We tends to forget things as we get older. It would be nice to have something to reflect upon."

Nathaniel contemplated what the old man had just told him before he spoke. "My word Jack, you are a deep old soul. I would like to think that one day you may consider me special enough to allow me to know some of what that old hat had has seen."

"Maybe you will and maybe you won't son. All you can do is ask. You have every right to ask and I have every right to say no. We will just have to wait and see, won't we."

"Yes, we will." Nathaniel knew the old man was toying with him and so he let it go.

Both men sat in silence. Nathaniel digested what he had heard.

As Jack stood to leave, he turned to Nathaniel and said, "What a man sees and feels, both good and bad, gives value to what he succeeds and fails at. The man is as important as the journey. There are plenty of journals to be had in the Plantation store. You have a fine evening young man." Then, they went their separate ways into darkness.

Nathaniel returned to his little dwelling and pondered what he had heard. He decided to keep the record-keeping and personal observations and feelings twined together.

***

With the help of Jack, Nathaniel built up a simple toolkit and used one of the smaller storehouses as a workshop. He would shoulder lumber from old dwellings to the workshop, where he would work on it through the heat of the day. Every morning at sunrise, he would take his efforts from the workshop to the site of his project for the day, returning by noon the next day to repeat the cycle. He systematically deconstructed the old buildings, categorizing and storing their pieces in a warehouse for future use. His system would minimize the search and allow his findings to motivate his creativity.

On bad weather days, he could be seen, rain-soaked, beachcombing for anything of use. But one area of beach, he religiously kept clear of all debris all the time, and he would move native plants into it to create what he called his oasis. Some nights, he would sleep at the oasis to be away from everything just to clear his mind and think about what he planned to do next. Away from the oasis, around his simple cabin, he kept an array of finds and a chicken yard, and while this was clutter, it was still, for him, a useful and essential area.

Nathaniel made a habit of going down to the docks whenever he saw an interesting ship come in. As time went by, he went to the dockside less and less.

***

Over time, Nathaniel had become more interested in looking at cargo and how things were being done.

"When you first arrived at Statius, you told me that you had a task to do and you hadn't been told what it was," said Jack. "I think Mr. Cane wanted you to find your own way and you have found it."

Nathaniel spent the next year building a large residence at the water's edge of his oasis. First, he employed local labourers to dig a large hole into the rocky ground at the sand's edge. Local craftsmen, with experience sealed the inside of the hole with a mixture of shell, soil, and ground rock, which formed a cement-like slurry. This was to be the cistern for storing rainwater. Soon he found the need to hire two strong young local men to work beside him. These men were to be paid by the plantation and Nathaniel would be charged with the debt. Using large, old beams, they built a platform over the top upon which he built the dwelling. There were two sleeping rooms and a large day room. The walls were constructed of rocks and boulders, smoothed over with the same slurry used in the cistern and whitewashed. Large arches opened out to reveal the beach and the sea. The side walls had tall, narrow, arched openings to create a cross-flow of air as the breezes changed direction. By purchasing items from the Plantation, he furnished the dwelling, his Oasis, with linens and furniture. All this, he did alone.

There were a few inns in the capital town of Oranjestad, and Nathaniel offered them the opportunity to provide refreshments. He offered Jack's eldest daughter the opportunity to provide carriage rides to and from the Oasis on call. Her mother believed that wealthy passengers who had been at sea on a long voyage would be willing to pay handsomely for a carriage ride to the oasis, being driven by a pretty lady and to spend one night off of a ship, It worked. So determined was the mother for her daughter's success that she had her other children spend two days walking the route from the docks to the Oasis, picking up any stones or rocks she felt would impair a smooth ride.

Nathaniel would approach the captains of larger ships and offer his Oasis for rent by the day. The demand was bigger than the supply. He hired one of Jack's other daughters to come to the Oasis every day and prepare it for the next guest. Within the year, ships arrived with passengers requesting a stay at the Oasis. In six months, Jack announced that Nathaniel was now carrying a credit on the books and no longer a debt, even after paying the housemaid and the workers hired for various projects and tasks.

When Nathaniel was told of the regular dispatches that Jack sent to Judd, he arranged for Jack to advise him when the next one would be leaving so he could write to his parents.

There was a constant flow of information going in both directions that was eagerly awaited by both of them. In one letter, Agatha asked if he thought that she should learn about hotel business and bookkeeping. Nathaniel readily agreed and realized that he had stumbled upon his career path.

The year leading up to his return to the deck of the *Mary Jane* had been a hectic one. More beach front had been cleared and five more units had been erected, for a total of 12 cottages. The notoriety had so grown that people who lived on other parts of the island were coming to stay at the Oasis. Nathaniel was careful to keep two units available for ships' passengers. He believed his future lay more with outsiders than with the local population.

Upon arriving to pick up Nathaniel, Captain Barnes presented him with a small article he had seen in *The New York Times*, which sang the praises of the Oasis, suggesting it as a refreshing break from the city's chaos. At last, Nathaniel had proved something to himself. The letters and news were the constant thread that tied his activities together. He now had made something of himself and had 'become some-one.' He felt that now he had proven himself capable and was worthy of Agatha. He could not wait to go on bended knee before her

Chapter 27

Standing on the deck of the Mary Jane, as she slowly edged away from the dockside at St. Eustatius, filled Nathaniel with a sense of pride, accomplishment, and sadness. The people who lived here had become the central part of his life. He wondered if Judd or Dickey Lemon or any of the sailors 'really' knew them. On the voyage back to England, Nathaniel spent countless hours recounting his exploits to Dickey, Lezza, and anyone else who would listen. Jumbo Barnes was impressed with what he heard. He knew Judd would be pleased. One of the sailors jokingly tossed a copy of *The London Times* at Nathaniel and suggested he get in touch with the outside world. Studying the business section, Nathaniel was intrigued by the 'writing' machine. It was a simple machine that could be operated by anyone who could read. The typewriter would revolutionize business. From his days in the village smithy and the shipyard, Nathaniel had seen huge changes in the use and perfection of metals. He had unfailing faith in steel and engines. Before long, big steel ships would run on something more effective, more efficient, and cheaper than coal. He couldn't wait to get home to Agatha and see how much things may have changed.

Standing on the quarterdeck, looking out at the rolling waves and swell of the ocean, he thought about Ojukwae. Oj had told him many stories of his time at sea with Judd, and many of them came back to him in a kaleidoscope of images. He was anxious to reconnect with Oj. The *Mary Jane* sailed East to the Canary Islands then North to Gibraltar, where fresh water and supplies were brought on board. From Gibraltar Nathaniel sent a cable to his father, announcing his pending arrival home. He didn't think that the whole of Mucking and Lower Mucking would already know of his return.

Nathaniel had often made fun of Oj when Oj spoke of the magic of Channel Night. But in living the same experience, watching sea-hardened men soften at the sight of England, he saw how shallow his mockery had been. Many of the sailors could point out Cornwall, Devon, Southampton, the Isle of Wight, Portsmouth, the White Cliffs of Dover, and the landmarks of places they had never been to. The very sound of these places' names tugged at him as well as them, and he didn't really know why. The emotions were infectious.

As they left the English Channel, the boat turned northward. Much to Nathaniel's surprise, they were going to be sailing up the River Thames. It was at the shifting of the wind, as the huge, full sails leaned to starboard, that the *Mary Jane* glided around to enter the Thames Estuary. He knew that, very quickly, Lower Mucking would appear on the starboard side, and he wondered if they would draw near enough on this wide river for him to see clearly. He felt the difference between the sea and the river. Sails were trimmed as seaman busily went about their business.

When the *Mary Jane* slowed, Nathaniel knew it was going to stop. He sought out Captain Barnes and asked what was happening. "Pilot," said Captain Barnes, disturbed and brusque. "They don't trust us up the river. Got to wait for the Pool of London pilot. Get your gear topside. You're going off with the pilot launch." Nathaniel thought this must be normal.

As the ship dropped anchor and swayed around to face the tide square, he saw a small craft with six oarsmen pulling in perfect unison. As the men leaned into the stroke, their oars dipping into the water, bent behind the power, the front of the tiny craft lifted up and out of the water, surging forward. What power these men had.

It took almost half an hour for that pilot launch to reach the Mary Jane. The launch was made fast to the side by the lead bowman, and in fast succession, as the pilot climbed the rope ladder lowered for him, the jib swung out over the side and lowered Nathaniel's gear to a waiting coxswain. Nathaniel, told to be quick about it, barely had time to thank the men around him.

On the launch, the order to cast off was given, and the launch drifted away from the ship. The crew sat silently, awaiting their orders as they lowered their oars, leaned forward, and dipped them into the water. Nathaniel recognized one of the crew from Lower Mucking—a fisherman and eeler. Nathaniel spoke to the man, but was told promptly not to speak to the crew while they were under the command of the coxswain. So Nathaniel withdrew into himself, watching the shoreline grow nearer. The brown, murky Thames water slipped by the launch, with its flotsam and debris, that was jettisoned by the filthy dock areas of London.

Nathaniel was shaken out of his trance by an unfamiliar noise, which transformed from a buzz into a loud cheer from the dockside of Lower Mucking. Nathaniel stood.

"Sit down," said the coxswain. "Do you want to drown us in all this filth?" Rebuked, Nathaniel sat. He visually searched the group awaiting his return. At the front and center of the group was Agatha, flanked by Judd and Mary, his parents, and Ojukwae. Cane International had been closed for the day, as was the blacksmith and the bakery.

The coxswain gave Nathaniel the signal to mount the dock. As Nathaniel turned to pick up his gear, the coxswain said, "Go to it, lad. We will get everything up to the village for you." Nathaniel needed no further encouragement. He climbed the simple wooden makeshift ladder fixed to the side of the dock, and with strong, masterful, confident strides, went from the docks edge into the crowd. Then, he encompassed Agatha in his strong arms and smiled over her shoulder at his parents.

Judd leaned over to David Blacksmith and said, "I think we have a very different person here than the one that left us."

Jane spoke to her husband, David, "Oh my, he has become a man. That sun tan glow and sunbleached hair, I do declare, I hardly recognized him."

Nathaniel raised his hand in the air in an attempt to quiet the crowd. It was when he pulled away from Agatha and dropped to one knee that the crowd fell silent. He withdrew from his pocket a small velvet pouch made by Jack Freeman's wife.

Opening it, he spoke to Agatha with tears in his eyes. "It is custom where I have been living to give a symbolic token of yourself to the one you love," he said. "I think that I have become the man I want to be. I have gained my strength from those who love me." He wiped away a tear. "As Samson's strength was given to Delilah in his hair, so I offer my strength to you in a lock of my own." He removed a delicate ring of his blond hair from the pouch. It was so tightly woven that it was rigid and looked like burnished gold. "Agatha Cane, will you?" He waited for the crowd noise to subside before he continued, "You know that I love and respect you. It is a happy man that you made me by waiting so long for me. I would be honoured and blessed if you agree to be my wife. Will you marry me?"

"Of course, I will marry you. Leave you to the mercy of all these eligible village wenches? No way."

The crowd cheered, Mary and Jane hugged and, Judd and David shook Nathaniel's hand. As their mothers admired the delicately woven hair band Agatha whispered in Nathaniel's ear, "Yes, yes, yes.

"Then tell the world, not just me."

In an uncharacteristic move Agatha said to him, "Lift me high on your shoulders, please." As her head and shoulders rose above the throng she shouted out, for all to hear, "I Agatha Cane am going to marry Nathaniel Blacksmith. He is mine and I want everyone to know it." Raising her voice even louder she shouted, "Hear that, world? I am going to be Mrs. Blacksmith." She slid down the front of Nathaniel's body and planted a kiss on each cheek and his mouth. "Does that do it for you Mr. Blacksmith?"

The greetings, hugs, and good wishes flowed thick and fast and seemed to last an eternity. Gradually the crowd shifted into a procession that wound its way up the hill toward Mucking. "This better not be my wedding ring," Agatha whispered to her mother.

"Consider yourself lucky he still wants you," said Mary. "Any fool can have a gold ring. Not everyone receives such a personal token of love. What the hell are we going to do with you?" Agatha flanked by her and Nathaniel's mother was quiet for the rest of the journey. Judd and Ojukwae walked with their arms around each other's shoulders, Oj slipped Nathaniel a small package and said, "I got what you asked me to. Don't worry about the money right now, we can settle up later. I've picked something that I would be proud to give my love," he said.

"You have a love?" asked Nathaniel.

"Yes, and a child. He is two months old. We call him N.J.—Nathan Judd Mielman. Quite a ring to it, don't you think?"

***

A few mornings later, before the rest of the world was awake, and life around Nathaniel and Agatha had settled down into the usual rhythmic village pattern, Nathaniel sat with Judd in the offices of Cane International. Judd said he had spent the night reading the four journals given him the previous evening. He praised the meticulous records and, especially, the journal of personal thoughts and feelings. Nathaniel proceeded to fill in some gaps.

At nine o'clock, Mary and Agatha intruded upon them with fresh tea and buns from the bakery. Judd suggested Nathaniel and Agatha go off and begin making arrangements for their wedding, as he wished to discuss some business with Mary.

"There is something I want to say to you all," said Nathaniel. "These past three years, you have given me opportunities which I can never repay. Mr. Cane, I understand why Oj speaks of you the way he does. In many ways, you both gave him the same opportunity."

Agatha rolled her eyes and looked away. Nathaniel turned to Agatha and spoke sternly. "Ojukwae wrote to me and offered to obtain something for me that I could not get in St Eustatius. I sent him back a drawing, and he had this made for me."

He took a small, highly polished, rich golden brown, mahogany box with a gold letter 'A' set into the lid. He opened it to reveal a wedding band and a simple, elegant engagement ring.

"Oj had Mappin & Webb make these to my specifications. He has kept them secure for me for nearly a year. Agatha, I am happy to leave all of the arrangements for our wedding to you and our mothers. I will object to nothing you wish to do, but I have one condition from which I will not under any circumstances be swayed. There is no finer person to be my best man than Ojukwae Mielman."

Agatha stood silently, looking on. Putting the box in Agatha's hand, Nathaniel led Agatha down the wide staircase and out of the offices. The doors closed behind them as Mary said to Judd, "What are we going to do about Agatha's attitude?"

"Nothing," said Judd. "There are some things they will have to sort out for themselves. I do believe that Nathaniel is just the man to do it."

Outside the offices, Agatha pulled Nathaniel to a standstill and said in earnest, "Is our marriage going to be like this, you laying down the law and me obeying? Because if it is, this will not work out."

"Agatha, I don't know what you have against Oj. As a man, it is my choice who will be my best man. That's the tradition and I don't aim to change it. Just as you have the right to pick your bridesmaids without my interference, I have the same rights."

"But Nate," said Agatha in a soft pleading voice.

"No buts! No buts. I am willing to bow to you in many things, but not this one. What is your problem?"

"Ojukwae, is not one of us. My pa brought him here and planted him into my life. I did not have any say in the matter. Now you are planting him in our life and again, I don't have any say in the matter."

"Ojukwae is part of your life, part of my life, he is part of your life. That's the way it is, and I personally, am grateful for it."

"Well, I am not happy about it."

"So, who would you pick to be my best man?"

"Oh, I don't care, pick anyone you like."

"I just did." Nathaniel took Agatha's hand and led her across the green to her parent's home. She went along submissively, brooding.

The village justice gave permission for the village green to be used for the celebrations. The whole of Mucking and Lower Mucking were invited. The village women sewed bunting and the men planted flowers. A stage was erected for the wedding party so that they could be seen clearly by all.

While the town was busy, Judd had lengthy meetings with Nathaniel, discussing the future of the young couple. It was clear to Judd that Nathaniel had already made up his mind on his plan of action.

Nathaniel wanted them to spend a year planning further development of the Oasis on St. Eustatius, as he called it. In that year, they would acquire building materials, linens, furnishings, and everything necessary to add more dwellings and elevate the existing ones to fine Victorian standards. Agatha was unenthused at first, but as she told Nathaniel of her experiences at a London hotel, and the other business administration experiences, she felt him open up to her input. This greatly improved her attitude and she became far more excited.

Judd secured a warehouse close to the East India Docks where their purchases would be stored as they awaited shipment. Agatha expressed the desire to start at once setting up the system to be used for bookkeeping, suggesting that the St. Eustatius project be a separate set of books. Judd asked why.

"If you expect me to go into this plan with my fullest commitment," said Agatha, "I can tell you that Nathaniel and I will not stop with St. Eustatius."

Judd and Mary relaxed. They did not know what had transpired between their daughter and Nathaniel, but suspected that they had crossed the invisible hurdle of Ojukwae's colour being a significant factor in Agatha's thoughts. Either way the two had arrived together as one, and appeared to be getting very deeply involved in their own futures.

The weekend before the wedding, Ojukwae brought his new wife and baby N.J. to the village. Mary cleared Ojukwae's old room of Agatha's overflow of possessions and prepared it for the couple. Nathaniel met them at the railway station and took them directly to Judd and Mary's home. Entering the kitchen, Oj saw Agatha sitting straight-faced at the table, her hands clasped together in her lap, but Judd and Mary's excitement at seeing Oj and his family, soon over powered Agatha's sullenness.

Ojukwae introduced his wife as Colly. He added, "Colly, like in lolly pop, because she's so sweet," he said. Her real name was Columbine. A light-skinned black woman of exceptional beauty and poise, Colly spoke of how her parents, the children of freed slaves, had been so grateful to England and the life they had that they had named their six daughters and three sons after English flowers: Columbine, Hyacinth, Rosemary, Daisy, Mimosa, Blossom, Fraser, Laurel, and Ash.

"I'm pleased my parents didn't use vegetable names," said Colly. "I could have been Cucumber." Even Agatha laughed, and she softened more when she held the gangly-limbed child in her arms. Later, with the baby left in Agatha's care, Mary and Columbine left. Agatha was entranced by the baby and did not seem to be bothered by his colour. In her mind, she kept repeating, he is just a wee baby, it is not his fault.

***

Mary and Columbine walked out on the village green as Mary said, "I am so glad that you came down for the wedding."

"Oj and I wouldn't miss it for the world Mrs. Cane."

"I have never had any reason to speak of this before, but feel that I must do so now."

"What is bothering you, Mrs. Cane?"

"Please Colly, if I may call you that? It sounds so pretty. You must call me ma, or Mary. I know that you were not raised that way, but I will take no disrespect from you doing it, besides, it will help me relax a little better."

"Then, ma, it is. Something is going on between Oj and Agatha and I don't know what it is. I feel that this is what is bothering you."

"I know, Judd and I know that Oj loves us as family. I can see that no matter what Agatha does, Oj cares for his big sister. He allows that to cloud his judgment of her behavior toward him, and frankly I don't like it."

Columbine thought for a minute before she responded. "If we, Oj and I, were to take offense at everyone that looked sideways at us, we would be taking on unnecessary battles. In London those attitudes are common. We both know that Agatha has a good heart. Oj says that she would have treated a white boy in the same manner, if he had come between her and her father."

"But Oj didn't come between her and her father."

"No, he didn't, but she doesn't see it that way. There is nothing anyone can say that will change that. So, why bother? Sadly, that is her demon."

Mary squeezed Columbine's hand in a gesture of acceptance and warmth. A bond was formed between the two wise women.

***

Meanwhile, Oj and Nathaniel headed straight for the Weary Traveler, which had been recently modernized from a country pub into something more upscale. Ojukwae announced, "Gotta tell you, since you went to the islands, I have been made a welding gang leader in the shipyard, and it looks like I could be offered a shift supervisor position soon. Things are looking up for me."

Nathaniel laughed as he replied, "That's only because I left and they had no else to choose."

"No way. It was because I fixed all the cock ups that you made before you left."

"They are only being kind to you because I asked them to."

David and Judd approached the two of them and David said to Judd, "You can't leave these young boys alone for a minute without them arguing."

179

Turning to Ojukwae he continued, "So my boy, a wife, a baby what's next, a house?"

Ojukwae burst out laughing as he answered, "to late Mr. Blacksmith, me and Colly already got a house over in Rainham, just the other side of Tilbury. I have to catch the train to work each day, but it doesn't take long, besides, I like the relaxing ride home." The man was a picture of contentment and pride. The two boys, who had now become men, sat across the wooden table from Judd and David. Judd remarked to David, with an air of pride in his voice, "Who would ever have thought, that we would be sat out in front of The Weary Traveler drinking ale with our sons." Ojukwae let out an embarrassed chuckle, to which Judd commented, "You might not be mine by blood but you bloody well are by sweat and tears. You make Mary very happy by coming to the wedding. Me, I couldn't care less."

Ojukwae put his fingers in his mug of ale and flipped them at Judd splashing him with froth, as he said, in a sarcastically humorous tone, "I only came here because Agatha desperately wanted me to." The group laughed. Nathaniel commented, "I never realized how much better the taste of English bitter ale could be. I had more than my fair share of beer on St. Eustasius, but, my God, this is a good ale." They sat long into the night supping ale and listening to Nathaniel regaling some of the more memorable moments of the past three years.

***

The September wedding was the highlight for the Canes, Blacksmiths, Mucking, Lower Mucking and all the surrounding villages. Nathaniel Blacksmith and Agatha Cane. The affair attracted so much attention that it was listed in small print in *The London Times* as "The Country Wedding all the South East Counties are talking about." The six lines detailed the bride, the groom, and the size of the event.

The celebrations lasted through the night, a few hardy revelers lasting until dawn. The next morning, half the community showed up to return the village green to its original condition; the other half were under the weather. Farmers were found under hedgerows, behind sheds and outhouses, and under wagons, sleeping off the revelry. The village constable spent his day keeping the local larrikins away from the recovering sleepers, as they would tie the sleepers' bootlaces together and attach tin cans to their coat tails.

Nathaniel and Agatha, meanwhile, stayed at her parents' house, as the tenants of the cottage that they would share for the next year had left a mess to be cleaned up. As they threaded their way around the debris and sleepers toward the cottage, Agatha commented to Nathaniel that, if one didn't know better, one would say there had been a huge battle on the village green. "Yes," said Nathaniel, "and it was us who caused it." They laughed as only lovers do.

Later that week, Nathaniel brushed and painted while Agatha washed, scrubbed, and cleaned. In the afternoon, furniture was brought from both parents' houses to get them started. Agatha said she did not want any embellishments to their home, as they would only make it harder to leave within the year.

***

One day, when Agatha and her father went to London to handle the finances, Nathaniel worked at the rented warehouse by the East India Docks, sweeping and removing unwanted debris. Using paint, he marked the walls off into sections, labeling each area with what was to be stored there: wood, machinery, heavy lumber, furniture, etc. He made a list of materials needed to build shipping crates.

For the next nine months, Nathaniel and Agatha worked as a team. Nathaniel would work out his requirements and Agatha would order them. He would arrange and receive delivery. Gradually, the warehouse began to fill. They arranged for the *Clan Macleod* a four-year-old three-mast iron-hulled barque involved in the tramp trade, to be available for cargo in January.

Chapter 28

With the Clan Macleod riding low in the water due to the weight of the cargo, the Atlantic crossing was slow. The cumbersome dipping of the ship's bow into the troughs between the huge waves that plowed through the crest kept a steady rhythm. White caps of surf decorated the tops of each wave. There was very little rolling from side to side though, so Agatha felt little discomfort. The couple spent many hours sitting atop the capstan, wrapped up against the cutting wind. The further south they traveled, the warmer the winds and the calmer the ocean. The Clan Macleod's navigator gave them a daily update on their journey. Approaching America, close to Virginia, the ship took on a southern route, passing Georgia and Florida. Much to Nathaniel's surprise, Agatha recognized Jakeskill Island as they passed. In fact, she pointed out all the different places Cane International owned property. With the passing of each island, Agatha's excitement increased.

St. Eustatius came into view and appeared as a craggy, sparsely populated island. The trees and growth seemed short and spread out. Nathaniel pointed out Boven and Venus Bays, with Little Mountain in the background. He explained that this side of the island, the windward side, was very different from the other, as it caught the brunt of the Atlantic storms. When they rounded the southern tip of the island at Buccaneers Bay, the landscape became noticeably lusher and more populated. Dropping anchor in Gallows Bay, they sat fourth in line for a dockside berth. Nathaniel informed the captain that they would not have to wait in line. Cane International had its own docking facility at the Plantation.

***

As the buggy bounced along the dirt road from the plantation dockside to the Oasis, the driver, Jack's Freeman's eldest daughter chatted away gaily. She updated Nathaniel on who had gotten married and who had new babies. She pointed out the large, white-painted rocks that had been added to the roadside. Shrubs and small trees around the island had been replanted here, forming an avenue to the Oasis. The dockside workers had made these improvements on their own time for no pay.

Nathaniel's spirits were high. Agatha was quiet.

Dismissing the buggy with the drop of silver florin into the girl's hand, Nathaniel turned to Agatha, who had walked through the Oasis's main house to sit on the veranda overlooking the sea. Nathaniel went and sat beside her. "Today, you are experiencing what I did when I first came here," he said. "It's the same thing Ojukwae went through when he came to live in our village—the feeling of what it is like to be on the outside looking in."

"But you never told me there are only blacks here. You never told me there were no white people. Why?" she angrily spat at him.

"I had no more reason to tell you than if I took you France and said in some parts there are mainly French people. Some things do not need to be said," said Nathaniel. He watched her break down into tears. Kissing the top of her head, he decided to check on the other cottages in the Oasis. Turning towards her as he went to close the door he said, "You need to work at controlling your tears when you are frustrated or something doesn't suit you. It can be taken as a sign of weakness. Let's put on a strong united front to the local people." He closed the door and left without waiting for a response.

***

Upon seeing three of the other cottages full of guests, white guests, and learning from Jack Freeman of pending guests, Agatha quickly adjusted. In the coming months, Agatha used the skills she had learned from the London hotel to convert the Oasis from an island cottage, bed and breakfast style, into a highquality luxurious island retreat.

Agatha was also quick to point out that there were almost no recreational places for the guests. In the center of London, a large percentage of hotel guests were not there only for business, but were also anxious to relax and enjoy the city. With the climate of St. Eustatius, the potential for exploiting holidays could be unlimited. While Nathaniel supervised the unloading of the construction supplies from the ship Agatha set about investigating each of the cottages. She paid attention to the construction as well location, views and amenities.

Two days later, at breakfast, Agatha asked Nathaniel, "In which order did you build the cottages?"

"Let me think for a moment," Nathaniel responded, only to be interrupted by his wife saying "I bet that I can tell you the exact order."

"Oh really, and how do propose to do that?"

"Give me a week to check on my observations, then, if I get it right, what do I get?"

"You get me to answer to your every whim, without question for one week. But, hold on. If, you are wrong by as little as one cottage out of order, I get you to submit to a night of passion, every night, for a week, without questions."

"Mr. Smarty Pants thinks he is going to win. What makes you think that I wouldn't want nights of passion?"

"Well, if you do, I win either way."

For the next six days Agatha reviewed her list carefully. She devised a system of grading each cottage. Her criteria included cottage size, layout, view, construction skill level, and progressive change. On the seventh day she left her list at their cottage and carried out a reaction inspection. This made her change the order of one cottage only.

That evening after Nathaniel completed the storage of the supplies Agatha greeted him at the cottage door with instructions for him to bath and clean up as they were to take a picnic to a small cove that she had found. Leading the way Agatha carried herself with a bounce in her step. Very quickly Nathaniel knew where she was taking him. The tiny inlet had a beach of no more than fifty feet wide heavily cloaked with lush palms that obscured the island behind them. He had often gone to this place where he would swim naked without fear of being seen by prying eyes. He put on an act of surprise when she held her arms open and said. "Voila. This can be our special place." Nathaniel did nothing to disillusion her enthusiasm.

After spreading out the blanket, Agatha served a simple meal. Standing up she drew her light linen dress over her head and showed off her swimsuit. The pants went below her knees and the top was neatly laced at her throat. She was the epitome of Victorian style. Nathaniel stood and disrobed, standing naked and unabashed. Agatha giggled as she said, "I can't believe you. Standing there for the whole world to see in all your born glory."

"There's no world here to see, just you and me. Join me in the way nature meant us to be. I dare you." She stood completely still, in a shocked state for a moment before she moved to lift her swimsuit over her head.

"You didn't think I would, did you?" she said.

"No, I didn't, but I would love to see you do it." Before he could blink an eye, Agatha had stripped off her clothes and ran ahead of him into the waves. Taking his time, he waded into the water. Agatha turned, watching his torso gradually disappear below the water before he swam to her. It excited her. As he got close ,she stood up, with the water only up to her waist. He stood and looked at her pert breasts, nipples erect from the cool water, and whispered, "My god, you are beautiful. Could you imagine if we were to do this at Mucking Flats?" They both laughed. The late afternoon sun was slowly dipping to the horizon as they made their way to the shore, stopping only to kiss, deeply and passionately.

They lay in a tight embrace after making love in a manner they had never imagined possible, speaking only of their hopes and desires for their future. Nathaniel whispered quietly in Agatha's ear, "I love you from the bottom of my heart, no, from even deeper down than that." To Agatha's smile of understanding he stood up, took hold of his manhood and shook it, saying, "I didn't mean from this far down."

"I bet you didn't, but there's nothing lower than that, on you, anyway."

Walking back through the undergrowth Nathaniel said, "You didn't get to show me the order in which you think I built the cottages."

"It didn't take long for you switch from my body to my brain. I think I'm offended. Wait 'til we get back home and I will show you. Walking back towards their cottage they noticed a stiff breeze was coming in from the sea.

Nathaniel commented, "It seems as if there is a storm on the way, I'd better check with Jack to see if he has heard anything."

"Why, how would he know?" Agatha was curious.

"Because the islands let each other know if it looks like a storm or hurricane is brewing."

"A hurricane? What exactly is a hurricane?" Agatha sounded alarmed.

"It's an extremely strong storm with high winds that batter the living daylights out of everything in it its path. It can be powerful enough to destroy an island and yet leave the next island with not even a hair disturbed. It's very scary."

Nathaniel settled Agatha in their cottage, then took off for the plantation offices where he found Jack Freeman sitting in his usual rocking chair watching the darkening evening clouds batter each other around.

"So, tell Jack, have you any reports of what is going on with the weather?"

"I got a cable about three hours ago and couldn't find you to tell you."

"Tell me what," he asked concerned.

"Calm down young fellow. The cable I got was cut off, so I'm guessing they lost power. Anyway, there is a hurricane spinning around out there, and I believe that it's headed straight for us on the weather side, so our side of 'statius is going to get the force of it, right here." Jack delivered the news in a calm, relaxed tone.

"So, what about our guests, shouldn't they be moved?"

"One step ahead of you my boy. My daughter packed them up and moved them over to Oranjestad. They are staying at the Old Gin House Inn. It's far enough inland that they should be safe there. Do you want some help in buckling everything down? I can get you a couple of men to help."

"Do we know where it's coming from and how long we have?"

"It devastated Kingston, Jamaica around 9:00 am this morning and dropped south. It looks like the eye is moving our way. It was last seen south of The Dominican Island heading east towards us around three o'clock. That's when the cable from Beata Island got cut off."

"Where's Beata Island?" asked Nathaniel.

"The southern tip of The Dominican Republic. So, it's headed straight for us. Judging by the wind strength right now, my guess is that we should see it within the next two hours."

Nathaniel thought for a moment before he replied. "Yes, I would appreciate all the help I can get. If you could get the men to start at the cottage closest to this end of the Plantation, I will start at the other end and hopefully we can get everything possible lashed down safely."

"Remember Mr. Nathaniel, you are going to lose something. We all did, in the last hurricane. We have been spoiled for two years now. It's now time to pay our dues."

Nathaniel quickly returned to Agatha and gave her the news. "We need to act swiftly. Get a pair of my pants and put them on. Also, put on a warm jacket."

"I will not wear men's pants or jacket," stated Agatha.

"Well then, let your skirts blow around your head so that you can't see what is going on. For all I care right now, you can freeze your rear end off. I have more important things to do. If you want to help then do as I say."

"What exactly are we going to do?"

"Go to each cottage as quickly as possible then move, stack and tie down everything to prevent it being blown away. Now, let's go."

For the next two hours as the wind grew from strong to a lashing, biting force, the two worked as a team. Periodically one or other would get blown off their feet only to stand, lean into the wind, and continue with their efforts. Exhausted after two and half hours, all the helpers, Jack Freeman, Agatha and Nathaniel sat huddled in one of the large storage warehouses that had withstood previous hurricanes.

For six hours the winds shook and clattered the sheets of tin that made up the roof, but they all held. The constant flapping of the loose tin sheets soon became a repetitive background sound. The noise of objects being tossed around, hitting the sides, and top of the shed violently, frightened the inhabitants. The wind kept up an unabated scream as it found its way through every crack and hole in the building's structure. Agatha could not work out what was cracking, snapping and swishing. She was terrified.

The sun rose at 5 am, shining on a silent, calm, scene of destruction. The occupants emerged to see fishing boats tossed far inland on the hillside. There were bigger fishing boats lying in the sea by the dock with water over their decks. Trees with every leaf gone stood like silent sentinels. Crates, boxes, timber and all manner of debris was scattered around. The silence held them all in awe. As they stood surveying the devastation, Agatha let out a piercing scream that startled them. "Oh no! Oh no! Nathaniel! We have lost everything."

Nathaniel's reply seemed odd and it surprised her. "No, we haven't. Our home is fine and we have four cottages left. We can rebuild. It could be worse."

"How can we start all over again? All the work that you have done is wasted."

"No, not wasted. Let's go and see what we can salvage. Repair will be easier then rebuilding from scratch. I will just have to work harder and longer."

***

The first day after the hurricane the two of them spent going from cottage to cottage inspecting the damage. Agatha was awestruck at the scope of the carnage. One of the cottages, one that Nathaniel had built completely of stone, was unharmed and looked exactly as they had prepared it. The adjacent cottage had boards ripped from the outer walls, pieces of a boat inside one room and everything else was gone. It was as if someone had played a trick on them. Agatha was at a loss to understand Nathaniel's calm appraisal of the situation. They met with Jack Freeman to review how the plantation's business has fared.

Agatha asked, "Was much damage done elsewhere on 'stasius?"

Jack replied, "Only this side of the island was hit. Our guests at The Old Gin House are safe."

"Has a hurricane ever hit the rest of the island?"

"Oh yes. This side rarely gets hit because we are on the lea side. The top of the mountain, at Oranjestad, right down to the Atlantic, gets pounded regularly."

"You mean they rebuild frequently?" Agatha was confused.

"Well, not that much damage is done over there. We had a hurricane two years ago. You should remember that one well Nathaniel. It was your first. Before that we haven't been hit in twenty years."

Turning to Nathaniel Agatha stated firmly, "I don't know how their buildings survive and ours don't, but, Mr. Nathaniel Blacksmith, we are going to find out."

Jack interrupted, "Concrete, Miss Agatha. They use concrete. Mighty expensive but it works."

"Then we shall use concrete. The one-time cost to build, balanced against the risk to our guests and the occasional minor repairs, must be better for us. Jack, when we are back to normal could you please find out what is involved in us getting concrete?"

"I know now. It comes as Portland Cement in bags of powder. We mix it with sand, water and stones to make the concrete. Do you want me to contract for a few bags?"

Agatha excitedly replied, "No, get a whole bloody ship load. If we can use it so can other people. We can reduce our cost by selling off any extra. Once the local people see us building with it, they will want some."

Nathaniel interjected into the conversation, "Before you do anything Jack, see if you can get any from the docks over at Oranjestadt's port." They exchanged goodbyes and left the plantation building.

Agatha looked at Nathaniel and asked, "Can we go over to Otanjestadt before we do anything else and take a careful look at the buildings? I think we can gain some good ideas." They did just that.

***

The balance of the day was spent in the capital town of Oranjestadt. Agatha would boldly walk to houses, shops and other buildings and closely examine the walls. Soon it became evident that two methods of construction were being used. It appeared that one was stone held together with a cement mix that had no small pebbles in it. The other method was the use of a coarse mix of the cement and larger sized stones. This looked as if it had been poured into a form of some sort to allow it to harden. She deduced this from the imprint of wood grain that could be seen in some places.

Nathaniel, after listening to her thoughts made a suggestion. "I know what we don't know. That's our weakness. We are going to contract a builder from over here to build a cottage for us. You and I will pay close attention and ask a lot of questions. I'm sure we can do it ourselves once we have seen it done." On the way back to the plantation Nathaniel could see that Agatha was deep in thought. After a while he could hold his questions no longer. "So, tell me what is going on in your pretty little head."

"Forget about my pretty little head. If we watch something small being built, we can build something small. It doesn't mean that we could build something big. But, if we watch something big being built, we can build something big and then, if needed, scale it down and build something small. We would not have to rely on anyone else."

Nathaniel laughed and said, "I knew there was a reason that I married you. What is the big thing you want to build?"

"A club house," Agatha told him.

"A club... house...what the...?"

"Just think about it. At home the pubs are places for men to gather. Each pub has its snug bar, for the ladies. There are lots of gentlemen's clubs in London. What if we built a group of large rooms in one building? One for a library, one for a cigar room. One for larger gatherings, maybe serve evening cocktails, even evening dinners. We could make tennis courts. Don't you see? We can provide more than one reason to visit our cottages and perhaps stay longer."

"Why do that first?" asked Nathaniel.

"I told you. We would learn the construction method. If we got that set up, by the time we have rebuilt the lost cottages we should have a line of people wanting to stay with us."

"That's a mighty tall order, but I do like the sound of it. Firstly, we will have Jack locate a builder for us, he will probably have access to the concrete, cement stuff. In the mean time we will get on repairing the less damaged cottages and keep the business going."

Agatha added, "By building the walls of the new buildings with stone and slurry, the supply of timber we brought with us will go much further."

"Great idea, let's get on with things."

Within two months, Agatha had selected a site at the highest point of the Plantation and convinced Nathaniel that a large central building, to act as club and meeting center, would be a good location as it would be visible to any passing ships.

It took the rest of that year and well into the next to see the completion of the main building. The less damaged cottages had been repaired and fully occupied. Nathaniel's workers had labored alongside the builder of the new structure and learned the art of making forms, and mixing and pouring solid concrete walls. There was a great deal of interest from the islands' inhabitants in the activity on the planation. The addition of a kitchen area to the central building was the talk of the lea side of the island. It looked like big changes were taking place.

Chapter 29

By 1877 Agatha, at the age of 28, was getting restless. There were now eighteen There were now eighteen individual cottages, fully completed and regularly occupied. There were ten large luxury suites built onto the main building. The clubhouse concept had proved to be a huge attraction. Many islanders had signed onto a waiting list for an empty cottage or suite. If one became vacant from a travelling guest, the list would be used to offer accommodation. This proved successful. Much to Nathaniel's surprise the tennis courts had to be increased within the first year as a tournament concept had been requested by other places on the island. Many smaller hotels from across the island rented time on the courts for their guests. To separate the Plantation from the hotel and cottages Agatha suggested a new name which Nathaniel happily agreed with. So, *The Gallows Bay Retreat* was born. She renamed the Oasis with the slogan, "You don't need to be a pirate to hang around here." Nathaniel was not so sure about the name, but Agatha insisted that this should be a fun place.

Coincidently, as if by some unknown force, on the same day, Agatha made another announcement to her husband. "Nathaniel? What do you think about being called papa Nathaniel?"

"I think that would be a grand idea. When do you plan on doing something about it? Tonight? Maybe, I could be convinced to start this afternoon?"

"A little bit late my darling. You have already done something about it."

"I did? When?"

"I wasn't keeping track, but I am with child - now."

"Are you sure?"

"I have missed my cycle twice and my breasts are swelling."

"Let me see." Nathaniel reached out to touch her breast. She quickly flipped his hand away and said, "You don't miss a chance, do you? I am like this because you can't control yourself."

"I can't help it if you stir my bones."

"Not your bones, my dear. Will you be pa, or as they say round here, daddy?"

"I don't care because I am going to be a father. So, you think we can expect the baby pretty close to Christmas?"

"I think then, or very early in the new year." The two of them spent the day talking about what they were going to do and if they should build a larger cottage for themselves.

Agatha took the opportunity to bring up the subject of moving on to a new project. Taken by surprise Nathaniel showed some confusion. "You want to move on, to where, why?"

"I told you when we were planning to get married and come out here that this would only be the beginning."

"Yes, but that was then, this is now. Look what we have created."

"All the more reason to move on. This is successful, so let's do it again."

"I'm not sure that I like the idea. With you being pregnant, it's not a good time to travel and start anew."

"There will always be a reason not to do something Nathaniel Blacksmith. If I thought that you were a stick in the mud, you would not have appealed to me in the first place."

"Well, Agatha Blacksmith, I never knew that I had it in me to do the things I did."

"My love, you not only had it in you, look what you have done. I bet there's more where that came from."

"Are we back on the baby subject?" Nathaniel laughed, to ease his discomfort.

"You men are all the same. You think from the south and not the north. No, I don't mean now. It's wise to stay here for the baby to be born. There's a hospital in Oranjestadt. But I want you to give some thought to making a move after the birth. "Although," she hesitated before carrying on, as if to choose her words carefully, "I'm not happy about our child being born here, in a Dutch country."

"What are you saying, where would you rather the child is born?"

"England of course."

"That's not happening. First, I don't think we could arrange a voyage that quickly. Second, you are safer here than being at sea if anything should happen."

"I know." Agatha grudgingly agreed.

In the months that followed Agatha was kept busy improving and training the staff. She had given thought to approaching Jack Freeman's daughter, Rosemary, who had recently got married. She and her husband were living with her parents. Rosemary jumped at Agatha's idea. The idea was that Rosemary and her husband should move into one of the cottages so that she could be on hand to undergo intense training to take over management of Gallows Bay Retreat when Agatha and her family moved on. Rosemary's husband, Kenny had been working for Nathaniel since he first arrived and was well trusted. Nathaniel felt this was the thin of the wedge. Was she preparing him for bigger changes? Was she getting him used to going along with her ideas, at her pace? As was Agatha's bent, she forged ahead with her plan regardless. It took four months for Nathaniel to build a large residence above the main club house for, 'a manager to live comfortably in,' as Agatha described it.

With her child rapidly developing into a large bulge, Agatha kept about her daily business. October turned into November and the area's hurricane season carried on all around them. Just as Jack had told them, the windward side of the island got battered by a couple of small hurricanes and countless season torrential rainstorms. It was during one of these rainstorms, that Agatha felt the tug of the restless child in her womb. In the middle of the night, she urged Nathaniel to take her to the hospital. She felt something was not right. The hospital was between Gallows Bay and the only doctor. With no experience in these matters, Nathaniel rigged the trap and they set off in the dark. The water-logged, slippery road up the side of the mountain created a stressful journey. The trap would slide from side to side as the horse would stumble. The trap jerked and jumped and Agatha cried out in pain. It took two hours to make the half an hour trip. As they trotted into the forecourt of hospital it became clear. The place was deserted and in darkness. The forecourt was awash with small streams that had eroded channels into the once packed earth. Nathaniel jumped down and ran, splashing around, to the front of the trap to assist Agatha. He startled the horse and it reared into the air standing up on its hind legs. Agatha, who was attempting to exit the trap, slid off the now steeply angled step, and went under the trap. It rolled backward, and it's huge iron bound wheel, lurched and bumped as it rolled over her outstretch arm, pushing it deep into the mud. There was a piecing scream and all went silent, except for the continuous tapping of the rain on the carriage. Nathaniel froze. Unable to lift Agatha from under the trap he dragged her toward the outer edge. Kneeling in the mud he lifted her head, cradling it in his arm he shouted at the top of his voice. No one came. He lifted his head to skies and bellowed. Still no one came. He removed his jacket, rolled it up and placed it under her head to keep it out of the mud, and then shouting for help ran.

A door opened to what was the caretaker's cottage and a man emerged holding a lantern high above his head. "The hospital is closed down sir," he said. "The hurricane destroyed the electric generators. Things should be back to normal tomorrow."

"My wife.... There has been an accident. She is with child. She fell and has been run over by a horse trap. Please help."

"I cannot sir, for I am not a medical man. I do not know what to do."

"Neither am I, she is by the entrance to the building - we must do something." Nathaniel was sounding desperate.

"Let me fetch the keys to the building. Wait here." The man closed the door behind him as Nathaniel stood helplessly waiting. The man came out carrying a huge iron ring of keys; and holding the lantern high above his head they set off back up the drive to the main building. Both men slipped and fell twice in the mire before reaching Agatha. Picking his unconscious wife up in his arms, Nathaniel carried her through the door the man had opened. He stopped at the first bed he found and laid Agatha down gently. It was then that he noticed the large bloodstain on her dress mingling with the muddy water dripping off her lifeless body. "Fetch help man. I do not know what to do. Now, now, go get someone."

The man placed the lantern on top of a cupboard to spread its light and took off running. Nathaniel found a sink and some towels and tried to clean Agatha's broken body, taking care to avoid her mangled arm. After a few minutes she roused, her eyes flickered and she whispered, Nathaniel, I hurt so much. What happened, where are we? Please stop the hurting."

A tall gangly black man entered the room and said, "Step aside. Let me take a look. What happened?"

Nathaniel explained. The man was not a doctor but had more knowledge than himself and had birthed children for the villagers, Agatha had no choice but to listen. "The bleeding has stopped and your wife is conscious but sleeping. I can give her laudanum for the pain and splint her arm to stop her moving it, but's that's all I dare do. The doctors will be here in the morning, which is only a few hours away. We have been told that the electricity will be restored by then. I am going to leave and I will stop at the doctor's residence and tell him he should come as soon as possible. He can do nothing until the morning anyway." With that the man left. The two of them were to be alone for the balance of the night.

The last few hours till dawn passed slowly and quietly with Agatha sleeping. He kept wiping her brow with a wet, cool cloth. He checked to see if she had been bleeding, and it appeared she had. The sheets on the bed were a mess of mud, water and blood. It was frightening to Nathaniel. She would wake from time to time and complain of the pain in her arm, and then fall back to sleep. As he sat beside her bed and kept vigil he ran through a myriad of emotions.

As staff started to arrive Nathaniel had to relive the whole nights, horrific events. Agatha had her arm broken in two places and her shoulder was badly bruised.

"Nothing that won't heal in due time," the doctor said.

Nathaniel asked, "What about the baby, is it alright?"

"It is hard to tell at this point. I wish to observe your wife for a little longer, but I would suggest that you prepare yourself for the worst. We are unable at to detect the child's heartbeat. It may be there just faintly beating. As your wife calms down it may pick up. We do not know just yet.

"You mean the baby could be dead?"

"I'm afraid that's a strong possibility. We will do all we can."

"But if the baby is dead, what happens to it?"

"We have to hope that your wife's body is strong enough to give birth in the normal manner. That's the best that could happen."

"And the worst?" Nathaniel asked frantically.

"Let's wait and see, shall we?" was the doctor's calm reply. Nathaniel decided to wait at the hospital until he heard something more positive to clear his mind.

***

By mid-day the waiting was over for Nathaniel, as Agatha had started to give birth. The labor lasted three agonizing hours. Nathaniel could hear the muffled cries coming from the birthing room, and they bit into his thoughts.

Suddenly, the door opened and a doctor approached Nathaniel. "Mr. Blacksmith, I'm sorry, we did everything that we could. Your wife put up a valiant effort. It was not her fault, or due to the accident. It is apparent that the child has been dead for a while. That is where her pains were coming from. Instinctively, knowing the child had died, her body was trying to expel it. She is a very lucky lady. Not many survive this type of trauma."

In shock and sorrow Nathaniel asked "May I see her now?"

"Indeed, but you must be careful, she has been through a lot. She needs to rest. Don't be shocked at her appearance. The worst is over. We would like to keep her here for a few days to be sure that she is on the mend." With that the doctor turned and left, giving instructions to the nurse as he went.

Standing beside the bed were two nurses who were washing Agatha's limp form and moving her to a clean bed. One of them turned to Nathaniel and said, "You probably don't recognize me Mr. Blacksmith, I am Lilly Bongolo. I am married to Jack Freeman's wife's brother. Your wife is in good hands. She will be fine. She isn't aware of what is happening right now. She has been sedated. I will stay by her side and keep vigil for you. You should go home and rest."

"Is she in pain still?"

Nathaniel told Jack of the whole night's occurrences. The telling was somewhat cathartic for him, and by the tales end, he had composed himself. On arriving back at Gallows Bay Retreat, Jack hoped off the cart and invited Nathaniel to come to his house for something to eat when he felt up to it. "Or, if you just want to come down to the Plantation office and be with me, I would welcome it. But, if you would rather be alone, I understand. Don't worry about Miss Agatha too much. Women are strong creatures, stronger than we men give them credit for." Jack touched the peak of his cloth cap in a sign of respect and strode of towards the plantation office.

Nathaniel sat on the verandah of his home looking out at the sea as thoughts tumbled through his tired mind. He was exhausted. How would he tell their families that the baby had died? Was it his fault for scaring the horse? Could he have done something to prevent the accident? He tortured himself. It was only the week before that he received letters from Judd and Mary expressing how excited they were about the upcoming birth. He drifted off into a fitful sleep. He woke up three hours later, still leaning against the verandah post, where he had slept. The mid-morning sun was scorching his legs. In a trance like state, he washed himself and wandered off to the Plantation, to be with Jack Freeman.

***

Agatha remained in the hospital for a week and was excited when Nathaniel arrived to take her home. She was reserved during the doctor's discharge visit. As soon they were in the trap Agatha burst, and let go of her pentup emotions. "Nathaniel, they told me that the baby was dead when we got to the hospital."

"That is what they told me as well."

"Well how do they know? If I remember correctly no one was there. And, how did my arm get broken?"

"When I came round the front of the trap to help you down, the weather, or something, spooked the horse, and you were tossed out of the trap. You fell under the wheel, that's what broke your arm. How is it feeling?"

"Forget about the arm. I just have to live with this sling and splint thing for about six weeks. I'm telling you the baby was not dead. I think he was being born quickly and the doctor messed it up."

"Now why would you think that? You were in pain and the doctor said that was probably your body trying to get rid of the dead baby."

"Of course, he would say it was already dead. They did something wrong. This would never have happened in Mucking, not where there is a white doctor. I was fine until the pain started. One time when I was laying in the room waiting for the doctor, before there were any lights, I remember a black man doing something to me. Maybe he made the baby die."

"How can you say that? That man helped us. He splinted your arm and checked to see if you were still bleeding and then went for help."

"Somebody made the baby die, I know it."

"Enough. Agatha, you have had a very difficult time. If it was God's will the baby should not live then so be it. We can have another."

"What? Go through this again so that 'God' can decide if it will live or die? I don't like that plan."

They rode in silence back to Gallows Bay - Nathaniel, not knowing what to say, and Agatha being angry." Nathaniel trod softly around Agatha for two weeks before she woke up one morning as if a burden had been lifted. She wanted to move ahead with the construction and completion of the Gallows Bay development. There were guests and the daytoday business to take care of. Rosemary and Kenny had taken on more and more responsibilities, and were practically running the complex. This allowed Agatha to focus on making sure that the standards were much higher than those of other hotels and inns across St Eustasius. She immersed herself in the work, rarely speaking of the baby.

Chapter 30

In November of 1880 Nathaniel and Agatha returned to Mucking on the Mary Jane. They both noticed that Judd had lost very little of his energetic persona. He kept himself busy with business and spent a lot of time at the forge with his friend Davey Blacksmith. Both sets of parents commiserated with the young couple on the loss of their baby, but, in true country spirit advised them not worry. If it was meant to be for them to have a child, it would happen. Judd and Nathaniel spent many hours discussing the progress at The Plantation, or Gallows Bay Retreat, as it was now known. The subject came up of what the future plans were. Nathaniel said to both Mary and Judd, "I think it is time for us to move on. Jack Freeman's daughter and son-in-law are doing well running the place and Agatha needs a change of scenery. I think the memories of our child haunt her still. She blames the local doctor, who is black, for the child's death. Irrational I know, but what can we do?"

Mary suggested, "Agatha has her own personal demons with black people. Best not to dwell on it." She whispered in Judd's ear and then continued, "Why not go to another property, and expand their achievements?

"Expand their achievements? Don't you mean build their own empire?" Judd slapped his thigh laughing and said, "I don't know what you wanted to prove to yourself, but you definitely proved your worth. Mary, I think we should reward their efforts. Why don't you arrange for the transfer of Gallows Bay Retreat into Agatha and Nathaniel's names?" It was more of an instruction than a question.

When Nathaniel told Agatha of her parent's decision it appeared to lift her spirits instantly. She said, "I think we should go to Beruka Fields in Dominica next. She described the property to him. "The property is comprised of two parcels of land of twenty-five acres each. They are strips of adjacent land that ran from the ocean up towards Watt Mountain. Both are fairly steep and have sea frontage of nine hundred feet."

"Oh my, someone has been giving a lot of thought to this," joked Nathaniel.

"It will be wonderful. We can take what we have learned from St. Stasius and go one better," Agatha said excitedly.

"One better, I didn't think we could do any better."

"We can always do better. Shall we stop at Statius on the way back? Do we even have to go back to Stasius?" There was a pleading tone in Agatha's voice.

"I believe that we need to spend a little more time at The Gallows so that we can instill how important it is for Rosemary and Kenny to carry on alone, with full responsibility. They need to run everything for six months as if we are not there. You know that you are a perfectionist. Bring them up to your standards. It's only fair."

"What will you be doing?" Agatha queried.

"I think that I should go ahead to Beruka and build the first cottage for us to live in and evaluate the potential of building a funicular up the slope. That is a railway sort of thing that runs on cables from top to bottom. It will make construction and everything easier."

"We can talk about it on the way back to Stasius." The two of them set about arranging for their return trip with an eager excitement. It pleased Nathaniel to see Agatha's renewed energy.

"I know what a funicular is It's a tram that goes up slopes" Agatha smartly told Nathaniel.

***

The White Star line took them to New York where they took a trading schooner to St Eustasius. The trip took four weeks, during which they experienced a renewed romantic connection. They frequently made love as if newly married. For Nathaniel, he had gained his old, wife back. For Agatha, the adrenaline rush of a new challenge was invigorating. Arriving in July of 1881, Agatha saw St. Eustasius through more mellow eyes. She quickly set about laying out the plans for a more intense training schedule for Rosemary and Kenny to get them to be fully autonomous in the running of Gallows Bay. After three months of planning and organizing, Nathaniel was ready to head for Dominica.

One afternoon as he was preparing to meet with Jack Freeman to arrange his passage, Agatha greeted him with the news. "I am with child again. What are we going to do?"

"Celebrate, of course!" was his joyous reply.

"No, I mean because you are not going to be here," Agatha retorted with trepidation in her voice.

"I promise that I will be gone no longer than six months. How far along are you?"

"Two months, I believe, no more than that." "The sooner I get going the sooner I will be back. This one is going to be alright. I just feel it."

"It was your feelings that got me this way," Agatha sighed, which signaled to Nathaniel that she was at ease with what was happening.

***

When Nathaniel returned from making his travel arrangements and proudly announcing his pending fatherhood, he took Agatha to their private beach. They sat quietly and watched the sun slowly fade from view. The brilliant shafts of red, gold and orange gradually turned to black, to be replaced by thousands of twinkling stars. Walking back to their cottage Agatha told Nathaniel, "Our child will be English. I will not have the child be considered a colonial. I do not care how you do it, but the child will not be born here. This is Dutch land, not English, and I do not want anyone ever thinking our child is black."

"Why would you say black?"

"I just want our child NOT! to be born here. That's it."

"Let me see what I can do." They continued in silence to the cottage.

The following morning, Nathaniel sat down with Jack Freeman and laid out his problem with the upcoming birth. Jack gave him a solution that was simple and foolproof. He explained, "If the child is born of English parents it would be English by birthright, as both parents were English. There is a risk however, of foreign born children getting caught up in sloppy governmental bureaucracy. You can avoid that. Here's how - if Miss Agatha could give an approximate date of birth, I should be able to arrange for the *Mary Jane* to be in port. If a child is born on the high seas," Jack said, "he is automatically the nationality of the ship as well as the nationality of the parents. All those factors being English the birth would then be registered in England without any issues." Agatha and Nathaniel were happy that a solution had been found.

***

In November of 1881 Nathaniel landed in Dominica with a determined plan of action. He quickly made his way to Beruka Fields and was impressed with what he saw. The fifty acres of land was a perfect rectangle from the sea to the top of the mountain. It was centered in a large cove. Both arms of the cove stretched out to the left and the right of the property. Lush stands of giant palms lined the hill tops and ran down to the water's edge as if they were arms embracing the spot.

The construction supplies he had calculated that he needed were being unloaded and brought to the site by a dependable contact of Jack Freeman.

On the tenday trip from St. Eustasius to Dominica, Nathaniel was befriended by a jocular French sailor. The man was gregarious and had spent many years aboard traders in the Caribbean. He gave Nathaniel much useful advice about Dominca. "Beruka Fields," he said, "that's on the southern-most tip of the island, and while it was not on the lea side of the island the cove offered some protection from the windward side storm potential." He went on to say the island had been a French possession, that they had given to the English. Now it was ruled by an, all black government. He claimed the local people were very friendly and hard workers. This Nathan had noticed when he was arranging transportation of his cargo to Beruka. He decided to name the property 'Frenchman's Cove.' He liked the sound of it.

It took the next three months to build a suitable cottage for his family to live in and to lay the base construction for the funicular. He decided to run it down the center of the two parcels of land thereby allowing him to develop it in a couple of different ways. It could start at the top, the bottom, or on one side at a time. The location of the track kept his options open. There was something about this place, with the sun rising from the left as you looked out to sea and setting on the right - it was a striking vista. If carefully laid out, every dwelling would have a view of sunrise and sunset.

***

Nathaniel arrived back on St. Eustasius earlier than planned. As his ship tied up alongside the dock Jack Freeman greeted him with, "You are just in time. The *Mary Jane* is due here either tomorrow or the next day."

Two days later, it was now three weeks before the due date Agatha had given, the *Mary Jane* rounded the southern tip of the island under full sail and entered Gallows Bay with great fanfare. Nathaniel offered to take Agatha down to the docks to greet the ship, but she felt tired and said she would go down in the morning. Nathaniel went to the Plantation warehouse offices to watch the ship come alongside. Jack asked where Agatha was, and when Nathaniel told him, Jack asked him to go quickly and fetch Agatha, as Judd and Mary are to be on board.

That night, Nathaniel, Agatha, Judd, and Mary went to Gallows Bay Retreat, where they sat long into the night, talking about many things. Later, Nathaniel took Judd on a tour illuminated only by moonlight. Judd was impressed. His imagination could never have produced what he saw before him. "I missed the birth of my daughter," said Judd, his words fraught with emotion. "I wanted to be here with you and share in the birth of your child. You have done us all proud."

The next day, as the morning sun shot over the horizon, Gallows Bay Retreat was already a scene of hectic commotion. Judd was awoken by Nathaniel, asking him to send for the trap, and ready the *Mary Jane* for sailing. "I think the baby is on the way," he anxiously cried. In what seemed a blur, Nathaniel found himself standing alongside the gunwales of the *Mary Jane* beside Judd. In the background, the wails of childbirth punctuated their conversation. A local midwife and Jack Freeman's wife had all come to assist in delivering the child. The cabin seemed cramped with all the women. The air was still and humid. Agatha would whimper from time to time as her contractions increased. She kept asking, "Is the baby alright? Is this what is supposed to happen? How will I know if the baby is alright?" The midwife kept swabbing Agatha's sweating brow as Mary held her hand tightly. "I want Nathaniel here, please get him."

"This is no place for a man. Birthing is women's work. Men don't have the stomach for it. We will call him when it's time. Just relax." The midwife had a low calming, monotone voice. She did not allow herself to be interrupted; she just kept talking quietly to Agatha, and at the same time busily ministering to her.

As the *Mary Jane* did a long low roll from port to starboard, Agatha let out a long low throaty groan and the midwife called out, "Here we go ladies. We got us a baby coming." In a heartbeat there was tiny cry from the blood covered little form. The midwife held him up for all to see as she said, "We got us fine young boy, a fine young boy. Mrs. Blacksmith, you is a mommy now." She finished the delivery and placed the baby in Agatha's outstretch arms. Agatha sobbed and sobbed. She had done it, and everything was all right. Out on deck in the distance, St. Eustatius gently rose and sunk on the horizon.

Putting his arm around Nathaniel's shoulder, Judd said. "I don't know how to comfort you my boy. I have never been involved in childbirth. It is a strange thing the birth of a child, while it belongs to both parents, it is kept distant from us men."

That's when Mary approached them with a tiny form in her arms. "Let me be the first to introduce to you. Nathaniel, your son, and to you, Judd, your grandson, Desmond Cane Blacksmith. Blacksmith Cane, however you want to say it."

Judd spoke first, "He is Desmond Blacksmith. That's it."

Nathaniel timidly took the baby and went inside to see his wife. His heart was fit to burst.

***

It took almost a year for mother and child to be ready to move to Dominca. The next chapter of the Blacksmith family had just begun. It took another four years to complete their plans for *Frenchman's Cove*. Many of the latest inventions had been incorporated. The retreat, as Agatha called it had its own power source. All the cottages they built were completely furnished with the latest in furniture, drapes and accoutrements of the Victorian era. Looking back at their work, Agatha and Nathaniel felt they had indeed progressed to a position where duplicating their original property was just a matter of organization and planning. They did little of the physical work in the last four years and mastered overseeing construction. Right from the beginning they had involved a local man to help them with their vision for the property. They had chosen well and by 1886 he was independently running the property for them and they were ready to move on.

Chapter 31

In 1887, Nathaniel and Agatha returned to Mucking with Desmond. After discussions with their parents Nathaniel brought up the subject of Desmond's education, of which there was none of any quality in the Caribbean at this time. Mary and Jane responded in unison, "You are not thinking of putting him in boarding school!"

Nathaniel spoke first, "Not boarding school, so much as, 'your' schooling. Think about it, ma. The village school can get him started. We don't know for how long. We'll make that decision later."

Agatha jumped in the conversation. "If he is staying with you, family, he can learn to read and write - something he must be able to do. We don't want to be apart from him, but we do have to do what's best for him."

"Mary, how do feel about this?" asked Jane.

"Well, he is beautiful little boy, and who wouldn't want to help him?"

"How do you think he will take it? You two leaving him here and going away?" Jane asked Agatha.

"I don't know ma. Do you think it's a bad idea?" asked Agatha.

Judd spoke, "I think that you are to be commended for putting Desmond first. I don't know if I could do that. You have your mother's strength.

Mary looked at Judd as she said, "You did put a child first, Judd, Ojukwae."

Judd nodded in agreement as Agatha commented, "This isn't about Ojukwae, It's about Desmond."

Judd looked away as Mary said, "Let your pa and I talk about this."

"We will help you. I think it will be good for Desmond to get to know both sets of grandparents well before you trot him off around the world," Judd added.

***

In what seemed like a whirlwind, arrangements were made for Desmond to stay with Judd and Mary and commence his schooling. Desmond appeared quite unperturbed by having to stay, which surprised all of them. Judd offered the couple the next property to move on to, which was East Caicos, part of the Turks and Caicos Islands.

They arrived by steamer that needed a local pilot to navigate the offshore reefs to successfully enter the anchorage at Breezy Point. Laid out in front of them in an orderly fashion were many small homes. These were the homes of the workers at a huge sisal operation, The East Caicos Sisal Company. The Cane property was situated at Drum Point, adjacent to the sisal plantation. The plantation appeared to be a thriving enterprise. Drum Point was connected to Flamingo Hill. This was the base of a beautiful reef harbor know as Jacksonville. The onehundred yard quay at Jacksonville caught Nathaniel's imagination. It supplied work for the huge salt production facility as well as the export of guano. The area was a bustling hive of activity.

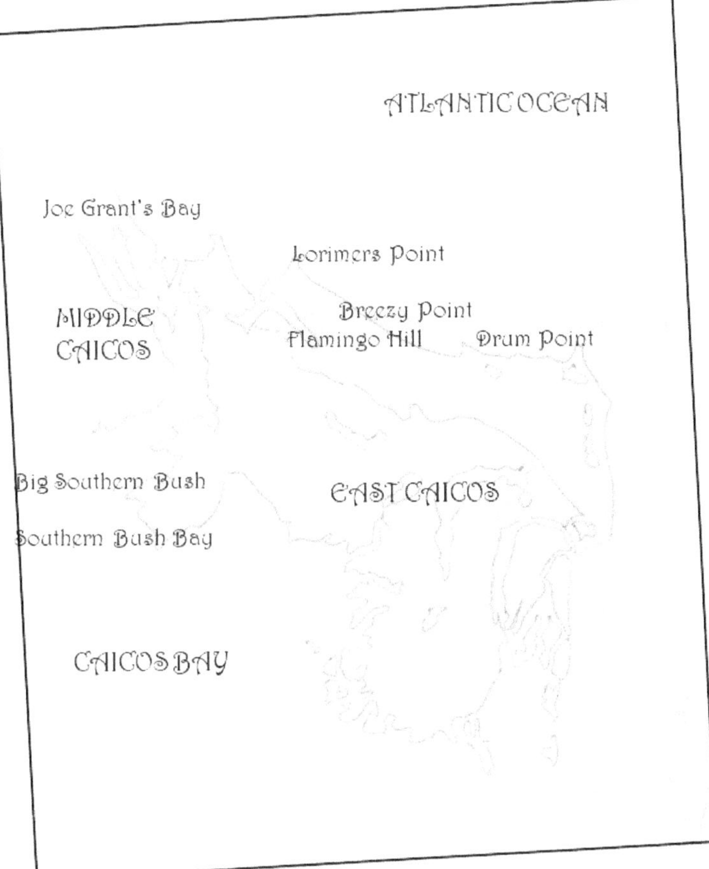

The Cane property was ideally situated to capitalize on the business already abound. Sitting on the verandah of their rented cottage, Agatha and Nathaniel discussed a new direction for them to take.

Agatha broached the subject. "With the amount of activity here and the people that live here I think we should modify our concept to suit them."

"What are you thinking about?"

Agatha was pleased that Nathaniel showed no opposition, so she continued. "There are many, many small boats coming and going from here. It is almost a nonstop stream. It seems like the local workers just work and sleep. I was thinking that we should build a sprawling cluster of simple cottages aimed at the less affluent visitor."

"How do you see that making very much money?"

"Two different economies are side by side in every city. Why not here? If we provide a place for relatives and friends of the workers to stay at a reasonable fee, give them a small marketplace to bring their things to sell, I think it could be lucrative due to the volume."

"That brain of yours has been working overtime again. A big part of our costs in Stasius and Frenchman's has been the level of luxury. Let's look into the idea. While the island was the smallest of the Cane properties and offered only limited potential, there was still some profit to be made. Nathaniel reasoned that as this tiny chain of islands was near America, and ships were developing rapidly. Times would change and get better. It took two years for the concept to take a firm hold, but when it did, the mass exodus of people leaving after a days work, made the Flamingo Hill Market and Resort come alive. Its notoriety grew rapidly. The ability to enjoy one's self after working had never been considered, and was welcomed with open arms. Often into the night one could hear the sounds of ethnic music floating over the reef. Agatha and Nathaniel become celebrities in the area. The Irishman, Mr. Reynolds, who owned the salt business, became a fast friend, offering advice and tips as they went about the development.

***

It was in the summer of '90 that they sent for Desmond to join them. Desmond came on the *Mary Jane* to Miami, in America. There, Nathaniel collected his son and returned to Caicos. With the way the child held himself, the way he walked, and the way he could look at you and speak with his eyes, the boy was a miniature of his grandfather, Judd. At eight years old, he was rambunctious and inquisitive and remembered everything he was told.

One morning at breakfast Desmond announced, "Oh ma. I met Uncle Ojukwae and Aunt Colly - that's Uncle Ojukwae's name for her."

"He is not your uncle!" was the snapped reply.

"If he is your brother, doesn't that make him my uncle?"

"I am white, he is black! Didn't you notice that?"

"But grandma said he was your brother."

"My father adopted him. They are not the same as us, you must see that."

"Ma, I don't understand. Should I ask pa to explain it?"

"No! He will only tell you the same thing I did. Now let's get on with the day." The subject was closed, but Desmond was still confused.

***

Life went back to normal as Agatha took on Desmond's schooling with the basic subjects, while Nathaniel exposed him to problem solving in the physical world. There were no toys—only tools for helping papa fix things. Desmond learned how to find the solution with the most chance of success before starting to work. He learned how to stop when things were going wrong and devise an alternative solution. Desmond became so adept at this method he was soon proposing solutions before his father could. Nathaniel quickly came to the conclusion that his son should be placed where he could gain the best education possible.

It took Nathaniel a year to broach the subject with Agatha. He expected resistance, and got it, as she raised a wall of resistance. Nathaniel stated that Desmond would go to boarding school in England and return to them for the summers.

Agatha objected strongly, "Desmond is now just nine years old. We have had him with us for less than half his life. Where are your feelings?"

"Think about this, he can have weekends and short holidays from school with our parents, and the entire summer with us. You must see that it will make him a well-rounded child. What other children get those opportunities?"

"I don't care about well rounded. I want to enjoy my baby."

"Your baby, look at him, he is growing so fast. I want him to have the best opportunity available."

"We have had good opportunities without being taken away from our parents."

"Do you realize that all our opportunities have come to us because your father was taken away from his parents?"

"That's not the same."

"No, it isn't the same - it is far better. It is for his future, not ours."

Agatha, who knew the feeling of not having her father around, was uncertain. Nathaniel pointed out the benefits of public school education and the possible connections to be made. He raised the point that Desmond might not want the lifestyle they have. "If he only knows island life, how can choose anything else? It will make life more difficult as he grows older. It is our duty to expose him to the choices that are available to him." Agatha capitulated. Within the year Desmond was returned to his grandparents and public school.

***

In the year 1892, Nathaniel and Agatha, having completed work on East Caicos, moved on to Mustique in Saint Vincent and the Grenadines. Their stay on this island was short-lived, as the sheer beauty and isolation of the place along with its tiny size compared to neighboring islands created a cocoon-like feeling. They agreed to leave the unpopulated island in its natural state, with one exception. Borrowing some workers and supplies from Gallows Bay, they set about clearing a road from the where their ship was anchored up to the highest point of the island, upon which a dwelling could be built. The idea was to create a highly visible building so that ships passing by might be interested in stopping there.

One morning, a small tramp trading ship dropped anchor and a small boat was rowed to the shore. A man jumped from the bow into the surf and waded the last few yards, to be greeted by Nathaniel.

The man spoke first.

"Are you Mr. Nathaniel Blacksmith sir?"

"Who is asking?" replied Nathaniel.

"I am Marcus sir. I trade these parts. Jack Freeman from the Plantation on St. Eustasius asked that I bring you this letter."

The man handed Nathaniel a letter, which Nathaniel read, with some trepidation. News received in this fashion did not usually bode well. When he finished, he just stared at the man, who spoke first. "Jack said that the news might put you in a position of needing help. Is there something that I may be of assistance with, sir?"

"Are you to be in this area for long Marcus?"

"I am headed north. I am expecting to be passing here in about two weeks. Why do you ask?"

"I have things to attend to here, then my wife and I will need passage to The Plantation."

"Happy to oblige Mr. Blacksmith. I can wait and transport you directly, tomorrow, or, return in about two weeks. My other business has no urgency."

"We can be ready by noon tomorrow if that is convenient, and we shall go St. Eustasius."

***

It had been ten days since Marcus had handed them the letter advising that Mustique had been sold and was no longer theirs. Agatha and Nathaniel arrived back at St. Eustasius to be greeted by Jack Freeman waving a telegraph form in his hand. "Am I glad to see you! I was quite worried about how you would receive the news and how much work you had put into the island."

Agatha replied, "We were surprised, but, we did not plan to do a lot there. In fact, we have just finished building a cottage. The new owners have a nice little house ready for them. Would one of your girls take me to Gallows Bay so that I may see how things are going for myself?"

Jack called out some instructions and quickly a trap arrived. Agatha went off to inspect the retreat, leaving Nathaniel to take care of things at the Plantation. Jack invited Nathaniel to the office, and handing him the telegraph he said, "I think that you will like what Mr. Judd proposes. I have been to that place, and like it very much." The telegraph read :

TO: AGATHA AND NATHANIEL BLACKSMITH. STOP.
SORRY ABOUT THE SHORT NOTICE REGARDING MUSTIQUE. STOP.
BEFORE YOU BOTH DECIDE WHAT YOU WANT TO DO NEXT TAKE A
LOOK AT ANGUILA. STOP.
WE OWN SPICE REEF AT PLEASANT COVE. STOP.
YOU MIGHT LIKE TO WORK YOUR MAGIC THERE NEXT. STOP.
DESMOND IS DOING VERY WELL AND MISSES YOU. STOP.
WE ALL SEND LOVE. STOP.
JUDD CANE

MUCKING ESSEX ENGLAND.

The two men discussed the wisdom of going to Anguila this time of the year. They were well into the hurricane season and knew the risks. During the afternoon Jack sent telegraphs to many of the Windward islands, seeking weather information. The general consensus was for them to wait until the new year, as there had not been many hurricanes so far this season. This could suggest some were to come.

The next three months Agatha and Nathaniel busied themselves between making preparations for Anguila and being at the Gallows Bay retreat, mingling with the guests. This was a time for them to relax and prepare themselves for their next endeavor.

***

By the spring of 93, the couple had arrived on the British Protectorate of Anguilla, a small island off the coast of the French and Dutch colony of St. Maarten. The proximity of the neighboring colony created regular traffic, which meant large exposure. The British had done little to Anguilla, other than maintain it as an outpost of the empire in a strategic location. They had built a few roads and installed electricity. There had once been a thriving cotton industry with its own cotton gin and mill, but it was in a fast decline.

The beauty of this island was twofold. As a long, narrow island, it had an abundance of pristine, white, sandy beaches, and a single road running right down the middle, with branches off to the beaches. Second, there was a well-developed port and infrastructure. It was administered by the English from the neighboring island of St. Kitts.

At twelve years of age, Desmond had been at Charterhouse School in England for three years as a weekly boarder, returning by train to his grandparents for the weekends. His grandparents on both sides rejoiced in his company and independent personality. He refused rides to and from the station, preferring to discover the fields and country lanes. Saturday mornings, he would spend in the forge alongside Grandpa Davey, asking a thousand questions and pointing out which tools and pieces he should send to Papa. One weekend, as summer fast approached, Davey took him to London, to a large machine and smithy equipment supplier. As Desmond wandered around the cavernous warehouse full of machines, strange tools and engines, he told Grandpa of his wish list of things for his father. The bond between the two was very strong.

Traveling on the Cunard steamship, RMS *Campagnia*, Desmond was excited to be returning to his parents. As a first-class passenger, he was free to roam the ship, and he spent his time aboard investigating the steamship from top to bottom. After all, if his ticket for his voyage was seventy-six pounds, he was going to get his family's money's worth. The captain, a Mr. Walker, a lieutenant in the British Royal Navy Reserve, now in the merchant navy, took Desmond under his wing. Every afternoon, the captain would show Desmond various parts of the ship and introduce him to the officers. He would leave the boy with the officers, who would answer his innumerable questions. He fascinated everyone he met. He would write busily as they spoke, sometimes asking them to wait a moment while he finished his notes. Everyone was usually relieved when he reached his final destination.

One evening at dinner Captain Walker engaged Desmond in conversation that to any observer was casual. It wasn't to Captain Walker. He approached his quest cautiously.

"Would you believe that I am seventyeight years old? I have been at sea for almost fifty years."

"Wow! No sir. Are you going to die at sea?"

"I certainly hope not. So, tell me young man, where are you going at the end of this voyage?"

"St. Eustasius sir, then on to Anguilla to my parents."

"You remind me very much of a young man I used to know many years ago, long before you born."

"Really Sir. Can I ask who that is?"

"Man, or he was a boy then, cabin boy. He became a navigator. Name of Cane."

"My grandpa is Cane, Judd Cane." Captain Walker put his knife and fork down and leaned back in his chair and gasped for air, as he went red faced.

"Judd Cane, oh my, oh my. Very interesting. I wonder if it is the same Judd Cane."

"I don't know sir, Grandpa is old. He has his own ship, The Mary Jane. I have been on it many times." Desmond was quite pleased with himself. "I don't know if grandpa was a navigator."

"What does he do now?" the Captain appeared to relax.

"He is retired sir. I don't think he has been a sailor for a long time. His friends Mr. Lemon and Mr. …Trott, I think it is, still work for him on the Mary Jane." The captain coughed and spluttered splitting out his tea. "Do you really think it could be the same Judd Cane?" Desmond asked innocently.

"No, I don't think so. It was Cane's fault that I am no longer in the 'Royal' navy. The Cane I knew was an evil, nasty, ruinous beast of a man. Destroyed my life, he did. But it sure would be a coincidence, wouldn't it?" The captain brushed himself off, excused himself and went to his cabin.

Sitting in his cabin Captain Walker replayed the experience of almost half a century ago over and over in his mind. He attempted to write a letter outlining his discovery, not knowing where to send it. As time passed with his writing, he continually sipped a brandy as he replayed that life changing night many years ago. It was the eight bells ringing out at the end of the evening shift that found Captain Walker on the deck below the ship's bridge with his sheath of papers in hand, muttering drunkenly to himself long into the night, until he slipped to the deck in an exhausted state where he slept until the morning sun woke him.

Chapter 32

Nathaniel and Agatha waited dockside at Marigot, St Maarten, as the steamer dropped anchor offshore. Through his trusty old spyglass, Nathaniel spotted the little figure climb down the rope ladder, as his belongings were lowered into the launch. Handing the spyglass to Agatha, he set off to find help in transferring everything to the fishing boat that would take them the three miles to Anguilla. Meanwhile, the small, steam-powered launch chugged out from the ship, bringing the lone passenger ashore.

When Nathaniel saw his sixteen-year-old son, he saw a strapping young man in the image of his father-in-law and over six feet tall. Nathaniel told him that he was now on Caribbean time and could simply relax.

On the small fishing boat that was ferrying them to Anguila, Desmond spoke of school. While he didn't dislike school, he complained that there was so much thinking, writing and reading, and very little doing. Nathaniel understood what the boy was going through.

Agatha came down on the other side of the fence. Without book knowledge, she said, he would be limited to his own experiences, and he needed to be able to consider the experience of others.

Desmond showed his parents the journal that he had written on his journey home. Both parents were fascinated by the scope of their son's curiosity. He seemed to have a leaning toward anything nautical and mechanical. Agatha sensed that the boy may be taking a similar route as her father Judd. She had read somewhere a saying that said 'Sons of men go down to the sea in ships, as their fathers did before them.' It made her nervous.

Blowing Point Harbour came into view, with a small jetty protruding out into the water and a few huts and buildings on either side. Everything was off-loaded onto the dock, and the fisherman bid them farewell in his odd, clipped English accent. Leaving Agatha and Desmond sitting atop the packages, Nathaniel went in search of someone with a cart or dray. Desmond told his mother that he and Grandpa had built the wooden chest he'd brought with him and filled it with new tools for his father. His pride was evident and his mother basked in it.

Soon, Nathaniel returned with a donkey and cart, and a helper. Between them, they struggled to load the packages and crate before setting off for Little Harbour.

Little Harbour lay about a two and a half miles down a well-worn trail between George Hill and Long Ground. The shape of the cove was like a horseshoe laying on its side, the open end to the right. The top side was shorter than the bottom. A large reef extended from the tip of the shorter arm to the tip of the longer arm about three hundred yards offshore. The reef was slightly visible in places at low tide as the surf broke over it. The longer bottom side was the mainland, and that was where the family entered the property. The shorter top side was a long, narrow peninsula that projected out into the ocean. Along this side stood a few cottages scattered randomly along a steep ridge facing the ocean on one side and the cove on the other. It was the ridge and the reef that protected the cove.

Agatha and Nathaniel spent the first few days on Anguilla reconnecting with their son, listening to his report on Mucking and their parents, the smithy, Ojukwae, and Charterhouse School. Desmond felt he would not have liked the school if he was not able to visit his grandparents on the weekends. "The other boys all have sticks up their arses, Dad," said Desmond. "Oh, Ma, really, they're toffs." He described the prefects and head boys with whom he had nothing in common and detailed how they would bully the smaller boys and brag about what their parents were and had. But he also said that, for some reason, none of these things happened to him. "Well, it did once, and I punched him right in the face. Grandpa Judd taught me not to wait, get the first punch in."

"Human beings are just another animal," said Nathaniel. "They can sense who are the weaker among them. Some animals will not attack anything they fear. Boys are the same. You're probably as big as them. Word gets around quickly in large groups. They know that you've travelled more than they have. It's called fear of the unknown. That's why you don't let anybody know everything about you. A wise man keeps a little piece of himself for himself."

***

As the summer break from Charterhouse drew to a close, plans were discussed for Desmond's return to England and a university education. Desmond resisted the plans, but Nathaniel stood his ground. It was during a heated discussion about Desmond's future that Agatha reminded her husband of the time their son spent in the ocean, exploring the reef, and the amount of time he'd spent over at Sandy Ground and the dockside, watching the trading ships coming and going. She sat Nathaniel down, holding his rough, construction-calloused hands in hers. "My papa spent hours down at Mucking on the river, watching the big ships come and go. He got dragged away to sea, pressed he was, when he was eleven," said Agatha. "As a result, our family has pulled itself up by its bootstraps, and look where we are—property around the world, a fine young son. I'm not saying a university education is bad. I'm just saying following our hearts has been good to us. Let it be good for Desmond."

"Are you proposing the Royal Navy?"

"No. You don't listen to me, do you?" said Agatha. "I'm saying, let's ask him what he wants and then talk."

Standing on front veranda, Nathaniel hollered at the top of his lungs and listened for the sound to echo around the cove. "Oi! Oi, Desmond!" He saw his son stand up out on the partially exposed reef, look his way, wave, and start toward him.

Chapter 33

While celebrating Desmond's sixteen birthday his father and mother instructed him to sit down, with stern expressions on their faces. His father talked about university, which simply did not appeal to him, while his mother was prying away, trying to find out what he wanted. He knew that the right answer was somewhere, but didn't know what it was. This was all just too intense for him. In an attempt to be vague, and not commit himself, he told them what he really liked about coming out to be with them was the journey—how the old sailing ships, meeting with the iron ships, enabled him to straddle two worlds.

Nathaniel started to tell him about his grandfather, "your grandpa Judd was very young when he was abducted, stolen, taken away, whatever you call it. Back in those day's it was called press ganging. He was only eleven and they put him on a ship in the Royal Navy. He learned to become a navigator and that."

Nathaniel interrupted, "Pa, pa, I met a man, the Captain of the RMS Campagnia, Captain Walker. He knew grandpa when he was a navigator."

"How did he know that? Grandpa Judd is Cane, your name is Blacksmith, I don't see how he made the connection."

"He told me that I reminded him of very young boy about my from a long time ago. He said that the boy's name was Judd Cane. I told him that was my grandpa's name."

"That captain had to be old. That was nearly fifty years ago, or more."

"He was old pa." Agatha and Nathaniel marveled at the coincidence for a while and then got back to their previous conversation.

"Remember when you told me how you needed to prove yourself to yourself before you would marry Ma?" asked Desmond.

"Hold on, young man. I was a working man when that happened," said Nathaniel.

"But you've told me many times that I'm never too young to learn. I have watched many sailors as young as me working, and I know I can do what they can do. Doesn't Grandpa own the Mary Jane? I could work on that and learn to prove myself."

"Maybe we could do something closer to us. The *Mary Jane* is a sailing ship. Wouldn't you rather go on one of the iron ships, like the trader that brought you to St. Maarten?" Nathaniel asked.

After some time spent talking around in circles, Agatha convinced her husband to go down to the dock at Sandy Ground and speak with some of the trading ships' captains to see what he could come up with. Nathaniel considered that, instead of fortnightly shipments of supplies from America, he could combine some into a monthly trip and find his son a position on one of the ships. It was something they could all agree upon.

Quietly that night, cuddled with Nathaniel, watching the sun set over the reef, Agatha told him that he should mark her words—Desmond was a chip off the old block.

Two days later, Desmond came running down the dusty road toward Agatha, yelling. Breathlessly, he told his mother that there was a trading ship leaving Sandy Ground on the evening tide, and that it would arrive in Virginia two days before the ship bringing building supplies to his father would leave. This would allow him time to switch ships.

Agatha was stunned. It was all happening too fast. She told him to go and find his father, who was out on the point, working on a cottage. Agatha said she would pack some things for him, but Desmond was halfway out of the door before she finished her sentence.

At five o'clock that evening, Agatha and Nathaniel stood and watched as the trading ship released its hawsers and drifted away from the dock on the evening tide. Somewhere on that ship was a cabin boy, their son, and they couldn't see him. Agatha wept, and Nathaniel, more out of fear than anything else, told her, "You should be careful what you wish for."

They slowly walked the mile and a half across the island into the sunset, kicking up dust in their wake, hand in hand.

The following morning, Nathaniel was in the work shack he had built for himself, removing the new tools that his son had brought for him from England. Wiping each one with the oily rag that protected it, he felt the sharp teeth of the saw, the finely honed chisel edge, as his emptiness overwhelmed him. His thoughts were running amok in his head. Did he do the right thing letting his son go off into the world? The world was changing so fast that he felt somewhat removed from it, living on these islands. It was only when Agatha brought him his mid-morning pot of tea that he snapped out of it.

The boy was gone. That's that. What will be will be.

Chapter 34

On the morning of August 1st 1901, Anguilla was cloaked in mourning for the death of Queen Victoria, as were all of England and her colonies. She had died while Desmond was on his journey of self-discovery. The somber mood that enveloped the ships was typical of England's. The colonies, however, displayed the requisite respect, then, went about their daily business. There were always a few die-hard loyal royalists, civil servants, and dignitaries who behaved as if they had lost a child, but they were in the minority. Out here, the struggle of day-to-day existence was foremost in the scheme of things.

The next afternoon, a barefoot boy came padding down the dusty track and handed Nathaniel a small, yellow envelope—a telegram. As Agatha and Nathaniel sat with their feet in the cool blue water, Nathaniel read out loud the ticker-tape-style message:

SORRY TO REPORT THE PASSING OF MRS. JANE BLACKSMITH
(MOTHER). STOP
THIS SATURDAY MORNING AUGUST 1 1901. STOP.
DEATH BY NATURAL CAUSES. STOP.
SHE PASSED PEACEFULLY IN HER SLEEP STOP.
SORRY. STOP.
LOVE YOU ALL STOP.
DAD. STOP.
SIGNED DAVID BLACKSMITH STOP.

Agatha held Nathaniel close and sobbed. Looking at his wife, Nathaniel calmly said, "My mother was good woman."

"Nathaniel, your ma is dead. Is that all you can say?" Agatha demanded.

"We are who and what we are, because of what she gave us. We have lost nothing." Placing his hand over his heart, he said, "I might be feeling a bit different if I was in Mucking, seeing her every day. But I've carried her with me in my heart and she will always be alive here in my heart. We will name whatever we build, here in Little Harbour, in her memory." We shall call it *English Jane's Bay*.'"

Not quite two years later, in September of 1903, English Jane's Bay held eleven private cottages, all sharing an incredible view of the bay and the ocean beyond. The main building, with a bar and dining room and a large library, was a long, low structure nestled into the side of the hill. Nathaniel had utilized the skills he had learned from his previous construction experience. He was now buying the bigger, locally, unavailable construction materials, from America. The shipping was faster and less costly.

***

Desmond, now an experienced traveler with seven years behind the mast, had grown into a handsome young man. His contentment and joy with life at sea relaxed his parents' fears. He had graduated from cabin boy on the tramp traders to working on the transatlantic steamers, first as a cabin steward and then in the galley. He was still employing his habit of keeping meticulous notes. As he filled a journal, it would be sent to his mother, who had an old, black, wooden seaman's chest in which they would be stored after her husband had finished reading them. Both his parents knew Desmond was finding his direction.

At the same time, Nathaniel could see that his wife was losing her fire for their travels and exploits. He decided to take her back to England for a rest and to reconsider their lives. It took about two months for arrangements to be made and staff put in place.

On a cold September afternoon in Boston, Massachusetts, they boarded the RMS *Saxonia*. As they settled into their first-class accommodations there was a knock on the cabin door, and an immaculately attired steward handed Nathaniel a small, yellow envelope and took his leave. Agatha and Nathaniel sat side by side on the bed and cautiously opened it. Agatha read it:

SORRY TO REPORT THE PASSING OF MR. DAVID BLACKSMITH. STOP.
FRIDAY SEPTEMBER 9 1903. STOP.
DEATH BY NATURAL CAUSES. STOP.
SO SORRY. STOP.
SEE YOU SOON. STOP.
LOVE MA AND PA. STOP
DAD. STOP.
SIGNED JUDD CANE. STOP.

The trip across the Atlantic was a sorrowful affair, with time spent sharing childhood memories of parents and the village life. Now, Nathaniel was the only male Blacksmith. He decided that if his sisters had no interest in the forge, he would sell it, share the proceeds with them and close the books on that portion of his life. The solemn air stayed with them until they landed in England and made their way to Mucking, and to the safe harbor of Judd and Mary. Meanwhile Desmond was quickly maturing as a seaman in his life at sea.

Chapter 35

Desmond had become tanned, well built, and handsome. He was now working as a steward on the big passenger liners of The Cunard Line. As the chief steward handed out the cabin assignments, each steward would quickly read their passenger list looking for special instructions, as this usually meant bountiful tips. Desmond Blacksmith was different from other sailors in that he was quietly self-confident and somewhat aloof from his shipmates. He did not possess the brashness often connected with these sailors. He was quiet, self-assured and confident. Protocol of the day required that he behave in a gentleman like manner and so he kept his thoughts to himself when he first saw the attractive Miss Angela Rose St. John-Brown. It took almost the entire trip to England for him to broach anything other than polite discourse.

One night, as they sailed up the English Channel, she let her guard down and asked about his background. Sitting in her suite they talked long into the night. She found the steward was no ordinary sailor. His family was from Essex on the East coast of England and he had lived in places she had never heard of. In her head she envisioned him as a swash buckling handsome pirate, not a steward. He told her of his family's properties and how he had wanted to get a better understanding of the ships that tied these properties together. He believed that to work on the ships for a while was the best way to connect everything. She shared with him her desire to know more about many things and if he thought going to college was the wrong way to do it. He told her that college was never available to his family and that he believed that he should learn by hands on experience It had suited his family well, but he encouraged her to go to college as nothing learned is ever wasted. She liked this young man. They shook hands and parted, all the better for having met. It was the first time the steward, Desmond Cane Blacksmith, had ever felt uncomfortable taking a gratuity for his efforts.

Chapter 36

By the summer of 1906 Desmond had been spending time between his life at sea and his grand-parents in England, as well as regular visits with his parents. In September of that year Cunard launched The Mauretania, the pride of the fleet. He signed on as Assistant Chief Steward. Very quickly into the voyage he discovered that the Captain was a Captain Walker. Desmond made it his business to find out if the he was same man he remembered as having said terrible thing about his grandpa Judd. It was. The man's reputation was a surprise to him. The captain had joined the Merchant Navy, a reason for which nobody seemed to know. He was apparently a hard drinker and known to avoid passengers. This was not popular among the crew as they were often faced with explaining his lack of socializing. Wealthy passengers expected to dine with 'The Captain'. It was a sign of prestige. Desmond spent the entire journey from Southampton to New York avoiding the man. It was the end of the evening watch as darkness fell that he was summoned to the lower bridge. It was a cold night and the decks were deserted. The rain, which had just started was being whipped by the wind into stabbing points of water. Desmond arrived at the top of the gangway to see Captain Walker standing there, waiting for him. In a slurred speech the captain said, "So, you thought you could avoid me."

"No sir, why would I do that?"

"You might have changed your name Mr. Cane, but I know who you really are."

"Sir, my name is Blacksmith, Desmond Blacksmith. It always has been."

"One look at your sorry face and I know you are a bloody Cane."

"What is your problem Captain?" Desmond was careful to keep his tone calm.

The captain mopped the rain from his brow and replied, "The Canes are my problem, Judd bloody Cane, to be specific."

"What did he ever do to you?"

"Ruined my career in the Royal Navy, that's what."

"And, just may I ask how did he do that?"

"Stole a ship I was captain of, that's what."

Desmond's voice started to rise. "Stole a ship you were Captain of. Stole a ship you were Captain of? Some bloody fine Captain you must have been to let that happen."

"No better than a bloody pirate. Piece of shit pirate. I hate you Canes. The whole bloody tribe of you."

"Excuse the expression sir, if it's a piece of shit you talking about, I suggest you look in the mirror." Desmond was becoming agitated. The rain started to soak through his uniform as he stood staring at the raving man in front of him.

The Captain screamed at him, "You think I don't know where Mucking is, well I do. I have been there twice since we last met."

"What for?"

"To destroy your lovely grandpa," he bellowed.

At this, Desmond grabbed the captain around the throat and slammed him against the steel bulkhead. He then banged the man's head against the bulkhead and pulled him close. He shouted in the Captain's ear, "That was for grandpa." He smashed the captain's head again. "That one's for my pa." He smashed the captain's head again and said, "This one is for all the Canes that ever lived." He then continued slamming the captain's head against the cold wet steel bulkhead until the man slumped in his hands. The only thing stopping the man falling to the ground was Desmond's strong grip, holding him up. Desmond saw the bloody mess made by the destruction of the back of the man's head. He dragged the captain to the ships rail and flung the limp body overboard shouting after it, "Now who's a piece of shit?" He turned and leaned against the rail trying to recover from the extreme beating he had just delivered. He looked back into the black of the night that was only broken by the fluorescent glow created by the ship's bow wave reflecting the ambient glow of the ships' lights. What a serene picture to follow such a horrendous incident, he thought to himself. As he turned to leave, he saw on the steel bulkhead the remains of blood and matted hair slowly being washed away by the incessant rain in red rivulets. The magnitude of what he had done hit him. He thought aloud, "oh….my…God. I have just killed a man." He staggered back across the deserted deck, bent forward into the lashing rain, to his cabin.

***

Desmond spent the rest of the night sitting in his wet clothes reliving the horror. He was torn between the Captain's vitriolic attack on his family and numbing thought of having just killed another human being. As dawn broke, he showered and changed into a clean uniform and went on deck. There was a group of passengers standing on the deck as it was drying in the morning sun's warmth. There was very little evidence of last nights' storm as the Second Officer addressed the group. "You will notice some unusual activity on board this morning. Our Captain has gone missing. We have searched all the common areas of the ship and request your assistance. We want you to return to your cabins and to stay there until you hear from the duty officer. Should any of you see the Captain please contact a crew member immediately." A woman passenger called out. "I saw him last night at about ten thirty as I was returning to my cabin."

"Where did you see him?' the officer asked.

The woman pointed to the lower bridge and said, "He was shouting something over the ships rail." Desmond's heart raced in panic mode. He stood immobilized.

The officer asked, "did you see anyone else?"

"No, it was raining so hard and the wind was blowing me around. I didn't stay around in fear of being blown overboard. I couldn't hear what he was shouting, so I thought he was just letting off steam or was drunk or something." Desmond relaxed as the officer sent the passengers to their cabin. He did his best to appear calm and normal, as went about his duties. However, his mind was, in a turmoil.

***

In the spring of 1909, Angela Rose St. John-Brown, now twentythree, had booked passage for America on the SS Ivernia. The ship was only three years old and was amazingly advanced compared to the Campania. The difference was so huge it drew Angela Rose's attention. When she was introduced to the Chief-Steward she was impressed at the level of attention that she was getting on the voyage to New York. She asked, "Are all the crew new to the Ivernia?"

"No Miss Saint John Brown, we rotate crews around our ships to allow them time to be with their families and to keep them on their toes. In fact, Madam, I believe that you know our Assistant Chief Steward, Desmond Cane Blacksmith, he recognized your name on the passenger list." Her heart skipped a beat. "He oversees all the staff assigned to the FirstClass accommodations. He will stop by to assist your settling in to your suite as soon as we cast off."

"If you don't mind Sir, our family name is pronounced Sinjon Brown. I would appreciate it if you could inform yours staff of that."

"My apologies to you, Miss Sinjon Brown."

A steward showed her to her cabin, which carried all the luxuries one would expect in a firstclass hotel. Polished brass, mahogany paneling, crystal ware, gleaming mirrors and plush velvet curtains draped the portholes. Angela flung herself on the bed and gazed up at the bulkhead above her. "Fate, could this be fate?" was her thought. From the moment he knocked on the cabin door, until they docked in New York, they shared every spare moment together in deep conversation. They employed the utmost discretion as they met in the ships' library, lounges or up on deck in the stiff Atlantic breeze. In the six days it took for the crossing, they crammed in each other's family background, their likes, dislikes, hopes and dreams. Their eyes locked into each other as if searching to find out everything they could about each other's inner self. When Desmond spoke of feeling like he knew her from the inside out, a little alarm bell rang loud and clear inside her head. Grandpapa William's words kept running through her head repeating themselves over and over. 'I'm not sure if I gave my heart away or if it was taken. The man you love must let you keep a part of yourself for yourself so that you may both flourish together.'

She did not need to ask herself if she was in love, she knew it. When he would put his hand on top of her hand on the ship's rail she would tingle at the very point of connection. Her heart would leap whenever he walked into her space. The very sight of him would render her surroundings invisible as if he was floating toward her. She decided to confront him head on about her feelings. She instructed her cabin steward to summon the Assistant Chief Steward to her cabin at his earliest convenience and she waited. In accordance with shipboard protocol. He knocked on her cabin door and waited. She opened the door and bade him sit. Before she could start, he spoke. It was as if he knew what she was going to say.

"My dearest Angela Rose, if I may be so informal. My life's ambitions and goals are as important to me as I hope yours are to you. I admire your independence and value of family. We can go through life with each of us achieving those goals, as I know I will and, I am sure you will. With respect for each other's goals, I see no reason why we cannot do this side by side, in support of each other."

Angela put her hands over her face, closed her eyes and took a deep breath. Coming to her side Desmond apologized and told her that he did not mean to hurt or offend her. Dabbing her eyes, she replied, "I am neither offended nor hurt. My thoughts have been about you since we met on the Campania. I am soon to be twen-tyfour and know my own mind. Let me share with you something my Grandpapa William told me that has become so imprinted me. "He told me that he was not sure if he gave his heart away or if it was taken. He said that the person you love must let you keep a part of yourself for yourself so that you may both flourish together."

Desmond sat and thought about what he had heard and slowly and deliberately he told her, "I do not want all of you as I do not want to give you all of me. The part of your life that you are willing to share with me is all that I want. The part of myself I want to share with you, will be unconditional and I hope it will support and benefit you."

"Does this mean we are planning to get married? Are you asking me to marry you?"

"I know better than to tell you we are getting married," he said with his joyful laughter. "I should ask your parent's permission first."

"I want to go to Brown University and finish my education, do you mind?"

"If it's part of your plan for yourself, then do it." He agreed to meet with her parents while the Ivernia was in New York, before he had to return to England to complete his contract with Cunard.

***

The hustle and bustle of the great passenger ship SS *Ivernia* arriving in New York appeared chaotic but was instead, a brilliantly choreographed ballet of cargo coming on and off, people meeting, greeting and leaving, and sailors threading it all together. Michael and Penelope St. John-Brown were in the city on their way to Buffalo, from 'The Estate at The Royal Palisades'. Angela Rose told them that she wanted them to meet her new friend. They settled on dinner at Delmonico's Restaurant on Forty-Fourth Street at eight o'clock that evening. Michael stayed behind and made arrangements for Angela's luggage while Angela took off to await Desmond, as arranged at The Royal Line offices. Her mother pulled her aside as she was entering a carriage and asked, "Is this young man serious about you, and you about him?"

"Mama, you will meet him. I know I am serious about him and, I believe he is about me. He makes me smile on the inside. Mama, that's good. I am excited for you to meet him." With that said, Angela closed the carriage door, waved to her mother and instructed the carriage where to go.

By the time Angela arrived at the shipping company offices, Desmond was already standing outside waiting for her. They embraced and Angela was surprised that as she turned her cheek to him, he kissed her lightly. She felt a tingle of excitement and returned his kiss, on the lips. This was their first kiss. He was equally surprised, and happy. He returned her kiss, passionately. They were all smiles as they made arrangments to meet at Delmonico's Restaurant on Forty-Fourth Street at eight o'clock in the evening

.

***

Delmonico's dated back to the mid-eighteen-hundreds, surviving by means of dependable quality and good management. Upon his arrival, Desmond was shown to a private dining room where the St. John-Brown family waited. As Angela Rose sat quietly, she watched her parents firing questions in rapid succession at Desmond.

"Where did you meet my daughter?"

"I told you earlier papa," interrupted Angela Rose, "We first met on the Campania when I went to England."

"Wasn't that the passenger liner whose captain disappeared at sea?" Desmond panicked inside, but kept a calm visage. "Yes sir, it was. They never did find out what happened."

"Made the newspapers here. Damn strange if you ask me."

"Well, nobody did ask you dear, and mind your language if you don't mind." Angela's mother said in a stern, rebuking tone.

"What do you do for a living young man?" Her father appeared to ignore the instruction.

"I am Assistant Chief steward on the SS.Ivernia sir."

"Does that pay well?"

"Sufficiently sir. It is a stepping stone for me."

"Stepping stone to what?"

"I have not planned my whole life out just yet sir."

"Don't you think you should?" Michael's tone was concerning Angela. She looked her father right in the eye and said, "Papa, this is not a job interview. Please be kinder."

"What's wrong? Any young man that pursues my daughter better be ready to be vetted."

"Vetted, vetted, papa, please. Be nice or I shall leave."

Angela's mother leaned over to Michael and said, "Take it easy on the boy. He seems a likeable enough lad. Give him a chance."

"Chance at what? That's what I want to know." Turning back to Desmond, he softened his tone. "So, what do you intend for yourself? How are you going to make your mark on the world?"

Desmond found himself on the defensive and Angela-Rose caught in the middle. Desmond raised his hands as if warding off the barrage. "Mr. and Mrs. St. John-Brown," he said in a soft and confident manner, "I am here to seek your advice on behalf of Angela-Rose and myself. We find ourselves faced with a situation for which neither of us quite know how to proceed." He looked directly at Penelope. "You must have seen Angela-Rose's face when I approached," he said, "and I wish you could see the way my heart is pounding in her presence, but you can't. I fear that my background and age do me no justice, but we do not seek justice—just guidance in helping us get where we wish to be. That is, to be married."

Angela's mother gasped. She glanced quickly at her daughter and said, "Is this what you want? Why didn't you tell me about this earlier today?" Angela held her mother's gaze without flinching.

"Because mama, I didn't know."

Desmond took hold of Angela's hand and said "I didn't ask you because I was too busy working up the courage for tonight." Desmond took a deep breath before continuing. "I know that we spoke of obtaining your parents' consent, but I suggest we follow your plan to go to Brown and complete your education, however long it may take." He removed a small velvet pouch from his trousers with the name "Tiffany" embroidered on the front. He placed it before her. "If it pleases you, and your parents approve, we shall become engaged this evening and plan to wed on your completion of your education." Angela-Rose opened the pouch to find a diamond ring. The simple single-stone setting was tasteful and modest, yet clearly was no bauble.

Michael spoke quickly, "Now hold on a minute! Show me that thing." He reached out to take the ring. Desmond looked at Michael without flinching and said, "All respect due to you sir, I am offering this token to your daughter. If she accepts it is for her to show you. I'm sure she doesn't need your approval for that."

"So now the boy's got a backbone, do you?" Angela's mother interrupted, "Michael, what is wrong with you? Let the young man have his moment."

"Moment, have his moment. He wants more than his moment. He want's our daughter, and everything that goes with her. Don't we have some say in that?"

"Actually, my dear we don't. If you calm down you will recall they have come to us for advice. Let's hear them out."

Angela spoke up. "Thank you, mother, and as for you Desmond Blacksmith, yes I would like very much to marry you." There was hush that dropped over the table as mother and daughter embraced.

Michael looked at his wife for her acquiescence before he spoke. "I know of your family," he said to Desmond. "In fact, I conducted business with your grandfather some twenty-five years ago, when I purchased land here in America, on Jakeskill Island."

"You know my grandpa?"

"A fair man, I would say. When Angela Rose told us about you a while back, I made some enquiries. My inquiries find you to be in the same mold."

"Enquiries, what enquires have you made? Why do you need to make enquiries?"

"Because you have shown interest in my child. It is a father's duty to protect his children. Until I made enquires. I knew nothing about you. For all we know you could be attracted by our money."

"Your money! I have no need for your money. Our family is quite independent of anyone else's wealth."

"Now take it easy young man. One day your will understand my actions. I admire your spirit, now let's talk of other things. Your suggestion to our daughter shows maturity and consideration, and we respect you for this. What is it you propose to do with yourself for the next three years?"

"I will spend as much time as possible with your daughter," said Desmond. "I aim to complete my contracted time with the Cunard Line. Then, I'll work with my parents for Cane International."

"Have you no plans further than that?"

"No sir. I want to be able to adjust to what life throws at us and move forward as opportunity presents its self."

"See papa, I told you there is something special about Desmond. Don't you just love him?"

"Apparently not as much as you do my dear."

Penelope lifted her glass. "Then if we are all agreed," she said, "let us drink to success!"

"Do your parents know of this plan?" Michael asked Desmond.

"No sir I am of an age that does not require their consent. However, I am anxious to tell them."

"Then when you do, have them contact us. There are other matters for us to discuss. I have no objections to the engagement. Young man, be advised that I shall be keeping a keen eye on you, so be sure that you do the right thing." Raising his glass, he stood and toasted the young couple.

The rest of the evening went smoothly, or so Desmond thought. Michael stood back as the doorman held the door open for everyone to leave. Desmond was the last in line and Michael leaned over and whispered, "Captain went missing eh. Mystery that. Missing at sea, or murder, not much of a choice. I'm sure my people will get to the bottom of it. After all, fifty odd years at sea, and he just goes missing. Didn't think I would hear about that, did you?" Desmond looked over his shoulder and replied, "It was a shock to all of us on board. I actually didn't find it that relevant to the evenings agenda sir"

"Might be, might not be, as long as you had nothing to do with it. Family reputation. Stella, doesn't need tarnishing. I'm sure you understand." Desmond's nervous thoughts ran riot in his mind.

***

As the RMS Ivernia pulled out of Pier Seventeen in New York City, bound for Liverpool, Assistant Chief Steward Desmond Cane Blacksmith had found the course of his life had now taken on a completely new track. His connections to his fiancée and to Cane International were quite clear, but it was where his fascination and love for the sea belonged, that baffled him. He decided to sign off from this ship upon reaching Liverpool and return to Mucking in Essex. Breaking his contract with The Cunard Line did not concern him. He had bigger fish to fry.

***

Mucking, he found on arrival, had grown into a small town, with its own police station and a network of telephone wires stringing their way around. There was a grand railway station right on the town's edge, resplendent with huge steel girders, brightly painted and embellished in the most ornate cast-iron decorations. The entire station was surrounded by wrought iron fences worthy of London. The main street from the station to the town square, which used to be called the village green, was now cobbled with heavy granite blocks. The forge was still called David and David Blacksmiths, but it now had the very latest in machinery and equipment and had expanded to include a large storage yard full of all types of steel and iron. The current owners had opted to keep the original business name because of the reputation and respect it had garnered. Alighting from the train, Desmond wandered around, reorienting himself with the places he could recall. It was as if Mucking had become a foreign place to him, after so much time overseas.

Desmond was surprised to see how his grandfather Judd had aged since they last saw each other. His father and mother were excited to see him and hear of his engagement to Angela-Rose. After his family's curiosity was satisfied, the conversation came around to Cane International. Agatha and Nathaniel believed that the Caribbean as a whole was yet underexposed, with the wealth of America soon expected to rival England's.

Judd asked Desmond if he needed a stipend upon which to live as he pursued his own direction, but to his parents' and grandparents' astonishment, he declined. He had heard from fellow sailors and seen itineraries that the Cunard Line had prepared about cruises for pleasure in the Mediterranean a long time ago. He believed a similar thing could be done in the Caribbean for the American market. He wanted to work for Peninsular and Oriental Steam Navigation, which had originated such cruises, for a while to learn more about the concept of cruising for pleasure.

"Can you imagine, one day, that we could be blending Cane International with Global Enterprises? It could be a perfect fit for cruises in the Caribbean," Judd said.

"What's Global Enterprises grandpa?" asked Desmond.

"That's what the St.John-Brown business empire calls themselves these days. It is shipping, Land development, mostly in America, and a vast food business, the Co-op and Mother's Fine Foods. They have their finger in a lot of pies. '

"You have to admire our Desmond he is thinking really big," replied Mary. "I like it."

"Hang on a minute grandpa. I haven't even married Angela Rose, yet."

"No, but it is obvious you will and we need to take stock of our holdings. It might not hurt for us find out as much as we can about their family and how they operate."

***

The Pool of London was home to an organization that worked with shipping companies to regulate and place sailors and maintain records. Desmond went with Judd to explore the potential. Within the week, Desmond was offered a position in the P&O's head office, dealing directly with the sailors and the Pool. Most workers at the P&O were experienced administrative personnel, very few having any nautical background. Desmond's background helped him rise very quickly to a supervisory level that afforded him access to almost one hundred years of records and files.

For the next two years until January of 1912, Judd, Nathaniel and Desmond worked in harmony crafting the future of Cane International. They had common ground in their visions and planned to enter the cruise business. They logged many hours researching the innovations of the huge iron ships being developed, paying particular attention the RMS Titanic. The Titanic was due to go into service in April of this year. This new behemoth of a ship was changing the public perception of travel by sea. While expensive, it was quickly becoming a tool of immigration and opening frontiers to the common man. Desmond was anxious to return to New York and Angela Rose so he booked his passage on the maiden voyage of the newest all iron, most modern ship the RMS Laconia. It was rumored that she was so up to date that in the eight months of final outfitting for her maiden voyage, updates and modernizations were frequently made. Her gross tonnage was over 18,000 tons and was sight to behold. On January 20th, Judd and Nathaniel stood dockside as the maiden voyage of The Laconia commenced. She slowly cast off her moorings and glided away as if she weighed nothing, just sitting majestically on the water's surface, gently being carried away by the tide. Suddenly the huge propellers hidden out of sight beneath the surface, churned the sea's calmness into a cauldron-like froth and the ship surged forward. The crowd on the quay side cheered at the spectacle. Judd turned to Nathaniel and Agatha, and in a quiet emotional tone said, "Not in my wildest dreams, when I found myself in a dark hole in the bowels of the British Navy, did I ever, ever, imagine standing here and witnessing something so incredible as this spectacle."

"Pa, three generations of Canes have gone down to the sea in ships. It has served us well," said Nathaniel. The two men stood in an awed silence until they were the only three people left watching the faint image of the ship slowly disappear on the horizon.

Chapter 37

April 16 1912, Judd Cane opened the morning newspaper to be greeted by the glaring headline,

J.J. ASTOR LOST ON TITANIC
1,500 TO 1,800 DEAD

He had read about the tragic disaster two days earlier and, like the nation, indeed the world, there was stunned reaction in everyone's mind. Reading on, he found there was a passenger list of those missing, or presumed dead inside. Without any particular thought he started to read the list and stopped at two names. Mr. and Mrs. Ronald Surtees. He called out to Mary, "Mary, Mary, come quickly." Mary entered the parlor wiping her hands on a towel and responded, "Whoa, what's all the fuss about?"

"The Titanic, you remember Ronald Surtees, the man that came here with Sir Michael St. John-Brown when he bought Jakeskill Island? He was on the Titanic with his wife. Dead, they are both dead, or at least missing."

"Sir Michael?"

"No, Surtees, Ronald Surtees, and his wife."

Mary dropped into a chair and said, "I think they were very close to Sir Michael. Do you think you should telephone him?" Judd thought for a while and, composed in his head, what he might say. He had been speaking regularly with Sir Michael discussing the upcoming wedding plans for Desmond and Angela Rose. He felt that they were a little more than cordial and so he picked up the phone and asked to be connected to the St. John-Brown household in Bath. After waiting for an inordinate amount of time for the switchboard operator to make the connection and an even further length of time for the St. John-Brown maid to find Sir Michael, Judd responded to Sir Michaels greeting. "I have just read the news Sir Michael, that Ronald Surtees and his wife were on the Titanic and they are missing."

"Quite so, quite so" was the curt response.

"I am so sorry. Mary and I offer our most sincere condolences. Is there anything we can do?"

"What do you mean, man? Anything you can do? They're dead. Nothing can be done for them now." The tone was rough and abrupt.

"I understood that you were close to them. This is a tragic and trying time." Judd tried not to show any reaction to Sir Michael's curt replies.

"You know nothing. They were employees, nothing more. Look, I have a lot on my mind right now. I will call you in a few days. I'm sure I don't know why, but if you want, I will send you the funeral details when they are available. I'm not even sure if it's any of your business."

Click the phone went dead. Mary watched as Judd held the phone out in front of himself and stared at the hand piece.

"What was that all about?" asked Mary.

"I'm not sure. I think the man must be really upset, still, there's no reason for him to act like a pompous bastard." Mary stood, and as she turned to go back to the kitchen, she said over her shoulder, "We should feel for the man. He has a wedding and two funerals to face all within one year. That must be hard."

"Just because he is a "Sir" is no cause to be rude. He is no better than we are, the pompous bastard! Makes me wonder just what sort of family we are about to become tied up with."

From the kitchen he heard Mary laugh and say, "We will find out soon enough." She repeated, "We will find out soon enough."

"Makes me wonder, just who he thinks we are," said Judd as he placed the hand set back on the hook. "Maybe *he* will find out just *who* he is getting tied up with."

To be continued.........

PLAYING THE CARD'S YOU'VE BEEN DEALT TRILOGY

A Royal Flush

The St-John-Brown Family's Hand

This family has built its status on dubious origins. While wealth and Royal family connections appear to come with un-written and perceived privileges, they are often abused, and are displayed with belligerence and arrogance towards the lesser recipients. The St-John-browns have a mixture of decency which tends to color their true character.

A Royal Flush
The St. John-Brown Family's Hand
Playing The Cards You've Been Dealt Trilogy
REX PATRIA FAMILIA
by Peter C BonSey

Coat of Arms (*Legend*)

The Catholic Cross is a symbol that Henry VIII granted lands to others upon dissolution of the Catholic Church in England.

The Tudor Rose denotes, 'The Crown's (Henry VIII's) approval and acknowledgement of the acquisition of Catholic lands by the St.John-Browns.' The very basis of their wealth.

A Coat of Arms

A coat of Arms is traditionally issued and approved by The Royal College of Arms. These are awarded to persons who have achieved acts of merit. Each symbol represents concepts and ideals held dear by the applicant for a Coat of Arms.

As time has evolved there have been many Coats of Arms produced that do not necessarily convey fact so much as the owners' perceptions or ideals that they would like attributed to themselves.

There are a great many Coats of Arms that have been produced without sanction from the Royal College. The St. John-Brown's is one of those.

This Coat of Arms image designed and produced by:
andrewmcnaughtoncreative@gmail.com

Use of red flowing silks symbolize the silks used to keep knights in armor cool. Red was usually used by Royalty but was not exclusive.

Ermine denotes the family's trading skills in expensive and exotic goods.

St George's cross on sails denotes Patron Saint of England.'

Crossed keys denote the family's connection with the City of Bath and it's Patron Saints.

Three lions denote loyalty to England.

Center shield of three peacock feathers denotes superiority and power.

Gold roundels in the tip of feathers denote trust and moral superiority.

Wheat sheath denotes trade, commerce and prosperity.

Ship Denotes commerce and trading on the high seas.

Helmet denotes flamboyance and great wealth.

Pennant's five circles denote Unity. Ships helms denote Control. Entire pennant denotes Royal Shipping Line's first five ships.

Flushing of playing cards denote the author's sense of humor.

The portcullis denotes The Royal stamp of approval for the St.John-Brown family.

Rex, Patria, Familia.   King, Country, Family.

Coat of Arm Designed by Andrew McNaughton
andrewmcnaughtoncreative@gmail.com

St.John-Brown Lineage

```
Sir William      Lady Veronica        David          Regina
St.John-Brown     Chartwell          Mowbray        Blackstone
  1820-1905        1830-1916         1835-1917       1840-1912
     I                  I                I               I
     I----------1848------I          I-----1858------I
              I                             I
              I                             I
           Michael                       Penelope
         St.John-Brown                   Mowbray
          1852-1926                      1851-1931
          I-------------------1875----------------I
                             I
                       Angela Rose
                      St.John-Brown
                         1915-
```

Chapter 1

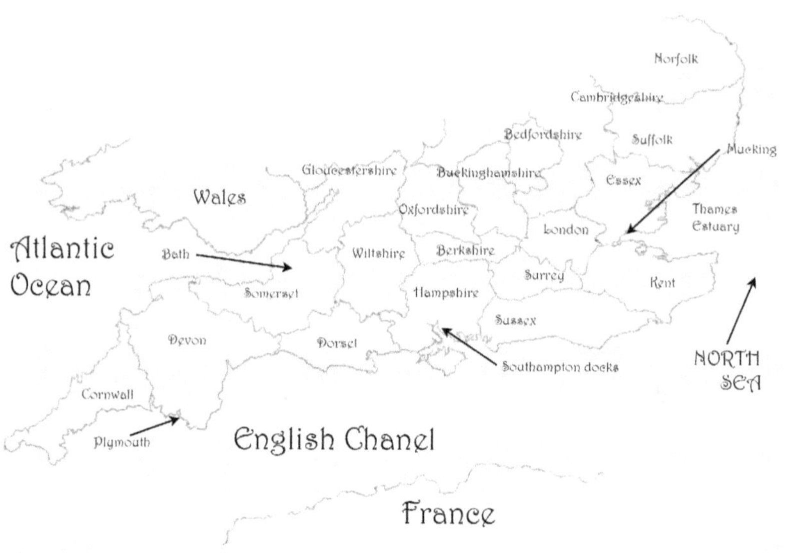

1820, the City of Bath, in Somerset was the scene of great celebrations. It was the family seat of the St.John-Brown family. The birth of their first and only child, William St.John-Brown had raised this aristocratic family to the highest of aspirations. This wealthy well connected family had a male heir. This was a fine reason to expand their empire. That same year had also seen the death of King George.

Bath is conveniently situated between the English Channel seaports, the Bristol Channel and the Atlantic Ocean seaports. Since the late seventeenhundreds, many of Bath's visitors were considered to be the upper crust of society. Much of London's upper class maintained second homes in Bath. This allowed the ladies of society to mingle with those of the Royal Courts in a less restricted fashion. The fresh sea air from both directions was an invigorating change from London's putrid streets. The spa waters were the reserve of the wealthy. The origins of this wealth were often obscure and, indeed, sometimes less than pristine. The origins of the St.John-Brown's wealth were proudly traced back to days of King Henry VIII. In 1534, King Henry VIII dissolved the Catholic Church, and the government passed the Act of Supremacy, which enabled the king to absorb the immense Catholic assets into his own purse. Around this time, the St.John-Brown family lore had it that the patriarch William's great-great-

grandfather's ancestors, obtained vast tracts of land and properties around Glastonbury Abbey. Often these tales carried an air of righteous indignation that they did not get the Abbey itself. That did not stop them from accepting the land grants and every benefit they provided.

As time went by, they sold, traded, and generally parlayed those holdings into magnificent and opulent residential properties in Bath. There was Queen's Square, built in 1728; the Circus, built in 1754; and the most prestigious of all, the Royal Crescent, completed in 1774. These magnificent structures, were built from highly prized local stone from the Mendip Hills and the Cotswolds. They were of such substance and style that they were the envy of every connected family that wished to join the London summer society at Bath. This family's initial investment was less financial than it was groveling at the feet of the King. The returns however, they believed, promised a secure future for their heirs.

The family business interests gradually shifted toward commerce, with a particular interest in shipping. In 1771, William's father was invited to join a breakaway group from Lloyd's Coffee House, a group of wealthy businessmen who united together to underwrite shipping investments. He became a founding member of the new Lloyd's of London, which eventually became owned by nine subscribers. The original owner, Edward Lloyd, became a member rather than supreme power.

Being well positioned at Lloyd's enabled one to be in a position to discover new emerging opportunities. Sir William's father soon gave birth to the Royal Shipping Line. In 1776, a 150-ton sloop, was renamed The Prince of Wales in honor of the family's royal connections in London. Smaller ships like this one were able to hug the coast and often outrun any trouble. They could quickly duck into safe harbors to avoid treacherous channel storms. A big factor in the selection of this ship was that its intended journey would not require arming it for protection from piracy or the feared French raiders. Though the Prince of Wales was the only ship in the Royal line, it was the beginning of a dream that was to control the family's future.

William's father believed it was God's grace that had set him on the path to wealth, and so his second entry into mercantile endeavors was to be The Grace, a 120-ton brig built in Cork, Ireland, with oak and spruce. It drew an eleven-foot draft, which made it useful in moving large cargo purchased from the oceangoing galleons that plied the world's seas. Cargoes purchased in Highbridge Port in Somerset, Poole Harbour in Dorset, and Bristol, were moved through the English Channel, up the River Thames, and into the heart of London. The Grace and The Prince of Wales carried not only the family inventory, but also that of other merchants who did not like the risk associated with huge cargo-carrying hulks getting plundered by the hostile Frenchmen.

In 1783, the 850-ton Duke of Richmond became available, and was a good fit for the international ambitions of the Royal Shipping Line. Built in 1769, she had been updated with a copper sheath in 1782, and her three decks were outfitted for the transportation business, including transporting criminals to work in Australia and moving slaves from the African Continent to the Americas and back to England.

International sea trade was booming, and in 1793, the 142-ton The Princess Royal, a single-deck brig with beams, was added to the company. She was built in Cork, Ireland, and was destined for the Caribbean trade. Her maiden voyage to Dominica was one of the most lucrative the Royal Line had yet seen. The world was growing more accessible, but the pirates seemed to capitalize on any circumstance that put ships in their path. So, in 1814, the Royal Shipping Line's requirements for bigger and faster ships saw the addition of the 355-ton Duke of Marlborough. She was the first new ship, built for the Royal line, which was now able to boast a fleet. A single-deck with beams, her hull was sheathed in copper and drawing sixteen feet, she was built on Prince Edward Island in Canada and was designed for the Americas trade. The Royal Shipping Line and St. John-Browns were established and making their mark on the world.

Chapter 2

William St.John-Brown never really understood his father's fascination with royalty. To have been named after King George III's son, Prince William, was just his father's way of currying further favor with the king. When Prince William became King William IV, there was no stopping William St.John-Brown's father. He carried on about the good fortune that would surely follow his son.

The family's strong belief in the paramount importance of education was at the forefront of everything they did. William's father had introduced tutors to William's nursery at four, and by age six, William could read, and was well on the way to writing. In 1827, at age seven, his father announced, "William, it's off to school for you my boy. Time you got out into the world." William's mother was as shocked as he was at the announcement.

"But, father, I am doing school here with my tutor," the boy cried.

"Not the same, not the same. You are doing school things but we are having you go to a real school."

William sat almost paralyzed with fear as his mother spoke up and said to her husband "Robert, don't you think he is a little young to go to school? Where did you have in mind?"

"I don't have anything in mind my dear, he has been enrolled in Charterhouse, a well-respected boarding school for boys in Godalming, Surrey, a quiet town south of London. You know it my dear. We pass through there often on the way to the coast. It is all settled, then."

"But don't I have some say in the matter?" was William's mother's plea.

"Say, say, you have had all the say, for the past six years, now it's high time we got on with his education properly. Must get the boy away from those apron strings." William's mother was stung by the retort and obediently reverted to her expected, subservient role to her husband.

***

Looking back, William remembered the whirlwind experience that followed the announcement of him going away. He recalled being taken in a carriage by his parents, first to London, where they stayed overnight in the elegant Savoy Hotel. In the morning, the carriage packed up and left for Charterhouse. It wasn't until they arrived at the school that William became really nervous. In the carriage, his mother, on one side, gripped his hand so tightly it hurt, and his father, on the other side, told him that he was going to be mixing with the right types. "Make a man

of you," he said. "Meet the right people here. Make your mother proud, my boy."
William fought to hold back the tears as he gazed at the great spires on the towers,
his head so far backwards he felt a little dizzy. He sat staring out of the carriage
immobilized by fear.

When they finally came to a halt the throngs of young boys that seemed to
be just milling around all had the same clothes that his parents had purchased
for him, at his father's Saville Row tailor. All his clothes were handmade and fit
perfectly. The coachman opened the door to reveal three gentlemen with flowing
black robes atop their suits and and mortar boards on their head with a boy, bigger
than William, standing to one side. The most imposing of the gentlemen introduced
himself as the headmaster. The other two were to be William's housemaster and the
last man, who was to be his father. For a panicked moment, William thought that
his parents were giving him away, until the headmaster explained it is the school's
father's role to show the new boy the ropes. He said, "Your son will not get into
any trouble for the first two weeks. By then, he should know the ropes, and then
be responsible for his actions. We are honored to have your son follow in your
footsteps Sir St.John-Brown." The man was careful to pronounce the family name
correctly as, Sin-jen Brown. He recalled William's grandparents firmly correcting
him many years before.

Orders were given, and trunks unloaded and hauled away. William's new school
father showed him around the huge school complex. It took most of the afternoon.
When he ended up at his dormitory, or house as it was called, his trunks were
already at the end of what was to be his bed for the next four years. His parents were
gone. There had been no goodbye, no hug from his mother, and no gentleman's
handshake from his father. They were just gone.

There was so much to remember. His new father's name was Mr. Michael
Mitchell. He was warned, 'Mr. Mitchell not Mickey or Mitch'. Words filled
William's mind. 'Crown' was the tuck shop, 'Banco', a study period. 'Calling over'
was when his performance was reported to the headmaster. 'Hash' was schoolwork,
'homebill,' the evening meal. 'Adsum' was roll call, which was taken twice a day.
So much to remember and so quickly. Yearlings, that was the worst. Every boy
started his time at Charterhouse as a yearling. As a yearling, the older boys in his
house would bully him for the slightest infraction of the rules with the threat of
reporting him for caning. They never seemed to get into trouble for bullying. For
a brief while William was terrified, but being big for his age, he quickly learned
and handed out a few bloody noses to bullies. He soon discovered that a threat was
often more effective and did not draw as much attention to himself. The only place
this did not work was with the masters, who would delight in intimidating any boys
they chose to. A master as a bully was a different story. A ruler whacked soundly
across the knuckles had to be endured in silence.

Some of the boys reveled in being able to 'fag' young boys, which allowed them
to make the weaker child their servant, to do whatever they were bid, no matter how
unsavory, disgusting, or demeaning. This always fell on the smaller, less confident
children. As he got older, William distanced himself from these activities. He did
not want to be bothered. He believed power by physical strength and size was too

much work, especially when power by threat was easier. Later, William would recall this as the year that he began to realize where he fit into scheme of things. He learned that his family's wealth and position afforded him a pass card in many situations from boys who perceived his station to be higher than theirs.

One summer afternoon he discovered a dormer window that overlooked the laundry building. It was from this position he could see the corner of the building where the laundry maids hid from sight of the prying eyes of curious little boys. One particular girl would leave behind the steaming heat of the laundry, and after checking to make sure there was nobody around, remove her sweat soaked blouse. She would lay her blouse in the sun to dry and bask herself in the warm afternoon air. William was enthralled by the way her breasts would hang down as she knelt on the grass to spread the blouse, and as she turned and lie on her back, how her large breasts would part. William was fixated by this spectacle. Soon he began to know when to go his 'special place' and what to expect. He would unbuckle his belt as he entered the tiny dormer space high above the fourth form dormitories. He knew seeing the young girl's breasts stirred something in him. He soon began to pleasure himself. It wasn't long before he was going to the place primarily for this pleasure. By the time the laundry maid would appear, in full expectation, he would be fully aroused. Often the results of his climax would fire off into the air and sometimes land on a small windowpane. He left it there to dry. Soon the collection of smudges hung on the windowpane as if they were his trophies.

One afternoon, as his breath returned to normal from its hectic, post-sexual rhythm, he smoked his customary cigarette, which the boys called a fag. Blowing smoke rings into the hot, static air, satisfaction and sheer bliss enveloped him when suddenly a yearling boy walked in on him. He quickly stood, head and shoulders over the boy, and was about to threaten him when he saw the fear in the boy's eyes. "Don't be scared you little shit. Take a look at out of the window. Having been instructed, the boy timidly approached the window and saw the laundry maid. William could tell from the boy's reaction, that the boy was no threat. William cajoled the boy to pleasure himself. He could see the boy was aroused "Go on play with yourself. See that on the window?" he said pointing to the murky splotch on the window, "that's me, see if you can do better." After following William's instructions and climaxing, the boy asked for puff on one of William's fags, and William accommodated him. William gave the boy a silver florin, a full two shillings, and made it plain that if any other boy ever found out about this place, there would be blood flowing. The boy was cowed, and believed him, and promised to ask permission before visiting the dormer again. William agreed. It was soon after that both boys would meet and watching the young girl they would masturbate. One time the boy said "would you like me to wank you off?" William did not object. William wondered if he would ever have been able to get the girl to do it for him. For now, his imagination would have to suffice.

***

Midterm breaks, exeats (special days off from the rigors of study), and end-of-term breaks allowed William to go home to Bath six times a year. Looking back, he knew these trips were what enabled him to survive the absence of his parents while at school. He felt as if he did not quite fit in either world.

Did he learn anything? On the one hand he learned to watch people carefully and to see how they behaved. This knowledge, he felt, gave him power. He learned that he could control his feelings so that others could not read him. More importantly, he learned that his family's position and wealth was a strong weapon and that it could be used to his advantage.

On the other hand, he learned that religion was a crafty package of actions, attitudes, and rhetoric, masterfully used to control others. He noticed that its' authority was rarely questioned. He was not ready to blindly accept this 'God.' The only physical scar he carried away from Charterhouse was the one given him by an infuriated minister trying to teach the bored boys religion. When William dared ask for proof of God's existence, a glass paperweight was thrown with such force and anger that it shattered on his desk, smashing William's inkwell, and a large shard of glass embedded itself in his cheek, along with a healthy smattering of jet black, India ink. He was sent to the infirmary with a firm caution. 'Remember boy, when asked, you fell on the corner of your desk.' William never went back to that study class, and he passed with honors. Yes, he certainly learned something there.

The school had its' elite element on the one hand, fostered by the wealthy and connected, and on the other hand, were those whose parents strived to have some of that societal influence rub off on their children. The hypocrisy surrounded William continuously. He was quick to notice it.

Chapter 3

By seventeen William had developed an arrogant stance in life. It was his schooling after Charterhouse that enriched William's appreciation of London. It was so easy to be anonymous there. The year that King's College's junior department had accepted him was 1837. Situated right in the heart of London, on the Strand, Kings was deemed to be the preparatory school for the college's professorial rooms, and though this was not what William or his father had in mind, it was a fine stepping stone to Oxford or Cambridge. As the Royal Shipping Line had much business in London, William's father had plenty of opportunity to spend time with his son. But, rarely did so.

William had no illusions about why his father wanted him to go King's. The Duke of Wellington was most influential in the formation of King's College, and his father Robert, believed that the connections of the Duke, who had recently been the Prime Minister of England and the leader of the House of Lords, could prove invaluable, and they did.

Drinking and bedding wenches was as much part of college life for William as it was for many of the young students. Dreams of easy money allowed William to disassociate himself from his own downward course. It amused him that, on more than one occasion, as he braced a lady of the night against a grimy back-alley wall, his always frisky manhood pounding into her, he would look skyward to see the iron girders and beams of some railway truss, bridge, or some other construction. This, he found reminded him of Charterhouse, with its great hall's roof, constructed out of timbers skillfully jointed and interlocked. How much more simple this iron and steel was than the intricate woodwork. Then he would unload his manhood secretions into the useful body in front of him He preferred to take his wenches from behind as he didn't have to look at their faces.

On another occasion, while repeating his debauchery in a dimly lit alley by a railway siding, the shrill screech of a train's whistle, as it pulled into a station, caught his imagination. His body working at one task while his mind worked at another. The train stirred him to think of other places, faraway places. He felt that here, in London, he was more at ease than he would have been in Oxford, Cambridge, or any other university. His thoughts, even here, were of the world, of shipping, travel, and exotic lands. He thought of change. He thought of family. He thought about how infrequently he had seen father since being at school. This was his second year and he could count on the fingers of one hand the number of times his father had visited him. William seemed to drift away from his father. Mother always had an explanation for her husband's absence. This would go wrong in the business, or that is happening in the House of Lords. William understood what a huge catastrophe that the huge fire at Lloyds of London, the shipping register, to which his father belonged, had been. But that was just things. The familyowned ships, but they weren't destroyed. Why did father always have something else to do? William sometimes felt that Lloyds meant more to his father than he did. It didn't seem fair to a young boy. Even when William would be off from school on holidays and was staying at Royal Crescent, his father would be gone before he arose and back after he was in bed. William managed to keep his mind off that subject with his carousing.

In 1840 at twenty years old, William completed his time at King's College's junior department and earned a well-respected accounting of his skills. All his instructors and classmates expected him to rise to the next step. Though senior professors, family friends, and even Arthur Wellesley, the Duke of Wellington himself, urged William's father to encourage William to pursue a professorial career, William agreed with his father that the family business was where he belonged

Chapter 4

The Royal Shipping Line offices were situated in an old, red brick building on Canons Way, adjacent to Hanover Quay. The offices had banks of clerks with mounds of different-colored paper, each with a weight holding down the stack. The clerk's workstations were overlooked by managerial offices that cantilevered out over the heads of the clerks. On the other side, equally cantilevered out, was the President's office suite. William and his father had arrived early this morning, and there was sense of purpose in the air.

The large easel set out in front of them displayed a list:

The Prince of Wales	150-ton sloop, built in 1746	Age 94
The Princess Grace	120-ton brig, built in 1775	Age 65
The Duke of Richmond	850 ton, built in 1769	Age 69
updated with a copper sheath 1782		
The Princess Royal	142 ton, built in 1785	Age 55
The Duke of Marlborough	355 ton, built in 1815	Age 25

Discussions between William and his father were cordial. William, now nearly twentyone, felt as if he were ready to step up and run the business, alongside his father. His thoughts were aggressive and as of yet unpolished. "Sir, the average age of our ships is about sixtyone years. If we sell The Prince of Wales, the average age will drop to fifty-three years."

"Why do think that so important? his father asked. "Eight years is nothing in the age of a ship."

William quickly responded with an air of excitement, "If we could afford to buy all new ships, we would be the talk of the town." William felt it was time to acquire more ships and show the world what the St.John-Browns and The Royal Shipping Line were made of.

His father leaned back in his plush, Chairman of the Board, office chair and pondered his response to his son. "I think that would cost far too much. We need to consider more important things than image. Think about what is going on around the world that could affect our ships. For example, the South African conflict with the Dutch, that although not a sea conflict, is closing off routes at Cape Horn." His father waited for a reaction, which he got quite quickly.

"How does that affect us?" William was trying to impress his father.

"It is foreseeable that the Admiralty could requisition ships, *our ships*, for troop transport. That could become a financial burden, as the Admiralty will pay, but, I fear, very slowly, some say, if ever."

"But they do pay, and, the more ships we have the more they will pay."

"Be careful my boy. Nobody can live on promises of payment, particularly government payments. That could break our bank, so to speak."

As more and more ships were being clad with copper or iron for durability and strength, William's father could see the use of iron and steel becoming used in other areas. "I can see machines that will hoist our cargo out of holds from the dockside much faster than is being done now. I can even foresee structures on ships themselves, replacing the derricks. These will be expensive but will use less manpower. That will allow ships to offload and reload cargo very quickly."

William was impressed that his father was thinking ahead, but was still impatient. Finally, they agreed that, with three of their ships rarely in English ports for any length of time and considering the selling of one, that only left one that was local trade. With the Princess Grace doing coastal work, their base in Bristol seemed poorly located. The coastal work of the Princess could easily be managed from anywhere. William was charged to meet with their ships at whatever port they next arrived, hire marine carpenters and ship surveyors, and conduct complete surveys of each ship, looking for rot, and signs of hidden decay. This could be done efficiently without interrupting the trade of the ships. His father wanted an accurate evaluation upon which to base his decisions. In other words, he let William know that he was still running the company. He further charged William with the task of considering new locations for the company's London office. He did not expect this report to be taken lightly or quickly. He promised that, if the report was well considered, he would make decisions based upon it and that William would be starting to influence major decisions.

***

Soon, William was spending much of his time in and around London, inspecting properties and potential office locations suitable for the RSL, as he called The Royal Shipping Lines. He relished the time that he spent in and around ports and shipyards as it exposed him to the seamier side of life and plenty of young women who were impressed with his title and connections. For a young, handsome man of his standing sex was readily available. When he wasn't working the docklands, he was carousing with his old college connections in London. It was not long before word of his dalliances reached his father. Sometimes, his concentration on his between the legs gymnastics, overrode his responsibility to the business. On more than one occasion his father had to reprimand him on these issues. One summer evening William arrived at Royal Crescent, responding to his father's summons to present himself at his father's house. William's father, was red faced and angry when he said, "If you don't have the pox my boy, you are damn lucky from what I hear. You are twenty, you had better wake up and be a man and stop being a child. Trash, just plain, common street trash, that's what you have been sticking yourself into."

"How would you know father? You are never around to..."

"I don't have to be around. You seem to forget I know a lot of people and there're many out there that enjoy sullying the reputation of their better's. God, boy, wake up will you."

"So, it's your reputation that concern's you, not me." William was getting hot under the collar as the discussion got more heated.

"Gentlemen do not behave the way you have been. If your sordid behavior reaches your mother's ears, you might as well go to sea, my boy."

"That would suit you fine, wouldn't it?" William snapped at his father.

"And what is that supposed to mean young man?"

"You would have me out of the way. I mean that it will be difficult for you to keep sending me away for much longer, will it not sir?"

"What do you mean, send you away? *Send you away!* I have been building your future for you, boy."

"First you *sent* me away to 'school' when I was still a child and every time we get together, you '*send*' me off to do some bidding or other."

"It's all for your own good, for the family business's good. William, the family business is growing very quickly, and I will not always be around to head everything. I want for you to be able to hold your head high. Bring honor to the family, bring honor to yourself, and all that kind of thing. I'm sure you want your mother to be proud. Just don't spoil things for yourself." His father was calming down and William grasped the opportunity to try and make peace.

"You mean to tell me sir that you didn't have some misspent youth?" He grinned at his father as he spoke.

"Well actually I did, but the big difference was that that I kept it private. All I ask is that you do the same."

In a humble tone William replied, "Father, we can be so much more. The opportunities that are out there are immeasurable. I don't think I am being challenged enough."

"Well, I'm glad that you brought that up. I have every faith that you will rise to the occasion and take our business to even greater heights. I have been working behind the scenes on your behalf."

"Pray, tell me more father."

Much to William's surprise his father appeared to change the subject when he said, "You have never been in the presence of her Majesty. Do you have any idea when you might actually meet her?"

"What are you talking about Father?" was William's confused reply.

"Your name will be the top of the list on this year's Times of London."

"For what?" William was uncertain of what his father was saying.

"The Queen has seen fit to…You are to be knighted."

"Me… knighted… for what? When did this come about?"

"I have been using a few connections and I think you are ready and so does her Majesty. It has not gone unnoticed just how much we have aided the country in our shipping endeavors to move cargo safely around England's shores. This honor has been earned, not inherited like some we know. So now what do you think of that?"

"I didn't earn it father. This is incredible. I don't know what to say."

"The family earned it. Isn't that enough? Say nothing my boy, just make the family proud. Remember, power attracts power." William now understood just what power his family had and what it could do for him personally. It had recently been announced that Queen Victoria was to marry this year and a spate of Knighthoods and peerages were being given as a celebratory act. William's father had managed to get his son on the list.

***

The knighthood was celebrated in grand style at Royal Crescent in Bath, as well as in the city. While London's wealthy, created many dilettantes, William believed this was not the case for him. He fully understood that his involvement in Lloyd's and his father's contacts were the reason for him gaining the knighthood at the young age of twenty. His parents were proud and to celebrate, a great bonfire was built in the center of Royal Crescent. Many of the Crescent's residents were unhappy about the ruckus the celebrations would cause, but their societal drive to rub shoulders with the 'connected' prevailed. Not only, was the Royal Shipping Line setting trends, but now the family had cemented their genuine royal connections. 'Sir' William was busy scheming, but he welcomed the trappings. They certainly would open doors for him.

Chapter 5

William had been industrious since his earlier rebuke from his father. Between time spent visiting Lloyd's of London Insurance and creating a list of possible new offices and ships that had captured his imagination, he was busy shagging any female that took his fancy. He had matured enough to know that his peccadillos should be more discrete, and he tried to keep them that way. He enjoyed the power he felt in dominating his sex partners. He once uttered to a partner, "You are just as passive and pliant as my mother."

He was taken aback by the response, "Shag your mother then, do you…*Sir*, or are you just punishing her?" The emphasis was on the *Sir*. This was the first time he had thought about his carousing as power based and wondered if there was more to his motives. He had to exercise restraint to prevent himself from striking out at the girl.

When his mind was on his work, he excelled. He soon proposed the purchase of new ships: There was the George Canning, built in France in 1811. It was a three hundred and thirty-nine-tonner with a single deck and beams. She was sheathed in copper and was equipped with four nine-pound and two eighteen-pound guns, as well as twelve twelve-pound cannonades. She had been busy trading on the North and South American coasts. The ship was valued at eighteen hundred pounds. Then there was the Pacific, built in New York in America in 1831. She was 537 tons and had two decks. Sheathed in copper, her main trade had been in the North Atlantic. The ship was valued at twenty-eight hundred pounds. Next, the Governor Raffles, built on Prince Edward Island in Canada in 1827, was 512 tons, sheathed in copper and built solidly of black birch, oak, and hackmatack. The ship was valued at twenty-two hundred pounds. Next, The Pallas, built in 1826 in New Brunswick, Nova Scotia, Canada, was a 316-ton copper-sheathed barque. Little was known of her background, but she appeared robust. The ship was valued at nineteen hundred pounds. Then, the Palmer, built in 1834 in Newcastle, Upon Tyne, was 334 tons, and had done just one transportation run. She was Virtually a brandnew ship sheathed in copper, it was valued at twenty-six hundred pounds. And, finally, the Palmyra, built in Calcutta, India in 1820 with teak, was 602 tons, sheathed in felt and copper. The ship was valued at three thousand pounds.

William's father was impressed. Each ship's description was accompanied by a surveyor's report and carpenter recommendations, along with both carrying recommendations as to actual purchasing price. The reasons for sale were varied and suspect. Businessmen could not afford a whisp of negative chatter, as many owners, members of Lloyd's, knew a bad rumor could eliminate their stature overnight. If

William had his way, the Royal Shipping Line would spend in excess of fifteen thousand pounds, including taxes and legal fees.

After the sale of their oldest ship and the purchase of the new, the fleet would stand at ten ships. William suggested that they should plan every two years to dispose of the oldest ship until the oldest they had was no more than ten. New ships in top condition would be more efficient to maintain and run than old ships in need of constant repair. He also identified that the shipping business was rapidly expanding with the advances being made in mechanization and production When William's father wanted to discuss the renaming of the ships, William backed away, his hands in the air. "Father, you enjoy the royal connection," he said. "It doesn't matter to me. But I think you should name one of them after mother. She is, after all is said and done, your queen." His father was taken aback by the unexpected gesture. "So! what do you think?" William asked. "The Palmyra is the finest of the ships, although not the youngest. She is solidly built, and I believe she will make a fine flagship. Choose the title and have mother's family crest carved for her renaming."

The Palmyra became The Royal Consort. The Royal Shipping Line set about the business of acquisition and expansion as father and son began to unite in family enterprises. That was all that was needed. William had buckled down to his responsibilities.

Chapter 6

William St.John-Brown was twenty-one. The term 'idle rich' definitely did not apply to him. The early days of his youth placed him conveniently among the wealthy and connected members of society. It was with great interest that he listened to the conversations of the gentlemen in their clubs. The discussion of Lloyd's of London was a frequent subject as many of his friends were members. Although three years earlier, Lloyd's royal exchange had been destroyed by fire, the members soon rebuilt, and it had now reopened. Many an idle summer evening was spent with gentlemen, smoking cigars and drinking fine French brandy from his father's stock. It was the responsibility of members to ensure merchants and make them whole after any losses, and William's family's vast wealth enabled him to join in these pursuits. The knighthood had changed how he was perceived and now new doors were opening for him. The St. John-Brown holdings in London and the West Country gave William many opportunities to mull over his experiences while traveling to and from the coast. It was clear that the landed gentry looked down their noses at rural folk, and rural folk looked down their noses at city folk. This created a chasm of opportunity. Sir William had a keen eye and was always looking for opportunities in the system. He once hypothesized that if one knew beforehand of a potential disaster, it would be easy to spread the risk amongst one's business associates in the city and share the spoils with friends and confidants in the country. There were hardly any trading merchants who did not turn to Lloyd's for insurance. There must be an opportunity to capitalize on them he thought. Masterminding a brisk and lucrative trade of shipwrecks that stood a step above the fishermen and coastal dwellers who quickly seized opportunities to scavenge cargo from wrecked ships, could be a challenge, but not impossible. The rocky treacherous English coastline along the English Channel, was frequently the site of shipwrecks. Those ships returning from fruitful journeys to the far flung reaches of the British empire were bursting at the seams with all sorts of valuable goods such as gold, silver and spices. To ship owners the speedy disappearance of their valuable cargo was stunning. Some of the local population survived from farming the rich fertile farmland in Devon, Cornwall and Somerset around the coast while others were seafaring folk and fishermen. Life was not easy for these people, and William knew many a tenant farmer and crofter who would not hesitate to a few extra pennies to afford themselves some of the finer things in life. He was a quick study in the business of controlling the tenants of his fathers' many land holdings. It was said that his father owned seventy five percent of free hold farms in the county and ruled his tenants with an iron fist. There was always someone waiting to be granted the privilege of renting an established running farm if its previous tenants displeased Sir Williams father. With farms dotted along every country road that led from English Channel inland to the towns and cities. There was a ready built infrastructure he could utilize. On occasions his thoughts would return to this idea, but he never acted upon it. Probably because he was afraid of the consequences.

There must be an opportunity to capitalize on them he thought. Masterminding a brisk and lucrative trade of shipwrecks that stood a step above the fishermen and coastal dwellers who quickly seized opportunities to scavenge cargo from wrecked ships, could be a challenge, but not impossible. The rocky treacherous English coastline along the English Channel, was frequently the site of shipwrecks. Those ships returning from fruitful journeys to the far flung reaches of the British empire were bursting at the seams with all sorts of valuable goods such as gold, silver and spices. To ship owners the speedy disappearance of their valuable cargo was stunning. Some of the local population survived from farming the rich fertile farmland in Devon, Cornwall and Somerset around the coast while others were seafaring folk and fishermen. Life was not easy for these people, and William knew many a tenant farmer and crofter who would not hesitate to a few extra pennies to afford themselves some of the finer things in life. He was a quick study in the business of controlling the tenants of his fathers' many land holdings. It was said that his father owned seventy five percent of free hold farms in the county and ruled his tenants with an iron fist. There was always someone waiting to be granted the privilege of renting an established running farm if its previous tenants displeased Sir Williams father. With farms dotted along every country road that led from English Channel inland to the towns and cities. There was a ready built infrastructure he could utilize. On occasions his thoughts would return to this idea, but he never acted upon it. Probably because he was afraid of the consequences.

Somerset. As a county, at this time was enjoying a prosperous life style. The duties expected of being a member in the House of Lords did little to impede Sir William. The tedious and boring tasks were often delegated to folk from his estates. The time that he was required to spend in London could provide him with many contacts wanting to purchase products from the colonies and the orient at agreeable prices. One might consider that William was no different from the grubby little shopkeepers of his estates who often toiled late into the night just to survive, but one would be wrong. Sir William never dealt with the little people. While they sold basics like food and clothing through The Royal Shipping Line, he could be selling silks, gold, spices, oriental rugs, and Persian carpets, fetching more money per item than his tenants earned in a year. Little people were just that, '*little people*, with '*little thinking*' and '*little doing*', of '*little worth*'. They were worth, to be exact, '*little*' of his time. Even so, Sir William became increasingly aware that numbers were the key to any enterprise. The more he traveled between London and Bath, taking his circuitous route, he realized that his reputation among the few in London could be easily destroyed by the many, namely the people he would have to use if he acted upon his shipwrecking plan. It became evident to him that he would become more vulnerable to "*the 'little'* people." He did not savor that risk. He wouldn't risk ruining his family's name. It was at this point he decided to completely abandon the idea of shipwrecking and concentrate on the legitimate opportunities in front to of him.

He started looking at what was going on around the country as he travelled. It never ceased to catch his attention that there were vast numbers of people who were barely surviving, barely eking out a living. There were even more that believed they had the good life. Compared to his existence many of those who believed they were living the good life were only fooling themselves.

Chapter 7

Traveling between ports and the City of London in the name of the Royal Shipping Line, Sir William noticed he was probably the only person generally disinterested in the royal coming and goings. Every tavern, every gathering of people, every business, discussed the damn wedding. Queen Victoria and Prince Albert were on everyone's tongue. It was as if nothing else mattered. His father would continually bring up 'Her Majesty' at every opportunity, even more than before the Royal bloody wedding was announced. On one visit to the docklands of Southampton he was turned away from one of his regular resting places due to a local town meeting regarding '*the wedding*', despite his indignant protestations at being forced to use a less than appropriate resting place for a gentleman of his standing.

The Duck and Feathers was a public house, and it set something ticking in his mind. He could not be sure what was waylaying his concentration, but something was brewing. His first evening at the Duck and Feathers grated on William's sensitivities. The surroundings, while comfortable were less than he was used to. When the maid came to his room with fresh water William notice her youthful complexion. Sitting in an armchair he studied her as she carried out her task. She was tall for a girl and slim with flared hips and fiery red hair that framed her soft pink skin. Her curls bounced as she turned to him and said with a wide disarming smile, "Is there anything I can do for you sir?" Her tone was full of innuendo.

William felt his loins stir and replied, "There are needs a man has, and you, are very beautiful.

The girl smiled and blushed. "Why thank you kind sir."

"Do you know what I desire?" William watched her face very closely looking for some sign of understanding.

"I do sir, but it is not permitted for staff to socialize with guests. I could not risk my position here," was her coquettish, knowing reply.

"Then where my girl? What is your name?"

"I am called Adelaide, sir. I am from Marchbrooke, over the river, on the west side of the river, but I am staying at Millbrooke Station."

"I am not familiar with the area. Could I interest you in a fine dinner? Somewhere special maybe, that *you* would enjoy?" William was trying not to show his rising ardor and frighten the young girl off.

"I would like to dine at The Duke of Wellington sir. It's a rather grand old Inn on Bugle Street in the center of town, that's off of Main Street. Do you know it?" William relaxed. He had set the right bait. Tonight, he would not be lonely. "I can be there by seven. That will give me time to change from my work clothes and pretty myself." She curtseyed and left the room. William was ecstatic as he adjusted what had now become a full erection.

***

Arriving at the Duke of Wellington at six o'clock, William took a room for the evening and roamed the old public house scouting for an appropriate place to wait. The pub was very old and intrigued him. Its décor was simple and clean and displayed it's well worn, aged fittings, with what felt like pride to William. The attentive staff appeared to be used to clientele of Sir William's standard, so he did not feel out of place. The local area was a busy, bustling part of the city that, even at this time of the evening, showed no signs of quieting down. Right at seven on the dot Adelaide entered the main bar of the pub. William jumped to his feet and escorted her to a quiet corner. "You look absolutely beautiful."

"Thank you, kind sir. Isn't this place grand?"

"Yes, yes, it is. I enjoy places with character. Shall we dine or would you rather have glass of wine or something?"

"Why don't you choose? I am not used to imbibing, not that I am an abstainer." Adelaide blushed as she said this.

"Would you rather we take our refreshment somewhere quieter?" To his surprise she suggested a more private place. Taking the cue William quickly ordered that wine and food be sent to his room. He then escorted Adelaide to the suite. William was intrigued by the girl's open, friendly personality. Slowly, as they dined, Adelaide became relaxed and more open. William smiled inwardly at the ease with which the situation evolved. Bedding her was no challenge but it excited him. She gave herself to him more than once through the evening and late into the night. In the early hours of the morning when she was dressed and ready to leave, William gave her a perfunctory embrace, kissed her forehead and said, "I look forward to seeing you tomorrow." After she left William thought about what had just happened. Adelaide seemed to be a pleasant enough person, but she showed no personality, no strength or weakness. He compared her to his mother, and then to his other sexual daliances. She did not fit either choice. She was, in his mind, a nothing. In a moment of uncharacteristic thoughtfulness, he decided to show her a small act of kindness before moving on and leaving her behind.

The following morning, he returned to the Duck and Feathers after stopping at a milliner's to purchase a pair of fine white kid gloves. He inserted a large, five-pound note into each glove and had the milliner wrap the gloves in delicate paper, and tie them with a pretty ribbon. Summoning Adelaide to his room he offered the gift.

"I cannot accept a gift. Last evening was most enjoyable. That is enough, or do you think you are paying me off?"

"Why would you say that? Do you usually do that for money?"

Her outburst shocked him. "What do you think I am? All you toff's look down on us country folk. We can enjoy the same pleasures that you do. It doesn't have to be about money. And I thought you were quite the gentleman. Just shows how wrong a girl can be."

"Calm down, calm down, young lady. I was trying to be nice for once in my life and look where it gets me." Holding out the small package he said, "I insist. I will hear no more about it, now be off with you." She had been summarily dismissed.

William was about to turn away when Adelaide, standing on tip toe, slapped him hard across the face and shouted, "try bedding people of your own age and class, you might get more of what you want, or should I say deserve. I bet your mother would be really proud of you." She snatched the gloves from his outstretch hand and stormed out of the room. Her last comment stung William to core. He wondered why, when women got upset, they always had to bring your mother into the discussion. He thought that even thinking about his mother and sex in the same sentence was odd. Why would someone say that?

Chapter 8

Action was something the wealthy paid others to do, but not in this case. The local gossip was all about a Guildhall meeting the next day. It appeared that plans were going to be made for festivities for Victoria's Royal Wedding celebrations. He decided to investigate further. At sunrise, William inquired where the local guildhall was and he was given directions. Upon his arrival, he found himself being challenged for entry. The Guildhall chairman, an alderman, obviously important in his own way, barred Sir William's entry. "Sir," he said, "The Guildhall is closed today for special sessions. Is your business with the sessions this day?" Sir William was used to dealing with upstarts, common or not. Despite his superior demeanor, he was aware that his youthful appearance often caused others to see him as self-inflated. "My contributions, Mr. Alderman, shall be discussed on the guild floor and not out on a public street with a ne'er-do-well," he said.

Ignoring the disrespectful reply, the man said, "May I ask of which contributions you speak, sir? We have many contributors, and we're holding a number of sub-sessions, which will then be laid before the floor." Sir William was caught off-guard and did not have a response. The alderman, seeing this, quickly added, "The Royal Wedding celebrations in our town can use all the assistance they can get. We want this to be so big even London will notice it, Sir. Transportation is in the lower west chamber, sir, perishables in the lower east chamber. Non-perishables will be in the main chamber, anteroom number one, and general or open contributions, by that we mean those wishing to assist but with no specific notions will meet in main chamber, anteroom number two."

"Thank you kindly, alderman. May I attend any session I wish?" said Sir William, handing to the alderman his gilt-edged personal card.

The alderman took the card, glanced at the '*Lord*,' and in a single motion of respect signaled an apprentice, who stood behind him. "Bradley, boy," he said, "take Sir William St. John-Brown to the gentleman's cove, where he may refresh and be more comfortable, and find him a suitable seating place in each of the meetings. Find another apprentice to sit in those seats until Sir William requires them."

The building was a solid stone and brick hall that rose four levels into the air. Great windows skillfully displayed brilliant leaded glass designs, incorporating all the many trades officiated from the hall. The chambers were tall, airy rooms with the craftsman's work evident in the plastering, coves, beams, pillars and columns, the woodwork, the floor, and even the heavy plush curtains and linens. Every one of the hundreds of people milling around appeared purposeful. Sir William bade the apprentice to sit with him for a moment and detail his understanding of the purpose of the meeting. The boy, in his innocence, spoke of plans for the celebration of the Royal Wedding. There were to be exhibitions and entertainment and feasting. The carpenters would build and erect temporary structures for the masses to eat throughout the celebration, while other guilds would help with transporting, feeding, and generally maintaining order. At this point, Sir William felt as if a switch in his mind had been turned on. "How much trouble would you get into if you dodged your master and spent the day showing me around the sites being used for the festivities?" he asked. "There are ten shillings in it for you, and I will pay your master for your time."

The boy thought for a moment and said, "let me fetch my master for you, Sir," he ran off into the mass of bodies. He returned with Ted Ballard, a diminutive, suited man with his hair slicked down the center. A jet-black handlebar mustache appeared to cut his face in half. He dipped his head, almost in mock reverence, and asked after the lord's needs.

"*You*, are a master carpenter, sir? Not what I expected," said Sir William in condescending fashion. "All *my* carpenters are men of burly size, great strength, and force."

"With all respect due to your lordship, I am not a carpenter," said Ballard. "My carpentering days are fifteen years past. I am a master, sir. I employ and oversee carpenters, fifty-one, in fact. Each of my carpenters has at least two apprentices. My employer is developing an area to the east of the port. It is going to be the Eastern docklands. It is expected to be a two-year project. What is it my apprentice, young Bradley, can do for you, sir?"

Sir William told him about the Royal Shipping Line. "Our fleet is at sea, and we have found no need to have a home port," he said. "I see that changing. We do not intend to be dragged forward by this great industrial progress that is happening. We are going to ride it like a horse. Two years, you say." He hesitated, as if pondering the years. "I would like to hire young Bradley to orient me with the sites of the upcoming festivities, so that I might find where I may make the best contributions. Southampton has the potential to become the Royal Shipping Line's homeport. This, of course, will require buildings. Your two-year project and your experience could make you our man." Changing the subject, he continued, "What do you say? Ten pounds to cover the cost of your boy for the day, and I will pay his wage." Sir William thought this would impress the worker. But to his surprise, Ballard handed back Sir William's card. With a cold stare, he said, "I thank you kindly for your offer, sir. In the spirit of the occasion, you may make use of the boy until eight o'clock of the evening hour. The monies you offer can be contributed to the guild to assist in the festivity's cost. As for your other thoughts, sir, I am a man of honor. I work for one master at a time. My remuneration dictates that my loyalty and my attention must stay focused. If your lordship requires it, I can find another master to assist you. No disrespect, sir."

"Indeed, indeed. None taken, I'm sure." With this, Sir William removed his pouch and extracted five large five-pound notes, handing them to the master. "Please add this to the guildhall's funds with my thanks. Please, retain my card and contact me if I, or the Royal Shipping Line, can be any assistance to you in the future, or indeed, when your tenure with your current employer expires." The men shook hands and parted ways. The balance of the day was spent studying the arrangements made for the Royal Wedding and sitting in on some of the meetings at the guildhall. During the meeting, a comely woman caught his attention. She was greeted by many men who appeared to be in good financial standing. Her reaction to all was aloof. She looked ladylike, but Sir William could tell this was an affectation. He was intrigued. At the end of the day, Sir William gave young Bradley the ten shinney, shilling pieces, along with four pieces of individually wrapped sweetmeats that he had got from a Mr. Tom Smith, a London confectioner, who had given them to him just days before. "These are the sweetmeats of the future," he said, referring to the individual eye-catching wrapping, a highly unusual practice. "*Oh my . . . oh my . . .*" The boy's face radiated wonder as he unwrapped a piece of candy. "This is incredible," he said as he carefully rewrapped it. "I like it, and I will share it with me sister and me mum."

As Sir William was about to give the boy his leave, he asked of the boy, "Do you know who the woman is that I keep seeing in all of these meetings?"

"That's Madge Dugan sir, Mrs. Madge Dugan," said Bradley. "'Er 'usband got killed in the dock riots or a storm or sumfing like that, drowned he did, and she took over 'is business. She's a tough un. Ain't no man will *not* step aside when she comes passin' by."

"And her business is what?" asked Sir William.

"She 'as the biggest ship chandlery in Soufampton, Duggan Ship Chandlers. She gets stuff off the ships afore anyone else gets a look in, and she sells it wif costamongers from 'ere to London. Mainly different an' exotic stuff. Some's fruit and 'at, but mostly rich people's stuff. She's rich, big rich, beggin' yer pardon, sir. But she is," Bradley said with respectful awe.

Chapter 9

Tom Smith was one of London's most prolific sweetmeat and sugar candy producers. He employed an idea he had seen in France, which was presenting sweetmeats in a way that was more dramatic than the current practice of large jars, from which people bought small amounts. The current practice was often a sticky, messy transaction. Value was often overlooked when people were presented with a more delightful and interesting package. If the package concept of the sweets was used on the larger-scale food industry, Sir William thought, the economy of scale would create potentially huge profits. As he sat that evening in his less than desirable lodgings, he started to formulate a plan.

A day-old London newspaper had been left in his room. One article covered the Chartism movement and how it was gaining respectability, this so soon after the deportation of the Tolpuddle Martyrs from Devon for doing virtually the same thing. Those six men had been found guilty of breaking a law over thirty-five years old, designed to prevent men from swearing an oath to each other. The grouping together of workers against their bosses was repugnant to Sir William.

Another article discussed the hiring of Henry Maudsley by the Royal Navy to mass-produce armaments and blocks and pulleys for the ships. Machines . . . men . . . money. Unions, mass production, fast transportation. Sir William thought of all these things combined, added food into the mix, and arrived at a conclusion. It struck William how little attention he had been paying to what was going on around him that he was now discovering in the newspapers.

In 1800, the English population was about eight million. Now it was closer to twelve million. Large public gatherings were commonplace. Couple the needs of a burgeoning population with the improved abilities of modern-day inventions, and add the fact that his family's ships were bringing hundreds of tons of raw material to England on a regular basis, and there was a lot of money to be made, a lot of legal money. He liked the low risk of this idea relative to his somewhat risky earlier thoughts about shipwrecking. Indeed, he felt that his father would not only approve his plan, but would fund it. He decided to discuss his plan with someone else first.

After resting, Sir William went to the snug bar and called for the landlord of the Duck and Feathers. William asked, "Do you really think the town will be able to support so many people for the celebrations?" he asked.

"The Guild Hall Sir, they are getting volunteers to come together. Yes, I believe we can do it."

"Yes, yes, I know about that, but, the volunteers themselves have to be fed, and from what I see of the huge crowds now, it's hard to imagine them all eating, sleeping and celebrating as well in this one place."

"What with the port being here and the big crowds the number of ships bring, we have gotten used to doing things on a big scale. It seems like England is either getting more crowded or it's shrinking." The landlord laughed at his own humor, but it added to William's thoughts about his future.

"So, tell me man, the Duggan woman, what do you know about her?"

"Madge, sir, Madge Duggan has turned this town's idea of business upon its' ear."

"Meaning what?"

"Her husband died, some say an accident, some say he was helped, but be that as it may, he drowned. Terrible, sir, 'twas, terrible how he treated that poor girl. Bog Irish she was, knew nothing when she came here and married him. Arranged it was you know. Things was bad for her for a while. When he died, would you know it, she upped and turned herself around. Became a lady. Kept the Irish smarts and before you knew it she had a hold on the trade here at the docks. I tell you I have seen ships that will wait at anchor for a space on her wharfs rather than go to other chandlers. They say she treats everyone fair, that ain't common around the docks. I've got a lot of respect for her, I have. Would you like to meet her?"

William quickly accepted the offer, and then kept probing. "When you say became a lady, wasn't she one before?"

"Don't rightly know sir. Mick Duggan used to keep her under lock and key, so to speak, when he wasn't trying to bed another wench. No one was allowed to have much to do with her. She was always in the room when Mick was doing business. I guess she must have kept her eyes and ears open."

"But became a lady, that's the thing I don't understand."

"Figure of speech sir. She was always prim and presented herself well, but seemed to be meek. When old Mick kicked it, sorry, died, she went off to London for a while and came back a changed woman. She never remarried or even looked like she was interested. I bet you can't find anyone to say a bad word about her. Well maybe some of the other chandlers, but that's just jealousy. She's a fine-looking woman. Got a lot of respect from everyone round here." The man's comments about Madge Duggan provided William with a more adult perception than the young apprentice had given him earlier. The knowing winks and nods the man gave as he spoke were so much more descriptive. Strangely enough, the same awe was present. The landlord turned as he left the room and said, "Let me see if I can arrange for you to meet with her, would this evening suit you sir?"

***

Later that evening, Sir William received a knock on his chamber door. He was informed that his guest was awaiting him in the inn's private bar. Upon entering the 'snug', a private bar, he was surprised to see that the woman who stood before him carrying the deportment of a lady had a disdainful expression. At five feet ten, Madge was taller than most women. Her hair was a fiery spun copper red that reflected the bar's gaslight glow with every turn of her head. Her complexion was a soft, milky white cream color, with tones of natural pink that surpassed the added rouge so commonly worn by women in the courts. She was a contradiction, the air of a young girl with the robust, full figure of a woman and the confidence of someone well beyond her years. Softly, with a strong undertone, she said, "If you are a, *Sir*, William, you should know that a lady does not meet a man, even a gentleman of your standing, in a public house for dinner. In fact, a lady does not meet anyone in a public house if she wishes to maintain her reputation. If I did not have an open mind to a business opportunity, I would not have responded to your request at all. The landlord tells me that you believe we may have some business together. Please elucidate."

As she spoke, Sir William felt his childhood blushing creep up his neck until his whole face glowed, not in her pleasant pink, but in a ruddy, blood-pumping shine. His gaze, he realized, was fixed upon her cleavage. The ample breasts were obviously pushed up, he thought, as he watched them rise and fall in unison. He switched his gaze to her stance. Her feet were placed squarely apart, hands placed firmly on the parasol before her. It was as if she was challenging him, which he saw, she clearly was. In what seemed like an eternity to him, he evaluated her sexual being in a brazen scan, which he could see she noticed. 'She has to be forty, my God, forty. That's nearly my mother's age', he thought. 'I bet her patch is red. I bet . . .' He stopped his cranial gymnastics and fought to gain control of himself, only to realize his bulge in the front of his breeches could give away his thoughts.

"William, if I may call you William," said Madge, "I believe that our business is better suited for discussion in private, where the ears of ruffians and rogues cannot filch any secrets." With a flourish of her parasol, she called for the landlord and instructed that a meal to be taken to Sir William's room, along with a bottle of French champagne and paper, pen, and ink. They would eat in one hour. "Let us take a walk in the evening air and allow that juvenile manhood of yours to subside," she whispered to him as she turned and left the bar.

They walked around the town center, where it appeared all sexual undercurrents were put aside. He spoke of his family's shipping interests and, with abandon, explained his ideas for moving the family into the business of food. He displayed a youthful, foolish recklessness in revealing his unsolicited business thoughts to a woman he had known so briefly But, she read the excitement in his voice and encouraged it. In return, he learned of her business empire. Small though it was compared to the Royal Shipping Line, she showed remarkable business prowess and was clearly a power to be reckoned with. It soon became evident that between them, they had similar ideas for future business opportunities. By the time they returned to the Duck and Feathers, her arm was looped firmly through his. He knew now that she was forty-one, and this only served to further arouse his ardor. He felt the electricity. But did she? There were no signs, and she gave none as they entered the inn's small reception area. She instructed the meal to be held until she called for it. The Landlord advised that paper and pens were already in the room, along with the champagne that they had requested.

Madge led the way to his chamber. As they stood outside the door, she smiled at him and said, "No, I have never been in this establishment and it doesn't seem like you have been in many like it either. Public houses usually have only one room they would allow a gentleman of your stature to stay in, and it is always at the rear of the top floor for privacy. In the future, your family will always be welcome at my home." With a flourish, Sir William opened the door and stood aside for her to enter, anticipating a lively evening. He was not sure if she was all business or, if his charm could move her in a more personal direction. He was not prepared for what was to happen next.

She closed the door, turned the lock, and, as she turned back, she slowly untied the ribbon that held her feminine lace bodice. As the ribs stitched into structure loosened, her breasts fell. She shook off the top and lifted her camisole to reveal the most magnificent breasts William had ever beheld, not huge, but ample, and each was supplanted with a rich, dark, ruby nipple standing erect. He thought, 'they are waiting to be kissed.' She interrupted his thoughts with, "Are you going to just stand there and ogle."

"Miss Duggan er….. Madge, I am not ogling. I have seen many such a sight, but none that can compare. I'm sure I don't know what to do."

"Then let me lead you." She held her hands out toward him. Without taking his eyes from her heaving breasts, he approached. 'A woman in control.' This was a different experience for William. Madge pulled him to her. She took his hands and placed them on her breasts as she felt for his breeches' belt and discovered he was already aroused. "My, my, we are quick out of the gate, aren't we?" William could not answer. As they fondled each other, they moved toward the bed, by which time she had his breeches around his ankles and his manhood, although not big, was hot, swollen, and damp, in her hand. They stood beside the bed, exploring each other. William tried to turn Madge around to push her on the bed. She resisted. His fingers found their way into her warmth. He moved close to place the tip of his erection between her legs, seeking entry. She did not allow it. She stopped him, by pushing him away and onto the bed. He lay on his back, his feet still entangled in his breeches, hung over the edge. His erection pointing upward, she gently pumped him until he fired his seed into the air, and she laughed. He was not disappointed but wanted more. "Let me pleasure you Madge, I'm sure I can."

"I believe that you may be able to but, I never tryst someone that I do not know if I can trust. I do not make a habit of bedding men. You must give me time. You must earn that trust," she said with a teasing tone. "Tonight, we shall start to build our relationship."

"Believe me Madge, your reputation precedes you. Are you sure that this is what you want?"

"What reputation? Who have you been talking to about me?

"Oh, don't misunderstand. You are held in the highest esteem. I would not want to do anything to sully that reputation."

"I learned a long time ago that when it comes to men, I don't believe that anyone can ever be sure. You shall never be in a position to do anything to me that I do not allow you to do. Do you understand that?"

"I do, at least I think I do. It sounds like you want to be in charge of things."

"Just in charge of my own life, and that's not a request, it's a condition."

"It sounds fine to me." William was getting interested in this woman's personal strength. It aroused his curiosity.

Madge continued, "I think that I am willing to take this risk. It is time that I moved on with my private life. We can bed each other, until such times as it has run its course. Hopefully we will move on to another level in our relationship. One that can survive all others."

Chapter 10

They sipped champagne and talked long into the night. William spoke of his observations with regards to feeding the masses. With each idea he put forth Madge would elaborate and build upon it to make it better. As they talked, discussion turned to the various ways of dealing with the large volume of products that arrived into the country. They exchanged ideas for ways to become involved in the potential changing of the manner in which these products, namely food, were made available to the masses with limited funds. Idea upon idea began to merge into viable plans. It soon became evident that they shared similar hopes and aspirations and that they could possibly work well together. While they were agreeing to forge a partnership both their demeanors became more relaxed and warmer towards each other. Fire embers slowly turned to black and they found themselves in bed. Williams' hand found its' way to her feminine warmth, only to have it pushed away.

"There will be no intercourse until I deem it right," said Madge softly. "It will be the right time soon."

"Would you care to share with me where your strength and determination come from?"

"Can I deem it to be the right time?" asked William. "Yes, you could, but not with me. I am in control of my body, not you, or indeed any man ever again will make that decision for me, no matter how charming, handsome or title bearing they may be.

"Would you care to share with me where your strength and determination come from?"

"Life. Just from life. If you go through life's trials and tribulations without learning something, then more fool you."

"Well, you certainly don't appear to be anybody's fool. Do you care to tell me more about yourself?" She did.

***

Madge told William of the time she had been discovered watching her mother and the local priest as they gasped in unison with each thrust. Father O'Shea, the most respected of the local Catholic clergy, and her mother were fornicators. At least that's what the bible would call them. The year was 1815. The pair of fornicators, for they were not lovers, discovered Madge watching, and Madge was stunned at the furious torrent that befell her. While acting innocent to what she had witnessed, she knew from the village lads what fucking was, but she bet none of them knew her thrill of actually witnessing it. She had never indulged, as she had no time for the coarse demeanor of the boys. She noticed Father O'Shea seemed to be very well endowed, not that she had any frame of reference. Her mother had certainly appeared grateful for his ministrations. Madge's existence was of dubious origins, and the lack of a father placed her mother in a very precarious position. If the village women of Clonmel were to hear what had happened, Father O'Shea would have nothing to fear other than rigorous pursuit from some of them, whereas Madge's mother would be run out of town, if not out of Ireland by the overly pious or jealous womenfolk. Madge was kept under close watch at the rectory as her mother and the priest tried to work out what to do about her. The very first night she slept at the rectory the priest came to her room in the dark of night. Madge was awakened by the man's hand under the blankets, touching her inner thigh near her pee pee, as she called it.

Startled, she spoke first, "What are you doing?"

"I'm giving you God's blessing in a special way." All Madge could think to say was "Why?"

"Because it was God that had you see your ma and me. I was giving her the special blessing, my child. I believe that God wants me to bless you."

"You was fucking, me ma - that's not God. That's you and yer willie. Fucking ain't no blessing. It's what gets girls with a baby. I don't want no baby. You, try's to fuck me and I'm going to tell all the lads, that's what I'm going to do."

Quickly the hand was removed accompanied by the admonishment, "If you are telling anyone, my child, it's your ma that'll be sorry, not me. Your ma and them other fatherless bastard children she has, will be."

"Then I'll tell me ma. What do you think of them apples?" The priest stormed out of the room. The next morning brought a furious tirade down on Madge, from her mother.

"Trying to fuck the priest, you shameless little brat? You're not old enough to even think about it."

"But ma, he tried to fuck me!"

"I knew you'd say that. Father O'Shea told me you would say that. Your mouth should be washed out for such disgusting things.'" Madge knew at this point there was no use in protesting any further. Within the week, during which Madge was kept within her mother's sight at all times, Madge overheard Father O'Shea's conversation with her mother. He was telling her that a Mick Duggan of Dungarvan, had a thriving business in the port of Southampton connected to shipping, had expressed to a Father O'Shea, of Dungarvan, who happened to be the one of his brothers, that he was in search of a good Irish lass to wed. Within that fateful week, Madge's betrothal had been arranged and announced, and she had been shipped off to another Father O'Shea the third brother in Southampton. This Father O'Shea was yet a third brother. It was the third Father O'Shea. He was one of three O'shea brothers who were all priests that she was to stay with, pending the upcoming marriage. Three brothers, all fathers, what a happy coincidence, for some, not, as it turned out, for Madge.

The marriage turned out to be a brutal variation of her mother's life. Virginity, dignity, and all hope for Madge seemed to have been left in the care of Saint Patrick back in Ireland. The wedding ritual, ritual as opposed to ceremony, bordered on barbaric. It was more of a drunken display of bad manners and poor breeding. Mick Duggan was indeed a successful man, but his rise to prosperity had come on the backs of, and spilled blood of, others. His bullying fists were his persuasion, his notorious drinking his downfall. At fourteen, Madge looked toward a marriage as a means of escaping her lot in Ireland, and the idea of sex, so enjoyed by her mother, held promise. But promise it was, and nothing else. Mick was twenty years older than Madge and twice her size. He controlled her days by working her at his business long into the night, having her manage his bookkeeping and any other task he deemed necessary. He controlled her nights by forcing her to accompany him in his carousing in local public houses. Many a night he hired men to help her get him home, drunk and legless, and many nights she found herself left alone in a public house as Mick went off with his latest conquest. She frequently had to fend off drunken advances from the opportunistic men Mick had assigned her to. This went on year after year, never getting any better.

One horrendously stormy black night in 1835, as Madge was walking with Mick, across a narrow canal pathway in the docklands, she pondered that if slavery had truly been abolished two years earlier, why did she feel like a slave with no chance of freedom? The rain ran down her face and straggling hair into the neck of her garments, soaking her to the bone. She stumbled, as her tightly laced boots caught in the front of her long, wet, dragging dress. She grabbed for Mick to steady herself, but still she fell down onto her knees, sliding in the mud, grabbing at Mick's heel. As he lifted his leg to shake her from his trousers, his other outstretched foot lost traction and he slid forward, grabbing at air. His face dropped down into the thick mud, sinking until only his ears stuck out. He pulled his face up, coughing and spluttering, and as he shook his head, he lost what little balance he had left. As he jerked to catch his breath, he hit his head on a stone abutment and disappeared from view with an almost inaudible splash. Madge sat atop the embankment and watched Mick slide down until he lay still, face-down in the water's edge, his head resting on the stone blocks. Madge walked away looking for help. It was too late. The accidental death, as it was ruled, was mourned by none and in fact, welcomed by many.

The dilemma Madge then faced was a welcome challenge. She had observed over the previous twenty years that while Mick was no saint, he was cunning and clever. He dealt with everyone in business by force or coercion. He had taught her that everyone had their own perception, and whether you liked it or not, that was their reality. She had seen him succeed in many situations because he knew how different people would react in any given situation. Madge smiled as she told William that manipulation is no different than friendly persuasion, if handled correctly. "Society has us women on a pedestal," she said. "We have our place, and as long as men believe that we accept that, we can tread their world with a strong advantage."

Through careful manipulation and mending of some of the relationships Mick had destroyed, she offered the perception of reward to his injured parties for having stuck by Mick regardless of his treatment, while at the same time garnering the obligatory aid offered to Mick's poor widow. Many offered support to her that they would not have dreamed of offering her dead husband. "The Madge Duggan you saw today, being courted and having favors curried, was my business persona," she said. "At times like this, while I lie with a real gentleman, and I mean gentle man, I feel I might be able to trust. You may be curious as to why I may be trusting you, when I have only known you these past three hours. I met your father a long time ago, a few months after he took possession of his first new ship, The Duke of Marlborough. My husband Mick, had found the ship unfinished due to lack of funds and passed this knowledge on to your father. Mick, had a successful business relationship with the Royal Shipping Line until your father discovered that Mick had caused the financial hardship that left the nearly completed ship unfinished. Your father said that someone who would destroy one man's reputation to curry favor with another was a disaster waiting to happen, and that he did not intend to be around that type of disaster. I have never met anyone that treasured his reputation that way. I would like to think that you have some of that quality in you. I had never been exposed to well-born people, and the politeness and respect that your father had shown, even though I was a mere slip of a girl, has never left my mind. "I think it was the professional, firm, respectful way that he conveyed his displeasure with my husband that made its mark on me."

"I am aware that reputation is everything in business these days," William interjected.

"Reputation is everything in life!" Madge was firm in her conviction. "Let my reputation be a warning to those who would do me wrong I say. I may not have been high born," Madge said, "but I believe a lady is a state of mind, an attitude. I demand of gentlemen that I be accorded respect, and I will give respect in return."

"So, you never remarried or desired a man?" asked William.

"Men, I have desired, but not acted upon. As for remarrying, I carry no illusions about what you men creatures are like. I am steadfast in never being slave, subservient, or dependent on a man."

As they lay in the warm, flickering shadows, thrown off by the gaslights, William was quiet. Madge's warm, soft hands had been gently exploring his shoulders and neck, and down his spine. A gentle squeeze of his buttocks followed by a gentle grasp of his manhood kept his mind from other things. Soon, she was in control, and William was experiencing a type of sex he had never imagined. Every time he tried to enter her, she controlled his entry by rising up. It was so different from shagging the wenches, as he had in the past. Use them selfishly, then cast them aside. Finally, Madge sunk down onto him. She shuddered one more time, holding an almost statuesque pose before collapsing on his sweating, heaving chest. Silence ruled, only to be broken by a sound running through William's head: 'William my love, William my love, William my love.' Madge rolled off of his spent frame and lay beside him.

"You said, 'William, my love," William whispered quietly.

"For that brief moment in time, you were my love. Does that bother you?"

"Is this for just a brief moment?" he asked somewhat subdued.

"I can never belong to a man, never be a wife, or a mother, again," said Madge. "The beatings Mick gave me left me unable to bear children. One month before I was to give birth to our son, Michael, Mick kicked me in a rage of jealousy, claiming the child was not his." She sighed. "Who knows what tomorrow may bring? Perhaps we shall be lovers forever. Who knows? I do know that you shall one day have a wife and family. Where will I fit in? Who can tell?"

William turned on his side, took hold of her hand and said, "I wish you could have met my mother. She passed away unexpectedly earlier this year. I think she would have liked you."

"Were you close to her?" Madge asked.

"Yes, I suppose so. One always loves one's mother, doesn't one? I never got to spend much time with her. I am sad about that."

"Why didn't you spend much time with her? Where was she?"

"Oh. No, she was at home. I have spent most of my life in boarding schools and college since I was very young."

"I have never fully understood the rich and how they treat their children. In Ireland we keep our children very close, even into their adulthood."

"I thought you said your mother sent you away to be married. That doesn't sound very close to me."

"I don't blame her as much as I do the church, the priest and the situation. Mother was in a difficult position in our village. I try to understand that. That's why I will never let a man control my life again, priest or not." William embraced Madge and held her close with a tight, protective hold. Madge let out a deep sigh of surrendered comfort.

Soon, dressed once again, they sat in silence by the fire's dying glow and shared the champagne. There was a peaceful silence as both their minds were busy. Madge turned to the small desk and folded some sheets of paper and put them in an envelope, which she closed after satisfying herself that it felt bulky enough. Pulling her bag aside, she withdrew a seal and wax and sealed the envelope closed. She wrote on the front the name of her lawyer, Mr. Pettigrew of Mesrs. Pettigrew Lumley, and his address. In a serious, business like tone she said, "I am proposing that we share our ideas for new ventures. If we find common ground, we shall join forces to maximize our chances of success. I require that once we enter discussions all others shall be precluded from joining our venture unless we both agree, and we commit not to take any ideas, that come from our partnership, and develop them under our own banner." She straightened her dress and rang the service bell before continuing. "As we both see some potential in feeding the masses, let that be our first endeavor." William nodded in agreement as he wondered what she was doing with the envelope. The door was gently tapped. Madge stood and opened the door. Then she turned to William and said, "Sir William, our business is conducted." She turned to the boy, who had entered. "Boy, here is sixpence. Take this package to the address on the front. It is by the south dockside. Now, be off with you." The boy bowed, took the envelope, turned and ran off. Madge turned to William and said,

"We cannot have the boy running off with an empty envelope, it might arouse his curiosity. We can have our lawyers draft an agreement in the morrow. I shall expect you at my place of business at 10 a.m. to meet with Mr. Pettigrew." With that she strode out of the room.

William sat in silence as he finished the bottle of champagne. Thoughts spun in his head like the fine threads of a spider web getting foggier and denser until he slid into a state of sex and alcohol induced euphoria. As men are want to do, his post sexual glow became his sleeping draught. The last embers of the fire went out, removing the last traces of light from the room.

Chapter 11

When the London daily newspapers began to focus on the pending marriage of Queen Victoria and Prince Albert, William was not exactly excited so much as fascinated by the huge public outpouring of the common man toward those who looked down on them. This marriage was going to change the royal household from that of Hanover to Saxe-Coburg and Gotha. Sir William's father could talk of nothing else. He even had hopes of being invited to the wedding. Indeed, the entire St. John-Brown family, were among the privileged few who got to attend the great wedding in Westminster Abbey on February 10, 1840. William St. John-Brown could not hide the fact that the awesome spectacle caught even him in its sheer magnitude. He felt as if London was calling him away from the family seat in Bath. As he sat, quietly observing the event, he reflected on the direction that his life was taking. Suddenly, a thundering roar of applause came from the crowd as Queen Victoria, solemn of face, entered the great abbey, following in the footsteps of many kings before her. Slowly, she glided toward the throne placed before the altar. The whole aura of Westminster Abbey was now pungent with pomp, awe, tradition, and spectacle. William crashed out of his reverie long enough to be absorbed into one of the great moments in history. His father's elbow jabbed him in the ribs as he whispered, "Welcome back, from wherever you were."

"I was thinking about how widespread and huge the festivities are across the country for this wedding. I don't believe the country has ever been this enthusiastic, of its own accord, for a royal occasion."

"The people have always loved their Royal Family. It's what we English do well."

"No father, it is like the common man worships the very ground Victoria walks on. She is only human after all."

"*Queen* Victoria. I'm not sure worship is the right term but we all hold her in high esteem, my boy. It would do you well to do likewise. Wonderful woman, wonderful woman." The two men sat in silence as the ceremony slowly wound its way to its conclusion. The peeling of the abbey bells broke the spell and England burst into one of the biggest organized celebrations ever seen in the country. City, town and village streets were thronged with partygoers. Dignitaries from foreign lands, from commonwealth counties, and heads of state from everywhere descended on London like bees to honey. The revelry continued for a full week before life started to settle back to normal. Signs of adoration dwelled in at least one corner of every home, office, shop and factory. Huge portraits, souvenir mugs, glasses, tea towels, the list was endless. The industrial revolution had given birth to poorer classes being able to collect memorabilia, and that they did with great enthusiasm.

Chapter 12

The cool evening air had seemed to invade every crook and crevice of the carriage, and William vowed he'd never to use a common carriage again. The company owned numerous carriages, and he intended to have his father place one at his permanent disposal, or so he'd thought. Upon his arrival back at 54 Royal Crescent Bath he was surprised to find a summons to attend his father at the earliest opportunity. Though William generally acted on his own, his father ran the Royal Shipping Line with an iron fist. William could not recall anything that should cause such attention. He sent his houseboy to his father's house, which stood on the opposite side of the crescent, with a hastily scribbled note advising that he would attend his father after dinner, at seven o'clock. This was eating away at William. He knew something was amiss, and yet nothing presented itself. That evening, his growing concern about what his father wanted was playing on his mind and it affected his appetite. He dismissed his butler and maid for the evening and noticed on the front page of the morning's paper that Beau Brummel had passed away. Syphilis was the reported cause. For a brief moment William's mind returned to his past sexual dalliances and pondered where Madge Duggan may fit into his private life. He stood and admired himself in the hallway mirror. The black, full-length overcoat with the astrakhan collar and his white Chinese silk scarf topped off with a black beaver top hat had him cut a dashing figure. William closed the door quietly behind him as he stood on the front step between the huge Mendip stone columns, like those paired on either side of every front door around the entire crescent. They stood as giant white sentinels, reaching up to the fourth-floor eaves, reflecting an ambient light that made them glow. The night air was cool and damp, and yet was more mysteriously inviting than the cold coastal winds. The evening mist settled gently over the tall buildings, gradually masking their rooftops from view. It was invigorating.

Lighting a cigar, William trod the great slabs of black granite that formed the steps that traversed the open green grass space that sliced the crescent in half. He noticed the light in his father's study was on. All the other lights in the house were dimmed. This meant only one thing: His father was disturbed about something, and the parlor was no place for discussion. Since the death of William's mother some six months ago, his father's disposition had changed. He'd become more combative and quicker to lose his temper. William's mother had never lived to see his admission to the House of Lords.

William had no illusions about his fortunate position in life. At twenty, to be the youngest ever to be admitted to the House of Lords, the heir to the Royal Shipping Line, and one of the principal shareholders in Lloyd's of London meant things were going well for him. Then there was Madge. '*Madge. Oh my God,*' he thought. '*Madge, that's what this is all about tonight. How the hell does father know?*' Pausing on the front top step of his father's house, he saw the front door swing open. The upstairs maid bowed and stood aside for him to enter. It struck him as unusual for the upstairs maid to be carrying out a duty that was clearly not hers. After taking his hat, cane, and coat, she directed him to his father's study. When the parlor maid opened the study door, he saw his father standing with his legs spread apart, balancing himself before the fire in an openly hostile stance. With a nod from William's father, the maid went over to the intricately carved sideboard and poured a brandy, picked up the mahogany cigar humidor, and offered both to Sir William. Having just thrown his unfinished cigar away, he selected another, took the drink, and waved the maid aside. She quietly left the room.

The aroma of burning coal mingled with pungent cigar smoke as it hung in layers. William looked around the room, taking in the overabundance of finery and heavy decoration. '*There's nothing in this room that didn't come on one of our ships,*' he thought, as he sensed his father staring at him. Breaking the silence his father said, "Welcome home my boy, I trust all is well with our business." He looked down at his feet and then fixed a firm stare into William's eyes before commencing. "You know my position on integrity. It is with great concern that I bring this subject up."

"Father, I have no idea what you are talking about."

"If you wait, I am about to explain. People are quick to believe what they see, no matter how untrue, or true it may be. It is important that we are always honest with each other. I took care of a problem that you have created, the like of which I never want to be involved with again." William was perplexed and becoming agitated.

"What problem is that father?"

"What does the name Adelaide, Adelaide from Marchbrooke mean to you?" William suddenly began to feel uncomfortable. He said nothing and waited for his father to continue. "Damn you, boy. You got the girl pregnant. She turned up here with the start of a swollen belly, seeking you. Looking for what I neither know, nor care. Consider yourself lucky your mother was not alive to witness the degradation."

"What did you do? You said that you took care of the problem?"

"Paid her off, you nincompoop! Handsomely I might add. Had her sign a document I drafted, denying you were the cause of her pregnancy. Well, she couldn't sign, she made her mark. Play, if you must, within your own field my boy. Stay away from the common folk, they can be your undoing." He threw a document on the desk in front of William. "Don't bother to read it, she won't be back. This type of behavior has to stop. The family business does not need this foolishness. Keep your peccadillos to yourself." William made no move to respond. His father picked up the document and put in a drawer. Folding his arms across his chest he continued, "Well boy! Speak up, what do you have to say?"

Recalling the stinging slap on his face received from Adelaide, William, with a smirk, replied, "Father it was nothing, just a pointless, meaningless, moment of aberration."

"One look at her belly and it obviously meant something to her. Though I believe it to be about money. Scared her off a bit, I did. Next time though it will be on your head, not mine or the family's. Do you understand that?"

"Yes sir, I don't think you will see any further behavior of that sort from me."

"Indeed. Don't think, boy, make damn sure. Well, that's enough of that. Don't ever bring anything of that nature to this house again." There was a confrontational silence hanging in the air. William decided to let his father make the next move, for, he was sure, there was more coming. His father spat out the next question with obvious hostility.

***

"*Now*! Exactly what business do we have with Pettigrew Lumley?"

William stared his father in the eye and calmly replied, "Sir, we do not have any business with them. *I*, have business with them."

As William tried to decide what he should share with his father and what he should not, his father said, "We will not undertake any business with the Duggan's under any circumstances. I have not built this business on anything other than the purest of motives, the finest integrity, and I, we, enjoy a reputation that I will not have besmirched by that man, you, or anyone else. I don't know what he thinks he is doing, trying to reconnect with the Royal through you, but it will not..."

William interrupted his father, "Mick, Mr. Duggan has been dead some six years or more. His widow enjoys a remarkably stellar reputation and it appears that she is supported and admired by many people in the shipping industry. Father, I believe the widow Duggan possibly holds the key to what could be the next lucrative opportunity to increasing our fortunes." At this, William's father's shoulders noticeably relaxed. He took a wooden taper and lit it from the hearth, offering to relight the end of William's cigar. They both puffed a huge cloud into the air and settled into the deep, plush, wing-backed fireside chairs. The fire's, bouncing flames, lit up the ruby golden glow of the brandy as they tipped their glasses to each other. The cigar smoke hung in layers just as the smoke does from burning autumn leaves in the cool, still evening air.

William proceeded to discuss his experience in Southampton, discreetly omitting his liaison with Madge. The conversation continued well into the night, William's enthusiasm energizing his father, who promised his support. William told him of the plan and some of his own thoughts elaborating on it. One being that Tom Smith's concept of individually-wrapped sweetmeats could be used to reduce the huge amounts of sugar, tea, and general day-to-day requisites that people were forced to purchase, into small, easier-to-handle packages that common folk could afford. The concept appealed to his father. "You seem to have given this some considerable thought."

William replied, "Father you had to see the masses of common folk at Victoria's celebration."

"You mean, *Queen* Victoria, don't you?"

"Yes, yes, *Queen* Victoria. If we could profit a penny, just a penny off each one, each day of the week, the numbers are immense. Food for the working classes is where the huge profits are going to come from in the future."

"You seem to be enthused by this new concept."

"Just the food the government is buying for the army and navy, that alone shows the potential. You know what we sell to the government every year."

"Then I wish you well. Keep me informed. It will give me a refreshing change to follow your own first enterprise. Remember to protect yourself from the unscrupulous."

"I am going ahead with the idea and it is separated from 'The Royal Shipping Line' for now."

When William's father stood to bid him goodnight, just before pulling the servant's bell, he put his arm around William's shoulder and said, "I hope this woman, or, indeed you, intend to keep this a *business* relationship, my boy. We should be looking toward a lady of breeding to honor your mother's memory, when you are ready."

"Sir, I have no intention of marrying at this time," said William, "and I shall choose a lady to honor yourself, mother, and, most importantly, myself."

"I sense a little defensiveness there, William. Just be careful. You speak of this woman with fervor, for someone you have known for such a short time. Women are wily creatures. Keep in mind, in today's world, just where a woman belongs. It is not in the business world, much less one of her kind in our family."

William wended his way across the dew laden grass of the green in the early hours of the morning to find the mist had become a light fog that hid his own home just across the way. He felt as if his life was taking on a new direction. He kept thinking of food, large amounts of food available to the masses, yet only small amounts of money. It occurred to him that small shopkeepers and costermongers, were forced to buy supplies in block and volume. It was they who apportioned it into smaller amounts for the poor to buy. The whole venture with Madge was making more sense and its huge potential was taking hold of his imagination.

Chapter 13

The contracts prepared by Pettigrew Lumley were sworn to, and signed by William as promised, without change. It had been well over a month and the whole of England was still recovering from the festivities of the Royal Wedding. William's father concluded that the poverty and unpleasant aura of London made him less willing to visit it in the future, deciding that William could take care of family investments and business there and at Lloyd's. He marveled at how the grounds at Hampton Court could be kept so well with the workhouses and factories in such close proximity. Street beggars and prostitutes seemed to appear on every corner. Even the carriage drivers had to fend them off with their whips.

Besides, it was very clear to William's father that the business his son was contemplating had huge potential. The network of railways grew daily, and saw people in London from all over the south of England. Even the visitors to the Royal Circle's great homes were becoming more frequent. William was right about change coming. He had great expectations for his April meeting with Madge, and had maintained a self-imposed celibacy in expectation of her pleasures. His abstinence had been in response to a recent situation that he was trying to wipe from his mind. On a visit to Southampton, he had stopped in at the Duck and Feathers to find that the young pregnant girl, Adelaide, had been removed from her position. Upon questioning the man further, he was told by the landlord, 'She was caught stealing. Stole a fine pair of kid gloves from a guest. We could not find out who they were taken from. Then would you believe she gets herself in the family way. Not good for business.' William was shocked and asked, "If she is with child how is she managing?"

"Don't know, don't care. Got enough on me own plate," was the curt reply. Walking away from the public house, William's thoughts troubled him until thoughts of Madge took over in importance and pushed those into the background. He was just relieved it had come to nothing more than an embarrassment.

***

Madge and William met at the Savoy Hotel, one of London's finest, and over the next three days discussed their arrangement. They spent time in the new London store, Harrods, which catered to the large city, metropolitan households, and country estates. Harrods was described as a department store, with a department for everything from food to lavish soirees, from goldfish to elephants, from sewing desks to elaborate antique furniture. Madge proposed that if an establishment as opulent as this could be so successful when limited to the very wealthy, then surely a similar method, on a more affordable scale, would attract poorer folk and produce a much larger volume of business. A place where they could buy almost everything they needed at low prices. William agreed that this successful business model could easily be applied to the other end of the wealth scale. So many cities across the country were now connected by rail and could be utilized for their benefit. As their excitement grew for their project, Madge told how she had used one of her smaller warehouse sheds in Southampton to break down large shipments of sugar, salt, pepper, cinnamon, dried beans, biscuits, nutmeg, dried dates, and figs into smaller sizes as they arrived off the Royal Shipping Line ships. They both became aware that they had to decide upon an appropriate, business name. "While we are willing to sell to anyone," said Madge, "we must not do it at the disdain of anyone."

"Indeed," said William. "What if we state on the printed packaging, 'By appointment to the Royal Shipping Line'? That way, we use the word *royal* without saying the royal family uses the products, and it is obvious how the masses connect to royalty. Madge's reply was firm and decisive. While she liked his suggestion for the label, she offered her own thoughts.

"People associate food with women, as they prepare most of it. I think a simple name such as, 'Mother's Fine Foods' makes a clean statement."

William responded with, "I know all about the women thing, but I still think we should use the 'by appointment' line. It impresses people."

"Firstly, I am not interested in impressing people. I just want to sell them products and make a profit. Secondly, I know your father is very heavily engaged in the 'Royal' thing, and believe me I have every desire to please your father. I respect him, but to be very honest, there is a huge part of the population that is far too busy with the business of surviving, Queen or no Queen."

"So, what are you saying, don't use 'by appointment' at all?"

"I'm saying, this is your venture not your father's. We can gain his approval later when we have succeeded, by adding the '*by appointment*' thing."

"I'm not suggesting it for my father's sake. I think it is a good sales angle."

"Again, right now, there are more people worried about feeding their families than there are wanting to curry favor with the queen."

"Alright, I see your point." William resigned himself to Madge's persuasive style.

"In the early days we should be appearing to be on the side of the poor people. When we have established our financial goals, we can then add 'by appointment'. Then it would look like even the Queen approves. It may be slower but I want to get the largest customer count as we possibly can, and quickly."

As the noon hour slipped away into afternoon, they relaxed, satisfied, and found themselves alone in the dining room of Harrods. William said what he had been thinking all day, that they should retire to somewhere more private. Madge allowed him to touch her hand across the table, but only briefly, before she withdrew it. William was perplexed. "I thought that we were…." Madge touched his lips with her lace-gloved fingers and whispered, "There will be time enough, but not here, not in Harrods, where walls have ears, waiters have eyes, and gossip is brutal. Call me a carriage and meet me at the Savoy later."

Chapter 14

By the time William's carriage arrived at the bustling forecourt of the Savoy, William had become tired, and was getting irritated by the clopping of the horse hooves and the rattle of the iron rims of the carriage wheels as they bounced on cobblestones. London was noisy compared to the countryside. Seeing the Savoy ahead, he bid the carriage to pull over and alighted, finding himself seven carriages from the hotel's entrance. The cool air revived him. The uniformed doorman was busy scattering begging children from the sidewalk as William arrived. "Sir William," he said. "Good evening to you. There is a message for you at reception, sir." William thanked him and pressed a silver florin in the man's open palm.

Approaching the reception desk, a boy came over to him and held a silver platter, upon which was a small, square envelope with a wax seal on the back. William took the envelope and waved the boy away. Walking to his suite, William smelled the perfume on the envelope and broke the seal, which he did not recognize. The message was simple: "The Cadogan suite. Seven sharp the door will not be locked." He had half an hour until the appointed time. With base thoughts, he went to his suite, shaved, perfumed himself, and donned his fine silk hunter-green britches and his handmade cream silk shirt, over which he wore a cashmere sweater of soft lime green. In the open throat of his shirt, loosely tied, he wore a hand-painted French silk cravat. His light topcoat had tails buttoned at the back and was edged with gold rope twist with tassels. He admired himself in his dressing mirror and patted his hair in place, which was parted down the middle, before heading for the Cadogan suite. The hallways were softly lit by flickering gas lamps, that gave a rich hue to the carpets, and ornately papered walls. The polished mahogany banisters and intricate cast bronze rails, threw sentinel like shadows on the stairs and walls. This fine hotel exuded wealth and elegance.

Standing outside the door of the Cadogan suite, he lifted his hand to knock, then decided against it. The door handle felt cold in his hand as he took a deep breath to quell his fluttering heart. He quietly opened the door and entered. Sitting in front of the window that framed the black night sky, was Madge, in a high-back Queen Anne chair, a sight as erotic as any could be. He turned, closed the door quietly and latched the lock. Turning to face her he stood admiring what he saw. The lady was beautiful. She was elegant, and he knew that he was in love with her. In a blood red lace chemise slightly opened at the front to reveal white stockings held up by a black garter belt, she was a tantalizing picture. The soft pink thighs above the stockings, where should have been nickers, came together in a patch of flaming red hair. Her full breasts were the sight men fantasized about. He felt over dressed as he approached her. He stood in front of her and she leaned toward him. He was becoming aroused. Not a word was spoken as she undid his buttons and lowered his britches. His undergarments now stood out in front of him. She pulled them down to release his stiffness. It flipped up, in a comical salute, as it was released from the material.

Still nothing was said. Madge placed her hands around his buttocks and pulled him close. Her face was level with his manhood, which she slowly enveloped with her warm mouth. She felt him throb inside her. He pulled out of her mouth and he gently lifted her by the shoulders and turned her. Compliantly she followed his direction. Holding onto the arms of the chair, she waited. Deliberately she lifted her own chemise over her back to reveal her buttocks, creamy pinkish white and firm. He nudged her legs apart and moved closer without entering her. He felt her warmth. Remembering her control of him the last time, he slowly backed away, his stiffness flipped up as it became free, he paused before he slid deeply into her, pulling her back onto himself. He had been practicing his self-control when masturbating by holding himself in a firm grip, just as she was holding him now with her tightness from within.

Unexpectedly she spoke. "Just stay there my love, do not move. Make love to me with your mind. Imagine your mind is on the end of your erection." For a few brief moments he stood perfectly still with closed eyes. He felt his passion rising as she tightened her insides and moved slightly, and it came. Out of the blue, like a bolt of lightning, his unreleased passion spurted. He felt himself rise and fall with each firing as he finished deep inside her. When he slowly withdrew, he watched himself exiting, shiny, slippery and still hard. His feeling of bliss, euphoria and sheer joy made his heart pound and his brow sweat. He had never experienced a woman so completely, so tenderly and uninhibited. He wanted this feeling of oneness to never end. Their breathing slowed as they gradually became separated. Madge did not display her own reactions to what had just passed. In an unexpectedly detached manner, she spoke as she was dressing, "I think we should use messengers for our communications, as they will be faster than the penny post. I think things are going to be moving quite quickly for us."

"I am sure they will. The more we discuss the future, the more excited I become about what is going to happen." William turned, as he was about to open the door, he bowed deeply and blew her a kiss as he left. They parted each other's company with an air of respect and gentility, typical of Victorian times. The fast and furious liaison was not what William had expected. It was tender and yet animal. Madge had not seemed as connected as he. Any casual observer would not have suspected what had just passed between them.

Chapter 15

The success of Mother's Fine Foods had exceeded William and Madge's wildest expectations. The initial feedback from the costermongers and small village stores was nothing short of pandemonium. Not one costermonger could complete his route without returning to Southampton for more supplies. None of the initial products met with resistance from the public. Many grocers clambered for a greater selection. At Sir William's father's suggestion, they made contact with Ted Ballard, the master carpenter from Southampton that William had met at the guildhall. He suggested that they commission the building of a production plant on land adjacent to Duggan Ship Chandlers. Much of the product would come right off the Royal Line's fleet into the new building, where the printing presses would run appropriate labels for whatever was required. When Ted Ballard was approached, he was attracted to their idea and made many useful suggestions. He was hired and soon capably ran the construction for an astonishing nine months from beginning to end. His reward was a handsome bonus and the ongoing responsibility of maintaining the plant and equipment. William believed that with Ballard's impressive talents and the loyalty that was developing, it could only benefit them to have this man close by. Although unions, now free of the legal restrictions that had been lifted the previous year, had called a general strike, the relationships that had been formed between Madge, the costermongers and their customers overcame all obstacles. Madge never missed an opportunity to advise William: "We are dealing with common folk, so put your bloody top hat away and get the plum out of your mouth."

William took her jocular manner in his stride as he replied, equally in jest, "I guess you would know more about those types of people than I do."

"Your loss, not mine," was the curt reply.

"I can deal with that as long as we are making our profits."

The sum total for the business in 1844 was a gross income of 750,000 pounds, with a forty percent profit margin. The safety of foods had improved, preserved in glass jars with the use of cork and wax stoppers, but there was still the problem of breakage. While the loss was high, use of these preserved goods gained great popularity, as it enabled the working classes to avoid daily trips for perishables. The clever use of in-house printing enabled Mother's products to stand out from others. Bright pictures assisted those who could not read. Soon, metal containers were starting to replace glass jars due to ease of transport, even though the attraction of seeing the items would never die out. Many of the poorer classes did not trust things they could not see, and that was particularly true of the new 'tin' cans. Even so, Mother's quickly embraced the new technology.

William looked ahead to the growing British Empire and saw huge opportunity in the needs of the many colonies that now formed the Empire. Steam-run machines reduced production costs for the tins. William wanted to start another business producing the cans, but Madge held him back, arguing that the success they were enjoying was on a very predictable path and there was no need for risk. With the Army and Navy buying huge quantities of tinned food, their market was stable. She reasoned, "Food will always be in demand, but tin cans - let someone else take the financial risks facing production. Who knows, something else may come along even better."

"I doubt that," replied William. "There is something about this tin can idea that is very clever in its simplicity. The cost to make it is so low, I think we should get involved."

Madge's tone changed to a strong, assertive style when she replied, "William, there is an invisible line between greed and good business. You will never see that line, but a good businessman knows when to stop without crossing that line. We are making excellent profits doing what we know and if you want to involve yourself in that go ahead. I am not greedy and will not put everything we have built at risk by jumping into every new thing that comes along."

William's pouty reply was, "I might just do that. I consider myself properly lectured. Thank you."

***

Although child labor laws were passed in 1844, there remained a large supply of young men and children willing and able to work. The poor houses and workshops offered nothing more than a meager subsistence. Mother's Fine Food Company, on the other hand, benefited from Madge's approach to business, whereby every employee was treated fairly and with respect. They were fed while they were at work, which, for many was their only meal of the day. With her personality and kindness, she developed a loyal and productive staff.

The product line had grown to thirty products, including syrup, molasses, and five varieties of biscuits. Dates, figs, cake, puddings, spices, oranges, lemons, and other exotic fruit brought the more unique products to the common table. Madge proposed that they reconsider the arrangement they had with the costermongers. Her reason was, "We seem to be taking on more and more costermongers who are self-employed and less and less under our control. It concerns me."

William offered a simple solution, "We already have systems in place and our employees are content, or so it would seem. Why not bring sales people, coster-mongers into the company fold where we would have more control? That could help create more of a family atmosphere among our workers. There does seem to be a 'them and us' feel between employees and independents. These union ideas are worrying to me." Madge appeared to be contemplating the idea. William con-tinued, "As we take on new employees that would deliver products directly from the plant to grocers, I expect that this will be met with some resistance from the independents, but they will soon see that they stand to gain more from this idea."

Madge suggested a unique proposal. "Railways are now well established across the country, and it will be only a matter of time before the costermongers, with their small carts and barrows, will not be able to keep up with demand. We can offer them two options: one, to stay with Duggan's or Mother's Fine Foods with their main trade as haberdashery and household items; or two, to sell off their routes to other entrepreneurs or even hire someone to take over their routes at Duggan's, and then they can join Mother's as supervisors for a direct delivery system. There will be no conflict of interest, and for those who join Mother's, there will be opportunities for promotion."

William followed Madge's comments with, "For each railway station, Mothers' can hire porters whose job it will be to off-load incoming deliveries and get them to the local stores. A lot of these porters can work their duties in a secondary role. They can be railway porters by day and Mother's porters by night." Ideas flew fast and furious between William and Madge. They were both apprehensive about the move but decided to go ahead with the ideas.

Ted Ballard was fast becoming an important contributor to the company's expansion. He frequently proposed innovative suggestions, like adding a central hostelry maintenance building, which could keep all horse and carts in good working order. Shoeing and cart maintenance that were needed in emergencies could be contracted out to local blacksmiths as needed. Many of his proposals were carried out quickly. Sales representatives were employed to open up new customer outlets. Ships grew more efficient and safer with their cargo. Contracts were made with The Royal Shipping line for fast movement of products from nearer ports in the Mediterranean and Europe.

***

Over the next few years, Mother's Fine Foods grossed over two million pounds, and was becoming a household name across the south of England. Everything was running smoothly until 1847, when one of mother's smaller plants that produced products in tin cans experienced a catastrophic accident. The area that became known as Canning Town housed many such small factories. Steam was the main source of power that was garnered from huge central boilers. The heat from the boilers was used to process the food being canned as well as creating energy to run the huge leather belts that operated machinery. This particular cannery operated twenty-four hours a day. The night duty was to maintain the boiler's pressure and clean and ready the facility for the long day shift. It was never properly established who was at fault for an explosion. Sixteen, night shift workers died at 1:00 am as the factory disappeared from the face of the earth. Seven surrounding, similar plants were severely damaged, fortunately only causing injury and no further deaths. Madge found William sitting at his desk with his head in his hands, over a newspaper's blaring editorial headlines.

EXPLOSION
KILLS 16
MOTHER'S FINE
FOODS'
CANNING TOWN
FACTORY
NOT SO FINE FOR SOME

Explosion at Mothers Cont.

In the early hours of this morning an explosion of a Henderson twentyfive ton boiler killed many workers. Among the sixteen killed were seven young boys under ten years old and two girls, eight years old. This horrendous accident highlights the lack of protection and disregard that factory and mill owners have for workers. It is not uncommon to see factory workers die in avoidable accidents around the country. It is becoming more prevalent that we are seeing multiple deaths in single locations. It is time to stop the disregard and abuse heaped on workers, especially our young people. Children should not be allowed to work a sixteen-hour day in intolerable conditions. It is time the workers united and forced the government to regulate these practices.

Public pressure should be brought to bear on the combined wealth of factory owners to aid these victims. The writer was unable to obtain any comments from the St. John-Brown family, and Mother's Fine Foods, owners of this business. It is no surprise that the rich go to ground, to avoid exposure, in times such as these. But rest assured, this paper will not let the matter go so easily. St. John-Browns, Mother's Fine Foods or whoever is morally responsible, take note, we will keep this story in the public eye until you stand up and bear your responsibility. It is time for you to do the right thing.

Madge sat across the desk from William and spoke firmly. "William, look at me. William,pull yourself together. We need to act. Now!"

"What do you mean? Father will be furious that the family name is being dragged through the mud."

"Sixteen workers *died,* nine of them *children,* died in one of our factories and you are worried about your *father*? I am more concerned about the wives and mothers. You get hold of the newspaper journalist and tell him what we are going to do."

"What are we going to do?"

"Mother's Fine Foods, just like its name, Mother's, is saddened by the tragic loss of these lives, particularly the children. We intend to take care of, and provide for, those families left devastated in this tragic time of loss."

"How do we do that?"

"Sometimes, William, you surprise me. Money is what we are going to do. We will do it publicly and fast. Get Ted Ballard over here, *now.* Give him sixteen checks and have him go to each family. He can tell them we will be helping them out until their lives return to normal."

282

"How much shall I give?' In an exasperated tone Madge said, "*I don't know. We could spend time calculating the value of each poor soul, but that will take too long. I want that nasty little journalist present, at each family home when the cheques are handed over, and I want to see it reported in tonight's paper. We have to try and change his attitude towards us. Let's start with one hundred pounds for each family.*"

"Madge, you never cease to amaze me. Thank you. I'll deal with father when the opportunity arises."

"*Forget* about being amazed. *Forget* about your father, for once. Just act quickly to quell what could be a great problem for us.

***

Under Madge's watchful eye, public outcry was averted and skillfully turned into praise for the company's acts of kindness and considerations displayed. There was no evidence that William's private largess, shown to the journalist, had any influence on his about face.

Even in the midst of this trouble, Madge could see that William's strong attachment to her was getting out of hand, and she felt that she needed to redirect his feelings. She needed to stay in control and deflect a potential collision of class distinction barriers. Waiting a respectable amount of time until the attention had died down from the accident, Madge put a plan into action.

Chapter 16

In August of 1847, while staying at one of the St. John-Brown mansions in Bath for the summer season, Madge threw a soiree, inviting the cream of society. It was here she intended to introduce William to a Lady Veronica Chartwell. Madge had spent a lot of time over the previous year seeking a potential candidate for William to marry without his knowledge. Her choice was Lady Veronica. At sixteen, Lady Veronica Chartwell was the elegant, only daughter, of the Chartwells, a family of landed gentry from Kent, deep in the English countryside. Her deportment and confidence were considered the hallmark of fine, young English ladies. Her family owned Chartwell, a country manor where Henry VIII was said to have courted Anne Boleyn. The Chartwells had significantly enlarged the red brick structure into a mansion. With its tile-hung gables, it was known derisively, in society circles as a grand example of the least attractive of Victorian architecture, but that did nothing to impede its popularity. Lady Veronica's parents were no strangers to the elite of London society, and Veronica's reputation made her a prize for any fine gentleman. Her charming, witty, and outspoken manner made her a favorite among the royals, so much so, that she was chosen to be a lady in waiting to Her Royal Highness Queen Victoria.

While receiving her guests, Madgie, as William's father called Madge, had him at her side. Madge had no parents, and proper society functions often required the presence of a man. William's father had accepted the honor, partly because his admiration of her had grown considerably through her friendship with William and the expansion of their business, and also because she told him the purpose of the soiree was to introduce Lady Veronica Chartwell to William. The man was suitably impressed with Madge's recognition of the class distinctions. Acting as host, William's father toasted the guests, including a flattering address to Lady Veronica and her parents. The St. John-Brown's support for the royals helped him bond with the Chartwells. Much of the evening was spent developing a closer relationship with the family, and he included Madge and William in gentle discussions of light topics, as much as he could without appearing pushy. He acted almost fatherly with Madge, no longer seeing her as a threat to his plans for William. William on the other hand, basked in the acceptance of Madge knowing that, secretly, she was his. Still, when guests talked of the beauty and poise of Lady Veronica, William heartily agreed. "I find Lady Veronica quite a charming lady, don't you agree father?"

"Indeed, indeed, don't you think?"

Madge deftly turned the conversation away from his father's direction by saying, "I think she is very comfortable in this company. Quite a lady, befitting of your hospitality, I would say." William's father sensed that Madge was steering the conversation and allowed it to pass without further comment. The evening was winding down and Madge whispered to William's father, "You have done well to plant the seed that I brought to you, in Lady Veronica. You must be careful not plant it too deep. Let William feel he has a part in its nurturing."

"You, Mistress Madge Duggan, are a wily woman. Thank you for guiding me." It was at this point he knew that his family's lineage was not to be threatened by Madge's existence in their lives. At the end of the evening, when the guests had left, Madge, William, and his father had a nightcap, and Madge deftly played politician. Every time his father brought up the subject of Lady Veronica, she would change the subject. She knew better than William's father that William would see through the thinly veiled attempts to draw him out on this matter. She knew William had to arrive at the marriage idea at his own pace. Besides, the seed, had already been planted.

Chapter 17

Robert, Sir William's father had on many occasions had a private audience with Queen Victoria and Prince Albert. Often William would go with him. When his father was in audience, William was able to observe Lady Veronica's demeanor close up, as she was Queen Victoria's lady-in-waiting. While William had felt a growing attachment to Lady Veronica over the last year, it was not the same feeling he had for Madge. Mrs. Duggan, or the Widow Duggan, as she was referred to in the presence of company, went to great lengths to assuage his fears and confusion. "In society, a wife's role does not require love. A wife is required to be respected, and respectful. She is required to run a house in the style and station expected. She is to give her husband children." Madge extolled the virtues and position of Lady Veronica and she started to encourage William to seek Veronica's hand in marriage. She could only see benefits. And as with everything Madge turned her hand to, it happened. William's father became emotional when told of William's plans to marry Lady Veronica, but his joy was tempered severely by the fact that his wife was not alive to share it. He puzzled over which lady could stand beside him at his son's wedding. William offered the perfect solution,

"Why not Madgie…our Widow Duggan? She is well accepted, and besides, who can go wrong with a good-looking woman on their arm?"

"What of possible gossip? Do you think it fitting?" asked his father. "Madgie is young and vibrant. I wouldn't want any unsavory connotations whispered about myself and her."

"It was Madgie who brought Veronica and I together. I think in this situation it is more than appropriate." Suddenly, William started to worry about offending his lover by asking her to be at his wedding. His father very eloquently ignored and calmed his fear, without knowing his son had any.

"You are right, she's a fine friend to the family, and we do have her to thank for the happy event. I know she will be happy to accept the honor." His father was brought back to earth when William told him he had not yet asked Veronica's parents for her hand, or even Lady Veronica herself. It was at this point William's father introduced another spoke to the wheel. It was, he believed, proper etiquette to ask the Queen for her permission, as Lady Veronica was her lady-in-waiting and thus in her service. There were protocols to be observed. "I shall request an audience for that purpose," he stated.

***

The next day, William took off by train for Kent and the family home of the Chartwells. Upon entering the great hall at Chartwell William was greeted by Veronica's father. "Sir William, what an unexpected surprise."

"Please sir, William will do. I have come to speak with you and your wife about your daughter."

"Oh my, what has she done now? She isn't with child, is she?" As soon as the words left his mouth Veronica's mother surprised them both when she said,

"How base you can be. Let Sir William speak his piece before you go jumping to conclusions."

"Well, you know what a little tear away she is. If you come to ask permission to tame her, my boy, you have it." William took a deep breath and spoke, "It is not taming her that I want. I came to seek your permission for her hand in marriage."

"Veronica has spoken well of you. I sense a fondness on her part." Veronica's mother said, "I think it more important that you love her. Do you?"

"I find your daughter to be a fitting candidate to be my wife, and my feelings are strong. Love her? Yes, I think I do. I do know that it will be easy to fall more in love with her as our time together passes."

"My, what a silver tongue you have young William," said Veronica's mother.

"Take her hand in marriage. Take her off our hands is more like it. What do you think of that my dear?" Veronica's father chimed in.

"Nobody needs to take her off our hands dear. How rude you are sometimes." Veronica's mother approached William with open arms and said, "Don't listen to the old bore. He is only happy when he is with his men friends doing whatever it is that they do. Yes, yes, you have our blessing and permission, doesn't he dear?"

"Yes, yes. Does she know about this? Does she agree?"

William responded, "I believe that I have to ask The Queen's permission, as Veronica is in service. I admit to being a little confused to whom I should be asking first, The Queen, you her parents, or Veronica."

"Well, you have crossed one bridge, I would say you only have two left," laughed Veronica's father. "It is for you to decide which one to cross next. Knowing women like, I do, I would think you should discuss this with Veronica herself."

"Martin," he beckoned the pageboy over. "Show Sir William to the library and have Lady Veronica present herself." "Best of luck my boy," he added. Veronica's mother added, "You will stay with us for the night, or however long you wish, I hope."

"I have business in the city tomorrow. But I gladly accept your hospitality for this evening."

"Then we shall see you at dinner," both parents said in unison as William was led to the library.

***

William, while waiting, marveled at the old establishment aura of the library. A musty, cool air of knowledge seemed to emanate from the books. Reaching to select a book he was surprised at the lightness of the tiny hand that touched his shoulder. Turning, he saw Veronica, and he realized that this was the first time that he had ever been alone with her. She appeared taller than she did in a group setting. No clever words came to him.

"Shall I speak first?" she said.

"Yes, yes please do. I am sorry I didn't hear you enter. I was so engaged by such a beautiful library."

"I'm sure mother and father welcomed you to our home. Shall we sit for a while?"

"Yes indeed. There is something very special about this room and I cannot put my finger on it. Tell me what it is."

Veronica smiled, blushed, and said, "I bet you cannot guess."

"And if I do, what do I get?"

"Anything of your choosing that is within my power to give."

"I think," putting his finger to his lips in a pensive gesture, he paused before saying, "I think this room means something very special to two people. Something very private, am I close?"

"Yes" was all Veronica would answer.

"Is, or, has this room been used for something other than what it was designed for?" William was quickly working out how to frame the answer that he thought was correct. "Let's put some words out there for you to respond to so that I may obtain a clue."

Veronica thought for a moment and replied, "No questions just words. I will allow you three words only, and if you get it wrong, what do I get?"

"Anything of your choosing that is within my power to give," William replied with a lilt of laughter in his voice, as he threw her phrase back at her.

"Then go ahead," she said.

"Love, intimacy," then, without waiting for her reaction, he quickly added, "sex...so give me your answer." Veronica knew he had worked it out. In a slow deliberate tone, attempting to titillate Veronica, William said, "This room has been a secret place where two people, possibly lovers, possibly more, indulge in their desire, or fantasies of an intimate nature, away from prying eyes."

Veronica shrieked with laughter that seemed to bounce off the books and walls as it echoed in his ears. She said, "William, my dear William, you have such a polite, delicate way of phrasing things. Mother and father like to fuck in here." Taken aback, by the coarseness of the reply and that his little game had backfired on him, William asked, "How do *you* know that?"

"I've seen it. Martin, the pageboy, once showed me a spy hole the servants use to see if the room is empty before entering to clean up. He showed me my mother and father. They were going at it."

"You were not shocked?" asked William.

"Well, I was a little shocked. I know about sex because I read a lot. I have been around the stables and the sheep, so I knew what was happening."

Without thinking, William, asked, "Have you had sex?" Quickly he added, "not that it is any of my business."

"Not very delicate, are you?"

William went to apologize and Veronica raised her hand to interrupt him, "No I didn't mean that rudely. You are just so forward. To answer your question, I am still intact. I think, as they say, a virgin. Why, does that bother you?"

"No, indeed it does not. It makes the subject that I came here to discuss with you all the more special."

"And what subject may that be?"

William moved his chair closer to her and reached out, taking her hands in his. "We have spent a lot of time together and every time we part, I feel a little loss. That bothers me."

"Me too, I have an emptiness."

"I want to see more of you. Have you around more. I want to be special to you."

"You mean permanently, as in married?"

"I have been thinking along those lines and do not wish to impose on you in anyway. I felt that I should seek your permission before I go any further forward with this.

"I think you should kiss me first. I might not like the way you taste, the way you kiss. You might be a brute for all I know." She rose quickly and sat on Williams lap, placing her face upward for a kiss. Holding her face between his palms he softly kissed her forehead, the tip of her nose, and then, very gently, her lips. The kiss lasted while each savored the other. Veronica pulled away and said, "I will consider your suggestion with great earnest. When do you need to have a reply?"

"When you are ready. Just don't keep me waiting too long. I might have to go down my list of waiting maidens."

There was knock on the door and the pageboy entered to inform them that dinner was being served. William held the door open for Veronica to leave the library. As she passed him, she stood on tiptoe and whispered, "Who knows, one day, we, may just fuck in the library."

William was lost for words. Veronica was a feisty little creature. He whispered back, "That may be the prize I choose for getting your question right about the library. I find it so exciting when you use the word fuck."

"I'm sure I don't know why, that's what our grounds staff and farm hands call it," she replied coyly.

Once her parents were told of Veronica's willingness to think about the proposal, discussions took place, and it was decided that her father would arrange with William's father an approach to the queen's equerry to sound out how to go about the situation. The response was simple. While the queen herself did not get involved in such trivial matters, Sir William would have to request an audience with Her Majesty and make the proposal personally. The meeting was duly arranged to take place at the Easter celebrations at Windsor. William was concerned, as Queen Victoria had a reputation for being dour and selfish, and the Chartwells often spoke of how the queen kept her servants and ladies-in-waiting up all hours of the night at her beck and call. Lady Veronica had told them that for every moment of sheer pleasure with the queen, there was a dark moment of frustration and torment, and often regret and humility.

***

When the day for the audience with the queen arrived, William waited patiently. He was apprehensive as he waited to be summoned. Looking around the exquisitely manicured gardens, William saw a pageboy come across a great lawn that fronted the royal residence inside the ancient Windsor Castle walls. The pageboy directed William where to stand. His turn with the Queen was to be next. Soon one of the queen's entourage beckoned William over to join the Royal party. The queen turned to face him.

"Sir William," she said. "We meet again. Wanting a sword for the other shoulder, are you?" She laughed at her own humor. "Your father speaks highly of your endeavors at the Royal Shipping Line among other things you are achieving for my people. Quite impressive. Stand over here in front of me man. The ground slopes that way, I don't like the sun in my eyes."

"Thank you, Your Majesty."

"What is it you wish of me?" The Queen turned her head slightly and whispered to her aide, "As if we don't know."

"If it pleases Your Highness, I wish to ask your consent for the hand of Lady Veronica Chartwell."

"What is it you want with her hand?"

"To marry."

"You want to marry her hand?" The queen watched Sir William's face intently, as he scrambled for what to say next. She smiled.

"I wish to obtain your consent to wed Lady Veronica, Your Majesty."

"What does Lady Veronica think of such an idea?" she asked with a serious expression. "Can she be exchanged, as if a possession?"

"No, Your Highness. If it pleases Your Majesty, I seek your consent before I seek her acceptance of my proposal."

The queen raised her hand and gestured Lady Veronica crossed the lawn and took her place behind the queen. "Come here, child. What say you of this man who wants me to give him your hand? I think he actually wants all of you."

Lady Veronica blushed with a soft, ruddy glow. She curtseyed. "Your Highness, I have not yet decided."

"If I give my consent, what would be your reply?"

"Do you think him a suitable match?"

"My child, he is asking my permission. Let's cross that bridge first, shall we?"

Sir William's face gave away his shock. He looked from one to the other, trying to understand what was happening. Why was Lady Veronica asking the Queen if she thought William was suitable? He had forgotten the Queen's sense of humor. Usually, this was only exhibited in close circles.

"Well, he does have a few ships," said the Queen. "I enjoy his father's company when we are at Bath. He is not a bad-looking fellow. I think we have made him squirm enough. Sir William, name a ship after me and she is yours." The entourage laughed, and the queen waved Sir William away. Lady Veronica came over to Sir William's side and dipped her head in respect.

"Her Majesty will have her moments of humor," she said. "Thank you for rescuing me, William." Without waiting to be asked, she said "and yes, now that we have the proper permission, I would be happy to be your wife." Her face glowed.

Chapter 18

The summer saw Royal Crescent in the City of Bath, a hubbub of excitement. The marriage of Sir William St.John-Brown to Lady Veronica Chartwell was carefully planned to take place at the height of the summer social calendar. It enabled the family to display their opulence and Royal connections for all to see. There would be no doubt, if ever there ever was any, that the St. John-Browns were a powerhouse family. The huge oval grassed and treed area between the two long magnificent residential structures was to be the chosen location for the ceremony and celebrations. The two buildings on either side of the circle stretched from one end to the other leaving an entrance and exit at either end. It was reminiscent of the Roman and Greek amphitheaters. Each building was an arcing terrace of large homes with magnificent stone pillars stretching from the foundations to the roof, four stories high. There would be plenty of room for what was expected to be a vast number of carriages. As huge marquee tents were being erected, the bustle of servants, from the staff of many attendees as well as the St. John-Browns own households, scurried around like worker ants, oblivious to any tasks but their own. There had been much discussion about where the actual ceremony should take place. Madge recalled the conversation with William's father who wanted it to take place in the Bath Cathedral in Wells due to its historic significance and seat of power. It was the seat of the Bishop of Bath and had a grand lineage going back to its early construction in 1175. He felt the majestic and religious power suited this wedding. During a discussion with William, he put his foot down stating, "I want this occasion go down in history. It will be at the Cathedral." Madge's levelheaded comments eventually won him round when she pointed out a more convenient location, Bath Abbey. "Bath Cathedral is some twentytwo miles away. Yes, I know it would create excitement, pomp and be a wonderful spectacle but just think how long it will take the guests to arrive here at the house. Also, Bath Abbey, which is closer, is where your family worships and is just as splendid."

"If we use Bath Cathedral, we can have the reception and festivities the next day." William's father said, firmly holding his ground.

Madge smiled at him, put her arm through his folded arms and said, "I can't imagine a bride wanting to wait until the next day to show off her fine new husband. Us women do like to show off, you know that. Bath Abbey is a stones' throw away. You want history, that started off as a monastery in the seven-hundreds. It was restored in the fourteen-hundreds. Now *that* is history. Edgar, the first King of the English, was crowned there. I could go on, but just think, the wedding in the morning and within a short time everyone gathered here to see what the St. John-Browns can do."

"Madgie, you know how to persuade an old man. So be it, Bath Abbey it is."

***

So much had happened since that conversation. The evening before the wedding, Madge and William were three stories up looking out over the circle from a guest room window. Invited guests had been arriving for a few days and the festive air was mounting. There was a steady stream of messengers returning accepted invitations and tradesmen delivering all manner of supplies. Both William and his father's cooks had hired extra help for the preparations. A band of stalwart men had been engaged to keep the riff raff and undesirables out of the circle. The local constable was ready to oversee his own men to keep the expected crowd in order. Madge put her arm around William's shoulder and said, "You seem on edge. Everything will happen as planned. What ails you?"

"You seem not to be concerned that I am actually going to be marrying someone else tomorrow."

"You know, dear William, that this is the way it has to be. I have made it clear that you must marry within your station, so has your father. This is for the best."

"Do you really care for me so little that you are not bothered at all?"

"How *dare* you say that. If you do not know by now that I care deeply for you then it's your loss. It is because of my love for you that I support the marriage. You and I can never be together, in that way."

"Are you saying our closeness and special moments are over?"

"No. I am not and have never said that at all. I must now take second place in your personal life and we must both be satisfied with that."

"But you don't have to! Just say the word and it can be changed. I will, change it."

"For such an intelligent man, you can be such a fool sometimes. I once told you that I would never be dependent on a man, no matter what my feelings are."

"But you are not dependent on me, nor ever would be. You are wealthy in your own right."

"You speak of financial dependance, I speak of emotional dependence. Believe me when I say, I will be here for you as long as you need me." In an attempt to lighten the mood, she slapped his rear end and laughingly said, "How could I ever do without your passionate lovemaking?" She ran out of the room and down the stairs.

***

Dawn the next day gradually lit the summer morning dew laden grass of the circle. It was like a curtain rising on a stage play. The wedding ceremony took place with military precision. The Abbey had been decorated by many volunteers with an over-abundance of flowers, and ornamentations, making it appear fairytale-like. William stood at the altar accompanied by his groomsmen. Constant glances at the entrance of the abbey door did little to calm him. The abbey's massive organ pipes projected a powerful yet soft background of music meant to calm the anxious. It wasn't working on William. Suddenly, the music paused for a brief moment. The pregnant pause was broken by the organ, playing at full volume, the music Veronica had chosen, the 'Bridal Chorus' from the popular 1850 opera, Lohengrin. This was becoming popularly known as Here Comes The Bride. The entire congregation rose and turned toward the door. A tumultuous gasp of admiration could be heard as Lady Veronica appeared. Much to his own surprise William felt his heart flutter as Lady Veronica came into his view, escorted by her father.

He noticed her spectacular dress with its plunging bodice that must have reached below her navel he thought. The ivory silk pleats of the skirt were narrow at the bodice and flared out to wide bases where they touched the ground. This glorified her tiny waist and gave her the appearance of gliding. The bodice was topped with an exquisite cape style covering of French lace that ended just below her breasts. The sleeves came from under the cape and were of the same lace. They were gathered at intervals with petite silk ribbons holding the material close to her arms. Short cuffs framed her delicate hands upon which she wore matching ivory gloves. A dainty wreath of lily of the valley with tiny rosebuds sat inconspicuously atop her head and held her veil in place. William had to admit to himself that she was a magnificent creature. All thoughts of Madge temporarily left his mind. That was until he saw her with his father. This woman who had come to be such an integral part of his life carried herself with such elegance and posture that nobody could have guessed her humble beginnings.

Before he knew it, the ceremony was over and Veronica and he were on their way to the reception. It was a whirlwind of prayers, sermons, hymns and well wishing. The journey from the Abbey to Royal Circle was lined with spectators. Veronica asked, "I thought our family knew a lot of people, but I cannot believe the number of guests here. Does your family know all these people?"

"I suspect that most people in Bath have been or are affected by our family and the business in one way or another. Look around, can you see all the men watching you? You are so beautiful and you are a radiant picture. If I didn't know better, I could be jealous."

"Why, thank you kind sir," Veronica mocked. "It makes my father's family and connections in our part of the country seem so insignificant."

"Our properties in and around bath, and the spas, have so many visitors for the summer season. I daresay a lot more of them know more about me than I know about them."

Looking up into William's face his wife asked, "do I make you happy today? You make me very happy."

"You make me very proud and so happy I could burst. I am indeed a lucky man." William could see that Veronica was thinking about something, and so prodded her. "What's on your mind? It seems like you are trying to work something out."

"I am. Why is 'that' lady escorting your father?"

"She is not 'that' lady, you have met her. She was the one that brought us together. I expect that you will not refer to her as 'that lady' any more. Madge Duggan is a close family friend. If it weren't for her, we would never have met. I suspect you owe her as much as I do. You will be seeing a lot of her. Since mother died, she has been great comfort to father and indeed to us all. I would thank you to be more accepting of her."

"Is your father her beau? She does seem so much younger than he."

William had to control himself from an angry outburst. He chose his words very carefully. "My parents were extremely close. Father is a man of great integrity and was floundering without mother. Madge helped him put his house back in order when mother was no longer around to do it. He is a private man and would not appreciate such scandalous suggestions of impropriety."

"Oh, William, I meant nothing of the kind. Your father is a dashing man and mistress Duggan such an attractive woman, one can't help but speculate." She emphasized the word '*mistress*'.

"Well don't. Whenever she is in Bath, she assists father with the house, as she did with my house. Now that will be your domain. You should find it in yourself to befriend her. She is not going away." They sat in silence for the rest of journey, watching the crowds from their carriage as it entered Royal Circle.

***

The waiting crowds parted to allow the first carriage of the long procession to enter the circle. In the middle of the left side of the circle, in front of William's house, a large stage had been built for the wedding party. On the opposite side of the circle was a similar stage, in front of his father's house, where an orchestra was in place. Cheerful popular music of the time was playing. Rows upon rows of linen covered tables were set out and occupied by guests. The tables were elaborately set with silver service and candelabra and colorful flower arrangements. It was as if the St.John-Browns were powerful enough to command the winds to stay away. Even if they weren't, the winds stayed away. It was a perfect summer afternoon. In the center of the circle a large wooden dance floor had been assembled for the festivities. Each end of the circle was a small village of tents that housed the food that was being prepared since dawn. Appropriately dressed men and women were hovering among the guests serving food and drink. It was a giant carnival.

When all the guests that were at the Abbey had arrived and were seated at the head tables for all to see, a round of speeches took place. Jokesters and slightly inebriated guests could be heard calling out, in good humor. At one stage, William leaned over and said to Veronica, "Breeding certainly shows, at times like these doesn't it?"

Her reply was simple, "Relax dear William, everyone is having a good time. My papa and mama seem to be enjoying your father and Miss Duggan's company. I think all is going well." William glanced over at his father's table as she leaned over and kissed him on the cheek. The crowd roared their approval.

"Why, I do think you are blushing."

William stood and offered his open hand to Veronica saying, "Come let's let our hair down and dance some."

The reception went long into the afternoon and continued until well after dark maintaining an orderly yet festive tone, the decorum was befitting their place in society.

Chapter 19

William and Madge frequently, utilized his father's study to review the business's progress. Back in 1847, the Fry's Chocolate Factory had found that by mixing cocoa butter with cocoa powder they were able to make a chocolate bar. Mother's Fine Food Company purchased large wholesale amounts of this invention, packaging it under their own label. They found that, the smaller they made the individual packages, the faster they sold. They started giving samples to the grocery stores and village stores as rewards for their purchase of other products. Soon, they offered stock that had gone out of demand as incentives as well. This way, they were able to move stock that had been returned from the costermongers. It surprised them how the clothing and general products were so sought after when perceived to be free. Along with their growth came acceptance. Some of their products were now being used in the royal court, and this gave them the slogan, 'By appointment to HRH.' This replaced their previous line, 'By appointment to the Royal Shipping Line,' which was phased out.

Ted Ballard devised a plan for developing a warehouse and distribution system. He suggested that drivers could be paid a finder's fee for locating sites where a company store could provide more sales than the current local store that was not a mother's store. If the company built one of their own stores close to a current local store and put a manager in that store, they would have control. If that store sold only Mother's Fine Food products, they could pay some of the profits back to shoppers. He believed that everyone would join, as they would be getting free money.

By 1851, with a gross income in of 5.5 million pounds, Mother's Fine Foods was awash with cash, and this year promised the same growth rate. Almost four years had passed and now that William was married, his familial responsibilities were coming to the surface. Neither he nor Madge had taken any money out of the business from the start. William felt now was the time for a big move, so he suggested, "It is about time we took some profit out for ourselves."

"Why? You don't owe money right now, and neither do I. If we leave the funds in the company, we will be able to grow faster, and without mortgaging anything. Cash rich is very strong."

Madge made a strong case, to which William responded, "We should protect ourselves by taking a promissory note each from the company for a certain amount. They can be cashed in should either of us see the need. I do understand your point, so, let's agree not call our notes without each other's knowledge."

Madge liked the idea and said, "Fine, then let's back Ted Ballard's suggestion. His idea was to create a situation where the stores customers could earn a portion of the profits, albeit a tiny portion. It would be heralded as the company sharing their profits. It would create a strong bond of loyalty between each town's store and the customers."

Ted Ballard's proposal was accepted and put into action, with a modification. For the time being Mother's Fine Food Company would operate as it was. They would form a new company whose name would have a more businesslike feel and appeal to customers as they became involved. The new company was to be called The Cooperative Company, or the Co-Op. Mother's Fine Food Company, as the financial backer, owned twenty-five percent of the A-class stock, Sir William and Madge each individually owned thirty percent of the A-class stock, and Ted Ballard was to be given ten percent of the A-class stock, with five percent held for his personal performance rewards. Ballard's stock was tied up, so it could only be sold back to the company itself. At the right time, Mother's Fine Foods, stores were to be changed over to the Co-Op company thereby creating an instant presence of size.

***

1853 saw the Co-Op open ten stores in the south of England, specifically in Taunton, Salisbury, Portsmouth, Southampton, Brighton, Winchester, Market Lavington, Glastonbury, Poole, Yeovil, and Bath, all close enough for word of mouth to promote trade and far enough apart to prevent intra-store competition. While there was opposition from local traders when the first store was opened, very quickly, as news of a new store got out, the nearest grocer would approach the Company to buy out his business. This quelled close competition and put a manager, who knew the local trade in the store. The managers were paid a decent wage and shared in the profits of the store they managed. The properties being purchased in this manner were to be owned by Mother's Fine Food Company, which used the premises as temporary storage places for products being dispersed.

In the matter of private lives, there grew a twisted web of emotional attachments caught up with matrimonial obligations, neatly tied into the strings of Victorian propriety. William loved Lady Veronica as a husband was expected to, and she rose to her role in family life. He spoke with pride of her whenever the subject arose. Lady Veronica took William's father under her protective motherly wing, adequately running both households and brooking no sway from her rules. It was evident to all who lived on the Royal Crescent in Bath that, when Lady Veronica crossed the open park between the two homes, the servants would scurry like ants preparing the nest for inspection. Her breeding had taught her how deal with the subordinates, in or out of her station in life.

Lady Veronica had seen the sadness in William's father's face at her wedding, and thus went to great lengths to become the daughter he never had. For his part, William's father doted on Veronica and accepted her control of his house. This allowed him more time in pursuit of his business interests. It was not uncommon for him to host gatherings at his home. As time passed Veronica had come to supplant Madge in many things in William's father's house.

Over a quiet dinner one evening Veronica asked, "We seem to be seeing a lot of Madgie socially these days. Does your father really need her around so much, or do you need her around?"

"Silly question my dear. Father has never really gotten over mother's death and Madgie was always there for him. It is wonderful that you have done so much in running his house, but Madgie is his friend."

"Then why doesn't he make an honestwomen out of her?"

"She is not that kind of friend. Shame on you for even thinking of her that way."

"They why do *you* need her around?"

"I do not need her around. She is my business partner and a family friend. You sound threatened by her presence."

"No, I'm not threatened. I just wonder why she doesn't have a life of her own. Have her own man, men, whatever."

"She has a vibrant life of her own, in which she includes father. For me it is just a business relationship. She has chosen not to remarry since the death of her husband. That's her right."

William believed he was doing his duty by the marriage, but his love for Madge never faded. Though they appeared on the surface as proficient, effective, and capable business partners, Madge knew William's love for her was a constant torment in his subconscious, as it sometimes was for her. At times, when she allowed her acceptance of class barriers to drop, she would ponder how different it would be if society would publicly accept a union between her and William. From time to time she would overhear whispered comments questioning her place in the St. John-Brown household. She knew that she could never surrender her person as completely as a Victorian marriage required, and she understood that the highly charged sexual encounters between her and William meant different things to each of them. Her love for William was one founded in respect, admiration, and a sincere desire to make his world the best she could. The sex was almost a separate entity between them, stoking both their fires and warming them for their individual lives apart from each other.

William and Madge had become masters at keeping their affair secret. They avoided any implications of impropriety and met often. William's private office suite at the Royal Shipping Line was elegantly furnished with all amenities afforded a gentleman. The boudoir in an anteroom was accepted without comment, as he often would stay overnight in pursuit of business. The same accommodations were annexed to offices at Mother's Fine Foods and Duggan Ship Chandlers, as well as the new Co-Op head offices in London's Blackfriars wharf. The sex was the fire that burned between them and kept them welded together, forging a bond that no man could break.

Chapter 20

The new offices of the Royal Shipping Line had now been open for one year. Pall Mall was fast becoming the home of all of England's major shipping companies. When Sir William spotted the trend, he managed to secure superior accommodations adjacent to the fledgling Peninsular and Oriental Steam Navigation Company.

Back in 1848, the oldest ship in the fleet, *The Princess of Wales*, had been sold. Within the year, she had foundered on the Lizard Sands of Dorset and was lost. The timing could not have been better. The move to London from Bristol had put the company in the heart of burgeoning economic growth. Sir William and his father began to acquire the ships identified by William. It took them five years of waiting for the right opportunities. By waiting, they managed to acquire all six ships at a cost of 12,600 pounds, not the total asking price of 15,000 pounds. The company's move to London was accompanied by great excitement with Veronica giving birth to a healthy baby boy.

However, the company's move to London did not sit well with Madge at first, as it kept William away from her more than she liked, but she knew this was the way things had to be. William met with Madge at The Cadogan suite, where he announced that his son had been born the day before. He was bursting with pride. Madge allowed him to regale her with all the details as she waited, seeking to find the right moment to discuss her feelings.

She asked,"I suppose this means that we will have even less time together."

"Why would you say that? Haven't I always been there when you want me?"

"Why is London so much better a place for the offices than Southampton?"

"Because London is where most of the shipping business is carried out. I need to be where there are the most opportunities to be had."

"I would have thought being where the most ships are on a regular basis would be better."

"Then I could be in any number of ports. I think London is best."

"It is starting to lessen the times we can have together. Are we drifting apart?"

"Oh, Madge, I am never far away from you." Putting his hand over his heart he said, "You, are always with me, here. I know that I get caught up in the daytoday business, but all you have to do is let me know when you want to be together and I'll be there. I never want to disappoint you." Madge quietly accepted William's words.

It may not have been as often that their paths crossed between Bath, Southampton and London, *but*, when it did, their passion would unleash itself as if they had never been apart. William's marriage to Lady Veronica had worked out well in Madge's eyes. She often felt the intrusion of Veronica as being the 'other' woman, and particularly with the birth of a son, she felt even more pushed out. William, as always, had the ability to hold Madge's emotions in check. As they lay side by side in their favorite Cadogan Suite, he took the opportunity, as Madge contemplated what he just said. They had both hastily undressed and climbed into the giant four poster bed. Preliminaries had been dropped. William held Madge close, feeling the warmth of her body. He was relaxed as he asked, "What do you think of Michael?"

"Michael who, I'm not sure I know a Michael."

"You once told me about the child you lost."

"Oh, that Michael. I often think about him and what might have been."

"I have never forgotten the great loss you suffered when you lost him. You were so sad when you told me."

"Why do you bring him up at this time?"

"Because I want…. would you permit me the honor allowing me to name my son, Michael? I would like this child, whom you had a great part in bringing into this world, to carry that name, your son's name." William watched Madge sob for the first time. He held her close until her hurt subsided. He knew that he was inside her guard. He had suspected it. Indeed, she had told him often, but now, he knew it. The closeness of the moment slowly evolved into an afternoon's intense, passionate lovemaking that was reminiscent of their earlier days. The intimate knowledge that had been gained through countless passionate moments, culminated in a fiery, release of urges and desires.

***

The extended family, William and Veronica, Madge Duggan, and Sir William's father and son became intertwined both in business and social events. William's father began to look upon Madge as his lady escort at social functions, taking her guidance in many matters. The bond between them became so strong that some thought they were father and daughter. In Madge's eyes, he was the father she never had.

Lady Veronica came to accept Madge as part of the St.J ohn-Brown package without question. At times, when Sir William entertained on a large and lavish scale, Veronica would turn to Madge for support, which was always tendered warmly. It sometimes fascinated William, however naively, that Veronica never suspected what he had with Madge and that Madge never begrudged his time with his family. There was one time that William overheard a conversation between his wife and Madge. Madge was staying at William's father's home and returned with Michael after taking him out for stroll in his perambulator. Veronica was seated on a garden bench under the shade of a large mature oak. She jokingly said to Madge, "You could be mistaken for his mother, the loving way you talk to him."

"I love him as if were my own. Does that bother you?" Madge's tone was firm and defensive.

"His father is my husband so, that would not be possible for you to love him as much as I do."

"I was not implying that I love him equally as you or William do, but I do love him in my own way."

"Why have you not remarried and had a child of your own?" Veronica's tone was more curious that challenging.

"One marriage and one lost child was enough for me. I will never be owned by a man, and I do not believe that it is possible to own a man either."

"You don't think that I belong to William?"

"There is a difference between belonging and owning. Yes. ,I do believe that you belong to William. I believe that William thinks he owns you. If you are both happy with the situation then that is all that matters."

"You sound so cynical, why is that so."

"Sounding cynical doesn't make me that way. I believe many women go through life thinking that they own their man but, I know from experience, human ownership is tenuous at best in all matters."

"Do you know something you are not telling me?"

"All I am saying is that it is not always wise to force issues if you are not sure of their outcome."

Much to Madge's surprise, Veronica stood and embraced her and said, "William is fortunate to have such good friend in you. I wonder what the man does to deserve it." Both women turned to see William exiting the potting shed by the lawn's edge.

He smiled and said, "how nice to see my two favorite women getting along so well." He turned and averted his attention to Michael, who was just waking up from his nap.

***

The next morning as William was escorting Madge to the train station he broached the subject he had overheard the day before.

"Yesterday, you and Veronica…that was a strange conversation."

"You heard what we were saying?" Madge asked.

"Yes, I did, it concerned me as to where the conversation was going. Do you think she suspects us, our liasons?"

"I don't think she knows. I *know* she knows."

"How do you know that? did I miss something?"

"Some things do not need to be said. I not only know she knows, but I am sure that she is aware that I know she knows."

"So, what now? What am I supposed to do?"

"Dear William, not everything is about you. Your wife and I appear to have reached an understanding. It would seem in this game you are but a pawn. A very big, nice pawn, but still a pawn."

"Have I just been put down?"

"No, I am comfortable that Veronica and I have an understanding. You will continue to treat your wife the way a husband should, and you and I will be respectful of that relationship."

"Are you at ease with that scenario?"

"Until I let you know otherwise, you are safe to assume so."

Chapter 21

During a huge tuberculosis outbreak in England, which affected seventy percent of the population, causing over forty percent of working-class deaths, William stayed out of London as much as possible. The lack of sanitation and the filth in the streets frightened him. For the first two years of William's son Michael's life, he rarely left Somerset and Dorset. Madge visited Bath frequently, and whenever William was forced to go London, he would stay away from Michael for periods of time to be sure he wasn't bringing the disease to him. But shipping was a business relatively unaffected by tuberculosis. More and more cargo, was moved between Canada and America and the colonies. The success of the *Sirius* in crossing the Atlantic Ocean with the power of steam promised even bigger changes. All of the Royal Shipping Line's ships were booked for voyages a full year ahead. With the introduction of better winches and steam-powered equipment, ships' efficiency and dependability was improving. William proposed developing a timetable for planned routes. If governments and business knew when a ship was leaving and arriving, it would encourage them to book space. *The Duchess of Kent* was fitted out for special cargo, like plants, with decks divided to prevent the fragile cargo from shifting and great barrels fixed throughout the decks filled with fresh water, the company's idea of changing ships' holds for particular uses distinguished it from its rivals. Often now, when William approached his father with new ideas previously discussed with Madge, they were accepted far more quickly. But still, his father believed that steel and iron would be the biggest influencers of change for the future.

When the British defeated Russia in the Crimean War in 1856, it appeared to signal peace and times of economic focus at home. This was not to be, as the very next year, the Indian Mutiny began. But typical of business at the time, Mother's Fine Foods and the Royal Shipping line pitched in and made huge profits. As for the Co-Op', the most memorable recent acquisition was that of licensing rights for the patent of the tin can opener. It surprised Madge that this simple piece of equipment had been so long in appearing. All sorts of accidents had been reported from people trying to open cans. When the patent was granted in 1855, Madge was the first person to contact the inventor, and he had happily agreed to a royalty for any she produced. Ted Ballard had a forge in the stables, and in time, he would produce these items. He had a local foundry produce the handle, and at the forge, he inserted the triangular sharp blade and riveted it in place. The molded handle displayed the Co-Op insignia and name. It was to be given away with the upcoming Co-Op dividends at the end of the month. The response was huge. Pretty soon, these items were available for purchase, or with membership application to the Co-Op.

The acceptance of the tin openers created such publicity that it steered the Co-Op into a full line of tools. The new line offered brooms, shovels, mops, cleaning supplies, and garden tools. The Co-Op became the first place to go for home needs as well as staples. An additional warehouse was built at the Southampton complex to deal with acquisition and distribution.

The British biscuit maker, *Peek, Frean and Company*, caught Madge's attention. Its products were not as costly to produce as tinned goods, and therefore could be sold for less. William established the contacts through his gentleman's club in Belgravia, and very quickly, biscuits appeared in all the Co-Op shops under their own label, and were often sold out the day they were received. Soon, Ted Ballard suggested that Mother's take advantage of their factory in Southampton and build its own biscuit factory. Because of this idea, Ted was awarded the further five percent of stock that had been held back.

Sales of Mother's Fine Foods grew from 5.5 million pounds in 1847 to 9.6 million in 1858. The Co-Op now had seventy-five stores between London and Cornwall. The factory complex at Southampton included a bakery, a print shop, stables for carriage-building, the ship chandlery, two warehouse-distribution buildings for dry and canned goods, a warehouse specifically for hardware and cleaning supplies, and a packaging and labeling building. Madge and William had paid for an extension of the Great Western Railway's track into their area, and this paid off as well. Train carriages were loaded with non-perishables for the London market, and when ready, the railway company would pick them up for delivery, dropping them off along the way at their stations. This proved very cost-effective, as roads were often impassable or obstructed in wintertime.

Madge Duggan spent most of her time running both the ship chandler's business and the food company. Periodically, she would meet with William in London, and their meetings would go long into the night. Sometimes, the meetings were in Bath, at the home of William's father. Celebrations often followed, where Madge would spend time with Lady Veronica, checking on Sir William's treatment of his wife, and son Michael, of whom she was very fond. She also spent time with William's father, who was now seventy-eight and ailing. He did not get to London so much anymore, and clung to her visits with great joy.

Chapter 22

In the late summer of 1860, much of Madge Duggan's traveling was done by the incredibly safe and efficient railway system. London was building its own underground rail system to connect all outlying stations. Mainly, Madge would use the Great South Western Railway to Fenchurch Street station, and then the underground to Pall Mall. As the Great Western Railway also served Bristol and Bath, it was to her benefit. It was fast, clean, and inexpensive. William returned to bath after having completed a two-day business meeting in London with Madge, which had culminated in a bout of unbridled passion. Madge was to follow after attending to her own business. Late in the afternoon she rode alone in a first-class carriage toward Bath, William's family, and young Michael. As the carriages clickity-clacked over the rails, swaying gently from side to side, she recalled the previous evening with a nostalgic calm. The gentle way William had caressed and raised her to a level of arousal that he had become so adept at. The way he had learned to satisfy her urges before having his way. First, he was soft and in touch with his feminine side, the second time, he was masculine, strong and demanding. The third time, yes, she thought, we were in sync…three times we made love. Closing her eyes, she recalled the firm way he held her buttocks, lifting them slightly off the mattress so that he might plunge deeper into her. My God, she thought, I was so wet. That night he seemed as if he could ravish her until morning. She was getting wet again, just reliving that degree of passion. She reasoned, that despite all her efforts to stay aloof, she really did love him. This sometimes intolerable, man, had a special place in her heart. One part of a conversation the previous night stuck with her, "You do know I love you not as a lover," William had said, "for in my mind, you are my chosen wife of heart. You were right that I should marry appropriately. Sometimes I wish you weren't right, but you were. But it is as if you and I are the ones who have a child together in Michael. He is lucky to have two mothers: Veronica in flesh and blood and you in spirit."

Madge could not remember how she had responded but did recall the inner warm feeling his comment had given her. She opened her eyes and was watching the sun setting out of the window. The lush English countryside was rushing past, broken up by a river, a field of cows, and some farmhouses. Madge felt a warm glow of contentment. The train attendant had come round and lit the gas lamps earlier. The lamps in the carriage flickered as if in time with the swaying, the rails clickity-clacked, and the carriage swayed and bumped. The steam engine whistled, hissed and shrieked. She heard its whistle blow somewhere ahead in the distance signaling an approaching tunnel or bridge. The carriage compartment, furnished in luxurious velvet seats with brocade-tasseled curtains, fine leather trim on the door and lights reflecting from outside in the long, beveled mirrors, above the seats, was a cozy, protective cocoon. *Clickity-clack, clickity-clack, clickity-clack.*

Suddenly… everything stopped and went black. Silence ruled supreme, cutting out all other noise.

Chapter 23

At fifty-four Royal Crescent, Bath, Sir William was awakened in his bedchamber by a commotion downstairs. The chambermaid met him on the stairs.

"Sir William, your father…."

"What's wrong with Father?"

"The doctor sent for you. Go at once, sir," she said, handing him his heavy winter coat to put over his pajamas. As he ran across the green island between the two huge rows of stone mansions, he spotted the doctor on his father's front entry. As he bounded up the stairs, the doctor greeted him solemnly.

"I'm awfully sorry Sir William," he said. "It was too late by the time I arrived. It was painless. I left him as I found him for you to see before I take care of his body." Struck numb, William entered the house, and the housekeeper waved him into the conservatory, where the bistro table was laid for breakfast.

A broken glass lay on the floor by his father's body, his hand laid open, a shard of glass propped open a gash in his finger. The blood had mixed with the orange juice in a swirled juxtaposition of red and orange, flowing around the grout groves in the tiled floor.

"What in God's name happened?" he asked. The parlor maid told him that his father had summoned her to serve his breakfast in the conservatory and to bring him the morning paper.

"I sent the boy out for the paper and made up his tray. When he returned, I put the paper on the tray and went to the conservatory. I handed your father the paper, and when I turned round to pour his tea, I heard a crash. When I looked, your father was on the floor."

"There, there, my dear," said the housekeeper to the maid. "Take yourself off to the kitchen and get a nice cup of tea." Then she turned to Sir William.

"I felt for his pulse, sir. He was dead. No heartbeat. I'm so sorry sir. She bent down, picked up the newspaper, and handed it to Sir William. The headline screamed at him.

**TRAIN CRASH
ON GREAT WESTERN RAILWAY
THIRTY PEOPLE DIE**

Iron bridge fails, wreckage crushes express London to Bath train. Thirty-one dead 142 injured. This is the ninth bridge failure this year. Is iron bridge construction, the great invention of our time or, has it's time come and gone? There must be something safer out there that will not risk the lives of passengers.

William glanced at the names of listed dead. He read down the alphabetical list. The first name in the 'D's was, Duggan, Madge, founder of Mother's Fine Foods, businesswoman of Southampton. William slumped to the floor and passed out alongside his dead father's body.

Chapter 24

Upon reflection, looking back upon his grandfather's and Madge Duggan's sudden death, Michael recognized that that was when his father had changed. It had been Madge who tried the hardest to persuaded his father to keep him close when father wanted to send him to Charterhouse. Between his mother and Madge, he had felt protected from his father and grandfather's more stern and austere ways. But now, Michael had witnessed his father's total emotional shutdown with some confusion. Prior to Aunt Madge's death, business associates from Mother's Fine Foods and the Royal Shipping Line frequented the family home at Bath. His father would spend hours behind locked doors in meetings with Madge. They would stay for dinner and retire to a local inn, only to return the next day and repeat the routine. Since the macabre exhibition of grief, Sir William had left Bath only once. That was to take Michael to Charterhouse. The train ride to London, the visit to the bespoke tailor, and the carriage ride to the school was accompanied by long stretches of silence. These silences were punctuated only by brief statements of praise for the school, and, of how Michael should make Madge and, of course, his mother proud. The death of Madge as a companion had caused his mother to withdraw from the world. It was as if Madge had been the link that connected his father and mother together. She maintained his grandfather's house as if he were still alive. The servants followed the same routines, and his mother would check on everything daily.

Michael wondered to himself why, if everyone was so unhappy, why were they sending him away. He wasn't the reason they were unhappy. How was he supposed to prepare himself to run a shipping company, or even Mother's Fine Foods, or the Co-Op? His father had told him that he was now half owner. Mistress Madge had left him her share. None of this actually meant anything to him. A visit to the Co-Op's head office at Blackfriars Bridge in London was the extent of Michael's knowledge of the business. This knowledge was of no significance to him.

Michael understood the importance of going to a "good" school. His father often reminded him that he himself had gone to Charterhouse at age seven. So in that way, Michael was not as confused, but still he felt he was being sent away. His father's old cricket bat and tennis rackets went with him. It was if his father was going back to Charterhouse himself. The headmaster, Form Master, and housemaster greeted his father very obsequiously. Their bowing and handshaking looked almost comical to Michael. Both the headmaster and housemaster were the same as when Sir William had been at the school.

Their conversations faded into the background as Michael observed many boys' comings and goings across the square. Maybe it would be fun to be with other boys. The excitement in the air, the laughter among them, could this be a good thing?

"Father, I hope my funds will permit me to visit your offices," he said. It was more statement than question.

"Hold your tongue, boy," Sir William said. Turning to the headmaster, he said,

"Michael is to be accorded your consideration in these matters. I expect that he will be held to the school's standards and disciplines with no special allowances." Turning to Michael he said, "you can spend time with me in city on the summer break." Sir William made it clear that Michael was to be channeled in the direction of business. With a perfunctory hug and a simple bow, he climbed back into the carriage and left. Feeling left alone and abandoned, Michael would never forget that parting.

***

The summer of '61 was a little disappointing to Michael as he expected to spend the entire summer with his father. Upon his arrival at Euston station, he was met by a dour looking man with a high starched collar, that looked as if it was choking him. "Master Michael, Bourne's the name, Michael Bourne. They sent me to pick you up and take you to The Royal. Fancy that, sending Michael to pick up Michael."

"Where's my father Mr. Bourne?"

"He is coming up from Bath. Will be here by lunchtime. Let's get you over to the Royal. Have you had breakfast?"

"Yes sir. We ate at six thirty, although I was the only boy left, so I ate with matron. She treated me really well."

"Good, good. Is there something you would like to see on the way to the office? Big Ben, House of parliament maybe? That's where Guy Fawkes tried to blow the place up you know."

"Yes, I know. I would like to go along the embankment and see the swans."

"Then off we shall go." Bourne held out his hand for Michael to hold and it was ignored. They stopped and brought a loaf of bread on the way for the swans. Bourne offered it to Michael who once again ignored the gesture.

"What do you do?" Michael asked.

"I work for your father, Mr. St. John-Brown."

"Doing what?"

Bourne, was taken aback by Michael's tone. "I am your father's personal aide. I do things that would be a waste of his time. That allows him to do more important things."

"So, you are his servant."

"I suppose you could say that. But in a way we are all servants to a higher authority."

"Not me Mr. Bourne. *I, am a St John-Brown*, we are servants to no man."

"Well, be that as it may young Mr. Michael, we all answer to God."

Michael stopped, turned around, and looked the man in the eye and said, "*you might believe in God, but I don't. How much further is it to the river?*"

Bourne, feeling that he had been put in his place by an eightyear old boy, pointed ahead and replied, "down those steps over there."

The feeding of the swans and the subsequent carriage ride over to the Royal Shipping Line offices was surrounded by the busy noise of London streets and no conversation.

Upon entering the offices Michael heard, "Welcome to RSL Mr. Bourne, nice to see you again, who have we here?"

"Master Michael St.John-Brown Alice, he is yours. Keep him busy 'til his father gets here." Leaning across her foyer counter he whispered, "snotty little bastard for sure." He turned to Michael and said, "It was a pleasure Master Michael. I hope we meet again soon." He turned and strode off.

Alice came round the side of the counter she said, "Well young man is there something particular you would like to do?"

"You may call me St. John-Brown, that's what they do at school."

"Do you like that? Wouldn't you rather be called Michael?" Alice was surprised at the boy's tone.

"I suppose. Show me where Papa's office is, if you don't mind. I will wait there."

Alice in a cold tone said, "Follow me St. John-Brown, I'll take you Sir William St. John-Brown's private office." She was offended by the boy's abruptness.

Without knowing it, Michael had set the tone for the way his summer was to be spent. He was passed from one secretary, assistant or worker to another of some kind. Naturally his reputation as an arrogant, rude little boy preceded him. He would lunch, most days with his father and have dinner at Sir William's private club. Their conversations were stilted and sparse. It was obvious that William was ill at ease with children including his own son. This summer visit lasted only two weeks before William packed his son off to his mother at Royal Crescent, Bath were the family staff and help were familiar to him.

***

The summer of 1862 Michaels father decided that he should go to Southampton because he would be exposed to the other side of the RSL's shipping business. This was an exciting time for him as he was able to have a much less supervised existence. It was arranged that he would stay with the Gratton family, whom his father knew well. They had a son, Willy, who was Michaels age. The boys would take off each morning after breakfast with a packed lunch and go exploring the docks. The connections the family had enabled them to go on board different ships. It was here that Michael became more aware of the world around him. He marveled at the vast array of ships that would come and go on a daily basis. The two boys spent days helping the workers with tying and untying the ships big ropes. They would run errands for the dockside workers getting drinks and cigarettes. They would come home each day tired, dirty, and excited to share their day's experiences with parents who listened and enjoyed them. While Michael was aware that these people's lives were working class and far different from his own, he was able to put that aside.

One morning Michael pointed out Duggan Ship Chandlers and asked Willy, "What do you know about this place?"

"Duggan's is a ship's chandlers. They have everything a ship could need before it sails away. It is their job to save the ship's captain as much time as they can. It is like a whole lot of stores in one place. The captain or who-ever it is that does it tells them what the next ship coming in will need and they get it all together in one place. They tell me the ships can buy everything from food to cooking tools, to sails, to rope, to clothes. That's a fascinating place to get into. But I was told not go there."

"Why, my pa owns that place?"

"I don't know. Do you think you can get us in there?" Willy seemed excited about the opportunity.

"I don't know, do you want me to try?"

"Oh yes. Do."

That evening Michael approached Willy's father and asked "Mr. Gratton do you know if Willy and I could go to Duggans."

"Yes, I do know. Your pa said for you to stay away from Duggans because that's where he is going to have you spend next summer."

"But that's not fair, I want Willy to go with me."

"Then I suggest when next summer comes, we should see if you can stay with us again while you are to be at Duggans." The friendly way Willy's father responded put the boys at ease and they became excited about the next year. "Have you boys spent much time at The Royal Shipping lines docks?"

Willy replied, "Oh yes, we usually go there every day and see what ships are in for the mornings and then we go to other docks."

"Make sure you have some things to talk to your pa about for The Royal.

"Oh, he doesn't care about that," said Michael.

"He most certainly does care. I am supposed to make sure that you pay attention to your own ships. If you want to stay with us next summer you better give your pa a good report." He stayed there the entire summer except for one week, which he spent in Bath with his mother. He really noticed the warmth and closeness of the host family, which he missed a great deal when he returned to Bath.

***

1863, Michael could not wait to return to Southampton, the Grattons' and Willy. The first thing Willy's father said was "You really did us proud last year when you told your father how your summer went. We are glad to have you back. You've gotten a lot taller in the last year. We were wondering if you had, because Willy is bigger than me now. When Willy returned, Michael was surprised. The boy had grown two inches taller than him.

"So, what are your plans?" Willy asked.

"I am supposed to spend a lot of my time at Dugans', other than that I don't know." The boys went together to Duggans' where Michael introduced himself. The cavernous shed that ran the length of the dock was a veritable Aladdin's cave. A man they referred to as the quartermaster told them, "Take the whole day and investigate the stores. You are not going to, but try and remember the things that you see and where they are. When you think you have it memorized, we will put you to work. Mr. Ballard says that I am not to overwork you. Mind you I was only expecting one boy. Never mind, off with you." As the boys turned to leave, the quartermaster called out, "catch this." Willy was the quickest as he caught a stick of chalk the man had thrown, "Each time you turn a corner, put a chalk mark on the floor. That way you will be able to find your way back."

"You think we might get lost?" Michael asked.

"I don't want to send a search party out for you at the end of the day. Here is a simple trick. Look up at the roof and see the long roof ridge. Well, in the morning the sun shines through the left side of that. In the afternoon it shines through the right side. The office, where we are now is at the north end of shed. So, if you little buggers know that the sun rises in the east and sets in the west and, the offices are at the north, you should be able to find your way back without the chalk." He watched the boys walk slowly away as they periodically would stop, look up then left and right before continuing their walk. He knew that it always took a while for people to get used to his navigation advice.

At the end of the week the quartermaster called them into his office, which was stacked with pile upon pile of paperwork. His desktop could hardly be seen. He handed each boy a small manila envelope, which both boys opened instantly. "What's this for?" asked Michael.

"It's your pay. Not much I know, but you done some work this week. As you get better, I will increase your pay. It's not a man's pay but it's something for your efforts."

"What's all this paper for?" asked Michael.

"Oh, this lot," the man spread his arms as if to encompass it all, "this is the orders we get down here from the office upstairs to get ready for the next ship coming in. I try to have it pulled to one side so we can get the ship in, unloaded and then out as quickly as possible. The top copy the Captain signs and that goes upstairs for them to collect the money. These are my copies I try to keep them in some semblance of order in case I have to find them for some reason because I make my notes on my copy."

"Why?" asked Willy.

"Because some captains aren't quite as honest as they should be. If they say something was wrong with what we gave them I can check my notes. Helps us try to keep them honest."

As they walked home Willy said, "I never expected any money. My ma will be thrilled."

"Why would she be thrilled?" Michael was curious.

"Because I will give it to her, that's why."

"Why would you give it to her, it's yours?"

"Because it will help the family to have a little more money."

"Don't you want it for yourself?" Michael didn't understand.

"Not really. Ma will give some of it back for me to spend as I want, I know. Ma and pa have rent and food and other things to pay for, I don't really mind."

"Do you want some of mine?" Michael offered.

"Not really, if I need something I'll ask."

By the end of the summer Michael left for Bath, a tired, hard worked, but different person. His mother was upset that her son had been doing hard work instead of enjoying his summer break. "No child of mine should be doing manual labor. It just isn't the thing. That family should know better. Wait till I tell your father."

"But mother, I really had a good time and didn't mind. In fact, it has been the best summer ever." He proudly offered her some of his saved earnings.

"I don't want any of that filthy lucre. Take money from a child! What will you think of next? Your only ten years old for God's sake."

"I'm nearly eleven mother!" Michael left the room feeling rejected.

***

1864, brought a different experience to Michael. Now being close to twelve years old he had developed a more acceptable demeanor. He was to stay at his fathers' club and spend time at the co-op. The hustle and bustle of the factory setting was less stiff and proper than the business environment at The Royal Shipping lines. Michael would rise in the morning and have breakfast with his father who then put him in a carriage and sent him over to the co-op. The big building had four floors of places and things to see and do. Machines to watch in the basement, barges being unloaded by the rivers' edge, clanking machines in the print shop, and people scurrying around with purpose. A gentleman who introduced himself as the production manager told Michael, "'Tis a big place this. Would you like me to show you around Master Michael, or would you like to discover it on your own?"

"I think I would like to find my own way around, if that's alright." Having learned at school that every place had rules and they had to be obeyed he asked, "Is there anything I should know or do while I am here?"

"Indeed, there is young man. You must not touch anything without asking first. It is not that '*you*' need permission, it is that some things are dangerous, some are very hot. It's just our way of trying to keep you safe. Trouble with hot is that you can't see it. Can take the skin of your hand in a flash. Then there's the river. Dirty bloody thing the river round here is. All sorts of things floating around in it could make you real sick. But look here, don't worry about a thing, just ask if it's alright to touch. Now be off with you and have some fun."

It took three weeks of investigating every nook and cranny of the building before Michael became weary of the place. Evenings spent with his father in the club were punctuated by long periods of quiet where his father would be reading. Sometimes Michael would try reading what his father had brought from the office but they did

315

not interest him. The daily newspapers were Michael's escape. At the end of three weeks, he was packed up and sent off to his mother

***

1865, Michael now thirteen is spending the summer at Mother's Fine Foods in Southampton. The first thing he did when arriving was to visit the Grattons. Mrs Gratton opened the door and was surprised to see Michael standing there. "Come in come in, there's no need to stand on ceremony. It's good to see you."

"Willy's father was seated in the parlor reading the morning paper when Michael walked in. "Surprise, surprise, how nice to see you, young man. Are you down here for the summer again?"

"Yes sir. Father has arranged for me to spend time at Mothers Fine Foods."

Mr. Gratton asked, "So where are you staying this summer Michael?"

"I though, that I was staying here. Why, is something wrong?"

"That's no problem for us. I haven't seen your father in over two months. He must have just forgotten to tell me."

Michael was embarrassed when he said, "Maybe I should check over at Mothers in case he has made arrangements over there."

Mrs. Gratton, said, "You will stay the night with us and tomorrow we sort things out." After dinner Mr. Gratton left the house and went to Mothers Fine Foods. He soon returned and spoke to his wife, "Can you believe they send the boy down here and didn't even make arrangements for his accommodation."

"How do you know that? That's silly the boy is only thirteen."

"They knew over at Mothers that he was going to be there for the summer and assumed he would be here with us. I guess Sir William forget to ask us."

"That's not right, we should have been asked."

"I know dear but let's not take it out on the boy."

"Do you think you might have forgotten he asked you, after all you are very busy these days."

"To tell you the truth, I think his father just plain forgot about it. Not that I could understand forgetting your child. I mean to say, he even put him on the train to get here."

The next morning Michael left for Mother's plant taking Willy with him. On the way Willy asked, "Do they know I will be there? What will I do?"

"I don't know but leave it to me. I know Ted Ballard, he is the man that runs the place. Do you want to earn some money or just check things out?"

"It would be nice if I could earn something like we did the summer before last." Willy was apprehensive.

The two boys marched into the front offices of Mothers and were greeted by an aproned lady of later years. "Can I help you young gentlemen?' If you are looking for work, we are not hiring right now."

A side office door opened and Ted Ballard walked out. Seeing Michael, he said to the lady, "I'll take care of this Miss Fotheringay." Turning to Michael he continued,

"Master Michael. Good to see you. I was expecting you yesterday. Where are you staying this year?"

"If there no arrangements made, I will be staying with Mr. & Mrs. Gratton, the same as last time."

"Good. Your father never spoke of any arrangements so that will be fine. I will let him know where you are. Introduce me to your young friend."

"This is Willy Gratton. It is his family that I stay with. He is my friend. I would like you to find work for him while I am here for the summer. Will that be a problem?"

"No, no indeed not. What hours will you work young man?"

Before Willy could reply Michael said, I stay with his family because Willy keeps me safe and out of the bad areas around the docks. He will be here the same hours that I am."

"Will he stay with you all the time?"

"Oh no, when I am doing whatever it is, he can work somewhere else." Michael was quite proud of himself taking charge."

"Miss Fotheringay, please take young Willy and get him some working overalls then show him to the packaging shop. Thank you."

Michael spent the morning with Ted who asked a myriad of questions about what he'd been doing the last four summers at other St.John-Brown companies. The man was trying to find out what he could do with the boy when his problem was solved by Michael, who in as mature a voice as possible said, "I have been looking at what our family business's do so that I might decide which one I want to be involved in."

"Have you found one yet that appeals to you?" asked Ted.

"I have been finding them all interesting in such different ways. Mothers Fine Foods is the last that I am going to see. So far, I have come to the conclusion that looking at them for the brief periods that I have been, does not give a really accurate picture."

"So, what would you do differently, I mean how would you go about getting a better picture of the business's?"

"I'm not sure. Mother says that I should go University and Father thinks I should go straight into the business."

"So where does that leave you?"

"Confused. If I please father it will anger mother. If I please mother I anger father, not that I am sure he will notice."

"If you want my advice," Ted held up his hands to show Michael that they were dirty. "I have found that I have learned more by getting my hands dirty and giving things a go than by just watching. You are young, young enough to spend one year in each business working among the workers. They will soon forget that you are a St. John-Brown. That's when you will see the dynamics of each business."

"Do you really think people will take me seriously?"

"Oh yes, we have a lot of people working for us here at Mother's that are dedicated to their job, or as we call it, their role in the business. If you want to learn they will show you, and, actually you are lucky because they will be showing out of pride and that you are no threat to them."

"Why is that?"

"Because one day you will be at the top of this company. I can hardly see you trading that for one of their roles."

***

On the way that afternoon Willy chatted nonstop about what he had been doing and how happy he was that he had work. When they reached the house, he rushed indoors and excitedly told his mother what had taken place that day. She calmly responded by saying, "I really didn't want you to work this summer. It won't be long and you will be working for the rest of your life."

"I'm sorry Mrs. Gratton, that's my fault. Willy said he wanted to work and I just helped."

"And ma, the extra money will come in helpful."

"Yes, I know, but."

Michael interrupted, "Mrs. Gratton Willy only 'worked' today because it is *my* first day. We are going to be learning all about Mothers Fine Foods and we shall do that by spending time in different areas and seeing what they do."

"Won't he get into trouble for not working?"

Michael proudly said, "Willy will be working with *me*. He will get paid, for being, shall we say, my personal assistant."

"You young people, I just don't understand you." She turned her attention back to cooking the evening meal.

One evening halfway through the summer, Willy and Michael sat on the front porch watching the summer sun slide out of view behind a mighty oak. Willy comment on it disappearing just before, Michael said, "It went to down to Australia."

Willy said, "You know Michael, we have spent the last five summers together and in another few weeks we will go our separate ways. It is so strange."

"What's strange about it?" asked Michael.

"I wonder how many friends know ahead of their time that the friendship is going to end."

"Don't all friendships end at some time?" Michael was genuinely curious.

"Well think back to friends you knew from childhood, where are they now?"

"I don't have any friends, well only you."

"But you must have had friends when you were younger, like before you went away to school."

"No, no friends. I'm not even sure that I am *friends* with anyone at school. I mean, they think we are friends, but I don't."

"Aren't you, don't you, get lonely?"

"Sometimes but it goes away."

"So, you think we are friends? How do I know that?"

"The first morning that we went to Mothers, if you remember I introduced you to Ted as my friend. Do you know, that is the first time I can recall ever having given anyone that title?"

"Wow. Wow."

Michael said, "I have known you now for five years. That's longer than I think I've known anyone else, who isn't family." The boys sat in silence digesting their thoughts.

***

The last few weeks of summer Michael immersed himself in the departments and details of work at Mother's. Willy and he would point out things to each other and together they would ask about the how, where, and why. They would follow the bulk cargo coming off the merchant ships through the weighing house to the unpacking sheds, into the repacking shop, then to the printing of the labels and out to its' final destination as it left the warehouse by train for places unknown to them. The precision and planning reminded Michael of the grandfather clock at Royal Crescent. Upon opening the door on the front of the clock he could see the big wheels would turn the big cogs, which would turn the smaller cogs, which would turn other cogs and cams and everything just kept going along relentlessly. Mothers Fine Foods worked like clockwork. He loved it.

***

Michael was back at school and now fifteen years old was only a boy, and yet he bore the carriage and confidence of a young man. He quickly learned that any requests he made to spend time at his father's businesses were met with swift approval. He discovered that, if the requests coincided with what he considered laborious sports activities, they still met instant approval. He knew his father was being kept informed, so he expressed interest in various parts of the business. Though this whole routine was initially just to get away from school, Michael quickly became intrigued by what he was seeing. His world consisted of the routines of school mixed with visits to Mother's Fine Foods, the Co-Op, and the Royal Shipping Line. This mixed bag of experiences opened his eyes to the diversity available to him. While he mostly just wandered around the businesses aimlessly watching what was going on, it shaped his focus on where he wanted to go in life.

The teachers either fawned over him because of his connections or looked down on him because of his privilege. It was the new Form Master, a Mr. Surtees, who held no sway in either direction, who spotted a commonality in the variations of Michael's life. Each time Michael would take leave from school to visit a business, he was charged to provide a brief report on his experiences. Mr. Surtees had obtained the exclusive use of a carrel, a private study cubicle, for Michael's studies. They would meet for evening banco, which was the study period, where Michael would be required to read aloud his report. A discussion would then take place about its content and merits.

Mr. Surtees was a diminutive man, twenty-two years old and somewhat posturing. He dressed immaculately in bespoke tailored suits with starched white shirts, stiff collars and cuffs, and silk ties and kerchiefs to match. His hat was a light tan felt with a taper from the top to the brim and a sweeping, wave-like brim edged in fine silk. He kept abreast of the fashion of the times, in the style of Beau Brummel, the well-known dandy around London. He would place his gloves and cane on an empty chair and sit the hat proudly atop them. To all who saw him, he was a fop, a dandy, but this was his shield. It once entered Michael's mind that the man might be one of those men who preferred other men over women, but then, as if on some unseen cue, he shared a likeness of his betrothed with Michael and promised him to secrecy. (Michael did not know what betrothed meant, but the dictionary solved that problem.) The girl appeared very young, but Michael asked no questions other than the occasional, perfunctory, "How is your betrothed, sir?"

The answer always started with the energy of a potential conversation, but quickly ended with, "She is well, thank you, Michael. You may refer to her as Lady Penelope." The relationship between Michael and Mr. Surtees was mixture of formal teacher-pupil and friends, even confidants. They both knew that they liked each other, but there was a barrier of Victorian propriety between them, which was as it should be.

The first time Michael took time to visit one of the businesses with a critical eye was in 1867, and it was the Co-Op he chose. Blackfriars Wharf was less than a mile from Charterhouse in Smithfield. Mr. Surtees advised him to write what he saw, and then what he thought about it and what his thoughts were about the place as a whole. He was warned to pay attention to detail. "What you think you see is not always what is really in front of you." Mr. Surtees said. As an example, he removed a locket with Lady Penelope's likeness, done in silhouette style. He asked Michael what he saw, and received a bland description.

"I see a girl, sir."

"What I see," countered Surtees, "is a young, vibrant girl with a youthful smile full of promise. I see the elegance and posture of breeding. That is how you can look at something and see beyond the immediate."

"I don't understand. What am I supposed to do sir?"

"Keep your eyes and ears open and question what it is you are seeing."

"Won't that start to annoy people sir?"

"I don't mean ask questions. Just in your own mind ask yourself what you are seeing and consider other ways to interpret what you see. Do you understand now?"

"Yes sir, I think so." Michael never forgot the last words 'consider other ways to interpret what you see'. This was to become one of Michael's guiding rules.

***

Michael arrived at the Co-Op building at nine o'clock on a Friday morning and was greeted at the door by Ted Ballard. They shook hands, and Ted asked, "Master Michael what would like to see first?"

Michael surprised Ted when he replied, "As I have not had the opportunity to know much about the building, I would like the plans, if I may. Then I would like to learn the journey of a product from its arrival to its departure." Ted Ballard, who split his time between Mother's Fine Foods in Southampton and the Co-Op here in the city, assigned a production manager to arrange for Michael to be handed off to a supervisor through each stage of his interest. Michael was treated respectfully at each stage due to the manner in which he was introduced. To everyone he met it was said, "Mr. Michael St. John-Brown will be your boss one day. Show him what happens here." Michael was exhausted upon his return to school. Feeling overwhelmed, he requested to be excused from Banco. He met with Mr. Surtees the next afternoon, deftly dodging the dreaded rugby match planned for that day. Michael started to speak. "Mr. Surtees…"

"In the privacy of this carrel, you may call me Ronald," said Mr. Surtees, "as I fear we are to spend much time together. Now, why do I not see a report? I allowed you to reschedule this meeting to provide you time."

"The day passed so quickly, and there was so much to absorb," said Michael. "To write it all down would take forever. I just don't know where to start. Then there's the dream I had last night."

Smiling, Mr. Surtees said, "Let us break things down. Tell me about the dream."

"Well, sir, it's not really clear. Along the back of the Co-Op building is a large, cobbled yard and wharf, where the barges unload and carts take product away. It's just wide enough for a cart to turn around and pass another. In my dream, I saw a figure bowling a large hoop down the side of the building, only it wasn't a hoop, it was a giant copper penny, a head on one side and Neptune with his trident on the other side. They were quite clear sir. I tried to stop a figure that appears from behind me as it rolls the hoop…penny, and it dodges past me and flips the penny into the river. Suddenly, the figure disappears, then, reappears again in an upper window and flips another penny hoop that bounces on the wharf and into the river. The penny was huge sir, up to my waist, it was. The figure then appeared again from the other side of the building, bowling a penny hoop across the wharf and up the other side of the building, and then it fades into the street." With a perplexed look, Michael hesitated, then added, "The odd thing is, instead of there being 'Queen Victoria's head on the other side of the penny hoop, there's a bust of my Aunt Madge, Mistress Duggan, that is, the dead owner of Mother's Fine Foods and the Co-Op."

"Let us say deceased rather than dead. It is more respectful." Mr. Surtees thought for a moment and then said, "Let me ponder that one. Quite a strange dream, on the surface, that is. Let's change the subject for a moment. Tell me what you saw going around the Co-op building yesterday." From the description he received, there didn't seem to be much control over the employees. In fact, it appeared that the workers were controlling the work. The school had a system and hierarchy, but the building did not appear to. It was as if the product dictated the work, a fact that the teacher had wanted Michael to discover for himself. He was very excited about what his pupil had learned without realizing it. "What your mind did was recognize the immensity of the task and shut down your focus," he said. "That's why you came upon the idea of the building plans. Your brain was telling you to focus on something smaller. It reinforced that concept by only allowing you to see confusion. What do you think, Michael?"

"What, about the dream?" said Michael.

"I want you to discover the symbolism for yourself. There is an excitement to be found in education, when the realization of a concept takes root in your brain. Be patient. You will discover what an unusual dream you have had."

"I thought it could mean that I see money being lost, wasted, or even stolen from my aunt Madge, the Co-op or even both."

"Oh my God! Pardon me. You already have it worked out. I see a similar interpretation as you do, but that is a conclusion." Mr. Surtees said. "You cannot start out a study with conclusion alone. It has to begin with a goal. For example, if we already know the conclusion, we need to find out what is the question. Enough for one day, we will get into your approach later. Now, off with you, and enjoy your weekend. By the way, did you see any pretty girls at the building?"

"No not really." Replied Michael as he felt himself blush. "Not as pretty as you find Lady Penelope." With that, he dashed from the carrel.

Chapter 25

The first week of a longer, school-approved study found Michael at the back of the Mother's warehouse at 6:30 a.m. Two river barges sat alongside the wharf, and numerous heavy-duty horse-drawn wagons stood silently waiting. The drivers and watermen were gathered at the water's edge, smoking and stamping their feet. The morning was cold, and a thin fog hung over the river.

Appearing out of the top of the haze were the giant steel girders of Blackfriars Bridge, which carried trains in and out of London. The hissing of the steam engines and the *clickity-clack* of the train wheels on the iron rails filled the air as they echoed across the river's surface. Michael walked over to the water's edge. What he saw bore no resemblance to the River Avon near his home in Somerset, which was fast-moving and clean. This river eddied and swirled, with all types of rubbish and detritus fighting for space in its coffee-brown, smelly mass. The men spat into the water contemptuously, aiming at the floating rat bodies. Standing away from the men, Michael looked back up the cobble side road to see a carriage stop at the top, and from it,

Ted Ballard emerged."I hear you're going to spend some time here with us, young man," he said. "That's good. A fresh set of eyes will always see things the everyday viewer misses. This bloody place is supposed to be busy right now." As Ted approached the wharf, he saw the men standing around. "What the bloody hell is going on?" he shouted. "Get the tops off those bloody holds. Get your wagons lined up where they should be. Why the hell aren't the gantries working?"

Galvanized into action, the men ran in different directions. Before anyone could answer, a steam whistle atop the building let out a shriek, and the loading bay doors rolled open on their steel tracks and wheels. Second and third-story doors flew open as the ornate gantries swung out over the river and clanked into place. A rotund man with grease on his face and sweat on his brow hung out of an open doorway and shouted, "Mornin', all! Tis a luverly day to be a werkin'. Les 'ave yer now, boys. Ooh. Sorry, boss, didn't know you was 'ere."

"I can see that. Get your arse down here now. These barges are supposed to have been unloaded by now, and the wagons should be leaving here," said Ted. Turning to Michael, in an exasperated tone, he said, "These buggers know when I come and go. I wasn't planning to be here today, but when I was told that you would be here, I wanted to help you settle in. Looks like I caught them napping."

Michael asked if there would be any punishment for the workers, and was told that he would change their time cards to reflect when they actually started work, and that would be that. Then Ted took him into the building and up to the second floor where his office was and showed him the space he would set aside for Michael's use. Ted handed him a white dustcoat with the Co-Op logo embroidered on the pocket and 'Michael St.John-Brown' in gold lettering underneath. He explained, "Each person's name is embroidered in a different color according to their seniority in the chain of command. They might as well know right from the start that you carry some weight around here. Are you comfortable with that?"

"Not only am I comfortable with that, sir, but my father has always said that you are responsible for your actions. Am I permitted to take the clock cards to the men on the wharf and have them sign for the correct time?"

"It's a ballsy little bugger you are, to be sure," said Ted Ballard. "I can see your father in you, son. Mistress Duggan always said she had plans for you. I can see why, although I suspect you will soon have plans of your own. Go for it, only don't stand to close or one of them might just '*accidently*' knock you in the river. Odd sense of humor that lot."

Each worker Michael approached to correct the time card stared at the name on his dustcoat, looked him in the eye, and grudgingly signed the change. Within the hour, the fire alarm sounded, and quickly, all the workers gathered outside the building. From a first-floor open doorway, Ted Ballard looked down on the group. "This is a fire drill, as our insurance requires us to have. If you could pay attention to me instead of glaring at young St.John-Brown, I will tell you what is happening." He waved for Michael to join him in the doorway. Michael ran to join Ted, and soon looked down on the large group of men and women. Ted carried on: "Master Michael St.John-Brown is an owner of this company. In my book, that makes him a man to be reckoned with. He may be young, but to me, this young man has always been big. Here's the bad news - he lives less than a ten-minute walk from here, and you can expect to see him at any time. I will, and I repeat, *I will*, take his side in everything. You have been warned. Now, get back to your work."

The group dissipated quickly, and Michael returned to a desk that had been allotted to him. He found copies of the floor plan, with a note attached that read, "Use these for your working notes. The quality ones have been sent to Charterhouse for you."

The plans were covered with hand written notes detailing the number of workers and how they were broken down. There were work flow descriptions, that had obviously been put there for his information. He wandered around the building connecting the notes to places and faces. There were burly men on each floor managing the heavy lifting, and an engineer in the basement who kept the boilers that heated the building and operated the winches and gantries. There was a night watchman Michael hadn't met.

The fourth floor was divided into two sections. Half was the bookkeeping section, which employed thirty girls and women and four dour-looking men. This section handled payroll, billing and collections, membership records, dividend calculations, and all other administrative duties. One quarter of the floor was a print shop producing all labels for Mother's Fine Foods as well as The Co-Op, from design to production. It had a master printer, two apprentices, and ten heavily ink-stained girls. The final quarter of this floor was set aside for purchasing and sales. This department was staffed by three matronly women, two, overly rotund men, and a boy. Besides these sales people, there were thirty outside sales people employed.

The third floor was the designated labeling and packaging area. Here, product was brought to be repackaged and new labels added. Products manufactured by the company were packaged, labeled, and boxed for delivery. Outgoing deliveries were assembled for shipment, and quality control was exercised. There were forty men and women workers, four clerks, and two supervisors.

The second floor housed shipping and receiving. Its cavernous open air facilitated the movement of large volumes of items. There was a network of rails, upon which sat steel carts, which could easily be towed around by four burly young men. A set of doors opened out onto the rear wharf, each with a swinging gantry. There were also twenty men and women workers, plus three clerks and four supervisors.

The first floor was divided into two halves, the first comprising design fabrication and construction. Here, stores were designed and test construction carried out. One half of the remaining space served as a training section for managers and other employees. The final portion was the company personnel department and managerial offices. Altogether, the floor employed two designers, a construction manager, four carpenters, with four apprentices, four foremen and four other apprentices, two plumbers with apprentices, and two electricians with one apprentice each. It also had twelve clerks and eight trainers. The staff bathrooms, break rooms, and kitchen were on this floor, along with a cook and two assistants.

The ground floor held the bakery, with a staff of ten, and also an infirmary with a doctor and a nurse. It also housed the bottling and canning section, with twenty men and women workers, four supervisors, and four apprentices. The company shop for the public opened onto the side cobble street, and had a staff of five girls and a manager. The total employee count was 324. Having now seen the whole building, Michael became fully aware of its' enormity. Later in the day, Michael's handwritten notes had been added to the existing ones. The break bell rang throughout the building, and Michael, deciding he had done enough for the moment, went outside with the younger workers. Many of the other workers stayed in their areas, drinking tea and eating biscuits.

As the sun hit Michael's face, he realized how quickly the day had passed. The morning dankness had given way to a radiant sunny day. Many workers sat on the ground with their backs against the sun-warmed wall, their eyes closed and faces pointed upward to the sun in a brief escape from the reality of life.

***

Michael recognized a young girl he had seen in the print shop, he walked over and spoke to her, "May I sit with you, um . . ." He looked at her name tag atop her full breast. "Melita," he said, blushing as he saw her, watching him look at her bosom.

"My name is pronounced 'Meleeta,' and yes, Mr. Michael you can sit with me." Her eyes were black and matched her hair, which peeked out from under a simple cloth wrap that covered her head. Michael thought her skin the most beautiful shade of brown, like the feathers on a tawny owl, and it shone in the sunlight. The girls he was used to had milky white skin like Aunt Madge. He had also seen the black servant girls, but Melita was very different, and he couldn't keep his eyes off the gentle rise and fall of her bosom. Her name was embroidered in black. He knew she was either new or of the lowest level of employee. He thought that she looked a little older than him. She was very aware of his watching her every move. She placed a delicate, small boned hand on her arm and slowly slid it down her forearm, observing his eyes following the movement. "You like my skin?" she teased.

"Yes, it is very pretty. Where are you from?"

"I am from the print shop." She laughed at his reaction. "Señor Michael, I am from Bethnal Green, but my mama was born in Madrid. My papa is from Morocco. My grandparents were from France. I was born here, so I guess I am a mixture. Where are you from?"

"I see your surname is Harrison, that's not French or Moroccan."

"My father's name was Hassan. My parents felt that they could make their origins a little less obvious by making their name sound more English."

His mind raced so quickly, trying to interpret her slight accent that he had to think carefully before he answered. "My family is from Bath," he said.

"You must be so clean," she said with a lilting laugh, still continuing to tease him.

"I guess I must be," he said.

"I think you want to steal my heart with your smile. You are a wicked, handsome boy." Michael stood to leave. "Why, thank you, ma'am," he said with a deep theatrical bow in an attempt to hide his blushing face and embarrassment. "We will meet again."

"Do you live at this Charterhouse school?"

"Yes, when I'm at school I do. Other times I go to my home."

"I think it is not good for you to be in school, away from your mama and papa. I think you might like to come to my house for a home-cooked meal. You let me know. My papa is the best cook, an' my mama, she is going to give you a big hug." As Michael walked away, he thought about Melita's bubbly personality and sense of humor. She made him feel a little uneasy with her forthright confidence. She had a friendliness that was difficult to ignore. He had not mixed very much with the common working class and decided to find out more about her. The offer of a home cooked meal, he just wasn't quite sure what to do about that. He felt sure that his father would not approve. Waving as he walked away, Michael knew which floor he would start on in his investigation of the Co-Op.

***

Following the visit to the Co-Op, Michael's meeting with Ronald Surtees went smoothly. Michael told Mr. Surtees that, while each floor was well utilized, there seemed to be little logic in the placement of departments. Product brought into the building went from cart or barge to the department where it was to be used first, creating a multitude of locations for recording the receiving of product and, thus, a lax reporting system. Similarly, when product left the building, it left by various means that again was suspect for poor recording. There seemed to be no one person in control. Also, Michael felt that, while the retail shop for public use had its benefits, it allowed too many people to access the building uncontrolled.

"You seem to be very focused on dishonesty," said Mr. Surtees.

"I'm very conscious of honesty. My Grandpapa and my father say that an honest man has nothing to fear, and a man's integrity, once lost, is almost impossible to replace. A man's word is his bond."

Mr. Surtees thought for a moment and said, "Michael, your father instructed Charterhouse to prepare you for your role in the family businesses. Is that what you want in life?"

"I think so, sir. Our family empire has been in shipping. I am interested in finding out even more about the family's shipping line, along with my father's businesses Mother's Fine Foods and the Co-Op, and any other businesses we own. I want to find out all about how they work." After a few moments of silence, Michael took a deep breath and said, "Ronald, Sir. Lady Penelope, you speak of her with a certain calm about you. May I ask how you met?"

"Ah ha. I asked if you had seen any pretty girls at the Co-Op." Ronald smiled, stroking the flat top of his immaculate top hat. "In our society, every man has his place. Each strata, in our society requires a particular behavior of its members. Knowing your place in the scheme of things is important, but our society is evolving, and as it changes, so do attitudes. Lady Penelope is not a lady in the literal sense. She is a lady in my eyes. She is the daughter of the Viscount Mowbray, The Earl of Essex, and her mother is the Viscountess Elizabeth Regina Blackstone. They are the cream of society."

"My father is a Lord you know. Sir William."

"Quite, quite so you understand these things. My station in life is not the same. He paused as if about to say more but seemed to change direction. "To answer your question, I was one of her tutors. She is twelve years old, and I am willing to wait for her. So, I must wait, to disclose my feelings for her until she is of age, and, hopefully, I am closer to her class."

"How can you change class?"

"By becoming a headmaster. In the eyes of many, education is perceived to transcend the boundaries of class. That is my hope, anyway, with Lady Penelope."

Chapter 26

On the following Monday, Michael arrived at the wharf of the Co-Op to find a river barge pulling away as another moved into position to unload, while a third was tied to a massive black tree stump projecting out of the water about fifty feet from the bank. The watermen sat on upturned buckets, waiting their turn. On Michael's right, the relentless cacophony of the overhead trains carried on, and to the left, the adjacent building stood out over the river some thirty feet further than the Co-op's. This created a swirling eddy, which deposited and held in place the rat carcasses and detritus washed down by the mighty river tides. The early morning fog swirled around on the light breeze, as if waiting for the sun to burn it off. This time, he was greeted heartily by the workers he passed.

The previous week had been full of school studies and mechanical routine. Every spare moment, his thoughts had turned to Mother's and the Co-Op. Now, he went directly to the office, spread out his floor plans, and scanned for the fourth floor, where he planned to start, the print shop where Melita worked. Donning his dustcoat, he headed for the personnel department on the first floor, only to find that it didn't open until seven o'clock. He had five minutes to kill. Leaning back against the glass-paneled division, he observed the large range of ages of the workers, from young eightyear old children, to wizened older workers. He thought of how his age affected if he was being taken seriously here. He wished he could be at school one day a week and here the rest of the time. The clatter of machines and tools working against wood and metal emerged from the fabrication shop, while fragrant aromas emanated from the employee kitchen. A rotund, ruddy-faced woman entered the doorway with a mug of tea in her hand. The white apron that girdled her stout frame was awash with stains of many colors. "Young Mr. St.John-Brown, get this nice cup of tea insides yer. It'll get yer engine running."

"Thank you, cook. Please, just call me Michael." Over his shoulder, Michael heard the sounds of gossiping women heading for the personnel department. With the cup of tea in his hand, he followed them into the office. As one of the girls spotted him, the chatter subsided to a whisper. The large ornate time clock clanged as each one punched a hole into their paper time card. An older woman wearing a long, matronly black dress trimmed at the collar with cream lace at the high neckline, approached Michael as she buttoned up her dustcoat. She introduced herself as the senior clerk. "Mr. St.John-Brown, I understand that you are to be honoring us with your presence on a regular basis. May I assign you one of our junior clerks to take care of your needs?" Some of the girls giggled in the background, but he put on his deepest voice, stood as tall as he could and made his reply, sounding, he thought, authoritative: "Madam, at this time I do not require an clerk. Should you wish to assign one, then, so be it. The alternative is for me to bring my requirements directly to you. I require you to provide me with a list of employees on the fourth floor, broken down by department and employee status. I will wait outside."

Soon, armed with the list, he took off for the fourth floor, taking the steps instead of the cargo lift. He wanted to observe before being observed. In the front were the book-keeping and purchasing departments. While the former was a model of quiet industry, the latter was babbling chaos. The confident voices of the salesmen were filled with bravado as they flirted with the girls and women. While the purchasing and sales department was noisy, it appeared as productive in its noise as the book-keeping department did in its silence.

This left only the print shop. Sliding open the heavy, wide oak, steel bound door on its track, Michael noticed the rails set into the floor, upon which sat an iron cart stacked high with paper and cardboard. A boy who looked younger than Michael greeted him with "Allo, guvner." The boy placed one hand on the cart and rolled it effortlessly toward the back of the shop. There was a tall, dapper man, on the thin side, with a giant handlebar mustache and brown, pomaded-down hair parted straight down the middle. His dress was tailor shop-window precise, and his deportment was militaristic. As he placed his sharply pointed pencil behind his ear and his pince-nez glasses in his breast pocket, he walked toward Michael. "Benjamin Loring, sir," he said. "I am the master printer here. How may I be of assistance to you?"

"I am going to spend some time in the shop, in hopes that I will understand what you do, how you do it, and why you do it the way you do. Would it be possible to have a guide for the day? I do not wish to be a nuisance or get in the way of production," said Michael.

"A junior will probably not be able to answer all your questions," said Loring. "We are training all the time, and this could disrupt our team approach, but I understand that you've already met one of our brightest finds, Melita Harrison. But no, perhaps not such a good idea, as she has such a strong spirit. Would you prefer Kenny, one of the…"

"I am happy to work with Miss Harrison," Michael interrupted as he gave way to his adolescent urges. Mr. Loring gave Michael a large bench and pushed aside its contents. He soon sent over a smiling Melita. "Señor Michael, happy I am to see you again," she said. "Mister Loring, says I am to spend the day with you. I hoped to see you again. You asked for me. This must be fate." She laughed as if to confuse Michael. She leaned across the large work surface, her hands on either side of her face, her blouse hanging to reveal her breasts and gave him a wide smile.

And so, it began. sixteen-year-old Melita showed Michael around, and Michael took copious notes, often asking Melita to repeat herself as he got lost in her enthusiasm and her gesticulating performance as she spoke. She was passionate about everything she said. Michael knew his mother would not take to Melita's joy of life. She would say Melita was of the common classes and to forward. On the other hand, he felt that Aunt Madge would have embraced the character in Melita. And what would father think? Michael felt this would never be an issue as father so rarely left Bath, other than for business. At these times he would summon Michael to meet him somewhere, usually his Gentleman's Club, in Belgravia. His mother spent her time between Bath and Essex with her family, so chances of them meeting Melita were negligible.

When the morning bell declared tea break, Michael and Melita went outside with the girls from the shop and sat in the late morning sun, chatting. The girls all hung around Michael as if he was a celebrity. Michael named each girl and, recalled what they did in the shop. When he finished, Melita shook his hand and said, "You did so good! You don't have your notes, it's all from memory! I am so proud of you." He was the hit of the hour.

*****

Back in the print shop, Melita spent the rest of the morning explaining each station's role. She took Michael to one of the smaller presses and showed him how to set the print, ink the rollers, and make prints. By the time lunch came, Michael was very comfortable in the print shop. All jobs followed the same process. They just varied in size. Michael went over to the master printer and asked, "Why is it that Melita appears to have risen above the others in the shop, and yet still wears the lowest color name tag?"

Mr. Loring said, "What young Melita has is *passion*, passion for life and everything in it. She will never reach the top of the mountain for two reasons, one, she is a woman, and, two, more importantly, because she does not believe there is a top and she will never stop achieving. Sadly, the first obstacle is the one she will probably not conquer, society is a hard taskmaster. Oh, that I should have a daughter like that. Her father knows how lucky he is, although I do believe luck is such a small part of it. He brought her up well and taught her to keep going. I am led to believe that he was the son of an African slave in Morocco. He somehow escaped that dreadful life. He once told me that his wife was an outsider in Spain, as she was of French origins. He was an outsider because of his origins. So, they came to England to live with her parents and start a new life. They could then share a common ground in being outsiders together. That's character for you. Ballsy if you ask me. I don't think I could move countries just like that."

The shrill lunch break whistle ended their conversation. Michael bounded down the large, wide-open staircases set into the center of the building. The ornate filigree and cast-iron rail supports steadied his descent. Six people abreast could go down these stairs. Michael burst out of the open doors to find Melita sitting at the wharf's edge. He approached her and asked if everything was all right.

She looked up at him, and in a soft, pleading voice, she said, "I don't want to be seen sharing this place with you for lunch. Too many people talk and say nasty things. What they don't see they don't know. Sometimes, we all need to go to our own special place. You want to see mine?" Michael nodded silently. "You go up the side wharf to the other side of the railway arch, go through the arch and back down the other side. I will meet you there."

She made sure he was watching her as she walked along the river under the Blackfriars' Bridge. He turned and walked up the wharf along the side of the building. He crossed under the huge railway lines through a stone tunnel and he saw what Melita had meant. Where the offshoot of the river created a wharf on the Co-Op side of the railway bridge abutments, on the other side, a narrow path ran down to the water's edge, where a wrought-iron gate closed off the river from the path. He had almost reached the end when Melita appeared from under the arch. She opened the gate and beckoned him. He followed her through.

"I think we can't be seen together by the workers. They talk a lot. You go one way, I go the other way. Nobody can tell." She pointed out where the sun streamed out on the cobblestones under the arch, causing a large arc of warmed surface. As she crept up the slope to the highest point, he followed her until they were crawling. Then they sat side by side idly chatting and basking in the sun. Soon the factory whistle sounded and they had to return to work.

***

"You are late Mister Michael. I have been waiting for you." Michael blushed thinking that everyone in the shop new his secret. He could sense the smile in her as her expression stayed serious. She was all business as she handed him an envelope from the heap of large manila envelopes in front of her. He spread its contents out on the large desk. In the background the wheels of one of the larger ornate presses were spinning with each clank of the press plate pounding down on the flattened cardboard box waiting for an impression. The wide leather belt above the press ran across the ceiling on big iron wheels that connected to other belts on other pulleys until it reached the sidewall of the building, where a steel cable on the final pulley disappeared in a hole in the floor where it descended to the boiler room. The steel cable and pulley driven by the steam boiler in the basement, spun relentlessly all day. When the press operator pulled a lever, a wheel moved to tighten the leather belt and the press would spin into action. The press operator and an apprentice worked in unison. The press would pound down on the cardboard then open up and spit it out with a hiss. Then a large rubber roller would apply a thin film of ink and flip out of the path of the plate. The apprentice would throw the next piece of cardboard in and line it up against stops and quickly pull his hands out of the press jaws. This routine was repeated until the run was finished or the press needed adjusting as the pressman monitored the progress. Bang, hiss, clank-clank, bang, hiss, clank-clank, on and on. There were soon four presses running this afternoon at different speeds and so the quiet of the morning was a distant memory. Michael leaned over the work surface and whispered to Melita. "Remember who is the boss around here."

With a smile she replied, "In the print shop you are not the boss. Mister Loring, he is the boss. You cannot have two bosses." Michael smiled in submission. The rest of the afternoon was spent with Melita going through job files and explaining the differences in jobs. The use of various inks was covered. Why different presses were used for different jobs and how jobs were assigned priority was reviewed. She demonstrated a thorough knowledge of the print shop, which was impressive. Just before he was about to leave Melita asked Michael, "Would you mind if I give you a test? I want to see if you have understood what I say to you and that you are not just looking at my," she leaned over and whispered, "titties all afternoon." Michael laughed and agreed. She took out a blank job order and filled in a fictitious job. "I want you to walk around the shop and fill in all the steps with the things that might be done. You bring it back to me and we shall see if you get it right."

It took almost an hour for him to pace his way around the shop tracing the path of the job. When he had completed the task and returned to Melita she went through it step by step and pointed out where he had things out of order, where steps had been missed. He questioned why certain items that she had said he missed needed to be there. He felt some of the points were common sense. Her answer was remarkably simple and direct. "If you are doing a job you have to think that the person that you give a piece of the job to, doesn't know anything. Sometimes he does, sometime he doesn't. There are no excuses for you if the job goes wrong."

The explanation showed Michael that the advice given him by Ronald Surtees about looking versus seeing was very important. He felt that if you just looked at Melita you would have a totally different picture than if you looked and listened to her. The latter gave you a picture of a person who was a diligent, and clear thinking, who did not let her diminutive size hinder her effort. This warmed her to him even more. He asked her to complete a task for him. He wanted her to draw a simple sketch of the floor plan of the print shop once more and place everything in it where she thought it would be more effective and to consider if it would be better suited in another part of the building. She agreed and with great speed took pencil to paper.

The hour was getting late and presses were being shut down as they completed their assigned runs. They were then being cleaned and readied for the next day's work. Michael went to the corner office occupied by Mr. Loring. He expressed his appreciation and they discussed Melita's contribution. It was evident to Michael that the man held her in high esteem as he said that she had the ability to do whatever she wanted in life. It was his next statement that was to prove a valuable life lesson to Michael. The man said, "As I sit here with all my training and experience, for me to decide when Melita has reached or not reached as far as she can go would be arrogant. Her achievements are set by her goals and I have no right to decide them for her. As a man and father of two girls, my heart wants for Melita many things, but my brain tells me to want for Melita, what Melita wants for herself. For the Co-Op and the print shop, I want for her to stay here. I hope she will want that as well. But who knows what she will set her sights on." The two shook hands and parted.

Turning to leave the man's office he saw Melita waiting for him. Melita had completed her suggestion and sketch. They were folded and in a manila envelope with Senior Michael artistically written on the front. It was not proper for a gentleman to touch, let alone kiss a woman in public, so Michael thanked her for her valuable guidance, picked up the envelope and dipped his head in a respectful bow. Turning to leave he said, "I look forward to seeing you next week." He left without looking back and he felt a certain pleasure in his connection with this girl.

***

Every time Michael went to The Co-op, he and Melita would share their lunchtime under the arches of Blackfriars Bridge. They entertained each other with tales of their background. It was at the fourth such lunchtime that their relationship accelerated. She reached over and took his hand. It looked so pale against her delicate skin color. As if by some unseen sign they turned towards each other and embraced. The warmth Michael felt was so different to the sun on his back. Very gently she placed her lips on his. Not kissing, just gently brushing. This was not the tongue plunging torrid sexual kissing Michael had read in the more sordid novels of the time. Melita parted her lips and touched his again. He could not find words to describe her taste. It was sweet, warm, wet and yet cool. It tingled and calmed. He felt an erection starting. He tensed.

"You like to see my titties?"

Without hesitation, he quietly responded, "yes."

She unbuttoned her dress front and lifted her chemise above her heaving chest to release herself. Michael stared in wonder. The silken tawny skin rose to mounds of warm flesh topped by chocolate colored areola with firm button nub nipples standing upright. "You can kiss my titties. They swill stand up for you. I think of you at night and they stand up. I want so much for you to kiss them, okay."

Michael gently placed his lips around her nipple and ran his tongue around it. She emitted a low deep murmur. "Please she has a friend." Michael repeated his attention on the other nipple and received the same results. Without warning she pulled her bra down and put her heaving chest away. Having finished correcting her dress she gently pushed him on his back and placed her hand on his now throbbing erection, through his trousers. Suddenly she stopped. "You have made a wet spot on your pants. I fix it." She unbuttoned his pants parted his drawers and his erection jumped out at her. "Turn on your side" she instructed. He obeyed as she cuddled into his back. She reached her arms around his side and held his erection in her fist. Slowly she moved her fingers to his tip and spread his seeping juices over the engorged end. Her hand slid tightly down the shaft where she would stroke him, then repeat the actions getting faster and faster. He stiffened, jerked and grabbed her hand, held it tightly around his shaft as it spat out a stream of semen followed by lesser spurts. The streaks lay on the hot flagstones and bubbled as the sun quickly dried them away. They lie huddled together for a few moments. "You should go back to work. I will go my way. She held his face in her hands and gently placed her lips on his. I think you are my special lover."

"God, I feel good!" said Michael, with a grin. With that, Melita left. Michael strolled back into the print shop with a relaxed confident air. He had been irrevocably changed forever.

***

Upon returning to Charterhouse, Michael went straight to his Form Master's chambers to request an audience. He was invited into the tiny quarters Mr. Surtees occupied. After showing him his notes and sketches, he began to elaborate, but the teacher stopped him. "You have done a remarkable amount of work with what appears to be a great deal of diligence," he said. "It is clear you need more time. I am not sure how much leeway the headmaster will give us, but I will speak with him. Well done. Go and relax, I will find you later on." When Michael left, Mr. Surtees collapsed into his well-worn, deep armchair. He closed his eyes and pondered the fortunate position he now found himself in. *This young boy could be just what I need to advance my career and could be my ticket to getting closer to Lady Penelope*, he thought.

Chapter 27

Reality set in the following morning when Ronald sat in the Headmaster's ante-chamber waiting for an audience. It came to him in a flash of inspiration. To fight the Headmaster head on, no matter how clever he was, would be foolish. He had to be more circuitous in his approach to slaying this dragon. He was called into the sumptuous study of the Headmaster with a condescending air and was met with, "You have fifteen minutes Surtees. What is it you want?" The Headmaster was gazing out of his leaded glass window at the boys milling around below on the grassed quadrangle.

"If you are too busy for me headmaster, I can seek assistance from someone else," Surtees firmly stated. The Headmaster spun round, put his fists on his desk and leaning forward with face full of rage spat out, "Who do you think you are? You little jumped up peon. You are only here because of your connections. There are many more standing behind you waiting to fill your fancy shiny boots and Little Lord Fauntleroy fashion."

"Excuse me! Sir." Ronald surprised himself at his bravado. He took a deep breath and carried on. "I am here by the grace and decency of the people that I know who contribute to the fiscal stability of Charterhouse. As are you! I am sure that there are people waiting in line to fill *your* space. I am here, for just that reason." The Headmaster sat with a thump in his chair, his fury clearly showing.

"This better be good Mr. Surtees. Go on."

"Sir, first allow me to apologize for my outburst. I came to see you, full of excitement and enthusiasm, for an opportunity that presents itself for the school and took umbrage at my reception." He waited for a response.

"I accept and offer my apologies in return. I am always under pressure these days. What opportunity have you found?"

Ronald took a deep breath to compose himself and then spoke, "The St.John-Brown family gave us young Michael to educate. I have had the bursar's office do some research and even though Sir William himself passed through our school and sees fit to place his son here, there have been no donations made from the family."

"Interesting point. I wonder if approaches have been made?" mused the Headmaster.

"It is an accepted fact that if you can get people to offer on their own, it reaps bigger rewards than if you ask them to give. I agree that its semantics, but it works. If you recall, when Sir William came to us with his son he asked us to prepare him for the family business. You have since authorized the one day a week that Michael can spend at the place of business. That has turned out to be the source of my plan. Last evening young Michael came to my chambers to request more time to prepare his report on his efforts at the business. I usually would not bother you in this matter but the rough notes that I saw were way beyond his years."

The headmaster's demeanor softened and he sat back in his chair and unfolded his arms. "Go on."

"The quality of Michael's work has always been good. He presented me with charts, notes, and diagrams that appear to be the prelude to a high-quality report at the level of a consultation. What I am suggesting is that you invite Sir William to come to Charterhouse in one week to review his son's work. I feel confident that the father will be so impressed that we shall not only have Michael for at least three more years, but that he can be encouraged to perhaps endow a chair of business. This would be first for Charterhouse, indeed any preparatory school. I also feel that with careful development of Michael we could see the St.John-Brown Empire sending us more pupils."

The headmaster took a replenishing gulp of air and sat back. "Jolly good form. Bring the boys work to me to evaluate tomorrow and we shall give it serious consideration. I see only one stumbling block. Sir William has declined invitations over the past two years to come to functions at the school. Rumors have it since the death of his father, and top that off with the death of one of his business partners, the Duggan woman, he has become somewhat of a recluse. Damned odd, that one. How do suppose we get him here?"

The Form Master thought for a moment. Then slowly his thoughts were spoken, "I had thought for the work to be revealed to both yourself and Sir William together. The element of surprise to both of you at the same time will eliminate any suspicions of a devious agenda. I was not aware of Sir William's hesitation to travel. I suggest that young Michael arrange this himself. He can ask you to meet with him as well as asking his father. Both of you will be equally surprised at the other's presence. I can spearhead the proposal for more specific studies while you stand your ground for the classics, mathematics, science and the arts to be maintained thereby tying the business and the school together."

"I like your idea though it might be better to have you send the cables in Michael's name and have Michael himself surprised thinking he is going to be presenting just to me. In fact, don't even tell him that he will be presenting to anyone other than you."

"I am a little concerned about the dishonesty of my masquerading as Michael to his father in a cable."

The headmaster's response was firm. "Well in that case I shall simply contact the father and request his presence to discuss the boy."

After the details were worked out, both men shook hands and parted on more co-operative terms. The headmaster dismissed Mr. Surtees with a tepid compliment, "If your little scheme works out you will have done well for the school. And maybe for yourself." It was time for Ronald to put the plan in motion. Telegraphs were sent and Michael was instructed to prepare his notes and presentation for his Form Master's approval.

***

One week later, unbeknownst to Michael, the plan that Ronald Surtees formulated was about to be played out. It was early in the morning when he was summoned to the headmaster's office. His nerves were on edge. He was scheduled to be giving a presentation to Mr. Surtees in an hour, and he had misplaced the floor plans of the Co-Op building. But, as he walked into the anteroom of the headmaster's office, he found Mr. Surtees waiting for him, "I took the plans and have them set out in the headmaster's study. He requires that he sit in on your presentation today," said Mr. Surtees. "Remember to take your time and breathe deeply between thoughts. It is not out of order to respectfully request that he hold any questions until you have finished. The floor is yours, until *you* ask for questions. Best of luck, young man. I am excited to hear what you have done."

They entered the overly large study with its ornate vaulted ceilings and arcing wood struts that peaked like the lining of schoolboy's cap. Before the headmaster could speak, Mr. Surtees turned to Michael and said, "Where would you be most comfortable speaking?" Michael pointed to the conference table, which had two table easels set up. While Michael examined the plans on the easels, plans to the left and print shop layout to the right, he scanned the room. The morning light shone brightly through the leaded windowpanes throwing a myriad of rainbow colored, reflections on the polished tabletop. The round, swollen break point in one of the handblown, glass panels looked like a huge eye, watching him. Toward the back of the room stood a tall black-lacquered, four-sectioned, Chinese, rice paper screen. It cut off one corner off the room from sight. A huge vase of fresh-cut flowers commanded the center of the conference table. Michael picked up the vase and placed it at the end of the table so that it would not distract his audience.

"You may start when you are ready," the headmaster boomed in an overly loud voice, as if wanting the whole world to know. Michael followed his notes very carefully, reading some and paraphrasing parts he had committed to memory, and sometimes even ad-libbing. He spoke of the print shop, which, for efficiency, he graded a six out of ten. He suggested that some employees were underused while others were not working to their fullest potential and that the buildings space were being best utilized., and that one person in particular could be groomed to be of greater use to the company in other areas. He glanced at Mr. Surtees, and his cheeks flushed briefly. He got back to his evaluation, emphasizing that his work for the study had been carried out in a very short time. "I have only scratched the surface, and although I do not know everything, Mr. Surtees taught me to not only look, but to look beyond, and to ask questions. As a result, I know that I have probably been an annoyance to many but I have really gained a huge amount of knowledge about that part of the business. I know there is a great deal more to learn." He went on at length detailing every issue and his suggestions for improving or leaving it as it was. He nodded in appreciation to Ronald Surtees. "Thank you, sir," he said to Mr. Surtees, and to the headmaster, "Thank you for taking the time to listen to the report, Sir."

The headmaster looked at Mr. Surtees and said, "impressive work for the lad. It is of a standard far above that expected of the boy Michael's age. Did you coach him in any way Mr. Surtees?"

"Oh yes headmaster. I worked very closely with Michael to ensure he stayed focused."

The headmaster turned to Michael. "I invited a guest to listen in on your presentation, and would like to discuss it with him." He walked over to the Chinese screen and opened it. "I believe you know *your father*, Sir William St.John-Brown." The man was smiling at his own humor. Sir William stood up from an armchair and stepped toward Michael. Father and son shook hands and hugged. Then Sir William turned to Ronald Surtees.

"You have done a remarkable job, sir. I don't believe I could have done any better."

"Not I, not I," said Mr. Surtees. "Michael has put in the time and effort and followed the advice. The accolades are his, sir. It has been my pleasure. The boy must be encouraged to go further."

"How do you propose we do that?" Sir William asked.

"If I may, Headmaster?" the Form Master said. And the Headmaster nodded his permission. "I think we should design a course of study based around the St.John-Brown family business's and your holdings."

"I will not hear of it," said the headmaster with firm conviction. "The boy must continue with his studies in the classics, mathematics, the sciences, and other things."

Sir William interrupted, "I believe that I am the one to decide what my son learns. He is a chip off the old block, if you know what I mean. He apparently can learn anything he puts his mind to. Don't you think? Right proud of him, I am," William said as he slapped his son the back and put his arm around the boy's shoulder in a rare show of pride and connection. The Headmaster tentatively agreed, as Ronald Surtees picked up the line of thought.

"I agree, but there are some less important classes and activities that could be exchanged to allow for a dedicated course of study. I think one year at the Co-Operative, one year at the Royal Shipping Line, and one year at Mother's Fine Foods would give Michael an excellent business education. It would also provide Sir William an excellent analysis of his family's businesses."

The headmaster chimed in, "and young St.John-Brown, a fuller understanding of where his future may lie. How do you propose to get the chancellor and governing body of the school to accept such an unusual proposition?"

"I do agree it would be a wonderful opportunity for young St.John-Brown, but it will be an uphill battle. They are traditional-thinking men." The Headmaster appeared to be thinking. It was just as he and Mr. Surtees had planned it.

"Could we propose the introduction of a chair of business studies?" questioned Mr. Surtees.

"They will reject it instantly, as there is no provision for funding such a thing," answered the Headmaster.

"What are we talking about for funding?" Sir William interjected into the conversation.

The Headmaster stared long and hard at Sir William, appearing to be thinking. "This would be a huge undertaking Sir William," he said. "It would require a rather large endowment."

Sir William stood and drew out a business card. Handing it to the Headmaster, he said, "A letter of credit for one hundred thousand pounds will be on your desk by the end of business tomorrow. Get it done, my man." He turned to Michael, put his arm around his shoulder, and, turning to the two educators, he said, "My son and I are going to my club, where we will stay the night. Thank you, gentlemen. Oh, yes, I expect Mr. Surtees to be assigned to Michael for the duration of his studies." Looking the Headmaster directly in the eye he said, "And I shall require that the endowed chair be known as 'The Duggan Chair of Business Studies'." With that, father and son left.

***

When father and son were seated in the comfort of Sir William's private club dining room, Michael spoke in earnest," I did not know that you were going to hear my presentation father."

"It was best that way. I would have been a distraction."

"I'm not sure that I fully understand what took place. The *Duggan* Chair of Business Studies?" he asked questioningly.

"Just a little tribute to Madge Duggan. We all miss her you know."

"What does this mean for my studies, the business?"

"There comes a time when a man has to take charge of his own destiny. Hearing your presentation made me think about my own life and how circumstances have dictated the paths I have chosen. It seems to me that the Surtees fellow saw something in you and has been able to guide you well. You would be learning many things at school that would not necessarily serve you later in life. This way you will be focusing on what is important. I expect that you will spend the next three, or four years learning our business from top to bottom. You must understand how things are done. As none of us know how long or short our life is, so it's better to get on with it as soon as you can."

"Are you ill father? Is something wrong?"

"Oh no, not at all. Your grandfather's death was so sudden. It shocked me. Then Madgie, no one saw her death coming. I want you to do something with your life that will make you happy and not someone else happy."

"Happy? Father, do I get to say in what makes me happy?"

"Not until you are old enough to know what life is all about. Then you will be qualified. What was good enough for your grandfather and our ancestors was good enough for me, and you, I suspect."

"So, am I going to still be at school?"

"Oh, yes. The big difference is that we are going to channel your efforts to achieve the best end results. I have every hope that you will champion the family and The Royal Shipping Line well."

***

The chancellor and governors of Charterhouse were quick to embrace the concept of the chair of business studies. The endowment was of such large proportions that they happily named the award given to student recipients 'The Duggan Chair of Business Studies'. It became known around the school as 'The Duggan'. Much to their surprise, the number of applicants for scholarships quickly surpassed the funded positions. Ronald Surtees was elevated to 'Master' of the program. A lot more students entered the program after Michael as the school readily used the donations made by applying students to become part of the decision-making process. The department quickly became not only financially independent of the school, but also the model for new departments.

Chapter 28

By the end of 1867 Michael, now nearly sixteen, completed his time at The Co-Op. Over the following three years Michael was to move through the other family businesses. The move to Mother's Fine Foods required that he apply the lessons he learned at the Co-Op. His meetings with Melita had to be restricted to weekends, but their stolen moments were as passionate as ever, pushing the boundaries of discretion though never fully consummating their union. Though Michael wanted to move Melita to Southampton to be with him, he realized the attention it would draw to himself was not advisable. Besides, what would her parents would think? Never the less, Michael selfishly proposed that she be relocated to Southampton. Melita seized the opportunity to gain more experience and to be close to Michael. The fall of 1870 saw him completing his study of Mother's Fine Foods in Southampton and move back to London and The Royal Shipping Line. At each new location he was able to get permission to take Melita along as his assistant. Her shrewd ability to observe and delve into the heart of things, was, quite often, more intensive than Michael's.

***

Michael found his studies at Charterhouse and the family businesses gave him more flexibility with his time, but less to spare. It wasn't until Michael's eighteenth birthday in 1870 that the relationship between Michael and Melita's moved from passionate foreplay to a more consuming level. Melita was fully aware of the bond developing between them. She was now nineteen and had developed into a vibrant young woman. It happened one summer afternoon on the bank of the River Thames at Henley. They had been attending The Royal Regatta and they were both intoxicated by the summer warmth, the good wine, and the relaxed fun filled atmosphere of the rowing races. The fresh country air was exhilarating. Late into the evening with the sun slowly setting, the revelers litter scattered the field around them, they found themselves alone. As the sun silently slipped from view, the quiet and excesses of fine champagne lulled them into another place and they fell asleep. It was Melita who woke first, studying Michael's face. Thinking he was sleeping, she whispered to him, as much to herself, "I wonder if you know that I do really love you, my foolish little boy."

Michael opened one eye and smiled as he said, "Yes, I know you do. I wouldn't have it any other way." Pulling her on top of himself he kissed her forehead with a lingering passion. Like statues they held each other tightly, not moving. Melita shifted her position and kissed him with repeated pecking kisses that ended with their hungry, moist lips locked. Without warning Melita suddenly sat, straddling Michael and started to unbutton his shirt. In a throaty sounding voice she said, "I think now is the time for us, for love, to finish what we have started so many times and yet held back."

Michael's now growing erection dictated what followed. "Are you sure you want to do this?" he asked in surprise, having been held back so many times.

"Why, don't you want to?"

"I have wanted to for a long time, but I want you to be sure."

"Then stop talking and make love with me." Melita rolled off of Michael and touching his erection through his trousers she said, "Oh my, someone is ready. Kneeling, she pulled her summer dress over her shoulders and Michael was fully aroused, both physically and mentally at the sight of her naked beauty. He ran his hands over her silky, smooth skin that was cooled by the night air.

She whispered, "Be gentle with me. I may seem forward but I have never given myself completely to a man, or good-looking boy for that matter." She laughed to cover her nervousness. Quickly Michael undressed, laid Melita down and kissed her lips, then her neck. He moved to her breasts and then her tummy, marveling at how erotic her cool skin was. He parted her legs with his shoulders and she quickly held his head between her hands saying, "No, not this time. I want *you* inside me, deep inside me."

"But I enjoy kissing you."

"I like it too, but this day has been special. This place is special. I am ready." Michael slowly moved up the body the way he came, kissing every inch. Without warning he quickly thrust into her. She flinched.

Concerned, he asked, "Did I hurt you?"

"Yes, no, ooooh. Stay there." She lifted her ankles around his waist holding him in place. Without warning Michael climaxed, jerking with each ejaculation. He went to pull away and Melita held him firmly in place with her heels.

Michael whispered, "I couldn't wait. It felt so good. Were you ready? Did you finish?"

"I don't have to. You don't know how much I have thought about this time. To feel you inside me doing what I have watched us do, by my hand, by your hand, and my mouth. This is so different. We have to recreate this dance, and end on the same note. But, for now this was wonderful. They lay side by side watching the stars move across the sky, talking long into the night. Michael believed that he possessed a high degree of integrity, charm, and charisma and that was what he felt made him attractive to her. Melita, for her part, was becoming increasing invested in Michael as a lover, a friend and a promise of a better future for herself.

During the years Michael spent at the various family businesses, Ronald Surtees would occasionally make the trip to Southampton to receive his reports and to monitor Michael's progress. When Michael was in London at The Royal Shipping line he spent more time at Charterhouse, where he had become something of a celebrity. With each meeting, Ronald gained an extensive, working knowledge of the St.John-Brown empire and it's workings. Slowly a strong friendship developed between the two that moved beyond the student teacher realm. Ronald quickly observed the connection between Michael and Melita. He could see why Michael wanted her close. She radiated youth, joy and fun, and exuded a mature sexuality. This fact was not lost on him. He thought about the risk of Melita interfering with what he was starting to see as an opportunity for himself to possibly change his own future. He felt the need to find out just how serious the relationship between Michael and Melita really was. After some of these meetings, he would press Michael to share the details. Did he take her from behind? Was she on top? Did she climax? Did she suck him? What did she taste like? These questions, though quite uncomfortable for Michael, gave him a feeling of superiority. Michael found himself very aware that not only had Ronald not had sex with Penelope, but had probably not had sex with anyone else. In many ways, Michael viewed his teacher as a sad, pathetic little man, but in no way did this diminish the pleasure of his company. Michael did not understand the man's infatuation, or was it obsession, with Penelope. It still passed through his mind periodically whether the man was a homosexual, or just a frustrated pursuer. It was not important enough for him to dwell on though.

***

While at Mother's, Michael had plenty of opportunity to learn more about Madge. Her offices at Duggan's Ship Chandlers next-door had been kept the same as the day she died. Many of her personal effects, such as clothes, traveling portmanteau, pictures, and ornaments, had been placed in a shrine like setting. Michael saw quite a number of masculine touches and items that he recognized to be his father's. Sometimes, he would stand and stare at the scene and see, in his mind, his father and Madge there. It unnerved him. He could never work up the courage to share his thoughts with his father. Any probing questions he asked the workers were met with a reverent stare and silence as if they were sworn to secrecy by some higher power.

The big difference he saw between the Co-Op and Mother's Fine Foods was Ted Ballard, who was clearly more effective in Southampton. The stables, machinery, and plant were immaculately kept, and everyone appeared to be busy at all times. Duggan's required little of Ted's time, as he had set things up to be independent and they worked that way. Michael at this time did not know that the chandlery business had been left in trust to him, and that he would own it in its entirety when he reached the age of majority, twenty-one.

In the ensuing years Michael gained an extensive knowledge of the Royal Shipping Line, The Co-Op and the management of the family's large property portfolio. He took Melita with him as his paid personal assistant. The pair developed a bond that each understood differently, in their own way.

Chapter 29

In 1872, as Michael turned twenty, his father announced that, having completed his time at Charterhouse, and the study of the Royal Shipping Line, he should put it to good use. "I want you to go to America and take a good look at what is happening there, son. There is a lot of business to be had, and I am thinking we should enter the fray a little more aggressively. Feet on the ground type of thing, you know."

So, Michael was faced with having to go to America. Without giving it much thought he stated, "I would like to take my assistant, Miss Harrison with me father."

"Who the blazes is Miss Harrison? Word has reached my ears about her. Is she the young factory girl from the Co-Op - Spanish, French or something?" Sir William questioned.

"Miss Harrison, Melita, has been assisting me for the last four years in each of our businesses, father." In a fleeting moment of bravado he continued, "I met her at the Co-Op print shop during my studies there and she has moved to each business with me. You could say Melita is *my* Madge Duggan."

"What the bloody hell is that supposed to mean?" his father spat out. "Explain yourself."

"Father, Melita has been my sounding board through all my studies. She is the person who stood by me as I grew up in Charterhouse and the family businesses. She makes me see reason when I become a little complacent."

"But she is a common factory worker? The St. John-Browns do not marry beneath their station. You would do well to remember that. Do you love her, boy?"

"Who said anything about marrying father? I don't know what love is. I don't even know if she's willing to come with me, but I wouldn't hurt her feelings by asking her to come only for you to deny my request."

"You have your own funds," said Sir William. "You do not need my approval. You need her parents' approval. I do have one condition. I have that right. Do not marry without seeking your mother's blessing."

"That's not even in the equation Father, so your condition is easy to meet. Agreed, father." With that, Michael headed for the Co-Op building and went straight for the personnel office, where he pulled Melita's employment card and found her information: Melita Harrison, 14 Nichols Square, Bethnal Green.

***

The hansom cab pulled up to the front of the red brick, semi-detached house. At the end of the street, or siding as it was called, was a railway line that abruptly ended the street. When Michael paid him, the cabbie offered to wait, but Michael declined, as he had no idea what reception he would meet. Not knowing what to expect, he was surprised by a house that had a small front garden full of brightly colored flowers. Michael approached the front door and was startled by the resounding thud that echoed through the house when he let go of the heavy brass knocker.

The door slowly creaked open, and a pair of deep brown eyes studied him carefully before a shriek split the air. "Michael, Michael, all the times that I have invited you over to eat with us you never came. Now you come to see me! Is anything wrong? You will stay for dinner, yes? Mama, Papa…Mama, Papa, come, come and meet my friend!" Melita stood back and pulled him inside and kissed him deeply. Over her shoulder, Michael saw a slightly built black man and a short, full-figured, olive skinned woman, who smiled at him as she looked at his outstretched hand.

The woman came forward and hugged him with more strength than her daughter. "We only shake the hands in business. I think you are more than business." She laughed and kissed him on both cheeks in the Mediterranean style. Papa just stared at Michael, and Michael became a little nervous. Her father whispered something to her mother, who turned to Michael and said, "Melita's papa wants to know what is the relationship between the two of you?"

"Mr. and Mrs. Harrison, your daughter has been my personal assistant for a long time. I have a great deal of respect for her. I care for her. She's a true friend." He was careful to avoid the word 'love' which did not go unobserved.

Melita broke the awkward air that hung over them by speaking as she led them into the parlor. "So, Mr. Michael, what brings you to our home?" Michael spoke slowly and deliberately as if speaking to a child. All the time he was studying the parents. Her father was so black and her mother so olive skinned. He surmised it must be the mother's French heritage that gave Melita the lighter skin, which he so admired. He explained what he wanted to do with Melita. Her job would be as his personal assistant at almost twice what she was earning now, plus all her living expenses would be paid. Some of her pay would be sent to her parents every week. The huge smile never left Melita's face as she went through everything once more in French, to be sure that her parents understood everything clearly. Michael picked up the word *marry* and saw her reply in the negative.

As Melita spoke with her parents, Michael noticed the bright colors used in decorating the room, and especially an exquisite silk tapestry hanging on one wall, taking up most of its surface. Ornate cloths were draped over the furniture. Melita's mother saw him looking and explained that her grandparents had settled in this house from France sixty years ago. They were highly prized silk weavers, and had taken in a family of weavers from Spain who had fallen on hard times. The house was currently home to three families. Melita's mother hoped that Michael would show her daughter a better life. She spoke, "Come in and sit with us. This is a big thing you ask for. Melita, she wants to do this?"

Melita responded quickly, "Mama, this is a good opportunity for me to learn. Yes, I want to go."

"You don't interrupt your mama. I want to know more about this man."

"What would you like to know Mrs. Harrison?"

"You may call me mama. That's ok. Melita, she has been happy all the time she worked for you. Papa and I don't know you. We know only what our daughter, she tells us."

"I am pleased that she has been happy working for me. I have been happy and very impressed with her as worker, as a friend, and as an advisor. She has a good eye and a strong mind. I think she would do well in a bigger role in our family business."

"As her mama I worry for my little girl."

"Mama, I'm not a little girl. You and papa have taught me many things. Papa often says that you and he gave me life, gave me wings. Now is the time to let me fly."

Melita's father's eyes started to well up as he said, "I think maybe I teach you too much."

"Papa, don't get upset. I am very excited about the opportunity that Mr. St.John-Brown offers me. You and mama did very big things when you came to this country to start a new life. This may be my big thing. Please, papa."

Melita's mother responded, "Your papa and I don't want to lose you. You may get to America and never come back. What do think that would do to your papa?"

Michael joined in the conversation. "Oh no, Mr. and Mrs. Harrison, It is my plan to go to America and see what opportunities lay there for our shipping line. In the future, who knows, but for now this is a journey, with a beginning and an end. Melita will return, I promise. I have to return and there is no way I would leave her behind."

"I worry for her safety, I'm sure you understand." Her father still had a look of sadness as he spoke.

"I promise with everything my family holds sacred that I will protect and care for your daughter, and bring her home safely."

Her father stared at Michael intently before he replied, "Mama, do you think we should let our little girl go? Do you think he is a good man?"

"I don't know if he is good or not, but papa he did come to ask our permission. That's good. Should we let Melita go? I think that maybe she has made up her own mind and we both know she has a strong will."

"That she gets from you, I just go along to make you happy."

"Let's have something to eat while papa and I think about this for a moment."

"Mama, papa, I am not a child asking to go out to play. This is my life you are wanting to think about."

"Hush girl, your mama has spoken," papa chided her. A pleasant afternoon was spent as the family got to know Michael a little better. The family history was proudly explained as Michael showed great interest. To Melita's joy, her mother filled everyone's glass with her home-made wine, raised her own glass and said, "brindemos por nuestros America."

"What did she say?" asked Michael.

"Mama said, 'a toast to America'. I think she approves." Glasses clinked. Smiles were all around followed by applause."

"Gracias," said Michael, and the family all laughed together. Michael was ready to leave and Melita's father embraced him in the traditional Spanish style, kissed him each cheek and whispered quietly in his ear, "If you hurt my little girl, no matter how big and important you become, I will hunt you down and kill you, like a dog."

"It is because I want to take care of her that I wish to have her with me Mr. Harrison."

"Just as long as we understand each other." Slapping Michael on the back he continued, "God go with you, and be safe."

Michael held Melita close for a moment and then left.

Chapter 30

The Duke of Kent, built in New York in 1831, was a relatively young ship. At 1,537 tons, she was a substantial craft and one of the few steam powered ships to cross the Atlantic Ocean. Here she was waiting dockside at Poole Harbour in Dorset. Her holds were full of a mixed cargo, everything that was in demand and was trading well in America. The American Civil War had been over for a couple of years, so the settlers had resumed the business of developing the country. Michael and Melita arrived dockside late in the September afternoon sun. Upon boarding with all their possessions, the captain, an obsequious little man, sought permission from Michael to cast off, which was granted. "Captain, this is your command," he said. He was excited about the opportunity to go the America. The Royal Shipping Line had, in his mind, been progressive in updating its fleet.

The crossing to America took thirteen days, during which Melita and Michael spent many hours making love, and soaking up each other's company without any outside interference. It was as if they were honeymooners, which one might observe, was how one of them felt. Michael discovered the powerful intellect Melita had and had only shown him the edges of. She once expressed that men were quicker to accept beauty than brains. But this didn't prevent her from thinking. In fact, it often spurred her on. One of their discussions explored the way of things in England. Michael's view was that men, particularly older men, were prone to be stubborn and resist change, and they were certain they were always right. He cited an old article about the SS *Great Eastern,* a massive steamship built to circumvent the vagaries of nature's weather. They put on it, not three masts, but six, which made no sense. He blamed this on the old school, stubborn attitudes that never stopped to consider the 'what ifs' or 'whys'.

Melita had her own example. She once approached the master printer, having been at the Co-Op only a short period, with her idea of improving the layout of the shop to reduce the amount of labor needed. She told him, "I have a lot of respect for Mr. Loring, but his response was brutal. He said you are *only* a woman. You have only been here a short while. If the owners felt the layout was right, then it's right. It is not our position to question that. He also reminded me that I was *a bloody foreigner.* If I wanted to keep my job, I learned, I must keep my thoughts to myself." She went on to say, "It was a long time before the old man came to accept my thoughts. He was indeed slowly becoming one of a new breed of thinking Victorian men." So, when Michael asked for her suggestions, she was totally enraptured by him.

Michael laid out his unfounded assumptions and ideas for America, a place he had not even been to. A colony with the temerity to challenge the great English

Empire had to have some different philosophies. He wanted to look into the ship-building and iron industries, and at the possible opportunities to expand Mother's Fine Foods. And lastly, he wanted land. If someone had had the foresight to acquire land in London early enough, they would be very wealthy today. He described to Melita his family's holdings, how the family had gained vast tracts of land from the Catholic Church by way of King Henry the Eighth, and how they had bought and sold property, becoming richer with each move.

She was intrigued by how far back his family went and their connections to Royalty. Michael could live well off the family assets. If he put any additional gains into areas of land that could become prime in America, the family could become a force to be recognized on both sides of the Atlantic.

At the end of the long voyage, the captain announced that land had been sighted, and that their cargo was bound for Manhattan. They would be going to old slip number fifteen. Michael said that would suit him fine. Final preparations were made as the SS *Duke* wound around the tip of Manhattan and turned northward around Battery Park, toward the slip.

***

Michael and Melita stood looking out at the view in awe and disbelief. Both of them were familiar with London's cramped and bustling dockside, but that had not prepared them for the enormity of what lay in front of them. There were piers stretching out into the river as far as the eye could see. Almost every one of them had a ship alongside, and many had two. The foreground of the cityscape was a forest of masts. Michael had been to many English seaports and was used to seeing large numbers of ships. This was bigger and stretched further than his eye could clearly see. His excitement began to rise as he pointed out the sights to Melita.

After the ship was secured, the captain asked if he could be of any service to the couple. Michael expressed his awe to the man. The captain told him that he had been trading on the east coast of America for thirty years, and what he saw was always difficult to comprehend. One never had to ask what was 'new' in New York, it was always visible. "Head office tells me that they're looking to open an office here in New York," he said.

"Where would *you* put it?" asked Michael.

"Either right down here where the shipping activity is or on Wall Street where the money is, or as close as you can get," said the man without hesitation.

"Why? Do you have family there?" said Michael in a joking tone.

"I wish I did. That's where I've seen more and more big money going. It sort of makes London's banking center on Threadneedle Street small by comparison. The way this country is going, it'll be the stronghold of financial power," said the captain. He continued, "They refer to America as the New World. It is a world unto itself. It is almost too big to be just a country."

"We're going to be staying at the Fifth Avenue Hotel, and we need transport," said Michael. With that, the captain directed a seaman to place their baggage in a waiting handsome cab. A short while later the captain returned with the newspaper Melita requested and wished them good fortune.

"Should the Royal need a man based out here who knows a thing or two," he said, "I would appreciate a word in the right ear, sir."

"You mean you would give up the sea?" Michael asked curiously.

The captain thought for a moment and said, "Many a seafarer thinks they are married to the sea, sir. But I've had a good life behind the mast, and I have no regrets. A man must decide for himself where life is going to take him. I think the least risk is to go where there is the most opportunity to use what skills you have. An office for the Royal would be just that, particularly here in New York."

"I respect your frankness," said Michael. "A man of your background and service to us, should be utilized."

***

Soon, they were at the hotel. It stood six floors high and a full city block wide. The Fifth Avenue Hotel was just ten years old, and looked it. The huge reception area was a bustling, seething mass of people coming and going. Ladies in the latest Victorian fashion evening gowns and men in top hats and tails interspersed with bellboys moving luggage and supervisors calling out instructions. It was a visual cacophony to Melita. In London, everything was so tall and closely knit, that its sheer size was hidden from view from people. Here, everything was so tall and so open one could see just how many buildings there were.

When they got to their suite, Melita whirled around as if some dancer on her own invisible stage. Stopping by Michael, she whispered in his ear, "You are my prince, and for that, I thank you." She kissed him tenderly on the cheek, not a kiss of passion, but one of heartfelt happiness, and that gave him joy. Melita sat in a plush, deeply cushioned armchair and asked, "Would you like to know what I think?"

Michael replied, "One of the reasons I wanted you along was that I value what you think."

"As big as this city looks, it feels alive, like it is still growing. The streets are as busy and full as the streets of London, but there is an aliveness, a feeling of purpose. It is quite exciting. In London people are busy going about the day-today business of living, but here, it just feels different. It is almost like a giant is waking up."

"I agree, there seems like there is just so much to take in all at once."

"Michael, if we cannot find opportunities here, for your shipping business and anything else, I will be amazed. I just want to go out and talk to people, find out about them."

"That is just what we will do as soon as we get settled." Melita's thoughts were an incredible composition of foresight, intelligence, and astute observation. It was simple, precise, and brilliant. Michael was starting to get the germ of an idea about what he wanted to do here in America.

Chapter 31

Michael and Melita awoke early the next morning, dressed in their best finery, and went down to the sumptuous and ornate dining room of the Fifth Avenue Hotel, where they ate a huge breakfast, not knowing when they would eat next. Melita asked for the *New York Times* newspaper, but Michael pointed out that it was not proper for a lady to read at the table.

"Does that mean you do not think I am a lady?"

"No, it just means that well-bred people do not read at the table."

"So, I am not well bred!"

"Please, we are building an image here. It doesn't matter what we are. It matters what the perception of us is. I'm sure you understand that."

Melita replied, "Then enjoy your breakfast. I am more interested in the paper." With that she folded the paper and left the dining room. Michael was shocked. While Melita sat in the lounge area absorbed in the newspaper, Michael arranged for a cab for the day. As they set out, their cabby was instructed to show them the library, Wall Street, the local shipping offices, the railways, and the shipping passenger terminals. Their list kept them busy late into the evening. The cabby, a tall, slender Irishman by the name of Liam Lang, accepted their invitation to dine with them. He took them to an Irish public house to get the flavour of the city. He proved to be a wealth of local knowledge. When he dropped them off at the hotel, Liam agreed to pick them up again the next day and continue showing them 'his' New York City, as well as the places they wanted to see.

*****

At 8 a.m. sharp, dressed in the less obtrusive clothes Liam had recommended, they set off to see the working-class side of life. Michael soon saw the equivalent of Mother's Fine Foods and Melita could see the immigrants' way of life. They stopped at many ethnic shops, delicatessens, and clothing stores, and ate in working-class establishments. Michael asked about gentlemen's clubs and was surprised at their absence. There was no 'society' as he knew it. But the working and lower classes were very similar to England's, albeit much more spread out. That evening, as Michael paid the cabby for his time, Liam offered Michael his opinion. "If you'll be askin' me, sir, havin' spent two days wit you I'll be a-t'inkin' you'll be barking up the wrong tree." Michael was intrigued. "I'll be askin' meself," said Liam, "why would chew want to jump in the pond wot's got all the sharks in it? No siree, you should be a-lookin' at Chicago. Now that's a growin' city. Maybe California, they's been findin' gold there. South, now there's the land o' opportunity, and there ain't a lot of folks down there yet." This short statement captured the early days of America and contained a wealth of information if carefully considered.

Over dinner in one of the hotels sumptuous dining rooms, Melita noted that if you looked around, there were so many people trying to be something better than they believed they were. "You look at that man over there," she said. "He's got a big cigar. He talks in a loud voice. He has a girl on his arm and she is dressed pretty, but she is a prostitute. Why does he want to make a big noise? I think he does not have a good self-image." She let her gaze wander round the vast dining room. "You look at the tables in the corners. Why do they have the curtains? I tell you why, when men come in here, they want to make themselves look important, so they ask for the raised corner location so that all the people can see them close the curtains. This is all a big act. Please, Michael take, your hand off my knickers. I am trying to be a lady. I don't think ladies would allow that at the table." Feeling suitably reprimanded, he removed his hand from her thigh under the tablecloth and she carried on speaking. Inwardly he smiled at her knowing that she had just thrown his comment of the morning back at him. "It looks to me like all people want to be something or someone they are not," said Melita. "You should make a place for them, help them live their illusion. They want to feel important, then help them. What do you care if they are not important? I think these people will spend a lot of money to be seen as important. It looks and feels like there is a lot of big money in America. I mean '*big*' money. Everything is on so much bigger a scale than England. Maybe I think we should go for the biggest money of them all. Let's catch the biggest fish." Michael just smiled and listened as she continued, "When you think of the railway barons in England and the size of America, these people must be wealthier than we can imagine."

Michael added, "I suppose you could view all the industry here the same way. Look at the market here for steel, travel, even something as simple as food. I think we did the right thing coming here." Michael stopped for breath and they both said in unison, "What a team we are!" Nearby diners stared as the two laughed out loud.

All the time she had been talking Michael had been watching her face intently. She was indeed beautiful. The movement her sensual lips made as she made her own unique sounds of language aroused his passion. Her confidence oozed through every pore. She radiated her excitement and was exciting him. He could see men around the room glance at her again and again. In an age when so many of the women he had been exposed to used rouge and powder to make themselves more attractive, here was a young woman who was naturally beautiful. He put his hand beneath the table and adjusted his swollen erection.

"My dearest Melita," Michael whispered, "I hear what you say and it makes me want to take you to bed and ravish you. I want to enjoy your body. I want to enter you many times. Only then can my mind be clear enough to discuss your brilliant observations." She mocked him by putting her hand under the table and fondled his erection.

He mimicked her previous tone. "I don't like for people to see our sexy." She giggled, and they left the dining room arm in arm, amid the envious glances from male patrons, which both of them were fully aware of. It added to their excitement.

***

Michael opened the door to the suite and let her in. She went directly to the bedroom and stopped in the doorway. Turning, she offered up her face. Throwing his jacket on the floor he approached her and held her face gently between his hands and kissed her lips softly and fleetingly. They stood there locked in a ritual of gentle attack and submission of each other. Lips exploring each other's as they felt the softness graduate to firmness and then probing. As if in delicate choreography, the movement from door to bed was a fluid drifting of two bodies disrobing each other, exploring and exciting each other. Melita laid herself on the bed and watched as he admired her from head to toe while her hand reached over the edge of the bed and grasped his erection. He stood still, closed his eyes and savored the cool of her hand against his heat. Placing one hand on her flat tummy he slid it slowly down to her pubic mound, his finger probing her wetness. She gasped and arched her back to allow him better access. Taking his hand away he lifted her hips and swung them round to the side of the bed. Dropping to his knees he put his head between her legs and placing his hand on her flat tummy, gently pushed upwards. This action better exposed her. He thrust his tongue. She writhed and groaned the faster he went. Suddenly she clamped her thighs around his head with extreme strength and shuddered violently three times, gradually subsiding. When he felt her relax, he gently freed his head and stood beside the bed. He said in a mocking tone, "what did you say? I couldn't hear you. My ears were covered."

As he rose up, she slapped him on the top of his head and replied, "You didn't need to talk, or hear." He lifted her hips and pulled her closer to the bed edge and he lowered her onto his aching manhood. She lay back and put her hands behind her head and watched his enjoyment of her. Deep inside her he twitched. He withdrew only to pause and then thrust deeply. He felt her move with each ejaculation. His scrotum tightened and his juices sped along his shaft into her. They remained together in this position savoring each other. She raised her arms in the air triumphantly, as he collapsed on top of her where they stayed locked, as their passion and breathing slowed and returned to normal.

***

Later, as the evening gave way to darkness, they lay together with Melita's head resting on Michael's chest. She quietly mimicked him "Is your mind clear enough to discuss my brilliant observations?"

His reply, "Oh yes my dear." He took her thoughts one at a time and discussed the merit of them. She had been doing the very thing Mr. Surtees taught him long ago. While he was looking at the big picture, she was carefully breaking it down and studying each portion. Her observation of the behavior of people and the way business dealt with that behavior was succinct. The social culture here was based on very different things compared to England. There really was no 'Old.' The divides in England were breeding, connections and money, usually in that order. As Melita pointed out, in America there was connection and wealth. The lack of the equivalent of England's breeding left a gaping need to be filled. The breeding here had no standards or requirements as the English did. The old families here were just old families, not '*old*' families. It appeared everything here was inter-racial and inter-cultural and had no obvious signs of class. Michael decided he was going to develop something based on the English model but more suitable to the American way of life. It felt strange to be talking about England and the English as if they were someone else, not them. Based on the very private London Gentleman's Clubs, he wanted to build an exclusive retreat for members only. Membership could be based on wealth, connections and family. The family component would replace the 'English breeding' that was a requirement of that society. Michael sat up and ordered champagne to celebrate. The only question now was where should he do it? They decided to go south, where, they were told, there were not a lot of people, *yet*. It was the *yet* that appealed to him.

***

They had spent two weeks investigating New York City when they decided that it was time to delve deeper into America. October was getting chilly and winter would soon be setting in. The days had a chill and the nights were outright cold. Darkness was arriving in the early evening. Many people had spoken of the warmer south of the country. If they were going to travel, they should waste no time. Michael planned their route plan as Melita packed their baggage, arranging for the majority of their belongings to be held in storage at the hotel, pending their return from the South.

A short cab ride to Fourth and Twenty-Third Streets took them to the railroad terminal. They settled in the first-class Pullman carriage. They found it to be of an acceptable standard to which they were accustomed, which surprised Melita. The Pullman was luxurious and well appointed, with attentive porters and waiters. The first short train journey put them in Elizabethtown in New Jersey. Passing through Philadelphia, they headed to Baltimore and then down to Wilmington, North Carolina where they had to change their mode of transport. The train journey had been arduous and was frequently interrupted at state lines. The change in track gauge required changing from one train company's carriages to the next states carriages. While this was tiresome, it allowed Michael and Melita to mix up close with Americans and observe them as they went about their business. The changing countryside was fascinating to Melita who was continually pointing out her observations. Their education of America was an ongoing, evolving experience. There were distances of nothingness, and then populated towns and cities. Melita had purchased a journal so she could record some sights and experiences that may be of use to them later on.

One evening, upon returning to their sleeper, as Michael lay in bed and dozed, Melita wrote late into the night of her reactions to New York City and the train. This trip to America was energizing her. The vibrancy and vitality of New York amazed her. At two o'clock in the morning, she left on a mission to find a newspaper. According to the night porter, she could only obtain yesterdays. She'd have to wait for the next station for the current edition. Back in the quiet of the compartment, she cut out the social and business sections of the paper, and anything else that caught her attention, paying close attention to any references to the lives of the wealthy. Each article was neatly folded and tucked into her journal. It was 3 a.m. by the time she crawled beside Michael's warm body and slept.

Melita slept solidly each night, exhausted from her tireless observations of everything they passed. Michael was awed by the vastness of what lay before him. It dwarfed England's countryside. The areas between cities seemed so sparsely populated. Hills and valleys continued endlessly. The train staff was attentive, and provided a valuable supply of anecdotes and information. One craggy old black porter regaled them with effusive pride for his home state of Georgia. He spoke of its beauty and less frenetic lifestyle, and the warm weather and welcoming people. Brunswick, he said, had a huge port, with ships coming in from all over the world. "Our biggest problem is that the railways from up north don't quite get down to us just yet, we are hoping they will soon."

Melita asked, "if there are so many ships coming here why haven't the railroads got here?"

"I guess the owners feel that there is more business for them to go west, what with the gold and everything going on out there. There was a time when the rails were coming south that we thought they would reach us, but no, west they went."

"So why do the ships come here instead of going north?"

"Because the little lower prices they get here is easily made up for by the speed with which they can unload and get back to sea."

"So that means everything unloaded here has to go north by wagon?" Michael seemed surprised.

"That's about the size of it, but very little of it makes all the way north because much is sold on the way north."

The old plantations were dying out with the abolition of slavery, which meant labor was plentiful. His enthusiasm convinced Michael that Georgia could be the end of his journey. But for today, Wilmington in North Carolina would be their last stop. Tired but enthused, Michael and Melita arrived late at night. They rose early the next morning to prepare for the final part of their journey. He was now faced with having to travel the last four hundred or so miles by carriage as there were no trains from this point on. It took all of Melita's patience to control Michael in his dealings with the local business's that offered the service they needed. There would have to be transfers as they would be passed from company to company.

She quickly realized his limitations as she pulled him aside and said, "My dear, you must calm down. These people could not care less about your position or stature in England."

"I will not put up with second rate service, I am entitled to more." Michael snipped.

"I'm afraid right now we have to put up with whatever service is available, *or*, abandon your plans altogether."

"Are you happy with all of this?' Michael was clearly agitated.

Melita saw a way to calm him down. "What you see happening around us is exactly why you are making this trip, to find opportunities upon which to build. Rubbing these people up the wrong way will only make them defensive instead of helpful."

"How can these bumpkins be helpful? They can't even provide the basics?"

"But that's exactly my point, they are only *able* to provide the basics. You want to bring your expertise and experience to bear." She waited a moment watching Michael calm down and then added, "That fellow told us about this place we are going to see, because he appeared to like you and wanted to help. We can always use more of that type of help." Michael was considering Melita's words of wisdom.

As if a switch had been flipped, he said, "Bees to honey I suppose. Yes, you are right. Let's get on with this.

***

Of all the advice given to them there seemed to be a common feeling regarding the time the journey would take. The owner of a transporting business gave them a choice, "If you are willing to travel light, and I mean with one portmanteau, the journey could take four to five days depending on the weather and roads."

Michael shot a glance at Melita as she spoke, "If we desire to take all our baggage, would it make a big difference?"

"Your journey's time is dictated by what strain we put on our horses. The more strain, the more rest they will need. We will still need to change horses about every 25 miles or so, depending on how they hold up. Not many horse owners are willing to put their beasts at risk. This can add an additional four to five days on the journey, and increase the cost considerably."

"How do *we* do that?" asked Michael.

"No sir, not you, us. We have reciprocal arrangements with hostelries along the way. We leave our horses and take theirs along the way. We have people that we trust and that trust we will provide for the beasts well."

Melita's curiosity kicked in as she asked, "Doesn't that put horses all over the place? How is ownership of the horses kept?"

The man laughed and replied, "Some of us more reputable companies can be trusted to reverse the process on the way back, so everyone ends up with their own animals. In essence they have rented out the animals. It works well as we use the finest of drivers who are willing to be away for extended periods, thereby they get to know the horses and their individual traits. It works very well. Which method would you be using Ma'am?"

Melita was quick to reply, "I think we should forgo much of our comforts and go for speed. What do you think?"

Michael was slow to reply, "If you don't mind, I will go along with it. I would like to make this as short as possible and get back to civilization."

"Michael, this is civilization, just not your kind of civilization." Turning to the owner she added, "I do apologize, we are just used to a more genteel lifestyle. I thank you for your kindness and valuable guidance." Over the next five and half days, their journey took them through Columbia in South Carolina, Savannah and Brunswick in Georgia, where they rested. The city proved a thriving metropolis built around shipping. It was bigger than anything Michael had expected, being so far from New York City. It looked like a thousand ships were anchored in the expansive Columbia River, waiting for dockside space. Some unloaded onto barges that ferried the cargo ashore. The whole city was alive, with an open feeling New York did not have. The wide mixture of races and creeds seemed to have a greater proportion of black, oriental and the native Indian people.

The buildings dated back as far as the late seventeen-hundreds, and the weather appeared to have been kind to them. While dining that first night, everyone they spoke to recommended they see Jakeskill Island for its sheer beauty and lushness. The notoriety of the island piqued their curiosity. It was suggested they contact the Sapelo Company, a group of Frenchmen thought to be the most influential on the island. Finding the hotel accommodations in Brunswick substantially less luxurious than they had experienced to date was a disappointment. They wasted no time arranging to leave for Jakeskill the next morning. The coachman had spent the previous evening asking the locals who told him interesting stories of the island's past. When he learned they wished to be taken to the Sapelo Company, the coachman offered an alternative. Over half the island, he said, belonged to an Englishman. The man had the property being taken care of by a trustworthy local merchant. The merchant, a Josiah Mielman had lived on the island longer than anyone in memory. His trading post had seen others come and go, and provided a modest living for a man who desired nothing excessive

Chapter 32

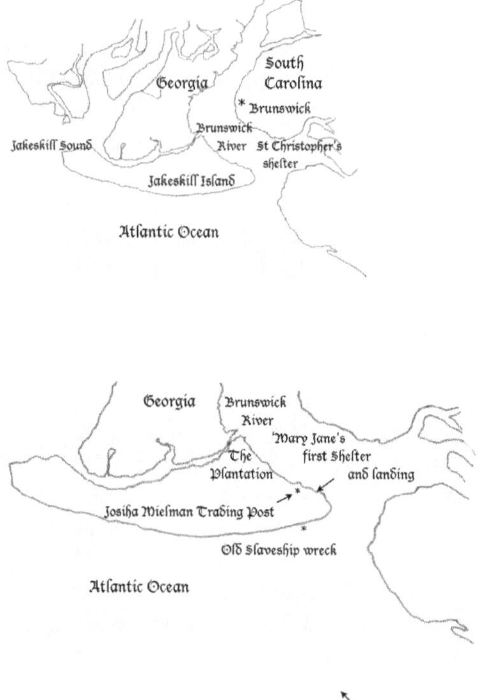

The journey took most of the day. The coachman said there were no hotels on the island, but Josiah had been known to take in guests if he liked them. The sun slowly turned the sky a brilliant fiery red, gold, and orange as they arrived at the trading post. Behind the merchant's store stood a large but simple plain two-story, red brick residence, surrounded by flowerbeds with all manner of tropical flowers. While Michael was being greeted by Josiah, Melita examined the flowerbeds, then returned to tell Michael excitedly, that the colorful vines climbing up the front of the house were bougainvillea.

Josiah was noticeably pleased with Melita's interest. Josiah advised the couple, as the coach was preparing to leave, that if the coach left there would be no transport out until the following day, and he was willing to provide them simple accommodations if they wished it. Michael asked if it would be possible to stay for a few days, as they had a lot of things they wanted to see. They were willing to pay for any inconvenience. When Josiah agreed, Michael, arranged with the coachman for his return in a few days and bid him farewell.

Josiah took them on a tour of the house and grounds, speaking of how he had moved his family up river to Brunswick, where there was a large Jewish community, for safety reasons. He now felt that circumstances had since improved and he wanted the family to return. Melita told Josiah that she had been exposed to Jewish people back in England and would be happy to cook him her version of a Sephardic, Spanish dinner with a French twist. The old man's face lit up with joy. When they arrived at Josiah's kitchen garden, Melita told the men to go and leave her alone to cook.

The two men went to the store, where they sat and talked. Josiah told Michael the history of the island, through to the sale of the Palisades plantation by the General, and up to the present time. "The present owner is a Captain Judd Cane from Mucking in England. I have found Mr. Cane to be an honest and trustworthy man, indeed he is a man of great compassion."

"What do you mean great compassion?" asked Michael.

"There was a young, orphaned, slave child that he took back to England to give the child a better chance at life. I don't know many, if any, men that would do that." The two men returned to the house, seduced by the aromatic smells emanating from the kitchen. The three sat around a large heavily scrubbed kitchen table. Its whitened planks showed a history of use. As they ate, Michael asked Josiah to share with them the story of Captain Cane. They sat enthralled as they listened.

"Indeed, he must quite a special person," Melita said, obviously moved. "Our children are such a special gift."

"Children, they are what life is all about. God's gift, which I might add, as parents we seem to be continually paying for. But then, what else would we do with the fruits of our labour?" The evening wound down with the setting of the sun bringing on darkness that slowly invaded the small group. The pleasure the old man received from his company was evident in his chatter and frequent big smiles. "You are such a grand cook Miss Melita," Josiah told Melita.

Michael added, "I had no idea that you were so talented in the kitchen my dear."

"You never asked. I didn't think you were interested in food when I am around."

"Maybe I am and then maybe I am not," Michael laughed.

Soon tiredness overtook and, exchanging warm wishes for a good night, Josiah showed them to the bedroom they would use. There was a comforting silence in this place. Melita lay on her back with her hands behind her head. Michael could sense her staring into the air, for he could not see her in the dark room. He spoke, "I can almost hear your mind at work."

She quietly whispered, "If the rest of this place is as peaceful and beautiful as what we have seen so far.... I find it magnetic, alluring, calming."

"Alright I get your message. There is a peace about it that I find attractive. Let's hope there is more of the same when we see it tomorrow." In an unspoken word, they reached out and held each other's hands, falling into an exhausted, deep slumber.

When Michael was awoken the next morning by the brilliant rays of sunlight streaming through the window, he heard from the kitchen the sounds and smells of cooking. Upon entering the kitchen, he found that Melita, who had been cleaning meticulously, had coffee and eggs ready. Josiah sat at the end of the room with a huge smile and a cup of steaming coffee.

Michael said, "There is no need for you do all this work my dear."

Josiah added, "I told her the same thing. It is my place to take care of my guests."

Melita held her hands up to silence them both and said, "In my culture, the women take care of the men and it is their pleasure to do so. So, that ends that. Now sit and eat."

"And take care of us you did. That dinner last evening was the finest I have had since I do not know when. If I was a younger man. I would not let you get away."

"You haven't mentioned your wife." Michael was cautious as he asked.

"Being alone and away from my wife, I find it better to keep her in my heart, than on my tongue."

"Tell me more about your wife, your family, if you don't mind Josiah."

"Oh yes, indeed, Miriam is my wife and I have four fine young daughters. Quite grown up now, three of them are, well, you know, young ladies."

"Where do they live, why are they not here with you?" asked Melita.

"It has not always been safe here. Our family home is in Brunswick, up river. The schooling is there and we have family there. We came here to start the trading post for those ships that didn't want to deal with the large port problems. One thing led to another as the girls grew up and Miriam wanted to stay close to her family. So, they returned to Brunswick. Now I frequently get home on one of the many ships that pass. It is not so bad to close the business down for a while. It provides well for the girls and soon I hope move back to be with them. I must give thought to parting with this place, one day. I like the peace and tranquility down here and it worries me that I won't fit into the city anymore."

After they ate, Josiah offered to take them around the property, but Melita suggested the men go alone. She found Josiah a gentle, kind man and wanted to do some things around the house to add 'a woman's touch that makes all the difference.' The men agreed. Arranging for one of his workers to take care of the store, Josiah borrowed a second horse. He and Michael rode off into the distance. Melita turned her attention to the house. The men rode from building to building, and Josiah inspected the wooden planks that boarded up the doors and windows. As they went along he explained what was, and what now, is the function of each building. He introduced the workers who assisted him in taking care of the property. Much of the land had become overgrown, but around each of the buildings, brush was cleared away. Around the dwellings used by the workers were vegetable gardens, neatly kept. Josiah told Michael that Mr. Cane paid for the upkeep of the property and had for many years. It was late in the afternoon by the time the men had returned to the house. Freshly washed curtains flapped in the breeze, and all the windows were open. Melita had been very busy. Josiah stood silently, his emotions clearly showing on his face. Melita put her arms around the old man and whispered in his ear, "I think it is time for you to bring Mrs. Mielman home, or for you return to Brunswick to be with your family."

The man sobbed uncontrollably. "You don't know what you have given an old man," he said. "I got stuck in my private fears born in the past. You have shone a light and breathed a new air into my home. I will consider my future more carefully since your visit." The three of them spent the rest of the evening relaxing and getting to know each other better. Michael and Melita planned to leave the following morning for New York City and promised Josiah that he had not seen the last of them.

As they rode the coach off the island, Melita said to Michael, "Josiah is a grand old man. He carries himself with such dignity in this lonely quiet place. We should try to do something special for him. I enjoyed his company very much. He reminds me of my grandfather."

On the return journey to New York Michael went into great detail explaining his vision to Melita. He had developed many ideas while riding around the property. He explained that the Victorian gentlemen's clubs in London were a place that every successful man wanted to belong to, where he could flaunt his wealth and connections. While here, many of the new settlers were busy earning livings and had little time for politics. There was no way for the successful to flaunt themselves to their peers. There needed to be a way for the male peacock to display evidence of his own success's and perceived social importance. This was to be his focus. Melita asked, "What are you thinking?"

"Josiah said there are approximately twelve square miles of land that takes up more than half of Jakeskill. We could build a gentleman's club for the sake of a better description. This will be a place like no other. It could have private suites of up to eight rooms owned outright by select members. There could be smaller suites available for use by other members. If we took about twenty acres around the main building and landscaped them in the style of formal English gardens, with orchards, and growing gardens, we could supply fresh produce for the residents."

"That sounds like a huge undertaking. Who would build it?" Melita queried.

"I'm getting ahead of myself. On the one hand I think of us building it, and then I think that there's a lot we don't know about how things are done over here."

"Maybe you could find an architect to start on some plans, or even better, have one of your connections in London start the design for you," Melita interrupted excitedly. "In the New York paper the other day I saw some pictures of a building that is nearing completion in Buffalo, New York. It sounds just like what you are describing. I can't remember what it is called but the man's name stuck with me."

"Who was it?"

"H.H. Richardson. He is an American, but you must take a look. It could be a good starting point." Michael saw Melita was paying close attention to his every word and nodding in agreement to some of his ideas. "I like it. American built for the American upper classes. Shall I carry on or would you like me to be quiet for a while?"

"No, no keep going. I am amazed that you thought out so much. You seem very excited about this project. But *upper classes?*"

"Yes, upper classes, or those who want to be perceived as upper class. Those who are superior. The plan is for the club to be run along the lines of true Victorian hierarchy. It is expected that staff will be minimally visible. The training and control of staff will be overseen by experienced, English professionals. I think that I would prefer an all English staff, be brought out to America specifically for the job."

"My word, you are staffing it before it is even built. I think your tone is a bit snobbish and aloof, you must be careful not to offend anyone."

"I don't care who I offend, as long as it isn't potential members. These are all just ideas at this point, although I have come up with a name."

"Don't tell me – you are going to call it 'Michaels Victorian Gentlemen's Club."

"Now you are mocking me?"

"Yes, I am. But I also see your passion about this idea could make it work."

"So, do you want to hear the name?"

"Of course, I do. If you ever get round to sharing it."

Holding his breath for effect, Michael pompously announced, "The Royal Palisades. Nothing else, no description, just complete anonymity."

"Why are you leaning so much on the Victorian theme when this is a different country, a new country? Will it not offend the American sensibility?" Melita posed.

"Possibly, possibly. But if you think about it, everywhere you look there are people doing things the way we do at home. Most of the architecture is the old style. I believe there is deep seated desire to belong in everyone. The Americans are no different. I plan to give them something big to aim for."

"I do say that you are very ambitious with this. Keep going."

Michael took the cue and continued. "The design of the building itself will be of Victorian splendor down to the last detail. It will resemble the large imposing entry of some English stately homes. Large stone lions will grace the pillars every tenth step up to the entry. Its sheer size will be American in every essence. The grounds will contain miniature versions of many trees that will add to the impression of the immensity of the building. As times change the club will steadfastly cling to its charter of elegance, wealth and exclusivity. While subtle changes will be made to accommodate huge technical advances such as plumbing, electrical improvements and the desire to stay modern, the whole aura will remain intact."

"How will you make money from a project like this?" asked Melita.

Michael could see Melita was already thinking about more in-depth considerations. "Money will never be discussed. Costs are never discussed and the members take care of their obligations privately and at other times. Money has no visible currency here, but money will be the key. I plan that class and character will control the club. From the moment one enters the property the quiet, understated elegance will envelope one into submission."

"I think you know what is best, and I like it. It is a very large undertaking. I think the size is hard for me fully comprehend. I support you in everything you do and I am getting excited about this one."

"Do you think I am being too ambitious? Not that it would stop me, I'm just being curious." Michael sat down in a deep, plush chair and waited for Melita's reply.

Melita spoke, carefully picking her words. "Michael, you know my background and where I come from. Before meeting you, my world was the print shop at the Co-op and Bethnal Green. You have opened up a whole new world to me. I love the excitement and discovery, but the speed makes me nervous. I know that we are here together and I do believe that we will work together for a long time. I suppose that I think about what you will be like when things get bigger. Will you still need, or want me around?"

"Where did that come from? Whatever made you think of such a thing?" he asked.

"There's my world, your world, and our world, and I see the edges are getting blurred. What will happen when you have achieved all that you set out to do? What will become of our world?" Michael leaned forward with his elbows on his knees, took hold of Melita's hands, and sat silently for a moment searching for the right words.

"You are right of course. There is yours, mine and our worlds. I hope that you see me as a man of honor and integrity. Comes with the family you know. I can assure you that there will always be an '*our world.*' It is silly to think that its form will never change. Life goes on and things do change, but I will always be here to protect and watch over you. I could never abandon you. I care for you."

"I care for you and love you Michael, please don't think me a fool for having these thoughts."

"I don't think you a fool for one moment." Almost coldly, Michael changed the subject, "Your idea of the architects is good. I shall have one from England and one from America work together. We shall have the best of both worlds. Melita shrunk back in her chair. She could not believe what he had just said. In the same breath he switched from personal, emotional warmth to business. That thought was to bounce around in her head for years to come.

Chapter 33

Michael and Melita returned to London in the spring of 1873, and Michael summoned Ronald Surtees to The Royal Shipping Line's offices. Ronald immediately saw that Michael was excited so he asked, "To what do I owe the pleasure?"

"Sit down, sit down, I have a proposal for you that will change your life."

"I am all ears, please explain."

"We have known each other for, how long, five, six years, maybe more."

"A long time. Closer to ten years, I would say."

"You have told me that your reason for advancing in the field of education is your desire to be worthy of Lady Penelope. I have a potential solution for you."

"What might that be?" Ronald was curious.

"All women admire success. In the academic field your success is always hidden under the bushel of your students' success. Now, in business, there is success that can be openly seen. In other words, how would you like to be a successful businessman? It's could be quite lucrative you know."

"Michael, what the hell are you talking about?"

"In the time you have known me, while you have been teaching me things, you have also been a student. You know more about the St. John-Brown business empire than any non-family member ever has. I propose that you leave the academic world and we will set you up as a commercial and industrial consultant. We, Mother's fine foods, The Co-Op, The Royal Shipping lines and the family properties will contract with you to work for us on a consulting basis."

"Michael. I don't know what to say. What does this mean?"

"For one, it means your pay will easily increase your present income, and could be even higher. It could improve your chances to gain the hand of Lady Penelope, particularly when your reputation starts to become public. What do you say? Can we shake hands on it?"

"What about my accommodations, duties...?"

Michael interrupted, "I have never steered you wrong. We will take care of everything. I want you by my side as my businesses grow, so will you grow to?"

"Yes Michael, yes. Should I now be calling you Mr. St.J ohn-Brown, since you will be my employer?"

"No man, you will be your own employer. You will never have to cow tow to anyone, ever again. Good, so that's settled. You have a week to separate yourself from Charterhouse and get settled into an office here at The Royal. I will have it ready for you. We will have the contracts ready for our signatures by then. I want you to accompany me on a special trip next week."

"Where are we going?" Ronald was curious.

"We are going to buy a piece of America. Michael said with a laugh.

Chapter 34

Two weeks later, Michael, accompanied by Ronald Surtees made their way to Mucking to meet with the owner of the Jakeskill Island property that Michael so coveted. On the journey, Michael outlined his ideas for that property. Ronald was intrigued. "You seem to have put a lot of effort and time into this project and you don't even own it. Is there a chance you may not get it?"

"There's a chance, but not if I have anything to do with it." Nearing Tilbury station, the conversation between the two men became focused. Michael brought up the subject of the negotiation to take place. "My informants tell me that this Cane fellow is a very shrewd and street wise fellow. I believe that he may have an attitude towards people of my standing."

"What do you mean people of your standing?"

"He is a country yokel. He has had a tough life and is very strong willed. I don't think he is used to the landed gentry, if you know what I mean."

"Then I believe that I should make the introduction, as I am more of his class."

"I didn't mean you. *Your* one of us Ronald," Michael said. "You're not country folk…. far better."

"I can probably talk more at his level, I think."

"Don't be a fool, man. I wasn't meaning class, so much as wealth," Michael responded.

"Then let me introduce you and stand back so that he feels superior to me and closer to your equal."

"Don't care what he feels. I just want that property."

"Then, as you know, money speaks Michael, you must get right to the point with the man."

***

Judd and Mary Cane were making plans with their daughter, Agatha and her husband, Nathaniel, when they saw two finely dressed gentlemen present themselves at the offices of Cane International. They were shown to the first floor waiting area. Judd, looking over the wrought iron railings, saw the men below and knew instantly they were of high degree by the quality and cut of their clothes. The heavier-set of the two removed his hat and gave them a slight nod of a bow as he called up to them, "I bring you warm wishes with a genuine desire to find you both in good health from a Mr. Josiah Mielman."

"Josiah, my God, is he here? Is something wrong with him? Does he need my help?" Judd then called out to one of the offices girls, "Please show these gentlemen up to my office, immediately."

When the two visitors arrived at the second level, Ronald was first to speak. "Mr. Mielman is well. I, sir, am Ronald Surtees of Commercial and Industrial Consultants out of Bath, Bristol and London. Allow me to introduce my business associate, the Honorable Michael St. John-Brown, one of the principles of the Royal Shipping Line, Mother's Fine Foods, The Co-Op and various other interests."

Judd studied the business cards of both men as he spoke, without looking up. "I am familiar with The Royal Shipping Line and indeed with your chandlers, Duggan's. My ship trades through them and we have taken many of your products, Mother's Fine Foods, to the colonies." Mary invited the men to be seated and called for refreshments. "How did you make the acquaintance of Josiah, may I ask?" said Judd.

Michael spoke, "I was visiting the area and had the good fortune to be directed to the place. Your man, Josiah, gave us a tour of the property, on Jakeskill Island. My company has an interest in purchasing the property."

Judd replied, "With all due respect Sir Michael, we have another party that is very interested in purchasing the property. We are currently in discussions regarding the terms of sale. We are not even sure if we are interested in selling at this time."

Ronald and Michael glanced at each other. "I am in a position to make an offer to you today, if you are in a position to commit," said Michael.

Playing her unspoken role, as if on cue, Mary smiled and said to Judd, "We did say that we are in no hurry to sell."

"Yes, we did, and indeed, and we are not. But these gentlemen have traveled a long way," said Judd. "I believe we should show them the courtesy of hearing them out."

"Yes, dear," said Mary.

"We came from London today and wish to return before the day is out if that is possible," said Ronald.

Michael said, "America is still suffering from the aftermath of the Civil War, and there is still a lot of dissension in the south over the slavery issue. Jakeskill Island is off the beaten track, but I am willing to take a long-term gamble on its future possibilities." Judd parlayed with his own observation of the beauty and location, pointing out that the fast advances made with iron ships made the island even more accessible. Besides, the two of them were not the only people interested.

Sensing the men already had plans for the property, Judd said, "If you are ready to make an offer, we will compare it with the other before making a decision."

"One hundred thousand pounds today, by letter of credit." Michael watched Judd's face for any sign he could interpret. There was none. "As a deposit," he quickly added.

"We own numerous properties throughout the Caribbean and are fully aware of the value of our property overseas, particularly in the Caribbean. The Jakeskill Island property is by far the finest of our properties. We are willing to start negotiations at one million pounds." To his surprise, neither of his guests showed any reaction. The four of them sat in silence, each waiting for the other to speak first.

At last, Michael broke the silence. "As I said Mr. Cane, one hundred thousand pounds today, by letter of credit, as a deposit. And further, one hundred thousand pounds by letter of credit on the first day of each month for the next six months." Again, there was no reaction from Judd.

"Gentlemen," said Mary, "If I understand you correctly, you are offering seven hundred thousand pounds. While we respect your offer, our other offer claims to be able to complete a contract within two months. Should you not be willing or able to complete a contract in six months, we could find ourselves tied up in the courts, a situation to be avoided. Michael quickly parried her thrust with, "Yes Mrs. Cane, and if you take the other offer and they don't consummate, you could still find yourself in court and my offer will have evaporated."

'I agree that there is that chance, but I think not."

Michael noticeably relaxed. "Mr. Cane, I have benefited from the counsel of wise women on many occasions, so, I respect your wife's foresight," he said. "Can we shake hands on my offer if I agree that should I back out of our arrangement at any time I shall forfeit any monies paid to that point?" Turning to Mary, he said, "I require the time to form a corporation for this purpose, and move monies from some of my other business interests to fund my plans."

Mary openly said to Judd, "So Mr. St.John-Brown has plans. If, for some reason the sale is not completed, we will have gained a minimum of one hundred thousand pounds, plus any other payments he may have paid. With the interest there is in the property, I am happy to wait for either outcome."

"Sounds fair to me, but remember if we take Mr. St.John-Brown's offer we must decline the other," Judd replied as he stood and shook hands with Michael. "I wish you well with your endeavors, sir. Let's put pen to paper."

Michael, in turn, handed the envelope to Judd and said, "I am one step ahead of you sir. Here is the letter of credit I spoke of. I had the liberty of having it prepared so that I would be able to assure you of my sincerity." Contracts were to be signed within the week. The sale of Jakeskill Island was agreed upon, and the closing of the deal took place much quicker than expected, in fact, the full price was paid within three months.

Michael and Ronald returned to London. In the privacy of the carriage Ronald brought up the purchase of the property. "The sum paid for that land suggests that either you are truly smitten by the property or that you have grand plans for it. That's an awful lot of money."

"I did, shall we say, fall in love with the property, or rather, I fell in love with the huge potential it has for us. You should ask Melita about it, she was with me when I decided to make the property mine."

Ronald asked, "Did she see what you saw in the property's potential?"

"She did indeed, in fact we spent a lot of time discussing it and you shall have the files when we reach London. This is going to be a big thing for us all." The men spent the remainder of the journey home congratulating each other on job well done. Upon reaching the city, as they parted, Michael shook hands with Ronald and said, "That's our first big deal together and there will be many more. You need to send your invoice for services to me personally, as this deal is outside of the family's business."

"Invoice you? Isn't that covered by our contract?"

"Indeed. Your contract is a retainer for you to be available when we need you. That financial arrangement is the cornerstone of your consulting business. When you actually perform a service, you are entitled to be remunerated and you should invoice whichever of the companies you provide the service for. Don't worry man, you'll get the hang of it."

"I'm not sure exactly what service I provided you."

"Moral support, advice, and you allowed for a powerful front instead of a singular one."

Chapter 35

In an act of gratitude, Ronald was due to visit to the Mowbrays and he invited Michael to go with him as a guest of the Earl of Sussex, Viscount Mowbray, at the family estates in Crowborough Sussex. The two men travelled together from London by train. They were met at the station by the Earl's man in a pony trap. Their journey wound its way around the villages until it reached the Earl's estate. They passed through the two local stone pillars that were capped with aged verdigris copper turrets. The pillars held the massive wrought-iron gates and there was as of yet no sign of the house, just a tan and brown gravel road curving out of sight over the hill in front of them. The trap stopped at the top of the hill, revealing rolling downs neatly divided into fields and pastures dotted with sheep and cattle. The road veered off to the right, ending in a large circle before a stately white sandstone mansion of a home. The pony trap lurched forward as a gun sounded nearby. In the distance, stood alone was figure, with a gun over his shoulder. "Gamekeeper," said the pony trap driver. "That's so they know you is a coming." Looking toward the house, they saw two liveried figures positioning themselves at the foot of the wide-splaying stairs that led up to the front entry.

As soon as they were ushered into the home, Michael knew something wasn't quite right. There were only servants present. Ronald was greeted with indifference until he introduced 'Sir' Michael, and then the attitude became more cordial. "Welcome to Crowborough, Sir." Michael ignored the fact that it wasn't clear who it was aimed or the incorrect addressing him as '*Sir*'.

When Ronald asked after Miss Penelope, he received a curt, "She is not at home, sir. I believe she will be returning tomorrow morning. The Earl is expecting you for dinner at seven in the main dining salon." Another servant stepped forward and took their bags, instructing them to follow him. Once they were shown to their rooms, the servant left, and Ronald came to the door of Michael's room and offered to take him on a tour of the house. Michael noticed how at ease and familiar Ronald was in this setting. There was a quiet air about the place. Ronald showed Michael the elegant home from top to bottom, even leading him up onto the great flat roof, which offered a panorama of the English Channel in the distance on one side, over to the wooded hills and winding rivers of Sussex, behind them. As he described every room and it's nuances it was plain to see that Ronald held this place close to his heart, but none of his oratory compared to what he displayed when describing areas in which he had spent time with Penelope, when he was her tutor.

Michael could not understand why the girl was not here to greet Ronald. When he broached the subject, Ronald brushed it off. The Viscount and Countess had made the invitation, he said, but Penelope would be here he was told. At dinner that evening, Michael was introduced to the Earl and his wife, the Countess Regina Elizabeth Blackstone, along with two other couples. Michael was introduced and his connections elaborated on, as if they were as important as the man himself. Ronald was simply introduced as Penelope's former tutor, to which Michael added "Mr. Surtees is my righthand man. He oversees some of the family enterprises and he is indeed my confidant." To this Ronald noticeably puffed his chest out and felt more recognized.

The conversation was spirited, and while Ronald tried to keep himself involved, Michael felt that every question and comment seemed to skirt around him. After dinner, when they retired to the billiard room for brandy and cigars, Michael watched Ronald struggling for an opportunity to join in. Finally, the conversation lulled. "I hope Penelope is doing well," he said, as if to the air and no one in particular.

"Yes, yes quite. She is always busy at something," said the Earl. "Damn girl never sits still. Sometimes I think she would have been better off if she were a boy."

The earl's wife interjected, "Well she is not a boy, and I, for one am happy about that. You must stop encouraging her manly pursuits. What man would want a lady that is spoken of in that fashion?"

"Damn fine shot for a girl, if you ask me," one of the other men said. The Earl blew a pungent blue smoke ring into the air and watched it fade away. "She will shoot herself in the foot one day, if you know what I mean," he said. Everybody laughed except Penelope's mother

One of the guests said, "I am surprised that she hasn't been shot by some angry spouse, the way she flirts. Good girl, that one of yours David," the man said to the Earl.

"She may flirt her charms around but I can promise you, my girl is as pure as the driven snow. Keep a tight chain on her is what her mother does." Turning to the billiard table the Earl said, "Let's finish this game gentlemen."

Around ten o'clock, as the men played their game of billiards, Michael wished them a good night and left. Passing the reading room, he saw the ladies gathered around, chatting and enjoying a glass of port. Standing beside the open door, he knocked gently and thanked his hostess for her gracious invitation. He expressed his pleasure to the ladies for their company and then spoke to the Countess, "Your ladyship, I am humbled and honored and thank you kindly for having me in your home unannounced."

The Countess said to Michael, "My daughter, Penelope has arrived home and is looking forward to meeting you. Perhaps we shall go to church together in the morning." Michael bowed and left them to their chatter as he heard someone say, "He could be a guest in my home any day, with or without an invitation." The comment was followed by giggles. He was very aware of their eyes following his every move as he retired. The atmosphere was full of loaded, sexual, double entendres, and blatant leering looks. Climbing the stairs, he realized that he was under the influence of the fine brandy that had been served with the cigars. He smiled. This was the way to live. He was tired of making do with some of the lower-class places he had found himself forced to dwell in on his journeys. From this night on, he would go first class or not at all. The whole experience brought to mind the less than salubrious surrounds that school and college had offered him. Those days were over. Nothing but the best from here on in. He swayed into his room, making a great show of trying to close the door quietly. He flung his clothes on the floor, crawled between the sheets, and slid into oblivion, thinking about his American project, and forwardness of these women, and any other thing that popped into his head.

***

Michael was awakened sensing his erection and it was wet. Semi-conscious, he lifted up the sheets over him and woke with a start. He looked down to see a small blonde tussle of hair atop a head busily engaged with his shaft. This person was so gentle he was inclined not to stop her, so he didn't. She was so intent on what she was doing, that she didn't register any sign of knowing that he was now awake. Suddenly, without warning, her ice blue eyes looked up at him, and she whispered, "Can I join in?"

"Please do," he said, somewhat shocked. She wriggled up from under the sheets and turned her tiny body, with her back toward him and lowered herself onto him. As if in two different worlds she used his body for her own ends and he, hers. Sated, she hopped off the bed and went to the washstand to retrieve a warm washcloth. He watched her as she walked toward the bed. She was a little over five feet tall, slender of build with full plump breasts, a tiny waist, and a bushy blonde patch of pubic hair. She washed his exhausted flaccidness, then climbed into bed and cuddled up to him. She held him close to her body so tightly that he had to fight for breath. "Hello," she said. "I am pleased, so very pleased to meet you. I think I could get used to this 'sex' thing. I am so glad I waited. No wonder papa wanted me to keep myself for the right man. He says it has to be special. Oh, yes. It was special." Half mockingly she added, "Oh yes! How rude of me, I am Penelope."

Michael sat upright, lost for words. She lay back on the pillow with her blonde locks framing her face and said, with an innocent smile, "Was it not good for you?"

"It was more than good, but, oh my God. You have never lain with a man! How did you know so....I thought it was supposed to hurt the first time. You were a virgin?" he asked apprehensively.

"No, it didn't hurt. They say that if you ride horses as much as I do that it changes your body. I guess that's why it didn't bother me at all. It did feel a little strange at the beginning though."

"But you seemed to know what you were doing."

"I read a lot. Not always what mama would call 'the right sort of books for a young lady' though. Mama and I read everything we can get our hands on. I have spent a lot of time around our stables and farm. You get to hear a lot of gossip and chatter among the workers. I worked a lot of things out in my head. This was so much better than reading about it, don't you think?"

"Indeed, I do, but why me, why now, you don't even know me?"

"I know a lot about you. When Surtees said you were coming, I asked around and learned quite a lot. Papa knows a lot of people in the city, it was easy to learn about you. Your family is very well known in the city, and elsewhere I would imagine."

"And to what end did you decide to research our family?"

"Papa says I should be thinking about finding the right man to marry, a man that could fit into our way of life. I haven't liked any of the prospects he has paraded before me to choose from, so I thought that I would take matters into my own hands. When I was told that you would be here, I decided to find out more. After all, we are getting quite progressive around here. Women of my position are more able to choose their husbands for themselves. I think you might just be that man."

"Do I get any say in the matter? Just what do you know about me?"

"I might let you have a say kind sir, if it suits me," Penelope giggled as she replied. "Surtees has spoken of nothing but you in his letters and whenever he has come to our home for a long time now. Father has been discreetly asking around and, believe me, if papa says you are good stock, you are good stock."

"What about Surtees, I mean Ronald?" Michael said.

"What do you mean, what about Ronald?"

"He is in love with you. He's waiting, hoping for you to one day become his wife. He's here, and he is my friend," Michael tentatively said.

"*Ronald Surtees, my old tutor*? *Oh God*! Yes, I know what he wants. He is a pathetic little man with aspirations above his station. Even if I wanted to, Father would never allow it. Please don't be concerned. I will wait until you are ready. You are my first, my only, and I hope you will be my last. I am happy." She pulled him back down and held onto him tightly. "I said that I am willing to wait to marry, but I hope you will not deprive me of this pleasure while I wait."

"Who says I am ready to marry or if your father would approve of me?" Michael asked.

"Who cares? I am of age. I do not intend to ask father. I will tell him."

There was a protracted silence as Michael processed what he had just heard. In a soft, gentle voice he said, "Now. Be off with you and let me sleep, I have a lot to think about." Laying quietly in the dimly lit room thoughts were flying around in his head. 'If father says I have to marry within my own station, this could be as is as good as it gets. Bloody close to Royalty, father will be impressed. What the heck am I going to do about Melita and Ronald? Why do I feel so elated at such a bizarre experience? She may be thinking differently by morning. But she is a goodlooking girl. 'He got out of bed and went over to the heavily curtained French doors that led out onto a balcony. He opened the doors and walked to the balustrades. Standing naked in the cool pre-dawn light, the air chilled his body as his mind was still racing along. 'Do I need to be married? So many people to please. Melita, Ronald, father...my father, what the heck will mother say, not that father will pay her much attention in these matters. 'His body getting cold broke his revere. He returned to the bedroom, pulled the drapes closed, climbed into bed and quickly fell asleep.

***

The next thing he knew he was being awakened by the sun shining blindingly through the windows, as the pageboy pulled the curtains apart. "Good morning, Sir, breakfast will be served in one hour on the terrace." Michael got up, dressed and made his way to the huge flagstone terrace, not quite knowing what to expect. Penelope greeted Michael by the closed French doors to the outside before he could go out onto the terrace. Putting her hand on his arm to stop him she said, "I went to Ronald last night and told him what had happened."

"I think it would have been my place to speak with him."

"I created the situation therefore it is my place to right it."

"What did the poor man say?"

"I sat with him for quite a while. It was hard to see him so hurt. I convinced him that I truly did not know of his feelings for me and how sorry I was to have hurt him."

"So, where is he now? He must be so embarrassed. I know I would be."

"He left for the city at dawn" she said.

Michael sternly replied, "If we are to go any further you should consult with me before you go destroying peoples' lives."

"He destroyed his own life! Well, not really, but could you really see him fitting into our life style? I just gave him the news. Believe me I was very apologetic and humble about it. I think he understands."

"Are you sure that this is what you want? How do you know that I will go along with you?" Michael watched her face intently as she replied.

"Some things you just have to get on with. I think we will make a wellmatched pair, don't you? Don't you want to marry me?"

"Well, you make a good point." Michael took a deep breath and continued, "I see no good reason why I should or shouldn't marry you."

"You could sound a little more romantic or enthusiastic about it."

"Be careful, young lady, what you wish for. I do find you intriguing and beautiful, and that's a good start I think."

***

Together, they opened the door and found all the other guests seated. Penelope led Michael onto the terrace. Everyone turned to watch them as Penelope said, "Mother, Father I would like you to meet the man I am going to marry, Mr. Michael St.John-Brown."

The congenial chatter was abruptly changed to a stunned silence. The Earl was the first to speak. "When did this," he stopped and ordered the staff to retire to the kitchen and await further instructions. The head pageboy led the staff out of the breakfast room and turned to close doors as he glanced at the frozen tableau in front of him. The Earl repeated "When did this happen?" he turned to his wife and added, "Talk about an arranged marriage. Did you have a hand in this?"

Lady Regina, ignoring her husband's comment, said to Penelope, "How do you know Michael? What is going on here?"

"Mama, papa, please listen. You have both commented many times that I should be looking for a husband instead of going off hunting and generally being irresponsible, as papa puts it. You have both given me everything a girl could wish for, probably the most important being a good brain."

"Doesn't seem to me like you used it here. Is this one of your *'here today gone tomorrow'* flights of fancy?" interrupted her father.

"Can you find a better or should I say a more appropriate husband for me?" She stood quietly and stared her father right in the eye.

Her mother spoke, "I am sure that Michael is a fitting prospect. I only wish you had discussed it with us. Let us hear what Michael has to say about it."

"Thank you, your ladyship. I have found that many things that we happen upon, rather than plan for, turn out to be the most fortuitous of situations." He could not believe what was coming out of his mouth. "If you feel that I am not worthy of your family, then you are going to have make some adjustments." He watched both parents for a reaction.

Lady Regina turned to her husband and said, "Now that's some backbone for you David. Not many people stand up to you, at a first meeting. I like this young man." Turning to Michael she continued, "Sit beside me Michael, so that I might get to know you better. I need time to absorb this turn of events."

Her father chimed in with, "I think Penelope should get to know the man better not us."

The whole mood around the table returned to an amiable, excited chatter and questions flew around the table. Soon Penelope and Michael were involved in fielding the barrage of questions. After breakfast was cleared away, the morning passed with traditional Victorian reserve and etiquette. Penelope circulated with ease and diplomacy, encouraging the family's friends to become more acquainted with Michael. The Earl suggested to Michael that they meet in his private study before lunch at noon, and Countess Elizabeth had a similar desire to meet with him after lunch, in her private chambers.

Penelope threaded her arm through Michael's, looked up at him, and whispered, "Don't worry, they like you. They are shocked, but they like you. My parents requiring private audiences is rare, you are honored."

"I'm not as sure as you are that they like me. They may just be being polite on the surface."

"Michael, believe me, my parents, particularly papa, do not put on a front for anyone. The only time they do is for the public. We are a family of strong-willed people. If I need to, I will convince them to be happy for us. I always get my way."

"I can see the strong will. If and when everything works out for us you must remember that *'I'* will be the head of the house."

"We shall see about that," Penelope quietly replied.

"Yes, we shall," was the simple response.

Later, as Michael spoke with the other guests and their wives, he watched Penelope with her mother. They could easily have been mistaken for sisters. The mother was fractionally taller than the daughter, but their mannerisms and gestures were identical. Even their laughter could not be told apart. As noon approached, a footman advised Michael that the Earl would take audience with him in the study and led the way.

***

Sitting behind his desk, the Earl was a picture of power and authority. He had an aura of confidence and privilege. He bade Michael sit in the plush Queen Anne high-back chair at the end of the desk, rather than the rigid straight-back chair in front of it. Michael, who recognized this as a subtle sign of acceptance, relaxed. The Earl pushed an envelope toward Michael, who made no attempt to touch it. Etiquette demanded he wait to be told to pick it up. "I must start off our meeting by saying that I am not happy with the way this situation has presented itself. As a father I expect things to be done in the proper manner. That having been said, my daughter always gets her own way and I hope you will be man enough to support her. Now, while in private, and in this house, you may dispense with 'Earl,' or any of the other folderol. I am David to family and friends, and so be it to you. I shall not bore you with intentions, threats, and promises. You have by now seen evidence of my daughter's strong will. It is about to become your duty to go through life with her, no longer mine. For that I thank you."

"You may have learned in your enquiries about our family, sir, that we do not back down from a challenge." He smiled as he responded.

"Indeed, indeed. I will not ask you what your plans are, as indeed you have not had time to make any. My sources at Lloyd's and others in London, tell me you are an ambitious and remarkable young man. Sometime soon, I hope you will share with me your plans and aspirations. This envelope contains something that I doubt you need, but it is a token that, should you ever need it or indeed desire to use it, you will not hesitate. It is an open letter of credit upon my private bank at Campbell & Coutts, my merchant bankers of London. I trust you will use it wisely and, please, inform me of its use."

"Sir, I, we, appreciate your gesture of good will. As you say, I probably won't need it but gladly accept your thoughtfulness. There is much to be done in the way of planning for the wedding and if you have no objection, I shall leave it in the hands of your wife, and my mother. Along, I guess, with Penelope. If you have any wishes or requirements, be assured they will be taken into account. I will arrange for our families to meet in the near future. I'm sure my father will look forward to that."

"Do your parents know about this proposed marriage?"

"No sir, they do not. I did not know last night. My father has always supported me in everything I do and I am sure he and mother will welcome my settling down, particularly with such a beautiful wife."

"You have quite the way with words. Now, be off with you. Penelope has more claim on your time. We must do the hunt together soon. You do shoot, don't you?"

"Not yet, but I will be happy for you to teach me."

"I will look forward to spending time with you, now off, off you go," instructed the Earl as he stood to shake hands. Michael thought to himself as he left, *"That man has class."*

***

By lunchtime, the other guests had left, and the four remaining adults sat in the warm summer sun on the large flagstone terrace overlooking an ornate tapestry garden with pristine gravel paths dividing the beds. A single, thick plume of water shot high into the air in the center of a formal raised pond and fountain. The tranquility was broken only by the occasional screech of a lone hawk, floating on the afternoon thermal air currents. They chatted about a potential wedding date and thoughts that each had regarding the wedding. Penelope's parents agreed that the planning and arrangements should be left to Michael's mother and themselves. It was when discussing the decision to marry that Michael could see the Earl trying to work out *'when'* last night the decision was made, knowing Michael had been with him until late evening.

Penelope's mother asked, "This has been awfully fast. Are you both sure this is what you want?"

Before Penelope could answer, Michael answered, "How could it not be right?" Penelope beamed. The parents left the couple to enjoy the sun. Michael asked, "Were we not supposed to be going to church with your family this morning?"

"Oh, that! Mama and papa always ask that when we have guest but nobody seems to follow up on it. I know quite a few of the house staff go to church. Why, did you want to go, are you a religious man?"

Michael leaned back with the sun beating down on his face and smiled before saying, "Questions, questions, I have had so many questions I feel like I am at an inquisition."

"Here's a question for you, would you like to meet me in your room in about half an hour so we can discuss last night more intimately?" She fluttered her eyes and in a mock demure way, and covered her face. Before he could answer a footman approached and told him Countess Regina would take audience with him in her chambers. Penelope said she was going to rest and would see him at afternoon tea.

***

The footman ushered Michael into the Countess's chambers, announced him, and quietly closed the door. Elizabeth sat on a chaise lounge, located in a large bay window that looked out over the terrace below. The sumptuous room was furnished with a writing desk and an ornate spinet, with exquisite marquetry inlays of different color woods depicting flowers, leaves, and nymphs. Chairs and couches dotted the room around a large, ornate, red brick, open fireplace. One wall was taken over, floor to ceiling, with dark, rich, red mahogany bookshelves, full to overflowing.

Small side tables held stacks of books, and every open space had fresh-cut flowers. It was the very essence of Victorian femininity and exuded a relaxed, intimate warmth. Elizabeth waved Michael to her side and patted the chaise beside her. "I shall be sad to lose the company, although it is less frequent these days, of my dear Penelope, for I fear you will live far away." She paused then continued, "She is my only child, which is in itself a miracle."

"Indeed, a thing of beauty is a miracle," said Michael. "For your husband to have two miracles in his house, he is fortunate, as am I." Michael impressed himself at just how smoothly that comment had come out. But Elizabeth's next comment stunned him.

"You are a silver-tongued devil, young man," she said. "The miracle I speak of is the fact that Penelope was ever conceived. If you are to become family, you must be trusted with private matters so that you will not embarrass yourself or the Earl. Our marriage was consummated but once, sadly, more out of duty, for you see, my husband enjoys the favors of others of his own kind." She watched Michael trying to interpret her words and could see that he did not understand. Her breasts heaved in a steady rhythm. His glances kept going back to them. "I know that you must be aware of the stigma and shame that man coupling with man brings," she said. "I love my husband and am happy that our one moment produced Penelope, for I would have it no other way. I trust that you will protect our family and its privacy, as you would your own. I tell you this so soon as Penelope is a bit of a rebel in her ways and I would not like you to think this family is trying to hide anything from you."

There was a projected silence before Michael spoke. Without thinking, he asked, "You mean that you no longer conjugate? No physical union? What do you do for…" He stopped suddenly, blushing.

Touching Michael's hand, she replied, "Since that night rarely do have the chance. I have asked you here, I'm afraid, for purely selfish reasons. I can most certainly see exactly what Penelope sees in you. You are a handsome specimen of manhood." Michael blushed as he listened. I think that you see Penelope in me. My husband sees little beyond our pageboys, footmen and his male counterparts."

"You mean that he…"

"There is no need to put it into words. I think you understand. Have you not noticed there are very few female staff besides the head housekeeper?"

"No, I hadn't noticed." Michael's mind was racing as she leaned over and placed her delicate hand gently on his breeches, over his growing erection.

"In our position, society would not look kindly upon a lady of my standing taking a lover, and indeed, the scandal is undesirable. I believe that you may be able to help me find another way." Michael sat silently as she moved her hand to unbutton his breeches and his erection sprung to attention being released from its constraints. Her hands were warm as she lifted him free. "You may touch them if you wish," she said, seeing his gaze, once again, on her breasts. She slipped her chemise up and over her head to expose her bosom. They were full and round with dark pink nipples and did not drop a fraction, which excited him.

"Is this some form of test?" Michael asked quietly.

"Do I look like I am testing? My attire might suggest otherwise."

He could sense his ardor growing and whispered, "Madam, might I ask what you are proposing?"

"That we shall not fall in love. We shall just enjoy each other. You can help me keep our fidelity within the family, and I can help you." With that she stood and went to the end of chaise, leaned over the curled padding of the chaise lounge and flipped her dress up over back. "Now, please slip that into me and have your way with me....please... please take me, for I fear I might faint with anticipation." She lay her bare chest over the chaise to further expose her womanly mound. Michael needed no second invitation. He stood behind her and spit on his hand to wet his shaft and slid into her waiting body. She was wet. She was tight. She was on fire. Looking down at her creamy white buttocks spread apart, the picture of Penelope from last night flashed through his mind, but it didn't stop him as he proceeded to ravish her. He stopped. She begged him to keep going. With one final thrust he held her hips tightly so she could not move and told her feel him inside her. She did. As he shuddered in climax, she shuddered in unison. They held this position for a moment before separating. Michael noticed her tears and questioned them. She whispered quietly to him, "A magnificent cock, and it works so well, thank you. I had completely forgotten what this is like. Please accept my apologies for my less than lady like language. I hope we can continue this arrangement from time to time with discretion." Without waiting for a reply, noticing his still erect member, she turned and knelt on the floor between his legs and said, "Let me clean you up." She took him in her mouth, and gently brushed her lips up and down getting faster and faster. Feeling his body tense, she held him firmly in one hand and gripped his rigidness with her fist and concentrated on the swollen end that was ready. He gushed and she swallowed, keeping him in her mouth until he softened. She stood up and smiled. "Twice in one day," she said. "Delicious. Far better than just reading about it."

Michael thought to himself, '*Far better than reading about it*', I have heard that expression twice in the last twenty-four hours.

***

Lady Elizabeth Regina Blackstone returned to her ladylike demeanor after correcting her attire and watching Michael dress himself. She expressed her willingness to be available for Michael as his desire may dictate. She also expected that as a gentleman their assignations would be kept discrete. "I would be honored should you agree," was her comment.

His reply, "I would be honored that you wish it so."

"Then, Michael, welcome into our family." She waved her hand toward the door, indicating that he may leave. Michael left the room and slowly made his way back to his guest quarters mulling over the last hour. Laying on his bed, looking up at the ceiling, he replayed the torrid sex he had enjoyed. It was the type one read of in the cheap penny pornographic publications schoolboys passed around. The big difference was the gentle, sensitive, sexual sharing he had experienced. There was nothing sordid in his mind about what had passed between them. He believed that the way she had motioned for him to leave after the coupling indicated that she would be an easy, willing, nondemanding, partner. His decision was to go along for the journey and hope it went well.

Chapter 36

It was the middle of the week by the time Michael returned to Threadneedle Street and the Royal Shipping Line offices. He was met at the door by Ronald Surtees, his hand outstretched to shake. Michael studied his face intently, looking for any warning signs of hostility, but there were none.

"What have I done? I have been a fool," said Ronald. "Please come to the coffeehouse, where we may talk in private."

"What have *you* done? You a fool? What do you mean? I am the one that should be apologizing." Michael was trying to understand where Ronald was headed with his comments. They walked together to the coffee house where they found a quiet corner.

Barely had they been served their coffee when Ronald blurted out, "If you wish to withdraw your generous contracts and end our business relationship, I will understand. You must think me a fool. For the entire length of our relationship, you have stood silently by, listening to my pitiful ramblings of love for Penelope and my goals of surmounting the class barrier, while all along you knew it was a quixotic notion. You stood with me as your teacher, your mentor, but more importantly as a friend."

"Stood by you, man, what are you talking about?"

"Being in the company of the Earl and people of breeding where I thought I wanted to be, where I thought that I was accepted and belonged, only to find none of them *really* knew or even liked me."

"Hold a minute Ronald. I do not believe that none of them like you."

"I now realize, I neither fit nor belonged. I want more from life. When Penelope came to me that morning and told me of your night together, I crumbled. I saw in her eyes the same thing for you that you have been seeing in mine, for her. My decision was made in an instant. Her desire to save my feelings was so genuine I had to respect it and just slip away."

"You have got this all wrong. As you know, my family expects me to marry within my class. I woke up to find myself being ravished, as odd as that may seem, by the girl. Her suggestion of marriage, you obviously knew as suddenly as I did. She announced it over breakfast, after you had gone."

"And you agreed to it? Michael, you are not usually a hasty man."

"She is quite the prize I'll admit. I think I can learn to love her. I should be settling down and having a family. My father will approve and I don't have to go through the tedious business of finding someone."

"That seems awfully heartless to me. Don't you want to love someone?" asked Ronald.

"Not heartless, just practical. I am sorry that it had to cause you discomfort, and pain. Now let's not allow a woman to destroy all that we have been working on together. I value your friendship and advice. What do you say to that?"

"Well, there's more," replied Ronald.

"Damn you man. You think I should end our friendship and business relationship? What more could there be?" Michael curiously asked.

"Wait," said Ronald. "When I returned to London, I met Melita, Miss Harrison, at the office and she saw that something was wrong. She took me aside and listened. She was shocked at what you had done and I had to console her, as she, was consoling me. You had done the same thing to both of us, and here was I full of self-pity. It was then I knew exactly how she was feeling."

"What do you mean, you know how she was feeling? What do you know?"

"I know it was not my place to share your private business, but at the time, all I could see was my world shattered. She listened to my pettiness and pointed out where I was so foolish. Melita said it was only natural that you should marry within your station. For me to try and place myself outside my station would invite only hurt and pain. She told me that, though she was hurt by the news that you are to marry, you are a good man and the part of your life you share with Melita belongs to her, as you choose to share it. She has every faith in you as a businessman and as a true friend. She sees no reasons that it should change."

"My relationship with Melita, like my relationship with you is my business. Our, my, private life is that, private. There is nothing to discuss. Why she should be upset about who I marry? Her opinion in this is between her and I, and it should be kept that way. I will talk to her about it." Michael was getting noticeably disturbed. It suddenly struck him that to this point Ronald had not been fully aware of the extent of his relationship with Melita. "I still don't see a reason to terminate our relationship," said Michael. "That would be cutting off my nose to spite my face."

Ronald blurted out, "But that night, Melita and I had sex. While wallowing in our individual self-pity, we made love."

"You did not make love to her. You fucked her, used her, and so be it. If she was willing that's between you two and that is the way it should remain. A gentleman does not discuss his private liaisons with others. Women are fickle creatures. If that was her way to console herself, or you, it has nothing to do with me."

Ronald sat quietly thinking about what Michael had said before speaking. "Melita changed my whole set of values. I find she is as close to perfect as a woman can be. In a rash moment I said, damn Michael, excuse my bluntness, if he doesn't want Melita, then I do. I asked her to be my wife."

"Damn me! Pretty strong stuff. What did she say?" asked Michael.

"She said that, if you approved, she would be happy to." There was a protracted silence as Michael was choosing his words carefully. "If you recall, Judd Cane gave me a sage piece of wisdom when he said 'Play the cards you have been dealt, not the cards you wish for.' Bit of sense there, if ever there was any." Michael took both of Ronald's hands in his and said, emotionally, "Let's both make the best of this hand we have been dealt, what do you say?"

Ronald attempted a smile and said, "You are quite the man Michael St.John-Brown.

"Let's put this behind us and get on with work."

Ronald asked, "Do you think we can go forward in such an uncomfortable situation?"

"As I said, these are the cards we find ourselves with. I most certainly can go forward, can you?"

"I will give it my best shot. I am just concerned about Melita."

"She has told you what she wants. It is not for you to decide anything on her behalf. Just support her. Now, let's change the subject."

***

Later that afternoon Michael summoned Melita to his private office, she entered the room, closed the door behind her and stood rigidly with her back against door, as if needing its' support, waiting to be told what to do. Michael stood and approached her with his arms outstretched and she burst into tears. "I'm sorry, I shouldn't cry like this, I have no right." Suddenly she pummeled her hands on his chest, trying to push him away. "I never expected us to end this way." Michael stayed silent letting her vent her feelings and crying on his chest before speaking.

"You, yourself have often spoken of how I must marry within my station." By now he was holding her close and gently rocking her in his tight embrace. "I had never given any thought to us ending at all. It just never seemed to be an issue. I'm not sure that I want it to end either but, we have to live in the real world."

"What are you saying?" came the muffled reply from her head buried in his chest.

He said, "Our relationship is something special. It does not have to end. What is between you and I, is ours, it's private. I see no reason that you and I cannot have our lives apart from each other as well as having something special together." He felt her stiffen and pull away. She stared at him as if searching his soul for an understanding. He pulled her head down and kissed her tenderly on the forehead. "I want you, need you, in my life."

"I want that as well. How? How would this work?" was her confused response.

"Between us we have three lives. Yours with Ronald, mine with Penelope and ours together, when we can snatch those special moments. Ours is private between us and will be conducted with discretion and consideration for the other two lives. Do you understand what I am saying?"

"I think that you want us to continue to be lovers after we are married to different people."

"That is more than a man can hope for, but, yes. That is what I would very much like." Melita was silent for a moment as she considered her answer, "You want to use me for your own ends."

"As indeed you will use me for your ends. It doesn't have to be so cold. You know that you provide something special for me."

"Yes, sex."

"Now come on. You mean more to me than just sex and you know it."

"Do I really? It just doesn't seem like that right now."

383

"You are hurting. I understand but, we are where we are." Michael sensed Melita trying to find the right words.

She then calmly said, "We will have to be very careful. I have never stopped to imagine my life without you in it. I don't know if I can manage it. Do you think we can make it work without hurting each other, or anyone else?"

"I do. Now dry your eyes. You can freshen up in my water closet. Then, let's move on with the next stage of our lives."

"I love you Michael, you do know that don't you?"

"Yes, I do my sweet Melita."

Chapter 37

Within the year Ronald and Melita were married in a quiet ceremony attended by her family and Michael St.John-Brown at the historic St. Martin in the Fields Church in London. Ronald's family was never discussed and remained a separate thing. The story was that he was estranged and that he had moved on. Tragedy struck the newlyweds early in the first year of their marriage. Late one evening as they were preparing for bed, Melita collapsed. Rushing to her side Ronald asked, "What is happening?"

"I have not been well."

"Why did you not share this with me?" Ronald was alarmed.

"I believe that I am with child, but not positive. I am getting pains in my lower parts. I am frightened."

"Pregnant, pregnant. How far along are you? When did you find out?"

"I don't know for sure. I think…ow….ow..." Melita held her hands tightly round her abdomen as she spoke. "I think that I am a few months."

"What do we do now?" Ronald's voice echoed panic.

"Call for a doctor, quickly. Help me onto the bed please...ow….ow... please, hurry." For what seemed like an eternity, Ronald mopped Melita's brow with damp cloths while they waited for the doctor to arrive. The man bustled into the bedchamber escorted by the maid. Dismissing Ronald, the doctor called for warm water and started his examination of Melita. "How long have you been with child Mrs. Surtees?"

"I am not sure. I did not want to announce it until I could be sure. I think about three months."

"When was your last showing? It seems to me that you are much further along than that."

"That cannot be, we have been only been married for four months."

"Humph. Four months you say." The doctor asked the maid to wait outside while he finished his examination. He then sat on the edge of the bed and spoke in hushed tones. "I fear Mrs. Surtees that you are more than four months with child. Before you say anything, listen to me carefully. Your child is not alive. We have to act quickly your life is at risk if we don't." Melita started to cry. "What have I done?" she blurted out.

"My dear lady, you have done nothing wrong. I must act quickly if I am to save your life." The man called for the maid and instructed her to fetch more help. He left the room to speak with Ronald, who was seated outside the bedchamber. "Mr. Surtees, your wife is with child." He emphasized the word *with*. "The child is no longer alive. I have to work quickly to save your wife. You will need to be patient while I do my best. If there is someone who can comfort you in this time, I suggest you go to them."

"Can I see my wife?" Ronald pleaded.

"I'm afraid not. I must get on with the task at hand right now." With that he turned and went back into the bedchamber.

Michael, who happened to be in London, was able to be at Ronald's side. He sat and listened to Ronald explaining what was going on. All the time Ronald spoke, Michael was doing calculations in is head. He began to realize that this could turn into an awkward situation, depending on the child's stage of development. All he could think of was the question of paternity and how this would play out. He put his arm around Ronald's shoulder and suggested that they wait in his study. Never having been in Ronald's home he waited for Ronald to lead the way.

Over the next few hours, the sounds of staff, assisting the doctor, coming to and from the bedchamber could be heard. Gradually Ronald, under the influence of fine brandy, slipped into a fitful sleep in a high back Queen Anne chair. Michael took the opportunity to go upstairs to see what was happening. He was greeted by the doctor outside the bedchamber. The man looked exhausted. Wiping his hands, he turned and handed the cloth to a maid and introduced himself to Michael. "A sad success, I must say, and who are you sir?"

"Michael St.John-Brown. I am here to be with Ronald in this trying time. What should I tell him?"

"Mrs. Surtees will be fine. She is tired and will need rest for a few weeks. She is a strong lady. Not many survive what she has been through, unfortunately the child did not."

"What is to happen with the child, should we be preparing for a funeral?"

"I would say not. The child was not full term. We shall take care of everything. There is no body to speak of and I think it better that Mrs. Surtees does not have to witness anything."

"How far along was the child?" Michael was hesitant to ask the question.

"I believe further along than the four months she suspected."

Michael shook hands with the doctor and returned to Ronald. When Ronald stirred, Michael told him the situation, keeping to the bare essentials and not mentioning the term of the pregnancy.

Michael stayed with Ronald until Melita woke and then left them to their privacy. Michael was consumed with anxiety. Would Melita tell Ronald that she had continued the affair with him, or, would Ronald work it out? He would just have to wait and see.

***

Melita was slow in recovering. It was almost two months before Michael was able to be alone with her. Throughout this time, he had regularly sent flowers and sweetmeats as offerings of his concern. Some weeks passed with Melita's absence weighing heavily on Michael's frame of mind. It wasn't until one afternoon,

Michael looked up and saw her entering his office, a picture of health, resplendent in the fashion of the day, along with a parasol and ornate hat, that his mood brightened. "Melita Surtees, sir, reporting for work," she cheerfully announced. Michael jumped out of his chair and moved swiftly to embrace her. Holding her close he drank in her warmth and presence. It was she who spoke first, "Enough of this, what are we working on now?"

"Do we need to talk my darling?"

"Nothing to talk about Michael, yesterday was yesterday and I want to get on with today and tomorrow."

Michael flopped back into his chair and said, "Well, I am glad to have you back. This place has not been the same. I am sorry for your loss. We must spend some time together and catch up on everything soon."

"Catch up, and well, you know what! I've missed you, Michael, but I need a little more time. It wasn't to be long before their lives settle back into the familiar routine.

Chapter 38

Michael's marriage to Penelope had been the highlight of 1875's social calendar. The ceremony took place in the spectacular, historic, Bath Cathedral and the St. John-Brown penchant for all things Royal was amply satisfied by the Earl of Sussex's, Penelope's father's connections. Dignitaries, socialites, the top echelon of the business world, as well as anyone well connected, came from all over the East, West, and South of England. The family did little business with Scotland and the North of England and so the lack of representation went unobserved. Michael's father, Sir William, relived many pleasant memories of his own wedding during the celebrations and festivities that took place in the confines of The Royal Crescent mansions. His wife, Lady Veronica was the epitome of Victorian elegance and orchestrated the lavish banquets and entertainment. Penelope had been affected by the preparations and demands of protocol being placed on her by tradition and equal pressure from both sets of parents. Still, retaining her individualistic style of pushing boundaries, on the afternoon of the ceremony she enticed Michael into the sacristy where she performed fellatio on him. He didn't protest. He was more concerned about being caught. When she finished, she stood, smiled and said, "I guess that's my last sex act as a single woman. Now, get out of here and let's get married."

The fast, erotic episode excited Michael, and as he left the sacristy, he said to a nearby altar boy, "I know why I am marrying that lady, for sure." He grinned to himself as he walked away. The choirboy nodded and smiled to hide his embarrassment, for he had witnessed the whole incident and could not wait to share the story with his pals.

***

The entire center of Royal Crescent was transformed into a spectacular arena of opulence. Seating for the eleven hundred guests formed an outer rim of the large oval lawns. Each table lavishly adorned with flowers and silver service embraced the event. Besides the staff employed for the event, many of the wealthy guest brought with them their own butlers. The butlers would lead their employers to the appropriate table and stand behind like sentinels. One end of the Circle was closed off where huge temporary kitchens and serving stations were established to allow a fast delivery of food. An orchestra comprising fifty musicians was off to one side and they had been entertaining the arriving guests. The gentle hubbub of the chatting crowd was silenced by a trumpet fanfare. The Lord Mayor of Bath led the bride and groom and wedding party to the raised head table. When all were seated the trumpets blared out again, demanding attention. A team of six Clydesdale draft horses entered pulling a huge six wheeled dray that had been modified for the occasion. Aback the dray was a huge spit being slowly rotated by a burly barechested man at each end. The heat from the fire beneath and the summer sun above, showed in the sweat dripping from the exertions of the men. The aroma wafting from the huge, cooked oxen created a hunger in the crowd, which was quickly attended to by the staff. The spectacular entry of the oxen was the signal that the celebrations were under way.

Penelope was a picture of feminine beauty, social elegance and pure happiness. She was happy that the openair setting had practically eliminated speeches due to its expanse. The more tedious side had her and Michael listening to the many repeated offerings of congratulations. Sir William, being observant, regularly broke up the small sessions with polite "We thank you so very much for your kind thoughts. May I steal my beautiful new daughter-in- law away for a moment?" It was during these brief exchanges that Michael got a rare glimpse at how dignified and socially skilled his father was. It made him realize that there was much about the private man his father was, that he really knew so very little of. He felt a pang of guilt about how his caustic comment long ago about Madge must have hurt his father. That emotion soon passed as the guests, music, and wine softened everyone.

Daylight seemed to just magically exchange places with a clear, star lit, deep blue night sky. The music softened in volume and guests dissolved into the night. The local church bells rang out the midnight hour and the scene changed from a subdued peaceful and calm emptiness, to a frenzied choreography of returning the circle to its usual sanguine, rightful setting by dawn.

***

After the wedding, Michael and Penelope had moved into his grandfather's house in the Royal Crescent, across from his father's home, much to his mother's pleasure. While Michael converted his grandfather's study into his planning room, his mother and wife kept a vibrant, full social regiment, the sounds of servants and household activities echoing comfortingly through the house. Sir William's spirits rose whenever his daughter-in-law cajoled him into participating. He even gained some of his old verve back. New life had been breathed into the house.

Melita and Ronald lived in London, but on weekends, they would stay with Michael and Penelope. On these Saturday afternoons, Michael would meet with both of them both in his war room to lay out his requirements for the next week back in London. Inevitably, when Ronald would leave the meeting, as he often did, to go to Bath Cathedral, a place he loved to worship in, it was not long before Melita and Michael rekindled their attraction for each other. These trysts were more sexual than amorous on Michael's part but he was fully aware that they meant more to Melita. Sometimes, it would be perfunctory gratification, and others times, with her eyes and gestures, she would have Michael ready to satisfy her every whim.

Both understood the unwritten rule to be considerate to one another and exercise extreme caution. Michael always exhibited a relaxed and calm persona at dinner, on Saturday evenings.

***

Two years passed before Michael had the plans completed for the construction of The Royal Palisades. He moved into high gear with the preparations for the work to commence. Ronald spent large portions of his time seeking out the finest tradesmen he could find; masons, carpenters, plasterers, plumbers, roofers, and gardeners who were willing to embark on what could be as much as a ten-year project in America. Those he located and approved would sign contracts that said they'd be ready to go at a months' notice.

There had been discussions of Melita and Ronald moving to Jakeskill, but Michael saw that as conflicting with the other businesses. Besides, neither seemed over anxious to be away for so long. As a team, they would provide advice and assistance to Michael, who planned to set up a permanent home in America. Ronald would keep his finger on the pulse of new inventions and innovations related to the physical building, while Melita would stay in society circles, observing fashions, trends, and styles. It was Michael's hope that, between them, they would be able to foresee and predict trends before they were common place in America. Melita suggested they find someone to duplicate some of their efforts in New York, where an American society was developing and demands for more exclusive surroundings were growing. Melita's fondness for Josiah Mielman had her offer the man's name as a possible candidate for the role, particularly as New York had a huge, wealthy, Jewish population. Michael liked the idea.

Christmas that year saw life at Eleven and Fifty-Four Royal Crescent the merriest and most spirited it had been since that terrible night in 1858, when Madge died. The celebration and love were flowing. Ronald and Melita stayed with Michael and Penelope while The Earl of Mowbray and Countess Elizabeth stayed with Sir William. The flurry of activity across the meticulously manicured gardens that lay between the two buildings wore a path in the lawn. Michael's mother-in-law, Countess Elizabeth made her desires known upon arrival, as did Melita. Penelope was oblivious to it all, busy as she was soaking up the family atmosphere. The evening was a joyous celebration of family and togetherness, and laughter echoed through the halls until the early hours of the morning.

During a lull in the conversation, Michael leaned back in his chair and surveyed the group. His wife, her look alike mother and Melita were together in one room harmoniously. The situation flattered his ego and raised him, in his own eyes, to the level he felt he belonged. He thought, *'There weren't many men who could claim to have a life like this. Life couldn't get much better.'*

Chapter 39

In 1878 it was as if history was repeating itself. Thirtyfive years a go, to the month, Mother's Fine Foods had experience rapid growth and expansion. Now, three new food processing plants were in full operation. Michael was being shown around a new plant that was due to go on line, when the unthinkable happened. A newspaper photographer wanted Michael to pose for photographs in front of a huge boiler designed to operate the machinery. Michael made a tragic mistake. The photographer suggested Michael reach up and put his hand on a valve, as if to operate it. As he held the valve lever, he asked the plant foreman, "what the purpose of this valve my man?"

Excitedly, the man responded, in an urgent tone, "don't touch that one sir, it is pressure relief valve. It's there for safety reasons, only to be used in emergency."

"I know that man. I'm not stupid, I own the place don't you know."

"Yes sir, but it's a very sensitive valve. I wish you would stand well clear of it."

"You do, do you?" With that the photographer shouted, "Look this way sir, and smile at the camera." As Michael turned towards the camera his hand pulled the valve control lever.

***

Two days later Michael emerged from a drug induced coma. His right side hurt like hell. He could see that it was heavily bandaged, and through a painful haze he saw that he was in hospital and surrounded by nurses. Penelope was by his side. He heard her say, "Doctor, doctor, he is awake."

"Thank God for that. Can you hear me Mr. St. John-Brown?" Michael slowly nodded his affirmative. The doctor leaned in close and listened to Michael trying to speak. It was barely audible.

A nurse spoke up, "Without a doubt doctor, he is asking what happened. It's always their first question when they come out of a coma."

The doctor turned to Penelope and said, "Why don't you explain. You were there and you saw what happened. He knows your voice. it will be less stressful for him."

Penelope stood close and gently lifted Michael's un-bandaged hand and kissed it before speaking. "It happened at the new plant. You were having your photograph taken for the newspapers. The plant supervisor told you to be careful of the relief valve and you turned it on. The blast of steam was so great it spun you round and knocked you off your feet. It badly burned your hand. Luckily you may only loose two fingers."

Angrily, Michael summoned all his strength and shouted, "Luckily? Luckily? Look at me! Do I look lucky to you?"

Penelope calmly replied, "Yes my dear, you were lucky. As the blast spun you away, the photographer and his assistant took the full blast of scalding steam. They both died, I am told, agonizingly slowly, from the burns."

"Will I lose my arm?"

In a detached manner his wife replied, "If you do, you will still live. Those poor men are dead."

"Whose side are you on woman? I am possibly maimed for life!"

"Michael I'm sad to say this but, you were told not to touch the valve. But no, you had to show off. You are lucky to even be here. *I* had to witness the whole debacle. It is going to be a long time before I am able to forgive you. You can't always be right." She gently placed his hand back onto the bed and turned and left the room. Michael's focus gradually returned and he was able to see Ronald and Melita seated at the end of the bed. They both stood and approached his side. It was Melita who spoke first, "You must relax Michael. It must have been horrendous for Penelope to watch you go through that and worry if you were going to live."

"For her to watch, I was the one going through it. How do you think I felt?"

"Nothing Michael, you felt nothing. You lost consciousness immediately," Ronald interjected firmly.

"You are all ganging up on me. I don't need any of you. This wasn't my fault. Bloody faulty engineering. I will find out who's to blame. I'm damned if I don't."

Melita took Ronald's hand and led him from the room. Ronald said to Melita, "I don't know why you stand so steadfastly behind that man. He can be so self-centered and cruel."

"Have kind thoughts my dear. He is in a dark place right now. He just found out how human and frail he is. He is just like the rest of us. He will come round."

***

It took three months for the St. John-Brown house to return to what was its normal pattern. Michael's arm and side of his neck would remain scarred for life. That was inconsequential to him as the loss of three fingers would always be a highly visible reminder and a source of curiosity to others. As was his usual demeanor, he would foist off questions about his injury with a simple, "Industrial accident you know. That's the risk of being a businessman. Must take the good with the bad you know." He would then change the subject as if it was never raised. He attacked the projects on hand with a new vigor and determination. The Royal Palisades was playing on Michael's mind the entire time he was regaining his ability to function without aid. Now it was on the front burner of production.

Chapter 40

Despite Michaels drive to be in America, his accident and the slowness of pulling everything together, it wasn't to be until the next year that the journey finally took place. With the spring of 1880 round the corner, and the Atlantic storm season fast disappearing, the first ship left for Jakeskill Island, carrying engineers, an architect, carpenters, construction labor foremen, and purchasing staff. It was decided that Michael and Penelope would follow later. Ronald and Melita would go ahead with the first shipment. The instructions were to establish private quarters for whenever the St.John-Browns were on site, along with accommodations for his guests. Penelope and Michael had agreed that they would arrive in New York in style to keep the public interested in them and what they were doing. They would bring in their fathers, the Earl and Sir William, to visit them in New York to play on the American public's fascination with the English aristocracy.

With the assistance of Michael's and Penelope's mothers a newly installed retinue was in Michael's house. The staff in Sir William's was upgraded. For each house, there was to be a butler and head housekeeper. William and Michael would each have a private manservant, a butler, and a secretary. Veronica and Penelope would each have a lady in waiting, an upstairs maid, and a downstairs maid. The general house staff consisted of cook, under cook, scullery maid, gardener, and houseboys. Countess Elizabeth set about training the staff to the level of the Earl's household. Michael and Penelope's staff prepared to move to New York when the time came. It was decided at this time to maintain both houses in America and England.

In September of that year Penelope cornered Michael in his study with, "You will never believe what is happening."

"What has gone wrong now? All I need is another problem."

"No problem, Papa."

"Papa, I'm not your bloody father. Tell me what you are talking about."

"No, you are not my father, you are this little one's father." Penelope rubbed her tummy and started to cry.

Michael stood and putting his arms around her spoke, "There is no need to cry. I'm sorry, I didn't mean to be so blunt. This is wonderful news. When did you find out?"

"I am crying with happiness. I have never thought of having a child. It has just never entered my head. I didn't even know if I wanted a child until I just spoke it out loud. Are you happy?"

"Great addition to the family. Bloodline and all that stuff. Sir William will be delighted."

"Why do you keep calling your father Sir William? It sounds so...so cold."

"Because, he is Sir William. He likes it and it doesn't bother me. He is my father, my papa, my daddy and we both know that. They say it's a wise man that knows his father. That's all that matters. When can we expect the child?"

"I have missed my last two showings, so I think we have seven more months."

"You need to take it easy my dear, use the servants. These are early days we don't want anything to go wrong."

"I won't let anything go wrong. Forget about a boy, this is going to be girl and she is going to be named Angela Rose," Penelope said with a giggle as she turned and left the study.

Michael leaned back in his plush study chair and watched his wife leave the room. With his eyes closed his mind wandered through a myriad of things, some disturbing to him, as if a play was taking place on the inside of his closed eyelids. The brief scenes included children running around his house shouting loudly and destroying things, broken bodies scattered among debris, large explosions, women shouting obscenities at him, and, a funeral procession, his funeral! He suddenly opened his eyes and the images disappeared. He broke out in a sweat as he tried to suppress those pictures. It was as if they had been burnt into his brain.

Chapter 41

By April of 1882, Josiah, had accepted Michael's offer to ingratiate himself into New York's high society, and had located a selection of desirable residences in New York City for Michael and Penelope to choose from for their new home. By June, Melita and Ronald had completed the setting up of the construction site on Jakeskill Island and returned to England to assist in the selection of furnishings for the St. John-Brown home. By the end of June, Michael and Penelope, along with the retinue of house staff, left Bath for New York. The subject of babies was kept to a minimum in consideration of Penelope's feelings. It had been about a year since the hopes of a child were dashed when Penelope announced that her showings had returned in the third month and that it had been a false alarm. Michael's harsh, unforgiving assault on her for embarrassing him with the false pregnancy had created a silent chasm between them that was gradually healing.

***

Standing on the dockside watching the loading of the ship bound for America, the gathering reminded Michael of the story of Hannibal crossing the Alps with slaves, staff, soldiers, and elephants carrying everything they would need.

"We still have time to get some elephants," said Penelope.

Boarding the White Star Line's RMS *Oceanic*, the St. John-Brown party took thirty of the sixty-six first-class accommodations and two hundred and fifty of the second and third classes' one thousand accommodations. Ronald had put together a list of workers that would be required to speed up the construction of The Royal Palisades. These people were gathered in the huge shed, waiting to board and start their new life. The *Oceanic* was only eight years old and promised a swift crossing. She was a steam and sail combination ship that impressed Michael.

***

Both Melita and Penelope spent hours on deck bundled-up against the Atlantic winds. They talked endlessly about America, the future, and where each felt their own lives were going. Penelope shared her hurt over the false pregnancy. She said, "Michael was so unkind. I did not know of such things. I was happy for us and yet he acted as if I had done something bad to him."

"Dear Penelope, we both know the world revolves around Michael, or at least he thinks so. We just have to navigate our way around him."

395

"But why? I thought that in marriage we were to be one, equal."

"Oh no! It will be a long time before men see us as their equals. We just have to accept Michael is the way he is."

Penelope was absorbing Melita's comment as she replied, "I may have to accept him for what he is. I am his wife. But you, why do you put up with it?"

This caught Melita off guard. She chose her next words, carefully, "I have known Michael for a long time. I have been with him since he was a boy, almost I could say a child. I have seen his life take many twists and turns. In my own way I love him as a close and dear friend, and, I suppose that allows me to see past his faults."

"It seems to me that the cost of friendship is almost as burdensome as the cost of marriage," replied Penelope.

Melita was uncomfortable at the direction this conversation took so she quickly changed it by saying, "I think all relationships throughout our life have costs. We just have to decide if we are willing to pay those costs."

***

Whenever it possible, Melita would bury the thoughts that arose out of her conversation with Penelope and meet with Michael where she would almost savagely use his sex to calm her demons, whatever they were. The sex was good for him, and seemed therapeutic for her. She always appeared to be so much closer to Ronald after her encounters with Michael. These encounters relieved her guilt feelings. Michael, on the other hand, had too much on his mind to worry about such petty things as guilt.

Chapter 42

Michael was even more impatient to get the construction of The Royal Palisades under way. As soon as the disembarking was complete, Ronald took over arranging transport for the tradesmen to Jakeskill. It took two weeks for Michael's family to settle into their New York home. Melita took care of her family's settling in and Ronald went ahead to Jakeskill with the second round of tradesmen. Michael met with Josiah and discussed the idea of his settling his family in New York and having them work the social scene towards the introduction of the Royal Palisades concept to the public. Josiah was paid handsomely for the trading post on Jakeskill. It was as if the old man had been given a new lease on life. The matter was put to rest and within the month Michael was to move into Josiah's home on Jakeskill as his temporary accommodation and offices on the island. Josiah spent that summer bringing his family back together around him and to a new home in New York. His daughters delighted at the move, and that invigorated the old man. He took on his new role in The Royal Palisades project with great gusto.

***

1886, Michael sat quietly in the attic of the old Meilman home, at the dormer window, looking out over The Royal Palisades and thinking back over the past six years. Michael was proud of the progression of his concept into a real, tangible property despite many time consuming delays. There had been problems created by materials not arriving on time, changes being made to original ideas, and improvements made that arose out of the craftsmen's suggestions. It had taken a year for the site for the main building to be cleared and the foundations put in place. The Architects went to great lengths to save and replant trees as well as bring three thousand new trees to the site to establish woods and a forest. The earth moving was done with military precision. As stone and other materials were brought to the site they were strategically placed for the minimum of movement. The foundations clearly stood out as a huge footprint.

In the second year the ground floor was completed which contained the structures utilities, and servant and staff accommodations. Kitchens, sculleries, laundry storage and a central staff command center were put in place. The thirty miles of road had all the bases laid and would serve to reduce damage to the surroundings. There had been a significant rotation of workers as some completed their role and others became homesick or disenchanted with life there. It was hard for many workers as the workdays were long and the schedule grueling. Those who brought their families with them fared better than others. Many in this position brought relatives over to join them as workers.

The architects had a two-year contract during which some completed their portion of the project as others took time off to explore America before returning to the job. The architects and the construction offices were housed in Josiah's house and store. Josiah had returned to Jakeskill twice since leaving. He wanted to be fully aware of the development he was touting. The old man had improved in health and demeanor since moving his family to New York. His improved financial status and assignment had lifted burdens from his shoulders. He even stood straight, felt stronger, and was excited about life. Michael credited himself alone for making that happen.

The third year the first and second floors were added. The Americans referred to these two floors as the second and third floors, Michael had to adjust to this different way of doing things. The heavy looking, huge, local red stone blocks that were the outer skin of the building visually gave the rising structure a solid earthbound stability.

It was in this two year period that national newspapers had started to take notice of the structure and the 'Royally connected Englishman, St. John-Brown' and his imprint on their country. It was the description of the future uses for The Royal Palisades that sparked inquiries. Josiah, Michael and Penelope, and Melita and Ronald frequented the construction of The Royal Palisades, escorting wealthy, interested members of the American elite. Under Melita's guidance there was always a reporter from some national newspaper included on a tour. Careful name-dropping of visitors increased awareness and desirability for the project. In early discussions with Penelope's father, the Earl had expressed a desire to own one of the top-level suites and if possible, it should be named 'The Earl's Chambers'. Michael liked the idea so he earmarked a space for Penelope and himself to be the St. John-Brown Chambers. These two chambers were to have irrevocable ownership in perpetuity. From that point on the upper-level areas were to be known as 'The Chambers'.

In the fourth year the final floor was added. As the carpentry, plastering, plumbing, and electrical installations were nearing completion things were becoming a frenzied mish mash of people, equipment and supplies. Everything was falling into place. It would soon be time to put the finishing touches to the place.

***

Josiah had located a French lawyer, Andre Leroi, who had experience both in Paris and London with many buildings that had multiple owners and was looking to move to America. It was arranged that he would be Michael's guest in New York with all expenses paid, with a view to acting as a consultant. Melita had suggested what she called 'a round table' meeting of people who could contribute to the development of an ownership plan. Michael quickly liked the idea of a meeting, but the round table idea was squashed. As a result of the entire investment in the project being made by Global Enterprises it was not right for this to be a democracy. Melita pointed out that she hadn't meant for ownership to change but to have a set of rules and conditions just as the gentlemen's clubs in England had, that gave the illusion of ownership. Rules that would create a hierarchical aura of rights permitted, but not carved in stone, was to be the plan.

Andre Leroi proposed a plan whereby there would be levels of membership to Royal Palisades. The top level would pay a membership application fee of forty thousand dollars. If successful in their application the lifetime membership fee would be two hundred thousand dollars. This would obtain for them the exclusive rights of use to one of the larger chambers. They would then pay an annual fee for the use of chambers, which would be used to cover the running expenses of the Palisades. Each time somebody would stay there they would pay a per diem service fee based on if the owner brought his own staff or not. This, he suggested, would create exclusivity and prestige. He did suggest that there should be strict rules of conduct and etiquette as well as defined renewal rules. Other owners should be allowed to buy lifetime non-transferable membership for a premium. This would create a hierarchy within the hierarchy. The lawyer went on to suggest a similar program for the next level of suites with the base sum being one hundred thousand dollars. This could raise sixteen million dollars to start, all running costs covered by fees plus usage fees.

The discussions ended in an agreement that there was more than enough wealth for the idea to work. Melita gave the example of selling oranges. If you only have five and ask for a penny each, you would earn five pennies. However, if you asked for an offer you may get offered more than a penny. The problem that she saw was that you could always get more oranges, but there is only one Royal Palisades. Why set the price before you know the market? She pointed out that between herself and Josiah they had a list of over one hundred people who had shown interest now, without any numbers being discussed. On that list were oil, steel, rail and telegraph magnates and then countless multi- millionaires, and America is still growing. Ronald went further to point out that there was England, France, Holland and many other countries with ties to America that had wealthy people also.

Michael commissioned Mr. Leroi to draft membership rules and conditions, without the fees that they would use, in advertisements to start the program. The lawyer said that they should keep at least two chambers and five suites available for high end paying guests. He also said that all dues and fees should paid by irrevocable letters of credit. This alone, he felt, was a substantial qualifier or disqualifier.

After the meeting had ended, Michael returned to New York to be with his wife for a brief break.

***

Michael was welcomed home by an excited Penelope, who had arranged a celebratory gathering. Standing in the foyer of their home the couple embraced, holding each other close, as if trying to make up for lost time by being apart. Suddenly

Michael pulled back and looked closely at his wife's protruding stomach. "Are you," he hesitated, "with child, for real this time?"

"Yes. When I visited you earlier this summer at Jakeskill you did this to me." She rubbed her stomach proudly.

"Why didn't you tell me?"

"I didn't want to embarrass or disappoint you."

"When am I am going to hold my son or daughter?" His tone was soft and pleasing to Penelope.

"I'm sure it will be a girl. I just have a strong feeling about it. So, Angela Rose is for real and she will be joining us in the next two months."

"You don't look big enough to be that close."

"My mama tells me that nobody even knew she was carrying me until a month before my birth. I must be following in her footsteps."

"Well, we really do have something to celebrate. A boy would have been nice, but, a daughter, who can complain about that?"

"Melita Surtees."

"What do you mean, Melita Surtees?"

"I know she is close to you. I fear she may view this as competition for your attention.

"That's because she is very close to us. There is no competition for my attention."

"I think she will be jealous."

"Why?"

"Because I have your baby and she doesn't."

Michael panicked as he said, "Why would she want my baby?" He was trying to hide any guilt feelings that he felt may show.

"No not your baby. She doesn't have her own baby girl. I know she and Ronald have wanted a little girl for a long time."

"She did lose a child when she and Ronald were first married. There's nothing to worry about."

"Oh, I don't know, she is…let's not talk about her anymore right now." Penelope took Michael's hand and led him into the parlor.

***

In September of that year, Angela Rose was born, the first St. John- Brown to be born in America. She was a feisty baby from the day she was born. She slept irregularly and demanded attention right from the beginning. Penelope had high hopes that the child would bring a softer, kinder demeanor to her husband's disposition. For the first six years of her life Angela Rose grew up in a pampered existence in New York City in a grand mansion overlooking Central park. She spent most of her young life with nannies and servants as her parents were frequently moving around between America and England. Gradually over time Melita became closer to Angela Rose who had taken to calling her 'Aunty Mel, or Mellie. It proved to be an uncomfortable arrangement as Melita was soon to find out.

On one sunny afternoon in Central Park, while resting on the cool grass under the shade of a huge maple tree, Angela Rose posed a question that surprised Melita. "Aunt Mellie, why do mama and papa always have to play kissy? It's yuckie."

"Mamas and papas kiss each other to show their love. Your papa kisses you a lot."

"Yes, but when they come out of their bedroom in the afternoon mama acts silly and giggles like a little girl."

"That's because she loves papa a great deal."

"I think. I think it has something to do with papa's breeches."

"Why do you say that?"

"Because he is always fixing his breeches and he is out of breath. Don't you think that's strange? Does Uncle Ronald fix his breeches when he kisses you?" Melita laughed and replied, "Young lady, you ask too many questions."

"Papa never fixes his breeches when he kisses me. He doesn't even kiss me like he does mama."

"Grown-ups kiss in their own special way. Papa's love for you is different to his love for mama."

"Does papa fix his breeches when he kisses you?" Angela Rose asked innocently.

"What do you mean?" blurted out Melita.

"Papa kisses you like he does mama. Does that mean he loves you as well?"

"When have you seen papa kiss me?"

"When you have meetings and when you leave from visiting us." Melita struggled to maintain an uninterested tone as she said, "Oh that, that is a grownups kiss of friendship. It means that two people care for each other. That's different from mama and papa's love." Fortuitously, a butterfly landed on Angela Rose's arm to which Melita commented, "there, see that? The butterfly is kissing you. He wants to be your friend. Now let's go and get ice cream.

As they walked to the man selling ice cream Angela Rose asked, "Aunt Mellie, do you know why papa's arm got hurt and he only has one finger and thumb on his hand?"

"Yes I do but I think you should ask him. Things like that are very personal and I am sure he will tell when he thinks you are ready."

Her questions kept coming. "Did somebody hurt him?"

"No, it was an accident. You must ask him about it." The ice cream vendor interrupted the conversation as he sold them a cone.

***

That next afternoon Angela Rose went to the zoo with a nanny while her mother was attending an afternoon soiree. Michael and Melita spent the afternoon enjoying each other's bodies. Laying cuddle in Michael's arms Melita related her earlier conversation with Angela Rose. "What should we do about it?" she asked.

"She is six, it's probably about time we got her interested in something to keep her prying eyes away."

"Michael! That's not why I told you. I don't want us to cause any grief to Penelope and the child."

"I know, I know. I have a possible solution. Leave things to me." All the time they were chatting, Melita and been softly fondling Michael's growing erection while becoming aroused herself, for the second time that afternoon. She whispered in his ear, "Take me, gently, slowly and fill me up. God, I love you when you are hard." They bucked and jostled with great earnest, climaxing together. In an attempt to calm Melita's concern, Michael whispered, "You know that I do love you more than just a friend, don't you?"

Holding his face between her upturned palms, she kissed him tenderly on the lips and replied, "Sadly, dear Michael, not as much as I love you, but that is our life, and we both have other lives, and my news for you is, that I am with child." Stunned, Michael asked, "do you mean I… we…a child?"

"No, I don't think we. Ronald and I, we are three months into it. I have kept it quiet until I could be sure. After the last time, I don't want to take any risks."

"You do not show any signs. Oh my. Do you think we should be doing this, the sex, I mean?"

Melita replied. "You don't get off the hook that easy Mr. St.John-Brown. I am safe now. We just have to be a little more gentle. I will let you know when we should take a break. I hope it's a girl this time."

Michael suggested, "At a time like this we should bring your mother over to America."

"I do miss my mother."

"I miss her too." As quickly as Michael said this he added, "She was always a great supporter of mine."

Michael," she said, "I will give it some thought."

"No, no, let's do it soon. Times like this, family should be together," Michael urged.

After she left, Melita thought about her conversation with Angela-Rose and her own liaisons with the girl's father. She knew that she loved Michael and that in his own way he loved her. But just *what* was his way?

Chapter 43

Michael concocted a plan that he felt would prevent any further risk of his daughter, knowingly or not, bringing attention to his affair with Melita. It wasn't long before he found the opportunity to bring it into play. Michael, while having breakfast served on their balcony overlooking Central Park, casually remarked to Penelope, "When I was in Buffalo this week. I spent a lot time with Kenneth, Kenneth Harken and his wife. They have a beautiful home. Buffalo is quite a remarkable city you know."

"That's the soap people, isn't it?' Penelope replied.

"I wouldn't use that description, my dear. While our business' have been focusing on food in England, here in America, they were achieving success with household goods, similar to our earlier venture with food and goods through The Co-Op, that reached England's poorer classes. They have put an interesting addition to the concept."

"Is it as lucrative?"

"Oh yes, you should see the lifestyle they have. Compared to the city here it is just as substantial but far less chaotic."

"Does that appeal to you dear?" Penelope was curious. She knew Michael always had an agenda when he raised discussions out of the blue.

"What did appeal to me was the freedom their daughter had. It is a much safer environment than here, or so it seems."

"Don't tell me you are thinking of moving us to the country."

"No, not us. Anyway, Buffalo is hardly country. It is a very wealthy city indeed."

"If not us, then who?"

"The Harken's daughter Tessie, is Angela Rose's age and to be frank an impressive child. She is so much more at ease around people than Angela Rose is. I think New York is somewhat restricting on our child."

"Michael, why don't you just come and tell me what is on your mind?"

"I am concerned about her not having younger people her age around."

"Are you suggesting that we send our daughter to boarding school?"

"Yes, well, no, not exactly. Not a boarding school."

"Then what exactly?" Penelope was getting a little agitated.

Michael related to Penelope, their daughter's conversation with Melita. "She was asking questions about our afternoon liaisons in the boudoir. A little bit too close to interest in sex, although, I don't think she has made that connection, just yet."

"So, explain clearly to me what you propose."

"I think we should try to arrange for her to commence an education that leads to preparing her for the duties that would fall to her from the family empire."

"Michael, she is six years old."

"I went to boarding school when I was six and I have not turned out too badly."

"You are not girl."

"Consider this my dear, you are travelling back and forth between England and here. The Royal Palisades needs a lot more of your attention. The Harkens have offered to help us out. I think day boarding during the week and staying weekends with the Harkens is a wonderful opportunity." Michael went on to promote his idea intensely. "The Harken family is well respected and lives in the wealthiest part of Buffalo in upstate New York, on the edge of Lake Erie. Their home is on the prestigious Lincoln Parkway, adjacent to Delaware Park, close to a Young Ladies Seminary on Bidwell Parkway."

"I will not permit this ridiculous idea." Penelope was trying to stand up to Michael.

"Now hold on, I do think we should consider relocating one day. Buffalo has a huge influence on the economy of this country. Grain mills, a huge shipping industry, meat and leather industry. The list goes on and on. Kenneth and his wife have been urging me to move for a long time now. You have met them at The Royal Palisades. A decent family."

"What does that have to do with us?" Penelope was becoming more agitated.

Michael decided to be blunt as he said, "I am the head of this household, and what I say goes. I have not considered this idea lightly. I have visited The Buffalo Young Ladies Seminary and think we should consider sending her there for an education. Their guiding philosophy is to provide a superior education for young women within a vigorous and participatory environment which emphasizes development of character, intellectual independence, creativity, service, and leadership for life. I also like the fact that it was an all-girls school, committed to full equality for women. The required curriculum would provide Angela-Rose with experiences in the arts, humanities, and sciences, and that would enable her to adapt in a world of rapid technological change." Michael watched his wife carefully for a reaction. It came forth fast and firmly.

"I repeat, you are not sending Angela Rose to boarding school. I will not have it. She is only six years old."

"And I repeat, I was six when my father placed me in a boarding school. I didn't turn out too bad, did I?"

"You are a man!"

"I was a sixyear old child. Those decisions were not made for my parent's comfort. They were made for my future."

"She is not going," Penelope spat out.

"Now hear me out. Kenneth and his wife were both enthusiastic about having company for Tessie, and felt that our daughter would enjoy a more relaxed environment."

"And that is what? I can't believe that you want to send our baby away. What has she done to you that is so bad?" Penelope started crying with frustration.

Michael's face flushed. It was a combination of anger at being challenged and embarrassment that his wife had touched a soft spot without knowing it - his affair with Melita. He waited until he had gained control of himself and his wife's crying subsided before he spoke. "Believe me, I am sure my parents went through the same emotions and I clearly recall my own trepidation, no fear, *shear bloody fear,* when I was dropped off at Charterhouse. We are not dropping her off where she does not know anyone. She has played often with Tessie at The Palisades. She is going to be staying with a family we know. Plus, I am in Buffalo on business so often I am sure I will see her more than my father saw me.

"So, it sounds like you have made up your mind."

"No dear, I have made up our minds. We will appear united on this subject, and that's the last word."

"Well, you can tell her. I will not."

***

Within the month The St. John-Brown family spent a week staying with the Harkens in Buffalo. The zoo, the boats on the lake at the Harkens beach house, along with the parks and myriad of things to do, soon relaxed the unsuspecting child. A brief tour of Tessie's school, The Buffalo Young Ladies Seminary prepared Angela Rose for what was about to come. The ground was laid with a carefully placed, 'wouldn't it be great if you could go to school here with Tessie?' started the ball rolling. Much to Michael's surprise on the last evening at dinner Tessie innocently asked, "Daddy, can Angela Rose come and live with us? We could have such fun together?"

Kenneth's wife replied, "If daddy says it is alright and Mr. and Mrs. St. John-Brown agree, I don't see why not." Turning to her husband she continued, "We have the room and you wanted another child." She reached out across the table and took hold of Angela Rose's hand and said quietly, "Do you think your mummy and daddy would let us borrow you for a while?"

"Please mama, and you papa, can they borrow, me? Pleeeease? I will come home sometimes."

Penelope joined the exchange with, "I think you can borrow her, but you must promise to give her back."

So, much to everyone's surprise it came to pass. It was agreed that the issue of boarding Angela Rose in the school would be put aside and that she would be a day schooler. At first, Angela-Rose, accustomed to getting her own way, was wary about the Seminary as she knew nobody, only Tessie Harken. She was quick to discover that the school was a relaxed, calm, quiet environment. The girls were from the best of Buffalo's high society and were recognized as such throughout the community. The air of entitlement was prevalent throughout the school population.

Tessie would often pull Angela Rose's leg about how she became embarrassed when the local boys would hang around the seminary flirting with the older girls. The innocent pulling of a girl's hair and name calling that was often followed by hand holding. She thought it strange and at first, she put it down to horseplay. She didn't however, connect the flushed faces and embarrassed giggles she witnessed as being the sex thing. It would be a long time before she would make the connection to sex. She would reflect on her conversation with Aunty Mel about mama and papa's kissy kissy. Why does everyone seem to act so strange when she asked these questions? She didn't really know what sex was. It wasn't important. She thought that she knew that her mother liked sex, because mama would say to papa as they adjusted their clothes, "I do like sex darling." And then she would kiss him on the cheek and run off to some other part of the house giggling as she went. That was the same giggle as the schoolgirls used.

In the years that followed, the less restrictive life in Buffalo than New York City enabled Angela Rose to flourish. Spending summers at the beach cottage on Lake Erie and being involved and absorbed in the social life in which she was surrounded filled her time and energies. Michael frequently visited Buffalo and would be escorted around, to be taught all the things his daughter had learned since his last visit.

Chapter 44

There was a prestigious Canisius Catholic High School, which was an exclusive, well respected, boarding school for boys. Being located on Washington Street in Buffalo, not far from the Buffalo Ladies Seminary, made it a natural magnet to the Seminary. The boys would congregate around the school, whistling and cajoling the girls to be with them.

Most of the organized social activities included Canisius Catholic High School pupils, but under close chaperoning. It was believed that the young blood needed to be controlled. Puppy love type of relationships sprung and died in fast regularity. Angela Rose would enjoy joking with the boys, but she had a healthy distrust of them. Tessie on the other hand was boy crazy. No amount of persuasion from Tessie could encourage Angela Rose to join her escapades.

Sunday afternoons 'Delaware Park' would be a hive of activities shared by families and groups of boys and girls. Often the groups would intermingle and wile away the pleasant summer afternoons. The park was close to the Harken's home and the girls would take walks and watch people. Tessie would point out the boys that she liked the look of and Angela Rose was more interested in the relationships between the different people. One such afternoon while sitting on a knoll observing the people, two young boys sauntered over and joined the girls. Tessie eagerly joined the boys in conversation. Teddy and Adrian were twins, the sons of a grain shoveler, who worked at the huge silos on the Buffalo River. They lived in South Buffalo and were of Irish descent. "We come here every Sunday to watch the toffs and see the pretty girls."

"Are we toffs or are we the pretty girls?" asked Tessie.

"Come off it. You is the pretty girls, of course." was the reply. The boys laughed. Tessie challenged them, "How do you know that we aren't toffs?"

"Because you are too pretty and you aint got no chaperone."

"Just because we don't have a chaperone doesn't mean we are not toffs." Tessie responded. The more forward of the twins said, "Give us a kiss and then we can tell if you are." Upon hearing this Angela Rose stood, turned to Tessie and said, "I'm going home." She started to walk away as the boy called out, "We can walk you home missy. What's your name?"

In a haughty tone Angela Rose said, "My name is for me to know and for you to find out. We are not staying around you common louts for you to find out. Come Tessie, let's go."

"So, we know you are Tessie, what about miss nose in the air, what's her name?"

"Bugger off, both of you," said Tessie in an uncharacteristic outburst. As she caught up with Angela Rose Tessie asked, "What's the matter AR, don't you like boys?"

"I'm not AR, I'm Angela Rose, as you well know. I like boys well enough. It's just that those two are common and crude. I don't trust boys or men. I don't know why, I just don't."

"You don't even trust my papa?" asked Tessie with surprise in her voice.

"Oh, no, I don't mean that. I love your papa. He is a very special person. I don't see him as man. I see him as your papa."

"Aren't you even a little curious about boys? Haven't you ever kissed a boy?" Tessie was enjoying the conversation.

"No, I haven't kissed a boy, and what's more I don't want to. Have you?"

"Oh yes, lots."

"What's it like. I mean isn't it yuckie?"

"No, it isn't yuckie. It really isn't anything. I don't know what they get all excited about.

"*Who* have *you* kissed? You're just bragging, was all Tessie could think to say."

"I'm not telling. A girl has to have her own secrets."

Angelo Rose spoke firmly as she replied, "The only thing I know about kissing is that it makes my mama act all silly when she does it. I don't want to look silly, not in front of a boy anyway."

"I do declare, you are one strange girl Miss Angela Rose. The two girls linked arms as they wandered back to their home.

***

The year 1900 saw Angela Rose's fourteenth birthday and her first real kiss. Her father was in Buffalo and had spent a week doing no business, just doing things with her. Aunt Mellie had arrived the day before her mother who came into Buffalo on the Friday. Angela Rose embraced Melita with a fierceness that surprised her. Angela Rose said, "Aunt Millie, I have missed you so much. This wouldn't be the same if you didn't come. Mama tells me your son Julian goes to school in England. Do you miss him?"

"I do, but parents do the best thing for their children. His grandparents are over there and he is happy. Did you know his birthday is next month? He will be six years older than you. I shall be going over to see him."

A large party had been arranged at the Harken household for the next day. Everyone was on their best behavior in front of the adults. Penelope and Michael sat on the patio and watched the youngsters playing. Penelope reached over and held Michael's hand as she said, "Our daughter has turned out so well. I have to say that you were right. This place has been good for her."

"She is just as beautiful as you my dear. I told you I would not steer her wrong."

"And she is more beautiful than Melita, isn't she?" said Penelope, sarcastically.

"Why do you say such things? What has Melita got to do with this?"

"She seems to be happier to see Melita than she does us."

"That's children for you. We are just parents to her. Don't let it upset you. You know she loves you."

"I haven't had much time to catch up with Melita and Ronald. How is their son doing? Where is he today? I thought he would be here."

"I believe that he is going….no, I *know* he is going to school in England. I should bloody well know. We are paying for him to go to Charterhouse."

"We are paying? Why?"

"Well, not we, the company is paying. It is a good investment in Ronald and Melita. If their son goes to the right school, he will have a good future. If their son has a good future it makes them better employees."

"Is that what they are, good employees?"

"Penelope, what is the matter with you? You know damn well that Ronald has been part of my life since I was six years old. I have known Melita almost as long. They have been by my side for the entire conception and development of The Royal Palisades, and long before that. But, in answer to your question, yes they are good employees, the finest, actually. Do you have a problem with that?"

Penelope rose and said to Michael, "No, but I think you might." She turned and left the patio in search of Angela Rose. Michael also got up and went in search of his daughter. Behind the stables was where he found her, she was with a boy. She was lying on a bale of hay alongside the boy. The boy's hand was on her stomach and both were laughing. Michael stood, frozen, watching and listening. His emotions were starting to rise.

The boy said to Angela Rose, "May I give you a birthday kiss?"

A birthday kiss, a birthday kiss, was all Michael heard. It bounced around in his head.

Angela Rose responded, "I have never been kissed, or kissed anyone." With that the boy leaned over to kiss her on the lips. As their lips touched all hell broke loose. Michael had picked up a pitchfork and had raised it above his head to strike the boy when a piercing scream stopped him in his tracks.

"Papa, papa, what are you doing?" Angela Rose screamed as she flung the boy from her.

"I am protecting you from this filthy beast," he shouted. "Get yourself out of here, before I do you serious damage," he bellowed at the boy, who rolled off the hay bale and was scurried away on all fours, trying to keep low to the ground.

Angela Rose stood, straightened her dress and brushing hay away from it marched past her father into the house. She stormed up to her room to find Tessie sitting on her bed with a boy. "What are you doing in my room?" she asked.

Tessie grinned as she replied, "Papa wouldn't look for me in your room. What's all the din about outside?"

"My papa caught me kissing a boy behind the stables."

"You kissing a boy, welcome to the real world. Tell me about it," she said as she pushed the boy that was sat beside her on the bed, telling him to go and get lost. "Was it good?" she asked Angela Rose.

"I guess. He only started to kiss me. His lips were soft and he tasted of apple, but papa broke it up. He went for the boy with a pitchfork."

"Now, that's what I call a party," laughed Tessie, "wait till I tell the girls at school. You are officially one of us now AR."

"I hate it when you call me AR. It's *Angela, Bloody, Rose* and you had better remember that or I'll be chasing you with a pitchfork." The two girls hugged and giggled about the uproar they had caused.

Chapter 45

Things had appeared to calm down between Angela Rose and her father by the time the summer ended. The next year, 1901, in the early spring after being shown the site where the great Pan American Exhibition that was to take place, Angela Rose and Michael were sitting under the shade of the great elms in Delaware park when she stunned her father with, "I never understood why you abandoned me so longago papa."

"Abandoned you? When did I abandon you?"

"When you sent me here to live. Do you love me papa?"

"Where did this come from? Yes, of course I love you. You asked to be allowed to live here, in fact if I remember it correctly, you asked if the Harkens could borrow you, that was your phrase."

"Funny how you remember the exact words, papa. I was six years old, only six years old. Didn't you want me anymore? I'm not sure if you even love me now."

"My dear daughter, every chance I get to be with you I take advantage of. Are you unhappy, do you need something?"

"Yes papa, I wanted you. I am on the outside of Tessie and her dad. I am on the outside of you and mama. When do I get to be on the inside? I am not unhappy, or upset with Mr. and Mrs. Harken, it's just that I don't belong, *properly belong*. I know they love me and they include me in everything. I am nearly a woman papa and something is missing."

"You are a young lady, that's a long way from being a woman. It will bode you well to be more respectful of your father. I have spared no expense in caring for you."

"Expense isn't the issue papa."

"Then what is?" There was a protracted silence between father and daughter as each absorbed the exchange. Angela Rose broke the silence and changed the subject. "How is Aunt Melita these days?"

"She is fine and her son is going to Charterhouse, my old school. She and your mother do many things together. She is often at the house."

"She always was papa."

Michael was becoming hot under the collar and so he changed the subject. "Mr. Harken tells me that you and Tess have been selected to be guides at the Pan American Exposition this summer. Quite an honor. Quite an honor. When that is over, if you wish to move back to New York after the summer we can arrange that for you."

"No, no papa, I will stay here.

***

Angela Rose, like her father, wanted to be where the action was. September 14 was a date that would stay with her and Tessie Harken on a permanent basis. The two girls had managed to get themselves accepted as volunteers for the Pan-American Exposition which was a coveted role and Angela Rose's first real job. During a short break from their duties, they were sitting on the long esplanade walkway that led to the Temple of Music when pandemonium broke loose. People came running out of the building, screaming and shouting. One yelled, "The president is dead! Someone shot the president! McKinley is dead!" It appeared that President McKinley had been in the Temple of Music, and an assassin had shot him. As it turned out, he wasn't dead, but he died a few days later, in a large private house on Delaware Avenue, the home of another friend of the Harken family.

Angela Rose's writings and telephone calls to her father, not just of the president, but of Buffalo and the sheer volume of people that passed through the exposition, reinforced to him the opportunities in the region that were yet to be capitalized upon. He believed that Buffalo had many of the dynamics and love for life that New York City possessed. Besides, it was the gateway to the American West. Many great things were happening there. It was the first American city to have electric streetlights. It's shipping and rail business was of huge proportions. The beef and leather industries, the flour milling, all were described in great detail. It was apparent that she had developed a great affinity for Buffalo.

Before the end of the exposition Michael, Penelope, Ronald and Melita visited Buffalo to see it for themselves. Michael was familiar with the Crystal Palace in London that had housed the *Great Exposition* and the growth it had instigated in that city. The four of them spent great lengths of time discussing the idea that good things would follow the Pan American Exposition and they saw a great potential. Penelope and Michael, or truth be known, Michael, decided to make this their new home. Many of the mansions reminded him of the splendor of England's finer houses. Melita was impressed by the vast ethnic enclaves that had taken over in various parts of the city. These groups staked their own territory and developed their own identities without generating open hostility among their neighbors, although the neighborhoods were clearly delineated by ethnicity.

Beyond that, the Erie Canal that ran from Buffalo to New York City had opened up the middle of America to the rest of the world. Cargo could be moved from one end to the other for ten dollars a ton instead of one hundred dollars. These were exciting times. Michael wanted to involve the Royal Shipping Line in trade on the Great Lakes. The company's experience in the early days with smaller ships would put them in good position here.

Angela Rose wanted to learn more about all of it. One afternoon while seated at her father's desk daydreaming about running the company, she noticed an open letter. Being inquisitive by nature, the English postage stamp further aroused her curiosity. She read the letter, which was from Melita Surtees. It struck her as odd because whenever her father received correspondence from Aunt Melita, she would hear him tell mother about it. She only read a part, as it seemed to be all about Mr. and Mrs. Surtees' son, Julian. She was not interested in the boy as she only had vague memories of seeing him when he was baby. He was of no consequence to her.

Chapter 46

Upon completing her education at the Buffalo Seminary, Angela Rose, at seventeen, found herself looking for a more challenging environment. Visiting her parents in New York, for it was, she felt, *visiting*, the subject arose of what she was going to do with her life. Standing outside the parlor before entering she overheard her father say, "I'm damn glad that she didn't come home pregnant."

"How could you say that? She is a sensible girl and has been raised the right way," Penelope said.

"Little bit too interested in sex if you ask me."

"How do *you* know that?"

"It's just some of the things I have heard."

The door was flung open and Angela Rose strode in and planted herself in front of her parents. "So, daddy where do we go from here?" she said in a scolding tone.

"It's papa to you, young lady, not daddy."

With a sarcastic tone Angela Rose replied, "That's right, daddy is for children whose father's love them. *Sooorry*."

"What is going on, what has got into your head young lady?" asked Penelope.

"Not a thing mama. I am here to receive my instructions on what to do next with my life. At least this time I will know the import of the words I use. Where's Aunt Melita anyway, papa?" Penelope sat in a dazed state at the exchange between her husband and daughter.

Michael announced, "It is high time you did something useful missy. You are going to visit your grandparents in England and reconnect with your roots."

"Do I have any say in this papa?" Angela Rose spoke in exaggerated tones.

"Well actually young lady, you don't." With that Michael got up and stormed out of the parlor.

***

Traveling on the ten-year-old Cunard Line passenger ship, the *SS Campania*, in first-class accommodations, she felt her first real stirrings of sexuality when she met a blond, tanned, well-built, handsome young man that was her assigned cabin steward. He was different from the other sailors she had been exposed to. He was quiet and self-assured. Though she found him extremely attractive, protocol and her straightlaced seminary upbringing required she behave in a ladylike manner. This did not stop the tingling sensation she felt whenever he stood close to her. It took almost the entire trip to England to broach anything other than polite discourse.

The last night of the voyage the steward invited her to join him on the upper deck and watch the celebrations. As they sailed up the English Channel, she let down her guard, as they stood at the ships rail, watching the festivities of 'channel night'. Being comfortably surrounded by passengers watching the twinkling lights on the cliffs of Plymouth, Southampton, and Dover pass by, she asked about his background. "So, tell me steward, can I call you by your name? Steward is so … stuffy."

"Please do Miss St.John-Brown. It's Desmond."

"Then you may call me Angela Rose."

"No ma'am, I can't do that. It is more than my job is worth."

"Will you get into trouble talking with me like this?"

With a lilting laugh he replied "As long as I don't touch or kiss you, we should be fine."

"You can't even touch me?" she asked.

"No ma'am. They call that tampering with cargo and that's a serious offense."

"So, it's cargo that I am. Well, I never did! Tell me Desmond, from where do you hail?"

"My family is originally from a little town on the River Thames estuary called Mucking, not to be confused with Lower Mucking. That would never do you know."

"Why not?"

"We are supposed to be better than the folk at Lower Mucking because we live close to the Great London Road."

"Sounds odd to me, a place called Mucking," Angela Rose posed.

"Sounds odd to me as well. My grandpa was pressed as a young boy into the Royal Navy."

"What's pressed?"

"It's where they take you either by brute force or devious tricks onto a navy ship. I think in the old days they used gangs of thugs to get men for the ships."

"How did they get your grandpa?"

"I don't really know. Grandpa Cane doesn't talk about it, so we just have to put pieces together to get the gist of it."

"Is he still in the Navy? What does he do?"

"Grandpa left the Navy and married a girl from his village when he was done with the sea. My grandpa is Judd Cane and granny is Mary. They are grand people, salt of the earth. Their daughter, my ma, Agatha, married a local man. Nathaniel Blacksmith - blacksmith by name and by trade, oddly enough."

"So, you were born in, what's it called…Mucking."

"Oh no, my ma was strong willed like grandpa. My ma and pa moved to one of the properties that grandpa owned in the Caribbean. They lived there for a while and then moved to other properties developing them. I was born off the coast of St. Eustasius, that's in the Caribbean. They wanted to be sure I would have British nationality. So, my ma gave birth to me on a ship our family owned, at sea."

"What an exciting life. My family owns ships. We own, well, my grandpa and pa own The Royal Shipping Line."

"No wonder they told me to give you the special treatment."

"They did? Why?"

"It's not every day we get shipping line owners as passengers."

"So, if your family has ships why are you working on someone else's ships?"

He told her how he loved working on the ships and that he was learning as much as he could about ships without the influence of his family so that he may be better informed as to the way things really worked.

"I think I might just have salt water in my blood," he said.

"If owning ships and liking the sea have anything to do with it, then we both have salt water in our blood in common." They stood watching the bubbling, eerie, iridescent foam wake of the ship, quietly taking in the cool night air. Angela Rose broke the silence by saying, "you seem very close to your father, you speak so proudly of him."

"Oh yes, my father and my grandfather are remarkable men. Why do you ask, are you close to your father?"

"I don't know. I think men are strange creatures. I respect and admire my papa."

"What about love, do you love him?"

"I suppose I do. But when I say that I'm not sure what it means."

"I am confused….. You *suppose* that you love him? Why don't you know?"

"He sent me away when I was six to boarding school."

"There's nothing wrong with that. I went away to boarding school at about the same age. I thought that's what all parents did. I see nothing wrong with that. How does that mix up your feelings about loving your father?"

"Well, I was told a long time ago that parents have a special love for each other. I was told that dear friends also have a special love for each other." At 'dear friends' she crooked two fingers on each hand and waved them in the air to connote skepticism. How do you know which is which is which?"

Desmond thought for a minute before replying, "You must know how you feel differently for different people."

"Oh, I do, but does that mean I love different people in different ways?"

"Well not quite. We are getting deep here," Desmond said, trying to lighten the mood.

Angela Rose said, in cold aloof voice, "Well, I'm not sure papa knows the difference."

"I'm sure he does. You just haven't understood the difference yet. It will come don't worry about it."

"Oh, I'm not worried, I just want to know why I am the lowest on the scale when it comes to Papa's love."

In an attempt to console what he felt was a sadness in Angela Rose, Desmond glanced about to be sure they were not observed. He put his arm around her shoulders, held her close and said, "You will find a man someday that will put you first in his love chart." Realizing that he crossed the boundaries of professional conduct, he quickly pulled away and said, "I'm sorry, I do apologize, that was less than professional of me, do forgive me."

"Don't be sorry, Desmond. There is nothing to forgive. I hope no one saw you so you will not get into trouble." The conversation turned to other things as they stood at the rail, talking long into the night after all the other passengers retired.

She shared with him her desire to learn and know more about her family and many other worldly things and asked if he thought college was the wrong way to do it. He told her college had never been available to his family in the past, and so the only option had been hands-on experience. But still, he encouraged her to go to college, as nothing learned is ever wasted.

Angela Rose liked this young man. Each time she would finish talking, she would let out a huge breath, as if she hadn't breathed the entire time. She was flushed and tired. This was strange. It was as if Desmond Blacksmith from Mucking had a spell on her.

Bidding each other good night Desmond said, "Goodnight. Look at the hour, it's more like good morning. When we dock in the morning. I will be very busy assisting you and other passengers in disembarking. We will not have any time alone so." He paused to choose his words carefully. "I just want to say how much I have enjoyed our time and conversations together. I wish you well and a safe journey. I hope your time with your family here in England will be a happy time. Lastly, I do hope that our paths will cross again one day."

In an almost inaudible reply Angela Rose whispered, "I do too. I really do hope we meet again."

Desmond strode off into the night air. His heart was pounding. When the voyage came to its end, they shook hands formally, lingering, not wanting to end the touch, and then parted, all the better, for having met. It was the first time the steward, Desmond Cane Blacksmith, had ever felt uncomfortable taking a gratuity for his efforts. Angela Rose found her steward was not any, ordinary sailor. His healthy sun tan and broad shoulders had her romantically imagining him as pirate, not a steward.

Chapter 47

Visiting her grandparents impacted Angela Rose's life tremendously. She realized she had been floating through life with the finest of everything and never stopped to consider where she came from. With her father and mother moving around so much, most connections had been tenuous at best. She found that The Royal Crescent, Bath, with its stately splendor and elegance, presented solid, grounded roots. The family coat of arms in the library was like a silent sentinel, declaring the family's origins and values. It was as if it was watching over the family and reminding them of their heritage. She had faint memories of her grandparents from when she was very young. She was having to learn them over again. The large portrait of Grandpapa William made him look such a regal and strong man, yet there seemed to be sadness in his eyes. Angela Rose thought it odd that there was no portrait of her grandmama Veronica. There were only posed, stiff portraits of the male ancestors, one going back to the time of King Henry VIII. Angela Rose knew that Henry VIII died in the middle of the sixteenth century. She had never stopped to consider just how far back her lineage went. Grandmama Veronica was quite the opposite of grandpapa. She was a social butterfly and full of fun. Together Angela Rose and Lady Veronica spent many hours mingling on the social circuit and shopping. It was at many of these gatherings that she gained a fuller knowledge of her parent's heritage, and indeed hers. She felt the sadness of having been so far away from these grand people.

One afternoon at tea in the exclusive tea room of Harrod's Department Store Angela Rose asked her grandmother, "Did you know that papa sent me away from home, to a boarding school when I was only six?"

"Now, now, my dear, your papa allowed you to stay with a family while you went to school with their child. You didn't *live* at the school."

"I might as well have grandmamma, he still sent me away."

"What is the matter with you child? Look at you, elegant, obviously well-bred and well educated, and here you are, at a young age, travelling the world alone. I would say your papa had done you proud. What ails you child?"

"Did you send papa away when he only six?"

"No, we did not, well not exactly. The family businesses' are large and need to be run by intelligent, strong, educated men. That's what we prepared your father for, and look at what he has achieved. We are all very proud of him. He went to a very prestigious boarding school, Charterhouse, and he has fared well as a result. The men in our family have always known what to do and when to do it. That's why we women followed their lead in all things."

"Grandmama, I will not just follow a man, not any man for any reason. I want to be in charge of my own life. Women in Wyoming and Utah, back in America can vote for themselves. Even women in the English colonies of Australia and New Zealand can vote for themselves, but not here in England, I don't understand that."

"I'm sure I don't know what the world is coming to. Why some women think they need that, I'm sure I just don't know. Just remember young lady, we come from a long tradition of very successful people. If it was good enough for them, it's good enough for me."

"Well not for me grandmama!"

"I am just an old lady, a very content and happy old lady, so let's not talk of such things. I'm sure you, young people will change things in good time." The conversation changed to discuss Angela Rose's plans for visiting her maternal grandparents.

***

When it came time for her to visit her maternal grandparents, Sir William offered to accompany her to London and make sure she caught the right train for Sussex. At the overnight stop in London's Savoy Hotel, in the Cadogan suite, Sir William expressed his desire that Angela Rose work with her father and prepare herself to take the family empire, Global Enterprises, to the next level. "There are things to happen that we cannot even dream of, and we must be ready to seize any opportunity. It will be the mark of the leaders in tomorrow's world," he said. "I read today on the daily wire that the Wright Brothers, a couple of young men in America, have got their damn contraption of a flying machine to leave the ground for an extended time. That's only the beginning there's far more to come."

"Don't you find all these new machines and things being invented are exciting?" asked Angela Rose.

"I find so many things that are happening today, that were never dreamed of in my day, to be exciting."

***

Over dinner in the hotel's finest restaurant, The Savoy Grill, they talked of many things. Angel Rose asked, "Has this hotel always had electricity?"

"Why do you ask?" Sir William enquired. "That's such an odd question."

"In America I have seen the use of electricity and it is getting more common every day. But in every room, in a place this big? Did you know grandpapa that Buffalo, where I lived, it was the very first city in the world to have streets lighted by electricity?"

"Yes, my dear, and did *you* know that this hotel, The Savoy, is the first hotel in the world to have electricity in every room? The first in the world, quite a feat, don't you think?"

"I do, I do, but what interests me more is the fact that there are so many new things happening all the time. Look at automobiles. I read in this morning's newspaper that they are giving them registration numbers."

"Why does this surprise you?"

"Papa has invested some money, stock, I think he calls it, with a company in Detroit Michigan that is building cars on an assembly line. It is called The Ford Motor Company and it is claiming to be able to sell four thousand carriages this year. That's a lot of automobiles."

"They call that mass production. It doesn't surprise me that it has happened to the automobile. Factories over here have been using production lines to make many things for a long time. Tell me young lady, do you have your eyes on a beau?"

"Grandpa!" Angela Rose gasped, blushing a little.

"Aha, so someone has caught your eye. May I ask who?"

"Oh no, not a beau. I met a nice young man when I was coming over on the ship. We became friends."

"Was he coming over here as well? Is he American?"

"He was sailor, actually a steward."

"You should choose your friends wisely. I'm not sure your father would approve of a sailor. He might approve of someone who owns a ship or two. By golly we have our own. Could always do with a few more." He laughed at his own humor and continued. "When you let someone inside your private self, you become vulnerable," he said. He seemed to be speaking to himself, as if trying to discover for himself what had happened to him. "When I was a young, inexperienced man, or perhaps just a boy, I allowed a person inside my guard, to the innermost me, without knowing the price I might have to pay. I'm not sure if I gave my heart away or if it was taken. It was before I met your grandmama. Love is like a magician's trick. You do not know for sure if what you see is what you see or if you are fooling yourself into believing you see something that isn't really there. I gave all my heart even though it was never asked for. I was very lucky that the woman encouraged me to keep a piece of me for myself, but I was too unlearned to see it. When it was all over, I had nothing left for myself."

"What happened to your first love, Grandpapa?"

"She died. I survived, *survived*, not lived, a whole life after that. You must learn from your father and mother," said William. "Your mother allows your father to be who he is. She doesn't demand all of him. The person you love must let you keep a part of yourself for yourself, so that you may both flourish together, like your mama and papa. Do not settle for anything less, my child."

"Mama and papa always seem so busy sometimes, alone, and sometimes together. I think it rather odd. I wouldn't want a husband that is always somewhere else."

"That works for them because they do not need to be tied to each other every moment of the day. Grandma and I live a similar way."

"Are you happy grandpa?" Angela asked in all seriousness.

"Yes, I suppose I am. Never did quite find chasing rainbows worthwhile."

"Chasing rainbows, what does that mean?"

"To me, it means knowing how to live with what you have and appreciate it. There's an old saying 'Life isn't always greener on the other side of the hill.' Damn true if you ask me. I like my side of the hill."

"You are funny grandpa."

***

The following morning, Sir William made sure that Angela Rose was comfortably seated in the first-class carriage of the train bound for Crowborough. As her grandfather hugged her tightly in a final embrace, she felt a special warm and closeness toward him, and tears welled up from inside her. She was experiencing an unconditional love, which was an unnerving emotion for her. To her surprise she shed a tear as the train pulled away.

Two hours later, amid hissing steam, clattering porters, and all manner of station noises and smells, she saw her other grandfather and grandmother. They were seated in their carriage on the other side of Crowborough station's ornate, wrought-iron fence, which declared, 'this side belongs to British Railways. Keep Out.' They were waiting for her. The Mowbrays presented a picture of Victorian upper-class, but though they sat erect and proper, when they saw their granddaughter, their faces told Angela-Rose that they were family and that in some way she belonged. The carriage driver took a circuitous route from the station to the family estate. Grandmama Elizabeth pointed out where Angela Rose's mother, Penelope, had grown up, where she had gone to school, and where she had shopped. The country village was an enclave of wealthy citizens mixed in with country and farm folk. During the ride, Grandpa David nodded and said little.

After a short while Grandpa David remarked, "It has been many years since you have been to Crowborough. I doubt that you even remember it." As the carriage rounded the gravel drive and the house came into view, she hoped some of her childhood memories would come flooding back to her, but nothing. She replied to the question, "I have been told many things about here and I am not sure if some of things are actual memories or remembered stories."

"Never mind child, you are here now, and right pleased we are to have you."

"David!" rebuked his wife.

"What, what did I do now?"

"*Right pleased* indeed. It is, *very pleased*. You are starting to sound like the country yokels."

Angela Rose spent two weeks with her grandparents rediscovering the English countryside. It was evident that her grandmama was tightly bound to her father, and she saw just how much her grandmama resembled her mother. They were both delicate, voluptuous, beautiful women who exuded femininity. Her grandpapa was a picture of Victorian upper-class stability and male superiority. He powerfully conveyed his feelings for his granddaughter with a gentle touch of her shoulder or elbow, sending strong emotional messages with no hint of impropriety. His stature and demeanor gave him such an aura, that he rose above his surroundings in Angela's eyes.

The long-curved gravel road that led from the heavy wrought iron gates up to the house made a calming crunch under the iron wheels of the carriage. The manor came into view with footmen standing and waiting at the large stone steps up to the front of the house. The carriage stopped and the driver quickly ran to the side and assisted the passengers with disembarking. The splendor and precise movement of the servants as they went about their business was far more controlled than she remembered the servants at home. Soon, seated in the cool comfort of the covered terrace the three people began to reacquaint. "Lady Regina, Elizabeth, grandmama, papa has told me so much about you and yet I did not imagine your home to be like this. You look so much like mama. Papa said that you and mama looked like you could be sisters, and golly, how true it is."

"Your papa, such a wag. Maybe that is why I liked him right from the start. You must just call me grandmama. The 'Lady' thing is just for non-family. How is your papa?"

"Oh. He is good. Very busy all the time. I don't see him that much."

"Why is that, child?"

"I have lived in Buffalo since I was six, going to school. I was staying with a family there. Papa visited when he could."

"Did you know that my dear?" Regina asked David, her husband.

"Yes of course I knew, and so did you. You are getting quite forgetful these days. An excellent school, some sort of lady's seminary type of thing I believe. Damn fine she has turned out if you ask me."

"If you say so my dear." Turning to Angela Rose she continued, "and what about Penelope, your mother, is she well?"

"Oh yes. Grandmama, can you show me around the house? I want to see mama's room. I want to learn things about mama that makes her my mama, I want to learn all about her."

Her grandfather laughed as he said, "I think I might like to do that tour with you, young lady. Learn about your mother, I might learn something."

"David, behave yourself. Angela Rose is but a child."

"Grandmama, I am seventeen. Not a child anymore."

"I'm damned if I know when a child becomes a woman. These days," snorted her grandfather.

"Then pay a little more attention and you might learn." Angela Rose enjoyed the badinage between the two of them. At this point she could not tell the difference between the serious and the humor, but she enjoyed the exchanges. She did observe the warmth with which her grandmother spoke of her father. It had a softer, more personal tone than when she spoke of her own daughter, Penelope. Angela Rose at this time was not experienced enough to understand the subtleties.

***

On a shopping expedition to the local town Angela Rose asked her grandmother, "Why does grandpapa keep referring to mama as a tom boy?"

"I think he always wanted a boy and so he taught her to do all the things boys do and she was a fast learner. She could shoot a gun, skin a rabbit and ride horses before she was six years old. She was very strong willed and did not hesitate to stand up to him when she disagreed with his rules or what he said."

Angela Rose was surprised as she replied, "Oh my, mama is not like that now. My papa rules the house. He is surely the boss."

"May-be she just grew out of the rebellious stage. She was young when she married your papa."

"I don't think I am rebellious. But I don't always agree with papa."

"And that's the way it should my dear. Men do know better. Well, they think they do and sometimes it is just as well not to disavow them of their inflated self-concept. Life is calmer that way."

"Do you love, I mean really love, grandpapa?"

"That's a strange question my dear. Yes, I do."

"Do you always obey him, do as you are told, I mean?"

"As long as he thinks I do, that is all that matters. We have found our own paths to living together in harmony. I believe that is the trick to marriage working. Such serious questions for a young girl, is there something you want to talk to me about?"

"I don't think so grandmamma." The two of them spent the next two weeks bonding. There was a formal gathering at the house where Angela Rose was introduced to many of the family, friends and acquaintances. It was a whirlwind of new and exciting experiences for Angela Rose. Soon it was time for her to return to America and start her adult life. The evening before she left Lady Regina threw a lavish farewell part in Angela Rose's honor. The affair ended around midnight with a firework display on the back lawn. As the guests returned to the house, her grandfather held her back until they were alone. With his arm around her shoulder, he turned to face the great manor, and with an emotional tone she had not heard before, he said, "My dear, dear, grand- daughter, all this you see before you will one day be yours. I hope we have planted a seed of pride in you for our ancestral home. Take care of it. Cherish it. I hope it will bring you the happiness that it has brought your mother. I guess this is a silly old man saying, I love you, child. You take great care of yourself, and those you care for." He pulled her in close and held her tight.

Without thinking she said, "I love you too grandpa." As the words came from somewhere deep inside, she felt a special heartbeat without fully understanding it. She was, very soon, going to understand the very thing she had been trying so hard to discover.

Chapter 48

Angela Rose's visit had been so busy with family that she hardly gave much thought to America or her trip home. The trip back to America came via the Cunard Shipping Line's offices in London, where Angela Rose booked passage for America on the SS *Ivernia*. The ship was only three years old and was far more modern and advanced than the *Campania*. When she was introduced directly to the chief steward, she was impressed by his level of attention. Without knowing why, she asked, "Are all the crew exclusive to the *Ivernia*?"

"No, madam," said the steward. "We rotate crews around our ships to allow them time to be with their families—and to keep them on their toes. In fact, madam, I believe that you know our assistant chief steward, Desmond Blacksmith. He recognized your name on the passenger list." Her heart skipped a beat. "He oversees all the staff assigned to first class accommodations," said the chief steward. "He'll stop by to assist you into your suite as soon as we cast off."

A steward showed her to her cabin, which carried all the accessories one would expect in a first-class hotel: polished brass, mahogany paneling, crystal ware, gleaming mirrors, and plush velvet curtains draping the portholes. Angela Rose flung herself on the bed and gazed up at the bulkhead above her. "*Fate. Could this be fate?*" she thought.

***

From the moment Desmond knocked on the cabin door until they docked in New York, they shared every spare moment in deep conversation that discretion and respect would allow. It was usually Angela Rose who started the subject matter. One evening, standing at the ships rail she said, "Because of this trip I now feel that I know my family roots."

"Did you not know them before?"

"My parents have travelled a lot and have business' in America and England. I have been at school or staying with family friends. Now, having met my grandparents, my world seems so different."

"Tell me all about your grandparents." Desmond showed a genuine interest.

"Grandpa and grandma of my father's side, Sir William St. John-Brown and Lady Veronica Chartwell are from Bath in Somerset."

"Sir and lady, different last names. What does that mean?"

"Oh no, grandma is now Lady Veronica St. John-Brown. Chartwell was her maiden name."

"Do you think your grandpa has a pet name for her, like knickers, you know, Ver-on-nicker, like lady's knickers?"

"You are terrible. It would be funny though, wouldn't it? They are such nice people. My grandpa took over the family business and my papa is going to take it over when Grandpa dies I think."

"What is the business?"

"We own, they own the Royal Shipping Line and properties in Bath, Bristol and London. My father owns a grocery business. Mother's Fine Foods and the Co-op stores. Oh yes, and he owns a property in Florida, well not actually Florida but down that way, the southern tip of Georgia. It's known as The Royal Palisades. It is a very prestigious Gentleman's club, family club actually. You don't hear much about it because it is so private. It is a wonderful place. you must see it some time."

"Oh my, quite an empire. Do you plan to go into the family business?"

"You know, I haven't really decided yet. I suppose I could do worse."

"What about your mother's side of the family?"

"My grandpapa is the Earl of Sussex and my grandma was Countess Regina Blackstone. Sounds quite grand, doesn't it?"

"So, what does that mean, Earl and Countess?"

"Titles, just titles, I think. It means they own lots of land and a great big manor house in Sussex. Sussex is just above where you come from in Essex."

"Thanks for the geography lesson."

"No, not a geography lesson, more it's just a sign that our ancestors come from quite close to each other."

"Is that a good sign?" Desmond laughed and Angela Rose joined in. Their conversation was interrupted by the ships bell ringing out in the evening air. "Six bells. I must go back to my duties. May I see again tomorrow?"

"You know where I live." Again, they both laughed together as Desmond walked backwards until he went through a doorway, and disappeared, as it swung closed.

***

They used the utmost discretion, meeting in the ship's library or lounges, or up on deck in the stiff Atlantic breeze. In the nine days it took to cross the Atlantic, they continued to learn more of each other's family backgrounds, their likes, dislikes, hopes, and dreams.

On the last evening Angela said to Desmond, "You haven't told me much about your family.

"Where do I start?" said Desmond.

"What about your grandparents, anything further than that will sound like a history lesson."

"My grandpa, Judd Cane, owns a ship, The Mary Jane. She is a trader. If you remember, I told you that he went to sea at a very young age and worked hard and was wise with his money. My grandmama, Mary, has a bookkeeping business. She takes care of all the legal and accounting things for them. They are from Mucking in Essex, the opposite side of England to half of your family."

"Well not really. As you know my mother's parents are from Crowborough, in Sussex."

"What the heck am I getting myself into here? Lords, Ladies, Earls and Sir's. I am starting to feel like a poor cousin." Desmond was joking but his comment disturbed Angela who said, "I am a person the same as you. If you don't hold my background against me, I won't hold yours against you."

"I'm sorry. I wasn't trying to be funny. It's actually quite impressive. My other grandpa, David, was a blacksmith. As a child I never understood that the the scale of his work was more than just shoeing horses. He also made the huge iron hoops that strengthen ships masts. My pa used to work in the shipyards as a welder and riveter."

"When you think about it, our two families cover the whole spectrum of English life."

"My ma and pa run the family business," Desmond continued.

"What exactly is the business now?"

"Oh, we own, they own, hotels and properties throughout the Caribbean. They have been developing land my grandpa bought a long time ago. We are even thinking of going into the passenger ship business. Maybe not as big as this one, but who knows. That's why I am learning all I can."

"Wow, that must be fantastic. I have never been to the Caribbean, have you?"

"Oh yes. I was born in the Caribbean, at sea, but still the Caribbean. I love the islands and the people and the way of life. They seem to know what is important in life."

Their eyes locked into each other's as if searching for everything they could ever know about each other. Desmond said "I feel like I really know you well."

A little alarm rang loud and clear inside her head. Grandpapa William's words kept running through her head: '*I'm not sure if I gave my heart away or if it was taken. The man you love must let you keep a part of yourself for yourself so that you may both flourish together.*' She did not need to ask herself if she was in love. She knew it. When he would put his hand on top of hers on the ship's rail, she would tingle at the very point of contact. Her heart would leap whenever he entered her space. The very sight of him would render her surroundings invisible.

Darkness had fallen and the ship was busy preparing for tomorrow's docking, as they bid each other goodnight. Angela Rose wanted Desmond to kiss her, but being a little scared, she held herself a safe distance away.

Safely back in her cabin, in her mind, she replayed the evening's exchange with Desmond. Lying on the bed, staring at the bulkhead, she summoned up the courage to tell Desmond how she felt. Quickly, she jumped up, opened her cabin door and instructed the first steward she saw to ask Desmond, the Assistant Chief Steward to please come to her cabin at his earliest convenience. She closed the cabin door, turned, leaned her back against its cold surface, closed her eyes, and thought, '*it's now or never,*' and then she waited.

In accordance with shipboard protocol, Desmond knocked on her cabin door and waited. She opened the door and bade him sit. Before she could speak, he did. "My dearest Angela Rose," he said, "if I may be so informal, my life's ambitions and goals are important to me, as I hope yours are to you. I admire your independence and value of family. We can go through life, each of us achieving those goals, as I know I will and am sure you will. But with respect for each other's goals, I see no reason why we cannot do this side by side, in support of each other."

"What are you saying? I don't think I understand," she coyly replied.

"Our families are so different. We are from opposite ends of the spectrum. I wonder of there could be a life for us, for you and me, us together."

Angela Rose put her hands over her face trying to hide her blushing and innermost thoughts from showing. Moving quietly to her side, Desmond apologized and insisted he hadn't meant to hurt or offend. "I feel a strong connection between us, as I hope you do."

"Oh yes, there is something. Dare I use the word?"

"Love," interjected Desmond.

"Yes. It sounds strange to say it out loud."

"May I hold you close and to hell with what anyone may say?" Without waiting, Desmond stood, reached out his arms as she rose, waiting to be embraced. He held her close and tightly. She laid her head on his shoulders and savored the moment. She drank in his masculine odor as she softly kissed his neck, to taste him. The two stood in a silent embrace, their bodies communicating in the way words cannot. The world stood still for them both.

"I am neither offended nor hurt," she said, dabbing her eyes. "My thoughts have been all about you since the day we met on the *Campania*." She told him of the words her grandfather had said to her.

Desmond sat and thought. "I do not want all of you," he said, "as I do not want to give you all of me. The part of your life you are willing to share with me is all that I want."

"Does this mean we're planning to get married?" said Angela Rose. "Are you asking me to marry you?"

"I know better than to tell you we're getting married," said Desmond with a smile. "I should ask your parents first."

"I want to go to Brown University and finish my education," said Angela Rose. "Do you mind?"

"If it's part of your plan for yourself, then, do it. Will your parents give permission for you to marry?"

"I don't know, but I am nearly eighteen and, by the time I complete my education I will be old enough not to need permission. My parents will be waiting for me when we dock. Can we tell them together?"

"I would want it no other way, but I have my duties when the ship docks, as you saw in England. I can meet with you and your parents this evening."

"I shall arrange it and let you know. What will you do about your work?"

"Right now, I do not know. Give me some time."

***

The hustle and bustle of the great passenger ship *SS Ivernia* arriving in New York may have appeared chaotic, but in fact, it was a brilliantly choreographed ballet of cargo moving; people meeting, greeting, and leaving; and sailors threading it all together. When Angela Rose left the ship, her parents were waiting for her dockside. They were on their way to Buffalo, from the Estate at the Royal Palisades, so picking up their daughter coincided well. After all the greetings were over, Angela Rose waited for the opportunity to tell them about Desmond. While her father's back was turned, she whispered to her mother, "I have met a young man, mama. I want you and papa to meet him. I am meeting my friend, Desmond at the Shipping Line offices. I will telephone you when I have let him know of the arrangements, if you agree."

Her father, who had not missed a word of the conversation, spoke "And, young lady, what if we don't agree?"

Her mother interjected, "Don't be such a bore Michael. It will do no harm to meet the young man."

"What's his name?" Michael demanded.

"Desmond Blacksmith, papa."

"I hope he isn't a bloody blacksmith," was her father's attempt at humor.

As quick as whip Angela Rose spat back, "No he isn't a blacksmith, his family was." She watched intently as her parents exchanged glances. Panic ran through her mind as she thought they might squash the relationship before it went any further. She spoke quickly, trying to ease the tension, "Don't worry papa, Desmond's family, his mother actually, is the daughter of a ship owner." She purposely left any further details out. She felt that she hadn't told a lie, it wasn't just as grand as she knew her father would imagine it. She waited excitedly for their response.

Her father said, "Why don't you set up something for Delmonico's for this evening, say around seven. We will take a look at this fellow. What's the family name?"

Angela Rose hesitated, trying to think of a way put Desmond in the best light. "His mother's family name is Cane papa."

Then off with you child. Meet your mother and me at seven. You know that I will not stand for sloppy punctuality." He waved his daughter off.

Michael stayed behind and made arrangements for Angela's luggage while Angela took off to await Desmond, as arranged, at the shipping line offices. Her mother pulled her aside as she was entering a carriage and asked, "Is this young man serious about you, and you about him?"

"Mama, you will meet him. I know I am serious about him, and I believe he is about me. He makes me smile on the inside. Mama, that's good. I am excited for you to meet him." With that said Angela closed the carriage door, waved to her mother, and instructed the driver where to go.

By the time Angela arrived at the shipping company offices, Desmond was already standing outside waiting for her. They embraced and Angela was surprised that as she turned her cheek to him, he kissed her lightly. *Her first, real kiss.* She felt a tingle of excitement and returned his kiss, on the lips. He was surprised and happy and they kissed again, passionately. They were all smiles as they made arrangements to meet at Delmonico's Restaurant on Forty-Fourth Street at seven o'clock in the evening.

Chapter 49

Delmonico's dated back to the mid-eighteen-hundreds, surviving by means of dependable quality and good management. Upon his arrival, Desmond was shown to a private dining room where the St. John-Brown family waited. As Angela Rose sat quietly, Desmond introduced himself. "Good evening Mr. and Mrs. St. John-Brown. I am Desmond Blacksmith. I am honored to meet with you."

"It is Sir, if you don't mind." Michael's tone and demeanor were pompous.

"Michael!" said Penelope, "Michael!" Turning to Desmond she continued, "Please feel free, I am Penelope and that man," she said pointing to Michael, "is Michael St. John-Brown, for now Mr. and Mrs. will be fine."

"I thought Angela Rose said your name was Cane."

"Cane is my grandfather's name. My father married Judd Cane's daughter.

Angela Rose continued to watch her father firing questions in rapid succession at Desmond. "What do you do for a living young man?" was the first of many.

"I am Chief Steward on the SS Ivernia sir."

Angela interjected, "I thought you were Assistant Chief Steward?" Desmond leaned over and spoke quietly to her, "That was when we first met. I am Chief Steward now."

Angela Rose smiled as she replied, "Modest little sailor, aren't you." Michael got right back into the interrogation.

"Does that pay well?"

"Sufficiently, sir. It is a stepping stone for me."

"Stepping stone to what?"

"I have not planned my whole life out just yet sir."

"Don't you think you should?" Michael's tone was concerning Angela.

She looked father in the eye and said, "Papa, this is not a job interview. Please be kinder."

"What's wrong? Any young man that pursues my daughter better be ready to be vetted!"

"Vetted, *vetted*, papa, please. Be nice or I shall leave."

Angela's mother leaned over to Michael and said, "Take it easy on the boy. He seems a likeable enough lad. Give him a chance."

"Chance at what? That's what I want to know." Turning back to Desmond, he softened his tone. "So, what do you intend for yourself, are you going to make your mark on the world?"

Desmond found himself on the defensive and Angela Rose caught in the middle. Desmond raised his hands as if warding off the barrage. "Mr. And Mrs. St. John-Brown," he said in a soft and confident manner, "I am here to seek your advice on behalf of Angela Rose and myself. We find ourselves faced with a situation for which neither of us are quite sure how to proceed." He looked directly at Penelope. "You must have seen Angela Rose's face when I approached," he said, "and I wish you could see the way my heart is pounding in her presence, but you can't. That may be your problem. It certainly isn't mine. I fear that my background and age do me no injustice, but we do not seek justice, just guidance in helping us get to where we wish to be.

"And where might that be?" demanded Michael.

"That sir, is to be married."

Angela's mother gasped. She glanced quickly at her daughter and said, "You are so young my darling. Is this what you want? Why didn't you tell me about this earlier today?"

Angela held her mother's gaze without flinching. "Because mama, I didn't know."

Desmond took hold of Angela's hand and said "I didn't ask you because I was too busy working up the courage for tonight." Desmond took a deep breath before continuing. "I know that we spoke of obtaining your parents' consent, but I suggest we follow your plan to go to Brown and complete your education, however long it may take." He removed a small velvet pouch with the name "Tiffany" embroidered on the front from his trousers He placed it before her. "If it pleases you, we shall become engaged this evening and plan to wed on your completion of your education."

Angela Rose became flushed with excitement as she opened the pouch to find a diamond ring. The simple single-stone setting was tasteful and modest, yet clearly was no bauble.

Michael spoke quickly, "Now hold on a minute! Show me that thing." He reached out to take the ring.

Desmond looked at Michael without flinching and said, "All respect due to you sir, I, am offering this token to your daughter. If she accepts it is for her to show you. I'm sure she doesn't require your approval for that."

"Got a backbone, do you?"

"Michael, what is wrong with you? Angela's mother interrupted her husband's outburst. "Let the young man have his moment."

"Moment, have his moment. He wants more than his moment. He want's our daughter, and everything that goes with her, don't we have some say in that?"

"Actually, my dear we don't. If you calm down you will recall they have come to us for advice. Let's hear them out.

Angela spoke up. "Thank your mother, and as for you Desmond Cane Blacksmith, yes, I would like very much to marry you." There was hush that dropped over the table as mother and daughter embraced.

Angela Rose's mother spoke calmly to them both when she said, "If I understand you both correctly, our daughter is going to finish her education, no matter how long it takes before you marry."

In unison Angela Rose and Desmond replied, "That's our plan."

"Waiter, I think we should see the menu's and order, demanded Michael." An aura of contemplation settled over the table as orders were taken and dinner served.

***

After dinner much of the conversation was taken up with small talk. Penelope could see that her husband was chomping at the bit to say something. The dinner table was cleared and Michael took center stage with his thoughts spoken out loud. He looked at his wife for her acquiescence before he spoke. "I know of your family," he said to Desmond. "In fact, I conducted business with your grandfather some twenty odd years ago, when I purchased land here in America, on Jakeskill Island."

"You know my grandpa, Judd Cane?"

"Yes. I found him to be different from most men who made the sea their life. Although, he was definitely an old salt. A fair man, I would say. My inquiries find you to be in the same mold."

"Enquiries, what enquires have you made? Why do you need to make enquiries?"

"Because you have shown interest in my child. It is a father's duty to protect his children. Until I made enquiries, I knew nothing about you. For all we know you could be attracted by our money. You could be some charlatan."

"Your money! I have no need for your money. Our family is quite independent of anyone else's wealth. We have a tradition of working hard and earning our way in life."

"Now calm down young man. There is no shame in being a hard worker, but there is work and, then there is *work*. It would be a strange world if one was to be measured by his work alone. One day you will understand my actions. I admire your spirit, now let's talk of other things.

Your suggestion to our daughter regarding her education shows maturity and consideration and sets you apart from most young men these days, and we respect you for this. What is it you propose to do with yourself for the next three or so years while Angela Rose is at University?"

"I will spend as much time as possible with your daughter," said Desmond. "I aim to complete my contracted time with the Cunard Line. Then, I'll work with my parents for Cane International."

"Have you no plans further than that?"

"No sir. I want to be able to adjust to what life throws at us and move forward as opportunity presents itself."

"See papa, I told you there is something special about Desmond. Don't you just love him?"

"Apparently not as much as you do my dear. Young man I think it would be wise for us to conduct our discussions in private, at your convenience of course."

"Yes sir, I will make myself available upon my return to New York."

"Father, there is plenty of time for that later."

"I have not finished young lady. Are your parents aware of your intentions toward my daughter?"

"I have to be honest sir I was not fully aware of my intentions myself until the last few days. I shall be informing them soon." Desmond turned to catch Angela Rose staring at him with a warm glow about her countenance. He turned to Michael and continued, "Sir I am of an age that does not require parental consent. However, I am anxious to tell them."

"Then when you do, have them contact myself and Angela Rose's mother. There are other matters for us to discuss. I have no objections to the engagement. Young man, be advised that I shall be keeping a keen eye on you, so be sure that you do the right thing."

Lady Penelope lifted her glass, "I propose a toast to Angela Rose and Desmond Blacksmith, may their plans, dreams and hopes be realized," she said, "let us drink to success."

Chapter 50

Michael then spoke directly to Desmond, "I read the daily shipping news and have many contacts. Know a few men in Cunard actually. Met Lord Inverclyde, the second, new chairman you know. I know my grandfather was chummy with the first chairman of the board, Samuel Cunard. The old man told many stories about him. I believe it was him who encouraged grandfather to found The Royal Shipping Line. The whole shipping business is changing so fast. Different type of man at sea these days. Don't seem to be the ruffians the sea had to take on anymore. Don't suppose you heard about the captain that went missing. Can't think of the ship." Michael stopped as if trying to recall the name.

"The Mauretania sir, it was the RMS Mauretania."

"That's it, that's it. I have heard many a story about crews in the old days throwing officers overboard and hellish stuff like that, but can you believe it in today's world?"

"I was on the Maruetania, sir, at that time. Tragic it was. The ship was searched high and low to no avail. They say a passenger saw him ranting on one of the ships upper decks. She thought he was drunk, but nothing came of that enquiry."

"I don't believe in mysteries. Everything has an explanation. It appears none of the crew had a bad word to say about the man." Michael's probing style was starting to unnerve Desmond.

"With all due respect, as a ship owner, I am sure that you know shipping companies rarely know everything that happens on their ships. It is my experience that when something tragic happens at sea, the sailors, close ranks. They are very protective of each other, even those that dislike a man will jump to his defense from another. A sort of brotherhood if you will."

Michael thought for a minute before adding, "Well I, for one, am glad they are not letting this one go. It's been a couple of years and they are still investigating it. Someone will find a chink in that brotherhood thing. Someone knows what happened. You need to take care of yourself, would be terrible if something like that were to happen to you."

"While life at sea can be dangerous, it has improved immensely. I never had much to do with the captain, but I do know that he was not a popular man. Now, the captain on the Ivernia, he is a man that is greatly respected and looked up to. Never the less I will take you advice to heart." Desmond waited for the conversation to move on.

The subject did soon change, and the rest of the evening went smoothly, or so Desmond thought. Michael stood back as the doorman held the door open for everyone to leave. Desmond was the last in line, and as he approached the door

Michael leaned over and whispered, "Captain went missing eh? Mystery that. Missing at sea, or murder, not much of a choice. I'm sure someone will get to the bottom of it. After all, fifty odd years at sea and he just goes missing, bit odd if you ask me. Didn't think I would hear about that, did you?"

Desmond looked over his shoulder and replied, "It was a shock to all of us on board. I actually didn't find it that relevant to this evening's agenda sir."

"Might be, might not be, as long as you had nothing to do with it. Family reputation. Stellar one it is too my boy, doesn't need tarnishing. I'm sure you understand."

In an angry moment of defiance, or guilt driven bravado, Desmond said, "I had no more to do with it than one could hope that *you* had anything to do with it, *sir*." Desmond's nervous thoughts ran riot in his mind as he dashed through the open door. He could not wait to get away from this man. Michael joined his wife on the sidewalk and whispered to her, "Cheeky little bastard, got to give him credit though, he's got spunk."

***

In the ensuing four years Desmond completed his contractual obligations with The Cunard Line and went on to work at the Penninsular and Oriental Steamship Company as Angela Rose accumulated acclaims of educational excellence at Brown University. The frequency of visits from Desmond concerned her somewhat but she understood that he was working for their future. She left the communications between her parents and Desmond's to the adults. The date was set for the wedding. It was to be held at The Royal Palisades in November of 1912. Angela Rose didn't want to wait that long, but she acquiesced to her father's decision on the matter. She thought to herself, '*this will be the last decision he makes that I do not have control over.*'

Sometimes she felt that the proposed wedding was being blown out of all proportions. As the time passed slowly for her, she felt that her papa was staying the course of holding her at arms-length. At least that was her perception. She began to feel the wedding was falling into place as just another task to be dealt with, but she kept her feelings on the matter to herself.

Chapter 51

It was early on New Year's Day, of 2012, that Angela Rose saw her father emotionally crumble for the first time. Michael St.John-Brown was seated in his study when the parlor maid knocked on the door. She entered on command and handed Michael a cable. In his experience nothing good could come in a cable on New Year's Day. He cautiously opened it to read,

SADEST NEWS STOP
DEAREST MICHAEL AND PENELOPE STOP
FATHER PASSED ON THIS MORING STOP.
HE DIED QUIETLY IN HIS SLEEP STOP.
DEATH BY NATURAL CAUSES STOP.
PLEASE COME HOME AND HELP STOP.
WE NEED TO BE TOGETHER AS A FAMILY STOP.
LOVE YOU ALL STOP.
MOTHER STOP
SIGNED LADY VERONICA ST. JOHN-BROWN

Michael called out, "Penelope, come quickly." They met in the hall as she came running.

"What's the matter? Is the cable bad news?"

"I'm afraid so. My father died early this morning."

"We must go to be with mother. She will be lost. Your papa was such a rock for, her."

"The White Star Line has the next Trans-Atlantic liner, The Baltic, leaving from New York in 5 days. I'll get the office to book us a passage. Unfortunately, we will not make it in time for father's funeral. I'll cable mother at once and let her know."

"We could have our London office start to make arrangements for a memorial service for when we are there. Do you think Angela Rose should go with us?" his wife asked.

"She will go with us! This is family. Can you take care of letting her know?" Penelope put her arms around her husband and held him close to console him. She could see he was trying hard to keep his emotions in check. It was the first time she had seen him cry.

He sobbed as he said, "I always thought my father was invincible, that he would never die. No, I never thought about death and father in the same thought. All he has done for so many people and now he is gone."

"Does one ever think of their parents and death in the same sentence? There will be many people whose lives he has touched that will want to pay their last respects.

The people that he knows in the House of Lords alone could fill a cathedral." They left Buffalo two days later for New York and the journey to England.

***

The memorial service took place in Westminster Abbey and was an affair of such magnitude that it was widely reported in local and national newspapers. The Times of London contained a two-page layout enumerating the achievements and giving accolades to Sir William's life. They printed condolences and comments from many people around the world who mourned his death. The ceremony was disturbing for Michael who felt it undignified to grieve in public, as he felt required to maintain composure. It took two days for Michael to arrange overseeing of the properties to reduce the burden on his mother. Michael was reserved and kept himself to himself on the return journey to America. Penelope kept her distance, allowing her husband his privacy. During this time, she made the most of the social events on the ship. The last few weeks had given her pause to think about her mother-in-law and her own parents' age's and when she would have to face the same losses.

Chapter 52

One of the greatest peacetime naval tragedies defies belief. The unthinkable just happened. The fas changing world of engineering marvels and inventions is to be set on its heels. As ships were getting bigger, the world appeared to be getting smaller and was becoming within the reach of the masses. April 14, 2012 was the night that shook the shipping world to its foundations. The newspaper headlines hit around the world with the stunning news.

RMS TITANIC SINKS
Iceberg rips open ocean liner on its maiden voyage

Titanic Cont.

In the early hours of this morning the RMS TITANIC, sunk after what is believed to be an orderly disembarking of many passengers. In what is being described as one of the most horrendous shipping incidents in history many lives have been lost. Adjacent ships are rushing to the aid of the survivors. The ships owners are not disclosing the passenger list at this time. It will not be made available until the survivors have been identified. The Titanic is known to have been carrying as many as two thousand passengers in first and second-class accommodations as well as steerage class

The previous morning Michael had spoken with Ronald as he and Melita Surtees were about to board the Titanic. Ronald assured him that everything was in order in the London offices of The Royal Shipping Line and that Mother's Fine Foods and the Co-op were prospering. Ronald even spoke of a number of wealthy English businessmen that had expressed interest in The Royal Palisades. Life had sounded good, and now this horrendous news.

***

April 15, nothing else was being talked about, no matter where you turned. Michael used all his contacts and was unable to find out if Ronald and Melita had survived. His wife asked, "what about their child, do we know where he is, how he is doing?"

"No, I don't know for sure. The company has been paying for his education and I believe that he is studying law in London. I will have someone in the London Office contact him. I am sure that his parents have provided well for him."

"I hope the company will finish paying for his education."

"Of course, we will."

"Why haven't they published a passenger list yet?" ask Penelope.

"They have. It is not the passenger list I am concerned with, it's the survivor list." Michael snapped at her.

April 16, 1912, the front page of The Times of London contained the headline:

1,500 TO 1,800
DEAD on TITANIC
J.J. ASTOR AMONG
THE DEAD

See page two for complete list.

To Be Continued...

Now! Who's The Joker
Julian's Hand
Playing The Cards You've Been Dealt Trilogy
by Peter C. BonSey

Playing The Cards You've Been Dealt Trilogy

Now!
Who's The
Joker?

One family is influenced by strong opportunistic women, while the other by strong moralistic men. It takes 150 years for a collision of their bloodline values in the mid-twentieth century to culminate with a shockingly ironic result. Murder is the act that changes an intense sibling rivalry into a spirited alliance. What some view as greed others, view as survival.

FOREWORD

April 15, 1912 the RMS Titanic sank at 2:20 am, taking with her the lives of more than 1,500 people. Julian's parents were among the missing passengers.

***

A private memorial service was taking place at St. Martin in the Fields church in London. The date was May 2, 1912. The service was in remembrance of the tragic loss of Melita and Ronald Surtees, Julian's parents, in the sinking of the RMS Titanic. The service was heavily attended by Melita's family. There were no members of Julian's father's family, as very little was known of them. Julian sat quietly waiting for the service to begin when he overheard a woman sitting somewhere behind him say, "That's the almighty's mistress's son." Someone else replied "For all we know, it's the almighty's son, the lucky little bastard, gets everything handed to him on a silver platter." Slowly, Julian turned to see who had spoken and saw the first woman as she said, "Wit what I am being paid to attend this funeral, I could go to funerals every day of the week."

The clergyman had pointed out the three women to Julian as he arrived and explained they represented The St. John-Brown family. Julian sat quietly throughout the service and his anger grew deep inside. All that kept rebounding in his head was, 'The St. John-Browns couldn't even be bothered to come to the service themselves. These people are just employees paid to be here, just for show. Just what did mother think *she* was to these people?'

In a cold state of disconnect he watched on as his grandparents sobbed throughout the entire ceremony. After the service was over, he respectfully declined the invitation to return to his grandparent's house for some refreshments. "I love you grandma, and you too, grandpa, but right now I just want to be alone."

His grandmother, with a warm, loving hug said "We know you do, my dear. We all handle this tragedy in our own way. You take care of yourself and don't, please don't become a stranger to us. Don't forget us."

"I won't grandma, I promise I won't forget you. *I will not forget anyone.*" The three exchanged emotional departing hugs, and then went their own way.

Chapter 1

Everyone at Rumsey Court had enjoyed a spectacular white Christmas. Cross-country skiers and children playing at building snowmen in Delaware Park created a picture book scene. But the cold did not sit well with Desmond Blacksmith, now thirty, as he had grown acclimated to a tropical environment. Spring has come, launching its welcome splash of color, tempered by bright sunny days. All conversations had become dominated by his upcoming wedding. It was only three weeks away. Grandparents and parents would arrive from England and be treated to the finest hospitality Buffalo had to offer. Due to the social status of Michael St. John-Brown, Desmond's in-laws, there were unlimited offers to host any overflow of guests. The Kelly's at 24 Tudor Place, the Howell's at 52 Lexington, and the Dorsheims' at 434 Delaware, had all made generous offers. The St. John-Browns finally settled on Mr. Gibson Williams, owner of the magnificent mansion at 690 Delaware Avenue, on the corner of North Street. The home was large enough to keep all the guests in one place, and would be more than adequate for the Earl of Sussex. In fact, this section of Delaware Avenue was known as Millionaire's Mile. Michael had been told about a new invention called "air conditioning," and was already making approaches to Mr. Haviland Carrier to try to install this wonder in his home in time for the wedding, to impress his guests. He remarked to Penelope, "What's the use of having all this wealth if we can't use it to make our lives a little more comfortable? Besides, my dear, if we're going to put it in our ships, we should at least have tried it ourselves."

The Buffalo Courier Express was the place to look if one wanted to keep abreast of what was happening in the cream of Western New York society. An article on the upcoming marriage took up a full half page, with the heading;

ROMANCE OR COMMERCE?
Is LOCAL UNION A HARBINGER
OF THINGS TO COME?
COULD THE ST. JOHN-BROWN AND BLACKSMITH
UPCOMING WEDDING BE SENDING
A SIGNAL OF A CANE INTERNATIONAL AND
GLOBAL ENTERPRISES UNION?

Desmond Blacksmith, hotelier, property owner of 'Cane International', and developer of the 'Classic Caribbean Cruise Line.' formerly of Essex, England, the son of Nathaniel Blacksmith and Agatha Cane, grandson of David and Jane

Blacksmith (nee Carter), and Judd and Mary Cane (nee Washerman), recently arrived in Buffalo for his wedding. The family business originated in Essex, County England in the early 1800s. Cane International, based in England, owns hotels and properties throughout the Caribbean. While the family maintains a private existence, we were able to develop an impressive property portfolio of the family.

Their known properties we were able to uncover are: 'The Plantation' on Gallows Bay, St. Eustasius, is a large hotel with suites and private cottages. This property also has a thriving ship trading terminal and dock. Hotels on Dominica, Mustique, The Turks and Caicos Islands and a large private cove and reef in Anguila. Once the family owned the now well known 'Royal Palisades at Jakeskill Island, Georgia which they sold, for development to Global Enterprises at an undisclosed sum. Cane International is expanding its hotel and vacation business and has its sights firmly set on the USA.

wedding Cont. pg 2

Wedding Cont. from pg.1

The bride to be is Miss Angela Rose St. John-Brown, 26, daughter of Mr. and Mrs. Michael St. John-Brown of New York City. The St. John-Brown family descends from Sir William St. John-Brown, member for the County of Somerset, in The House of Lords in the English Parliament. The family connections date back to King Henry VIII. Sir William's wife, Lady Veronica Chartwell, was a member of the Royal Household of England's Queen Victoria and the Queen's personal Lady in Waiting. Michael St. John-Brown runs both the British and American divisions of Global Enterprises.

Global Enterprises owns and runs, the giant British grocery store chain known as The Co-Operative, which has retail stores as well as it's own manufacturing and packaging plants throughout the southern part of Great Britain. Global Enterprises also owns The Royal Shipping Line and has a fleet of 25 ships that bear names indicative of the family's Royal connections. They specialize in immigration from Great Britain to Australia, New Zealand, Canada and the United States. Other family businesses include Mother's Fine Foods, a distribution and packaging food business that caters to private labels, packaging, and their own proprietary products. The St. John-Brown family also owns Duggan Ship Chandlers of Southampton, one of England's largest independent shipping suppliers.

The family's largest private development in the USA is situated on Jakeskill Island, Georgia. It is a twelve square mile private estate operating as 'The Royal Palisades, a members only private estate. It took six years and in excess of ten million English Pounds to build.

Global Enterprises holds a large portfolio of commercial and residential properties in England with the jewel in the family crown being the famous Royal Circle buildings in Bath Somerset. These properties have been the setting for many popular novels, particularly those of Jane Austen. A spokesman for Global Enterprises advised the wedding will be a private affair at an undisclosed location. The bride, Angela Rose, graduated from the prestigious and exclusive Lady's Seminary

Academy located in Buffalo. Miss St. John-Brown plans to further her education at Brown College in Massachusetts. The marriage of these two powerhouses of international trade and development will be an event to watch for. As for the union of the young couples' families, one can only sit back and watch. Will sparks fly between the establishment males, and the progressive, modern young bloods? Or, will their offspring create a force to be reckoned with and blaze yet another trail in today's fast paced changing world of development? Watch this column for updates

The balance of the page was taken up with photographs from the St. John-Brown family collection, which included The Royal Circle in Bath, the home of the Earl of Sussex, two of The Royal Shipping Line's ships, the 'Duke of Kent' and 'The Victorian Prince', and the construction site of The Estate at The Royal Palisades on Jakeskill Island, Georgia, along with an artist's rendition of the finished project. A photo of a Co-Op store and Mother's Fine Foods factory were also present.

The Cane family was equally featured with maps of the Caribbean showing where Cane International owned property, the Cane's first ship from the 1800's, 'The Mary-Jane', their hotels, and the 'Caribbean Queen' cruise ship.

Angela-Rose wanted to settle in Buffalo after the wedding, but Desmond was concerned about not being available on a more international scale. They both agreed that England was not worth considering, partly because of the unsettling news that trouble was fomenting in Europe. While Desmond preferred the Caribbean, he could see the value of staying closer to their customer base in America. Desmond had become interested in new automobile development. The Model T Ford helped calm Desmond's impatience while he waited to buy a Pierce-Arrow car for his stays in New York. They decided to base *The Caribbean Queen*, which itself would be handed over to Cane International a month before the wedding. Judd and Nathaniel had supervised her fitting and hired a crew to bring her to America. This was how all the English attendees to the wedding would be travelling. The balance of passenger accommodations was filled with other paying passengers and a festive air permeated the entire voyage.

***

The wedding was to be one of Buffalo's social event highlights of the year. While niether the Canes nor the St. John-Browns were particularly religious, the ceremony still took place in the magnificent St. Paul's Cathedral on Pearl Street. Built over fifty years earlier, its growth and size, was reminiscent of the cathedrals in England and Europe. For the guests who arrived in Buffalo early, carriages were arranged to take them on tours of the Pan-American Exposition site and then to the Frederick Law Olmstead Parks that encompassed the city, as well as to the great grain elevators, the waterfront, and Forest Lawn Cemetery, where many famous people, from presidents to pioneers in the development of Buffalo, were buried or interned.

Angela Rose greeted the friends and relatives as they arrived in Buffalo. She was most thrilled at the arrival of her grandmother, Viscountess Regina Elizabeth

Blackstone, who, she knew was very close to her father. She couldn't wait to spend some time with her. The opportunity came one afternoon as they sat in the private garden, bathed by warmth from the afternoon sun. Her grandmother spoke first, "So tell me child, this young man, Desmond, what of him?"

"What do you mean Grandmamma?"

"I haven't met him yet so you must tell me, is he handsome? Does he make your heart flutter? Have you laid with him?"

"Oh Grandmamma, how could you say such a thing?" Angela Rose blushed and bowed her head to hide her embarrassment.

"Now, now my dear, it is nature's course. Men are strange creatures and coupling comes to them with ease. For many ladies it is distasteful and to be avoided."

"Do you think it distasteful Grandmamma? I am not even sure I know anything about laying with a man."

"come on my dear, you either know about it or you don't. Hasn't your mother told about this?"

"No, she hasn't. I know some things I heard at school, but that's about it. Please tell me what to expect."

Her grandmother went quiet for a moment as she thought about how she might explain things. She was shocked at Angela Rose's innocence. "I suppose you know the difference between a man and woman?"

"Grandmamma, of course I do."

"Good, that makes this a little easier. The women in our family have always been blessed with the ability to enjoy lovemaking, copulation, sex, call it what you will." She smiled as she said, "there's no rule that says only the men can have pleasure from it." Angela Rose sat in a bewitched trance as her grandmother explained the act of making love from arousal to erection to climax. When she had finished, she asked, "Do you understand?"

"I think so. It sounds a bit gross if you ask me." There was a protracted silence before she continued, "So, if his thing gets so big and hard doesn't it hurt when it goes inside you?"

"Some say it does. I think some people just say that for effect, but no, I think it is one of the most wonderful experiences that I can think of."

"Do you and Grandpa still do it? Do Mamma and Papa do it?"

The grandmother held Angela Rose's hand and said, "There are some questions you don't ask my child, but in a healthy loving relationship, it should happen often. Men think it is their way of showing that they love you. I don't. I think it is simply one of life's pleasures. I will tell you one thing, should this young man of yours stop making love with you, something is wrong. Now be off with you and let an old lady enjoy the sun in peace and quiet." Angela Rose stood and kissed her grandmother and sauntered back into the house with all sorts of thoughts bouncing around in her head. She wondered why nobody had taken the time to explain these things to her before. She didn't know if she should be excited or frightened about what Desmond was going to expect to do to her, but if it was as good as Grandmamma says, she hoped it would be often.

Chapter 2

Angela Rose's plans to go to Brown University seemed to have been left by the wayside as, with a great deal of input from Michael, Angela Rose and Desmond settled into a new home on the corner of Delaware and Auburn Avenues. This prestigious location suited them, as it was far enough away from her parents and yet close enough when needed. The first year they stayed close to each other and reveled in each other's bodies. The sex was fast and frequent, much to Angela Rose's delight. As time went by, she became more the aggressor. Desmond was responsive on most occasions, but seemed to be holding back. There was one incident that Angela Rose thought might be the cause for her husband's apparent behavior change. Her periods were so regular and dependable that she was able to manage them with great privacy. Desmond was only aware of them when she told him of their presence. It was a warm early fall afternoon that found them in bed together. They lay side by side after a slow, passionate exchange of each other's bodies. Angela Rose thought that Desmond had climaxed an unusual volume as she felt wetness between her buttocks. Putting her hand between her legs she felt the warm liquid. With a sigh of satisfaction she raised her hands and put them behind her head and lay staring at the ceiling. Desmond rolled over with his eyes still closed and moved on top of her and kissed her passionately. He opened one eye and caught the sight of the blood smeared, white pillow. Grabbing her head with both hands he raised it and pushed it back down onto the pillow. Suddenly, Angela Rose was shouting at him, "What are you doing? Stop! Stop! Desmond, what's wrong?" As quickly as the violent episode started it, it was over. Amid profuse apologies, Desmond gently held her in his arms. As he looked over her shoulder at the bloody pillow, he saw a face. Not of his wife, but the face of Captain Walker as it smashed against the rain soaked, white bulkhead. It terrified him. He quickly closed his eyes, opened them again and the face was gone. Desmond went to great pains to avoid telling Angela Rose what he had seen. He knew what the reason was and that the glaring splash of bright red blood on the white pillow had clicked a memory in his brain. The incident had been pushed aside under the guise of a nightmare. Even that term frightened Desmond. He began to worry that he would indeed have nightmares about the incident. Her explanations of her period being a little earlier and messier than usual did little to assuage his fears of a re-occurrence.

By the end of their first year of marriage the images of the dying captain only happened once more, but Desmond was ready for it and managed not to react to the image in his head. It bothered him that the second time there wasn't any blood to instigate the image. He could only reason that the head against the white background had become the trigger. He henceforth made love with his eyes firmly closed, hoping to keep the demons in his head away.

They both agreed that a large hurdle they faced was what path to follow in their own careers. Desmond wanted to focus on his own family's holdings; however, his interest was being sparked by the inventions that were being unveiled almost every day. Just in the time that he had left the islands and been at sea, great changes were taking place. Men and machines were getting closer and closer. He had noticed that in New York City the construction was far more advanced in its methods than he had ever seen. He was fascinated that the inventions he was seeing in England and America had not yet reached the Caribbean. He felt sure that there could be an opportunity there. Angela Rose was torn about what she should do. She was not sure if she was interested enough in the family enterprises, covering two continents, or if she wanted to carve her own path. Her grandfather, Sir William had added fuel to the fire of her interest in things mechanical. Ever since their discussion that spoke of the incredible paces being made with the automobile, another subject had caught her interest - flight. She had started a scrapbook when she was fifteen, where she collected articles and stories about the development of flight. The first sustained flight by the Wright brothers in nearby Ohio spurred her into daydreams of airplanes replacing ships. It was Desmond's solid approach to life, with his feet firmly on the ground, metaphorically speaking, that enabled her to broach her thoughts with him. "I know my father wants me to be involved in Mother's Fine Foods and I suspect The Royal Shipping Line, but I'm not sure."

"Of what are you not sure, your father's thoughts or your own? Maybe you are a little on edge about your father's reaction."

"I think a little of each. Papa and Grandpa are such strong men and have such firm ideas about things. I worry that I might just be a instrument of them and not myself."

"I could not imagine you being anyone's instrument. If you are truly not sure, then why not take a little time and go to England and look at the businesses, on your own, without anyone looking over your shoulder trying to influence you."

"You wouldn't mind me doing that?" she asked.

"Oh no, not at all. My Grandpa Judd gave the same advice to my Pa. He sent Pa to a Caribbean Island on his own so that he could work things out for himself. Pa claims it was the best thing that ever happened to him. I was encouraged to go out into the world and find what I wanted to do. When you are away from the familiar you tend to look at things differently. I did."

"I think Pa will feel that I am pulling away from him."

"So, what if you are? That's not all bad. It's now, you and me. We are separate from our parents. Do you want me to talk to him?"

"No, no, I will do it. Just give me a little time."

"Well, now that you have brought the subject up, I have been thinking quite a lot about changing my direction somewhat."

"How? Doing what?"

"I want to investigate taking the hotel idea in a different direction. Although the final decision will be ours, I want to go and talk to my parents about it. I'll tell you more when I have formulated a firmer concept." Angela Rose felt a warmth and contentment in the comfortable way she felt when she discussed her thoughts with her husband. She wanted to end the afternoon's conversation with love making, but Desmond pulled away. She was starting to get used to him doing this.

***

Angela Rose soon approached her father and laid out her thoughts on her future. Much to her surprise, he was open to the idea. "Let me make some contacts. I will see if there is a dependable lawyer there that we can have assist you. Now that your grandma has passed away and left you some properties, it might be a good time to divest yourself of some of them. Madge Duggan left me some business interests which I would like you and Desmond to take charge of. It's about time we set this in motion and you take the reins."

"But, Papa, what if I don't want to take the reins?"

"It's a little early for you to make those decisions without seeing the big picture. Leave things with me. Let me change the subject, what is Desmond going to do?"

"He is out in the garden. Do you want to speak with him now? I can fetch him."

"That sounds like a good idea."

***

"Sit down with me for a moment Desmond. Angela Rose has told me what she wants to do and we are going to make arrangements for her to investigate her options."

"Thank you. Sir."

"Let's dispense with the '*sir*'. I think we can relax with formalities, after all you've been my son in law for over a year now."

"How should I be addressing you? 'Father' sits a little odd with me."

"It seems like the popular term these days with young people is 'Dad'. Would you be more comfortable with that?"

"I would Sir, Dad. So, what can I do for you?" Desmond asked, feeling a little more at ease.

"I am interested in what direction you are going to take with your life."

"That's a big question. My parents are very interested in me carrying on their plan to develop the properties that the family owns."

"Yes, most parents want that, but what do you want for yourself?"

"I am interested in what they want, but I don't know if Angela Rose has mentioned to you that I am interested in the modern world."

"The *modern* world?"

"Yes. When I leave the islands and travel, I see so many things that frankly, even you could not have imagined in your lifetime."

"Like what?" Michael was showing a genuine interest.

"Like, the Rigid Dirigible Airship is quickly being replaced with airplanes. The broom is being replaced with an electric vacuum cleaner. Then there's a machine that makes glass bottles. Color photography. Just think what the electric washing machine can do not only for women, but also for my family's hotels. Just this year, a hydroplane, that's a boat that can fly."

Michael interrupted, "Just a minute. Let's take the washing machine for a moment. Explain what it could do for the hotels."

"The amount of laundry that has to be done is done by hand right now. That labor could be used to do others things; as well as the laundry being finished much quicker. Just that alone is a big money saver."

"I understand the money side of it. So, are you wanting to go into washing machines?"

"No, no, I think that if one is to look at what the inventors are doing when they first create the inventions there will be opportunities."

"Keep going. This is interesting." Michael's interest spurred Desmond on.

"I believe that when someone invents something they are thinking of a specific problem. By the very nature of their mindset, they are focused on that problem. When I stand back and look at the invention with an open mind. I should be able to see one of two things; a bigger application of the idea or another use for the idea."

"You have an interesting way looking at things. Where did you learn that?"

Proudly Desmond responded, "When you are isolated, like our hotels are, you learn to look at things, not so much as what they are as what you can do with them. My pa calls that on-sight creativity."

"Not a very common skill, I must say. Not that I want to take over or anything, but I do have a contact in New York that has access to patents as they are approved. Do you understand how patents work?"

"I understand what they are for, but not exactly how they work."

"When a patent is applied for to protect an idea or invention, there is a period of time that it takes for the patent office to investigate whether or not the idea has been done before. The idea is given a provisional patent to protect it during this process. Once they are satisfied that it hasn't been done before it is granted a patent. My contact records and distributes the patents."

Desmond was becoming excited as he asked, "So what do you think my next step should be?"

"I can have my man keep you informed of the patents as they are issued. I think that you should keep on with your primary goal of your family's hotels and properties and have your skill of viewing things differently applied to a second business."

"And do what with it?" Desmond was a little confused.

Michael went on to explain how his family had taken ideas and developed them further. They bought the rights to them or used them on a huge scale. He said, "The creative brain is very different from the business brain. Few people are capable in both areas. It would appear that you are. I think you should keep your eye on what is new and decide if you want to do something with it. To give you an example, Angela Rose's grandfather bought the patent to the food can opener. He paid very little for it and used it in his own business as well as licensing others to use the idea. You can go either way. Would you like me to make the introduction to my contact?"

"Yes, please." Desmond was excited about the meeting with his father-in-law.

"If you need any seed money to work on these projects, don't hesitate to turn to me. Now, off you go and keep your eyes open when you travel. Always remember, something that might not have a market in a small country could have huge potential here in America."

That meeting was to have a lasting effect on Desmond.

Chapter 3

Michael St. John-Brown contacted Judd Cane with a specific request: that his daughter, Angela-Rose, should have her own personal solicitor. His tone was devoid of his antagonistic tone he used with Judd after the Titanic debacle. He was aloof yet cordial. He believed that his daughter should have independent representation on British soil to look after her needs. "After all, not everything is tied up in the business. Too many eggs in one basket, and all that sort of thing. If you can, old chap," he said, "see what you can find out about a certain fellow for me. Name's Fetters, JM Fetters, Solicitor. Black fellow. Heard some good stuff. Has chambers on Fleet Street in the city. A partner, I believe. Been away a long time. Out of touch, you know. Think we need some fresh blood to take care of the family things."

"I know JM Fetters well. He has done quite a bit of work for me. I like him. He is a straight shooter. I would be happy to introduce them. When do you think Angela Rose will be coming over?"

"Thank you, but I can take care of that. I will have my daughter contact you when she has made the arrangements."

"I do hope that she will visit with us. Is Desmond going to be with her?"

"No, she wants to do this alone."

Judd thought to himself that he had never noticed how Michael spoke in bursts. Just like the rapid fire from snipers, high on the rigging, as they would pick off sailors on enemy ships. This flooded him with colorful memories. As he replaced the telephone on its hook, he mused about the change in Michael's manner. Perhaps, he thought, it's time to move on.

***

By the end of the year, JM Fetters had been appointed to deal with matters pertaining to Angela Rose in England. Desmond & Angela Rose were the bridge that joined the families. In this union she saw great opportunity to build a bigger and more powerful empire. Her father's steadfast clinging to his English heritage appeared to her to be a little hypocritical, as his greatest achievements had been in America now that 'Mother's Fine Foods, The Co-Op and Duggan Ship Chandlers' were running independent of his day-to-day input. It was true that the family had long bloodlines running back through English history, but she leaned more towards her husband's hands-on style of life. She had no doubt that in the future these two great commercial entities would become one, and she was happy to let that happen when it may.

***

In February Angela Rose left for England on the Mary Jane, her husband's grandfather's ship. A meeting had been set up by her father with JM Fetters, the London solicitor with whom she would settle her grandmother's estate. She plunged into the ten days at sea with great abandon, observing the sailors and listening to their stories and sometimes sharing their meals. She began to develop an understanding of her husband's rugged pride in his family. She learned more about her father-in-law, Nathaniel, and the grit and determination he used to forge the Classic Caribbean Group with his bare hands. One old man onboard just sat around and smoked a pipe and sunned himself. He turned out to be one her husband's grandfather's original shipmates. Most of the crew treated the old man with a kindly respect and tolerance, as at this point, he was more a part of the ship than part of the crew. His memory slipped in and out of focus as he told her of the days of the *Gideon Rover*. In his words, the romantic history of the sea came alive. These were *men*; hard-working, tough men of the sea, carved out of stone and yet possessive of great tenderness and love for Captain Judd Cane. Before this trip, her picture of Judd had been that of a well-weathered, once handsome, retired sea captain who had settled back on land for his twilight years. In reality, it appears that he was a man who had capitalized on his ability to seize whatever opportunities life threw at him.

Another older man, whose name was Dickey Lemon, asked Angela Rose to mention him to Judd when she met him. He also told her that this was the final voyage of the Mary Jane. She was out of date. She was being replaced. With a knowing smile he said, "Ain't many ships like this un 'anging around anymore. Them iron one's is what's getting the business." Angela Rose felt a strange attraction to these old sea dogs. She had never been exposed to the masculine, self-confident aura they possessed.

***

Upon arriving at Poole Harbor in Dorset, Angela Rose's first steps onto the quay were aided by a six-foot-five, handsome black man attired in the height of fashion for city business. His lean, muscular build belied his profession. "JM Fetters, Mrs. Blacksmith, I am at your service," he said. But Angela Rose was distracted. Excusing herself for a moment, she entered the harbormaster's building and asked to use the telephone. She called her father–in–law, Nathaniel. After introducing herself she said, "Please don't get rid of the Mary Jane, she is in such wonderful shape. I would like to use her at one of the Classic Caribbean hotels as an attraction. She's is part of the history of the family business." He agreed that it sounded like a good idea and he replied, "Well my young lady, when you come out to visit us, we can talk about it. When do you think that will be?"

"I am here for a few weeks, so I'll contact you soon. I'm looking forward to it. Love you." She returned the telephone to its hook, and went to find JM Fetters.

Chapter 4

Fetters owned a Rolls Royce Silver Cloud, an impressive automobile. He proposed taking her to London, where they would arrive by nightfall. "What a beautiful car," exclaimed Angela Rose.

"It's the first Rolls Royce Silver Cloud sold to the public. Can you believe I was lucky enough to get it?" It was more a statement than a question.

"You must really have some influential connections."

JM laughed, "That and a lot of money. I have no illusions about my connections."

"Oh, you have connections. My father would never have suggested that I use you."

"Well, I do know your grandfather-in-law, Judd Cane, so I guess that helps."

Angela Rose felt there was an immediate connection with this man, and she felt comfortable. Angela Rose and JM spent the long trip to London getting to know each other. Angela asked, "What does the JM stand for?"

"I have always been JM. My simple answer is it stands for *just me*." He laughed with a pleasant a warm tone. "Maybe one day I will tell you."

"Is it James, John, Jack?"

"Let's just leave it at JM." His tone had finality about it and so she dropped the subject. He was a charming and eloquent man at ease with himself. He subtly changed the subject by relating his background to her. It appears that his grandfather had been a slave in the American colonies, whose master had returned to England and brought his slave with him. His master had died unexpectedly after being set upon by an angry mob in a dockside riot, as his ship arrived. The ship had the misfortune of being in the wrong place at the time. JM's grandfather had fought the group vigorously, trying to protect his master and he had received broken arms and legs and a head injury. Out of gratitude for his efforts, the master's wife granted the slave his freedom and a stipend to live on. He was allowed to live in the carriage house behind the family mansion in Bermondsey, London.

JM's grandfather only had a Christian name, but he was a proud man who told his son of how they came to be slaves by way of shackles, or fetters. He wanted them to never forget that. By the time JM's father sired him, his grandfather was dead and in the old man's honor, the child was named JM Fetters. "I decided at a young age to make something of myself for my grandfather to look down on and be proud." He went on, "As I grew up I saw that laws were used against my grandfather's people and I wanted to be in a position where I could use the laws. It took a long time, but that is how I became a solicitor.

The story sent chills through Angela Rose. She shuddered at the stark reality that what she grew up believing was merely romantic storytelling. In fact, reality was far more brutal. She realized that the maids and servants that she had grown up with were actually only one step away from slaves. She had never had a maid's history so graphically described, and yet here was this man quite comfortable with his history.

No sooner had they arrived at The Savoy when Angela Rose exclaimed, "I've been here before. My grandfather William and I stayed here."

"I am happy to see that you are acquainted with the finer things in life. We will be comfortable. I have arranged for separate rooms. But you must be hungry." He instructed the bellman where to take the bags and they went into the grille to eat.

All through the dinner, Angela Rose got the distinct feeling the JM was studying her closely. He asked many questions. So many that she asked, "Why all these questions? I don't mind answering them, but I feel like I am being interviewed."

"You *are* being interviewed. I spoke at length with your father and I know what he wants me to do for you. But you must understand that I am to be *your* solicitor, not your father's. If I am to serve *you* well, I must know what you think and feel. What your thoughts and desires are, or should I say, aims, are. My experience tells me that the better you know your master, the better you can serve, or should I say in your case, mistress." When dinner was over, they retired to their rooms. Standing outside her door, she looked across the hall at JM holding his door key and said, "You know so much about me and I so little about you. Would you mind if we talked a little more?"

"I would enjoy that Mrs. Blacksmith. May I simply call you Angela? Where do you suggest we go?"

"Yes, you may call me Angela, and my room will be fine." She said, After settling down in her room, across from each other by the fireside, they continued talking.

JM put coals on the fire to keep them warm. He asked, "So what else do you want to know about me?"

She replied, "From grandson of a migrant slave to a powerful solicitor. That couldn't have happened overnight, in London of all places."

Room service brought them a hot-chocolate nightcap and bid them goodnight, and JM spoke. "My grandfather's benefactor was a grand old lady. She took a shine to my father and paid his way through penny school. He learned to read and write. When she died, her will allowed my father to stay in the carriage house until he died. She had set aside an investment that was to pay my way through school and if desired, Oxford Law School, should I be clever enough."

"Is your father dead?" asked Angela Rose. "Were you clever enough?"

"My father is still alive, but ailing, and I guess I must have been clever enough because here I am. But the sad part of the story is what happened to her."

"What did happen to her?"

"My, my, are you always in this much of hurry?"

"No, seriously though, you tell your story so well it's touching. Go on, I will be quiet." As JM continued Angela Rose felt herself studying how he talked, how his mouth moved, the way he shifted his body. The man intrigued her.

It turned out that the lady's will that had been written for her was by one solicitor and what she had added, the codicil, was by a different solicitor. The first was a charlatan and he tried to wrest all her wealth, possessions and property for his own gain. The codicil was written by a man of great upstanding character and was rock solid. My parents were able to stay in the coach house and my education was paid for. While at Oxford, I brought the case before my professors and it became a 'cause celebre'. By the strangest of coincidences, it finally wound its way through the courts and was adjudicated at the same time I graduated."

"What did that mean?" asked the transfixed Angela Rose.

"It turns out the old lady had no heirs. The courts ordered that as my parents were the benefactors under the codicil, they became the benefactors under the full will. My parents became wealthy and hence so did I. Well, sort of."

"What do you mean sort of?"

"At that time, black folk like mine didn't fit well into wealth. They sold the property, coach house and all, and bought a small cottage in the country. The proceeds from the will, I manage for them. But the upstroke of it all is that it gave me an insight and an education, besides the legal one." He took a deep breath before continuing. "The extra education was that there must be many widows with poorly written wills that are vulnerable to the wicked legal practitioners. I had had the good fortune to advise wealthy people and was often more concerned with my clients' understanding of what they had than I was with my own well-being. So I set about contacting all those I knew from the old lady, and started reviewing their wills. I was amazed to learn the over half of them were either badly written, or written to enable them to be plundered."

"So, what did you do?"

"I set about correcting all those I could find. Most of my business now just walks in the door. In fact, in a four-year period, I had four wealthy widows pass away with no heirs. Each will, was written in such a way that if no heirs were found I would inherit everything. I had other solicitors advise the widows and they wouldn't budge from the way they wanted the wills written. I can only assume that they each appreciated the way I protected them while they were alive. Very quickly, clients were recommending clients, and as a large number were very old, in a space of another two years, seven more had died and left their estates to me. As diligent as I was, even I had not discovered just how wealthy some of the clients were," said JM. "I became even more wealthy overnight. The money follows the effort." JM surprised her by telling her that most wealthy people do not know enough about their wealth. That's how he'd become as well off as he was at so young an age.

"They were lucky you weren't the kind of solicitor that would kill them off for the money."

"I had thought about it." JM laughed at his own humor and then continued. "To be serious, believe me, there are plenty out there that would. I think the fact that I was wealthy myself put them at ease. Who knows?"

"So why did you take on something as mundane as my project?"

"Miss Angela Rose, neither you nor your project are mundane. I set out to be a respectable, honest solicitor. That's what I became. Judd Cane introduced me to his connections and that brought me to your father's attention. I must admit, America has always held a fascination for me, so I jumped at the chance to meet with you."

JM picked up a lace shawl and placed it around Angela-Rose's shoulders. She looked up at him, and he kissed her upturned face. Holding his hand, she pulled him in front of her and said, "You are one hansom man JM."

"And you are one very alluring woman."

"I can see that I arouse you." She said as she glanced at his groin and felt her own excitement increase.

He touched the bulge in his pants and sat in the chair and said, "Would you like to see how much you arouse me?"

Angela Rose blushed and in a horse whisper said, "yes, yes please." Pulling the tall-backed Queen Anne closer to her, he sat down and unbuttoned his trousers to reveal a thick, short erection. He lay back and slowly stroked himself. With his fist around his member, only the flange at the end protruded as he moved his fist up and down the length. She was mesmerized by what she was seeing, and watched him intently as dewdrop like spots of moisture appeared. His pubic hair was tight, curly, and black. She compared it in her mind to Desmond's soft blond tufts of pubic hair. "Shall I go on?" he asked. She did not reply. Slowly rising she lifted her dress and petticoats and removed her nickers. She turned her back to him and straddled his legs, lowering herself until she could feel him at her entrance. She put her hand between her legs and guided him to her warmth. Expecting pain from his girth, she hesitated, at which he held her hips and pulled her down, sliding into her. She sat perfectly still, feeling his warmth and throbbing. Suddenly his hips rose and she felt him ejaculate warm liquid into her. Feeling his thickness shrink and slide out of her she returned to her chair, faced him and watched him pull his trousers up. "Are you always that fast?" was her question.

"No! Rarely do I have to spend many hours looking at a beautiful woman and desire her without being able to do anything about it. This certainly was not a premature ejaculation. it was more delayed than premature."

"You really are a silver-tongued devil. Why were you not able to do anything about it?"

"What would you have done if I had pulled over by the side of the road and taken you on the back seat of my car?"

"Probably the same thing as we just did, except I would have been able to join in."

"Oh, my Lord. How selfish of me. May I pleasure you now?"

"You just did." She though how different this man was. He was at ease with his sexuality. That made him very attractive to her.

Later that night, lying in the darkness of her bedroom, Angela Rose relived the encounter in her head. What had she done? Dear Desmond was not as sexual a being as this man. He was a kind and good man, but his flame somehow belonged to the sea, the world, the islands. He was a practical, earthbound man, and he had not wanted her body as much anymore. Her grandmother's words just before the wedding about a man's desires kept bouncing around her head. JM wanted her and she wanted him again. The solid pounding of her heart pushed her into a deep and satisfied sleep.

***

The following morning Angela Rose awoke with a renewed vigor to what lie ahead. The journey from London to Crowborough was of the kind of luxury Angela Rose was used to. JM chatted away, pointing out the sights as they passed. Angela Rose asked, "Do you usually drive the car yourself?"

"Oh no. In the city I have driver, but when I go into the country I like to drive and enjoy the car." As they approached Crowborough Angela-Rose remembered her grandmother's house was running on a skeleton staff, but having called ahead, there was a welcome awaiting her. The housekeeper had prepared her mother's old room for her and a guest room for the visitor. David Mowbray held his granddaughter close. She could feel his sadness.

"Grandpapa, it was just like it was yesterday when you were at the wedding. How are doing?""I am alright my child. As well as one can expect under the circumstances. Your grandmother's presence is so ingrained in this home that sometimes it's too much. She just isn't here anymore. I still don't think I have grasped it."

"Is there anything I can do for you?"

"Just take anything you want from the home. Grandmama would like you to have what-ever you want."

"I couldn't take anything, just yet."

Turning to JM, David Mowbray said, "We have to go through my wife's will and be sure all her wishes have been kept.

"Have you not had the will probated yet, sir?"

"Oh yes, I just haven't done anything further, too painful you know. I would like you to advise me on what I should do. I would appreciate it.

***

The next morning the housekeeper woke Angela Rose and told her that the gentleman guest would meet her in the conservatory at her leisure. Within the hour, she walked into the conservatory, greeted by the fragrance of daffodils and hyacinths and an abundance of tropical foliage. The warm, earthy smell was something she was not aware she had missed.

JM sat at an exquisite, ornate wrought-iron table, reading the newspaper and sipping tea. He stood and pointed her to a small table set for breakfast. He told her that he had instructed the housekeeper to wait for her arrival to serve breakfast. Beside the table was a large leather case rather like a doctor's bag. JM opened it to reveal tightly packed files and envelopes. After they ate, he told her of the thirty-five properties in and around Essex and numerous other assets in London and Somerset that she had to examine. "We are going to spend the next two weeks inspecting the properties that you own," he said. "You will listen to my recommendations and opinions. I need for you to decide for yourself if you find me to be the right sort of fellow to act on your behalf."

The next week was spent inventorying and inspecting the properties in Essex and Kent. Angela Rose was a quick study and impressed the solicitor with her grasp of the intricacies and nuances of each individual situation. After inspecting the many small cottages in Crowbrough, that her Grandmother had left her, JM's opinion was that they should be sold. He suggested that the costs of having someone oversee and maintain them would not justify the returns. The proceeds could work better for her invested in other areas. From Kent, they moved through the southern counties of England, ending up in London. Both JM and Angela Rose found there was much to be learned about the Royal Shipping Line. Ronald Surtees and Melita had both been efficient in overseeing the business and the staff Michael had placed in charge appeared to be have been equally diligent.

The next week was spent with JM touring Mother's Fine Foods and The Co-Op and explaining everything that he and Angela Rose saw. He pointed out what he saw as positive and negative factors. Their days were spent in a professional business-like manner. Their evenings, however, were a whirlwind of wining, dining, and the most intense lovemaking that consumed Angela Rose more than she could have ever imagined. The bold forthright manner with which JM consumed her body excited her. His sexuality was not hidden under the pretense or guise of anything other than the fact the he wanted her. When his desires rose, she knew it and it kindled a desire in her that she never knew she had. The evening before she was due to return to America, Angela Rose, in a business-like manner that belied her laying naked with her lover said, "In all the time we have been looking at my inheritances and businesses, you have not once told me what I should do. I thought that you would advise me."

"It is my belief that my best service to you has been to explain everything that we have looked at, from my point of view. To tell you what to do would be presumptuous. My opinions are simply that; my opinions. I can be wrong you know."

"So, what do I do now? Am I supposed to instruct you with what I want you to do?"

"No, no. It would be unwise to make any decisions so hastily. You should remove yourself from this situation and give careful consideration to everything, even discuss it with your husband before acting."

Angela Rose became very emotional as she spoke, "why do you bring my husband into this?"

"Because, my sweet Angela Rose, you *are* married. It is only proper, though many men would argue otherwise, that decisions of this magnitude are shared by spouses."

"Does it bother you that I am married? What about this, us? Where do we stand?"

"Bother me that you are married? No. What about this, us? I would like for this to never end, but it will. You are leaving tomorrow. What would you have me do?" JM pulled her close to him in a tight embrace as if to prevent an answer.

There was a protracted silence before Angela Rose whispered, "you could come to America."

JM registered no physical reaction to her comment. He just calmly said, "and what would I do there? My practice is here in London. While I could afford to live without work, it would not be prudent." Before she could reply, he added, "Let's agree that you should go home. Our time together here is special and who knows what tomorrow may bring. If fate brings us together again, so be it. I hope it will. We will be in regular contact over your business affairs should you wish it. There's our starting point for the fates to work with. What do say?"

"I don't know what to say. I suppose at times like this one should say, I love you."

"You only say those words when you truly feel them. Goethe, a wise old German philosopher once said 'You will only know that you truly love someone when it is incomprehensible that it possible for someone to love your beloved more than you.' I don't think either of us are at that point yet, and it doesn't worry me, *right now.*"

Angela Rose said, in a tiny voice, "you always seem to know the right thing to say." Looking into JM's eyes. "What do you see for our future? Not generally. You and me."

"You have your life. I have my life," said JM. "When and if circumstances permit, we will cross paths and reawaken. I am your humble servant in law. I am your trusted friend and lover, if and when you deem it right for you."

***

Angela Rose left London and went to Mucking to visit with her husband's grandparents. She discussed with them the Mary Jane. The condition of the ship for its age was remarkable. When Angela Rose spoke of Dickey Lemon, Judd felt sure he did not want to just abandon those who he had relied upon for so long, but he didn't know if he even wanted to own another ship. Angela Rose provided a solution. He should send the *Mary Jane* to New York, where she would take delivery for Desmond. Her time in the villages and towns around Mucking revealed a country life so different from the West Country where her family was from. Angela Rose felt as if Somerset and Dorset were the thumb on her hand, while Upper and Lower Mucking were her little finger. The two lifestyles were firmly separated from each other by London, the palm of her hand. While her thumb could touch her little finger, it could do little to influence it, and vice versa. This was the way rural life in England had quietly trod its diverse roads, for centuries, and would continue to do so.

Chapter 5

Steam-driven ships were becoming the norm rather than the exception. Global Enterprises took its modernization one step further with the latest of advances such as oil fuel-driven ships. While Angela Rose was busy with her grandfather and JM, her father, Michael, returned to England early and undertook a vigorous plan of turning each of his business' public, starting with the Royal Shipping Line. It was the first of his companies to offer stock to the public. Retaining thirty percent of the stock for The Royal Shipping Line, the balance of stock sold in twenty-four hours. One of the largest new stockholders was the P&O Line. Next up for public offering was Mother's Fine Foods. It sold at a higher price with public knowledge of its connections to Global. The Co-Op was, in essence, already perceived as a public company, though only the company's B shares were used to control the dividends. Many dividend holders did not understand the concept of A and B shares. The release of the A shares was handled privately by a broker, and they again achieved a high price. Michael and his mother, Lady Veronica, held seats on the boards of these public companies for life. The family's on-hand cash at Coutts now exceeded one hundred million pounds. His solicitors advised that although he was Angela Rose's father, he did not have the authority to take Duggan Ship Chandlers, the Co-Op or Mother's Fine Foods public as he had transferred to Angela Rose Madge Duggan's share of these business's. He arranged a meeting with his daughter and JM.

***

"Angela Roses father said, "I understand that you now own a significant portion of Duggan Ship Chandlers, the Co-Op and Mother's Fine Foods. I think it best that I take care of taking these companies public. You will then own an equal amount of the shares and profit well from the conversion."

JM responded before Angela Rose could, "with all due respect Sir, I feel obliged to point out to Miss Angela Rose that she should take a close look at the suggestion before making any such important decision."

"What difference will that make? I have only the best intentions for her future."

"Be that as it may, it was your suggestion that Angela Rose has independent counsel. I believe that she has the right to decide for herself. If I have understood your daughter correctly Sir, she has not yet decided what direction her life will take. I feel it my duty to assist her in taking whatever action she decides will best suit her future, no matter what direction it takes."

"*I*, am the best judge of what is best for my daughter. You hardly know the girl." Michael's tone was condescending and abrupt.

"How well I know her has little to do with her ability to make decisions for herself. I think your suggestion for going public has merit, but it is not my decision. My opinion of what she should do will not influence my assisting her to take the route she chooses, and protect her while she does it." JM leaned back in his chair and waited for Michael's reply.

Angela Rose spoke next, "Father, JM has not steered me in any direction with my business affairs so far. He has laid out many alternatives and their potential outcomes and left me to decide for myself. I appreciate you wanting to take care of things for me, and I appreciate JM wanting me to understand the ramifications of any decisions that I might make. Papa, you should be happy that JM, your choice of solicitor, is so open and frank about things."

Michael accepted his daughter's comments.

Before he could respond JM said, "I would appreciate it if we could take a closer look at those business's with you while you are here in England. I am sure that Angela Rose can arrive at her decision quite quickly."

As if a switch had been flipped, Michael said, "Grand. Let's get to it then when you are ready."

***

Over the next few days, the three of them toured Duggan Ship Chandlers, the Co-Op and Mother's Fine Foods. On the final day, at dinner, Angela Rose finished her meal, folded her napkin and said to her father, "Papa, it has been very exciting learning about my share of your inheritance from Madge Duggan. JM has made some very valuable observations that I have considered. Probably the most important being my home is in America and my personal interests are not in the areas of any of the three business' we have inspected. I think, and JM feels, that for you to take the business' public, would be in my best interests."

"A wise decision my girl. Thank you JM for enabling me to see my habit of making decisions for everyone was running over my daughter's opinions."

"That, Sir, is what I am paid to do." JM replied.

"And you do it well, thank you." Michael told them that he would be leaving in the morning to address business at The Royal Palisades and looked forward to getting together back in America.

***

The Royal Shipping Line underwent a modernization project and sold all its existing fleet and purchased seventeen iron, steam and oil powered ships. Four of these were passenger ships to concentrate on emigration routes. The balance was medium-sized, fast, cargo carriers. The line's ensign and colors were changed to emphasize its new beginning. The newspapers were reporting unrest in Europe and Michael could not wait to return to America. It was a hectic year for the family, and as Michael returned to Buffalo, he felt a sense of relief. Most of the family's business assets were now in paper form, with the exception of the vast amount of cash deposited in Coutts, and the property holdings in Bath and Somerset. Michael had returned to New York by mid summer and Angela Rose soon followed.

***

The Estate at the Royal Palisades had developed far beyond expectations. Michael and Penelope spent the colder winter months at their suite at the Palisades. In early fall of 1913, Angela Rose returned to London not only to meet with JM and finalize the paperwork for taking the companies public, but also to be with him. Having completed the essential paper work, JM set out about rekindling his relationship's more personal moments with Angela Rose. His advances met with a welcoming passionate ardor.

Meanwhile, pending his daughter's return, Michael arranged with Nathaniel and Judd that they should meet at the Royal Palisades and investigate any possibilities that may have presented themselves with the marriage of their children. Michael arranged for suites to be set-aside for the Cane family. Lady Veronica would stay with Michael and Penelope. The only non-family member invited to attend was Josiah Mielman, now a sprightly eighty-six years old. After all, Josiah had become an important part of the Palisade's family, and Michael knew that Judd would welcome meeting the old man again.

Mary had never met the old man, but felt she knew him well from her husband's reports. Within minutes of arriving at the Estate, she presented him with a photograph of Ojukwae Mielman, his wife, and their children. The old man wept. He was humbled and proud that they had chosen his own family name for the child. He joked that Ojukwae was the first black in the Mielman family.

Judd saw a very different person in Josiah. His step was so alive and brisk as he held himself erect and proud. The first gathering of the men was more social and centered on what was happening in Europe. Nathaniel's penchant for keeping a journal had gradually changed to collecting newspaper headlines. He read through the more recent items, compiled in a large, leather-bound scrapbook. While opinions were varied the common thought was that Europe was on the brink of war. The unrest in Europe was clearly foreboding, and all shared concerns about where it might go.

The next few days were spent discussing the respective businesses and discovering the vastness, uniqueness, and enormity of the Estate. The Italianate and Japanese gardens were the clear favorites of all who toured them. The theme gardens had been designed and built with such attention to detail that one would believe himself to be in the different parts of the world. The self-contained farm, which produced for the kitchens, was so well organized for animal husbandry, rotational cropping, and greenhouses for out-of-season growing, it was an adventure just to tour them.

They were clean and the workers appeared happy and skilled. A large area of stables and grazing grounds for the horses was undergoing modernization. The courtyard was being cobbled with local quartz blocks for ease of cleaning. A new long, low, sleek building was being erected for the expected arrival of the motorcars.

One evening, sitting in the Heavens Above, the gentlemen-only salon, watching the sun settle over the horizon, Michael pointed out an area to the north of the estate that had been cleared of vegetation. "The Wright Brothers in Kitty Hawk have caught my Daughter's imagination with their flying machine," he said, blowing a cloud of pale smoke into the night air. "Gentlemen, there were horses, then trains, then cars. My daughter believes the airplane is going to be the biggest thing since ships gained engines. Although it is not proper to discuss other members of the Palisades, I can share with you that the space you see beyond the farms is where Orville Wright, one of our members, landed one of his flying machines. That was the site he suggested our members would fly their airplanes into. I don't know what will be needed to care for these planes, but by God, we will do it. These are exciting times we live in."

Within the week, Michael and Judd met privately. Michael's financial superiority was evident, but he admitted that, although his empire was bigger, he had started halfway up the ladder. He didn't know how Judd had achieved his empire, but he said, "From nothing. You did it from nothing."

The men appeared to have arrived at an unspoken respected toward each other. It was evident to Judd that he was more focused on what his family was building for their heirs, while it seemed that Michael was doing it for power. Judd had seen many injured and maimed sailors during his time at sea. Many wore the disfigurements like badges of courage. Michael appeared to do everything he could to keep his mangled left hand out of sight. Judd wondered why. There was a pompous air about Michael that unnerved Judd.

When Judd required that Mary be part of the meetings, Nathaniel and Agatha were also invited. Michael started thinking about how the world was changing to include women more readily into business. The Canes let their women have visible control and input. This was an alien concept to him. For him, women were an adjunct to his way of life, and yet to the Canes, the women were an integral part of the decision-making process. He rationalized, Madge was his father's dalliance that happened to be profitable and for himself. Melita was out of the same mold. This attitude stalled the progress of the meetings. Michael laid out his vision for his companics and gave the floor to Judd. Judd similarly described where thought his family's business interests were headed. Neither man made any suggestion as to where each saw the future of their interests working together. When the point was raised, Judd said, "There are some similarities but it's early days yet to consider anything other than that point."

Michael looking pointed at Mary and Agatha as he said, " Men have and always will run our businesses as women run yours."

"We, run our business as a family!" Judd bit his tongue as he responded. It was more of a statement than a criticism. He continued with, "Maybe some-day down the road we may see a reason to combine but for now things are fine the way they are."

It was eventually agreed that the two families would have a biannual summit to review the potential opportunities. They also tentatively agreed that if either one saw large opportunities they would involve each other rather than outsiders.

***

Nathaniel and Agatha, Judd and Mary and Angela Rose sat enjoying the early morning sun and fresh brewed coffee. They were gathered on the terrace of The Royal Palisades waiting for the carriage to take them away. Desmond had requested they all meet, as he wanted to discuss something with them. He arrived and sat facing them. Nathaniel asked, "What's wrong, has something happened?"

"No, quite the contrary. I wanted to tell you, Ma and Pa and Grandpa and Grandma, that I have been busy with a new project."

"You are always busy these days. What are you talking about specifically?" Nathaniel asked.

"After Angela Rose and I got married I had some discussion with her father about my direction in life. I had expressed an interest in all things modern and he gave me some good advice."

"Does that mean you are not going to stay in the family business?" Agatha shot out as she suddenly sat bolt upright.

"No Mother. It means that I have developed other interests as well that I am following." He went on to explain the thoughts he had shared with his father-in-law. The group listened intently. When he had finished, Agatha asked, "So, what does this mean in simple terms? That you are going to be spending less time in the family business?"

Judd interrupted, "If it does, my dear, it will be what he chooses and not what you choose."

"Papa, let the boy talk for himself." Agatha was getting irritated.

"Thanks Grandpa." Judd smiled at Desmond standing up to his mother. "To give you an example, the modernization of the hand washing machine to an electrically driven one is an opportunity for our business. By putting a few of these machines in each of our resorts we can save a lot of money on labor and speed up the laundry process."

Nathaniel commented, "I am not sure that I want to get rid of some of the workers. Many of our staff depends on us to feed their families."

Desmond's reply was very quick, "There is no need to get rid of anyone. Firstly, the laundry people will welcome their work-load being less strenuous. Secondly, those people can be trained to offer even better service than we currently do."

"What's wrong with the level of service we currently offer?" Agatha was clearly defensive, a point upon which Desmond jumped.

"Mother, and even you, Grandpa, have seen how much ships have changed in your lifetime. If we go around being defensive about every new idea that comes along, we will be in the same boat as everyone else. Excuse my pun. The world will leave us behind. I really do believe that we need to get on this movement."

For the first time since they had been talking, Mary spoke up, "This is all very interesting but what is your point? You seem so intense, there must be more to why you sat us all down."

"Grandma, there is. When you came to America on your first visit, you must have noticed how different it is from England. You have been to St. Eustasius, when I was born, and that was different again. Each of these places were ahead or behind of the others. That's where our opportunities lie."

In a prompting tone, Judd said, "And that means we do what?"

"Get involved grandpa, get involved. Angela's Rose's father has put me in contact with a man in the patents' office. I get to see brand new, approved patents, *before* the rest of the country. He has generously offered to finance my purchasing of the patents where possible. I declined his offer as I want to do it alone."

"Smart move," " Judd Cane said. "Smart move, profit from your own endeavors."

"I just want you all to know what I am doing. I want to be open about it."

Mary said, "If your washing machine idea is anything to go by, I think you are onto something great." Leaning over to Agatha, she said, "I would go ahead and act on that one right away. It will stand you out from the other hotels and they won't know why."

Judd added, "Maybe you could buy the rights to sell the inventions in other countries. In their early days the inventors will be so happy that their inventions are paying off, that you could buy at the right price. I would think that, in its self, would be lucrative."

In his enthusiasm Desmond went on to describe some of the things he had seen. "There was the I.R. Johnson patent for a bicycle frame, and wouldn't you know it, a Gottlieb Daimler invents an engine driven bicycle. John Thurman invented an electric vacuum cleaner. A Mr. Reno invented an escalator, thats a moving staircase! Boy could we use something like that at just one of our hotels. What about Mr. James Stewart? He invented a vacuum flask for keeping things cold. Nearly all these things we could use or variations on them.

Great Job young Desmond, you go for it. Should you need finance for anything, turn to family, *our* family. I'm sure we will all support you."

Desmond was happy with the outcome of the meeting and Angela Rose left with her arm linked through his, congratulating him, all thoughts of JM were nowhere in her mind.

Chapter 6

Desmond was excited about the completion of the Panama Canal. He saw the Caribbean as the crossroads of travel around the world. Every business wanted to be at the crossroads, and this was to be a big opportunity for Cane International, with or without the aid of the St. John-Brown Empire. At thirty-two years of age, Desmond had a wealth of experience and a drive and ambition his parents believed would take the business far. He did not fully understand stocks and bonds, but was impressed with his wife's ability to predict financial happenings. The previous year, she had described Henry Ford's invention of the moving production line as a turning point with far-reaching effects. So strong was her belief that she heavily invested in stock of the Ford Motor Company. Many in the family followed her example. Angela Rose had returned from England with a clear-cut sense of direction for her life. Desmond's trip to the Cane International properties and other international destinations had spawned his new direction. This was all to go on hold on the fourth of August 1914 when the headlines of English newspapers were wired to America. Angela Rose read them aloud to the family:

"Great Britain Declares War on Germany."

"Huge Crowds Cheer Their Majesties at Buckingham Palace."

"The King Calls on the Navy to Once Again Prove the Sure Shield of Britain and her Empire."

"Fortunes will be made and lost," said Angela-Rose, looking at the loved ones gathered around her. "Possessions will be destroyed and families torn apart. We must protect the family's fortunes and neither follow nor lead. Wait, watch, and learn from the mistakes of others."

***

From 1914 through 1918 the world was in upheaval. The St. John-Browns focus was on protecting their assets. The entire Royal Shipping Line was busy transporting men and machinery for the war effort. Those ships not moving personnel were involved in cargo work. The government, instead of requisitioning the ships, allowed the company to orchestrate the day-to-day running of the ships. This suited the family with the exception that as time went by the government debt to them was steadily growing.

Cane International was in a similar position, but on a much smaller scale. Early on in the war Judd summoned Nathaniel to a meeting. Sitting in the offices above Mary's business Judd spoke first. "You know that it is only going to be a short time before the government is going to want to take our new passenger liner for troop movement."

"Yes, I know. We can avoid that though."

"How do you propose we do that?"

"We have holdings throughout the Caribbean. We could send her there until this war is over. It is not our war, it's the government's."

Judd's reply was stern, "If it is the government's war, then it damn well is ours. I have served our country in The Royal Navy and I have seen our empire. It is our responsibility to protect our dominions from those that would destroy it."

"I understand that Sir, but Agatha and I seem no longer to be part of this. Your daughter and grandson know other lands as their home."

"Those other lands belong to the British Empire and by that virtue it is still our responsibility to protect. I must admit that I am happy that Agatha and Desmond are far away from this mess."

"So, what are you saying?"

"That we pull our horns in, settle down, and do what's right and when it is over pick up the pieces and rebuild. England will prevail."

***

October 1914 was two months into the war for the world, for Angela Rose it was something else. She had been home from England for three months when she discovered that she was pregnant. She was not sure if she wanted to be. Desmond's homecoming was passionate and full of warmth, which seemed to fade with time. He had been touring Europe and the Mediterranean looking at hotels and was flush with excitement. They had made love every night for a week before Desmond's flashbacks started occurring again. She thought to herself, "something is causing him to not want me, then my sex life must be over. I suppose I should be happy that it ended with a child." Fleetingly, in a short daydream of unbridled sex, her thoughts were of JM Fetters, but were quickly dispelled by Desmond's great excitement with the news, and soon both families greeted the news with joy. Judd and Nathaniel were happy that their grandson's family was now firmly anchored by the pending birth. Names were thrown around, but no decisions were made. The St. John-Browns were equally happy, but seemed more casual about the news. Angela's grandfather, David Mowbray, the Earl of Essex was quietly proud when he said, "Our blood, at the top here, is getting a bit thin. Glad to see you youngsters keeping it going."

In May of 1915, a ten-pound six ounce son was born. Even at birth, the child was robust looking. His fine downy hair was blonde and looked like it would have tight, frizzy curls. His coloring was not pink, but rather looked as if he had a pleasant summer tan. Desmond was firm the child be named Ojukwae, in honor of the Cane family's history. Grandpa Judd had rescued and adopted a slave child and named him Ojukwae. The child had grown up to become Desmond's father's close friend and indeed, the best man at his wedding. Desmond was very proud of how, despite society's slow acceptance of the black races, his family had stood by Ojukwae as an equal. Angela Rose was fixed on the name Brian. There was no reason other than the fact that she liked the name. A compromise was reached. The tiny offspring was to be named Brian Ojukwae Blacksmith. The name Ojukwae was ignored by Desmond's mother, as it was by Angela's father. Right from birth Brian was a restless, demanding child. He quickly learned to demand his mother's attention with tears and tantrums. Angela Rose found him exhausting and welcomed the nanny's ministering calm when she took control of the baby.

***

The summer of 1916 brought sad news to the St. John-Brown family, Lady Veronica, Michaels mother died quietly in her sleep. The war prevented any chance of a safe passage to England for the funeral. Michael refused to get involved in any discussions of his mother's death. It was as if it was being ignored. This bothered Angela Rose, but she was unable to discuss it with her father. She felt that sometimes her father could be quite cold on personal matters. She used her scrapbook collection of airplanes as an escape and, in fact, purchased shares in the newly formed Curtiss Wright Airplane and Motor Company. She now felt that she was actually a part of this exciting invention.

To make matters worse, the next year, 1917, David Mowbray, her grandfather on her mother's side died. Her father was equally as distant as he was when his own mother died. She recalled he had seemed far more upset when the Earl's wife, died. She was not aware of the sexual liaison he had shared with his mother-in-law. Upon reflection, she saw how different the men in her family were from those of her husband's family. She wondered if this had any connection to her husband's erratic sexual prowess, or lack thereof.

***

1918 as the world relaxed with the end of the war, Angela Rose had begun to think more about her own future. Brian had become an energetic handful. The live-in nanny was a blessing, as Angela Rose could not see herself functioning as anything other then a mother. Most afternoons would find her walking the baby in a pram into Buffalo's busy business section, where she would gather the Buffalo Courier Express newspaper and any other national newspapers she could find. Passers-by would admire her baby and comment on his head of golden blond tight curls. By the time she returned to the house she was ready to pass Brian off to the nanny. Retiring to her room, she would spread the newspapers out and go through them looking for anything on flight. Her scrapbook of cuttings on the subject was quickly getting thicker. There were a few articles on Samuel Langley's gasoline powered 'Aerodromes' from 1901, but her imagination was really fired up by the Wright brother's great invention of 1903. The papers were full of pictures, diagrams and photographs. Her 1905 favorite was 'The Flyer'. It was affirmation that flight was practical. She would run her fingers over the photographs of the Flyer above the ground as she imagined this machine being developed as fast as the automobile had been. Somehow, she knew her future would be connected to it, and she would own part of it.

***

Over the previous two years JM Fetters had carried out Angela Rose's instructions on her English holdings. As each task was completed, he followed it up with a warm letter of congratulations on her decisions. Sometimes she would read unwritten meanings and then she would deny them to herself. With some trepidation, in November of that year, she broached a subject with her father. "Papa, I know that the war is only just over but I have an idea for you to consider."

"About what?"

"Papa, don't be so curt. For the longest time, we seem to be having troubles finding a lawyer that you are comfortable with."

"What do you mean? We have fine Lawyers."

"Every time I see lawyers at the house, they are new ones. It has nothing to do with me, I know, but while the family has business here and in England, we are at the mercy of one side or the other."

"I suppose you have an answer to that problem."

"Actually Papa, you have the solution. When you found that English solicitor, JM Fetters, you found a clever, honest man. With all the government's debt to us in England it would be good to have a man familiar with their side of things."

"Go on, this sounds interesting." Michael relaxed as he realized his daughter was making sense.

Angela Rose said, "I had you look over the work he did for me and you were impressed. He even advised me soundly on the public offering of Madge Duggans's inheritance. You met him and you seemed to like him. He could be your man for the English matters. He could also be the man over here that helps you find the right lawyers here. He could oversee them. For all I know he could practice here. That I don't know, but isn't it worth looking into?"

"I do believe, young lady, that you have developed quite a head on your shoulders. You should contact him on behalf of the family and invite him over for discussions."

"Oh no, Papa. You are the head of the family. I think it's your place."

"Then so be it."

"Papa, there is one more thing."

"And what might that be?"

"I know that you would like me to get involved in the family business. I really enjoyed seeing Mother's Fine Foods and The Co-Op, but Papa, they don't excite me."

"What does excite you then?"

"Flying! Papa."

"You want to fly?" her father asked incredulously.

"Not me Papa, the whole flying thing is fascinating to me. Flying was just for birds, but not anymore. I think it is going to go the way of the automobile and iron ships. Ground floor papa, I see this as the ground floor. I didn't tell you, but I actually have shares in The Curtiss Wright Airplane and Motor company right here in Buffalo."

"I find this interesting. You are probably going through the same experience that I did when I faced your grandfather and told him that I was going into the food business, when all he knew was shipping. I must say you are turning into a chip off the old block if ever there was one. You must do what your heart tells you is right for you. I see you have been buying shares without telling me? Quite the crafty little thing, aren't you? Now get out of here and let me work."

"Thank you, Papa." Angela Rose walked behind her father's desk and kissed the top of his head. Much to her surprise her father uttered words she had never heard from him before, "I love you my child, now go." He waved his hand in an air of dismissal.

Chapter 7

January 1919, Angela Rose and Desmond stood in the Central Railway Terminal in Buffalo's East side, waiting for their visitor. The hissing of the steam locomotive slowly subsided as a tall hansom black man strode towards them followed by porters overloaded with baggage. Angela Rose embraced him and whispered in his ear, "I am so glad to see you."

As he shook hands with Desmond, he introduced himself, "JM Fetters, Mr. Blacksmith. I am pleased to meet you. Your wife has told me many fine things about you. My, I wish all my clients met me with such a warm welcome."

Desmond replied, "It is an honor that you do us, coming here to help our family. My wife's family is expecting you to stay with them while you get settled. I hope that meets with your approval."

"Indeed, it does." Turning to Angela Rose he continued, "You never told me what a handsome man you have for a husband. Your father tells me you have a fine son. I look forward to meeting him."

When they arrived at Michaels house there was an air of warmth as JM was introduced to Angela Rose's mother and he was shown around the house. Her mother, having instructed Angela Rose to show JM to his room, left for the kitchen. Holding the door open for him to enter, Angela Rose let him through and closed the door behind herself. Flinging her arms around his neck she kissed him passionately and said, "God! how I have missed you."

Holding her face between his hands he gently kissed her and then whispered, "Instant erection. You have not lost your effect on me. What shall we do with it?"

"Fuck me, please fuck me. We have plenty of time for love-making. I just want to feel you deep inside me."

"I have never heard you talk like this. What has got into you?"

"You, please, you get inside me." In a flurry of passionate thrust and parry she consumed JM sating her own desires. It was over as quickly as it started. He said, "Now, *that's* what I call a welcome." Straightening her clothes, which never were taken off, she whispered, "We must be careful, we don't want to get caught."

"Indeed, we will be." He smiled at the now closed door after she left. "When I am good and ready."

***

After that Angela Rose only saw JM for short periods, as her father and him were locked in meetings for many days. Whenever they met, company surrounded them.

After two weeks had passed, her father held a private diner where he announced that JM Fetters was to be the lead council for the family. It was stated that he would take up residence in Buffalo and represent the family in both American and English matters. The celebrations went on into the night. With this move Angela Rose began to accept that she now had JM in her life, as he had her in his. On the one hand, she was excited and on the other, she felt nervous. She accepted the situation. At least JM was to be a part of her life and maybe it would make up for the shortcomings of Desmond's performances, or lack thereof. She thought, I could have the best of both worlds here.

***

Soon after that evening, Desmond decided to share his thoughts on his own direction. Over a bottle of wine, he laid out his ideas. "When you were England, as you know, I went to Europe and the Mediterranean. I have been increasingly intrigued by the size of my family's hotels and development compared to what else is going on in the world. Our hotels and resorts are quite unique, although small. When I looked around, most large cities have many small hotels and just one or two really big hotels. They are almost palace like. Very luxurious and they cater to big money. Wealthy people, who do not care about what they spend as much as they care about what they get."

"I've seen many of the big hotels. I especially like the Savoy in London." Said Angela Rose.

"There are Savoy type of hotels around the world."

"Tell me more, what have you seen."

"I haven't seen a lot, but enough to make me read newspapers from around the world. I contacted Cook's, the huge travel company in London and have received quite a lot of literature. I decided to focus on those near the sea, or huge lakes. It is interesting what I have found. In England there is 'The Headland Hotel' in Southampton that overlooks the English Channel. It has hundreds of rooms it even has a dance floor on coiled springs that can hold two thousand five hundred people. Can you believe that? Then there is The Amsterdam American in the Netherlands. It has a hundred and seventyfive rooms and is a spectacular sight. The list goes on. The Hotel Negresco in Nice, France, The Carlton in Cannes, France. The Taj Mahal Palace and The Gateway in Bombay, India. The Peninsular in Hong Kong. The Hotel Mount Nelson in Capetown, South Africa. Even as far away as Melbourne in Australia has the Grand Hotel."

Angela Rose interrupted her husband, "They all seem so big, why?"

"It's all about size, and luxury. These hotels are connected in another way, water, namely the sea. But beside that, there are two huge hotels here in America, by the great Lakes. Michigan has two, The Book Cadillac in Detroit on Lake Erie and The Grand Hotel on Mackinac Island on Lake Huron. The other connecting thing is private families. They are all owned by private families not huge corporations."

"Why is that important?"

"Because it means the big corporations have not yet seen the potential. The hotel that I found out about is the one that got me really thinking about our properties throughout the Caribbean. It is the Hotel Santa Catalina on Las Palmas. That is a small group of islands off the coast of West Africa, on the way to Australia and the orient. It is such a big hotel, so far away from everything and yet it is always full."

"There is no disputing your excitement. So,what is your next step?"

"I plan to talk to Father and Grandpa about us going big in the properties that we have and seeking out new locations. I always thought that there had to be big cities for there to be big hotels. That's not the case. There are journeys and destinations. There is no reason that the journey can't also be a destination."

"So, what do you plan to do with our new passenger liner? Speaking of that, I asked your grandpa to save the *Mary Jane* for you to use at one of your hotels."

"We can still do that with the Mary Jane. As for the liner, I will have to see what they say. I believe that a new direction for the future will give our son something to work towards."

Angela Rose and Desmond had at last found their own directions to take in the business world while having their life together. Each one's choice would add to their family's earlier endeavors, thereby moving the empire into the next century.

Chapter 8

February 1919, Angela Rose announced that she was once again with child. Desmond welcomed the news, as did the rest of the family, except Brian Ojukwae, now four years old. He was vehement in his stance. "No baby. I don't want a baby." His parents put this down to him not understanding. They had never seen a rambunctious side to the child. He was highly spirited and seemed to forever be up to mischief.

Angela's mother, Penelope, gave her sage advice when she said, "children don't come with a care guide or handbook. You have to figure out what works for each child."

In frustration, Desmond said, "Handbook! This one would need a handbook as thick as a bible." Angela Rose's pregnancy was quite different from her first. She became enlarged very quickly in the the early days and had numerous difficulties. The doctors told her there was nothing to worry about. Her main concern was with Brian, who constantly slapped her swollen stomach since he learned that that was where the baby was. The nanny had kept Brian away from his mother as much as possible. That angered Brian all the more. Angela Rose was anxious for the pregnancy to be over. Desmond had ceased all sexual relations with Angela Rose, despite her protestations of safety. JM was always ready in the background to alleviate Angela Rose's stress. After one such coupling Angela Rose asked JM, "Do you think my mother is pretty?"

"Pretty, is not the term I would use, she is beautiful. I bet your father can't keep his hands of her."

"It's funny you say that. As a child I often caught them after they had been having sex giggling like schoolchildren. They don't seem to be doing that anymore."

"If I didn't have you making such huge sexual demands on me, I would do your mother in a flash." His comment was phrased in a joking manner.

Angela Rose replied, "I guess I will just have to keep you to myself." They both laughed, but Angela Rose was stung by the comment. The subject was soon put aside. A few days later, Angela Rose's mother, over dinner asked JM, "Why don't you have a wife?"

"I guess that I have never found the right woman that would put up with me. I am quite happy being a bachelor."

"Do you have a lady friend?" her mother asked.

"Oh yes, I have friends, but it is more accurate to say that I am married to the law, that is unless you are available."

Angela Rose cornered JM the next day and asked, "Were you trying to titillate my mother?"

Acting indignant, JM replied, "You are all the woman I need. Older women enjoy a little light banter, particularly of a sexual nature. You have nothing to worry about. Did it bother you?"

"It just got me thinking. What will I do when you do find a woman worthy of you?"

"Rest assured my dear Angela Rose, you are part of my greater plan. There is no one else." Changing the subject, he asked, "What is Desmond up to these days, I haven't seen him for a while?"

"He is busy with the hotels and he seems to be having some success with his invention ideas."

"Invention ideas, what has he invented?"

"Oh, he doesn't invent, he is rigorously following the news of new patents. He has acquired interest in a thing called the popup toaster. Also, he has interest in the escalator, moving staircase. One that I think is a bit odd is a thing called a separable fastener. It appears that the B. F. Goodrich Company uses the fastener on a new type of rubber boots or galoshes they call it the zipper. It is being used on boots and tobacco pouches. Desmond thinks this has great potential for other uses. It's his investment thing."

"So, he is doing quite well then?"

"Yes, he is."

***

Attention in the family home was soon to be focused with the receipt of a telegram from Judd Cane's wife, Mary.

SORRY TO REPORT GRANDPA DIED THIS MORNING STOP.
SATURDAY FEBRUARY 28 1919 STOP.
DIED AT THE HANDS OF A MOB BY THE *MARY JANE* STOP.
HE DIED DEFENDING HIS SHIP STOP.
I WILL WRITE YOU DETAILS SOON STOP.
HE WAS MY ROCK I FEEL SO ALONE STOP.
LOVE YOU ALL STOP.
GRANDMA STOP.
SIGNED, MARY CANE STOP.

Angela Rose and Desmond kept in touch with Nathaniel and Agatha as funeral arrangements were made. Two weeks later they received a newspaper cutting that detailed Judd's death, it read:

Obituary: Mr. Judd Cane. 1826-1919
Killed by angry mob in Port of London.

Mr. Judd Cane, 93 years old was brutally killed last night in the Port of London dockland area. Cane, the founder and guiding light of the Cane business empire, died at the hands of an angry mob, while visiting the Mary Jane, a merchantman owned by his company. He was there to oversee the preparation for the Mary Jane's final voyage to America where it was to be used at a Caribbean resort. Cane happened upon a demonstration by the National Sailors' and Firemen's Union, who were opposed to the plan to form a National Union of Seamen. It was apparently the plan for many ship owners to ally themselves with the new union and control access to work on ships. Cane was seen leaving the *Mary Jane* as it prepared to cast off. It was general knowledge that Cane and his crew had no quarrel with the unions, but did not support their endeavors. Mr. Cane's unique method of pay distanced them from the general discontent found commonly among seamen.

Many sailors vied for a position among his crew when one became available the mob viewed him as an obstacle in their collective plans.

Mr. Cane was killed outright by a thrown belaying pin that entered the back of his head pointed end-first and went through his brain.

Cane leaves behind a wife, Mary, a daughter, Agatha; a son-in-law, Nathaniel Blacksmith; a grandson, Desmond Blacksmith; a granddaughter-in-law, Angela-Rose Blacksmith; and a great grandchild, Brian Ojukwae Blacksmith.

A burial at sea funeral is expected as Cane was one of the few remnants of a passing breed of seamen. Tough men who endured the rigours of sea life and on whose backs this great empire of ours was built. We have lost a treasure. May God rest his soul.

RULE BRITTANIA

Chapter 9

For Angela Rose, the weeks and months following Judd's death seemed to fly by, what with family going to and from England, Desmond going to and from England and the properties in the Caribbean. Brian was a handful with no improvement in sight. Angela Rose was surprised when Lucy, the nanny asked. "May I speak with you quite frankly Mrs. Blacksmith?"

"Of course, my dear and please, how many times must I tell you to call me Angela Rose?"

"I can't ma'am. It is not respectful for me to address you in any other way than I do."

"Alright, what is the problem?"

"I am getting concerned about master Brian. He is a very angry young boy. I'm sure his tantrums are aimed at your condition."

"What do you mean aimed at my condition?"

"When he is angry, he keeps saying, 'me no want baby, me no want baby.' He uses baby talk and he is four and a half."

"I don't know what to say. What do you think I should do?"

"Well Mrs. Blacksmith, Brian gets out of bed during the night and walks around the house."

"What, why didn't you tell me this before?"

"Because it is no big thing. I am always there to steer him back to bed, but it worries me that when I ask him what he is doing he says. "I look for baby. Where is baby? His speech is more appropriate, so I know when he is speaking for effect."

"Oh my God! Do you have any suggestions?"

"Yes Mrs. Blacksmith I think we should prepare the nursery for the new child and put a latch, bolt, or lock up high on the door, out of a child's reach."

"Do you really think it's needed…?"

"No ma'am, but I just want be on the safe side."

"Yes, yes, we must do that. Angela Rose was alarmed, but felt helpless. It was at this time she understood why parents had nannies. When Desmond came home, she told him of her conversation with the nanny. His response was, "He is only a baby himself. He will grow out of it."

Angela Rose was not so sure and asked, "Do you think he might listen if JM spoke with him about the baby?"

"Why would JM make any difference?"

"Because children listen differently to people who are not their parents. I have noticed that when Lucy speaks to him. He obeys her quicker than he does me."

Desmond thought for a moment before replying, "I guess it's worth a try."

***

Angela Rose heard doorbell ring and called to the maid, "I will get that it's only JM. I am expecting him." Opening the door, she stepped aside to allow JM to enter, as he stepped into the hall he said, "What's wrong, what's the problem?"

Angela Rose replied, as she walked towards the study, expecting JM to follow, "Desmond thought it would be a good idea for us to discuss a problem we are having with Brian."

JM sat in a chair facing Angela Rose and said, "Problem with Brian? Desmond's idea? I don't understand."

"Well, it was my idea and Desmond agrees. We think that Brian is working himself up over my pregnancy. He is starting to worry me."

"Who, Brian or Desmond?"

"Brian of course. The boy will not listen to either of us and it is all he keeps talking about. He doesn't want a baby. Those were his words not mine." Angela Rose started to tear up. JM stood, walked over to Angela Rose, who was seated and put his arms around her to comfort her. With her arms around his waist, her head on his stomach, she started to cry. The pair of them just stayed in that position for a few moments, only to be interrupted by Angela Rose looking up and saying, "You are getting aroused. You have an erection."

"What can I say? You have this effect on me. Your hair smells good. Your warmth excites me. I guess this is inappropriate timing."

"Knowing that I excite you could never have an inappropriate time. Can we make love? I need to calm my nerves, and you do have a way of doing that."

"If you insist." JM unbuckled his belt as Angela Rose stood, lifted her dress and removed her knickers. She touched herself and showed JM her moist fingers saying, "See, I am ready."

JM took her hand and licked the wet fingers and asked, "Where do you want to do it? Right here on the floor?"

"Yes, like animals. Let's do it, but be quick, just fill me up." The room went quite except for the sounds of sex, only to be broken by JM's "OOOOh my, take it all my sweetheart." As quickly as the act began, it was over. Angela Rose's demeanor was distinctly calmer. She smiled as she said, "I love watching you get dressed after you have had your way with me. Or should I say I have had my way with you?"

"Oh no! I, have had my way with you." JM rubbed his lingering erection through his pants as he repeated, "I, have had my way with you. Now let me go and find Brian and have a chat with him."

"Shall I come with you?"

"No, let me do this alone." JM found Brian in his room. He was drawing. The picture was of stick figure of a girl that appeared to be falling down stairs. JM looked as if he was studying the picture. Instead of commenting on the subject matter, he praised Brian's drawing skills. This led into a lengthy discussion.

Angela Rose was in the kitchen when JM walked in, omitting the details of the drawing he said "I have had a talk with Brian and I'm not sure how much good I did, but we can hope."

"What did you say to him?" asked Angela Rose.

"I just told him about my sister and how I didn't want her and now we are the best of friends. I told how she had grown up and that we are very close."

"But you don't have a sister." Angela exclaimed.

"How do you know that? Just because I haven't told you about her."

"What else haven't you told me about yourself?" Angela Rose was starting to become indignant.

"Take it easy, I don't have a sister, but Brian doesn't know that. I just invented her for the situation."

"Quite the inventive soul, aren't you?"

JM laughed as he said, "You will never know just how inventive I can be. Now, I must get off to work."

Angela Rose changed the subject. "Before you leave, I have a quick question. As you know I have shares in The Curtis Wright Aircraft and Motor Company. I see that another company is being put together. It is to be called The Curtis Wright Aeronautical Company. I want to have shares in that company. Could you do that for me?"

"How much do you want to spend, or should I say how many shares do you want?"

"I will leave that to you. More than just a few I would say. Get enough for me to have some voice, should I ever need it. You have my power of attorney. I trust your judgment."

***

September 20th 1919, a scream broke the night air. A girl child was born into the Blacksmith family. At seven pounds, two ounces, she was smaller than her brother. At birth she had jet black, straight hair and a nose that looked as if someone had pressed it down and it never popped back up. Both families were happy that the pregnancy had been a safe, comfortable one for Angela Rose. Lillian Jane, as she was to be called was a beautiful, peaceful child. 'Jane' was in honor of Desmond's fraternal grandmother, Jane Blacksmith. Brian's life had just taken on a whole new direction.

Chapter 10

For the first few months of her life, Lillian was kept a watchful eye over by Linda, her nanny and her parents. Brian had only been allowed to see the baby in the presence of adults. He showed little interest other than trying to put things in her mouth or to vigorously shake the cradle, at which he was reprimanded. He had no interest in the baby at all. Both nannies had made attempts to introduce him, in quiet times to Lillian. On a few occasions, Lucy had let him push the pram along the upstairs landing without the baby in it. He became used to it and appeared to enjoy it. In the spring of 1920, Lillian at six months old was becoming quite vocal and was a calm and happy baby. Lucy was supervising Brian with the empty pram on the landing when Linda came up the stairs, slid the bolt on the door and went into Lillian's nursery. She left the door open. In the brief moment Lucy took her attention off of Brian, he pushed the pram across the landing between himself and Lucy and ran into Lillian's room. Linda had her back to the door as she was opening the curtains. Brian spotted the crib standing upright on its legs in the middle of the room. He rushed over to the crib, gripped the sides firmly and shook it before pushing it over. Lillian screamed as she hit the floor. All hell broke loose. Brian dashed out the door as Linda was shouting something behind him. Seeing Lucy coming round the pram at him, he turned and ran for the attic, where he locked the door behind him.

Fortunately, no harm had come to Lillian. Both nannies had been reprimanded for losing control of the situation. It took until late evening to coax Brian out of the attic, with promises that nothing would be done to him. For the next few days adrenaline ran high around the house and everyone was on full alert around the children.

***

In July of that year the British had successfully managed to cross the Atlantic Ocean in a dirigible, the R34. This excited Angela Rose. Her scrapbook was starting to get hefty. The acquisition of stocks in the Curtis Wright Aeronautical Company had been purchased and at JM's suggestion had been put into Lillian's name.

The summer was a long hot one and Brian spent much time in the cool shade of the huge elms in Delaware Park with his nanny. It was one such afternoon. upon returning to the house, he asked to be allowed to play in the garden. Seated on the ornate wrought iron bench under the huge beech tree Linda was gently rocking the pram with Lillian asleep in it. Beside her Lucy relaxed and they reminisced about

Ireland. They had both been brought to America in search of a better life. Both their fathers worked in the huge grain elevators on the Buffalo River and had aspirations for their daughters. Their chatter was interupted by Brian, who was standing at the back corner of the carriage house, waving to them. He had his finger to his lips in a gesture of silence. Linda stayed with baby Lillian and Lucy walked stealthily towards Brian. She approached the corner and peered around it. She gasped in shock at what she saw. There on the ground was the gardener with his pants around his ankles and his skinny white legs protruding from under and between, the large rotund black buttock cheeks of the cook. They were oblivious to the world around them as his hips thrust upwards and her hips thrust downwards. Mesmerized, Linda and Brian just stared. Brian, in his pre-pubescent high-pitched voice exclaimed, "What *are* they doing nanny?"

The copulating couple, finding themselves discovered, hurriedly dressed and in panicked tones said in unison, "Please miss Linda, don't tell the mistress. She will not approve of the gardener being with a me, me being a darkie and all."

Linda responded, "Miss Angela Rose does not approve or disapprove. She just doesn't want the children to witness any such thing." She walked away with Brian taking him by the hand she led him back to the garden bench.

As she walked, Brian said, "I think Cookie was trying squash the gardener. Doesn't she like him?"

"It's sort of like a game that grown-ups play."

"Does it hurt? Cookies bum is so big and the gardener, well..."

"No, it's just a fun thing. Let's keep it their secret." The subject was dropped and Linda hoped that Brian would soon forget about it. Linda told Lucy about what she had seen. Both girls laughed about it. Lucy, I think we can expect an extra nice dinner tonight with cook trying to keep on our good side." Both girls laughed. Brian started to return to the corner of carriage house. By now the cook and gardener had disappeared. Linda suggested they take the children to Parkside Candy and get Brian an ice cream. Brian wanted to push the pram but both nannies were hesitant. Linda started to lead the way with the pram when Brian said, "I don't want to be behind the baby. We should be in front. I am the big brother." To keep the peace, that is what happened.

***

Desmond spent the late summer and early fall in St. Eustasius, putting into action his plans to greatly increase the level of service for the Gallows Bay Retreat. He wanted to model it after the Hotel Santa Catalina on Las Palmas. The hotel's distance from anything else and the fact that it was so popular appealed to him. There was nothing in the Caribbean to equal it and he wanted to be the first. Upon his return to Buffalo, his excitement about his plans for the hotel on St. Eustasius was overflowing. There were materials and supplies to be obtained and shipped. Plans had to be prepared and the finest quality of furniture, and accouterments to furnish the improved Gallows Bay retreat purchased. At Angela Rose's suggestion,

Desmond decided to develop a plan that could be modified and repeated in all of their other Caribbean holdings. He set about his task with a one-eyed enthusiasm. Christmas came and went, as did Desmond. As he was preparing to leave Buffalo in February of 1921 for the islands, Angela Rose found him in the bedroom packing. She approached him and pushed him back on the bed. Straddling him she said, "We don't to seem to have sex any more, or very rarely."

"You mean we don't make love?" he asked.

"Make love, have sex, call it what you may. Don't I appeal to you anymore? Do you have someone else?"

Desmond sat bolt upright, nearly knocking Angela Rose off his lap. "Do I have someone else? No, I don't! It's just that we both seem to be so busy with other things. You being a mother and me with the hotels and the other investments. Maybe we should take some time away together."

Angela Rose quickly pulled away and got off of him, saying, "I wouldn't want to pull you away from your precious hotels." With that she stormed out of the room. Desmond fell back on the bed, putting his hands over his face he tried to block out the recurring image of heads, white walls, rain, blood running down in rivulets. He just couldn't understand why sex with his wife, who he loved dearly, dragged up these images up from deep down inside his past or was it his subconscious?

***

Three days after Desmond left for the islands Angela Rose received a cable from Desmond's mother.

SORRY TO REPORT GRANDMA MARY CANE
DIED THIS MORNING STOP.
WEDNESDAY MARCH 9 STOP.
DIED PEACEFULLY IN MUCKING STOP.
I WOULD LIKE YOU TO COME HOME FOR THE
FUNERAL STOP.
IT IS UP TO US TO CONTINUE THEIR LEGACY STOP.
WILL KEEP YOU INFORMED STOP.
LOVE YOU ALL STOP.
MOTHER. STOP.
SIGNED, AGATHA BLACKSMITH STOP.

The news shocked Angela Rose. It was as if everyone around her was dying. In 1916, her fraternal grandmother died. In 1917, her maternal grandfather died. In 1919, her husbands' fraternal grandfather murdered, and now 1921, her husband's fraternal grandmother, gone. The entire family tree line of grandparents, on both sides was gone. She was reading the cable when the maid announced that JM was at the front door. "Show him in, for heaven's sake, show him in."

JM knew as soon as he saw her that something was wrong. Noticing the cable in her hand he asked, "Not bad news, I hope. Cables most often mean that."

"Well, yes, it is bad news. Desmond's grandmother has died and he has just left for St. Eustasius."

"Were you close to her?"

"Not really, I am more concerned about how Desmond will take it. He was very upset when his grandfather died. I'm not sure what to do."

JM said, "Leave it to me. I will contact Desmond for you and assist wherever I can."

Angela Rose thanked him and asked, "What brings you here? I did not expect to see you today."

"To tell you the truth, the snow is melting, the sun is brilliant today and I'm feeling good about myself, and you of course."

"So, you have a spring in your step, or should I say your pants?"

"Oh yes, I want you. Even as we speak, I feel a twitch in my pants."

Angela Rose smiled and leaned back in her chair and smiled as she said, "Show me." Without saying a word, JM, undid his belt buckle, unbuttoned his flies and dropped his pants to the ground. He stood there smiling at her. She said nothing. He waited a few seconds and slowly pulled his underwear down. He had to unleash the erection. It flipped up in a mock salute. "Would you like to help me out here?" he enquired.

"No, I want to watch you pleasure yourself." Her tone was playful and seductive.

"Do I get some encouragement?" he asked as he sat on the front edge of a chair, spread his legs apart and slowly stroked his erection. Angela Rose, much to his surprise leaned back in her chair, moving her hips to the front and raised her dress. The sight of her tussle of pubic hair garnered JM into a faster stroke.

"Stop, stop, slow down I want to see you squirm. Go very slowly. Hold your thing tight. I want to see it slide in and out of your grip and imagine it going in me. I want to see what it looks like." The ritual played out slowly with Angela Rose orchestrating his every move. As he gasped for breath and spurted out his seed, she looked to see that his eyes were tightly closed. The sticky mess dripped through his fingers.

"See" she said, "You didn't need me at all. You did quite well on your own."

"Phew…that was good, not as good as when you do it though."

"But the end result was the same." she mocked.

JM cleaned himself up with a towel and asked, "What about you? Can I pleasure you?"

"You did, while you were busy with your eyes closed, concentrating on your own ends, I was busy. The nice thing is that this makes me look forward all the more to our next time."

"Miss Angela Rose, you never fail to amaze me. You exude a quiet sexuality that is impossible to resist. I don't understand why Desmond spends so much time away from you. I swear I would never get much work done if I was in his position."

Angela Rose started to speak, "Desmond and I, we, don't….." She stopped midsentence.

JM took the hint, "You don't have to explain to me. It's none of my business."

Changing the subject to save Angela Rose any further embarrassment, he said, "I think would be nice if I went to Desmond and took him the news of his grandmother. After all, he is alone out there, not with his own, I mean."

"I think he would appreciate that. Sometimes I feel Desmond to be a solitary soul and I know he likes you."

"Would you like me to take young Brian to be with his father? I would be happy to. It might give you a break and some one-to-one time with Miss Lillian."

"Let me think about that."

"I shall go now and see what arrangements I can make for the journey and allow you time to decide what you want to do"

***

Angela Rose had decided that JM could take Brian, now five, with him to see some new things and to give herself a break. JM declined the offer to take Brian's nanny with him. "Let's make this a male-bonding trip." was his suggestion. Stepping off the Aeromarine West Indies Airways flight in Havana Cuba, hand in hand with the child, JM made straight for the dockside to arrange passage to St. Eustaius. It didn't take him long to secure passage on a freighter bound for there. The trip took two days, during which Brian relaxed around JM. Approaching the island JM explained much of what he knew about the place and said to Brian, "We shall discover new things and see what your papa does for living." Desmond had received word that they would be coming and was waiting on the dockside to greet them. The gangway dropped and JM had to hold Brian back while the ships carpenter went ashore to read the ships Plimsoll line.

"What is a Plimsoll line?" asked the boy

JM said, "A ship never completely floats on water. A part of it is always submerged below the water surface depending upon how heavy the ship is. The Plimsoll line is a line drawn on the lower end of ships, marking the maximum level to which the ship can sink into water after its loading capacity is full. If the water level goes above the Plimsoll line because the ship is overloaded, it could be dangerous as the ship may sink."

"So, what does he do if it's wrong?"

"The carpenter tells the captain so that he makes sure it is right before the ship sails again."

"Oh. There's Papa, can I go now?" With that that, Brian ran into his father's arms. JM followed with their baggage and greeted Desmond. Shaking his hand, he held on to it for a little longer as he continued, "I thought it might be nice for you to have some familiar company at a time like this. I am so sorry for your grandmother's death."

"I suppose it is to be expected, she was ninetynine. She had a good life. I have to decide if I should go to England."

JM suggested, "Let's talk about this more when Brian is in bed tonight. I'm not sure if it is really necessary. You should find out what your mother's plans are and decide from there."

Brian interjected, "Papa show me where you sleep. Show me what you do. The sea is so big Papa. I have never seen the sea before."

"I will take you to a special beach. One that your mother and I know about. It was our secret beach, and I will teach you to swim in the sea." The rest of the day Desmond showed JM and Brian the hotel and the local area. It was not long before Brian became tired and fell asleep. JM and Desmond discussed business and Desmond proudly explained what his ideas were for the hotel and how he saw the family business developing.

Without thinking JM said, "It is amazing how things change just with the passage of time."

"What do you mean?" asked Desmond.

"There is no longer any one left alive in the family tree above Fingers. He is the oldest and head of the family now."

"My father-in-Law? Michael, why do you call him Fingers? Apart from the obvious fact he has half his hand missing. I have never heard anyone call him that."

JM quickly recovered his faux pas by saying, "That was his nickname. Well, that's what Melita and Ronald Surtees used to call him in fun. He took it in good spirit on the surface but, I think it hurt him deep down. I believe he was quite close to the Surtees."

"Oh, I never knew that."

Again, trying to soften his comment, JM continued, "Your father-in-law once told me of the nickname. Ever since the Surtees couple went down with the Titanic, he rarely mentioned it, or them again. He was a grand man and I hope he will run the family and involve you and Angela Rose a little more."

Desmond said,"I intend to make my own mark, as you see with the hotels and Angela Rose is quite smitten with the airplane thing."

JM pondered, "I do believe that she is quite capable, although I think she is looking more towards those interests as offering an alternative opportunity for your children." The two men talked long into the night only to periodically notice that Brian would wake, listen for a while and fall back to sleep.

Desmond discussed with JM how impressed he was with Angela Rose's interest in airplanes. "In fact, because of her, I have been paying attention to the plethora of new inventions. There appear to be many small flying companies forming all over the world. A fledgling industry I suspect. One should keep an eye on it and look for investment opportunities. It might be a good way of connecting your large luxury hotels idea together." The two men talked of the way the world was changing and how far both the family's businesses had harnessed the change upon which to build the fortunes.

The three males spent a few days fishing and swimming in the sea. They toured the island together and spent much time showing Brian interesting and exciting things. When it came time for JM to return to America, he approached Desmond,

"It has been grand spending this time with you and seeing you with your son. I do believe he idolizes you, which brings me to my question."

"Which is?" asked Desmond.

"Shall I take Brian back with me or will he stay with you?"

Desmond thought before he replied, "I would like him to stay, but I think he should be with his mother and sister. I am concerned about his relationship with Lillian and don't want them apart for too long. It might perpetuate the divide between them. I shouldn't say between them, it's more his attitude toward his sister. I just don't understand where that comes from."

"Then I shall take him and, Desmond, I have enjoyed getting to know you better. I feel that I can serve your family so much better." The men shook hands and Desmond stood on the dockside watching until the freighter was a tiny speck on the horizon.

On the voyage home, JM asked Brian what did he like best about his trip. He was disturbed by the reply; "I didn't have to share anybody with my sister. That was fun, and you know what JM?"

"What?" Responded JM.

"There was a lot of black people there. They was nearly all black."

"Were, it is were *nearly* all black. Why do you say that?"

"Because, black people like to hurt white people. Didn't you know that? Weren't you a little bit afraid of them?"

"No, I wasn't afraid. I think black people are quite friendly."

"That's because they are not the same as us and because we are better than them. They need us to like them." JM was shocked to see that it had not registered with Brian that he was partly black. It appeared as if JM's very light skin tone was what had confused the boy. He asked, "Don't you think I look like I could be black?"

"Oh no, Mama says you are Moccan. You parents came from Fr…Fr.."

JM helped him out, "France, my grandparents came from France and Mor occ o. You could say that I am Mor occ an."

"Well, there you are! You are one of us, not one of them." Brian was proud that he had straightened JM out on the facts.

***

Back in Buffalo, JM told Angela Rose about the trip and how he now felt connected to her husband. He also said, "I got close to Brian. I like the lad." Thinking it better not to mention that Brian enjoyed not having to share anything with his sister he continued " Brian never once mentioned his sister and we didn't bring it up. We just let him be a little boy and it was fun. I felt like a father for a short while and I enjoyed it."

"Have you ever thought about having children of your own?"

"There are things that I don't think about because there is so little chance of them happening. I am happy being around your children, that's enough. Besides, I have things I need to get done before I can give any thought to having a child." Later that evening when the house was quiet Brian slipped quietly into his mother's bedroom and clambered up on the bed beside her. She pulled a blanket over him and asked, "What does my little man want to talk about?"

"How do you know I want to talk mama?"

"Because, my little angel, that's what you want when you snuggle up to me. I don't know why you find my bed the place to chat, but that's ok. Talk to me."

"Is Mr. JM our family?"

"Well, he sortof is. He works for Mama and Papa. He also works for all of Grandpa Michael's family. We treat him as family because we all like him."

"Doesn't he like Grandpa Michael?"

"Of course, he likes Grandpa Michael. Why would you say such a silly thing?"

"He said Fingers? I heard Mr. JM talk about Fingers. He was talking about Grandpa Michael."

"Why would you think that?"

"Because he was talking to Papa and I heard that."

"I think he was probably just fooling around, because you know Grandpa has some fingers missing off one hand."

"So, is it joke mama? How did he lose his fingers?"

"I suggest that that if you need to know, you should ask him and I don't ever want to hear you call him Fingers. He is Grandpa Michael and that's all there is to it."

***

It wasn't long before Brian found the opportunity to ask the same questions of his grandmother, Penelope. "Grandma, how did Grandpa lose his fingers?"

"You are a little boy and you make decisions based on the things you know. As you get older, you make better decisions because you know more about the world and more importantly, you will know yourself better. Some of us make decisions that are not very wise. Your grandpa made a not so very wise decision one day and touched a piece of machinery that he was told not to. There was an accident and Grandpa got burned. It was very sad. We were all upset and angry with him for doing that. It's all in the past and we don't talk about it anymore."

"Do you think Mr. JM doesn't like Grandpa?"

"You ask the strangest of things. I think Mr. JM is very good man and if your grandpa didn't like him, he wouldn't be working for us. Mr. JM has always been very kind and helpful to your mama and your grandpa. Now, put your silly ideas out of your head. Do you like him?"

"I think so. Mama and Papa like him, so I should like him. Papa *really* likes him. He took me to see Papa on St. Stacie and we had a fun time." The subject was dropped and never came up again.

***

Brian's trip with JM did little to temper his attitude towards his sister Lillian. It was during the Christmas celebrations at the end of the year that Lillian fell down the stairs at home. Brian was playing with his new truck and cars at the bottom of the stairs when he called to his sister. She came running out of her bedroom to the top of the stairs and tripped headlong over a string Brian had tied across the second stair tread. The scream brought the whole house running, not before Brian had run to the top and removed the string. Lillian was more bruised and in shock than anything else. A small graze produced some blood, which took everyone's attention. Amid deep sobs, Lillian said that Brian had pushed her. Desmond pulled Brian aside and demanded to know what had happened. Brian sobbed as he said, "Papa I did not push her. I was at the bottom of the stairs when she fell."

"Then what were you doing at the top of the stairs when we came to see what was going on?"

"But Papa, I went up the stairs to see what she tripped on."

"How do you know she tripped on anything?" Angela Rose became involved.

"She fell Mama, she must have tripped." There was no getting to the bottom of what really happened. Brian's nanny, Linda, ushered him away while Angela Rose tried to calm her daughter down. She took her into her study and said, "I have a secret that I will share with you and you must not tell anyone one. It will be our secret." She placed Lillian on her bed and pulled out her scrapbook.

As she was explaining the pictures, Lillian saw a picture of the Zeplin and said, "Balloon. Mama. Big balloon."

"Yes, it is dear. It is so big that people can fly in that balloon, from one country to another country. Isn't that exciting?" When things had calmed down, she brought Lillian downstairs and whispered to her, before entering the parlor, "Remember our little secret, and don't tell anyone." This was to be the start of a bond between mother and daughter that would be based upon Angela Rose's own aspirations.

Two days later, when Linda, Brian's nanny, was preparing his clothes for the laundry maid she found a length of string in a pocket. It struck her as being odd and without knowing the reason why, she sat on the top stair and stretched the string across from rail to rail. She knew what had happened. Thinking better of it she took the string and went to basement coal burning furnace and threw the string in. She was not sure of how her discovery would be received, and decided to keep quiet about it. She valued her job too much to cause a problem.

Chapter 11

July 1926, The Buffalo Courier Express headlines announced that the US Government had formed the US Army Aircorps. This confirmed Angela Roses's belief in the future of air travel. Trans World Air had been formed in 1925 and Pan American Airlines was following close behind with flights from Key West to Havana, Cuba. Angela Rose's scrapbook had been steadily filled with articles and photographs. Lillian was now six and been comforted with the shared collection as a pacifier after frequent conflicts with her brother. The scrapbook had become her private connection with her mother that her brother was not allowed to penetrate. Brian, having seen her leave her mother's study after one such session, devised his plan.

Lillian often played in the garden on Sunday mornings while waiting for her mother to take her to church.. Brian, now nine, suggested playing hide and go seek. Lillian, always anxious to get into her brother's good graces, agreed to play. Brian was to hide first. He ran into the carriage house and took the key to the side door from the inside of the door and put it in his pocket. He climbed up into the attic and propped an empty, tall, large wooden crate up with a stick. Tying a length of string to the stick he threw the ball of string out of the upper window, where it fell onto the lawn behind the building. He quickly exited the carriage house and hid behind a garden shrub where he could watch his sister. She walked slowly down the garden calling out "I'm coming, I'm coming." Noticing the side door of the carriage house was open, she went in. Brian threw a stone onto the roof knowing that she would follow the sound. He slowly pulled the string and the loud clatter of the box enticed Lillian up the ladder to the attic. Brian ran out from the back of the building and locked the carriage house door. There was a cracked windowpane with a small piece missing in the door. He pushed the key back through the hole and ran indoors. "Mama, Mama, I was playing go hide and seek with Lillian and I can't find her. I think she went down the street. Help me find her Mama, please help me find her."

Lillian asked, "Why do you think she went down the street?"

"I don't know Mama, I've looked in the carriage house, behind all the bushes. I then found her hankie down at the end of the drive." Lillian called for the nannies and they went off in different directions calling out Lillian's name. Almost an hour passed before they returned. Lillian was distraught. Brian, sitting on the front steps of the house, was quietly watching the happenings. As his mother walked back up the drive Brian jumped up and said, "Mama I think she is in the carriage house. I can hear her shouting."

"Why didn't you open the door?" Lillian asked exasperatedly.

"I don't have the side door key and the front doors are too heavy for me. Please help me Mama." Angela Rose, with the nannies help, managed to slide the huge wooden doors aside on their rollers to release a sobbing, hysterical Lillian. Hugging her daughter to her breast, Angela took her inside the house while the nannies billed and cooed in attempts to sooth the child. Brian took advantage of the chaos to quickly remove his string trap. Picking up the key he went into the kitchen and said to his mother, "Mama I found the key to the side door on the floor just inside the door on the floor. I think that when Lillian went into the carriage house, she must have banged the door and the key fell out."

Linda, Brian's nanny quickly snapped, "How did the door get locked then?"

Angela Rose said, "Now, now, everything is alright. Lillian is safe. Let's not dwell on things.

Lucy, Lillian's nanny said to Linda, "I think we both know what's going on here."

Linda's reply was. "It's all over now. Nobody's hurt." She leaned over to Lucy and whispered, "Let's not rock the boat on this one. It could get ugly for us both." Soon things settled back to normal and going to the church visit was cancelled for that day.

Chapter 12

Two days before Christmas, the north bound No. 2 train, The Ponce De Leon express from Florida to New York was going full speed as it approached Rockmount in Georgia. Train No 101, The Royal Palm had stopped to take on water in Rockmount. The crew of the 101 panicked when they saw The Ponce De Leon express heading for them at full speed and jumped and fled from their stations. The wreckage and destruction were horrendous. The railway officials and engineers were blamed but that did little to usage the devastation as nineteen people died and a hundred and twenty-three were injured. On his way to Buffalo for the holidays from The Royal Palisades, Michael St. John-Brown was one of the dead.

***

Penelope St. John-Brown, Michael's wife, at age 75, was frail. The news of her husband's death drained her spirit. She was inconsolable. Angela Rose tried to cajole her mother with the fact that the children were excited about Christmas and she felt their joy would ease some pain. Not so. Brian and Lillian were oblivious to the tragedy that pervaded the occasion. Christmas night, when the children were in bed, Penelope sat by the fireside with her daughter and Desmond. She asked them to listen carefully to what she was about to say. "I have lived a good life. Your father, for all his stubbornness, his arrogance and his faults, I loved him. How I hated him when he lost his fingers at that infernal boiler. How I hated him when he wanted to blame others for his own faults. I was never blind to his downside, but my word, did he have a good, kind, caring side. I always knew when he was unfaithful to me, but I was able to overlook that because you know what? I worshiped the very ground he walked on. I know it sounds silly to hear an old lady ramble on, but these last few days have made me see that if you have something to say, say it. Tomorrow just doesn't come to some of us." She started to weep and Desmond and Angela Rose sat silently allowing her the dignity and time to compose herself.

Desmond reached out and held his mother-in-law's hand and said, "Is there anything I can do, we can do for you?"

Penelope composed herself looked directly at Angela Rose and continued. "You come from a long line of hard-working, intelligent, strong men and women, wonderful people my dear. Henry VIII, can you believe we are connected to that line of blood? Your grandparents, all of them, stood for something, they made something of themselves. I look at you children with your own families and I see myself, tired. I am tired and weary." Turning to Desmond she said, "I want you to take charge

493

with Angela Rose and do what you will with the businesses. I think you should probably keep the Bath properties for a little longer."

Desmond said, "I'm not sure that I understand what you are asking."

"I know that you will both look after me, so I am not worried. I just don't want anything to do, any folderol, legal or otherwise. I just want to relax and enjoy the rest of my life without concerns. I would like you to get JM to prepare a document that hands everything over to you two, worries and all. I just want to not worry any more. Your father was my rock, my warrior and my worrier; he did *all* that for me. I don't want to do it without him." Angela Rose spoke quietly and said, "Mama, whatever you want, we will take care of it for you after the holiday."

Chapter 13

The day after Boxing Day, Angela Rose telephoned JM and requested that he stop by the house for a business meeting. Having been duly summoned, he arrived. Angela Rose had the maids show him to her study where she sat at her desk sporting a serious expression. JM removed his coat and threw it on a couch. Sitting down, he spoke first, "My word you look so serious, what's wrong?"

"We need to get Father's body back here to Buffalo and arrange the funeral. I know it's a lot to ask, but could you take care of that for us?"

"Most certainly. I will get everything ready for your mother's approval as quickly as I can. There's something else, what is it?"

"I feel empty inside. It is difficult to focus on anything."

JM moved over to Angela Rose and took her hands in his and said, "It is very hard losing a parent and I feel for you. I wish I could bring you comfort, but I know that we all have to go through this at our own pace." Angela Rose suddenly burst into tears and JM held her close to his chest until her sobs were over.

"You are going to cry a lot more my dear. We should try and be strong for your mother, after all, she has lost her husband and for you that doesn't seem important right now because you have lost your father. Strange as it may sound, those two things are so different."

Angela Rose dried her tears, clasped her hands together in her lap and said, "That's not all."

"What more could there be?"

"Mother wants you to prepare, what I think is called a power of attorney."

"For what?" exclaimed JM.

"She wants nothing to do with any of the family affairs. The businesses, the properties in England, anything."

"What does she want?"

"She wants Desmond and I to take care of everything. For you to make it happen."

JM sat silently, contemplating what he had just been told before he replied, "Do you realize that you will now be running the entire St. John-Brown Empire, everything?"

"I do and it frightens me."

"I need to meet with your mother. Please understand that my first meeting with her on this subject should be private. I need to be sure that everything she instructs me to do is of her own free will."

Angela Rose looked confused at JM, "What are you suggesting?" she spat out.

"Nothing, absolutely nothing. It is important that I do it this way to protect you and of course Desmond, in the future. We cannot have any appearance of impropriety."

"Oh, I understand. We should take care of this quickly, as mother is very frightened about her future and will not relax until she thinks everything is in order."

JM smiled as he said, "On my way over here I was excited thinking you wanted to ravish me, or have me ravish you and was I ever wrong."

"No, you weren't wrong, but that just doesn't seem right just now, but don't be upset with me. It makes feel so good that you are here for me to turn to. I treasure you."

"And so you should. I understand. I would just be taking advantage of you at a vulnerable time. I wouldn't want you to know…think that."

Angela Rose said, "Then let me tell mother you are here. She is staying with us for a while until she adjusts to things."

***

Penelope asked JM to sit beside her in the parlor. Holding her cold hands in his, JM said, "These are hard times for you. Angela Rose has told me of your wishes. I need to hear them from you. I am going to take some notes to be sure that I fully understand your wishes and don't leave anything out."

"I trust you my dear, just as Michael did. Do what you have to." Penelope made it quite clear that she wanted Angela Rose and Desmond to have everything and to run everything.

"But Mrs. St. John-Brown, that can be taken care of with a will."

"No, no, not a will. I want it to happen now. I don't want to be bothered with anything."

"Please explain."

Penelope thought for a moment and then, choosing her words carefully, she said, "I want Angel Rose to have the final say in any decisions that are made. Dear Desmond is a fine young man, but he is from that *other* family. I'm sure you know what I mean."

Very quickly JM said, "What if there is some sort of conflict? I mean what if I feel that she is not acting on her own free will, but is being encouraged to do something that I feel is not in her, or your best interests?"

"You're a lawyer man, write it up so that cannot happen. Can't you make yourself a power of attorney along with her?"

"If that is your wish, it could be done, but I don't advise it." After thinking for a moment, he suggested, "I could become a adjunct power of attorney, no I still don't like that. What do you think of my having the authority to…? Let me think on this a little more. Now that I know what your wishes are, I will work something out."

"Then off you go young man. I can rest a little easier now, but please, let's make haste and get this burden off my shoulders."

***

Two days later, JM held a private meeting with Penelope at his downtown office, where he went over the document he had prepared. "Mrs. St. John-Brown, let me go through the form I have prepared for you. Would you like me to read through it or just explain the thrust of its meaning?"

"An explanation will be enough. The legal mumbo jumbo always confuses me."

"The document is a simple power of attorney whereby you are giving all your legal powers to your daughter, Angela Rose, without taking them away from yourself. In other words, you both, or either of you, have those powers. I felt this is sufficient as it does not preclude Desmond from his input, but what it does do, is have Angela Rose in complete control."

"I understand, but what about if he pressures her?"

"Do you really think that could happen?"

"One can't be sure about everything. I would like some safeguard."

"Good. That's what I thought. That is why I have a clause in the document that provides myself with a fiduciary power to implement any decisions that she may make on your behalf, or to veto them."

"What does that mean?"

"Simply put, it means that I would be given the legal or ethical responsibility of making sure that your confidence or trust is not being violated."

"That doesn't sound simple to me."

"In layman's terms, if I think that your daughter is being coerced or being forced to make a decision that is not her own, I have the right to prevent it happening."

"I like that. Let me sign this thing and get it taken care of."

JM called his personal assistant into is office and had her witness the signing. As he walked Penelope to the door he said, "I do hope that we will see more of you. You mustn't lock yourself away from the world. When you have come to terms with your husband's passing, you must not hesitate to call on me. I am more than willing to have the occasional dinner with you. Even beat you at a hand of whist. Sometimes just plain old company is comforting."

Penelope turned, offered her hand to him and said, "You are a good man JM. The family was so lucky to have found you." With that, she left. JM closed the door, leaned against it, closed his eyes and thought to himself, "That was easier than shooting fish in a barrel. Oh my, one step closer."

Chapter 14

1929, Brian had moved onto Canisius High School. The school was located at Main and Jefferson Street, walking distance from the St. John-Brown home on Delaware Avenue. Sometimes his sister would meet him on his way home from school to walk with him. She had never stopped trying to connect with him despite his rebuffs. Brian's friends would frequently taunt her about one thing or another. It was not every day. No sooner would one day pass, that the boys would be friendly and nice to her, when the next day one of them would taunt her. "Where did you get that squashed tomato nose? You're not Goldilocks, you're Blackilocks." The other boys would laugh at her features. The jibes poked at her appearance, her size, what she was wearing and many other things. Brian always stayed in the background, only coming to her defense as the group would approach their home.

Soon summer came and family rituals changed. Lillian was allowed to have her school friends over to play one day and Brian was allowed his friends the next day. Lillian was only allowed to have her friends around the house and garden, whereas Brian was allowed to go to Delaware Park or to the ice cream parlor with his friends, unsupervised. Sometimes the boys would just hang around the carriage house and play cards or talk boy talk. It was one of these carriage sessions that the gardener had overheard a disturbing conversation. The boys were up in the attic of the building as the gardener was cleaning his tools below. He overheard one boy say, "Alright Brian, time to pay up."

Another boy said, "I have been keeping a list." He then named each boy, "Kenny, 4 times, Billy, 3 times, Roy, 5 times, Michael, 7 times, he's the champion, then me, I did it five times. So, pay up." The gardener did not understand what the conversation was about but felt something was not right. He went to the kitchen and told the cook what he overheard. She went straight to Angela Rose and repeated what she had been told. Angela Rose was in her study with Lillian poring over the scrapbook of flight. She thanked the cook, who turned and left the room. As if to herself, but out loud she said, "I wonder what that's all about?"

"I know Mama, I know."

"How would you know what those boys are up to?"

I think it has something to do with me, Mama, because when I sometimes go to meet Brian coming home from school, his friends tease me."

In a puzzled tone, her mother asked, "Now why would you think that has any-thing to do with this?"

"Because when the boys tease me, the other boys would say a number. I never knew what it was for. I do know that Michael teases me more than the other boys. I thought it was because he likes me. That must be what the numbers are." Angela

Rose was angry. She wasted no time in having her husband and Brian in a meeting. In front of Brian, she relayed the story that came from the Gardener, via the cook.

Brian became obnoxious as he said, "They are the hired help. You can't believe everything they say. They don't like me."

Desmond said, "Why do you think they don't like you? That's ridiculous."

"It's not as ridiculous as what they do behind the carriage house," was the retort.

"Just what do they do behind the carriage?" asked Desmond

Angels Rose raised her voice in anger, "Don't try to change the subject. This is about you, not about the cook and gardener."

Brian stared out of the window with an insolent glare and said, "Animals, they go at it like animals."

"I told you, it isn't about them. This about you." Angela Rose's voice became agitated.

Desmond looked her and asked, "Did you know about this?"

Angela Rose replied, "Don't let the boy deflect this. I am more concerned about what our children do than what consenting adults do. Brian! Are you paying your friends to taunt your sister?"

"It's only in fun. Nobody's getting hurt."

"Your sister is. What about her feelings? Don't you care about your sister?"

Brian stood with a sullen look and said, "Not as much as you do."

Desmond, in a rare show emotion, shouted at Brian, "Go to your room! No friends for a week! No pocket money for a month, now get out of here!"

Angela Rose followed Brian to the door and slapped Brian on the back of the head as he left the room.

"Ow." yelled Brian at the top of his voice as he stormed to his room.

"What are we going to do with that boy?" she exclaimed to Desmond.

"That's your domain." Desmond said as he left the room.

Angela Rose shouted out after him, "Valentines' Day massacre. That's how the Al Capone thing got started. A gang killing people they don't like. A massacre. Our boy could end up that way. He is nothing better than a gang member. What do you think of that?"

***

Towards the end of summer, the previous incident slipped into being a memory. Angela Rose and Desmond's relationship was strained. Matters at home seemed to pale in comparison to the news that hit America in December of that year. The great depression hit the country and things were about to change.

Christmas celebrations were held at the family home on Delaware Avenue. Penelope, who was spending more time with her daughter, was there. Nathaniel and Agatha had come to America from *Cinnamon Reef* in Anguila, bringing the whole St. John-Brown and Blacksmith clans together. After the Christmas day dinner, with all around the table, JM proposed a toast. "I am always greatly warmly when all the family comes together, especially as you include me. As you all know times are taking a grave turn financially speaking. We are fortunate in that those of the family who are now departed have placed you all in a very fortunate position of being cash rich as well as asset rich. I have made a careful study as to where you all stand. Nobody knows how long this depression is going to last. I would like you all to raise your glasses and toast those of the family who are no longer with us." He raised his glass and said, "The family."

Angela Rose responded, "What do you see our position being in relation the our stocks both here and in England?"

"It is my recommendation that you sit tight and do not divest yourselves of any, and I mean any, stocks. This will pass, but no one knows when. Stocks will rebound. It might take a long time, but they will. You are going to hear lots of talk about their value dropping and how people will lose money. If you don't sell, you don't lose. Yes, the paper value goes down, but it is just that, paper. The value of that paper will go back up when things get better. The only people that will sell shares are those who need the cash to survive. This family doesn't"

Nathaniel asked, "Doesn't that mean our worth, or value goes down?"

"Your worth or value is perceived to be what you own. Who cares what you own? It is more important to weather the storm than it is to worry about what others think your worth is."

Angela Rose added, "That's an excellent point you make. In the light of your comments, it is almost embarrassing to have just enjoyed such a sumptuous feast. Do you think we should be cutting back?"

Nathaniel said, "Maybe not such a bad idea for now."

"I am just suggesting that you don't have any knee-jerk reactions to what is happening. Just be prudent."

That evening as Nathaniel and Agatha were preparing for bed, Agatha asked Nathaniel, "Where does this JM come from, do you think he is black?"

"My dear, you are 88 and you still have not waived in your thing about black people."

"I am just asking. That's all."

"For your information, Angela Rose tells me he is of French Moroccan decent. Damn nice fellow if you ask me. He certainly has his head screwed on the right way."

"I was just asking. That's all."

Chapter 15

1931, Angela Rose' flight scrapbook was so full that she started a second. It was referred to as Lillian's scrapbook. The previous year a whole new career field had been developed for the airlines, that of a stewardess. It was all Lillian could think about, working on an airplane. In May Amelia Earhart flew from America to Ireland. This firmly convinced Angela Rose that her growing passion for flight was well founded. She believed that it would not be long before airplanes would be flying all over the world. She started to consider that Desmond's shipping interests were insignificant. Had her grandparents' business, The Royal Shipping Line, not been so big and such an income generator, she would have sold out her shares in it. She was often reminded of JM's words that cash was important and Royal Shipping Line was bringing it in. It was sad news that made her wish the development of flight had evolved further. Her mother, who had been living with her at the Delaware Avenue home, died while Angela Rose had been to see the famous Greta Garbo in the film Mata Hari at the Shea's theater. When she opened the front door the cook, the maids and the housekeeper, were seated on the bottom of the staircase. She had noticed that the chauffeur was unusually quiet when he drove her, but thought no more of it. She was about to ask what was going on when JM walked down the stairs, he said, "I am so sorry. She went peacefully." She stood immobilized as she was told how her mother had been found. "Cook had taken her afternoon tea up to her and assumed she was sleeping. When she went to bring the tray down, she discovered the old lady was dead."

"I'm sorry miss, the only person I could think to fetch was Mr. JM.

"That's fine. Can I see her?" she asked JM.

"That should be alright. I'll take you up. We have called for the doctor. He should be here soon."

"Why do we need the doctor if she has already gone?"

"Death certificate my dear."

"She looks so peaceful. I do hope she didn't suffer. If only I hadn't gone to the show."

JM, in an effort to calm her down, said, "Look at the bed. Nothing is disturbed. It looks like she came in, laid down and died. There is no ruffling of blankets or anything. The doctor should be able to tell us how she died. I don't think even if you were here there was anything you could have done."

Penelope was laid to rest in The Forest Lawn Cemetery, not far from the family home. Desmond and JM, one on either side of Angela Rose, led her from the graveside service. She said the she would rather walk home than be driven. The three of them walked in silence, each to their own thoughts. As they walked through the huge stone edifice of the entrance, they decided to sit on a stone bench. The afternoon sun bathed them in a calming aura. Carriages and automobiles busily scurried by unaware of the sad tableau by the gates. As they sat basking, JM pointed to the Park Lane restaurant across Gates circle and said, "Why don't we go and have a quiet drink? I know someone there that can find a quiet corner for us."

***

When they ensconced themselves in a private corner with a cocktail, the obliging waiter left them to their privacy. JM said "We should talk about what you want to do now that your mother has gone."

"What is there to do?" asked Desmond.

"As you know," he said to Angela Rose, "The Royal Crescent properties are still in your mother's name. There is probate to be taken care of as well as for the other properties around Bath, plus there are other matters I need to look into for you that might take a few days for me to sort out." JM leaned back waiting for a response

"What about the stock in the other business'?" asked Desmond.

"The stock is held in a company trust that will not be affected." Turning to Angela Rose he continued, "It might be more efficient if you both go to England with me.

Desmond quickly said, "Oh, we can't do that. One of us can go, but one should stay with the children."

"Well, Angela Rose should be the one to go because she has the power of attorney to sign things." Suggested JM.

"She should go with you?" said Desmond.

JM became a little unnerved at the comment. He thought to himself, "Does Brian really know so little about the situation?" The subject was changed and they reminisced about the family's history. It was decided that Angela Rose would go and JM made the arrangements for the trip.

***

Lying beside each other in bed after the rough day, Desmond held Angela Rose close and asked, "Do you feel alright about going to England with JM, alone?"

"Yes, he is always a gentleman, and, I would like to get all the business put to rest over there. We are American and with my mother and father gone, as well as Grandmamma and Grandpapa gone, there isn't much reason for me to have ties there."

"We still have my ties. Well, my Ma and Pa don't go back much, but they have the businesses their parents left them, and they can be run from anywhere." Desmond lay silently as he thought about what he was going to say next. "The Royal Circle in Bath, I think that if you sell everything else, you should keep those homes."

"Why? It's just something else to be concerned about."

"When I look back at the Mary Jane, I see a tangible connection to where everything started for my family. It is the one thing our children can see, touch and feel that connects them to their past instead of just wealth."

"I suppose I could put the homes into a trust. Grandpa's for Brian and Papa's for Lillian. When they are old enough, they can do with them as please. I like that, a tangible connection." She leaned over and kissed her husband, saying, "I love you Desmond Blacksmith. Our lives have been quite a journey, haven't they?"

Desmond leaned over, pulling her close to his chest, and opened one eye to look at the pillow. To his relief there was no dead man grinning back at him. They made love, slowly and passionately and all was well.

Angela Rose lay in her warm bath, the next morning and replayed the previous nights' events in her mind. It was so strange how her husband could be so gentle and sensuous one time and them pull away from her as if she had the plague the next time. She thought, 'If only he would share what bothers him, is it me or something else?' JM never had any trouble wanting her. 'He was always ready willing and very capable." The two men in her life were such polar opposites. When it came to sex, one did only what he had to while the other did whatever he could when he could. JM was so comfortable with his sexuality, she felt blessed.

Chapter 16

1935, Brian was to spend his summer in between Buffalo and *Cinnamon Reef,* on Anguila with his grandparents. The hotel was nearing the completion of its upgrades and Brian enjoyed his grandparents' company. He knew that Grandma Agatha who was 86 and grandpa Nathaniel who was 89 were nearing 'being called' as they referred to it. Desmond, Brian's father had been spending a lot of time on the island, as if he was also expecting Agatha and Nathaniel 'to be called', and he wanted to be there. One evening back in Buffalo Angela Rose had their full attention after dinner as she said to Desmond, "Our son, what plans do you have for Brian?"

"If he wants to, he can follow in our footsteps and learn the business. I think he is quite capable of doing whatever it is he wants to. You have to remember my dear the young people of today live in a world so different to the one we are used to. I am happy to support whatever direction he chooses."

"Are you suggesting we do nothing?" Agatha was becoming agitated.

"You can't control everything, especially the young people. Let's wait and see where his interests lie. I suspect they will be with the business."

Brian had been studying business and had spent his previous summers at The Royal Palisades or in New York City. He fancied himself quite a man about town. Desmond would spend countless hours in his study with Brian going through his plans and what was happening with the growing hotel business. They now owned five luxurious hotels that catered for the incredibly wealthy. The dots on the wall map were in Sydney Australia, Naples, Italy, Istanbul, Turkey, Buenos Aries, Argentina and, Rio De Janeiro in Brazil. The style and elegance of these five properties were distanced from the Caribbean hotels by their sheer price. Desmond had decided that the smaller, more intimate style of the islands' hotels suited their locations. The very high-end properties were in major international destinations. He reasoned the customer base already existed in those locations. All he had to do was to make things a lot better than anything else that existed in there. "Give the locals something to aim for." was his favorite expression.

In the same summer, Lillian, now 16, was preparing to go to college and spent all her free time at Lake Erie summer cottage of family friends and so was not at the family home very much. Brian had only been at home a few days when one of his meetings with his father was interrupted by the parlor maid, "I'm sorry to disturb you sir, do you or master Brian know where miss Lillian might be?"

"No," answered Desmond, "I haven't seen her since, Sunday I believe she at the lake with friends. Why do you ask?"

"There is a young lady here to see her, A Miss Livingston."

"Show her into the parlor," interjected Brian "I will speak with her." He excused himself from his father and went to his room. Standing in front of a mirror, he combed his hair, straightened his clothes, admired himself and went to the parlor. When he opened the parlor door, he saw a girl he did not recognize. She was five feet eight, had long wavy blond hair and was well developed for her age. Somewhat set aback, as he was expecting a childlike friend of his sister, he struggled for words and came up with, "Miss Livingston, I presume?"

"Pretty close to something someone else once said, except, you, are not Mr. Stanley." The girl had an enticing laughter as she spoke. "You may call me Silla. That's short for Priscilla, Brian."

"I do not recognize you. You look so much older than Lillian. Was my sister supposed to be here to meet you?

"Oh no, I have just come back from Toronto with my parents and thought I would stop and see if L wanted to do something."

"I have never heard Lillian referred to as L. Maybe you and I could do something until she turns up." He suggested.

"That would be nice." Scilla said with a giggle.

They decided to go to the local Ice cream parlor. As they walked, Brian told her all about himself and what he was going to do, going to be and his great ideas. Scilla listened patiently. Every time she raised Lillian as a subject, he would change it round to himself. Periodically he would put his arm around her shoulder and she would shrug it off. He tried holding her hand at which she would move her pocket book to that hand. While they sat in Parkside Candy store enjoying their ice cream, Brian could not keep his eyes of her fine lace brassier that he could see through the light cotton summer dress she wore. She made no sign that she was aware of his glances. Slowly, they wandered back to the house and Scilla allowed Brian to hold her hand. By the time they got to the house, Brian had worked up the courage to ask, "Would you like to see my room?"

"No! Your parents are at home. You could show me the carriage house though. We could be looking at your father's new automobile." They went in through the side door of the carriage house and before them was the brand new 1935 Plymouth sedan. It was the epitome of luxury. Brian held the door open and Scillia climbed into the back seat. To his surprise, as the door clicked closed, she leaned over and kissed him. "Oh, this is sexy, don't you think?" Brian wasted no time on making his move. He touched her breast and when she did not object, he slid his hand down the front and cupped her warm flesh. In his mind, the god of sex had blessed him. He was hard and ready. He moved his hand to her crotch and she quickly pushed it away. "What's wrong?" he asked.

"Let me help you." she said. She moved her hand to feel his swollen penis through his trousers. Trying to undo his fly buttons, she struggled. He slid his bottom forward in the seat, undid his own buttons and proudly allowed his erection to stand in full view. Briefly, she held it in her hand. He savored he cool palm on his heat. She stopped and opened her pocket book appearing to look for something.

"What are looking for?" he gasped.

"My magnifying glass, I've never seen a willy so small. "Will it get bigger if gets hard?" she asked. Her words stunned him. Instantly he lost his erection. She giggled again and said, "Oh my look, it's getting even smaller. You need to tie a string to it so that you can locate it." Brian felt like he had been punched in the stomach. He launched himself out of the car, and out of the carriage house and strode into the house as he buttoned his fly. Preicilla straightened her clothes and walked down the drive with her shoulders held high and whispered into the afternoon breeze, "That one's for you, Lillian."

Later that afternoon, Lillian took the phone call from her friend Clarissa. "He thinks your friends call you L and get this, he thinks my name is Scilla, short for Priscilla. I even told him he needs to tie a piece of string to his willy so that he could find it." Both girls laughed. At the end of the conversation Clarissa said, "All we have to do now is continue with the plan."

***

A few days later, Brian had recovered from the sting of his incident with Priscilla when he heard his sister ask, "Can Clarissa come to dinner this evening? Her parents are going to the show and she doesn't want to?" Angela Rose agreed.

Brian asked, "Have you seen your friend Scilla lately?"

Lillian said, "No, I think she is in Toronto with her parents." Brian relaxed a little. He thought to himself, "A mans' got to save his reputation. I am going to fuck this one of her friends to straighten the record once and for all." At six o'clock sharp, as was the family ritual, they sat down for dinner. Brian was missing. Desmond sat at the head of the table. Angela Rose to his righthand side. Across from them sat Lillian and Clarissa sat with her back to the door.

"Ah there you dear." Angela Rose said to Brian as he entered the room.

Desmond, looking at his wristwatch, simply said, "Punctuality."

Lillian looked at Brian and said, "I would like you to meet my friend Clarissa." Clarissa stood up, turned and held her hand for Brian to shake. Brian recoiled as if bitten. He tried desperately to fight off the deep blush he felt creeping slowly up his neck onto his face until his ears glowed crimson. He turned and left the room without saying a word. Both girls quietly started singing, "Tea for two and two can tease." in tune with the popular song. Desmond cautioned, "No singing at the table girls, come on. Behave yourselves."

***

Desmond waited until later that evening before seeking Brian out. Knocking on Brian's door he called out, "It's me, Pa, can I come in?""If you must." was Brian's sulky reply. As he entered the room, Brian saw that he had box file under his arm. He watched his father put the box down on the bed and opened it saying, "You know that your sister and mother have been collecting articles and things to do with flight."

506

"So, what of it?" Brian was being difficult.

"I'm not here to talk about your sister. I want to share something that is mine, with you."

Brian swung round and sat on the edge of the bed, now he was ready to listen. Desmond started to lay papers out across the bed in small stacks. Brian noticed some of them were official looking documents and others were articles from magazine and or newspapers. "What are these?" His interest was perked.

"Just give me a minute to sort them out." Desmond continued until the box was empty. He then pulled a chair over to the bedside and started to explain. "Young people like yourself think that you have the world by the balls, and in many ways you do. Older people like me think we know better than you. In a way, we are both wrong. The only time that I see any difference between young and old is the realm of ideas. There is nothing wrong with old ideas, but many new ideas are better than the old ones. Some new ones are just plain stupid, but many are very interesting. For a long time now, I have been watching and following new ideas."

"Why Pa, what interests you in them?"

"It's all in how you look at them. Example; what do you think of when you see an automobile?"

"A way to get from a to b without much effort, in comfort."

"I see a machine than can make life easier, that saves money. I see something that can be used for more than traveling."

"I don't understand. An automobile is an automobile. What more can it do?"

"Consider for a minute if the engine drives the wheels, how hard is it to lift the back off the ground, put blocks under it and run a belt off the wheels? Now your automobile can run a generator or anything else that needs to turn."

"That's clever Pa. Why don't they use the automobiles to do that now?"

"Because they haven't arrived at that point yet. What I am trying to show you is that if you look at new inventions carefully, many of them have other uses besides what they were designed for."

"OK, so what are all these papers?"

"For a long time now, I have been buying rights to patents, or a license to use the patent. Let me show you some." Desmond went to explain each patent he had rights to, as he did, he would put each set of documents back into the box file.

"The electric washing machine; I have the rights to sell these throughout the Caribbean. This machine was designed to make life easy for the lady of the house. Think how many islanders can use it. Now think of the just the hotels alone that we own. I want to get one down to St. Eustasius and take it apart and see how we can refunction it. There has to be many uses."

"The Aerosol can. This is a fairly new patent. Anything can be put into an aerosol can under pressure. You can spray those things out of it without the aid of pumps. It gives a steady, regular spray. Paint is the obvious thing. But look around us, how many things come in bottles that could be better and less wastefully used. I see this thing becoming huge. I have limited rights of usage, but that doesn't bother me."

"The vacuum cleaner; that one I bought into, as I can only imagine the number of home-owners that would want one. This is a straight numbers game."

"Dirigibles; now, I know there have been a lot of accidents with them. I believe that is because they have been pushed beyond their limits. They have uses not yet thought of; after all, they are giant balloons. I'm not saying to do this, but if you wanted someone to find your home, your business or whatever, all you have to do is fly a smaller version of the thing. I have been watching your sister's airline interest and I can see that nudging dirigibles out of use. That should make the patent be really cheap at the right time."

"Air conditioning; now here's one that I am just not quite sure how to go about it. I can see it's uses, but I think the market might be gobbled up by the rich and powerful. I don't need to fight them. There are plenty of other ideas out there. I'm still following the concept though."

"Bicycles with motors; this I think has a great future. A powered bicycle is a lot less costly than an automobile; therefore, it has a much bigger market. Maybe not here, but in the islands and poorer countries."

Desmond spent most of the evening going through his collection with his son. Brian got caught up in the passion his father displayed. "Why are you showing me these Pa?"

"Because you are wasting so much energy in your battle with your sister. I think there is a better way to channel it."

"So, this is your way to get me off my sister's back?"

"Brian, grow up. If you are not interested in joining me on this journey, then that's your choice."

"Sorry Dad. I'm sorry. How can I get involved?"

"You can be my partner. Let me give it some thought about how we will do it and we shall talk some more." He stopped at the door, turned around and said, "This is just between you and me. Let's keep it that way for a while."

Chapter 17

Lillian had taken over the maintenance of the scrapbook. Her entries recorded Amelia Earhart's 1935 solo flight from Hawaii to California. How The China Clipper had flown 110,000 pieces of airmail from California to Manila. How, in 1937 Howard Hughes had set a record of flying from Los Angeles to New York in 7 and half hours. The large amount of news coverage of the devastating Hindenburg disaster in New Jersey. Howard Hughes had caught her imagination. The man was repeatedly appearing in articles about flight. She searched for articles about him in the papers, daily. He seemed to have his finger on the pulse of all things aeronautical.

Early in 1938, the population of Buffalo was consumed with a natural disaster that was to take center stage from January 23rd until April 12th. It all started with a tremendous windstorm that sent a deluge of Lake Eire ice downstream and over the Niagara Falls. The base of the falls quickly jammed up with such immense amounts of ice that the pressure pushing against the Falls View bridge abutments became severely damaged. On January 27th, the upper steel arch of the bridge collapsed into the river pulling the bridge off its Canadian side abutment. It was considered a dangerous situation. Early the next morning, a crowd gathered on the American side of the falls to witness the demolition of span using dynamite. Desmond, JM and Brian were on hand at what evolved into a party-like atmosphere. They were watching history being made. On April 12th and 13th, the remaining center section of bridge broke into two and slid beneath the lower falls. The three men were up early and were there to witness the final Canadian section drifting down the Niagara River on a huge ice floe. Very quickly, in a silent ballet-like salute to nature, it rolled off the floe and sunk into the deepest part of the river. It was never to seen again.

The great depression was lingering on and JM felt the need to bring the family together to review their financial position. Nathaniel and Agatha were unable to attend and requested a report on the meeting. They had also raised the subject of an agreement being made, similar to the one that Angela Rose's mother had put into place. JM met with Angela Rose, Desmond and the children, Lillian now 19 and Brian now 23.

"I felt the need to for us all to understand the position the family is in and to fully understand some of the fears that I am hearing around town.

"What fears?" asked Desmond.

"There are a lot of rumors that the depression is going to destroy our country. I don't believe so. There is much discussion about the war going on in Europe and we can say on the one hand it's not our war, but on the other hand, it is. We are closely tied to England, not only through our heritage but also through our assets over there."

"What are your thoughts on the companies we have an interest in in England?" asked Brian.

"As odd as it sounds, I have noticed a considerable spike in production at Mother's Fine Foods and at the Co-Op. I'm sure it's because of the fact that they are supplying the military effort. Does that mean they are making money? I think they are going to be in the same position as The Royal Shipping Line, and, your family were with last world war. They had to wait to get paid, but get paid they did. I feel if you are going to have debtor, you can't get better than the Government."

Angela Rose asked, "Do you see us getting dragged into the war?"

Brian jumped in with his opinion, "There is no way we can avoid it Mama. The sad business fact about war is that it will stimulate the economy."

Desmond quizzically asked, "How do you see that happening."

"War is a machine Papa. It needs to be fed, to be fueled. That means things have to be produced, sold, shipped. Many, many things."

JM held his hand up to intervene, "There is no need for us to worry. I don't ever see war coming to our shores, but I do see us having to do our part. I mainly wanted to get us together to allay any fears and to let you know that your positions are quite safe. Now, to change the subject, I think Brian and Lillian you may go, I need to talk with your parents privately." Under protest, Brian left and Lillian had no problem with leaving the parental decision to them.

"The other thing to discuss is that when I spoke with your parents, Desmond they raised the issue of a power of attorney arrangement similar to the one that your mother-in-law executed." JM waited for a response.

Desmond spoke slowly, as he looked from JM to Angela Rose, "Do you think there is a need for that? After all, Mama and Papa are still very active in the business."

"Desmond, your father is 90 and your mother is 98. 98, do you how many people live to a hundred? Not many. That having been said, I feel that you are more than capable of handling your responsibilities should they pass. There is the matter of assets the family has in England, many of which I am not privy to. You do need to make yourself aware of everything. I mean everything. I will be happy to help you in anyway. I think you should go to your parents and be sure of what they want. I can come out with you if feel it's necessary to prepare whatever paperwork may be needed. To this point my interest and focus has been on the St. John-Brown family because of what I am here to do. If you want me to slightly shift my perspective, I will.'

"I think JM is right. We do need to be sure your parents are happy with their position in things."

JM's predictions quickly came to pass when America became involved in World War II.

***

Brian and Desmond had been working together seeking out patents and ideas and developing a portfolio. Their time was spent between the hotel business and the portfolio. It was an exciting time for both. Desmond began to feel that he was connecting with his son. Their relationship was running on parallel, but separate tracks to Angela Rose and Lillian's. Frequently, both Brian and his father would go together to one of the islands on hotel business. Sometimes Desmond would send Brian off to pursue an invention or idea while he went to the islands alone. They had started to function well as a team. They secured interest in an invention by Edwin Land known as Polaroid Photography. It was the instantaneous availability of a photograph that they saw great potential in.

They had, by this time, acquired interests in a simple concept that Brian felt would storm the construction industry, The Phillips Head screw. The development of a digital computer by Bell Labs took them into stocks in Bell. Their stock portfolio increased with holdings in The Haloid Corporation, which had invented a photocopier. It was Brian that quickly related it's potential usefulness. He had frequently commented on the amount of paperwork and it's vulnerability. "Copies, Pa, copies. We could send copies of things and keep the originals." The advent of sound recording on magnetic tape in 1934 went partly unnoticed. To Brian's surprise, it was his father that brought his attention to it. He proposed that they watch this technology very closely. He compared it to rapid growth in technology that the radio had used. "It wasn't that long ago that our homes were quiet. Now, you can't go into a home that doesn't have a radio. That's how the world gets its news these days."

"But Pa, if the radio is so instant, who would want to record it?"

"I'm thinking more of music. Every time musicians come to Buffalo, they are mobbed with people wanting to hear them. Not everyone is able to."

"You must be living under a log Pa, that's what we have records for."

"I know, but there something about this tape thing that's.....I don't know I just have a feeling about this. Let's keep an ear to the ground."

In 1937, Brian got excited about the Russian invention of the Helicopter and discussed it with his father. He was surprised at the reaction he got. Desmond was firm and admonishing in his tone when he said, "Flight related things are your sisters' domain. We have a huge variety of other inventions to look at without stepping on your sisters' toes."

"Stepping on her toes, Pa? We could beat her to this one."

"Why might I ask, do you want to do that?"

"Because I can Pa, we can."

"I will not be part of it. This is not a competition between you and your sister."

"It is to me Pa. I want to be better than her." Desmond summoned the maid and asked her to fetch Lillian for him. When Lillian entered her father's study, she was surprised to see her brother there. She did not even know he was at the house.

"Hello Pa, did you need me for something?" She ignored Brian.

"Yes, we have been reading about this Russian fellow, Sikorski and his helicopter thing. Brian thought you should know about it."

"I did not Pa." Brian snapped.

"Thanks Pa. Ma and I have noticed, but thanks for thinking of us." As she turned to leave, making sure her father wasn't watching, she poked her tongue out at her brother and quietly closed the study door behind her.

In 1939, the looming event of war in Europe looked more and more as if it might drag America into the fray. America's involvement in the war effort put everything on hold. There was an ominous cloud gathering over America.

Chapter 18

It is now 1940 and President Roosevelt received the approval of the US Congress to finance the construction 50,000 airplanes. The morning the news had Lillian rush into her parent's bedroom waving the newspaper. She exclaimed, "Ma, Curtiss Wright over on Elmwood is looking for help."

Desmond sat up and said, "What the heck are you on about?"

"Curtiss Wrights over on Elmwood is looking for help. They are looking for women to work on the production line building airplanes. Pa, building airplanes. Ma and I could help the war."

"No way, not on my watch you don't."

"Wait a minute." Angela Rose sat up, and said, "Pass me the paper."

Desmond spoke while Angela Rose read, "I have nothing against hard work, in fact, I believe in it. But your mother, she does not come from a family where that would be approved of."

"Desmond Blacksmith, I can't believe what I am hearing. I don't have any family left to approve or disapprove, accept you and you just said you approve of hard work."

"I don't mind if Ma doesn't come, I'm going to go." Lillian stood with her hands on her hips.

"It's Mama, not Ma. That's so common. I won't let you go and work in a factory with all those men. I'll go with you."

Desmond threw his hands in the air as he said, 'Ma is common, but working in a factory isn't. I give up."

"Angela Rose got out of bed, turned leaned forward with her fists on the covers, started at her husband and said, "If anyone's family would not approve of a behavior Desmond Blacksmith, it would be your Grandpa Cane. He would be ashamed of you right now." With that she left the room to find her daughter.

***

Much to the chagrin of many Americans, on September 16th, The Selective Training and Services Act became law, 'The Draft', as it was to become known. Lillian and her mother were airframe technicians at the Curtiss Wright factory. Each afternoon as they walked home from their shift, they would excitedly discuss things about the building of airplanes. They were both proud of their exposure to airplanes. Lillian kept volunteering for new jobs in the factory and it was not long before she knew the aircraft from one end to another. When the Draft was announced they came home to find Desmond and Brian in a heated discussion. The discussion ended abruptly as Angela Rose entered the room. "What am I interrupting?" she asked.

"Pa wants me to join the Army." Was Brian's reply.

"I did not say the Army. I said the service."

"What's the difference?" sneered Brian.

"Let's back up a minute." Said Angela Rose, "Firstly, what the heck gives with you two children calling us Ma and Pa? Where does this come from all of a sudden?"

Lillian interjected, "Ma. Alright, Mama, we are both to old to be using baby talk. We sound like freaks when we are with our friends and we say, Mama and Papa. It's just not the way our generation talks."

Desmond lifted his hand, "Can we stay on the conversation at hand? I was telling Brian that as we are not going to be doing much travelling for a while, he should be a man and stand up for his country."

"*You* never did Pa." Brian said, rudely.

"There wasn't a war where I was needed."

"What about the first world war."

"America wasn't in that until the end and then we didn't have the draft."

"How convenient." Sneered Brian.

Angela Rose, asked, "Why do you think he should volunteer, if there is the draft."

"Because, he can volunteer for the service he wants. If he waits to be conscripted, he will go wherever they send him. I admit I don't want to see him go to a dangerous area, but I do want him do something. If he volunteers for a particular branch of the service, that's where they will put him."

Lillian sat down and spoke quietly and firmly, "Brian if you do not volunteer by the end of the month, you will be on your own. Every member of our family from my great grandparents to your father's great grandparents has fought for what they have and by God, so will you."

"Or what?" Brian sullenly asked.

"Oh, don't go there." said Desmond. He knew what his wife was going to say next. She did.

"If you are not willing to fight for what you have, then you will lose it. Do you understand me?"

"How will I lose it?"

"Quite simply. The family business will not employ someone who behaves that way."

"Disinherit me? You wouldn't."

Desmond and Angela Rose spoke in perfect unison as they said, "Oh yes we would."

Within 5 months, the Japanese had attacked Pearl Harbor and America was in the thick of the war. Brian volunteered for the Navy and by virtue of his business studies was sent to a naval supply base in Virginia where was to spend his time. He managed the victualing and stores for the supplies of ships. It was a detail-oriented management role. The clerical work suited him fine.

***

Every time Brian had leave, he would come to Buffalo to savor the comforts his family home provided. As time passed, he became more aggressive towards his sister. He had learned to be sneakier about his actions toward her. He would taunt her about being a common factory worker. It was obvious that he was jealous of the attention her fellow workers paid her and the admiration she received everywhere she went. She was always socializing with some young man. Her popularity emphasized his lack of friends. This he put down to the fact that he was stationed far from home. After a particularly offensive attack on her character, she confided in a male co-worker, who listened to her plan as she worked it out.

It took a great deal of control for Lillian to be nice to Brian for a week. When his guard was down, she said to him, "A few of the young men from the factory and their girlfriends are going out for drink, would you like to come?"

"You don't want me with your friends."

"Maybe I don't, but there a lot girls that work at the factory that just want to have fun and let off some steam. Come on, you don't have to be around me. Let your hair down before you go back to base. Wear your uniform and you won't have to buy a drink all night." she instructed.

On her insistence, Desmond drove with his sister beside him as they went to Ulrich's Tavern downtown on Ellicott Street. The tavern was bustling with activity and was spilling out onto the street. Lillian grabbed Brian's hand and fought her way into the bar dragging him behind her. Brian was glad that he had decided against wearing his uniform. What he didn't realize was that his haircut and stance gave him away as being military.

Before long, Lillian had disappeared and Brian made new friends. Kenny, who turned out to be a welder alongside Lillian, introduced him to every young girl that came along. Brian wasted no time on making his carnal thoughts known to each of them. They would quickly drift off, away from him. As Brian slowly became intoxicated, he became more and more amorous with each introduction, unaffected by the rebuffs. It wasn't long before he saw a woman who stood out from the revelers as she sat alone at the bar. She smiled at him each time she caught him looking in her direction. He soon went over and introduced himself. As night's darkness crept in, Brian started to become more suggestive with his comments and found no resistance. Eventually, he left with the woman and went to the car. "Nice car, this is, is it yours?"

"No, I am on leave and it's the family car." He held the door open for her climb into the back seat.

When the door was closed, she asked, "Shouldn't we wait for your sister?"

"No, she will have gone off with someone by now."

She leaned over and kissed him, pulled away and said, "We should move the car away from the front of the tavern so we can be more private." Brian clambered over the front seat and quickly pulled round the corner and parked in what appeared to be a quieter location. The woman was all over him. As she started to undress him and he laid back in anticipation thinking 'This is going to be easy.' She slowly unbuttoned his shirt, undid his belt without any objections. When she had him fully undressed, she started to massage his erection. She looked up to see his head lain back on the seat and his eyes were closed. Suddenly she stopped. She put two fingers in her mouth and let out shrill whistle. Lying back in stunned silence, he watched her throw his clothes out of the open window and then shout to the crowd of women now gathered and staring in at him, "Roll up, roll up and see the man with smallest dick known ever to be given to a member of the human race. Roll up, roll up, no charge." Brian was immobilized. Before he could react, she quickly bent down and took his erection in her mouth. She proceeded to perform oral sex on him. While she did the act, she tied a small piece of string around his scrotum. He did nothing other than just lay there, sated and confused. He became embarrassed as she pulled away for all the girls gathered around the car to see his ejaculation. She wiped her mouth and said, "That will be ten dollars sir."

One of the girls outside shouted, "Fair rate mister, that's what we all charge." Suddenly Brian understood he had picked up a prostitute. He could not wait to leave. Shoving her out of the car he climbed over the front seat and screeched the tires as he left. The group stood and waved him off. The woman gathered up Brian's clothes and walked back into the tavern. She approached Kenny and said, "Mr. Kenny, you know how to show a lady a fun night and I didn't have to take my nickers off. I haven't had so much fun since I don't when. I got a few of the other girls to gang round and watch. It was a scream."

"Shirley, I owe you one." Lillian will be pleased. "Now what did we agree to?"

She replied, "Twenty dollars, but keep it. I really haven't laughed this hard ever."

"Would you like to go to his house to collect the money?"

"Now there's an idea. Tell me where."

***

The following morning at nine am, the doorbell rang and Angela Rose answered it. She saw a striking tall, blonde woman, who she estimated to be about forty years old. The woman said, "I was told to return these and pick up my fee here."

"What are those, what fee?" asked Angela Rose.

"I gave someone called Brian a blow job last night and held his clothes for security."

"Wait here. Angela Rose closed the door quietly and in an uncharacteristic bellow, shouted, "Brian! Brian Ojukwae! Get down here *now*."

Brian came down the stairs in his dressing gown with red, sleepy eyes he asked, "What's going on?"

"Your, damned prostitute is here to be paid." She thrust a twenty-dollar bill in his hand and said, "Get rid of her. Now!" Sheepishly, he did as he was told, but inside he was furious and embarrassed.

Later that day as Lillian passed Brian on the stairs, she handed him has underwear and sang in a whisper, "Tea for two, and two can tease." and gaily laughed as she walked away. Turning at the top of the stairs she said in a firm, commanding voice, "*Don't you* ever mess with me again, Brian Ojukwae. You will live to regret it. Remember, hell hath no fury et cetera et cetera"

Brian left that afternoon without saying goodbye to his mother. The cook attempted to wish him well and was rudely rejected with Brian saying, " What do you know about anything? Women don't want anything from men but money." JM, who had just come in the kitchen door, saw what was going on, he said to Brian, "I once heard a man say that as you go through life, you should play the cards that you've been dealt, not those that you want. You, young man are fast gaining the potential to be the joker in the pack." Brian said nothing and stormed out of the door, slamming it behind him. JM looked up to see Lillian standing across the kitchen staring at him, "That's not very nice." She said and turned on her heels.

Chapter 19

The year 1945 saw the end of World War II. May saw the end of the conflicts in Europe and September put an end to the Pacific side of the war. The economic thrust the war production had given America had lifted it out of the depression. The demand for armaments and airplanes stopped. Many women that had entered the work force to help the effort, quickly resumed their domestic roles. Angela Rose sat in her parlor awaiting the arrival of JM. She wanted to discuss her children's future. She felt that she had done her part and was ready to welcome Brian home when he was discharged from the navy. She had been perusing Lillian's scrapbook and was marveling at the surge in development and innovation in airplanes. She knew instinctively that this would be where Lillian would concentrate her goals. Brian, on the other hand, she was not so sure about. There had been a strained relationship around him since the prostitute event. She needed some guidance, other than her husband's off hand, 'just forget about it. He will be different when he comes home for good.'

JM, entering the room, broke into her thoughts. She patted the couch beside her for JM to sit. He leaned over and kissed her cheek. "I would kiss you more passionately, but I can see that you are somewhere else."

"No, not really. Well, yes. I was thinking about where we all go from here."

"What do you mean where we all go?"

"I know it's a little quick to be thinking about these things. I don't want to find myself, or Desmond, in the position that our parents were. Eighty years plus, old and scurrying around, trying to put things in order. I think plans should be made more leisurely." All the while she was talking, JM was gently stroking her thigh through her dress. She lifted her dress to cover his hand and continued as she felt his warmth causing her to lose her train of thought. "I know Desmond can't wait to get back to his overseas building program with the hotels. The children will be moving off in their own direction with high speed." She stopped talking and laid her head on the back of the couch.

JM knelt between her legs and reached up to her knickers. "Lift up, for me." he whispered. She did, and he slid her knickers down, dropped them in the floor and lifted her dress over his head. He did not hear her low throaty murmur as shift lifted her hips and felt his tongue touch her point of no return. Clamping her legs tightly around his head she jerked up, arched her back, and climaxed. He stayed where he was gently flicking his tongue. When he sensed her breathing return to normal, he pulled away, stood up and removed his trousers.

She watched as his erection, flared at the end, looked angry. "How do you want to do this?" she asked quietly.

"From behind. I want to see myself enter you. I want to hold you in a position where I am master." She turned; flipping her dress up over her back she spread her legs. He thrust into her with a violent motion.

"You feel so big, so wonderful." She wriggled to try getting him deeper inside her.

"And you are so wet, so tight, I can hardly control myself."

"Then don't. Give it all to me." He suddenly stopped moving, pulled her hips back firmly against his thighs and climaxed.

"My god," she said, "I can feel that deep inside me. Wow. I can't tell where you end and I begin. Oh….JM, I needed that!"

He replied, as he pulled out and playfully slapped her bottom, "Wasn't bad was it?"

After correcting their attire, they discussed having a family meeting to assess what direction the family was going in and how the resources could best be used. JM's advice was, "Lillian is local, I understand that she has finished at Curtiss Wright, so she is available when we need her. We don't know when Brian is going to be home, but I do think he will be discharged before Christmas. So, talk to Desmond and let's see if we can have a family conference before the new year, say between Christmas and the new year. Everyone should be around." Angela Rose decided to follow his advice.

Chapter 20

The lead up to Christmas was a flourish of activity filled with an abandon that had long been missing around the family home. Spending suddenly became an unleashed pleasure. Desmond had spoken frequently of 'really working' as he described it. He spent many hours listening to his daughter's infatuation with airplanes. Brian was conspicuously absent, although promising to be home for the holidays. He had been discharged earlier in the month and claimed he had things to take care of in Virginia before coming home. He came home on the afternoon of Christmas Eve, loaded down with wrapped gifts, which he handed to the maid, and her new assistant. He quickly disappeared with his father, into his father's study. He instructed the maids that they were not to be disturbed. Desmond had requested that their dinner be brought into the study. Their conversation went on long into the night. When Desmond, took a break to use the bathroom, Angela Rose approached him and asked, "What is going on? Why are you both locked away? This is supposed to be a family time."

The reply was simple. "It just a father son thing. I told Brian about our planned family meeting after Christmas and he wants to investigate and discuss his options with me and not in front of anyone else. Don't worry, nothing is wrong."

"If you say so, my dear."

Christmas day was a quiet one in the house. Angela Rose woke first and poked Desmond in the ribs as she said, "Happy Christmas, my dear."

"You too." was his mumbled reply. Angela Rose, feeling a little amorous, gently rubbed her husband's stomach and moved her hand down to his growing erection. She enjoyed arousing him. As he slowly reacted, she thought about the first time they had made love. Her thoughts increased her ardor. Slipping beneath covers she took him in her mouth. She heard him groan. Peeking up from under the covers she asked, "Am I hurting you?"

"Oh no. It feels so good. You should do this more often." She continued for a few more minutes. Sitting up, she threw her nightclothes off and mounted him. Her hands on his chest she gyrated slowly and watched his pleasure. "I want you on top of me. Be my master, dominate me, take me."

"No, no. Stay where you are. I am about to lose control." He did. He bucked and thrust and she hung on to him enjoying his satisfaction. As they still, she felt him throbbing inside and she climaxed, a slow powerful ending.

Flopping beside him they lay quietly. She eventually spoke, "Why don't you like being on top of me when we make love? You never seem to be able to be satisfied that way."

"It's nothing to worry about. I guess it's just the way I am."

"But is it something I do when we are like that?" She kept pushing the point.

Without thinking he snapped, "If you must know it's the captain, the captain. I can't get rid of the god dam captain."

"What captain? What are you talking about?"

"Now in an agitated state, Desmond jumped out of bed and said over his shoulder, "Nothing, nothing. I will tell you about when I am ready." He left the room.

***

Presents were exchanged between Mother, Father and Lillian. Brian did not come downstairs until the middle of the morning. He kissed his mother and his father, wishing them a happy day. He handed his sister his gift and left the room to get some coffee. There was a strained atmosphere pervading. After lunch, Angela Rose went up to Brian in his room and sat the edge of his bed. She asked, "What is wrong?"

"Nothing is wrong Mother. Didn't you like your gift? I am fine. I just have a lot of things I want to read and I have some decisions to make for my future."

"I know that dear. That's why we are going to have the family conference next week. Now why don't you come down and spend the day with your sister and us?"

"I don't want to spend the day with my *sister*. I'd rather not be in her company. I hate her."

Angela Rose was stunned by the outburst. "*Hate* your sister. Why do you dislike her so much, what has she done to you?"

"Mother I don't dislike her, I hate her. I have since the day she came into my house."

"Firstly, young man, *this is our house*, not yours. Your father and I have not raised you to hate anyone. You are being very disrespectful."

"Mother, I love you and Pa and I don't mean any disrespect. I am only here today *because* I respect and love you both. Lillian, well, she is Lillian and I have no time for her."

"She is your sister, your flesh and blood. What's wrong with you?"

"Mother, that's all she is, flesh and blood, I decide who I will give my love to. I will not be told who to love. She has been nothing but a pain in my side and frankly I'm tired of it."

"Then what do you propose to do about it?" Angela Rose snarled at him.

"Stay away from her. That's what, stay away from her forever." Angela Rose started to weep as she left the room without saying another word.

Angela Rose went to her husband and told him what had just passed. When she finished, he quietly said, "I know my dear. I had to listen to the whole thing last night. That's why we were so long in the study. I tried to reason with him. Tried to find out why, but to no avail. I think we just have to accept the fact that they want nothing to do with each other."

"So that's where we leave it?" Angela Rose was shocked.

"The more we interfere the worse it's going to get. I feel sad for Lillian. She doesn't seem to have the same angst towards Brian that he does to her. She seems accepting of the reality of the situation and is just getting on with her own thing."

Angela Rose asked, "So what is the point of the family meeting?"

"It would appear there isn't a reason to have it. Brian wants to work alongside me, learning all he can about the hotels, construction and development. I think he has the brain for it. Let him be, see if he comes round."

"And Lillian?" questioned Angela Rose.

"Our daughter does not need anyone to help her. She is focused. She knows what she wants. I think we should just have a discussion with her and see where we can assist and guide her. It would seem to be a good fit for her to be in the airline business, I think you know more about that than I do. Maybe I should mentor Brian and you mentor Lillian."

Angela Rose flopped into a chair and said, into the air more than to anyone, "Merry bloody Christmas. Who would have thought Christmas would have turn out this way."

Chapter 21

Upon the advice of JM, a variation of the planned meeting took place. Firstly, Angela Rose, Desmond and Brian met with JM. The meeting was strained and yet cordial. JM started with, "The purpose of this meeting is for us to see where we can help you in your plan for the future."

"You mean Ma and Pa can help me." interjected Brian.

"Yes, quite, it will be my job to make sure that you are protected legally in every way. That is, unless you wish to have separate counsel."

"That is not necessary. Because we have such a complex situation, both here and in England, JM will be your lawyer." Desmond was firm.

"I don't need his help." Brian was being combative.

"I can assure you, young man, that if your father and I need his guidance then you do." Said Angela Rose.

Desmond joined in, "If you wish to go ahead with what we discussed the other day, then JM is part of my conditions."

"So be it." said Brian.

Desmond proceeded to lay out how his son was going to be involved in the business and how that would be handled. JM took copious notes and suggested that he draw up a memorandum for them to have a record of the agreement. "Nothing binding, just a record to refer to, if needed. It will avoid misunderstandings later. Before you leave," he said to Brian, "there is one other thing to discuss." Turning to Desmond and Angela Rose he said, "There's the matter of the Royal Circle houses."

Desmond said to Brian, "Your mother and I want to transfer your grandfather and great grandfather's father's homes to you children. Do you have a preference for which one you want? We don't want you two having something else to bicker over when we are gone."

In a removed tone Brian said, "I would like grandpa's, but I won't fight over it. Give her the one *she* want's, she always gets her own way anyway."

***

Lillian's meeting was totally different from her brother's. JM stood and hugged her when she entered the room and said, "So now young lady, what do you see for yourself?"

523

"Well, as you all know mother and I are interested in airplanes. I would like to be a stewardess, but I know that is all glamour." Turning to JM she asked, "My shares in the two airlines, should I keep those, or sell them?"

JM thought carefully before answering, "Those are stocks in manufacturing. Things are only going to get better and grow quickly if the past is anything to go by. Listening to your mother, I think you would be better off in the service side of the industry as it develops. I'm not saying a stewardess is quite the right entry point."

"What do you think of me buying, or even starting a small airline? Perhaps a local one maybe? Papa, what you are doing with building hotels for the very rich, what if a I started a small airline for the very rich?"

"Now, there you go." Said Angela Rose. "That's thinking for you."

Desmond spoke next, "Because Grandpa and Pa started at the bottom, doesn't mean that you have to. I'm not saying that being a stewardess is the bottom. All I'm saying is that you can learn more about service to the public by serving the public. You certainly know a lot about airplanes and how they are built. That's a good foundation. I'm wondering is there any other areas that you could learn about before taking the giant leap of owning or starting a small airline?"

JM added to that line of thought with, "I think your father is right and I think you are right. There is a way of connecting the two. I have learned that we learn more from mistakes than we do success. Knowing how to take care of something that's gone wrong is safer than not knowing and hoping nothing goes wrong. There is always something that can go wrong, and will."

"So, what are you suggesting?" Asked Angela Rose.

Desmond replied, "Buying an airline from the inside."

"From the inside?" said Lillian.

Desmond said, "You know JM has a good idea. We are financially stable enough for you to do that. Go out and find a small airline and get yourself a job with them. That should be easy with your knowledge of how planes work. Look for an airline that is struggling, see why it is struggling. Not by asking, but by being on the inside. Employees talk to each other. You will quickly find out the truth. Some of these people you will find it better to walk away from, other's you might see a way to solve their problems if you were in charge. Not for them, for you, after you have acquired the airline." JM pointed out that when many businesses are in trouble, they panic and cannot see what is front of them. Some get into trouble because they keep doing the wrong thing over and over, stubbornness."

Lillian looked at her mother and said, "You do understand Ma, and Pa, this will mean that I will be moving out on my own. I don't know where it will be."

"We will always be here for you." her mother replied. The meeting was about to be concluded with Lillian being very upbeat and anxious to get started.

"There is one other thing to discuss." Turning to Desmond and Angela Rose, JM said, "There's the matter of the Royal Circle houses."

Angela Rose said to Lillian, "Your father and I want to transfer your Grandfather and Great Grandfather's homes to you children. Do you have a preference for which one you want? We don't want you two having something else to bicker over when we are gone."

Lillian replied in an excited voice, "I would love to have Great Grandpa's, but I won't fight over it. What does Brian want?"

Desmond laughed as he said, "For once, you two have agreed on something. He wants Grandpa's, so it's all settled. JM get on to it."

***

By September of 1946, Lillian had worked for one small airline with three airplanes. Dakota Airways, which was run by a businessman with little knowledge of service, but a lot about aircraft. Lillian quickly saw his attention was one directional. When approaching him about the subject, he became belligerent, stating people should just be grateful to be able get into an airplane. She quickly moved on, knowing it was a fight she didn't want. Her second experience proved more fruitful. Kennedy Airways was a cross between passengers and cargo. The airline had found a niche market in moving urgently needed products to rural areas and filling their airplanes with passengers. Their offerings were not of comfort as much as cost effective. She quickly noticed that the airline was cost effective for the users and not the owner. By the time the owner realized he was in trouble, Lillian soon set up a financial solution that left her holding half of the company. She embarked on a journey of hiring and firing that turned things around.

Following news of everything aeronautical, she read in late October that the wealthy magnate, Howard Hughes, was due to take his Spruce Goose, the largest fixed wing aircraft ever built, on its maiden flight. She wanted to be part of this historic event. She contacted her mother and the two of them made the trip to California to be part of the spectacle. The flight took place on November 2nd and lasted eight glorious minutes. The celebrations of the successful flight however, went on long into the night. Sitting in the same restaurant was Howard Hughes having his celebration, Lillian had a plan, which she put into action as she watched the group surrounding Mr. Hughes. She waited patiently for her opportunity. Angela Rose noticed and asked, "What are you up to in your head young lady?"

"Ma, I'm going to get Mr. Howard Hughes to help me."

"Oh no you don't. He will chew you up and spit you out."

"Not me, Ma, you watch." With that she jumped up and ran. Intercepting Mr. Hughes, before any of his aides could cut her off, she said politely, "Mr. Hughes, I think I can help you."

He stopped dead in his tracks and looked at the beautiful, twenty-seven year old, raven haired girl with the funny nose and said, "And just how might that be young lady?"

"I am Lillian Jane Blacksmith from Buffalo, New York. I own stock in two aircraft production companies and stock in a small airline."

"Someone so young and attractive *and* it would appear smart." He waved his aides away.

"So how do you propose to help me?"

"Mr. Hughes, if I may call you Howard, I am willing to share my plans with you and help you turn my dreams, ambitions and assets into something huge in the airline business."

"And that is helping me *how*?" By now Mr. Hughes had become amused by the bravado of this girl.

"Mr. Hughes, wouldn't it make you feel proud to know that you have helped someone as driven as me to achieve something that big?"

"I'll tell you what." He turned to an aide and said, "Give Miss Lillian my private business card." Looking back at Lillian he added, "Not tonight my dear. Call my office. 9 am in the morning. You get one hour, that's it, one hour of my time." He waved her away as he spoke to his aide, "Good looking child, that one."

Angela Rose was flabbergasted when Lillian told her what had transpired. "Do you know what people would pay to get what you just did? You must be careful though my dear, he is thought to be quite a lady killer."

"Not this lady, Ma, not this lady."

As Lillian and her mother paid the restaurant bill, Lillian looked up to see Howard Hughes standing at the table, he proffered his hand to Angela Rose and said, "You madam, I suppose are the mother to this young force of energy, although you do not look old enough. I am happy to make your acquaintance." Turning to Lillian he added, "Nine o'clock, on the dot young lady and you may bring your mother." With that he turned and left, his entourage following behind like a circus procession.

Chapter 22

The meeting with Howard Hughes was burned into Lillian's memory forever. He had carefully listened to her descriptions of what she had done and was planning to do. His advice was remarkably simple. Follow your gut. Everybody has a right to his or her own agenda, as do you to yours. The trick is to find out what other's agendas are and respect them, but do not let them change or overpower yours. His example was, I have every right to want to make love to you, which I do." Angela Rose's eyes opened wide at that comment. The man continued, "You have every right to say no, which you do. There, we both know each other's agenda. Now that you know mine, is there a reason to change yours?"

"No, Sir." Lillian was quick with her reply. She could see his point, that another person's agenda is as valid to them as yours is to you, as he said; the trick was to know the other person's agenda. He went on to point out the potential pitfalls and positive aspects of her plan. He felt that she had a good grounding in the basics of airplanes and that she was learning more of the business side. He liked the idea of her doing a brief stint as an '*air hostess*', as he called them, but suggested she get into the administrative side quickly and master it. Continuing on, he said, "While I inherited one fortune, I made another, do you know how?"

"No sir," was her enthralled answer.

"Because I quickly realized that there are far more poor people in America than there are rich people. So, I got into the film business. Hundreds of thousands of people paying a quarter a time to see my films, that's big money. There is nothing wrong in catering to the rich. That's one market and it's lucrative. Us rich can be quite fickle to deal with, the poor folk, not so much. Choose your target and stay focused. You can have two targets, but they are quite different. Never let the two mix." His parting piece of advice was simple; "Everything small will eventually be taken over by something bigger, plan for it."

One hour after the meeting started, as if a pre-set alarm in his head, Mr. Hughes stood and shook hands with Angela Rose, who had not spoken a word through the whole meeting. "It was charming to meet you. You have a fine daughter. Mark my words, she will become something big one day." Angela Rose glowed with pride. To Lillian he said, "You have the right stuff young lady, go out and take on the world, it's yours."

On the way back to the hotel Angela Rose asked, "Do you think he is sexy?"

"Mr. Hughes? Oh, Ma. I was too busy listening to what he was saying to think about that. But yes, I suppose he was good looking."

"Do you have a young man in your life these days?" "No one special, Ma. Don't need anyone special."

"Really, don't you want to get married, have children?"

"Ma, remember Galena, the Polish lady that worked on safety belt installations with us at Curtis Wright? She had a saying; a woman doesn't need one man, she needs four men. One for sex, one for dancing, one for things around the house and one for money."

Her mother asked, "Do you have your four?"

"I don't need number four or three, and I don't dance much, so that only leaves me needing a man for the number one position and I'm not telling you any more than that."

Angela Rose 's response for that was, "I guess I must be out of the loop.

***

Upon her return to Kennedy Airlines, Lillian focused on her work. Old man Kennedy had taken a shine to her and she did her best to keep her distance. He was old and wrinkled. She was young and beautiful. She played to what she knew were his desires by flirting outrageously when then were alone. He was a widower and had a daughter from whom he was estranged. Lillian never asked him why. She didn't want to know. She felt that he was a lonely, kind, sweet old man. Late one night when the last flight had arrived back at the airfield and everything was locked down, she went to turn the lights of in his office and he was sitting there silently. She asked what was wrong.

"Sit and have a drink with me." he said, pushing a bottle of whisky across the desk. Lillian fetched a glass and poured herself a small shot. At this, old man Kennedy started to ramble about his life, what he achieved, how he lost his wife in a farm accident. That was what had turned him away from farming and into airplanes. She could feel his loneliness. He seemed tired and sad. She went round the desk and gently held his face in her hands and kissed him on the forehead. It was a tender kiss, which lingered.

"I must go, we have an early flight leaving first thing in the morning." she said. He did not answer.

She turned to leave. As she went back round the desk, she knocked his chair. His arm flopped to his side. She was paralyzed for a moment. Old man Kennedy was dead. His last act was to receive her act of kindness to an old man; a heartfelt gesture of kindness.

The old mans' will honored the arrangement they had made when Lillian purchased half the business. The survivor had the right to buy out the remaining stock. Lillian would now own her first airline.

***

Texas Oil and Air was Lillian next small airline. This airline specialized in moving oil drilling supplies around the southern states. Texas provided most of their business. They had four aircraft, which were always off working. Inevitably, one would need repairs or maintenance at an inopportune time. Lillian was able to show the owner, who referred to himself as 'Cowboy' and always spoke in third person, a solution. She had purchased an aircraft from a defunct airline and approached Cowboy with a proposal.

"All your aircraft are older and well worked. It is expensive when one goes down. Customers get upset and you lose income. I have a solution."

"What is it? I can see this is going to cost Cowboy money."

"No. it isn't. We develop a tight delivery schedule operating three planes. We use the third for parts when needed. That way, we don't have to wait for parts to get to us when we desperately need them."

"Girly, we have four planes kept busy full time right now. Cowboy can't take one of them out of service."

"With a set delivery schedule that all our customers know, we can manage that and do the same work as four, because you won't have one plane running around on emergency deliveries and being taken away from unscheduled deliveries. But here's where Cowboy makes his money, if a customer can't wait for a regular delivery schedule, he must pay a premium charge for faster delivery. This will take the pressure off and allow our planes to fly fully loaded. We save money and thereby make more money."

"How does Cowboy fly them premium emergency deliveries without no plane? You is using the fourth plane for parts." Cowboy was getting agitated.

"Here is my deal. I have a plane perfect for the job. I will lend it to you for one month free. If after the month, I have increased your revenue twenty percent, just by better schedules and premium delivery charges, you will make me a partner and the new airplane comes with me as part of the deal."

"Dang it girl. You got some mind on you. What about the cost of the new airplane, does Cowboy to have buy it after the month?"

"No. First of all, it isn't a never-used plane. It is just in far better condition than any of your four. I will sign the plane over to you as payment for partnership."

"Where's your plane right now, Honey?"

"It's at an airfield that I have an interest in. It can be here in forty-eight hours. If you are nervous, we can take a flight out there tomorrow and you can inspect it."

Cowboy shook his head in disbelief and said, "Don't need to Honey. Damned if you don't have bigger balls than a Texas Longhorn, and you're just as feisty. I like it"

The following morning, Cowboy announced that Cowboy had changed his mind. He told Lillian he should go and see the aircraft. Together they flew to Kennedy Air that afternoon. Cowboy was impressed with the reception Lillian got at the airfield.

"The plane is ready Miss Lillian," the mechanic proudly said, leading them to it for the inspection.

Looking at Cowboy, Lillian said, "Take as long a look as you want, Eddie here will show the log books. Kick the tire or whatever. I'm just going into the office to check on a few things."

"So, tell me Eddie, how do you know Miss Lillian?" "Why, she's the boss round here."

"I thought she works for me?" Cowboy was confused.

"She owns Kennedy Airlines and as far as I know a couple of other airlines in New York."

On the return trip to Texas, Cowboy could not wait to question Lillian. "You own Kennedy Air and a couple of other airlines in New York?" His question was more of a statement.

Lillian laughed, "No, I don't own a couple of airlines in New York. I own shares in a couple of aircraft manufacturing companies, and yes, I do own Kennedy Air."

"So, what do you want with little old Cowboy's outfit?" he asked.

"Every airline can learn something from other airlines. They are all too busy with their ends to open their eyes and see the future. It is my plan to take a number of small airlines and group them together. We will be more powerful together than alone. Every small airline is vulnerable to big airlines. Howard Hughes taught me that everything small is eventually taken over by something bigger, gobbled up, as he puts it."

"Goldurn it girly, you know Howard Hughes?"

"He taught me a lot in a very short time. So, what do you think of our deal?"

The old man smiled as he said, "Cowboy had better hitch himself to a wagon that's going places." Within the year, Lillian was a partner with Cowboy and was ready to move on to her next opportunity.

Chapter 23

By the time Lillian came home for the Christmas holidays in 1948, she had ownership of one small airline and managing control of another. She wanted to focus on her goal of learning more about the passenger business. She noticed as the welcoming hugs and kisses were over, the absence of her brother. "Ma, is Brian coming home for Christmas?"

"I don't think so dear. He is so busy these days."

"Doing what? He can't find time to be with family?" Lillian was curt.

Desmond interrupted, "It's not that, it's just that we have embarked on a huge project and he is seizing the holiday break to quietly obtain some property in the English protectorate of Tanganyika, on the shores of Lake Victoria."

"That's not on the ocean shores like all the other hotels, is it?"

"No, the lake is a growing tourist destination and it's close to the exotic country of Zanzibar. It offers great potential for a hotel rather like the Mackinaw Island Lodge in Michigan. I think he is onto something there."

"Does he come home very often?" Lillian was curious.

"About the same as you dear, once a year. But we understand he is quite successful in his efforts, as are you."

That evening Desmond sat in front of a raging log fire with a brandy and called out for Lillian. As she entered the door he said, "Come, sit with me a while. Why don't you tell me what your problem is?"

"Why do you think I have a problem Pa?"

"I'm your pa. I can always tell when your mind is on somewhere else."

"I don't have a problem, Pa, I just want some advice. I'm not sure how to go about something I want to do."

"Well, Pa, you know how things are working out for me, I'm sure. I asked JM to keep you informed."

"Yes, he has done me the courtesy of showing me the agreements that he has been preparing for you. Damned respectful, I must say."

"I think that I need to work in the airline stewardess role to round off my experiences."

"So, do it, what's the problem?"

"I am nervous about how to go about it without ruining the opportunity. All the girls that are stewardesses are much younger than I am. I am a bit concerned that my experience may be a little intimidating and hinder me."

"I don't think so, but consider this, my grandfather and father would often tell me to play the cards I have been dealt, not those I want. Think about your experiences so far. They are the cards that you have been dealt. Nobody ever said that when you play cards, you have to tell everyone what cards you hold. Keep some close to your chest."

"So, are you saying don't tell the truth?"

"Absolutely not. Spend some time close to an airport, a major airport, get to know a few stewardesses and find out about the application process. Get an application form from Pan American Air. They are getting quite big. You young ladies chatter quite freely amongst yourselves. Find a stewardess that will guide you through the form the best way possible. Just remember to not give too much away about yourself, just enough. You should avoid the appearance of bragging."

"Pa, you always seem to have the right answer."

"You have a lot to offer, much more than they need. Just offer what they need. Be anxious, but not overly so."

***

Within three months, Lillian found herself standing inside a Pan American flight to London assisting passenger boarding. The Chief Steward assigned her to crew care. This was where first-timers started out. She introduced herself to the pilot, a Captain Conway, a handsome, red haired Irishman. With the flight deck crew taken care of, she turned to leave and overheard the navigator say to the co-pilot, "That's one good looking woman."

The Captain replied, "Keep your hands-off boys, she will be mine." The men laughed.

The flight seemed to be over quickly. The myriad of duties tripped over each other to fill the time. It felt strange to Lillian to be on her feet for such a long time when all her previous experiences on flights were as a passenger. She reasoned that was why she was so exhausted by the time the flight had arrived in London. She soon found herself laying on her back on the hotel bed, still in uniform, staring at the ceiling. She was slipping in and out of sleep between thoughts. Her mind was processing the many things she had seen that she could improve upon. While the airline was providing a high level of service, she could see where they had placed the bar. She knew from growing up surrounded by wealth, the bar could be so much higher. Her thoughts were interrupted by a knocking on the door. She opened the door to see Captain Conway, out of uniform, looking quite dashing with his black Barathea blazer and red silk cravat. "Come on, get out of your uniform. Time for civvies, we are all going out on the town. You've got five minutes. We will wait for you in the lobby."

***

The evening was a whirlwind of bar hoping and dancing at Kings Cross, the center of nightlife in London. Despite being older than the usual crowd at the Cloudland Dance Hall, nobody paid them any attention. Lillian enjoyed the attention of the other crewmembers and was entranced by their stories of life in the air. Captain Conway kept close to her side as if marking her for himself. He was handsome and attracted much female attention, which he politely brushed off. Throughout the night other crewmembers gradually faded away with their conquests. The American accent drew the English like moths to a flame. It was 2 o'clock by the time bars were shutting down for the night. Riding back to the hotel, alone with the captain, Lillian guessed what was coming next. The taxi stopped at the hotel and the captain exited and went round to open the door for her to leave. He was about to get back into the taxi when Lillian spoke. Looking back on that moment, Lillian didn't know why she asked, "Aren't you coming in with me?"

Everything after that was a blur. Flashbacks of the seduction were of a muscle toned, tanned body slowly exploring her body. Warm lips kissing her flushed skin and feathery touches of fingers covered her all over. The pace was slow and deliberate and raised her to a tingling climax. Some deep-seated power took over as she lifted her hips to allow his entry. She lifted her legs round his back and arched to a receive him. Somewhere, at some time she slid into a deep satisfied sleep.

Lillian was awakened by the need to use the bathroom and the sun streaming through the huge picture window. Walking back to the bed and the sleeping man, she studied his naked, 'magnificent', as he called it, body, as it lay uncovered. Lowering herself slowly onto the bed she touched his flaccid member, then she held it. It was warm and small, about the size of her thumb. As she fondled him his erection slowly grew in her hand. Fascinated, she started to stroke his shaft. Curiosity getting the better of her, she leaned down and licked his now throbbing shaft. She liked the taste and wondered if it was his taste, her taste or both of their tastes. With a slow, deliberate motion she took his whole erection into her mouth and started to slide it in and out, in and out, of her mouth until she felt it touch the back of her throat. Noticing his balls getting hard she held him deep in her mouth, squeezed his balls and felt a sudden gush of warm liquid. She coughed, regained her composure and continued to suck on him until he finished spurting. She liked the control she was experiencing. It was a new sexual experience for her. She felt him move and looked up to see that he had been watching her as he said, "let me reciprocate."

"How?" she innocently replied.

"Come up here and sit over my shoulders." She followed his instructions and felt his head between her legs as she lowered her vagina over his face. She felt no sexual reaction until he parted her lips with his tongue. Slowly he worked his tongue into her. Suddenly she shifted her position slightly and leaned forward placing her hands on the headboard of the bed. It did not take long for body to respond to him. She no longer saw the print on the wall. Closing her eyes, she gave way to her animal instincts.

Gently, he rolled Lillian off his shoulders onto the bed beside him. He sat up and said, "That's all you get. I have places to be."

***

The Pan American, London to New York flight sat on the runway waiting for clearance to take off. Lillian had served the flight deck crew their morning coffee and was closing the cockpit door when she heard Captain Conroy say, "Nice, very nice. A good shag, that one. Good for a first time."

The navigator said, "First time, first time for you or her? Did she like it?"

"Her, you bloody fool. She loved it. She's yours now."

"You are one heartless bastard, Captain."

"Yep, that's me. When you're good, you're good."

Lillian stood frozen in her anger. Her thoughts were interrupted by the Chief Steward assigning her another task. During the flight, the co-pilot, taking a break, pulled her to one side. He put his arm round her shoulder and was about to speak when she shrugged him off angrily.

"Lillian, ignore the man. I'm sorry that you had to hear that conversation."

"How do you know I heard any conversation?"

"Because I saw you through the opening of the door. I was going to stop the conversation, but I wanted you to know what some of these pilots are like. I'm so sorry."

"It's alright. It's not your fault. Are they all like this?"

"Unfortunately, most of the men working on the flights are like that."

Lillian stared at him and said, "I suppose this is your line, to try and get some of what he had."

"I guess I deserved that one. I am married and only want to do this job for a while. I need the experience to move on to bigger things. I want the best for my family and this job is a stepping-stone. Plus, my wife would castrate me. Mind you, I think Captain Conroy's would do even worse than that to him. She is one Irish hellion."

During the flight Lillian formulated a plan. She slipped a note to the Co-pilot asking him to go along with whatever she said in the cockpit. He read it, smiled and nodded in agreement. Preparing herself for her plot, she stood beside the cockpit door, took a deep breath and entered. "Can I ask you boys a personal question?"

"Sure, said the Co-pilot. Will I be embarrassed?"

"Not as much as I will." Lillian waited a minute for effect and then said, "What are crabs?" She watched the three men's mouths drop open.

The Co-pilot quickly knew what was going on and played along, "You don't mean the seafood do you?"

Lillian picked up the cue; she wriggled her hips and rubbed her crotch area, as she said, "No. I have this infernal itching around my private parts."

"When did this start?" The Co-pilot was running with the act.

"This morning. Right after I showered." The pilot had gone very quiet and jumped as Lillian put her hand on his shoulder and innocently asked, "Is this what happens the first time?" without waiting for an answer she turned to leave and said over her shoulder, "I guess it wouldn't be so bad if I had enjoyed it. Maybe it was because his dick was so small." She heard two men laughing as she closed the door.

Her summation of her first time was a blurred memory. It was then she recalled her grandmother's words regarding how many men a woman should have in her life; 'One for sex, one for dancing, one for things around the house and one for money.' "I'm not even sure if want man number one." She thought to herself.

Chapter 24

It took only six months for the inflight work to satisfy Lillian's curiosity. She quickly transferred to administration. It was when she began to slowly reveal her experiences that she moved quickly up the ladder to head the personnel department. Her attitude towards men had become jaundiced. Had she used them to satisfy her curiosity or to confirm her opinion about sex? As time went by, she learned to separate sex as an individual act, as an act of pleasure rather than a demonstration of love. Her work at Pan American opened many doors for her and she was not averse to using sex to aid her quest. It increased her ever-growing list of business contacts. She spent a lot time of time in airports and mingled with the first-class passengers. She felt this was where she belonged. Soon she noticed that wealthy first class passengers appreciated being separated from the masses, and yet often, disliked being lumped in with other 'first class' passengers. It was her observation that 'first class' only meant that you could afford the price of the ticket and the luxuries that went with it. She knew instinctively that 'first class' was something other than that. This was to be her guiding mantra.

1951, three years after joining Pan American, Lillian left to pursue her own goals. Texas Air had been struggling without her constant presence and Cowboy was noticeably tired. This was when she made her move. She offered to buy him out and let him stay as the titular head only. No power, but big ego. He went for the deal. The oil business was booming and she saw an opportunity. Cowboy spent a week with her visiting the oil companies big and small. He sat in awe as Lillian pitched her idea to them. Her pitch was simple. Texas Airways will be a subsidiary of a new airline, Texas America International Airlines. The new airline will have a fleet of ten fast, small private aircraft. Luxuriously appointed with the latest technology. There will be office facilities, sleeping quarters and catering. All pilots will have up-to-date training and have the best experience available. These airplanes will be available on demand to fly anywhere that the clients wish. They will be private and only carry one client's people at a time. No mixing with the public and nobody knowing your business.

The idea was met with astonishing acceptance. Lillian had a charter business. She had an airline that she had built from the ground up. Over the next few years, she applied her oil industry experience and focused airline principles to the film business, 'Zoetrope Air'. Next was the music business 'Metronome International Airways'. Each time, the demand quickly increased the need to increase capacity. This gave her the idea of offering the same level of service to business executives, 'Executive Flight'. The charter business was growing in all directions. Lillian soon found herself being pulled from pillar to post. By 1959, she decided to pull the six charter companies under one umbrella. It was to be Global Charter Services. By having all administration under one roof, excessive passenger demand could be met with cross utilization of crews and equipment between her own airlines. The big boys began to notice her development and were paying attention. The major decision facing Lillian was; did she go public or sell off?

***

Christmas 1955, neither Brian nor Lillian made it home to Buffalo. Desmond, Angela Rose and JM spent an unusually quiet day reminiscing. JM posed a thought for discussion. "Now that you, Desmond, are 73 and Angela Rose, you are 69, I think you need to make some firm decisions on your English holdings. The company stocks that you own are safely in a trust fund and cannot be touched. However, the magnificent homes on The Royal Circle are increasing in value every day and you never finalized the transfer to the children. A potential problem I see looming is the English Death Duties that will become payable upon your passing."

"What do you suggest we do, is there a way to avoid them?" asked Desmond.

"Should we bother?" suggested Angela Rose.

"That is for you to decide. I do not see any point in giving the government any more than you have to. I have been researching what the difference might with you Angela Rose being American while Desmond is English. I understand they have a different and heavier tax code for non-nationals. I am waiting for better information as to whether they may lump you together, and if they do will they put you as both as English or American. This could create quite a tax burden."

Desmond said, "I thought we were going to give one to each of the children."

"We were, but we never got round to completing it." Angela Rose thought before continuing, "You know how the two of them don't get along. Whatever we do is only going to cause more problems between them."

JM said "Let me get the papers in order and I think it is time we made them sit down together as adults and take care of everything. Quite frankly, it doesn't matter if they don't like each other. This is business."

Desmond smiled as he said, "Best of luck getting them together."

Quickly JM offered, "I will manage it. I will contact them both and tell them there is a legal situation with the properties that is tangled in their historic origins and that I need them here. I will tell neither that the other is coming and I will arrange their flights."

Angela Rose suggested, "Tell them that we do not know they are coming as you want to discuss the matter with them prior to bringing us into the situation. That could arouse their curiosity enough for them both to come."

"I will get onto it right away." JM pulled out his note book and made notes.

Chapter 25

February 3rd 1956 was the scene of incredible volume of snow. Flights had been delayed for the last two days in and out of Buffalo, New York. Earlier in the flight to New York, the stewardess had spoken to Brian, "If I may interrupt you for a moment, Sir." Brian looked up from his magazine and nodded his assent. "It is quite unusual for us to have two people with the same surname on the same flight. There is a lady on board, a miss Lillian Blacksmith, do you know her?"

"She is my sister." Brian said in an offhand manner.

"I could move her up to be with you, if you wish." The stewardess was polite and trying to be helpful.

"No, thank you." Brian went back to reading. As flight 106, taking advantage of a small window of opportunity through the snow laden skies, approached the airport Lillian was watching her brother, Brian. They were seated at opposite ends of the first-class cabin and had not spoken to each for the entire flight from New York City. In the final approach, the aircraft was buffeted about and managed a safe, but bumpy landing. Standing at opposite ends of the luggage carousel, they waited for their luggage. An immaculately attired chauffer approached each of them, advised them that the family limousine was waiting for them outside the terminal exit. He collected their baggage and led them to the car.

***

The chauffer was exercising extreme caution as he slowly pulled away from the curb. The Limousine slid slightly to one side before being corrected. Waiting for opening in the slow crawling line of vehicles on Genesee street, the chauffer looked in his rear-view mirror to see the back of Desmond and Angela Roses' heads and facing them, Lillian and Brian sat icily, side by side, stoically ignoring each other. Taking advantage of an opening in traffic, the driver accelerated and turned right into the road. A resounding truck horn blasted out in the dark night. Brian looked out of his window and saw a small passenger car sliding and turning sideways across the driving lanes on the opposite side of the road. He leaned over to get a better view and gasped. He saw a huge semi-trailer, loaded with steel coils start to slide towards them as it turned sideways and crossed the centerline of the road. What followed wiped his memory clean from that point on.

***

Death came swiftly to Angela Rose, Desmond and the chauffer, as the limousine was crushed beneath the large semi-trailer. Apparently, the semi-trailer was hauling steel from the Lake Erie steel mills bound for The Carrier Air -conditioning Company in Syracuse. It appeared to have been loaded beyond its' capacity. The ice-covered road surface and excessive weight allowed the sliding combination of tons of steel rolls and immense horsepower to change the truck's center of gravity as its' driver tried to correct it's lethal trajectory. From the warmth of the passenger compartment, Brian saw the truck start to lose it's balance and roll. He thought it was going to crash in front of them and cause their vehicle to collide with the wreck. Lillian, upon hearing the squeal of brakes and sounding of the horn, quickly, and instinctively using her airline training, leaned over and pulled Brian to the floor. The eerie silence that filled that cold night air was broken by the sound of hissing steam, which abruptly stopped collapsing into nothingness. The Limo had come to a sudden stop, impaled on a light standard. Rescue and fire services found the chauffeur completely pounded into his seat, which had passed through the floor of the vehicle and was sitting on the road. The steel coils had crushed the engine compartment, the driver's compartment and the two seats that backed onto the driver's compartment. The rear two seats had collapsed and folded down onto Desmond and Angela Rose, folding them in half snapping their spines. Brian and Lillian were thrown forward onto the floor. Their parents' dead bodies had fallen on top of them cushioning their badly mangles bodies. Later, photographs were to show why the only survivors were the siblings. They were in the rear of the limousine that protruded out from under the wreckage like an obscene bubble poking out the side of a child's balloon.

Chapter 26

March 10 1957, it had been more than a year, an agonizing year, since the death of their parents. Countless surgeries and rehabilitation had been their individual, and sole focus. Brian had elected to have his treatment in Sisters Hospital because his sister, Lillian, was being treated at Buffalo General Hospital. There was little or no contact between them and what there was, was conducted through JM Fetters. It wasn't until March 3rd 1957 that they finally came face to face in the foyer of JM's office.

***

JM was preparing himself as he sat quietly in his corner office with the panorama of Lake Erie spread before him, while his clients, Brian Ojukwae Blacksmith and his sister Lillian Jane, patiently awaited his audience. He silently reviewed his life. Buffalo was the 8th largest city in the country and was a major railroad hub, the largest grain-milling center in the country, and the home of the largest steel-making operation in the world. His relocation to the area to better serve his major clients, The St. John-Brown family, had proven to be a lucrative and comfortable redirection of his talents. The St. John-Browns were his biggest and often his only clients and yet they afforded him a life style substantially less stressful than others in his profession. The timing of this move placed him in the dynamic business hub for which many of its citizens held great respect, awe and acceptance of the English people. The fact that he was a light skinned, black man of mixed descent seemed to have little effect when he spoke. His very correct English elocution, his proper attire, manners and way in which he carried his tall willowy frame seemed to wipe away any vestiges there may have been towards discrimination.

To be accepted as a client and to enter the opulent stained glass, polished mahogany and crystal inner sanctum of JM Fetters so over whelmed clients that their acceptance of his ministrations was a forgone conclusion. Their reaction did little to temper his illusions of superiority. While JM treated every visitor to his offices to a visual and overloaded sensory feast of what the English must be like, he never fooled himself. Often, he would privately ponder over old photographs and newspaper articles that went as far back as reporting his grandfather's heroism in saving his slave master's life. No, JM had no illusions. He was directed, focused and calculating.

Snapping out of his reverie, he quickly stood up and moved deftly around his large office and turned certain framed photographs face down. The only two pictures he left untouched was a pair of large gilded framed portraits. One was of Michael and Penelope St. John-Brown. The other was of Desmond Cane Blacksmith and his wife Angela Rose St. John-Brown.

The manila folder that JM's secretary had placed on his desk was remarkably thin for an attorney's file, but like all his files, there was one for each of the many tasks he performed for the St. John-Browns. This one was the will. Placing his hand on the closed file he closed his eyes as if reverently connecting to its contents. The assets contained in this will had been intertwined in his life since he was a thirty-year-old aspiring lawyer in England. JM still could recall his first meeting with Penelope. Her persona had enveloped his imagination and captured his loyalty from that very moment and it had never wavered. Since Michael died in a train disaster in 1926, JM had escorted Lady Penelope to many functions and had been her rock in the chaotic years that followed the loss of her husband. He had symbolically held her through the following years.

Looking through the cut glass Victorian styled office doors, JM studied Brian and Lillian as they sat silently ignoring each other's presence. Many aspects of their grandparents were evident in them both. His observations of their relationship made him secure in what was about to take place at their meeting. Right now he believed that he held the upper hand in his dealings with the two of them, but knew that he had to tread carefully if he wanted finish what he had set out to do, as both of them were successful and financially secure in their own right. With an air of professional aplomb, he opened his door and apologized for keeping them waiting and promised not to keep them much longer.

***

Standing up from behind his desk, JM walked over and embraced Lillian. His hug lingered. He held her at arm's length and drank in her beauty. When he looked at Lillian's face, he saw her mother.

"Nothing I can say can convey to you how I feel at your loss of your parents," he said, "so I will not offer platitudes, other than to say I hurt for your hurt."

"Oh JM, Mother's passing must leave such a hole in your heart. I know you cared deeply for her. Over a year, gone, just gone. I still cannot look at mother's and my scrapbooks with-out crying. It's like…it's like, something has been ripped away from me, something is missing, and yet, I am all here." Lillian's tone was controlled and emotional one.

"Physically you are, but it will take a long time for you to emotionally rebuild. How about you Brian, how are you holding up?"

"As well as can be expected. I just want to get on with my life. I need to pick up the pieces that fell on the wayside since Pa's death. I must get back to the hotels and construction in Tanganyika before everything gets too out of hand. I have been in contact with our people, but need to be there. Need to keep them in shape, you know how these natives can get if left unsupervised."

"You must take it slowly. I have had reliable people overseeing things in your absence and I am sure may of the staff and contractors will welcome you back."

Brian shifted the focus to the matter of the meeting. "As Pa would say, how about a gin and tonic, old boy?"

"At once, at once," JM said as he proceeded to mix the cocktail. He turned from his bar. "May I offer you something?" he said to Lillian.

"A Glenfiddich, if you have one, please," said Lillian.

Brian snorted, "That's a man's drink." Lillian ignored him. JM approached Brian with the drink in one hand, the other open to shake.

Brian said, "I know you loved my parents. It's just sad, very sad. Let's just get on with the business at hand and go our own separate ways."

Shocked at the attitude, JM returned to sit behind his desk. Picking up his gin and tonic, Brian moved into the center of the room and sat erect on a low coffee table, ignoring his sister.

The attorney looked good for his age, slow in movement, but his mind was still sharp. Although his eyes were rimmed red and his shoulders sagged as if loaded under a great burden, which indeed they were, his voice was strong. His attire, as always, was immaculate, right down to the silk kerchief in his jacket pocket. In a theatrical gesture, aimed to relax the mood, he stood, removed his jacket, put it on a hanger then returned to his seat. He removed his glasses, and polished them, wiped his eyes, and took a deep breath. "I can read your father and mother's will to you in its great length if you wish," he said, "but there is a codicil there which is of great importance."

Lillian spoke, "Why don't you deal with that first if you think it is important?"

JM continued, "During your recuperation and convalescence, a great deal of work has been carried out and has yet to be completed. There is the issue of death taxes, etc., and I will not bore you with the minutia, but as you both know, with the trusts that have been set up and the various corporate entities that exist, probate is going to be a drawn-out affair."

"What will be drawn out, this meeting, or the will?" Brian asked impatiently.

"The finalizing of the will." Replied JM.

Lillian asked, "What was it our parents wanted us back here for, something about Bath?"

"Unfortunately, it's too late to deal with that issue. That was about succession of the two homes on The Royal Crescent. I have that being sorted out as we speak. I have managed to slow down that process somewhat due to you both being incapacitated for so long. In the meantime, let's address the codicil."

"Yes, let's." said Lillian.

"I am able to tell you that you are both to share the estate in its entirety. It's estimated value is in excess of four hundred million dollars, plus the English properties. Everything is subject to one condition."

As JM took a deep breath, the siblings did something he had never seen before. They spoke in unison: "What condition?"

JM glared at each of them in turn and in doing so, seemed to gain strength. "You two have not said a civil word to each other." he said. "In fact, I have never heard you speak to each other decently, ever."

"What does that have to do with anything?" asked Lillian sheepishly.

"I believe that it has a lot to do with the very reason for condition in the codicil." said the attorney.

"I, we have no desire to become friends, so you can forget that right now." said Brian.

"There is a no time limit on what you are expected to do, but expediency is recommended." said JM. "Your parents have lost a lot of sleep over the way you two behave toward each other, and the codicil is clear, very clear indeed, in its language. It sets out for you each to complete a task and should you not complete the tasks given to you, the entire estate is to be inherited by an undisclosed third party. In plain language, both of you could end up gaining nothing from what should be your inheritance." He watched as Brian and Lillian proceeded to talk over each other, dictating loudly what they would and wouldn't do. He sat silently as they expended their initial rush of vehemence on each other. As a lull in their rhetoric opened up, they both looked at the attorney, who sat silently at his desk, observing them.

"Well," said both of them. JM found it amusing.

"Unfortunately, I am bound to give each of you your tasks individually and privately," he said. "There is no provision for delays or excuses. I am bound that should the tasks not be completed in a reasonable amount of time, to file with the probate court a notice of completion or lack thereof. Believe me when I tell you both that this is completely out of my hands."

Brian was becoming agitated when he said, "This is ridiculous."

"How do you know it's ridiculous, we haven't heard what the tasks are yet?" said Lillian.

"There you go, little miss clever clogs, always sensible."

"For Gods' sake Brian Ojukwae, you always have got to have the last word."

Angrily Brian snarled at his sister, "I'll thank you to drop the bloody Ojukwae."

JM held up his hand to silence their petty bickering. "Who shall be first?" he asked.

Chapter 27

Lillian stood and said, "Let him go first, I'm tired of his attitude." She left the room and sat in the foyer.

JM, after being sure the door was properly closed and that Lillian could not hear, spoke to Brian. "There is to be no joint effort between you and your sister in completing this task. The task is set out in simple, direct language."

"You can count on that." Said Brian. JM slid a document across his desk and instructed Brian to read, date, and sign it. It read:

I, Brian Ojukwae Blacksmith, do hereby agree to travel to Lagos, Nigeria. I understand that I am not allowed to use any money other than that which I earn from my labors directly connected to this task. I am to make acquaintances on the journey, photograph these people, have my photograph taken with these people, and write a brief report of their lives, background, hopes, and aspirations. I am then to travel a minimum of two hundred miles into the interior of Nigeria and become acquainted with a local inhabitant and repeat the same requirements for this person. All persons that I make a record of must read and sign the report and attest to its accuracy, as well as the photographs. I understand that I am to keep a journal of my efforts and submit it to JM Fetters for approval. There are no guidelines for the biographies, or the journal. I shall wait at my final destination for the approval of JM Fetters. The satisfactory acceptance of the completion of this task is the sole prerogative of JM Fetters. The required documents and photographs are to be sent to JM Fetters, and I shall await further instructions. I do further agree to follow any further directives then given to me.

Signed Brian Ojukwae Blacksmith,

....

Dated this....Day of........... 1957.

Brian sat silently, considering what he had read. He leaned back in the luxury of the armchair and closed his eyes. JM could see the bewilderment and anger in Brian's composure. The silence hung like a heavy cloud of cigarette smoke in noisy barroom. Suddenly, without warning Brian sat upright. "Well, I guess, I guess I had better get on with it." he said. He signed the space provided and slung the document across the desk to JM.

Taking the document, Julian signed his own name as witness and dated his signature. "I have known you long enough, Brian, to know that already you are thinking of ways to shortcut this task. I suggest you don't." he said. Nigeria was chosen because it will be easy to verify what you tell me. It is the spirit of this task that is important and both your parents have made it clear to me what is expected. I will not waver in my duty toward their last wishes and I hope you will not place me in a negative situation. I have great faith in you. God be with you."

"What is her task?" Brian asked, indicating his sister.

"It's got nothing to do with you. There is no reason for either of you to know the other's task unless both of you wish it so." At that, Brian stood, turned, and left the room. He passed Lillian, sitting in the foyer without speaking to her.

***

JM ushered Lillian back into is study. As she sat down, she said, "Brian didn't seem too happy."

JM said," He never seems to be happy, as far as I can tell." As he slid a document across the desk to Lillian he said in a professional tone, "There is to be no joint effort between your brother and you in completing this task. The task is set out in simple, direct language."

"I can't image he would want to help me." she said.

Lillian did not lift her head, but instead just kept reading her document:

I, Lillian Jane Blacksmith, do hereby agree to travel to Adelaide, South Australia. From there, I shall travel inland to Ayers Rock. I understand that I am not allowed to use any money other than that which I earn from my labors directly connected to this task. I am to make acquaintances on the journey and photograph these people, have my photograph taken with these people, and write a brief report of their lives, background, hopes, and aspirations. I am to travel into the interior of one of the major Australian deserts, or the Outback, and befriend a local inhabitant and repeat the same requirements for this person. All persons that I make a record of must read and sign the biography, as well as the photographs. I understand that I am to keep a journal of my efforts and submit it to JM Fetters for approval. There are no guidelines for the biographies, or the journal. I shall wait at my final destination for the approval of JM Fetters. The satisfactory acceptance of the completion of this task is the sole prerogative of Sir Julian Fetters. The required documents and photographs are to be sent to JM, and I shall await further instructions. I do further agree to follow any further directives then given to me.

Lillian looked at JM. "These seem to be very loose requirements," she said, "giving a lot of room for interpretation."

"Indeed, they are. It is your parents' hope that you will immerse yourselves in the spirit of the task and I have great latitude with which to give my approval. There is much to be gained in these tasks, and your parents hoped that you would benefit a great deal from them."

"I'm sure I will," Lillian said, moving to embrace JM. He held her close to his chest, a little longer than was professional, as if to absorb by osmosis, some of her connection with her mother, something he was beginning to miss.

545

Lillian had experienced this before and allowed him the comfort as she whispered in his ear, "I know you loved Mother. This must be just as hard for you."

The old man took a deep breath and held her out in front of him. "I have loved your mother since before you were born, you don't know how much I loved her." he said. "I see so much of her beauty, poise, and intelligence in you. You bring the same light into my life when we meet. Make her proud."

"What do you mean, I don't know, what else don't I know?"

"Time will tell, my dear, Time will tell."

Lillian left the office with her mind racing. She tried to make sense of what she had just heard. Loved Mother since . . . since when? This is a bit spooky. JM speaks in riddles sometimes.

***

Brian left Buffalo, New York, to commence his task on March 10th, without telling anyone. He was morose, but was motivated by the potential financial gain. He hoped his sister would fail. By the end of the month, JM was becoming annoyed with Lillian as she was still in Buffalo. He telephoned her constantly at the family home to urge her forward. The last conversation was somewhat abrupt. "Good morning Lillian, JM here."

"I recognize your voice, what can I do for you?"

"You should be making plans to carry out your parents' wishes, I believe your brother has started his task."

"I am making plans. Please do not keep on at me. There are things to take care of here at the house. *I have business's, as you know*, which need to be organized for when I am away."

"But we should try to abide by your parents' wishes."

"JM! There was no time stipulation. My parents are dead! I will do the task when I am good and ready. Is there anything else?"

"Well, no, I would like to take care of my end of the business."

"Your end of the business? You are the family attorney. You have no end of the business. It's the family Business. I will get started as soon as I responsibly can." With that Lillian hung up the phone. JM sat at his desk staring at the silent phone in his hand, shook his head and hung it up. He was starting to see a side of Lillian that was new to him.

Chapter 28

March 10 1957, I see that playing the game was to me, a way of life. Following the rules was an inherited essential, which I chose to do selectively. But at forty-two, having traveled the world extensively, I know that I do know a thing or two. I am beginning to think the world as I have seen it may have been colored by my family's privileged position, giving me a protected view, which can distort one's perception of reality. I have always been aware that you had to play the game to get anywhere, but I also knew that there was more than one interpretation of "the rules." I used my own version. For many years, I have travelled the world on luxury passenger liners and first-class airlines. The task that I face is a little intimidating, as I am not supposed to use my own financial resources. I have decided to see if I am able to secure a passage on one of the many cargo boats that travel the world. JM advises me that I cannot use one of our ships from Global, but that won't stop me using our contacts. I felt somewhat belittled asking the shipping clerks for advice, as they knew who I was and did not trust my story. Very quickly, I decided instead to avoid the familiar and head for the East River docks. Saying goodbye to the standard of clothes I am used to was difficult. If I wanted to fit in, I had to change my appearance. The Salvation Army was my outfitter of choice. I have to admit feeling a little theatrical. I hope my sister is experiencing this. No, I hope she is experiencing something worse than this.

March 30. O'Hanlon's Bar, in the dockland area of New York City, seemed like a place that sailors would hang out, so I summoned up the courage to go there. My first mistake was calling the bartender "my good man" when I ordered a whiskey. I got shot down very quickly.

"This ain't no place for a toff," he said, "and I ain't your good man." Fortunately, he still agreed to speak with me privately at the end of the bar. I don't know what compelled me to tell a story of running from New York to escape a jealous husband, and some very bad people with no money to my name. I enjoyed the theatrics of this. I told him I was willing to work for my passage to Africa. His directions took me to one of the lesser-used terminals that catered to the small freighters, whose owners weren't willing to pay the higher fees demanded by the better-located wharfs. The man I was to meet behind a wharf shed was three hundred pounds at least. He stood expectantly at the wharf gates. As I approached him, he proffered a piece of paper. "If you are the man who wants to work your passage to Africa, you can be a steward." he said. "Sign this and get your gear on board. We're due to cast off." I had only one small bag, as I'd expected to have time to have my belongings brought to me. Upon my cajoling, he gave me one hour to get some clothes together. I managed to return to the Salvation Army and get more clothes and was back behind the shed quickly. The heavyweight man grabbed me by my arm and pulled me round the corner just as the gangway was being hoisted. Then I saw the ship, well, not exactly a ship. It is a three thousand-ton, rust-ridden steel hull dented from one end to the other. It is a dirty, scary, small, very small, tramp steamer called the SS *Flowergate*. I don't believe Global Economy Ltd. or any of its predecessors would ever have owned a piece of junk like this. I feel as if I have just become a victim of the 1950's equivalent of the "press gangs" of olden days. But it is too bloody late, I have been well and truly had.

As hawsers were pulled and lines let go, we were soon pulling away from one of America's most sophisticated and alive cities and headed for, well, that seemed to be the problem. Tramp steamers by their very name often did not know where they were going. They just sailed into the night and waited until the ship owners had secured cargo and then went to load that cargo. The man I had met at the gate was the chief steward. His cabin was dark and dank and smelled of raw whiskey and eons of cigarette smoke. "Next stop, Livorno, Italy," he said, "where we're taking on a cargo of shoes." When I told him that I was led to believe we were going to Africa, he replied, "We might just be going there one day."

Our entire bloody cargo was shoes. To go where? We either did not know or were not to be told yet. *"This can't be too bad,"* said my ill-informed mind. *"It will at least be interesting"*

Comparisons usually come from examining similarities. My comparison was not that easy. On the one hand, my previous nautical exposure came from sleek, white, giant liners, like those of Cunard and White Star Line. They catered to the finest of first-class service and consideration for passenger comfort. Oh, yes, the liners carried cargo, but it was not the sort of thing one openly acknowledged. Generally, the cargo was "the royal mails," very top-notch, old chap. These shipping companies had no concerns about ordinary seamen tampering with the royal mails. They were too well organized.

The *Flowergate* looks like it is closer to the bottom of the barrel. The crew cabins smelled not of the last sweaty, unkempt booze-sodden poor soul, but of every sailor of the same ilk who had preceded him. The quiet, sedate calm of liners' passageways shared nothing with the raucous din of a six-cylinder engine standing over ten feet high. Each piston stroke shook the ship from stem to stern. This was disgusting, but it is to be my home for however long it took to get to Africa. God, I hope we get there sooner than later.

I can see plainly this is going to be rough. There is total crew of twenty-seven men. Only five of us are white, and the captain is an unwashed, smelly man, overweight by at least 150 pounds. There is a chief engineer who seems barely capable of riding a bicycle and yet he is an engineer. Another steward is an inveterate Scottish drunk, who relishes his desire to break my wee bonny nose with just one blow. Thankfully, he seems to like me and as he kept up his drinking, he soon lost his desire to maim me for life. The chief steward is nothing better than a washed-up bully. He certainly isn't washed. His cabin stinks to high hell. The rest of the crew is made up of Africans, Somalis, Laskas, wherever they come from, and other forgotten nationalities.

March 22. The SS *Flowergate* is 130 feet long and has aft, midship, and forward hatches to the holds. She sits very high in the water, as we are traveling with a light cargo. My first dawn on board is approaching and is accompanied by the hammering of the deckhands as they chip away the rust from the hull and the decks. I spent the night finding my way around this hulk. The idea of being onboard for any length of time does not sit well with me. The superior attitude of the chief steward is sticking in my throat. Nobody on this piece of shit appears to be clean. Even the bathing facilities were ancient and moldy, makes me suspicious of the cleanliness of the water. I will probably be lucky if I don't get dysentery.

The galley is run by a black fellow calling himself Ollie. Cigarettes hang out of his mouth as he cooks. He proudly announced that he was from Chicago. I swear; the mechanic garage bays at the Royal Palisades were cleaner than his galley. It's my job to wait on the captain, the engineer, the chief steward, and any passengers. What passengers? We don't have any. I can't work out where a passenger might stay. Ollie tells me that I would have to give up my berth, and I would be relegated to the storeroom. This is just too hard to imagine. These people are the scum of the earth.

March 29 It took us seven days to cross the Atlantic and round the Rock of Gibraltar. We bounced around like a shuttlecock with the less than melodic acoustic sound of steel straining at every wave. I imagined the rivets popping and complete parts of the hull dropping into the sea. I can only imagine the peace of the huge wooden sailing ships that Pa said his Grandfather Judd spoke of so lovingly. Nothing loving about this heap of junk. What I wouldn't give for that.

March 29. We arrived safely and have loaded a cargo of shoes in Livorno and are off again. I noticed the names Turnbull & Stott on the freight coming abroad. Apparently, that's the name of the company that owns this ship. Sailing west as best I can tell. There are rumors that we are going to the West African Coast.

March 31. We have changed course and are heading due south. I can see land off the port side in the distance. The weather is relatively calm and for once this old tub isn't making so much noise.

April 2. Roddy tells me that we should be getting close to The Canary Islands. It seems everyone is hoping we will stop there. I guess time will tell.

April 4. There's some excitement on board. We have changed course and appear to be heading straight for The Canary Islands. ....This afternoon we did indeed stop at Las Palmas. Well, we are at anchor. No one seems to know if we are going alongside.

April 5. I was woken up during the night by the sound of the anchor cable clattering up the hawser. At first it was thought we were going in. No such luck. At dawn the Canaries were nowhere to be seen. We were going due south again. I don't know how the crew can live with such uncertainty.

April 8. Four days and still none knows or will tell…After what passes for lunch Roddy tells me he overheard the captain talking about Capetown, South Africa. Roddy rekons that's another two days away. We are close to the equator and it is getting very hot. The deck is hot to walk on. We have gone right past Nigeria. I guess that's not a good sign for me.

April 10. Still sailing south. This afternoon we turned around and now heading for the coast. It is dark now and lights are appearing on the horizon dead ahead of us. Nobody is sure of our destination I can't understand why everything has to be so secretive. Around midnight we dropped anchor off shore. The word is out, we are at Luanda in Portuguese West Africa.

April 11. We go along side at noon. No one is allowed ashore. The decks are swarming with the local natives trying to sell us things, including their sister, or if you want it, their brother. It's disgusting. By the evening watch, some supplies have been brought aboard, the locals pushed ashore and we are leaving. I have been told that half our cargo of shoes was offloaded. Nothing came on except a plethora of bananas and some supplies. Ollie, the cook, will have one hell of a time serving those up for long. But it was good to taste fresh fruit. Everything on board is either tinned or frozen. At dinner tonight in the officer's mess there was talk of us getting a cargo of teak if we could get rid of the shoes quickly. The engineer suggested throwing them overboard, at which the captain severely rebuked him. The man was only joking. This whole bloody ship is a sub-culture unto itself.

April 12. Here we are back at sea, sailing northwest to who knows where. The captain announced this morning that we are going to Accra in Ghana where we will offload the balance of our cargo of shoes and we then are going Las Palmas. I don't know whether to be happy or angry. I am starting to wonder if I will ever get off this ship. Roddy and the chief engineer asked me if I want to make some quick money. We are to meet this evening and hear their plan.

I can't believe my ears. Roddy and the engineer said that the captain, the chief steward and first mate all have girlfriends here. They want to hide some of the shoes and when the officers go ashore sneak them off and sell them. I'm not sure about it. Roddy says that by the time we eventually get paid by the company, they will have made so many deductions, that we will feel like 'we' have been robbed. Their plan was to have one of crew lowered down the airshaft funnels and pass up the shoes before we dock. They are to be hidden in the paint locker until it is safe to take them ashore. I am concerned, but it seems half the crew is in on this. One of the deck hands is from Accra and says he can sell them to a middleman very quickly. It looks like I am going to go along with it.

April 13. We have secured the stolen cargo. I have to admit it was like something out of a thriller. Bodies being lowered down airshafts. Boxes being passed up on a rope and run off into the night to be hidden in the paint locker. I can't imagine that it will not be noticed. This all took place at 2am when we were at anchor off Accra. This morning when we went alongside, the captain went below decks and came up cursing. "Those thieving bastards in Lusaka. After I signed off on the cargo going ashore, they stole a shit load of shoes." Roddy smiled at me. We were safe. The captain didn't have a clue. After the midday meal, the captain announced that he and the first mate, along with the chief steward, were going ashore and the crew were to get the ship ready to sail at dawn. The pantomime of activity as stolen goods were moved ashore, was quite comical to watch. My share of the booty was a surprise, forty English pounds, 40 American dollars and a handful of Ghanian bank notes. I'm not sure of the total worth, but this will stand me good stead. The shoes must have fetched a good price. Roddy and guys wanted to go ashore and celebrate. I declined. These aren't my type of people. I just want to get the damned task of mine over and done with.

April 14. We sailed at dawn headed for Tenerife in the Canary Islands for a cargo of tomatoes. Where the hell next? A cargo of tomatoes!

April 16. We were in and out of Tenerife in eight hours. There was a rush to deliver the cargo to Marseilles before the tomatoes could become damaged. Nobody got to go ashore. It didn't seem to bother anyone, as the upcoming Marseilles apparently was a much better place to let off steam.

April 19. The three-day trip to Marseilles was uneventful with the exception of crossing the Bay of Biscay. It appears that the Atlantis Ocean currents collide with the Mediterranean currents and create a broiling cauldron of rough water. We lost half the cargo that was stacked ten crates high on the deck. They were smashed to pieces. The cargo below fared better. I swear I will be picking tomato seeds out of my arse for the rest of my life. The fascinating thing was, there was no mess by the time we pulled alongside. No crates, no tomatoes, that was, unless you looked behind and under anything on deck. When I opened my porthole this morning, bloody tomato seeds ran down the bulkhead. What a freaky experience.

April 21. We left Marseilles empty, bound for, believe it or not, Nigeria. My only hope is that something else doesn't crop up to change plans.

April 23. What a night I had last night. It was too rough for me to journal. I thought crossing the Bay of Biscay was scary when we were loaded. Going back across empty is enough to scare the strongest individual. We were tossed around like a shuttlecock. Move forward, bang, stop, lurch forward again, bang lurch stop. It was endless. The horrendous bang sounded like steel on steel. I was so sure we were going to sink. It sounded like the ship was breaking in half, or least chunks of deck were being ripped off. I went to my cabin and pulled the stinky blankets over my head and hoped for the best. Thank god it's over. I thought it would never end. I can't wait to get off this…this..

April 26. We left Marseilles. Roddy says it will be about five days before we get to Nigeria.

April 30. We are about to drop anchor outside the breakwater at Lagos, Nigeria. This morning I spoke with the chief steward about getting off the ship and them paying me off, hopefully. I told him that I was destined to go into the country. He said for me to wait. It could be a few days because the ship may be going up river. SO…wait for my next entry, says he, anxiously.

May 1. We are still at anchor off Lagos. The thing that seemed odd about Lagos is the lack of attention paid to the ship. No launches or contact has come from ashore. It's like we aren't even here. To pass the time, while the *Flowergate* bobbed lazily on the South Atlantic swell, I decided that Roddy, the Scottish steward, would be my first subject for the task I had been assigned. I photographed Roddy with Lagos in the background as he reminisced of Oban on the northwest coast of Scotland. His brogue, though broad, spoke of early childhood dreams, shattered by a drunken father and a strong, domineering mother. 'Me father beat the shite oot my ma. Twas nae a good sitiation. Wah wi me twae deed siblings and nae opportunity for me there. Sae I got oot I ran awa tae sea." He had been a cabin boy for many years and after ten of them, he attained the rank of steward, albeit only one station up, where he has remained for the rest of his life. I wrote two pages and Roddy was happy and willing to sign it without reading it. "I've lived the bloody drama." he said. "I dina wanna spend a second reading it." The bosun, a tall broomstick of a man from Somalia, took my photograph alongside "Jock," as Roddy wished to be called. It does seem sad to me that Roddy has resigned himself to mediocrity. Not that there is anything wrong with that, but I think he's destined to follow in his father's footsteps, if he isn't careful. *If this is how my project is going to be, it doesn't seem too hard*, I thought.

May 2. At last, some activity. The chief steward told me that our instructions were to proceed alongside Lagos and await further instructions. "Is that far enough inland for you my boy?" Not knowing any better I decided to go along with it. I have nothing to lose and any distance inland is a start and won't cost me anything. Apparently, we are going to get the teak logs ourselves. I'm not sure if he expects us to cut them down. Nothing surprises me anymore. Time will tell.

It took an inordinate amount of time for officials to come on board to clear the ship for docking and when they came, it was on a dingy with an outboard motor, not the style of launch I had been accustomed to.

I took my place at the rail with the rest of the crew, watching the shoreline rise and sink with the swell. It wasn't long before the six great big pistons began to rattle the hull as they coaxed the ship into the mouth of the river, with Lagos on the starboard side. I was not really impressed, but was interested to see what it was all about. After weeks chugging along on the *Flowergate*, being fed in accordance with maritime rules, I needed a change. (Incidentally, they tell me that maritime rules were written in the early 1800s for the sailing ships of the day and not for the 1950s. So, eight ounces of meat a week, a piece of fruit daily, lots of bread, and weevil-ridden biscuits were well out of touch with reality. Shit, this is ridiculous)

The river pilot brought us close to the city of Lagos and changed direction to the far side of the river. There was a heated exchange between the captain and the pilot. The pilot insisted, Appapa is Lagos, it's the port for Lagos. The captain lost the battle and we soon tied up at the wharf in Appapa. The ship was followed by hords of dugout canoes with small outboard motors perched precariously on the back ends. The owners touted their wares and offered passage to Lagos. Many offered their sister, brother, mother, or whatever you wanted. It was evident that, as sorry a sight as the *Flowergate* was to me, that to the locals, it was a business opportunity. We are to wait for our next instructions. I started to learn about Nigeria's history from the locals. England had magnanimously recently given Nigeria its independence and it's as if all progress just stopped dead at that time. There is only one crane and watching other ships being loaded and unloaded, with regular tea breaks and stoppages for discussion, usually not of anything to do with the work at hand, this is not the most vibrant daily routine to watch.

As for nighttime, well, that promised delight that a fertile imagination could only dream of. Perhaps it would have been better to leave it to the imagination. The night air is pungent with the smell of cocoa beans and hemp. (My God, I seem to be waxing poetic.) The huge burlap sacks that contained the beans are coarsely woven. My first few steps off the gangway were greeted by cockroaches the size of my childhood dinky toy cars. When I tried to step on one, it proved just about as rigid.

After I worked up some courage, I boarded one of the primitive dugouts to be taken to the Lagos side of the mighty river. It felt like I was taking my life into my own hands. Visions of being beaten and robbed fueled my imagination. But this was the only way to leave the pitch black of Apapa's cargo-laden dockside, which I imagined to be lurking with huge black Maasai or Zulu warriors, waiting to do unimaginable things to me. In the direction of Lagos were bright lights that not only lured one on, but also magnified what might be behind in the pitch-black night. As I pondered what lay behind those lights, I looked over my shoulder at the man paddling the canoe, and imagined a long-bladed dagger hidden under his loincloth. While steering the canoe with one hand, he gaily spoke to "Johnny", that's me, as it was for every sailor. I was only allowed off this skimpy craft after multiple promises to use only him to return. It was emotionally harrowing, to the point at which I think I would have willingly given my firstborn, if I had one, to be allowed off the canoe.

With one foot on the Lagos soil and the other hovering in midair, I worked up the courage to go it alone. A few of my fellow crew had wanted to go ashore as a group, but experience has taught me that a multiracial gang of rowdy sailors on their first night ashore looking for pleasures both carnal and otherwise usually invited attention and trouble. I felt I needed to be as low-key as possible, or at least appear that way. But maybe I was afraid to show my fear and weakness. Sailing the world in the confines of a tramp steamer with men of every conceivable race, attitude, and quality, that I had only known for a few weeks and with whom I had nothing in common, made me keep my cards close to my chest.

Wanting to explore this new place, I placed my life in a taxi driver's hands. The taxi I took was, by my usual standards, filthy, noisy, and damned lucky it got where it was going. All of the bars and dance hall places he took me to were open-air, populated by colorful natives with turban-like headdresses, wrap-around sarong-style robes, and boisterous demeanors. It was disquieting to be introduced by the taxi driver as his friend. I never actually saw another white person all night. There were dirt huts, iron-roofed shelters with upturned oil drums, and a plank acting as a bar. The raucous babbling made me feel like the butt of the joke. Propositions of "Want a good time, Johnny?" came so frequently that I quickly realized that it wasn't my charm that was working. Was everybody who came to Africa called Johnny? I decided that my constitution was not up to this. I had the driver bring me back to the river. It was as if he passed through only darkened streets. Great ditches lay open beside the roads with huge sewage pipes yet to be connected. Excrement oozed out unconnected seams. Apparently, the British had left projects unfinished and the locals never got round to completing them. I hurried back to my cramped, paint-peeling cabin on the rust bucket that offered me the only form of refuge I could find.

I learned from my father, always to pay attention to your surroundings and be honest with yourself, no matter what front you put on to the others, know your own truth. This may seem trite, but it helps you back down when you have to maintain face. But I didn't know these people, much less care about maintaining face with them. These black people were nothing like those in America. It was as if the warrior these people have in them, has been knocked out of their American counterparts. As I write this, I must wonder what in this experience did my parents hope I would gain?

May 26. The wait-time passed slowly, allowing me to relish the sun and little else. We soon learned where the *Flowergate* was going. We untied from the wharf and left Apapa to return to the ocean, outside of the breakwater. Here, we dropped anchor again and waited for confirmation of our next cargo. The Somali bosun screamed orders in his language, expecting to be understood by the international crew. Roddy, sorry, Jock and I passed the time by throwing each other overboard. This may seem extreme, but the drop to water level from the empty vessel's top deck was only about twenty feet. I was almost as fast returning to the rope ladder as I was hitting the water. Was I afraid of sharks? Sort of, but more than that, I was afraid of anything unknown in the water. Two hours later we pulled up anchor and headed to a place called Port Harcourt to await a delivery of teak logs from Sapele. The next day, no sooner had we arrived at Port Harcourt, when we were instructed to turn about and go directly to Sapele. It appears that we could wait for the logs that were at Sapele to be transported by road to Warri and then floated down to Port Harcourt, or we could go directly to Sapele. The *Flowergate* was small enough to sail up the Benin River to Sapele and tow the logs to deeper water. We are to be on the move. Maybe now, I can get my task out of the way

Chapter 29

May 6. The next morning found the *Flowergate* once again bobbing at anchor, offshore from sandy beaches lined by palm groves. Tourist brochures display such pristine vistas, but these are spooky, no people, no buildings, nothing. But in the intense, searing midday sun, a tiny speck emerged from between the groves. It was a small dingy with an outboard motor, slowly pushing toward us. Two hours later, a river pilot boarded and ordered the anchors hoisted. We are about to be going upriver.

We' shall be going upriver to Koko, where shall spend the night and change river pilots. There pilots will be changed before proceeding to Sapele. There the captain will oversee the selection of teak logs, which will be chained together and towed out to sea. This seems like a lot of work to me.

May 7. All I had ever read about the wildlife that live in Africa has not prepared me for this experience. From the moment the river pilot guided the SS *Flowergate* into the mouth of the river, things looked as if we would have no problems. Things soon began to change. Leaving behind the deep, clear, sparkling cerulean waters, we swiftly approached a broad band of sludge-brown water, *where the river and sea meet and mingle. Hanging around the ship's rail were some twenty or so local Nigerians. Nobody seemed to know who or what they were.* They're not passengers in the true sense, but firmly ensconced aboard as if they belonged. They are more like freeloaders. When I asked, one of the men told me, in weird, broken English, "We work the ship, help the pilot, do anything you need done, Johnny." They had cooking utensils and large packages bundled in cloth and tied with vines. It looked to me as if every one of them had his own supply of bananas.

Quickly, the ocean was was behind us and the wide river mouth narrowed at an alarming pace. Distant riverbanks now became muddy groves of tangled tree roots, so close one could almost touch them. Tree limbs would thwack the masts, the loading derricks and the funnel. Leaves rained down like large green snowflakes. This shit was too much for me. I retired to my cabin and locked myself in, attempting to hide and secrete away any belongings I thought would be attractive items to be stolen. This is foolish. Everything is an attractive item to be stolen to these barbarians. Satisfied I'd done enough, I opened the cabin door, and my heart rate went into overdrive. When I entered the passage, I saw three monkeys shrieking and jabbering, looking as if they were deciding whether or not to attack. Slamming the door shut, I opened my porthole and exited through it. From then on, for what seemed like hours, the riverbank would remain only a few feet, sometimes inches, from the port side, with everything growing along the bank brushing against the side of the ship. As quickly as this would start, the ship would lurch to one side as the pilot headed for the opposite bank to navigate a bend, only to have the same problem on the starboard side. All kinds of debris flew onto the deck. Monkeys, bugs, lizards, and small snakes and the occasional very large snake would thud onto the deck as well. The black fellows scrambled around with large tree limbs, clubbing the snakes. Every time they got a good-sized one, animated jabbering would fill the air. But their excitement is my misery. The exhausting pandemonium lasted all day until the river, at last, widened to about four times the ship's berth. Dusk had started in by the time we arrived at Koko. While it is good to get a break from the persistent noise, this place was like something out of *The African Queen film,* with natives running around half-naked, shouting at whoever was listening and canoes swarming the ship. Straw-roofed huts stood clustered together, interspersed among iron-roofed structures without walls. Smoke wafted around the settlement from what appeared to be cooking fires. This is not a town or village by my frame of reference; it is more of a settlement, like those of the Picts, Celts, Saxons and serfs of old England. But this is the nineteen fifties, and I, am not very comfortable.

As bad a cook as Ollie is, what he made was fit for a king compared to the culinary activities on the ship's deck. The self-appointed Nigerian helpers invited local natives onboard where the decapitated snake bodies and the plumper of the monkeys are being prepared for cooking. It is as if animals are eating animals. As night set in, the darkness got blacker and blacker and unseen night creatures brushed past my face. Some fly straight into my mouth. Creatures whose identity could only be guessed at supplied the orchestral accompaniment. Maybe they were frogs, crickets, mosquitoes, or cockroaches. There would be no going ashore for me in this place, thank you. Cabin door locked, lights off, head under the sheets, I was determined to sleep until it was all over, but so very little sleep was had.

May 8. The locals have risen early, and Koko settlement is bustling. Our temporary crew was untying the hawsers in aft and forward of the ship that had held us in place all night. The ship seemed to cough and sputter as the huge engine's piston turned and burst out a cacophony. We are underway. But the second part of the upriver voyage to Sapele was no different than the trip to Port Harcourt, with one exception: The river failed to widen periodically, staying close to one side or the other for the entire day. With each bounty of snake or monkey, the new crew becomes more selective about what to keep and what to throw overboard. They did not spare the lives of those they chose not to keep. I was able to corner and catch a small grass monkey without being bitten and I hid him in my cabin locker. I had no idea what I was going to do with the animal, but letting him be killed because he was not big enough to eat just seemed sad. After a time, I opened the cabin door slightly and placed a piece of banana inside. Surprisingly, the monkey had calmed down. One time, when I opened the door, the tiny creature was asleep in the drip well of the porthole. Perhaps things sane and normal do exist in this place.

The ship arrived in Sapele as the sun set. The river pilot went ashore. No shore leave was granted. That rule is for the crew, but it did not seem to apply to the black crew or locals. It was impossible to tell them from each other as they scurried about, jabbering nonsense. Two of the Ghanaian crew somehow had their wives with them. It was all very confusing. As I thought back to some of the tales Grandmother

Agatha used to tell of Great-Grandfather Judd, it was easy for me to see why there was the need for firm control over the seamen.

May 10. Sapele was a bustling place of industrious activity. The river widened to such an extent that, when the locals ashore secured the ship's bow to huge posts sunk securely in the middle of the river, the ship was able to slowly swing around with the river's current, ultimately facing the way we came and the way we wanted to go. The ship was now secured by hawsers from the stern to the shore in order to keep it aligned with the shore and anchored from the bow to keep it in place. Almost immediately after, huge teak logs were allowed to drift to the ship's side, where one of *Flowergate's* agents would approve it, tag it, and chain it to the next log. This operation continued throughout the night and all the next day. As primitive as this system was, in no time at all, we had amassed a huge armada of logs ready to be towed out to the open sea. These massive chunks of wood were linked together in such a way that when the ship moved, as long as it maintained a set pace, the logs would gracefully follow. We were informed that the last log in the line was around the river bend behind us and it had to be secured to the bank. Otherwise, the current would push all the logs to the front of the ship. The hawsers that held us in place were untied to allow the ship slowly be swung about by the river's current. When we were in palce in front of the logs, the rear log was freed from its' tether and we were all set to go. When we leave, I am told that there will be natives spaced along the long string of logs. Their job will be to fend the logs off from the banks on corners to prevent snagging. We had to stay the night, as the trip out to Koko was to be a nonstop journey. The second leg of the journey could be in darkness and put us in the ocean by midday. The captain informed the entire crew that the second leg, being in darkness, would require the entire crew, cabin staff included, to man a watch station at the ship's side for the whole night—no exceptions. Thus, early to bed tonight. I didn't mind, because Sapele was not on my radar as a place in which to satisfy my urges esoteric, carnal, or otherwise. But even more important, I had to accomplish my task. I needed to find a subject.

With all the logs chained and ready to go, I was assigned to stand the evening watch at the ship's portside bow. The evening watch suited me, as it lasted from four o'clock until six. There was still daylight left when I was joined by the Sapele harbormaster, who spoke with the most perfect English accent. His enunciation and grammar were spellbinding. Listening to him talk reminded me of JM Fetters, plumb in the mouth style of speech. I knew I'd found my next subject. Before daylight slipped completely away behind the giant palms, I encouraged him to climb down the ship's ladder and stand on the logs so I might photograph him with the *Flowergate* behind him. He agreed and posed and then posed with me, much to the amusement and excitement of the locals. After returning aboard, we stood at the ship's rail, smoking Lucky Strike cigarettes, which he took much pleasure in. The man opened up and told me his life story without any prompting. The situation could not have been better. I think JM will like this one. The man's name was Leslie Garunds Amabollo. He was the son of an English colonial rubber baron, Nigel Garunds, and one of Nigel's servant women, Hyacinth Amabollo. Nigel Garunds had exiled himself to Nigeria in protest of something long forgotten, leaving his wife back in England. His career had blossomed in local plantations to the extent that he eventually owned his own, leasing it to others for the collection of rubber sap. When the English pulled out of Nigeria, it created a catastrophic vacuum in the economy, with many plantation growers and businessmen leaving the country.

Leslie had been sent to boarding school in England in the more affluent days, an experience he regarded now with as much pride as sadness. "The English still call us wogs and all manner of unpleasant names," he said. "I don't think they hate us. They just treat us much better when we are in our own country." The vacuum left many locals striving to fill the vacant jobs, placing many unqualified people in top positions. Though Leslie's education had taught him much of an academic nature, he valued more what he had learned about life and people. He believed that top people come and go and bottom people are dispensable, but the middle core seems to escape the fluctuations. With this in mind, he focused on managing workers while remaining non-threatening to his superiors. This strategy had worked, as he had seen six bosses come go in seven years and not once, did he feel at risk. Nigel Garunds had long since sold out his holdings to a multi-national conglomerate. The change in ownership had not affected Leslie.

Leslie is married to a girl from the Yoruba tribe to which his mother belonged. Both he and his wife spoke Yoruba and Hausa, which gave them great flexibility in managing the workers. As Sapele harbormaster, he holds sway over everything that comes into the town, as the river is the only consistent and dependable route. His wife and mother both work in his office and so his family maintains as good a living as they'd ever had under English rule. He has two boys, six and eight, and speaks of the importance of their education. I wish that I could have enough time to get them altogether for a photograph. Leslie appears sad that the education he received was not available to his boys, he felt this was due to him via his English connection. He feels that he is invisible to the English, now the colonial era is over. In the eyes of the law he no longer warrants the privileges he once had. When I asked him if he minded if I made a record of his story for a project I was working on, he was proud, willing, and happy to sign it.

The ship's four-bells signaled the end of second watch, eighteen hundred hours rang out. While the watch change took place, everyone else started to gather at the bow, pointing at a large, bloated body of a black person, its leg grotesquely snagged in the anchor cable. It is as if the body has been inflated to stay afloat. The spectacle did not seem to have any importance to the local populace who are busy concentrating on their own daily routines. A small craft ferried across the river and dugout canoes attempted to ply any last-minute trade before we left. They were all uninterested at what is playing out before them.

Leslie left me and went to the bridge where he used the ship-to-shore telephone to summon the police, then returned to watch the spectacle play out. The response to his call came faster than expected. A well-kept motor launch with official insignia emblazoned on the colorfully painted superstructure sped to the *Flowergate's* bow, where the huge anchor cable links disappear beneath the murky water. The wave bow wave created by the boat made the dead body a dam-like obstacle, but this was quickly fixed by the man standing erect on the launch's bow. He used a long boat hook to untangle the body, generating a huge roar of approval from the natives that are travelling with us. The body quickly gained speed on its way downriver, toward the sea.

"Why did they do that?" I asked Leslie. "I would have thought they would have pulled the body out."

"No reason to. He is dead. Probably deserved to end up that way. Some pretty bad people upriver from here. Nobody is going to tell the police anything. All the local people believe that the police are still connected to the British Empire, and as such, they are greatly distrusted. The fish will take care of the remains long before the sea gets a chance." With that, the man turned and proffered his hand to me. The ship's watch was over and he was leaving. I took the opportunity to ask Leslie if he would send my journal and photographs to America for me. Leslie agreed and took the details, refusing any form of payment. He promised to have the film developed and sign the pictures before sending them. I don't believe I am taking any chances, as Leslie comes across as a very dependable man.

I am attaching this note for you JM, Hopefully, you will read it and contact me to come back to Buffalo. I will stay with the SS Flowergate. It can be reached via radio. The ship is owned by Messers, Turnbull and Stott in London. I think this should be easy enough for you to find out how to contact the ship directly.

It took two days to go up river from the sea to Sapelle and I thought that was nerve-wracking. The two days to come back out were horrific. There was no stopping at Koko. We kept going throughout the night. A man was positioned on every other log to fend off from the bank. They kept on shouting to each other. The noise quickly became tiring and quickly moved to damned annoying. I was never so glad to see the sea again. It took three days for us to load the logs into the holds and secure the others to the deck.

Chapter 30

Journal of Lillian Jane Blacksmith)

April 15 1957. Well, I am on my way. As I sit in the luxurious first-class cabin, that Qantas had generously delivered to my door free of charge. I have no qualms about using my connections in the airline industry to arrange a future consult with Qantas that happened to include my travel and hotel in Sydney. If I am breaking the rules of the task, it's a matter of semantics and does not bother me. Something is not quite right about this so-called task. Father, well I can see him wanting me to experience different things in this, but mother, I just don't connect the dots. She was so practical and down to earth. Everything in her life and her fathers' comes down to that, it has to have purpose. I don't see what practical purpose this is going to achieve. I know you are going to see this journal, JM, but that is not going to stop me from writing just how I feel. I am pissed off with you for riding me to do this task. You know bloody well that I do what I set out to do. Having said that, back to the task in hand.

While I am there, I am going to look at what the Australians are doing with small aircraft in rural areas. There may be a business opportunity there. My research shows me that the Australians are prolific travelers who think nothing of driving great distances at short notice. Their gregarious, outgoing personalities seem to equip them with a fearless ability to ignore risks and face whatever confronts them. "She'll be right, mate." seems to be a mantra to them. I am learning a lot about the people from the Aircrew, they are a very open people. The Australian attitude toward each other and to the outside world is interesting. It appears they are nearly isolationist in their attitudes, and yet extremely friendly. They do not tell the outside world much about themselves and yet, are fiercely proud of their country. "Mateship" is a prime driving force in their lives, so it seems. They help those who need it without ceremony or obligation. I think I might enjoy this task more than I expected to.

One of the damn good-looking stewards, an Irishman named Danny, suggested that if I was to travel the bush or go 'back of beyond', as he puts it, I would be wise to get a rifle for protection. I am not sure if he is playing with me or trying to frighten me. I sense a high degree of male superiority in him. He exudes an attractive masculinity that could be off-putting, but I find it very sexy. I might just see if he could be considered for the number one position.

Upon the approach into Sydney, I am mesmerized by what I see. The Kingsford Smith Airport was just as I remembered it. Other erotic memories, of Sydney, a pilot and payback. I wonder whatever happened to him. Danny tells me it is one of the oldest airports in the world. The Sydney Harbour Bridge connects two vast sides of the harbor, with houses and roads and factories that could compare with those of any American city. The fingers of the harbour's myriad of peninsulas are covered with homes and lush green foliage. The ferries darting about, are numerous as they slice through the deep blue waters like white ants running about their business. They leave white lines of froth as if to say, "See where I have come from." Large passenger liners shine white against the majestic skyline of buildings. The site for the proposed Sydney Opera House sticks out like a thumbnail waiting to beautified. The site surrounded by water the most alluring and complex shades of blue

The arrivals hall and customs and immigration were bursting with a welcoming air. While waiting my turn my thoughts kept jumping back to my first time here. If I didn't know 'g'day' when I arrived, I felt at ease saying it by the time I had cleared the massive hall. Talk about slang, 'g'day' is 'have a good day,' shortened. I guess they don't waste words here. It is as if something has pumped my chest with an exciting, euphoric air. I have experienced this kind of excitement before and I feel alive. All these people seem so upbeat, happy and energized. Perhaps my task will not be a bore.

I instructed my taxi driver to take me to The Hotel Australia. He suggested a tour of the sights; Kings Cross, Circular Quay and Piermont, but I told him to take me straight to the hotel. He had a Mediterranean look about him, and spoke with a broad Aussie accent. Reading his taxi identification, I saw that his last name looked Greek and asked him about it, saying that I could not understand much of what he was saying. "Lady, me family name is Nikol-ako-poulos", he syllabized it slowly for me. "My grandparents came to Stralia from Pitsa, a small town in Peloponnesuss, a part of Greece. I am second generation Aussie. There are a lot of us Greeks, Italians, and Pommies, thems is the English people, we call em pommie bastards. Did you understand that, lady?" he said with a huge smile. "I take you for a ride round the city center, and show you a few sights on the way, no extra charge." I just lay back in the taxi seat and drank in his excited and exuberant descriptions of the places we passed through. As I paid him, I asked him about the outback and if he thought I might need a gun. "Bloody right mate. Them 'roos are big buggers and it never hurts to show you mean business. A sheila should always protect 'erself." I paid him and gave a large tip. He happily shouted over his shoulder, "Oroo missus." I don't know what that meant, but it sounded friendly. This young man has put a positive spin on my project. It seems the Australian men refer to all females as 'sheila's.

April 19. This is very strange; today isn't the 19th as it should be. Australian is so far ahead of American time that today's date here is the 20th. It feels like a day got lost somewhere. Anyway, As I was leaving the airport terminal, my cabin steward Danny appears out of nowhere, very dapper in his uniform, and wants to know where I was staying. Who am I to resist a temptation? I told him. "The Hotel Australia on Macquarie Street."

"I know where it is. I will pick you up at six this evening and show you our town." Presumptuous man. He didn't even wait for an answer. Then he was gone. They don't waste words here and it looks like they don't waste time either.

(This note is for you JM. You want a report? You are going to get one. I am leaving nothing out and I bet mine will read better than my brother's.) What a night I had last night.

My suite in the hotel commands a spectacular view of the harbor. I don't feel tired as I slept most of the arduous flight. I almost feel like I am on vacation. However, I did fall asleep to be woken by the telephone. "There's is Mr. Hannigan to see you ma'am, shall I send him up or will you come down?"

Without thinking, I just said "send him up." When I answered the door, Danny stood there sexier than ever. Shirt open to his chest, beautiful looking man with a big smile, how could I resist? He walked in, closed the door and unbuttoned his shirt and pulled me toward himself. He slid his hand in the front of my dress. Cool hands, warm breast, result: responding nipple. Need I say more? Later that evening, sated, we went out to eat. I ached the ache of a completely satisfied woman. Me, an American of English descent, in Australia with an Irish lover. I have had my own international congress going on here. I like Australia already. I wasn't thinking of making Danny one the subjects of my task. He was just a digression. A very pleasant digression indeed.

We walked to Kings Cross and as the darkness of night settled in, the neon lights and party atmosphere blossomed. Everyone I saw was having fun and laughter filled the cool night air. This is the cleanest city I have ever seen. The colors were vibrant, and the people were so alive. Almost every person I spoke to wanted to know where I was from and how long I was visiting. This place had the energy of New York City with the joy of life of San Francisco. I'm not sure if my tiredness is from the flight or from the sex, either way I don't care, I'm happy. We stopped at a restaurant with street-side tables and ordered a meal. I did not feel out of place amongst the crowd. A group at the next table asked if we would like to join them, Danny agreed and we did. They were six young adults, all postgraduate university students. I digress, our waiter Stavros was very gregarious, we soon learned all about his family background. Stavros Politiadis was his family name and they had immigrated to Australia from Athens in the 1930's. His parents were farmers and had come to start a new life, a better life for their children. Being from a big city, they had dreamed of owning more land than they had in Greece. To assimilate they decided to change their family name to Politis. I don't see much difference. They purchased a large rural property in Balmain on the south shore of Sydney. They had become successful market gardeners. Stavros had grown up speaking Greek as well as English. I should say, 'Australian' because there is a difference between English and Australian. His parents insisted on an education, something that was not a big thing in Greece at the time. Stavros's bilingual ability was an advantage for him as a waiter, as Sydney had many tourists and huge multi-cultural population. Sydney reminds me of New York City, in that many languages are quite common here. I took a photograph of Stavros with the group and the big Kings Cross neon sign and then I had Danny take one of Stavros and me. I hope this covers JM's requirements.

Around Midnight, Danny had to leave due to a flight the next day. I asked him if I should leave with him. He suggested that I stay with the group and 'get to know the natives.' I did. There was no suggestion of meeting again. Oh well, there's plenty of men out there. I don't need a number one man permanently.

I stayed with the group for about an hour when the subject of my trip came up. When I mentioned Ayers Rock, they took a quick count of hands at the comment, "who wants to go to Ayer's Rock?" The count was six. "So, Lil, how are we going to get there?" one asked.

"What do you mean, we?" I asked.

One of the girls said, "We are on our summer hols from uni, so we are free. It will save us all money if we club together and rent a combi."

I asked them, "What's a combi? Why would you want to go with an old lady like me?"

One of the boys said that I sure don't look like an old chook to Him. "What are you thirty something?" He said that I seemed like a fun person. I didn't tell him my age. I liked the 'something'. It turns out that a 'combi' is Volkswagon combination van, capable of carrying twelve passengers. His thought was that the seven of us and our luggage would be fine. The point of the shared cost made sense if I was supposed to not be using my own money. They offered to show me around Sydney the next day so that we could get to know each other better. I took them up on their offer. We arranged to meet in my hotel lobby at 9am the next morning. By the time I got to bed I was too tired to think about anything and had completely forgotten about using Stavros for my JM subject.

April 21. I woke up early this morning and had coffee in my room looking out over the glittering spectacle of the city. I decided that, if the students appeal to me as a group, I would travel with them.

We met downstairs and as none had eaten, I suggested a breakfast planning meeting. Elvira, the oldest balked, she said they weren't rich enough to eat breakfast in this hotel. It was funny how she held her arms and pirouetted in a display of awe at the opulence. I tend to forget that not everyone is as fortunate as I am. I got the message and offered to treat them. For the love of me, I could not recall all their names. So, I had each tell me their story. The group consisted of three boys and three girls, aged nineteen to twenty-five. The oldest was Elvira, 25, a tall, buxom, no-nonsense, country girl from Dubbo, in New South Wales. Then there was Mario, 19, from Woolongong, New South Wales. Then came Martin from Geelong, Victoria, and Rosy, 21, also from Victoria, Warnambool. Followed by Mikos, 23, from Mount Gambia, South Australia and finally, Matilda, 20, from Calundra in Queensland. I am sure I will learn more about them as time goes by. Between them, they represented four of the six states in Australia. None seemed to have any romantic attachments to the others, although I do sense some connections. Martin, the youngest in the group, gave me the nickname Aunt or, as it quickly became, Aunt Lill. Just as quickly, Aunt Lill was shortened to just plain old 'Lill'. I offered to rent a 'combi' van so that we could use it for a couple of days to see if it would work for the trip to Ayer's Rock or 'The Alice' as they called it.

Today we toured the city center. I was impressed by the colonial architecture and life of the city. After lunch we went to Circular key. There, two P&O ocean liners were berthed along-side the modern terminal. The Orianna and the Arcadia.

These huge ships dwarfed the ferries that seem to depart nonstop. Six wharves serving twelve ferry destinations. It was fascinating to watch the movement. There is a strangely hypnotic effect just standing and watching everything. I sat and listened to the group talking as we sipped our frozen pineapple drinks. This was a new experience for me. They tell me that we are going to take a ferry tomorrow morning to Tarronga Park Zoo and some beaches in the afternoon. I had read about kangaroos and koalas, but seeing them, my word. I don't think many people who haven't seen a kangaroo understand just how many types there and just how big they can be. An amazing array of strange and odd animals here. I loved the zoo. The group was planning to go dancing tonight. I begged off. For no other reason than dancing just does not appeal to me. Plus, I needed to do my journal for today. I had taken plenty of photographs and I was tired. I did, however, say that we should make some firm plans for the trip to Ayer's Rock.

April 23. This morning I offered to provide the transport we would need for the trip, conditional upon them accepting me as the voice of reason, should it be required. They knew how to party and were vigorously proud of being Australian. Their energy and drive was infectious. I just wanted to be the voice of reason, should any conflict occur. Frankly, I don't expect it, but I need to be sure. My offer was received with excitement. I raised the issue of a gun for protection. I told them that I had been advised by more than one person, that for me to go into the bush without proper considerations such as water, food, spare parts, etc., would be foolish. I wanted to know what their thoughts were. The group erupted into a cacophony of discussion. When all was done, it was agreed that the presence of a firearm would be wise. Mario had a relative at the Pyrmont Wharves, where the nautical commerce was centered, and was sure the man would sell us a gun. His actual words were, "Well, sell a gun to Aunt Lill, I mean, with the right paperwork." He went on to say "As for tucker and stuff like Lill don't worry, she'll be right. "" It took us a couple of hours to accomplish the acquisition of the gun. I told them that the gun should be hidden within the vehicle. I spent the afternoon with them showing me the beaches. Coogee, Bondi, Manly, Mossman, there were so many of them. It suddenly hit me that the only thing I knew as a beach was Crystal Beach in Fort Erie, Canada, Wend't beach, south of Buffalo and Gallagher beach and they were all on a lake. The surf and salty water fascinated me. I hope to be able to take a swim in the sea before I leave Australia. Elvira pulled me to one side and said, "I saw you looking confused about what Mario said regarding food and supplies. She'll be right is just simply saying, don't worry about it. Us younger Aussies are more laid back and take things as they come. Between here and The Alice there will be plenty of small towns and places to get whatever we might need. The only planning we should really do is tents and stuff." I was grateful for her watchful eye over my confusion.

Over dinner, which ended up being a beach barby, the group agreed to pool their limited resources and have me handle the finances for the journey. They grudgingly agreed that I would have the final say in spending. I tried to make plans for our route to Ayers Rock and was met with a resounding, "No plans, that's for Sheilas.

Let's just follow the road." So, this being their country and them knowing more about it than me, I agreed to their idea.

Chapter 31

April 24. Alone in the hotel parking lot waiting for my fellow travellers, I sat in the van by the open door, studying 'the gun'. It was a Winchester Model 70, bolt-action rifle about ten years old. While the barrel was just metal, I found the stock captivating. The grain of the wood, with its deep mahogany glow seemed alive. The swirls of the grain, marred by continual use wearing off the finish, shone with what I assumed to be oil from the hands of the myriad of users. I wondered what this gun might have seen: A fight, a barroom brawl, fights over sheep or cattle, or maybe the slaughtering of rabbits in the big myxomatosis scare in the fifties. I resisted the urge to hold the gun and peer through its sights. After removing a lot of the luggage and belongings, I placed the gun carefully in a place where it could be reached quickly. To be honest, I am very nervous about the whole gun issue, but I suppose it's wise to listen those that know more than I do. I hope I never see it again.

Much to my surprise, everybody arrived on time with their entourage of well-wishers and friends. Personal effects were stowed. Mikos, the oldest of the boys, offered to start driving. I had no intention of driving. Right now, driving on the left was one of the few things that intimidate me, although I don't think it will be long before I try it.

The van was stocked with cases of beer, flagons of wine, and all types of munchies, Cherry Ripes, Violet Crumbles and crisps, that's what they call potato chips. With the honking of horns and jubilant shouts, Mikos pulled out of the parking lot onto Macquarie Street and headed out of Sydney.

He announced that we were headed through the Blue Mountains to Bathurst, a distance of 131 miles. There was talk among us that Australia will one day be converting to the metric system. They seemed divided on whether it will ever happen and if they liked it or not.

The orderliness of the outlying towns and villages of Sydney soon gave way to the majesty of the Blue Mountains. It is now Fall here, what they call autumn, although for us at home it is now spring. No wonder we think Australia is upside down. It is bit confusing, as our gardens start to grow in the spring, here theirs start to grow when the weather cools and becomes wetter. There isa myriad of wild flowers in every crevice and open space. Elvira points them out; Sour Sobs, which are brilliant sulphur yellow, Salvation Jane is a pale blue, Oleanda shrubs of bright reds, pinks and white, Agapanthus, which are a vibrant strong blue, the names are fascinating.

The plan is to stop for lunch before heading for Bathurst, then to West Wyalong, where we would spend the night. When I asked about sleeping arrangements, Rosy said, "Don't worry, mate. She'll be right." Another Australian phrase I am hearing a lot. Everyone here seems to be so laid back. It's not what I am used to. Soon, the mountains are behind us and before us is a vista of farm after farm, growing produce for the big city. Many are smallholdings, parcels of land as small as five acres and as big as fifty, farmed by single families. Most, I learned, were migrant families from Ireland, England, and nearly every Mediterranean country. The land looks so rich and fertile. This is altering my preconceived notions that Australia is one huge desert. The dense greenery and trees and lush vegetation are such a contradiction to my expectations.

The chatter in the van was endless, each passenger relating experiences and stories. I often just sat quietly, listening to their banter., often not understanding the slang they were using. Towns flashed by with strange sounding names like Katoomba and Lithgow, as did signs to places with even stranger sounding names such as Wollemi, Mudgee, Cowra, and Coolamundra. Every sign was spoken with the broad Australian accent, after I mangled it with my American accent. They seem to place the emphasis on different vowels than I would, and drag out the pronunciation.

Mikos likened the area to the orchards around the River Murray flood plains. He told how the regular flooding of the Murray kept the large tracts of land on either side rich in alluvial deposits. "It's always a big happening every year when the floods hit." he said.

I Started to warm toward Mikos, he was very knowledgeable and got onto the subject of the Queenslanders. Their family businesses are predominantly lamb and beef farming. The great outback stations that covered the country were an organized blanket of commerce, an interwoven mesh of nationalities, cultures, and traditions. This huge network, it appeared, was ready to drop everything in times of tragedy and need and come to each other's aid. Mikos simply said, "We are all Australians, mate."

"What are stations?" I asked.

"That's what we call these huge properties. They are way too big to be farms. That's why they call them stations." It soon became evident why the Australians were able to bond together to achieve a common goal on this trip. It was plain to see that in this group of youngsters.

We made good time and after a brief stop in Bathurst for lunch, we decided to press on. Rosy, from Victoria, took the wheel. I declined the offer to drive just then. I wanted to feel more comfortable on these roads. The van hummed with chatter and laughter between Mario, Rosy and Matilda while the others dozed. Small towns sped past with little comment. By the end of the day, we were twelve miles away from Cowra, which put us about where we agreed we would stay the night instead of West Wyalong.

We were about to stop when a lone traveler thumbed us down for a ride. Rosy stopped the van and all of us tumbled out to stretch our weary bones. The traveler was a sun-dried, wizened man, on his way wherever. It was very difficult to gauge his age due to his leathery skin. Mario asked the man, "Where you going cobber?"

"Where ever you want to take me. I'm on walkabout."

"You ok with us giving him a ride Lill?"

"If everyone agrees, that's fine." I told him. The man said, you lot look buggered. Do you want me to make a billy of tea?"

Elvria replied, "This is Aunt Lill, she has never seen anything like this. Let's do it." The man scurried around gathering sticks and before long he had a can of water boiling over a small fire. I was intrigued when he threw a small stick into the boiling tea, and I asked, "Why did you do that?"

"Stops the tea tasting of smoke." We gathered round and sipped the hot brew. The man regaled us with his background.

"Me ma was an abbo, and she tells me that me dad was an American airman. Based at Woomera, they say." he said. "Guess that's about right, 'cause she is a Pitjantjatjara, from Uluru. That's up the track aways from Woomera, and I aint exactly a full abbo" He had the unusual name of Ben Franklin. When I told him that we had left Sydney that morning for Ayers Rock, he laughed. "A bloody septic tank, Yank, going to the rock. Yer got yer own Ben Franklin. Bet yer never met 'im. Now you can tell yer friends yew ave met Ben Franklin." He laughs at his own humor without waiting to see if anyone else thinks it's funny. You made bloody good time, cobber. Me, I'm on walkabout. No hurry for me. Need a change, like. Me plates are a bit knackered. Glad you got room for one more for a bit, mate"

Thank God Elvira translated for me. "His feet are bothering him and he's out to see the country." she asked again, "Can we give him a lift?"

I was uncertain, but the willingness of the group encouraged me to go along with the idea. Elvira explained that it was very Australian to help a traveler along his way.

As night closed in, Ben suggested we camp where we were for the night. I had never done this before and was interested to experience it. Quickly, we set up a fire and tents, and before the night was completely black, we were enjoying a meal and gradually falling asleep. Ben Franklin refused the offer to sleep in a tent. Unfurling his roll, he mounded some soil for a pillow and promised to keep watch for the night. He pulled out a Colt revolver and tucked it under his roll. "You don't know what them bloody dingoes can do. Fire should keep the 'roos away, but they do get a bit dolally when they get excited." he said.

"Dollally?" I ask.

"Yep, that's a bit loose in the head, crazy like."

I was nervous that this stranger had a gun, but yet, as each member of the group quietly bade the others a good night and peace settled in, I relaxed. Oh yes, a roo is a kangaroo. I am slowly picking up the slang terms.

April24. The blinding sun forced me to cover my eyes as I awakened to the sound of gunfire. Looking around, I found myself alone among the empty sleeping bags. The fire still burned strongly, and a billycan was bubbling away furiously in the smoky flames. Panicked, I stood up and found the group surrounding Ben who stood astride a large, mangy looking, animal. "It's a dingo, the bugger took more than one shot." Ben said. "We better shift our bods and bury him before anything else gets a whiff of him. We don't want scavengers bothering us."

I went to Ben and demanded the gun, but he refused. Our heated discussion was calmed by the students, who were united in their defense of Ben. "We told you that a gun is an integral part of life in the outback, sometimes to defend and often to put an injured animal out of its suffering. Ben was protecting us. Calm down Lill."

Ben took me to one side and gave me the gun. "Life out here can be bloody rough." he said. "Roos get hurt, get hit by a car, sheep get injured, and then there's the human animals. Some real drongos go bush to hide from the law, or other things. The boys told me you have rifle stashed away. Lady, your gun often only needs to be seen to be useful." In a gesture of goodwill he said, "Keep the Colt. I have another in my kit. A Sheila needs a gun. By the time I leave you, you and at least one other person here will know how to use it. I'm pretty nifty with me boomerang anyway."

"Aunt, all of us are comfortable around guns." Elvira said. "We just thought you were nervous, so we all kept quiet. Besides, I bet Ben really is good with his boomerang." Elvira is clearly emerging as the dominant one in the group. We packed up and resumed our trip. Stopping briefly for lunch at Narrandera, we were soon back on the road again. We camped the night just outside Mildura, our last town in New south Wales. There was some debate between the boys and girls about going up north to Broken Hill or going west to South Australia. Both sides argued their case, looking to me for support. I simply told them that I was in no position to decide. I don't know enough about either way. My focus was to get to Ayers rock. As there was no clear consensus, I settled for Broken Hill, the name intrigued me.

April26. The drive north to Broken Hill took the entire day, then we set up camp for the night, just outside Broken Hill. I asked, "Why do we always camp outside of towns and not go into town, aren't there any camp sites?"

Ben's answer summed everything up. "Why pay to set up camp next to a lot of other campers when out here under the stars, you can experience the real Australia, not the sanitized version."

Mikos added, "There is something calm and peaceful about being in the bush. I love it."

Mario laughed as he said, "Holiday Inn is camping for me, although I do enjoy the camaraderie." Matilda, who didn't talk as much as the others said, "I don't care either way. I get just a bit nervous about spiders, snakes and creepy crawlies."

I said, "Ok, ok let's change the subject." To this point I haven't seen any spiders or snakes and the further they are from my mind the better. The mining town's welcoming sign boasted a population of thirty thousand. Mikos said it used to be a lot more than that, as the mining was now pretty much down to various minerals with iron ore being predominant. I got a brief history lesson on the place. After setting up camp, we decided to go into town, eat at a proper table, and look around. The group broke off into pairs after agreeing to meet up at the Royal Exchange Hotel for dinner. Mario asked, "Who's shouting?"

"Nobody. I didn't hear anyone shout." I said Everyone thought I was hilarious.

I asked, "What are you all laughing about?"

Martin told me, "Who's shouting means who is paying." I told them dinner would be my 'shout'.

We went our separate ways. Ben acted as my tour guide, as he had worked the mines as a teenager before 'giving up the normal life', as locals called it.

Ben said, "Picture books and mags, that's magazines, got my imagination going. I wanted to see it all for meself." His easygoing manner got me thinking about my own life and how simple it had been. I asked him about why he was doing a 'walkabout'. His description of how Aborigines had been treated by the British colonizers and then by the "new" Australians, evoked a sadness in me. It was plain to see the admiration and respect Ben had for his Aboriginal people. It was their truly nomadic lifestyle that he modeled his own life on.

"I want for nothing, need nothing, and want to take nothing from this country without giving something back. That's why I buried the dingo." He explained.

April27. With the aura of hangovers filling the van, we broke camp and prepared to move on. We were going northwest towards Uluru, the local name for Ayer'sRock. Ben told us he would leave us at Coober Pedy or Andamooka, as Broken Hill had reawakened his interest in his mining past, particularly opal mining. Nobody seemed to object.

On the way we agreed to go Woomera, where Ben would break away and head for Andamooka. Woomera was about 330 miles and we aimed to do it in one day. The small town of Buckaloo was our stop for fuel and 'coldies,' cold drinks. Noticing a strange rumbling sound that shook the ground beneath our feet, we gathered outside the gas station. From behind the station, six huge, red kangaroos, each well over six feet tall, bounded out of the bush, crossed the dirt road, and thundered into the bush on the other side. I could not believe that they could make this earth-shaking noise. I was amazed at the sight and size of these magnificent creatures. Ben told me they easily weighed in excess of two hundred and fifty pounds each. That was three quarters of a ton banging the ground in unison. Five minutes later, a semi-trailer towing four empty trailers in tandem, called a road train, came into view. Ben told us the kangaroos had picked up the sound of the empty trailers bouncing long before we could and didn't know what it was, so they'd panicked. We were lucky we were not in their way. The petrol station owner told us it was rare for road trains to come empty in any direction on this road, as the American air base at Woomera was always sending or receiving something. He warned us not to go near the base, as it was heavily patrolled by U.S. servicemen. As he spoke, a huge American military cargo plane descended from behind us, coming in to land. It flew so low, it left our field of vision, as if it was heading into the bush. Ben took the gas station owner aside and had a conversation with him, after which he announced he would be going on with us to Coober Pedy, not Andamooka.

Nightfall found us pulling into the township of Coober Pedy. The welcome sign was a simple steel frame holding a large lorry, that's what the Aussies call a truck, twenty feet up in the air. Mounted on the back of the truck was a fifty-gallon mechanism for dumping the waste brought up from the mines. The sight was surreal. Laid out before our eyes was the small township, much of it in caves, surrounded by mounds of red earth.

Ben suggested that the youngsters take off and investigate the town, as he wanted to spend some time quietly with me.

Finding an aboveground pub was easy. In a gentlemanly way, Ben pulled out a chair for me to sit. He picked up an old newspaper off the red dirt ground and showed me the headline as he spoke, "Your President Lyndon Johnson was here last year." he said. "Not at Coober Pedy, but in Canberra. Our government said Aussies would back up the Americans in Vietnam all the way. Not a good war in my book." He pointed to the front-page picture of a nurse from the Royal Australian Army Nursing Corps holding a Vietnamese baby. "It's the young'uns that pay for our bad choices." he said. "It's why I live like I do. Not sure I like the human race. Greed, power, control, for what?" He seemed to go into a pensive mode before he continued. Ben was quiet for a moment, as if deep in thought. He then continued, "You seem like a nice lady and I don't know why you're here or what you're doing. You yanks, You mother those university kids like they're your own. Given life on a silver platter. Ain't right. You are with these uni kids, you aint one of them. You are bit like me, hovering between two things and not quite connected to either as far as I can see. What's your story?"

The barman interrupted, asking what we wanted to drink. Ben asked what was available.

"Tooheys, West End, Southwark, Foster's, you name it, mate." he said. "We only serve schooners here. No time for midis." Ben ordered for us both, then sat silently, staring at me. He knew he had found a raw nerve.

I sat pensively, trying to determine what I should tell him. I said, "I came to Australia because I was directed to by my dead parents." "To find what, I'm not sure." I didn't tell him of the will or of my own wealth. His words about greed stuck in my mind. "I am to meet certain people, find out about them, and photograph them, then send the information back to my lawyer. It's a sort of test, I think. You know, you resemble my lawyer. He is part Moroccan, that's in Africa and part English." The more I tried to explain things, the more bizarre it sounded. "You have brought a new perspective into my life, and you don't even know it. The life you have chosen has more simple, pure meaning and purpose to you than mine does to me. I have always thought the people who come into contact with me were the better off for it. Man, am I blowing smoke or what?"

"Aunt Lill, what the bloody hell are you on about?" said Ben, finishing his beer and signaling for another.

I said, "I'm going to abandon my plans to complete this ridiculous task. I intend to fly home from Ayers Rock. I have a proposal for you."

"What might that be?" asked Ben.

"In exchange for the Colt you gave me, the 'combi' is a rental vehicle, I will loan it to you if you promise to take the kids back to Sydney, at your own pace and return it to the rental company."

"Can you do that? I will arrange for the rental to be paid when you or one of the students return it to the rental company."

"I'm not sure I like the responsibility it puts on me." Ben was clearly thinking this through.

"There is none. I don't care if it takes you two months to get it back to them. The students have to be back at university at the end of their holidays. What do you say?"

"I'm not sure."

"What if I give you some money?"

"I don't want your money. I have no need for it. I can take care of myself."

"You will need money for gasoline and other bits and pieces."

"Sounds like you have your side of the deal worked out Lill. Do you want to hear mine?" I was surprised at his next move. He opened his backpack and pulled out a small ornate wooden box, a little bigger than a cigar box. The box had brass corners, hinges and a keyhole. The lead edge of the box lid was rounded and the finish was worn off from years of contact. Inserting a key into the lock, Ben opened the box and turned it toward me. There was another Colt .45 nestled into the velvet interior, along with a space where the other gun had been and various implements for maintaining them.

"Keep its twin where it belongs and you have a deal," said Ben.

"Oh my. I didn't know the one you gave me was part of a set. Oh my. They must be important to you. They're the only tangible possessions you have. I couldn't."

"Whatever it is you think I've given you, is more important than material things. The twins are too heavy for me to carry around anymore, besides I have another smaller pistol." He smiled, rose, and signaled for more beer. Then he offered to have the guns engraved before I left.

"Just think, you can go home to yer cobbers and tell them that Benjamin Franklin gave you these when you met him in orstralia. Just don't tell them which year. Every time you see this gun case, you think of this dashing abbo called Ben Franklin." He was noticeably pleased with himself.

April28. We rose early and headed the four hundred and sixty miles to Ayer's rock. The miles of red dust road seemed as if they would never end. Either side of the road, the dust banks were three to four feet high with scrub growing on them. Looking in the rear-view mirror, I could see the huge cloud of dust we were kicking up block out everything behind us. I had worked up the courage to drive, as Martin, who had been here before, said that he would be amazed if we saw another vehicle at all. We did see a few and as soon as I learned to slow down, so that my tail wind cloud became smaller, the oncoming cars did the same and we passed without any mishaps. I must admit, I was scared the first time, but after that it was easy. I really enjoyed the driving. I'm not sure that I would want to do it in a city.

We pulled into Ayers Rock around four o'clock and the gang wanted to camp in the large area reserved for tents. After setting up tents, they all took off to look around. I think they might be tiring of me, what with the age difference and every-thing else. We sat around the campfire eating dinner and watching the sunset behind the huge rock. It was as if it was changing color before our eyes. It is a majestic sight. Slowly, as the campsite died down and the partyers slipped into a tired sleep, the blackness became quiet. Ben Franklin had chosen to spend the night alone in the bush outside of town. Only Martin and myself sat staring at the dying embers. Throughout our trip, he had put his arm around me, which I thought of as simple friendliness. He whispered, "You are leaving in the next few days." It was more a statement than a question. I did not respond. "I am going to miss you, you know?" I let him carry on. "I don't know how to say this." He was uncomfortable. I knew where he was headed with his attempts to express himself.

"Don't you think I am a little too old for you?" I asked him.

"No, not really. Don't I appeal to you? You certainly do to me."

"It's not that. It's just I hadn't thought about it."

"Well, I have. I have been thinking about it a lot." He reached out and took hold of my hand and continued, "I have thought about your breasts. Sometimes I see your nipples standing out and wonder if you are aroused or just cold. I can't tell you how much I want to free one of them and kiss it."

"Getting a little bit ahead of yourself, aren't you?" I watched his awkward manner as he stumbled on.

"I actually get a hard-on thinking about having sex with you."

"Are you saying you love me?" I was playing with him.

"Blimmey no. You don't have to love someone to shag them. It is nice if you feel something and I do for you."

"What is 'shag' and what do you feel for me?"

"I feel an attraction. Shagging is having sex." He leaned over and kissed me. I didn't stop him. I thought this could be fun.

I asked, "Where, right here?" There was no answer. By the glow of the embers, he slowly undressed me. He satisfied his curiosity of baring my breasts and kissing them. It was when he put his head between my legs that I weakened and really joined in. It has been while since I have had sex and I was enjoying this. After I climaxed, he moved my head towards his erection. Up until this point, I had not looked at his manhood. It was short and thick and glistening. I took it in my mouth and savored its saltiness. I stopped quickly and he asked. "What's wrong?"

"Nothing. Just put that deep inside me, I want to feel you cum. He did both things I asked and stayed inside me until he started to lose his hardness. I have to admit, this is one of the best sexual experiences I have ever had. He was so hell-bent on pleasing me, quite a novelty.

April 30th -The following morning Elvira commented on how "chirpy' ' I was. I don't quite know what she means by chirpy, and I don't care. The group split up and went about exploring all there is to see of the rock, even climbing to the top. Ben Franklin did not come with us; he went off on his own. I think to the aboriginal village. Naturally, Martin paired off with me. I suspect Elvira has picked up a vibe from him, but nothing is said. This evening around a huge campfire we cooked some of the biggest steaks I have ever seen and bangers (sausages) over the fire. It was the end of a really good day. Discussions soon turned to tomorrow. I brought up my own plans, "I am going into Alice Springs and I am leaving to go back home." I told them.

"What about us? What about the combi?" Rosy asked.

"Ben has agreed to stay with you guys and return the combi to the rental company. There is no rush, just be sure that you all get back in time for uni."

"What's the hurry Lill?" asked Matilda. She was the thinker in the group. She spoke very little, but was always studying everything around her.

"No hurry, I have done what I came here to do and I have really had a wonderful time with you all. The small slice of Australia I have seen really excites me and that's thanks to you all." We spent a lot of time chatting and it is heart-warming to know that they have enjoyed me as much as I have them. Slowly the group dissipated into their tents until only Martin and I were left by the fireside. I knew what he wanted and I told him that I wanted to be alone this evening. I asked him to drive me to Alice Springs the next day. I told him that we could spend some time together before my flight out, whenever that may be. He was happy at that.

As I sat out from the edge of the campsite, under the black night sky, the canopy of a million tiny stars, like a huge dome encompassing all around me, endlessly twinkled. The quiet, the calm, the peace, were humbling. I really enjoyed my trip, but still don't know what my parent's purpose was. The night air chilled and I soon called it a day.

May 1. Amid emotional hugs and kisses, we said our good-byes. Ben showed up as I was about leave. He walked towards the group with an upright confident air of a man at peace with himself. There is something about this man, ethereal maybe; I can't put my finger on it. His handshake conveyed so much in its strong, yet gentle grip. I didn't want to let go. Giving him most of the cash that I had left, as promised, to take care of the students, I climbed into the combi and Martin pulled away.

I said, "That was emotional."

"Farewells always are when you like someone." We drove in silence to Alice Springs. My thoughts were busy. We arrived at Alice Sprigs at 2pm and had missed the only flights out for the day. So, I booked us into a motel until the next flight at 11.50 tomorrow morning.

Martin couldn't wait to get his hands on me. We spent the afternoon in a delicious body-fest. The experience of having a man pay undivided attention to my body is one hell of a good one. The afternoon started off with what can only be described as a 'phew I needed that' coupling. Thank god for the endless energy of youth. Martin was able to slowly arouse me to want him, again and again. His fingers, tongue and cock are magic. Oh my. I though as we lay side by side spent and he asked, "Do you want to watch me wank off?" I nodded. He started to slowly play with himself. The more he massaged himself, the bigger it got. I didn't think that I had another round in me. I did. I straddled him and suddenly he stopped. "Do you have a mirror?" I leaned over to the bedside and pulled a small one out of my purse and handed it to him. Holding it on his tummy and turning it towards me he said, "Move it until you can see me entering you." I angled it and watched as he slid in and out, very slowly. Wet and slippery, it shone. To see myself open and absorb his manhood fired me up even more. It looked so big going in and yet the sensation was so erotically stimulating that when I climaxed, I just kept coming. This was a totally new experience. I want to wrap him up and take him home. I was going to write 'take Martin home' but I think I would be just as happy taking his cock home. I can't believe how base I am becoming.

May 2. Martin drove me to the airport this morning. After stopping at a bank, I withdrew five hundred dollars and gave it to him. I told him to keep the cash as a reserve for the group, should they need it. I also gave him seven of my business cards, upon which I had written on each one, the name of one of the students and the final one, Ben Franklin. I told him to be sure that they got them. He was to tell them that should they ever make it to America, I would welcome showing them the same kindness's they had shown me.

"You own an airline?" he asked

"I own six small airlines." Was my reply.

"Why didn't you tell us?"

"Because it had no bearing on our experiences together."

With that I boarded the flight and left.

JM! This is the end of my journal. I have decided not to send it to you as agreed. The futility of this task is lost on me and quite frankly; mother and father are not the type of people who would put me through hoops to get money. I just don't believe it. I don't need the money; neither does Brian, I suspect. I will courier it to you when I arrive back in America. You are a good enough attorney to work your way around the codicils.

Chapter 32

Sitting in the Boeing 707's first-class cabin, Lillian amused herself with thoughts of how JM would react to her not only failing to complete the task, but in fact, fragrantly ignoring the rules in the process. On the surface, he was a stick in the mud for rules and regulations, but she felt deep down, there was more to him than met the eye. Going through the collection of photographs she has amassed on the trip, she let each one, evoke a memory. Some she had taken and quite a few had been taken by the students as they passed her camera around. They thought that they should record things for her that she might not. There were scenes, road signs, people, the 'combi'. She was thrilled to see the combi with Martin at the wheel. She had thought of the photographs as being for herself rather than the task. The result had been exactly that. There was one picture that haunted her. It was of Ben Franklin. She thought it could easily be mistaken for what she imagined a young JM might have looked like. Even in a picture, Ben had an air of personal dignity that shone through his unkempt appearance. She drifted into a deep sleep.

Lillian was awoken from her sleep by the steward as he was readying her for dinner. As her mind cleared, Ben Franklin's photo was still on the top of the pile in her grasp. JM's image surfaced in her mind again. She knew something was going on in her subconscious, but not what it was.

***

After dinner, without knowing why, she decided to try and locate her brother before returning to Buffalo. She smiled as she tried to remember the last time that she had *wanted* to talk with him. It didn't come. She didn't even know where Brian might be or how she could contact him, even if he would bother to talk to her.

After the evening meal was served, the cabin lights were dimmed to allow those who wanted to sleep to do so. Lillian started to make some notes. She listed everybody she knew who knew Brian, to determine how to locate him. In a flash, she recalled her own airline connections and realized that, her brother's unusual middle name, Ojukwae, would make it stand out. Lillian explained the situation to the steward. She was told that the captain would be happy to radio ahead and have Qantas's customer services desk see if they could find any information for her. Soon, the steward informed her that the Quantas desk was unable to locate anyone of that name travelling. "The captain suggests that you wait until you arrive in New York and the international operations should be able to flag his name. It will only appear when he books a flight, if he does." He went on explain, "Giving out information is a sensitive subject when dealing with the public, however, Miss Blacksmith, if you do it through your own airline, you may have better success." He returned her business card to her. She spent the rest of the flight pondering if Brian had finished his task or not, and where he could be.

***

Upon booking into her hotel, she decided to take a gamble that Brian was still out there somewhere, carrying out his task. Contacting her offices at Global Charter Services, she instructed her staff to do a daily search for her brother. She carefully instructed them to be sure to draw attention to the middle name, as she felt it would stand out, if he used it. She thought about contacting JM and asking him if Brian had finished. On May 11th, after a week of fruitless waiting, she took the bull by the horns and called him.

"JM, Lillian here. Have you heard from my brother yet?"

"How are you?" he asked.

"Fine, fine. Have you heard from Brian?"

"Where are you my dear? So good to hear your voice."

"JM! Have you heard from Brian yet?"

"Calm down, no I haven't. Have you completed your task? Where are you?"

"I'm still out here doing my thing." she said and hung up. She rationalized where 'out here' was and turned her thoughts back to contacting Brian. She had taped the picture of Ben Franklin to her room mirror, where it kept staring out at her. Her wait dragged on for a full two more weeks. She was beginning to wonder if Brian had even started his task. That was a possibility. Just as she was about to give up, her office called. "Brian Ojukwae Blacksmith is currently in flight from Lagos, Nigeria to New York and is expected to land in two hours." The caller advised. She thanked the caller and hung up the phone. Her heart raced. She had forgotten to ask the flight information. She sat looking out of her hotel window at the Manhattan skyline and composed herself. She calmly called her office back and dictated a message to be radioed to the flight. Addressed to Passenger Brian Ojukwae Blacksmith, it read, 'Big problem. Do not return to Buffalo. Meet at Tavern on the Green in New York for lunch tomorrow, 1pm. Do not contact JM. Your sister, Lillian."

She knew exactly what she was going to do if Brian showed up.

Chapter 33

By May 26th, the spring was well under way in Central Park. Most trees were now in full leaf. The evergreens stood out majestically against the backdrop of skyscrapers. The midday sun provided for the needs of a few sun worshiping human statues, which stood lifeless, faces pointed skyward. There was a slight cool breeze. Lillian arrived at the restaurant early and was recognized and welcomed. The maître d' told her that her brother had called and would be arriving at one o'clock. He had requested a private table. Unfortunately, we don't have one open. The man took her to a table off to one side of the main dining room. "I hope this suits you madam."

Brian soon appeared. Tanned and immaculately attired, he sat down opposite Lillian. "What's all this cloak and dagger stuff about?" he said curtly. "Did you complete your stupid task?"

Lillian took a deep breath to prevent one of her typical retorts.

"Yes, it was a ridiculous task and no, I didn't complete it." she said. "That's why I'm suspicious about it. Did you do yours?"

"Of course, I did. Don't I always do what Father asks?"

"Are you sure Father, or Mother for that matter, came up with these tasks?"

"Who else would?"

Lillian paused as she searched for the right words to use. She knew that if she just came out with her thoughts, she might lose her brother's cooperation. "You know how strong-willed Mother was, just as our grandparents were. I can see the plan was for us to learn something from the task. I did learn something, but I'm sure it wasn't what was expected. In fact, I gained insight into myself from, of all people, an Aboriginal on walkabout."

Brian noticeably relaxed as he laughed out loud. "My, something I learned was also from a black fellow. A cast-off of the British Empire in a Godforsaken hole in Africa, Sapele, actually." he said. "Like you, I can't imagine what it was that that Mother and Father had in mind. Let's order. It is so good to see decent food. I'm starving."

Lillian pointed to the photograph of Benjamin Franklin she had laid on the table and said, "Who do you think that is?"

"Looks like a young JM to me."

"Exactly my thoughts."

"If it isn't him, who is it?"

"It's a half-cast aborigine called Benjamin Franklin. He is half aborigine and half white. He is the child of an American serviceman actually."

"That's a fine one, what's your point." Brian was becoming curious. He was quiet waiting for his sister to continue.

"Who do we know that is half white and half black, let's say Moroccan?"

"Get to the point, please. I don't see the connection."

"Think about this, JM and Benjamin Franklin look alike. If you consider the dilution between black and white that produced those two people, is it so far to think that out similarities to JM may be of a similar dilution?"

Lillian laid out her thoughts to an astonished Brian. She focused on how JM had followed the family to Buffalo. The closeness between JM and their mother throughout their own childhood was noted; as was the creepy way he hugs me. "It creeps me out, the way he hugs me." she said. "I sometimes get the feeling it's almost parental if not sexual."

Brian suggested, "Could it be more paternalistic? He has been known to say that he views us as the children he never had. For all we know, the man could be a pedophile." He grinned at his insinuation.

"If you only think about the way he treated us when we were children, yes. That doesn't explain his present attitude toward us. He wanted to hug you before we left on these damn tasks." Lillian stopped to regain her breath. "Just three months ago, he was touchy feely with me." Her bombshell was delivered over dessert. She said it simply and quietly: "Considering everything, I have been giving this a lot of thought, and I really think JM might be our father."

"Now hold on a minute. That's a big jump to conclusion."

"Brian the more I think about it. Look at your tight blond curls, not wavy hair, curly hair, then there's your olive skin tone. Look at my nose, as your friends call it, my squashed tomato nose. Look at my lips they are fuller than Ma or Pa's."

Brian banged both fists on the table and loudly spat out, "God no! That nigger? No, the bastard! I will kill him." A silent shroud dropped over the room. Other guests were shocked at hearing the outburst in such a dignified place.

Brian stood upright, his arms fully outstretched and his knuckles pushed downward on the white linen. "I am white, and so are you." he said. "That man is not even in the same class as us." Without another word, he turned and stormed out of the dining room.

The maître d' came over to the table and said, "Is everything alright Miss St. John-Brown, can I do something for you?" She replied, "No thank you, my brother has just had some upsetting news. He will be fine. I want to let him calm down, He will be back." She watched Brian outside through the parted curtains of the dining room as he chain-smoked one cigarette after another. She saw him wipe his eyes and pace up and down, stopping only to look up into the sky. He periodically waved his arms at the sky and would then put his head in his hands. She could see that he was trying to come to terms with things.

Eventually, Brian calmly returned to the table. He sat quietly, staring at Lillian, waiting for her to speak. For the first time in his memory, she reached across the table in an attempt to hold his hands. He pulled away as if stung, "What do we do now?" he asked.

"Let's think this out, before we sit down with him." said Lillian.

"I have some business to take care of here in the city. Why don't you make the appointment and book into the Statler Towers Hotel in Buffalo? We can meet on Wednesday." Brian said.

"Why the hotel? We can go to the house."

"No, he will know if we go home, the staff will tell him. He has kept a skeleton staff on at our house."

"Why shouldn't he know we are going to see him?"

"I'm not sure yet. We may find out more if we surprise him."

Lillian asked "Doesn't he expect us? I sent him my journal three weeks ago, from here. Did you send yours?"

"Yes, I sent mine about a week ago."

Brian was thinking before he said, "New York! Why did you send it from New York? Not that it matters. He will suspect something is happening if we arrive together. We are not particularly noted for being in each other's presence"

"I think he must already know because I never finished my task and my journal has a few things in it that may piss him off."

Brian smiled. "If what you say about him is correct the bastard should sweat. Let's meet in Buffalo on Wednesday." He flipped a business card on the table and left. Lillian was confused, no goodbye, no warmth, she thought this turn of events would have made some difference. He still was focused more on his own ends than anyone else's. She sat silently at the table brooding, was everything a lie? She hated lack of trust more than anything and this was shaping up to be a huge case of mistrust where JM was concerned. She just could not get her head around it.

***

May 28th, sitting in a corner suite at the Statler Towers, Lillian looked out on the skyline. The backdrop of the setting was Lake Erie and the foreground was the ornate center tower of the City Hall of Buffalo. The traffic island that ran around Niagara Square in front of City Hall held a constant flow of automobiles, like a giant merry-go-round. The early afternoon sun shimmered on the waters of the lake. Despite the myriad of activity below, the room was serenely quiet.

There was a knock on the door. Lillian greeted her brother as she held the door open for him to enter. She moved in an attempt to embrace him, but he brushed past her with such speed that she was left standing with open arms. He removed his coat and sat, looking out the window as if preparing himself for something. He didn't notice a small wooden case with its brass inlays and corner protections sitting by the window.

Lillian offered, poured, and served him a cup of coffee, then poured one for herself. She sat facing him, took a deep breath, and said, "I have been rehashing everything and frankly, I cannot imagine how we are going to approach JM."

Brians' gaze was almost a stare, devoid of any inclination of what he was thinking. "I don't know what difference our paternity makes or whatever is going on."

he said. "In fact, I damn well don't have a clue what the truth is, or even what we are going to do, or can do."

"Do you think it really is possible that JM is our real father?" said Lillian.

"No bloody way. We both know who our father is. I'm just not sure who fathered us." said Brian. "If that black bastard is our father, he must have raped mother. I'll . . . I'll!"

"Brian, you won't do anything. I doubt that he raped mother." said Lillian.

"You actually think Mother let him crawl all over her? The thought of him forcing himself on her sickens me."

"Right now, that doesn't matter. We have enough combined clout to achieve whatever it is we decide to do, if there is anything we can do. I want to know the truth. No more lies."

"Yes, I know but doesn't it make you mad? Mad and sick. I, you, we are not black, part black, mulatto, or whatever the correct term is."

"I am not so bothered by the black issue as I am about the deceit. The incredibly two-faced, ongoing deceit. Can you imagine what Great-Grandfather William would think about it? Or Grandfather Michael, he was emphatic about integrity and honesty."

Brian said, "I bounce between thinking about my middle name being a tribute to Great-Grandfather Judd's adopted son and that it may really have been suggested by JM. I don't give a shit about where my middle name comes from. Being sired by a blacky bothers me more. What is everyone going to say? Can you imagine the field day the newspapers are going to have with this?"

"Brian, you have to put those feelings aside. Speaking them out loud can only cause us problems."

"What problems? Am I going to be breeding a black child when I decide to? What a wonderful surprise for a new mother. Here, this one's black. He must be yours. We'll be the laughingstock of Children's Hospital."

"I hadn't thought of that. Not that I have any plans on having a child." said Lillian.

"You hadn't thought of that? What are you, crazy? Black people aren't like us. You'll tell me next that you socialize with them." said Brian.

"My God Brian, listen to yourself. We own hotels across the world heavily staffed by black people. My airlines have many black employees. I never stop to consider their color, as I am sure to this point, you hadn't."

"Not when they are servants or employees, I don't care. Okay, okay." said Brian. "So, what are we going to do?"

Lillian rose and poured them both another coffee. She paced the floor. "I haven't told JM we are in town." she said. "I didn't want to give him a chance to prepare for us because, frankly, I didn't think you were going to come."

"Well, I did. So, what's your brilliant plan, clever sister?"

"Let's just go over to his office unannounced. We will not leave until we are satisfied."

"You are so much like Mother sometimes, with your orders and smarter-than-thou attitude." said Brian as he stood and put his coat on. While his back was turned, Lillian opened her briefcase and placed one of the pistols from the ornate case inside, closed it, and followed Brian out the door. They shared the elevator ride down to the hotel lobby in silence. Crossing Niagara Square with their collars turned up to protect them from cool spring wind coming off the lake, their hunched-over forms, bent into the breeze, were silent and ominous

Chapter 34

The manila folder JM's secretary had placed on his desk was remarkably thin for an attorney's file, but like all his files, there was one for each of the many tasks he had performed for the St. John-Browns. This one was the will. Placing his hand on the closed file, he closed his eyes as if reverently connecting to its contents. The assets contained in this will had been intertwined in his life since he was a young aspiring lawyer in England. JM could still recall his first meeting with Lady Penelope, the children's grandmother. Her persona had engaged his imagination and sometimes threatened to derail the plan he had set out to achieve from his youth. It was from that very moment and he stayed focused on his revenge and never wavered. For years after Michael St. John-Brown had passed away in his sleep in 1926, and ever since JM had escorted Lady Penelope to many functions. He had been her rock in the chaotic years that followed the loss of her husband. He had symbolically held her hand throughout the years that followed and helped her survive the coming and going of the Second World War. A connection that had its foundations back in England in 1912, was rekindled. Looking through the cut-glass Victorian-styled office doors, JM studied Brian and Lillian as they sat silently, ignoring each other's presence. Many aspects of their grandparents were evident in them both. His observations of their relationship made him secure in what was about to take place at their meeting. Right now, he believed that he held the upper hand in his dealings with the two of them, but he knew that he had to tread carefully, as both of them were successful and financially secure in their own right. With an air of professional aplomb, he opened his door and apologized for keeping them waiting. He promised not to keep them much longer. He then returned to his cloistered office after telling his assistant that she could go for the day and to lock the office on her way out. JM glanced at the two files on his almost bare desktop. The top one bore only a number code on the front. Opening it, he began to read the will and his own notes written in his own distinctive handwriting. The two separate sheets of paper that were the codicils were paper clipped to the back of the document. He did not open the second file. He knew it's contents by heart. The foyer of JM's Law Offices reeked of pure colonial opulence. The highly polished wood paneling and ornate, stained, leaded glass doors conveyed an ethereal air supported by the silence. Lillian knew from her business experience that silence was used by some businesspeople to intimidate. The modern trend of piped music to calm was carefully avoided. She felt that they had been kept waiting long enough. As if by some unseen signal, they both stood and brushed past the protesting secretary. Both siblings then marched into JM's office and unceremoniously sat across from him. Lillian placed her briefcase across her lap. With a startled expression, JM stood and before he could offer a welcome, Lillian said, "Please sit down. There is something we need to discuss. Oh, perhaps you could get your file with our parents' will. We will be needing it."Julian studied them both, stood up, and heading through his office door, he spoke to his personal assistant, "Rosie, I said you may leave for the day. Be sure to lock up as you go." He returned to his desk slowly, as if he was trying to compose himself. He slowly spun his chair around. He glanced down, pulled the lower file and placed it on top. "Brian, how good you look." he said. "I was very pleased with the photographs and biographies you sent from Nigeria. It seems like you had quite an interesting experience."

"My experience did little to aid me in understanding what our parents expected us to gain from such childish endeavors. With all due respect to you, JM, what the task did do was reinforce my perspective on black people, if anything it strengthened it. Be that good or bad, who's to know?"

"I did not complete my task, as you well know by now." said Lillian. "I guess that means I failed, or whatever the term is."

JM leaned back in his chair and, interlocking his fingers, rested his chin on their up-pointed apex. He spoke slowly and deliberately, as if preaching. "My connection to your family goes back a long way, as you both know." he said.

"I'm not sure what we do know." Lillian said with a degree of vehemence.

Ignoring the comment, JM continued. "My services to the family have been twofold; as a lawyer and legal advisor and I have been the protector of the family's business interests. As a man, I have been a close and supportive confidant of your family's personal life."

"*Mother's* personal life, you mean. Very personal, if you ask me." spat Brian.

JM was set aback. He searched for some explanation. "As in all families of great wealth and public stature," he said, "there have been times when support has enabled problems to be kept to a minimum. It has been an honor to be involved with the family. Much of the time, I have been privy to your parents' innermost thoughts and concerns. It is this privilege that allows me to tell you both that your parents did not expect you both to complete the tasks. In fact, we all got it wrong by assuming that Brian would be the one to fail."

"What exactly does that mean?" asked Lillian.

"The general opinion was that Brian would fail and the family assets would not be divided between the two of you." Brian and Lillian exchanged glances. JM carefully studied their reactions.

Brian stated, with firm conviction, "Sir, as you say, I did not fail. I completed the task. My sister did not fail, as she chose not to complete the task. There is a difference."

"I understand, but you must remember that your parents' wishes are explicit. The final decision on completing or not, lies with solely with me. The will clearly states that should you fail in the tasks, the assets of the will are to be dispersed in an alternative manner."

"What manner? I have never even seen the will. What's going on here?" Brian said vehemently as he glanced at Lillian.

With a cold stare at JM, Lillian, while holding up her hand to quiet Brian, looked at the lawyer and said, "Are you my father? My brother's father? Our father?"

JM's demeanor suddenly changed into a stoic legal stare. "I don't know what you mean. Please explain." It was clear to Brian and Lillian that JM was fighting for space in which to phrase his answer. The protracted silence that hung in the air carried unspoken thoughts.

JM broke the silence, slowly. "My connection with your family started back in England, as you well know—"

"Connection, connection?" said Brian. "That's one way to describe it."

JM carried on as if nothing had been said. "I was instrumental in guiding your mother, the family, through a very intricate, financially trying time."

"Oh yes, you helped her all right. Helped your bloody self is more like it." muttered Brian.

"Brian, let him finish." Lillian said.

"Thank you, my dear." JM said.

"I am not your dear." said Lillian.

"Anyway," said JM, "your family has relied on my guidance and counsel over the years and I have not let them down. In fact, when your grandfather passed away, I became your grandmother's rock. She was able to lean on me. I was also very supportive of your mother in those trying times."

"Supportive, supportive? It sounds more like you were doing more than supporting amongst other things." Brian said.

"Do the terms honesty, integrity, and honor mean anything to you?" said Lillian quietly.

"Young lady, I have a reputation that is beyond reproach, from you or anyone else." said JM. "I understand that you are grieving and that can distort your perception, but please, be more respectful."

"Respect?" said Brian, glaring at the lawyer. "You are the hired help, and nothing more. You are not of our station and never will be. You, sir, should be respecting your superiors."

"Respect is based on trust." said Lillian. "Trust is based on truth. You have hardly respected my family's trust in you. It looks as if your whole relationship to this family is a sham, for what reason I am not sure."

"Oh, I know what for." said Brian. "He just wanted to fuck his way into respectability, and Mother was his chosen victim."

A pervasive silence hung in the air. Each waited for the other to make the next move. JM gradually lost his self-control. Years of applying the principles most basic rule of not disclosing one's own hand, flew out the window. Planting his hands flat on the desk top in an effort to be in control, he started to deliver a speech, which quickly disintegrated into vehement tirade. A long-awaited justification of his actions that had been brewing in his gut since his youth, flew from him as if he were in a demonic trance. "Your grandfather took an innocent young girl, Melita Harrison, my mother, he debauched and used her. When he had enough of her, he threw her aside and married into the so called, upper classes. Upper classes, what a joke. He pawned her off on one of his minions to become, Melita Surtees, wife of Ronald Surtees. The man I knew as my father, Ronald Surtees, was not my father, he was a stand-in for my mother's bastard child, me. Your sensitive, kind well-bred grandfather continued copulating with my mother until the very day she died. Very upper class, I must say. I had to grow up listening to my parents fight over how wonderful your grandfather was. Mother died believing in him. When he was finished with her, he put her and my stepfather, because that's what he was, on the Titanic, to be drowned and forgotten."

Lillian interrupted his tirade, "My grandfather did not put her, them, on the Titanic to drown. Everyone knows that disaster was an accident. Nobody could have foreseen it."

JM continued, "How very convenient, it doesn't change the fact they were drowned, in his service. They were off his plate. How *very* convenient. The problem is that I lived. I lived to see your grandfather pay people to go to the memorial service because he couldn't be bothered to go. Well, I was bothered. I was so bothered that I made a promise to destroy the St. John-Brown family and my task in nearly complete." There was a protracted silence in the room. JM continued, "The sad thing is that I never counted on growing fond of your mother. I respected and loved her as a friend, but I did not let that stop me from my pursuit of the goal to destroy your family. Fair measure I would say for what he did to my mother."

"Brian uttered, "That's downright sick, you are sick."

Unfazed by the comment, JM went on, " When each of you were born, I could see a little of my likeness in you. Fucking your mother, as you like to call it, was sweet revenge on the family, out of which something good came, you two."

Brian snarled at JM, "You ruthless bastard, you had sex with my mother to get back at my grandfather. You are one sick piece of shit.""I harmed no one, I just stopped the despicable St. John-Brown train dead in its' tracks. You two are Blacksmiths with a little dash of Surtees in you."

"So, you are not even JM Fetters? You are really Julian M. Surtees." Said Lillian. Your whole existence with our family has been a lie. You are nothing but a fraud."

"No matter what else I am doesn't matter. What really counts is that I am your father and you are my children. We can now move on with life."

"Did Father know what was going on?" asked Lillian, quietly.

With a superior air, JM leaned back in his chair, puffed out his chest and said, "Do you think that your father was stupid? Do you two really think that he was that blind, that he didn't know? Just look in the mirror, for God's sake. Look at each other. Open your own eyes for once."

Brian stared at JM with hatred emitting from his every pore. "*You*, my father. But, *You're* Black. That means…" His sentence trailed off into silence.

Arrogantly, JM replied, "Oh yes you are more Like me than you know. Fucking your mother was a project and one that I might add, was not easy. Haven't you noticed that I never married? Do you want to know why? It's simple, I prefer men."

Lillian covered her face in shock and Brian's face became even darker. Before either of them could say anything, JM continued, "Yes that's right I am what is politely referred to as a homosexual." He paused and said directly to Brian, "It hasn't gone unnoticed that you have never married either. You're probably more like me than you knew." Brian's face was frozen in a mask of hatred.

With a confused look, Lillian asked, "JM Surtees, Jullian, I get that. Where did JM Fetters come from? What about your 'slave' grandparents?"

"Oh, my dear child, that was designed to draw your grandfather and mother in. They might have been suspicious if I had kept my real name. Creating JM Fetters was the first step in my road to destroying your family. I had to be sure that I wouldn't be discovered. Your mother, God rest her soul, was nobody's fool."

"Don't you feel any remorse? Our parents died horrifically."

"That was none of my doing. That was God finishing my task for me. You were there. You had to see that it was an accident, an accident in which I had no part. I am only glad that you, my children, survived it."

Lillian slowly opened the briefcase on her lap, keeping the lid from exposing the Colt .45 to JM. She leaned toward Brian and touched his leg to draw attention to it. They looked into each other's eyes. She looked up at the attorney and said, "You spoke about my grandfather being despicable. Try this for despicable."

In a synchronized ballet of fury, pale blue gun smoke hung in the air as Lillian closed the briefcase and pointed the colt at JM's heart. Brian, recalling a childhood memory of JM ridiculing him as a joker, said, "Now! Who's the joker?" Lillian pulled the trigger. The bullet hit its mark on the white shirt stretched across the heart of the surprised attorney. A spot of blood quickly enlarged into a growing patch of vermillion. Brian leaned over, took the gun from Lillian's outstretched hand, took aim, and fired the gun a second time, hitting the exact same spot. The lawyer, with a look of startled disbelief and pain, slumped forward across the files on his desk and died.

Lillian said, "Hold the gun for minute." reaching into her purse, removed a cheap hand lotion, which she squirted into her open palm. She proceeded to rub the lotions into her hands. She told Brian to call the operator for help and ask for the police and an ambulance. "Say nothing more than, a man's been shot at Attorney JM Fetter's office in the Staler Towers. Then hang up. Quick, quick. Say nothing else."

She took a handkerchief from her purse and took the gun from Brian, opened the office door and threw it down the stairwell beside the elevator.

Brian, having done what he was told, said to Lillian, "Why did you use a kerchief to take the gun? Are you trying to pin this on me? There's only my fingerprints on it now."

"If you have never listened to me before, listen now. We don't have much time. There are my prints, then your prints and at the door I took the gun and held it with my hand that had the lotion on it. I held it and threw it. There is only to be your and my prints all messed up by my taking the gun and throwing it down the stairs. That is going to make a confusing mess of all the prints. We want them to find some prints, otherwise we can't throw suspicion on the unknown man."

"What unknown man?" The sounds of an ambulance could be heard in the distance.

"We were in a meeting with JM when two shots came from behind us. By the time we turned, all we saw was the elevator door closing. We don't know if it was a man or a woman."

Brian had become more composed as he said, "Stick to that story, but only tell it after Alan gets here. We want an attorney. They'll try to separate us. Just keep saying you want our attorney, Alan Goldfarb."

"Who is Alan Goldfarb?" said Lillian.

"I hear that he is, without a doubt, the finest criminal lawyer in Buffalo," said Brian. "Neither of us must say anything without his presence. If we stick together, we can beat this."

"I don't know how good you are at this, but we had better start acting. I am going to be very distraught. You should be angry at the time it took help to get here." With that, Lillian went round to JM and put her left hand in the growing pool of blood and touched JM's throat feeling for a pulse. She returned to her seat as the police rushed in with guns drawn, followed closely by the ambulance crew.

"Alright Brian, stick to our story and neither of us will speak without our attorney." With that, she started to cry hysterically and paced the room. Brian began berating the ambulance and police.

Chapter 35

The police took control of the situation and calmed Brian and Lillian down. Crime scene detectives soon arrived. "We will need you to come to the station to have your fingerprints taken, to eliminate you as suspects."

Brian spoke, "Eliminate us as suspects?" Lillian let another wailing cry.

"I'll get to you in a moment." The detective was getting forceful in his tone with Brian.

"I don't like your tone. You can see how distraught my sister is. She was very close to JM, and you want to talk about us being suspects."

The chief detective was being low key as he asked Lillian to tell what had happened leading up to the shooting. When she had finished, he said, "You told me that the palm print on the desk is yours. Now tell me why exactly is it that your palm print is in the blood, on the desk."

Before she could answer, Brian interjected "My sister told you she was trying to see if he was alive."

An ambulance arrived and was told that it had to wait for the coroner to come and certify that JM was dead. As soon as this was done, the body was removed.

"The detective resumed his questioning and was interrupted by another detective coming through the door holding the colt on the end of a pencil in his hand. "Look what I found chief. Down the bottom of the stairwell."

"Well, well. I don't suppose your fingerprints would be on the gun, wouldn't they?" He was speaking to Brian and Lillian.

Brian snapped back, "Of course they are, I told you, I went out to see if I could see the murderer. She followed me out and when she saw that I had picked up the gun, she took it from me and threw it towards the stairs. It obviously went down to the stairwell. Even a detective could work that out."

"Just take it easy Mr. Blacksmith. I am only doing my job." The chief was becoming annoyed.

"I'll tell you how you can do your job. If we are suspects we want our attorney. We are not going to say another word."

"Make the call. Sargent! Take them over to the station."

"Are we being charged with anything?" Brian asked.

"No! Mr. Blacksmith you are helping us with our enquiries. Now call your bloody attorney."

Brian moved over to his sister, put his arm round her shoulder and said, "My sister and I will talk no more until our lawyer is present."

***

The interrogation room was small and musty. Alan Goldfarb had arrived quickly and took control of the situation. Before the detectives entered, he instructed Brian and Lillian, "Do not offer any information. They are going to want to separate you two. I need to talk to you alone before we agree on anything with them."

The detective entered the room and sat opposite the trio. To the lawyer he said, "I'm sure that you understand Mr. Goldfarb that we shall be interviewing your clients separately. Please explain to them the reasons for this."

"Detective, let's not play games. We both know that you will probably try to turn one of them against the other. I need to talk to my clients alone before your interview proceeds." The attorney's tone was firm and left no room for objection.

The detective sullenly picked up his papers and said over his shoulder, "I'll be outside when you have finished." He sarcastically added, "One of them will turn, they always do."

Alan Goldfarb, spoke slowly and deliberately, "It is usual for the police and even the judge to want you to be tried separately. It's not essential, but is wise. There could be a time that I might be faced with a conflict of interest. That would be disastrous for one, or both of you."

"Why would there be a conflict of interest?" Brian asked.

"Because no matter that you are brother and sister, you are individuals and as such, one or both of you could be at risk of being turned upon by the other. Not that I am saying it will happen but, if the pressure put on one is so intense, it could create a situation where one decides to turn on the other."

There was silence hanging in the air as each waited for the other to speak. Neither did. Alan took his cue and spoke, "If I agree to take the case you must both understand that I will not be put in the middle. Should one of you turn on the other, I will step down from defending either of you. That is not a situation that will help either of you."

Brian looked at his sister and said, "While I cannot speak for you, I will not under any circumstances turn on you."

"Why would I believe you after all we have been through? I would have thought it would deliciously tempting, for you." Lillian gazed intently at her brother.

Before there could be a response, the lawyer spoke in a hushed tone, "Be very careful what you say. There is a probability that our entire proceedings are being taped. We don't want anything said that could be used against you."

With a knowing smile, Brian took Lillian's hand and said, "We may have had our own unique past together, but in the last few days I have seen a Lillian I never knew existed. You are brave beyond belief. We are all that's left of the St. John-Brown family. Together is where we must stay and rebuild our relationship."

The lawyer interrupted, "As long as you both understand my position, I am ready to move forward. You have raised some questions in me that will wait until we are in a more secure place. When the detective returns, I want you to only answer the questions. Do not elaborate on anything. Take your lead from me. They are going to want you to tell them what happened. I want you to be very careful and only start at the point where your conversation was interrupted. They are going to try and get you to reveal what the discussions were about. That is covered by what we call attorney client privilege, you do not have to disclose the conversation. I will get into that after you are out of here. Do you both understand?"

"So, what happens to us?" Lillian asked.

"As long as you have not been arrested, you are only helping them with their enquiries. I would actually prefer they charge you, because then I can get bail and we can get out of here and work on things. I think, right now the only way that can happen is if you give them enough reason to charge you. That's not really good. If we leave them to make a charge, we know what we are fighting."

The door opened and in came the chief of Detectives. Introductions being made, he said, "We are going to interview your clients individually Mr. Goldfarb."

"No Sir, my clients require that they be interviewed together."

"I'm not sure that they have any say in the matter, Sir."

"Well actually, I have a lot of say in the matter and it's going to be together or not at all. So, are we finished detective or do you wish to proceed?"

The detective adopted a sour expression as he said, "So why don't you tell me exactly what happened, and start from the beginning."

Brian started, "My sister and I were discussing business with our attorney."

"What is your attorney's name?"

"JM Fetters."

"What were you discussing?"

Alan leaned over and spoke into the voice recorder. "I have instructed my clients not discuss this as it is protected by attorney client privilege."

"They are the clients. They can talk about it if they want to."

"I am advising them against it." Alan stood firm.

"The detective said, "So you are saying that you don't wish to answer the question?"

Alan said in a firm voice, "Move along detective, you know their position."

Brian started to speak and Alan said, "Let the detective ask the questions."

The chief leaned back in his chair. It was obvious that he was trying to regain his composure before asking his next question. "How was your discussion with the deceased interrupted?"

Lillian said "There were two gunshots in fast succession."

"What did you do then?"

"I turned and saw the door swing shut and a figure running away." said Brian.

"Did you recognize the figure?"

"No sir, the doors have stained and leaded glass in them which distorts an image."

Alan leaned over and whispered, "Too much information. Just answer his questions."

"What did you do then?"

"I went around the desk to see if JM was alive or dead."

"Was he dead or alive?"

"Yes." Lillian said smugly.

"Yes what? Was he dead or alive?"

"He most certainly was dead or alive. More dead than alive though."

"Mr. Goldfarb, caution your client not to be flippant with me."

"You just did detective. Let's move on."

"What did you do to determine if he was dead

I leaned on his desk with my left hand to reach over and accidently put my hand in the blood." She lifted her hand to show the stains.

"After you knew he was dead, what did you do?"

"I went out to see what my brother was doing."

"What was he doing?"

"He was standing by the elevator holding the gun. He looked like he was in shock."

The detective said, "I think he shot Mr. Fetters and took the gun out with him."

The attorney interrupted, "Detective, let's keep our speculations to ourselves at this point."

Lillian continued, "No, he couldn't have shot JM."

"How are you so sure, if the gunshots were so frightening, you could have missed that."

"Enough of the theorizing detective. Lillian, tell why you don't think it could have happened."

"Because we were sitting close together and he had to move in order for me to get past him to go to JM."

Looking back at his notes the detective smiled and said, "You just told me that your brother had gone to the door."

"No, I did not, I told you my brother went to go to the door and I went to go to JM, he had to move for me to do that."

Alan said to the chief, "I think that about covers it for now. If that's all, you can either charge my clients or we are finished."

"Just a couple more questions. Do you have any idea why someone would want Mr. Fetters Dead?"

"No Sir." replied Lillian.

"And you Mr. Blacksmith?"

"No, none at all."

"Is there anything else detective?"

"Not for now. I require that you do not leave this jurisdiction and that you make yourselves available to us. This is far from over."

As they were leaving, Alan cautioned them not to speak until they were clear of the station. Standing outside, they shook hands and agreed to meet the next morning to discuss what was going to happen. Alan said, "Do not talk to anyone. Go home and stay there until we meet tomorrow."

Brian asked, "Do you want to know what took place at JM's?"

"No thank you. I only want to know the answers to the questions I ask."

Chapter 36

The next day was a tedious and exhausting experience for Brian and Lillian with their attorney, Alan Goldfarb. He started off by repeating the terms under which he would represent them and summarized it by saying, "If either of you have any reason to believe that you will turn on the other, you had better decide it now, so that we are all certain of my ground rules.

Brian said, "We have discussed it at length and stand united in this matter."

"Fine, let's get down to business. Explain to me the reason for the meeting with JM and what took place. I don't want to know which one of you shot the man." Alan was carefully studying his clients as they responded.

Lillian said, "Who said either of us did?"

"That's it. I want it to stay that way."

The long day covered everything they knew about JM's involvement with the family; from what they knew of his meeting with their mother, his moving to America and his relationship with their mother. It was this point he said, "I don't want to know what you thought, only what you know. You mentioned him seducing your mother, you don't know that."

"Yes, we do," said Brian, "he told us."

"That still doesn't make it true. Stay with everything you '*know*' about the man and his connections with the family. I want to hear about what he told you after I have a firm understanding of the family dynamics with him. This will help me build a timeline."

Lillian and Brian seemed to be at peace with each other. The bickering and tension appeared to be absent. Its presence could only be felt where parts of the family history involved it. The attorney was particularly interested in the codicil tasks they had been asked to perform. He asked many questions and asked for copies of their journals and the will. Neither Brian nor Lillian had copies, as they had been sent to JM and they said that they had never been given a copy of the will.

After Lunch, Alan instructed his law clerk to obtain copies of Angela Rose and Desmond's wills from the police. He gave specific instructions for the clerk to find the codicils. He suggested the clerk be creative as to where he might search, even to look for them under JM Fetters name and the name Julian Surtees as well. He also had her put in a request to England's Somerset House, the home of births, deaths, marriages and name changes. He wanted to know if Julian Surtees and JM Fetters were indeed the same person. He felt there was something unusual about it. They continued with details and it was mid-afternoon by the time they had given the account of what had taken place in JM's office. Both Lillian and Brian were getting restless when Alan said, "Now that I know that you have been through everything,

I want you to go through everything again step by step, starting from when you arrived at Fetter's office. Except this time, I want you to describe the shooting as you told it to the police.""But why? You have been making copious notes. Why do we need to do it again?" Lillian was almost pleading in her tone.

"If we go to trial, I want to be able to have such a clear understanding of what happened, that I will not need to turn to my notes. Preparation is everything."

Around five o'clock, Alan called an end to the meeting and as Brian and Lillian were leaving, he stopped them and asked, "Tell me the truth on this point. Is there any sibling rivalry between you two? I mean do you get on well? Are you both ok with each other?"

Brian put his arm round his sister and said, "We are fine. Of course, there is a degree of sibling rivalry in our business lives. We do try to one-up each other, but other than that, I'm fine. What about you, Lill?"

Lillian said, "I wouldn't be here with my brother if I didn't care about him. There is no way I would share an attorney with someone in this mess unless I was serious. I would be looking after myself. Brian is all I have left. He is my brother."

***

Walking back to the hotel, Lillian asked Brian, "Are we really fine, I mean is the rivalry over?"

"No quite."

"What do you mean not quite?"

"What I said, not quite."

"So where do we stand?"

Brian stopped took hold of Lillian's shoulder and turned her toward him, "Right now, no matter what you think, I have bigger fish to fry."

"Fish to fry?" Lillian did not understand what he was saying.

"Step one, that black bastard is out of my, our lives. Now the next thing we need to do is stick together to get out of this mess. Then and only then will I be able to address *our* situation." Brian was vehement.

"Do you want to continue with our relationship, or lack thereof forever?"

"Look, we are family. We can choose our friends but not our family. We must stay united until this is over. With what you have done to me in the past, I'm not sure if I want to have a relationship." Brian seemed to be still holding his life-long animosity towards his sister.

"What I have done to you! What about what you have done to me?"

"You don't listen too well. Firstly, we need to get rid of the stupid gun case you left in the hotel that you think I didn't notice. Then we must go to the house and get ready for whatever is to come." Brian let go of his sister and walked ahead of her.

"How do we get rid of it?" Lillian was confused.

Brian called out, over his shoulder, "The furnace., We use the furnace." He kept walking.

Lillian followed along, her head swirling with thoughts and emotions. They returned to the hotel room, gathered their belongings and went to the family home. Brian had the gun case under his raincoat to avoid it being seen. He suggested that they walk the relatively short distance to the house rather than using a taxi. He felt it better to avoid the chance of a taxi driver seeing the case. There was little to no conversation between them.

Chapter 37

May 30th, Lillian heard the house telephone ringing and the maid answered it before she could. The maid met her on the stairs and said, "Mr. Alan Goldfarb on the phone Miss."

Picking up the receiver, Lillian spoke, "Good morning Alan, what is happening?"

"Well, the train is leaving the station. I have just had a call from the police and they are going to charge you both with the murder."

Lillian gasped, "Are they coming to the house? What do we do?"

"I have arranged for you to surrender yourselves at the police headquarters at eleven o'clock this morning. I need you to come to my office by nine-thirty so that I may prepare you."

"Prepare us, what does that mean?"

"Just come to the office and only bring the things you need. Leave your purse, wallets and other bits at home. Here is what will happen: they have to formally file a felony complaint or put you before a grand jury and let them decide if there is enough evidence to charge you."

"Do you know which one they will do?" Lillian was confused.

"If they think they that they have enough evidence, they will go for the felony complaint. If they do this, we will ask for a probable cause hearing. This is good because they have to reveal their evidence. If they want to go the Grand Jury route, a Grand Jury hearing will be scheduled. Either way, we will gain insight into their course of action."

"What does all of this mean to us?" asked Lillian.

"I like the felony complaint route, as it moves things along quickly. What I don't like about the Grand Jury is that you will go before the jury without representation. I cannot be in there."

"So, when does the bail issue arise?"

"Either after the probable cause hearing or after the Grand Jury verdict."

"Verdict!" Lillian said, "You mean they decide if we are guilty or not?"

"No, they decide if they feel there is enough evidence to warrant that you will be charged with the murder, not if you are or are not guilty. They could decide that there is not enough evidence, in which case the prosecution has to decide if they want to come at you from another angle."

"So, could we be faced with the bail today?" Lillian asked.

"No, not that quickly, but you should be ready. Why?"

Lillian suddenly realized that they might not get bail and asked, "We will get bail, won't we?"

Alan replied, "There is no guarantee, but I have a good track record, even with accused murderers. The bail may be high it will be cash or property bond, but I assume that will not be a problem."

"How do we go about that? I mean getting the money, we don't know how much to bring."

Just leave that to me." Alan hung up the phone.

Lillian went to Brian in his room and told him what was happening. His response was simple, "From here on in, we stick to our story. You must remember Alan's advice."

"Which was?" Lillian asked.

"Only answer the questions asked and keep your answers brief and on subject."

"I am frightened Brian. What if this goes wrong?"

"Then we have a big problem. I think you were pretty smart with the way you handled things in JM's office. I have every faith this will work out."

"Thank you." Lillian's reply was soft and uncertain.

***

Alan ushered the two of them into his office and was smiling when he said, "You two look scared shitless."

Brian replied, "I am cautiously optimistic, but I would be lying if I said I wasn't nervous."

"Me too." Lillian's reply carried more conviction than her brother's.

Alan went into a detailed description of what was about to happen. "You will be a little uncomfortable in the cells with everyone else that has been arrested."

"In the cells? They are going to put us in cells with the riff raff?" Brian was disturbed.

Then *you* will be the riff raff. It is a very short time, as you will probably go before the judge before lunch. While you are separated from me, do not talk to anyone about what you are charged with or anything. Keep yourself to yourself. With any degree of luck, we should have you home by the afternoon."

"What about the bail thing?" asked Lillian.

"I want you to sign a check and give it to me. I will use it to go to your bank and obtain the funds. Are you paying your cash bonds individually?"

"How much will it be?" asked Brian.

"We will not know until bail is set by the judge. Why, is there a problem?"

Lillian asked to make a phone call, which she did, to her bank. She instructed them that no matter what the amount of the check that her attorney will bring, she wanted it honored and cashed. She told the banker which account to transfer money from if there were insufficient funds to cover it. Turning to Alan she said, "I will put up the cash bond for both of us."

"I appreciate that thoughtfulness, Lillian." Alan said as he suggested that they walk over to the courthouse, which they did.

***

When Brian and Lillian were ushered into the court by the sheriff, they saw the judge with his head down, reading. They stood in silence, waiting. The clerk of the court started to read out: "In the matter of the State of New York versus Brian Ojukwae Blacksmith and Lillian Jane Blacksmith…" when the Judge, S. Haron, held her hand up to silence the clerk. Looking directly at the siblings she said, "I would like to offer my condolences on the tragic death of your parents."

"Thank you, your honor." Brian replied.

The Judge spoke directly to the defendants and said, "This is a probable cause hearing for the court to decide if further actions are to be required by this court and if the prosecution has provided sufficient evidence to proceed. Do you both understand that?"

Alan spoke, "My clients understand, Your Honor."

The judge spoke to the attorney, "Mr. Goldfarb, am I to assume that both your clients wish to be tried together?"

"Yes, Your Honor."

"Do they understand they have the right to be tried separately and that there is an inherent risk if they are tried jointly?"

"They do, Your Honor. As they have been charged jointly and were together during the so-called commission of the charge against them, it is in their best interest to remain together."

Looking at the siblings, the Judge asked Brian, "Do you understand what your attorney has just said?"

"I do, Your Honor."

"And you?" he asked Lillian.

"I do, Your Honor."

"Then we shall proceed." Looking directly at the siblings he continued, "While you have the right to defense council of your choice, I cannot emphasize enough the folly of sharing the same council. I have no doubt that Mr. Goldfarb has pointed this out. I also wish it to be clear to this court that you have had advice on this matter and that it is your express wish that you be represented by the same council, namely Mr. Goldfarb. Please individually state your choice of council for the record."

Lillian in a clear loud voice spoke first, "I Lillian Jane Blacksmith confirm that Mr. Goldfarb is my council of choice."

Brian echoed his sister, "I Brian Ojukwae Blacksmith confirm that Mr. Goldfarb is my council of choice."

"Then let's move forward." The Judge commanded.

***

By mid-afternoon, the prosecution had laid out their case. After a short recess, the Judge addressed the defendants, "In the matter of the State of New York versus Brian Ojukwae Blacksmith and Lillian Jane Blacksmith, you are charged that on May 30th 1957 you did willfully murder, in the first degree a one JM Fetters. How do you plead?"

Alan whispered to Brian and Lillian before they spoke, "Not guilty, Your Honor."

The judge set a date for preliminary hearings and motioned for Alan Goldfarb to speak. Alan said, "In the matter of bail, Your Honor."

The prosecuting attorney jumped to his feet and interrupted saying, "The prosecution vehemently opposes any bail, Your Honor. This is a murder case."

"I am aware of what the case is." Responded the judge.

Alan spoke next, "Your Honor, my clients fully understand the gravity of this case. They have surrendered their passports and I have them for the court and they offer no flight risk. Their family is well respected in the community and their individual reputation is stellar. I am asking that they be released on their own recognizance."

The prosecuting attorney became irate as he said, "Your Honor, for God's sake they own an airline. They are stinking rich. You cannot."

The judge held his hand up as he said, "Mr. Chantwell, I cannot do anything for God's sake, your sake or my own sake. The matter of owning an airline is irrelevant and to what degree their wealth stands, I do not know, stinking or otherwise."

"But Your Honor, they could fly the coop."

"If, you are right about their wealth, they could own the *coop* as you call it. I believe that if flying was their plan, they would have done it, after all, you did say they own an airline. Now, let's get back to reality." Looking at Lillian he said, "Miss Blacksmith, if I were to consider bail, which I am not saying I am, what would you do while you await trial?"

"Work to defend mine and my brother's innocence." The attorney nudged her. She quickly added, "Your Honor."

The prosecuting attorney said, "The prosecution asks for a one million dollar bail to be set on each defendant."

The judge responded, "Seems reasonable to me, Mr. Goldfarb. What say you?"

"Your Honor, with all due respect, the defendants, roots are here in Buffalo. Their assets that are here have been in the family for generations and their reputations are stellar. I respectfully request a bond of five hundred thousand dollars."

"That doesn't sound like much respect for the victim, Mr. Goldfarb."

"No, Your Honor, it doesn't. The evidence you will see supporting the charges of murder against my clients, when the case comes to trial, also shows no respect. They are innocent until proven guilty. In the court of public opinion, they have now been branded."

"Very dramatic, Mr. Goldfarb. Your point has some merit, but I must remember this is a murder case."

Brian interjected, "Your Honor, my sister and I respect your position and are willing to pay the bond of one million dollars, in cash, *today*."

"Very noble of your client, Mr. Goldfarb, considering I haven't yet ruled."

The prosecutor snapped, "That shows you, Your Honor, they can anti up the cash at a whim. That's how unimportant it is to them."

Brian looked at the prosecutor and said, "I don't know about you, but we are not willing to walk away from a million dollars."

"That's enough. Mr. Goldfarb, control your client. One million dollars cash bond on them jointly and individually it is then." Looking at Alan, the judge added, "Your clients caught a very lucky break today, make sure they understand that."

The prosecutor was noticeably angry at the outcome. He slammed his files closed and went to turn and leave as the judge called out, "Mr. Chantwell, please respect my court." Waiting till the prosecutor returned to his seat, the judge set a date for the trial to begin and looking the prosecution right in the eye said, "The court is adjourned."

Chapter 38

It had taken six months for the case to come to trial. Judge S. Haron was the presiding judge. For a week, Brian and Lillian sat observing the tedious Jury selection. Rejection after rejection. At the end of each day, besides their input on the potential Jurors, they were full of questions for Alan. At lunch on the last day, Brian saw a pattern emerging and asked Alan about it."It is starting to look like you are stacking the jury.

"What do you mean? You seem to be leaning towards a heavily black dominated jury. Why?"

"I have left my choices until late in the jury selection so that the prosecution hopefully doesn't see it. I think it is working. Our prosecutor friend thinks the jury is going to lean his way."

"But why black?" asked Lillian, "You know Brian's position on black people."

"Exactly. If we balance the jury with Black and white, we stand the chance of a hung jury on racial lines. We can't afford that. It could lead to a mistrial. It should be easier to sway a majority jury of one color. If the prosecution feels they have the upper hand they might just stay on that track. We will come at the jury from another direction."

"But black?" asked Brian.

"I feel that if we can keep the prosecution going in one direction and then we show an equally reasonable, acceptable alternative we can plant seeds of doubt in the jury's minds." Brian still seemed confused, so Alan went on, " If your distaste for black becomes an issue, we could well loose. With the temperament of the country right now towards racism, we must be careful. If we can show that it is equally ridiculous to think that you *could* have been angry, not at black but at your black heritage being withheld from you, we stand a fighting chance. We will have started to muddy the water a little."

"But how? Isn't that giving them another possible motive?" asked Lillian.

"The more possible motives that we can offer the jury, the harder it will be for the majority to lock into anyone."

Simultaneously, Brian and Lillian said, "What about the inheritance issue; *Money*, as another probable motive?"

"I am thinking about that. I need to offer more obvious motives than the race one to really muddy the waters. We just have to hope the prosecution hasn't noticed what I am doing. I have been holding off reading your journals until I have gained a better knowledge of you both. I think it is time I read them.

"Brian became anxious. "If they have to give you everything they have, do you have to give them everything you have?"

"Not everything, only things I intend to use as evidence."
"Can they use our journals against us?" Brian asked.
"They can, why? Is there something I should know about?"
"Not in mine," said Lillian.
"I think mine might be a little borderline." Was Brian's answer.
"Let me read them and then we will decide."

***

Back at the house, Lillian asked Brian what he could be worried about in his journal. Brian was obviously uncomfortable speaking about his prejudice to his sister. "Like it or not, I don't know why, but I just don't like black people."

"But you have them working for you all over your businesses."

"I am able to distance myself from my employees, be they black or white, I see them all just as employees. I really don't have much interaction with them. The layers of authority keep them distant."

"Are you going to be able to keep your emotions under control during the trial?"

"I don't know, I just plain don't know."

"I really hold out some hope on Alan's approach, but if you loose it just once, you will have a majority of the jury go against you; against us."

"I know, I know. In a silly way, it doesn't bother me if the blacks go against me. I'm not ashamed of my position, I don't like them, but it shouldn't go against you."

"Brian if you lose control, that's exactly what will happen; it will go against me."

"I know. I know. What about your journal, is there anything that could harm us?"

Lillian sat quietly, as if ignoring the question. Brian could see that she was trying to formulate her answer. He spoke again, "Is there anything that could harm us?"

In a very slow and deliberate delivery Lillian replied, "There is nothing that could harm our defense."

"Then what are you holding back? I can see there is something bothering you."

"It's more a matter of," she paused before going on, "some things are private and should stay that way."

Brian said, "I think one's opinion on the black issue is private, but mine isn't going to be for much longer."

"Would you like your sex life bandied about for the public, for everyone to be titillated by it?" asked Lillian.

"No." was Brian's short reply.

"That's where I find myself. In my fight to be successful, I have had to use anything I can to win."

"You mean....you, you, are less than pristine"

"Don't ask. I am just not happy about my sex life being drooled over."

"It's really *that good* to make someone drool?" Brian was making light of his sister's dilemma. "Well, let's just hope it won't come to that."

Chapter 39

The morning of the trial, Alan summoned the siblings to his office. He had a serious expression as he spoke, "I have read both of your journals and yours, Lillian, I have no problem with. Brian, you probably don't remember all that you wrote in yours."

"No, I don't remember much of it, but there are some parts that might hurt us, I think."

"You think right. This is my problem. Do I try to get the journals excluded? I doubt this will even be possible, simply because the codicils are part of a whole document; the will. The journals are a direct connection to the will. If I do and fail, the prosecution could surmise that we are worried about them. If I don't, do I risk pieces being pulled out of context and used inflammatorily?"

"Do you think, as a whole, my journal is better for us than in pieces?"

"Of course, because I only have to justify your thoughts once for the whole document. In other words, if there is a highlighted negative issue by the prosecutor, I can put it into a softer, more positive, fuller context. One of your journals could be used against the other to try and point the guilty finger."

Lillian asked, "Are you allowed to have the journals read in their entirety by the jury?"

Alan's reply was, "We can request it, why?"

"If I am correct, wouldn't the police fingerprint report show the order in which he gun was handled?"

"Not necessarily. It shows two sets and a lot of smudges. Brian's and then yours were the only usable ones."

"Then if the prosecution tries to use Brian's journal against him, surely he should have been the one to handle the gun first."

"I have thought of that and it's fraught with risk."

"Oh." Was all Lillian could think to say.

Alan thought aloud, 'If the jury reads both journals in their entirety, they will give insight to you both as individuals. I'm not sure how that will play out."

"Let's get this show on the road. I want you both to only look at the jury when I signal you to."

"What's the signal to be?" asked Brian."

Alan showed them four file cards. Each had a comment on it. They were, Smile at Jury. Smile at black Jurors. Don't look at jury. Look of approval. He said, "I am going to have these cards in front of me most of the time. When you see me pick them up, the top one will face either one of you. Follow its' message.

Chapter 40

As the defense and the defendants approached the courthouse steps, a wave of reports rushed at them. The shouting of questions and requests for comments was silenced as Alan Goldfarb held up his hand for. He instructed Brian And Lillian to leave him and rush into the court as he spoke to the reporters. "Thank you all for attending this morning. At this point there is nothing to report. We will be happy to grant you all a press conference when this is all over." Someone in the crowd shouted out, "Guilty or not Mr. Goldfarb?"

Turning his back to follow Brian and Lillian through the door, he shouted over his shoulder, "Not for me to say or you to speculate."

The courtroom was a buzz of chatter awaiting the commencement of the trial. "Please rise. This court is now in session. Judge S. Haron presiding."

Judge S. Haron banged her gavel to command attention. "Before we start today's proceedings, I have before me a motion to suppress the private journals of the defendants. Counsel, approach."

Before reaching the bench, the prosecutor started to speak, "Mr. Chantwell, for the prosecution, Your Honor,"

"I know who you are, we covered that ground yesterday."

"We oppose the suppression of the journals, Your Honor, as they define the character of the defendants."

Alan Goldfarb spoke up, "Their character is not on trial Your Honor."

"Damned right it is." Chantwell was getting angry.

"Mr. Goldfarb, it is sort of relevant. Tell me why I should grant your motion. Besides what you have in the motion."

"It's highly prejudicial to one of my clients as well as misleading. Besides Your Honor, the codicil is an addendum to a will, the will of the defendants deceased parents and as such becomes part of a total document. It is highly improper to allow a portion of a document as evidence and not the full document."

"Your Honor, you are not seriously considering granting the motion?"

"Do I sound like I am considering it, Mr Chantwell?"

"But, Your Honor."

"Mr. Chantwell it's ten o'clock in the morning, please don't make me tired before my day gets into full swing. Your request has merit, Mr. Goldfarb." Looking up, the judge said to the defense attorney, "I think your client wishes to speak to you. Make it quick." Turning to the prosecutor he said, "I don't know what the fuss is all about, Mr. Chantwell, he has a request and you don't like it. That's the way it goes. Let me be the *'judge'*." She crooked her fingers in the air as a gesture of quotation.

Over at the defense table, Alan said to his client. "It's going well, just as we thought." Returning to the bench, Alan looked at the judge and said, "Your Honor, my client, Mr. Blacksmith has requested that I amend my motion before you. I have advised him against it and stand firm in my request to have the entire will, journals and codicils entered into evidence."

"And how would he like you to amend it?" the judge asked.

"This is highly irregular, Your Honor." Interrupted the prosecution.

The judge looked at the prosecutor and said, "As you said yesterday, Mr. Chantwell, *'for God's sake.'* Let me do my job."

"Your Honor, Mr. Blacksmith wishes to defend his sister's honor and privacy and asks that you suppress his sister's private journal and allow his to be introduced. I advised against such a request. My motion stands."

The judge smiled as she said, "Noble actions seem to be abundant in my court these days. I grant the defense motion to include the will and codicils into eveidence, as together they form the total will. The prosecutor stood immobilized. He could not believe the defense had played right into his hands. The woman's journal was worthless in this trial. He'd got the one he wanted. What was the defense up to? His reverie was broken by the judge saying, Mr. Chantwell, you can return to your table. Walking back to his table the prosecutor was confused.

The judge paused and then said, "I have a motion before me from the defense for dismissal, I am denying the motion. The prosecution may present its first witness."

While the witness was being brought into the room, Alan leaned over to Brian and said, "He took it in, hook, line and sinker. He even looks confused."

The judge ordered the jury to be brought into the courtroom.

***

The prosecution started their opening statement. Prosecutor Chantwell allowed a prolonged silence before approaching the jury.

"Ladies and gentlemen of the jury, the charge of Murder in the first degree has been made against the defendants. I believe it was a heinous murder. We intend to prove that the defendants, in a racially motivated act of aggression set out to take the life of their victim, a well-respected, *black* attorney, an attorney who had faithfully served their family for over fifty years. You may well ask; if they had known him for so long, why did they wait so long to act upon their distaste for his being a negro. The evidence will show that they had accepted the victim, as they had known him from childhood and never saw color; after all, the victim was of light skin, one might say of half black appearance. We will show how the tasks assigned to them by the codicils of their parent's will, forced them to confront their feelings about black people. We will show that how, fueled by anger and hatred, they contrived a situation that could show that together they set about building a scenario that could be taken to imply the introduction of a third party, who committed the murder. We will show that the only passion present at the time of the murder was the passionate dislike of the black race. We will show how this hatred was built over many years

605

and finally boiled over and left one-man dead. A black man. Their intent was to kill a black man and get away with it."

"You are going to hear thinly veiled, creatively imaginative, scenarios by the defense that are aimed to shift your focus off the two individuals and away from their murderous act. As a jury, be you black, white or mixed, I urge you to not only listen to the facts, but to listen to what is behind the facts. I promise you that you will see through the ploy."

"Remember the word mixed, it will come into play and will be used to divert your attention away from the finality of this murder. Are mixed origins a justifiable excuse for murder? We think not, no more than being black is a reason to be murdered. Murder as a crime, a racially motivated crime, cannot be tolerated. We have left the dark days of racial divide behind us. Do not allow some individuals to practice lynch mob justice. Thank you."

Alan leaned over to Brian and said, "So, they are going full head on for the race card."

***

Judge S. Haron looked at Alan and said, "Mr. Goldfarb, your floor I believe."

Alan stood, and making a show of it, took off his jacket and placed it on the back of his chair. He walked over to the jury and spoke slowly and deliberately, frequently fixing is gaze on the jurors, particularly the black ones. "I would like to thank you for your service. For some of you, this will be a difficult time. We welcome your attendance on this jury. You may have noticed that the jury is predominantly made up of black people. This is no accident. I am sure that the death of JM Fetters was not a racially motivated act. You are also going to hear the name Jullian Surtees, I want you to remember that name."

The prosecutor interrupted, "Your Honor?"

Before the man could finish, the judge said to Alan, "Let's move along Mr. Goldfarb."

"Ma'am," Alan carried on, "I intend to prove to you, a jury made up of many black people that are all intuitive, irrespective of color, that you will be able to see through the so called, 'manufactured string of incidents,' to find the truth. The prosecutor promised to show you evidence that he claims will prove the act of murder was premeditated based on the victims' color. We, the defense will show the fallacy of that presumption because that is what it is, a fallacy. What they will fail miserably to prove is, who owned the gun, where did it come from, and who fired it. What they will fail to show you is why the murder took place at all. There is no motive. Oh yes, murder was committed. What they will fail provide is a motive as well as a perpetrator."

"What we shall show is that the defendants were upset with the intense, prolonged and egregious level of deception JM Fetters/ Surtees used on them. Intense deception spread out over their entire lives. Not only deception against them, but against their parents and grandparents. The victim here was not the man who set out to destroy their family by changing his name around the turn of the century in his efforts to build his subterfuge. The true victims are Brian and Lilian Blacksmith. The prosecution will try to convince you by tying a string of feeble coincidences together, that this was a plan. Yes, there was a plan, not by the defendants, but by the victim. Why was Fetters murdered and by whom? The prosecution doesn't know and nor do I. May God go with you in your duty. I stand strong and urge you to find beyond a reasonable doubt that the defendants are not guilty. Thank you."

Judge Haron called for a brief recess and summoned the attorneys to the bench, she said, "Mr. Goldfarb, you are on thin ground with the use of the name Surtees. I expect you to strongly support its presence. Mr. Chantwell, I suspect that you know where this is going. If I feel it necessary, I will accord you same latitude."

Chapter 41

The first witness answered the prosecutor's question about his identity, "Detective Inspector Kowaleski. Detectives Squad Police Headquarters, Sir."

"Tell me about your duties on the afternoon of Wednesday March 5th."

"I came on duty at 2pm and an emergency call came in about a shooting."

"Where did the call come from, officer?"

"From a telephone operator."

"What did the operator say?"

The detective replied, "She said there had been a shooting in an attorney's office on the sixth floor of the Statler Towers. The office of a JM Fetters, I believe."

"When you arrived, what did you find?"

"Upon entering the office, I found two people standing there and a dead person laying on the desk."

"Let's back up a minute. How did you get into the office?"

"Through the door, Sir." There were titters of laughter in the jury box.

"Was the door locked?"

"No, Sir."

"Was there a key in either side of the door?"

"That was never established, Sir."

"Why not?"

"Oversight, Sir."

"Let's move on. Do you see the two people in the court today?"

"Yes Sir, it's those two, the defendants."

"What were they doing?"

"The lady was crying, bordering on hysterical and the man started berating myself and the ambulance people that followed. He was angry that we took so long to get there. His words Sir."

"How long did it take you get there? Detective"

The detective looked at his notebook and said "seventeen minutes, Sir."

"Seventeen minutes from when?"

"From getting the phone call, Sir."

"How far is the police headquarters from the Statler Towers?"

"One city block, plus the Niagara Square. I would say about eight minutes."

"What did you do for the other nine minutes?"

"Drove the car, parked it and took the elevator up to the office."

"Moving on, you say there was dead black man on the desk. How did you know the body was dead?"

"I checked for a pulse. There was none. I saw all the blood on the desktop."

"What did you do then?"

"I asked the man to tell me what had happened."

"By the man, you mean the defendant, Mr. Blacksmith."

"Yes Sir.

"Using your notes, take your time and tell the jury exactly what he told you."

"He said that they were in a private meeting with the deceased."

The judge interrupted, "The deceased wasn't deceased at the time I suppose."

"No Sir, Your Honor. They said they were in a meeting with the attorney when they suddenly heard two gunshots come from behind them. When they turned around..... no, Your Honor, when Mr. Blacksmith turned round to see who was there, Miss Blacksmith said she went over to see if the attorney was dead. She said that she had leaned over his body to feel his pulse, when her hand went into the puddle of blood. She then said that she rushed out through the doors to see her brother had picked up a gun that was by the elevator doors. She took it from him and threw it against the wall."

"Did you find the gun where she said she had thrown it?"

"No Sir. About ten minutes after we had arrived, one of my detectives found the gun in the stairwell."

"What did you do next?"

"The gun was bagged for fingerprinting. The coroner was called and we commenced to process the site for evidence."

"What did you find?"

"The only thing we found that could be evidence was when the body was removed. There were two files under the body, one was a will and one was some agreements signed by the defendants."

"Anything else?"

"No Sir."

"What were your observations about the crime scene Detective?"

"Observations Sir?"

"Did you ask the defendants if they saw or knew the so-called assailant?"

"Yes Sir, the lady said that she didn't look because she rushed to attorney's aid. The man said it was not possible to see through the leaded, stained glass doors."

"Did you agree with the defendant's description of the glass doors?"

"Well, no Sir. I could see through them."

The prosecutor turned to Alan Goldfarb and said, "Your witness."

***

"I only have a couple of questions Detective. Do you always use a car to respond to a call?"

"Yes Sir"

"Seventeen minutes to respond to a shooting. This morning, during peak traffic, I walked from Police headquarters to the Statler Towers. Four minutes, detective, four minutes and I was only walking, not running. Do you think it possible that if you had run from Headquarters to the attorney's office, those other thirteen minutes might have saved his life?"

"No Sir, the lady said there was a shooting and someone was already dead."

"Which lady detective?"

"The defendant."

"No, Detective, the defendant didn't call. Her brother called spoke to the operator. It was the operator who called you and said that there had been a shooting. She said nothing about dead. That is, unless your testimony is inaccurate. Did she say there had been a shooting or did she say someone was dead?"

"Objection, badgering the witness." said the prosecutor.

The judge overruled the objection.

"I ask again, did the defendant say someone was dead or that there had been a shooting?" Following a brief silence, defense counsel spoke again, "It's a simple question detective. Maybe you have a faulty memory, we don't know."

"That's enough." The judge said to Alan Goldfarb. To the witness she said, "Please answer the question."

"She said there had been a shooting." The detective was uncomfortable.

The defense continued, reiterating, "The operator said there had been a shooting, not my client. Moving on, you said earlier that the gun was found in the stairwell. You say the defendant told you that she had snatched the gun away from her brother and threw it against a wall, is that correct?"

"Yes Sir."

Turning to the judge, Alan asked to enter into evidence a diagram of the elevator lobby. The judge nodded to her assent. Placing the diagram up on the wall, he traced a trajectory and asked the detective, "Is it possible that a gun thrown from here, to this wall here, could have slid across the terrazzo floor and tumbled down the stairs here?"

"I guess it's possible."

"Would you say likely?"

"I suppose." the detective said grudgingly.

"Let me propose one more scenario. Is it possible that an assailant could, not, for some reason being able to use the elevator, had to run down those stairs, and have dropped the gun where it was found?"

"It's possible, but what about the finger prints?"

"Detective, you didn't know anything about the fingerprints at the time."

"Miss Blacksmith told us that she had handled the gun. There was no need to look any further."

In a scornful tone, the defense said, "No need to have looked any further? So, of all her story, you decided on the spot, that that part was truthful. What rules did you use to decide what else she told you was true or false?"

"Objection, Your Honor."

"I withdraw the obvious." Alan walked back to the table and paused for a moment before carrying on. "Tell me Detective, did you make any effort to trace the gun ownership?"

"Yes Sir. We found nothing that could substantiate the ownership."

The defense asked, "Was anything else removed from the crime scene and if so, what was it?"

"From under the body of the deceased we recovered two wills, both were registered at the county courthouse. There were two codicils also found, neither of which had been registered at the county courthouse. There were two agreements signed, for the completion of the codicils requirements, attached to journals documenting the codicils completion. None of those documents were registered at the county courthouse."

"Thank you, Detective, that will be all.

***

The prosecution's second witness was JM's personal assistand. She was a frail tiny woman, who carried herself erect and dignified. The prosecutor approached her with trepidation. When asked to state her name she said, "Mrs. Rosalina Burke, but you can call me Rosie, everyone does."

"Thank you, Rosie." The prosecutor looked at the judge for approval, She gave him another assenting nod.

"Ms. Rosie, is it correct to say that you were Mr. Fetters's personal assistant?"

"Yes Sir, it is."

"Have you ever worked for a black attorney before?"

"No Sir, Mr. JM was not black, Sir."

"Then how would you describe him?"

"Objection, on the grounds of relevance." Alan called out.

"Sustained. Mr Chantwell, let's stay on the subject." The judge ordered.

"Sorry, Your Honor. Ms. Rosie, do you remember the afternoon JM Fetter's died?"

"I do, I do. So sad."

"Where were you that day?"

"I was at his office, as I was there every day for the last fifty-eight years."

"That's one loyal employee, Rosie. You knew all of his clients?"

"Oh yes. Not that there were so many these days. Most of his work was for the St. John-Brown family. Wonderful people, you know."

"Did you see anyone come into the office that afternoon?"

"Indeed yes," she pointed to Brian and Lillian and said, "Young Master Brian, that's him over there, he came in with his sister Miss Lillian, that's her next to him."

"Can you tell us what happened that afternoon?"

"Master Brian and Miss Lillian came in to see Mr. JM and when they had been with him for a few minutes, he came out and told me that I could go home. I had to remind him to let me check his appointment book because he was getting a bit forgetful these days. He didn't have any appointments, so he told me I could leave early, so I did."

"Who locks the door when they leave?"

"When one of us leaves, we always lock the door. It isn't safe for one of us to be alone in the office. We are getting older you know. Well, I am anyway."

The jury box faintly laughed at the comment.

"So, you locked the door from the outside?"

"I think so."

"Can you be sure?"

"There was three of them in there, so I might not have. You silly boy, I'm eighty. I sometimes think that when I look in the mirror in the morning and recognize who I see, I must be going to have a good day." This created a roar of laughter from the jury box.

Judge Haron lifted her hand to silence the tittering.

"So, you know Master Brian and Miss Lillian very well?"

" I do." She leaned forward as if to share some confidence with him and said, "JM once told me that they were his children. Did you ever hear such foolishness?"

"Do you think they are his children?"

"If that's what Mr. JM wants to think, then God bless him. I do know he cared a great deal for them. Is it true, well, when you look at all them mixed up marriages and things, who knows these days? Strange world we live in. What does it really matter? What was your name dearie?" she asked the judge. Further laughter came from the Jury. The prosecution handed the old lady over to the defense.

***

"Mrs. Rosalina Burke, Rosie, if I may, what a pleasure to meet you. I am not going to cross-examine you, as I think you have done a grand job. As for your memory, I wouldn't worry about it. Just one quick question. Have you ever forgotten to lock the door before?"

"Sometimes my dear, I wonder how I get home, but I do and I am thankful. I have sometimes forgotten, but Mr. JM would always forgive me. So, it is possible that I forgot this time. I just can't be sure, my dear. If I didn't lock it, anyone could have walked in and shot poor Mr. JM."

"Objection, calls for speculation." The prosecution stood waiting for the judge's approval.

"Sustained. Strike from the record. Ms. Burke, you must keep your answers to what you know." The judge said softly to the witness.

Grasping the opening, the defense continued, "It is possible that anyone could have come in and shoot poor JM, but we are here to find out if it was my clients, Master Brian and Miss Lillian. One final question, do you think my clients could be Mr. JM's children?"

"Well, they are good looking children, aren't they?"

"Maybe one more quick question, you said Mr. JM wasn't black, what did you mean by that?"

"I meant that black people are black. Mr. JM was, well, he might have had some black blood in him, but to look at him, he looked almost white, maybe white, with a suntan. Anyway dearie, it doesn't make any difference, does it?"

"No, it shouldn't make any difference." The defense counsel turned to walk back to his desk and picked up a document before speaking. turned toward the witness. "Does the name Julian Surtees mean anything to you, Miss Burke?"

"Yes Sir, it does."

"Could you please tell the court what you know about Julian Surtees?"

The witness became noticeably agitated as she replied, "That was JM's real name sir."

The prosectution jumped up, "Objection. This is speculation Your Honor."

Alan Goldfarb held the document in his hand up in the air and said, "I have here a certified document from Somerset House in England. It is the repository for records of Births, deaths, marriages, and name changes in the United Kingdom. I wish to enter it into evidence."

The prosecution shouted, "We have no knowledge of this document. Why did we not receive it in discovery?"

"I, or indeed, no one in the courtroom is deaf, Mr. Chantwell. Please control yourself. Mr. Goldfarb, why is this document being offered into evidence so late?" The judge was firmly in control.

Alan Goldfarb returned to his table and picked up an envelope. He offered it to the judge saying, "I received it this morning, Your Honor, by special delivery." He walked over the prosecution and handed them a copy of the name change certificate.

The judge said, "I will allow this into evidence.

The defense continued with the witness, "I see that you are uncomfortable, Miss Rosie. How did you come to know about Julian Surtees becoming JM Fetters?"

In a whisper she answered, "One day when I was organizing Mr. JM's papers in the safe, I saw an envelope I did not recognize, so I looked inside. It was the original of the document you just showed me."

"Did you ever ask JM about it?"

"Oh no, my dear. It was none of my business. It is not my place to question Mr. JM's private things."

"I would like to draw the court's attention to the date of this document's filing. It is May 4th 1912, about one month after the sinking of the Titanic. The horrendous tragedy that took many lives, including those of Julian Surtees' parents."

"One final point I would like you to help us with." Handing Rosie, the agreements that both Brian and Lillian had signed, to complete the codicil's requirements, he asked, "Have you seen these documents before?

"No Sir. I do know that they were prepared in our office."

"How do you know that?" Alan Goldfarb sensed the importance of her answer.

"Because we have a fancy new electric strike font typewriter and Mr. JM choose an unusual font for his machine. I have not seen it used anywhere else. I just loved that machine."

Alan Goldfarb turned to the judge and offered both of the signed agreements into evidence. Turning back to the witness, he said, " Was it normal for you not to see documents that were prepared in your office?"

"My dear young man, I am amazed that Mr. JM made those documents. I never saw him even try to use the typewriter. He always referred to it as *my* private domain."

"Objection. The response calls for assumption on the part of the witness."

"Sustained. Miss Rosie, if you did not know that Mr. JM made those documents, you cannot suggest that he did."

"Sorry, Your Honor."

The defense had made their point. Alan said, "That's all, Rosie. Thank you for helping us." Alan quickly saw that no good could come out of keeping Rosie in the witness box any longer. As she got up to leave, she turned to the judge and said, "Judge Haron Its' been a pleasure and thank you for having me. I do hope Master Brian and Miss Lillian aren't in trouble." With that she straightened her dress, refused the bailiff's arm to help her down, and marched proudly out of the court, her skirt swaying like the kilt of a marching Scottish piper.

***

"Your next witness please, Mr. Chantwell." Judge Haron moved the trial along. The prosecutions third witness was a fingerprint expert. Answering the prosecutions first question, the man said, "Mario Cintalucci. I am a private fingerprint expert, contracted by the Buffalo PD for examination and preparation of fingerprint reports for court purposes. I have been with the Buffalo PD for twenty-six years."

"Are you a police officer?"

"No Sir."

"How many fingerprints do you estimate you have examined in your career?"

"We go by sets, Sir. I must have examined thousands."

"Thank you. Please walk the court through the process that you used to examine the fingerprints, on the afternoon of May 28th."

"I received the prints on June 5th at 2 pm. Sir."

"My apologies, why not the 28th?"

"You will have to ask the police that. I presume that the police were waiting to be able to send them with the arresting fingerprints for comparison and my examination."

"Certainly. Carry on."

"I first examined the three sets of prints taken from the firearm, looking for quality, clarity and definition."

"What did you find?"

"The prints were somewhat distorted and there were three sets."

"You say there were three sets of prints. Please explain."

"When more than one set of prints are present, they are layered. I tried to determine the order in which they were laid down on the firearm."

614

"What did you find?"

"I was able determine that the first set were smudged and unreadable the second set where from one person and the third set from another person.

"What did this tell you?"

"That person one handled the gun, then person two handled it and then person three handled it again.

"Thank you for your patience. Moving along, what did you do next?"

"I used the arresting set of prints to compare and try to identify the print's origins."

"Did you in fact make a match?"

"Yes Sir. The first are unidentifiable the second set is from Mr. Brian Blacksmith and third set is from Miss Lillian Blacksmith."

"I would like to enter the fingerprint cards and the expert's report as exhibit one, Your Honor." He turned back to the witness and said, "Thank you." He turned to Alan Goldfarb and said, "Your witness."

***

Alan stood in front of the witness and scratched his head before speaking, "It appears that you didn't address the fact of the distortion or smudging of the fingerprints you mentioned, why?"

"I was not asked, Sir."

"Could you please describe, the distortion?"

"Usually when fingerprints are overlaid on top of each other, they are not laid down neatly, a smudging occurs."

"So, would I be correct in saying that it makes them more difficult to read?'

"Yes Sir."

"Then would it follow that the top set are the only really clear ones?"

"To some degree that could be right." The witness could see that he was about to be challenged and quickly added, "But not impossible."

"What do you mean to some degree?"

"The prints are more overlapping than they are directly on top of each other, so I was able to pick out individual fingers. There was not a complete set of any of three."

"Thank you. Let's focus on the top set. Were they clear? Being on the top, one would expect that to be the case?"

"The top set appeared to show a dragging to the right."

"So, they were smudged?"

"A little, but not enough to prevent partial points of reference."

"In your expert opinion, could the smudge have come from the action of the firearm being held and thrown?" Alan held his hand to his chest and extended it in a throwing motion, saying, "Like this?"

"It is possible, but..."

615

Alan interrupted, "Thank you, Mr. Cintalucci. When you examined the prints taken from the firearm you gave no details of any other prints beside the top two sets. Is it correct to assume that there were none?"

"Yes Sir. That would be correct."

"Is it possible to detect fingerprints that were made, say, at some other time by someone else?"

"Yes sir. Older prints can become affected by a number of conditions, but they are generally considered to be less reliable, particularly if they have been exposed to the elements. I was instructed to only consider the clear sets of prints immediately evident."

"By who? Let me rephrase my question, whose direction was it for you to only consider the clear sets of prints reportedly taken from the firearm?"

"The detective sir."

"So, it is safe to say that you were instructed not to look any further than the sets given you?"

"Yes sir."

"One final question before we let you go, of the thousands of reports you have made for the Police Department, how many of them have been used in court cases?"

"I would estimate about half of them, Sir."

"Fifty percent of your reports must not have been good enough for the police to use. Thank you, Sir. I am done, Your Honor." Before the prosecution could say anything, the Judge said, "Let's take a lunch recess. The court is adjourned until 2pm."

***

During the lunch break, Alan discussed the morning's session with his clients. "This is going very smoothly. They have not given us any surprises and so far, all we have seen are things not in dispute."

Lillian asked, "How do you think we are doing?"

"I never get too confident when things go my way. Suffice it to say, I am waiting for the hammer to come down. There always is one."

"I think you got a few good points across though." Brian suggested.

"We need a lot of good points. I am waiting for him to bring up your journal, Brian. As far as I can see, it's their only big gun. I am thinking about bringing it up before he does. It might throw him off balance a little."

***

"This court is now in session." The clerk announced on the dot of 2pm. Alan stood and spoke to the judge, "Your Honor, if I may approach the bench."

The judge waved him over. "What is it Mr. Goldfarb?"

Halfway to the judge's bench, Alan stopped and appeared to be thinking about something before he replied, "I apologize, Your Honor, for wasting the court's time. My mistake."

Judge Haron smiled and said, "The prosecution may call their next witness."

***

"Please state your name and occupation Sir." Instructed the prosecutor.

"I am Leslie Garunds Amabollo. I am the Harbor Master at Sapelle in Nigeria."

Brian nudged Alan Goldfarb and whispered, "He is from my journal."

"I know, this bodes well for us, the prosecution is starting halfway through your journal."

The prosecutor asked, "Do you know anyone in the courtroom today?"

"You Sir, I know you."

"Yes, yes. Do you recognize anyone else in the court?"

Pointing to Brian, he said, "I know that man Sir, his name is Brian."

"Where do you know him from?"

"From Sapelle Sir, he was a crewman on the SS Flowergate when it was in Sappele to take on a cargo of logs."

"How did you meet?"

"He was standing watch just before the Flowergate left and I kept him company."

"What happened when you were standing watch with him?"

"We talked about my family and other things."

"What other things did you talk about?"

"We talked of a dead body that floated down the river and got caught in the ships anchor cable."

"The body of a dead black man floated down the river?"

"Yes Sir."

"Can you recall anything specific the defendant might have said to you?"

"Objection, Your Honor. The question poses suppositions, and hearsay."

Alan called

"Sustained.

The prosecutor tried again, "Did Brian talk about a journal?"

"No Sir."

"Did he ask you to do anything?"

Alan leaned over to Brian and said, "He wants the man to say something in particular."

"What?" asked Brian.

"I think he is taking a long way around to establish the authenticity of your journal. All he had to do was ask the court to ask you."

Mr. Amobollo replied, "He asked me to pose with him for a photograph and then took my picture on the logs."

"Did he say why?"

"He told me that he was doing a project."

"Did he tell you anything about the project?"

"Objection, relevance." Alan called out. He stood and said to the judge, "Your Honor, the journal is not in question. The defense has agreed to it's being admitted. I fail to see the relevance of this line of questioning."

Judge Haron replied, "Frankly counsel, nor do I. I will allow a little more latitude."

The prosecutor repeated his question, "Did he tell you anything about the project?"

"No Sir. He did ask me if I would be willing to mail it for him. I agreed."

"Where did he want you to send it?"

"I had to have the film developed and package it up and sent it to a Mr. JM Fetters in Buffalo, New York. That's here Sir."

The prosecutor, turning to the jury then said, "That's the black attorney who was murdered here in Buffalo."

Judge Haron spoke, "I'm getting a little tired of the use of the word 'black' all the time. Move on."

"But Your Honor, the victim was a black attorney. That's a simple fact." The prosecution was belaboring the point.

"I'll give you simple fact, Mr. Chantwell, if you refer to Mr. Fetters once more as black, I will hold you in contempt."

The prosecution showed no reaction to the judge's comment. Returning to the witness, he said, "Did you notice anything strange, odd, or different about Brian?"

"What do you mean by odd, Sir?"

Didn't you tell me on the telephone that Mr. Blacksmith did not like black people?"

"Mr. Blacksmith, no Sir. I didn't know anyone of that name when we spoke on the telephone."

"You said that *Brian* did not like black people and that he looked down on black people, did you not?" Becoming agitated he pointed at Brian as he spoke.

"Yes Sir, I did say that Brian appeared uncomfortable in Sapelle and I felt he looked down on black people."

"Why did you say he didn't like black people?

"I didn't Sir, like I said, Brian appeared uncomfortable in Sapelle and I felt he looked down on black people. That is what I said

The judge said, "Move along, Mr. Chantwell."

"Why did you agree to come to this country and testify against Mr. Blacksmith?

"When you offered to bring me to America if I would repeat, in a court, what I had told you on the telephone, I agreed. I have never been to America before. The offer was very generous of you.

The prosecutor appeared to study his notes as he regained his composure. "Mr. Amobollo, you said that *Brian* appeared to not like black people and look down on them, is that correct?"

"No Sir, I speak very good English. I was privately schooled in England and I do know the difference between what I told the court and how you changed it."

Now the prosecutor's back was up, "Please explain the difference."

The witness said, "I said that Brian appeared uncomfortable in Sapelle and I felt he looked down on black people. That is what I said. I never said he didn't like black people.The judge spoke. " Once again, that's enough Mr. Chantwell, move on."

The prosecutor realized that he was gaining no ground on this front and replied. "I have finished with this witness, Your Honor."

"Your witness, Mr. Goldfarb." The judge looked at her wristwatch as Alan spoke up, "It's been a long day, Your Honor. My cross may be lengthy. I have no objection to an adjournment."

"There we go again with this noble attitude. I like it. But it is my court Mr. Goldfarb and I will decide when recesses and adjournments take place. Continue with your cross."

***

The cross examination started out smoothly when the judge addressed the Defense. The defense began with Alan saying, "Thank you for your time Mr. Amobolla, I am not going tie you up in knots or twist anything you say."

"Mr. Goldfarb!" cautioned the judge.

"Sorry, Your Honor. If I may call you Leslie, Leslie, if I understand you correctly, yesterday you said that you spent an entire watch with Brian, chatting and exchanging backgrounds. It sounded to me as if you were at ease with my client. Would that be true?"

"Yes Sir, it would."

"Would you say that you liked him?"

"Yes Sir, he seemed angry at the world, but I understand him. At least I like to think so."

"That's good. Why do you think he asked you to post the package to JM Fetters and not someone else?"

"Objection, Your Honor, calls for speculation." Chantwell called out.

"Sustained. Rephrase, Mr. Goldfarb."

"In your own opinion, are you a good man, a man that people usually trust, an honorable man?"

"I like to think so, Sir. My employers, over all my years with them, have no reason to see me otherwise."

"Good, good. That's as it should be. In your role as harbormaster do you have much exposure to white people?"

"Yes Sir, although Sapele is many miles inland in Nigeria, the river brings us freighters on a regular basis. Many of the crews are white people."

"If you were to place all those white people on a scale of zero to ten about how you perceived their discomfort with black people, where would you place the average?"

"I have a simple scale Sir, about one third intensely dislike black people and show it. One third have no strong opinion one way or the other and the other third are almost color blind."

"Which group would you place Brian in?"

"Without a doubt Sir, he would fit in the group that have no strong opinion one way or the other. I suspect for that group the individual they deal with sets the tone."

"You seem quite sure about this. Why?"

"Mr. Brian was living with black people on the ship. His manner of speaking with any black person that passed us while we were on duty, was in the least, respectful. Sailors are very unforgiving people, Sir. It is my experience that they are straightforward honest men. I found Mr. Brian to be no different. To be sure, it would be difficult for him to hide such dislike."

"Why do you say that?"

"The entire crew was of varying races, with only a few white men among them. If he didn't like us, he would never have entrusted such an important package to me to mail."

"Good point. Thank you. I hope our Prosecutor's generosity in bringing you to our country gains you a pleasant experience. I have nothing further, Your Honor."

***

Back in Alan Goldfarb's office, discussions were well under way. Alan said, "If this is a ploy, I can't for the life of me see what it is. I have never seen a prosecution so badly handled. He hasn't called for a coroner's report. There are many little things he could have brought to light that am prepared for. Consider for moment, the fact that your parent's Will has not been brought up, the codicil has not been brought up. This is very strange. Right from the start, I felt the prosecutor's office has assumed that they have this one in the bag. Arrogant, I know. I wonder if that is why they didn't assign it to a top flight prosecutor."

"So, what do you think? Where do we stand right now?" Lillian asked.

"We are standing on a precipice. I suspect that our Mr. Chantwell is going to get a going-over when he returns to his office to prepare for tomorrow. He could come back in like a tiger. As things stand now, we are in a good place. I see a number of options. The first is to wait and see what he does and have a strategy to deal with whatever. The second is, if he doesn't come back with more backbone than we saw today, I am considering calling for a dismissal. The third is, I put Brian on the stand, which I do not want to do. At this point the jury is making up their mind about you without you saying anything. If you go on the stand, we would run the risk of the prosecution getting Brian to say something that puts him in a bad light. No, I am not going to do that. Putting Brian on the stand opens him up to cross-examination. That's not always smart. My fourth option then becomes resting the defense and going for a powerful closing argument. If I take that route, I will need to be very good."

"One way to interpret the journal as an anti-black tirade. The other way is read into it an angry approach at the world. I can dissect the journal in my closing argument. I don't think that either direction is safe."

Lillian said, "How will you decide which way to go?"

"Gut instinct, just plain gut instinct. I have a lot of homework to do. So, go home, rest up and let's get together in the morning. Early."

Chapter 42

The following morning, as the proceedings started, Judge Haron turned to the prosecution who said, "The prosecution rests, Your Honor."

Puzzled, the judge called for a side bar. Both attorneys came over and listened, "As the prosecution rests, Mr. Goldfarb, does the defense wish to make a motion to dismiss for failure to establish a Prima Facie case?"

"No, Your Honor. Thank you."

"Then so be it. Step back gentlemen." She spoke to the clerk of the court and the court reporter, who suddenly started to write furiously.

Banging her gavel Her Honor said, "The court has other business, we will adjourn until 2pm tomorrow, when we will hear closing arguments.

As they left the court, Alan said, "You both look confused."

Lillian asked, "What happened at the bench?"

"The judge asked if we wanted to make a motion for dismissal, on the grounds that we might think the prosecution had failed to establish a Prima Facie case."

"Of course, we do." Brian said.

"Not so quickly. One, the judge could deny such a motion. The risk there is that if she did, the jury might think the prosecution had proved it. I don't want that risk. Two, if she did dismiss it, the prosecution could possibly try for another trial. We want a 'not guilty' verdict from the jury. That will close this once and for all."

"There must still be a chance that the Jury could find us guilty." Lillian was on edge.

"Yes, there is but, I feel that we have the jury on our side. As wrong as it may seem, I am reading the jury to be leaning away from the prosecution. This is one of those times when you have to trust me."

Chapter 43

Alan spoke to Lillian and Brian expression, "We are at the point of no return. I fail to see why the prosecution has rested so abruptly, though I suspected it. We have a brief time for you to decide what direction you want me to take. The Amobollo fellow did you a great service with his testimony. Have you given any thought to the dilemma I laid out for your yesterday?"

Brian replied, "We discussed it, but I fear our ignorance could be our undoing."

"Don't play with me, there are no signs of any lack of knowledge in what you have done so far."

"Anyway, I am nervous about going on the stand. I know I could handle a cross-examination, but I think my bias might leak out if I am pushed." Brian thought for minute before continuing, "We feel that you interpreting the journal, in its best possible light, is our best bet. Something I don't understand; what was the judge referring to when she appeared to be trying to get the prosecution to keep going?"

"I can only guess what she was expecting and that's not worth wasting time on."

"So, what's the procedure?" Brian wanted to know.

"The prosecution's closing argument comes first, then ours, then they a get a final argument."

"And we don't?" asked Lillian.

"No."

Lillian said, "This is all very frightening to me. The possibility we could go to jail....oh....my. Do you really think this winnable Alan?"

"During the prosecutions, argument this afternoon, if I give you the signal Lillian, I want you to get sick, faint, do whatever you can. We should try to kill some time. I want to drag out their side until the end the day. That way, we will have a fresh, alert jury for our side in the morning."

"Do you think this will help?" Brian seemed skeptical.

"I do. My closing argument is going to be very long. It will last probably most of the day. I want to shut out the possibility of the prosecution confusing the jury. The danger here is for the prosecution, as a tired jury starts to shut off. I want that to happen on the prosecution's time, not ours. In fact, I aim for a lunch break in the middle of ours, to keep the jury fresh."

***

The jury was seated and waiting as the courtroom clock ticked its way past 2.15pm. Judge S. Haron was becoming agitated at the absence of the prosecution.

623

Mr. Chantwell rushed through the doors, his arms loaded with files and sheaths of paperwork. "Nice of you to join us Mr. Chantwell. You have left the territory of my good will and are now in no-man's land, fast approaching that of my bad will. Do I make myself clear?"

"My apologies to the court, Your Honor. Tied up at the office." was his simple response.

"Then let's proceed without any further delays."

***

The prosecutor carefully positioned himself central to the jury. He stood still for a moment, unbuttoned his jacket and started his closing argument. "You will have no doubt noticed that this trial, for a murder, has proceeded quite quickly. I imagine many of you thought that you were going to serve on this jury for quite some time. There is a good reason for the brevity." Looking directly at a black juror who appeared not to be concentrating on his words, he said, "That means short, Sir. It is rare that a case comes along where there is no need for courtroom dramatics. The matter of fact is that a man, Mr. JM Fetters, a very well-respected black attorney, not only here but also in England, is dead. A man who uprooted himself from his homeland to follow and serve his employer. That service, ladies and gentlemen, lasted over half a century; only to be ended by the decendants' of Mr. Fetter's employer. There has been no dispute that police found the gun used in the commission of this deadly act."

"There has been no refuting the prosecution's evidence that both the defendants handled the gun. The defense has offered no evidence to support the defendant's claims of a third party carrying out the execution. That is what it was, ladies and gentlemen, an execution. The gun was aimed so accurately that both bullets hit the same spot, on JM Fetter's chest and they sat watching his lifeblood drain out before doing anything. Then! What did they do? They fabricated the scenario that the defense laid out before you."

"The defendants were known to have entered JM Fetters office. His personal assistant was not challenged on that fact. The only attempt made by the defense to muddy the waters of evidence, was when they confused an old lady into saying it is possible that someone else could have committed the shooting. Many things are possible, but not very likely. We, here in America, are trying to land a man on the moon. Is it possible? I don't know. It might happen, but can we take a possibility and simply assign it into fact? I don't think so. If nothing else, you look like a very down-to-earth, feet-on-the-ground group."

"I would like to address the documents that have been entered into evidence. The Will; a will is simple document that sets out what is to happen to one's assets when one dies."

Brian leaned over to Alan and said, "Isn't he insulting the jury's intelligence a little?"

"Very risky, very risky."

The prosecution kept going, "The contents of the Will, no matter how upsetting, annoying or offensive they may be, are just that; the wishes of the deceased. I find the wishes to be so sufficiently unexpected that I am not surprised the defendants were angry. Angry enough to kill the messenger. I'm not surprised they took so long. They had to come up with a plausible, devious plan."

"The codicils are an addition to the Will. Let me explain what a codicil is. It is an attachment to a will that is often added at a later date. A codicil determines things like conditions or terms that must be met for the will to be executed. There is nothing unusual about that. Again, if you decide to look at *those* documents you may well see what I did, a pretty demanding set of tasks for the defendants to accomplish. Remember, both of the defendants signed those codicils of their own free will. I can see why they might have been angry enough to shoot the messenger. For once in their lives something was not being handed to them on a silver plate."

"The last two documents, those codicils are the smoking gun, if you will. They are agreements signed by both of the defendants, in which they agree to complete the tasks set out for them. The estate they were about to inherit suddenly rode on their compliance. Greed, ladies and gentlemen, sheer greed, made them sign. Sheer greed made them carryout the tasks and finally, sheer hatred for a black man, a black attorney, made them shoot JM Fetters, not once, but twice."

"I'd like to touch on one more point, a point that I am sure my colleague for the defense will address is the Fetters/Surtees issue. JM Fetters parents died on the RMS Titanic. He changed his name and came to America to build a new life under the auspices of his generous employer. I see nothing sinister in that. In fact, many immigrants came to our shores and changed their names. Sometimes for simple pronunciation and sometimes for anonymity, but I hardly believe any did so only to find themselves murdered."

"So, in closing, if we look at the whole trial so far and take a mathematical approach, my prosecution was fairly short, but the defense was even shorter. *You do the math.* You do the math. Guilty as charged is just as quick and as simple to find as this trial has been to conduct."

"You will recall, the judge instructed me to stop referring to the victim as black in my examination. It would remiss of me not to draw your attention to the fact that Mr. JM Fetters was part black, a fact that even his own personal assistant agreed to. She pointed out that the defendants bore some resemblance to Mr. Fetters. You have heard witnesses refer to Mr. Brian Blacksmith as being angry. Add to that, the fact that he found himself thrown amongst black people for almost three months and you have enough happening for that anger to boil over. We, the prosecution contend that was the straw that broke the camel's back. Together the defendant's arbitrarily decided to execute their family's black attorney. Thank you. Thank you for your attention. May God be with you in your decision. The prosecution rests, Your Honor."

Judge Haron leaned back in her chair, gently rocking back and forth. She was watching the defense counsel carefully as she said, "Mr. Goldfarb, three fifty, you have a choice, now or in the morning?"

Alan replied, "Your honor, the prosecution was as riveting as one could expect. I think the jury would welcome a night's rest."

"I wasn't asking them, but if you insist." She smiled and said, "We are adjourned."

***

Alan and his clients went for a coffee in the Docket, a small restaurant frequented by the local legal profession. As they sat mulling over the days proceedings, Brian, with a thoughtful look on his face said, "Everyone is talking about the Will. Did you know, Alan, that we, or at least I, never actually saw the Will?"

"Me either." Said Lillian.

"Hold on a minute! You both told me how much the value of the Will was. What do you mean you never saw it? Did you see the codicils?"

"The Will and the codicils were read to us. Then we were asked to sign the agreements."

"So, I, know the Will and the codicils actual contents, so does the prosecution, but the two of you don't? You only know what JM read to you, supposedly being the will. You cannot not say for sure how the Will read? And the jury, if they read them would know. You only know what you have been told? Do you realize you could have been told a lie?"

"What?" Brian and Lillian echoed each other.

"Why did you not ask to see the will at the reading?"

Brian said, "JM has been the family attorney since I don't know when, certainly before we were born. We have seen our parents sign many documents presented to them by JM without reading them."

"I have been raised always taking JM to be a trusted family attorney. It just never occurred to me to ask to read the Will. It was not the way our family operated with him." Lillian was becoming agitated.

"I was about to ask why should we even think that JM would lie to us, but now I know what the bastard was up to, it's a different story." Brian was visibly angry.

"That's it. That's it. I have my closing argument. I am going back to my office. I have the right angle for my closing." With that he put a five-dollar bill on the table and almost ran out.

Chapter 44

The court, having been called to order, watched Judge Haron as she spoke to the defense attorney, "Are we to expect as brief a performance from you today as you have given us the last few days, Mr. Goldfarb?"

"No, Your Honor. Packed lunch is probably in order."

"Really?"

"No, Your Honor. I expect to take most of the day though."

"Then let's get going, shall we?"

Alan stood, took of his jacket, adjusted his bright red suspenders, loosened his sulfur yellow tie and faced the jury. He spoke, "Ladies and gentlemen, I shall not insult you by explaining the terms I use. I have a habit of paying very close attention to you all. If you are unsure of something I say, please just raise your hand like this; he raised his hand to shoulder level and carried on. "I will know that you want me to clarify the last point. Thank you."

"Now let's move on to the codicil. You see, the codicil is a simple, but incredibly important document, in that it will often vary the terms of a will. This document requires each of the beneficiaries to perform a certain task before gaining their inheritance. Now, those of you that have been following along, must be asking yourselves, 'where is this going?' I would say '*exactly*' to that. The very presence of this document, you will note, unsigned, supports my contention that the defendants did not know what the Will actually said. That's right. I said the defendants did not know what the will actually said. If they did, they would never have signed the next two documents, the agreements to perform an unnecessary task. Now, we are beginning to see the tangled web that has been woven and not by the defendants."

"Now, as you know, the Will of the parents of the defendants will be available to you in the witness room, along with the codicil and the agreements my clients signed. I mention this because the prosecution provided an innuendo of their contents and a suggested motive. I have to tell you that as a motive, it is nothing more than a flight of fantasy. It is such a stretch of the imagination, that I can see some of you being offended by its suggestion. I will demonstrate how false it is. But first, let's address the prosecution's case. A case, which the prosecution itself, described as brief. It was not brief because the outcome was so obvious. It was brief because they had nothing but hype to play on your emotions. I was asked if I wanted to submit a motion to throw the trail out as the prosecution had failed to present a Prima Facie case. My response was no, absolutely not. My defendants need to walk out of this courtroom with a 'not guilty' verdict."

"Let us look at the crime scene. Take the arrival time of the police to the crime scene. They didn't exactly rush there. The chief could have run over while a subordinate followed with the car. A full nine minutes was wasted. Would it have saved JM's life? I doubt it. What it did do, was anger Mr. Brian Blacksmith. Why was he angry? Because he just saw somebody that he has known since birth, shot right in front of him and his sister. The police took their time in getting there. I think anyone of you would have been angry, given the same circumstances."

"Why was Miss Lillian verging on hysterical? JM had been her family attorney for over fifty years. He had been around her since before the day she was born. Here she was, recovering from an accident that put her and her brother in hospital for over a year, after it killed her parents. Then, she sees the man shot not once, but twice and collapse on his desk. Pretty scary stuff, I would say. I have been in the legal profession for a long time and I've never seen anyone actually shot in front of my eyes. I like to think of myself as a strong man and I think I might get a little hysterical. Not that the people of my faith, Jews, are known for our almost flamboyant histrionics." The jury chuckled.

"In his shock from witnessing the shooting, Mr. Blacksmith, ran out of the office after the assailant. Why? Instant reaction, that's why. Finding the gun, he picks it up and probably says to himself, what now? Miss Lillian, without thinking automatically goes to see if she can help her friend, JM. She leans on the desk and puts her hand in the puddle of blood while she is feeling for his pulse. The prosecution would have you believe that this was a clumsy mistake. Not a mistake, not clumsy, just the act of someone focusing on the situation that they see a family friend in. There was no clever discovery of the gun on the part of the police; Miss Lillian pointed it out to them. When she realizes her friend is dead, she runs out to see what her brother is doing, sees him with the gun, snatches it from his hand and throws it against the wall. Not cleverly seeking to hide it down a stairwell, just a clumsy, frantic throw. Just as you would snatch something poisonous from your child's mouth and throw it anywhere, just throw it away. A simple reaction, that's all it was. Did the clever detective work uncover all this suspicious activity? *NO!* The defendant's pointed it out to them."

"Now, to the gun itself. The colt forty-five is not registered to anyone in New York State. In fact, nobody can find any history of the gun anywhere. This is usually the practice of professional killers, not wealthy entrepreneurs that have just spent the last year and bit in hospital, recuperating. Ladies and gentlemen, the gun cannot be connected to anyone! *Not even Lillian or Brian Blacksmith.* If the prosecution wants you to *assume*, without any proof, it belonged to my clients, then ok, please grant me the same privileged and *assume* it belongs to someone else."

Before the defense continued, the judge said, "I think this might be a good time to take a recess for lunch. Sorry, Mr. Goldfarb, there's no packed lunch today." She stood and chatter erupted in the court as it broke for lunch. Walking out of the courtroom, Alan gestured to a man and woman sitting in the gallery. He excused himself from Brian and Lillian and asked them to wait for him. They watched as he stood away from the exiting group and huddled to one side, getting into a deep conversation with the couple.

After a short while, Alan rejoined the siblings and they went back to his office. Alan's personal assistant had arranged for sandwiches and coffee to enable them to have a private discussion without wasting valuable time and to be away from unwanted listeners. Brian could not wait to ask in an excited manner, "Alan, I think things went really well for us. What do you think?"

Lillian asked, "Did they?"

"The couple I spoke to, they are attorney friends of mine. I wanted an impartial man and woman to give me some feedback. The lady feels that we are on good ground, however the man, has been watching the jury and feels that we are probably holding about a fifty/fifty ground with them. They both agree that we should come out strongly on the 'black card'."

"What does that mean?" Lillian was a showing some concern.

"Our last card to be played is Brian's journal. If I do that, it is going to be uncomfortable for you Brian."

"How so?" Brian responded.

"We both know, that journal has a distinct flavor that could be taken as racial bias. If I just paint you as a good guy, it is not going to be an easy pill for the jury to swallow. On the other hand, if I take the path of you being angry, which the jury has already seen, we stand a chance. I must tarnish your image to start with and then turn their opinion around to one of understanding."

"I'm not sure I understand." Brian was studying Alan's face as he spoke, looking for clues.

Alan said, "Just let me do my job. I am going to take my direction from the jury and the signs that my accomplice gives me. His job is to study the jury's reaction and advise me on how he thinks they react to my words."

***

At two pm sharp, the court was called to order and Alan took the floor again. "Ladies and gentlemen, I hope you are well replenished. I shall endeavor to make the last part of my closing arguments as brief as I possibly can."

"You will recall the prosecution's annoyance at my using the reference to JM Fetter's as JM Fetters slash Surtees. They did not like that because JM Fetters is also known as Julian Surtees. In a strange coincidental turn of events Julian Surtees parents worked for my clients' grandparents and parents and his parents were among the hundreds that tragically perished on the RMS Titanic. Julian Surtees continued to accept the largess of my client's grandparents, who paid his way through law school. At a time when a young man should turn his thoughts to his future Julian Surtees suddenly decided to become JM Fetters. There must have been a purpose. I am suggesting to you that purpose was the birth of a twisted plan of revenge against the St. John-Brown family. I believe that he held their grandparents accountable for his own parent's death as they put his parents on the RMS Titanic. I think JM Fetters not only inveigled his way into becoming the St. John-Brown family counsel and friend, but he also set about seducing his way inside the private life of the defendant's mother. I will be kind enough to leave the sordid side of that to your imagination."

"This man was clever enough to keep his identity secret and yet his emotions toward his offspring, he could not subdue. I urge you to read the journals of the defendants carefully. His manner of physically hugging Miss Lillian was far more parental than professional. I urge you, look at Brian Blacksmith and Lillian Blacksmith. They clearly bear the signs of being born of two races. Even JM Fetter's personal assistant acknowledged that fact. Who didn't know this fact? *My clients did not suspect it*. Now, respecting your individual abilities to reason things out, I know that you must all be wondering, 'what does this have to do with anything?' This is a good question. The answer, I suggest to you, is integrity, honesty and character. Was JM Fetters victim or perpetrator? What this brings to question in this case is, were my clients being manipulated into discovering their true paternity? I think so. Now, let me digress to make the dastardly cunning being used against them easier for you to follow, but before I do, allow me to urge you to keep your minds open and avoid falling into the trap of racial bias. It will appear, as I go along, fingers could be pointed at Brian Blacksmith as having grounds for wanting to kill JM Fetters. To tell you the truth, if a man that my family trusted had kept my paternity from me for my entire life, I think I might have wanted to kill that man. Keep in mind, the evil path of destruction being heaped on the St. John-Brown and Blacksmith families by JM Fetters. The path has been one of revenge, manipulation and destruction."

"Let's consider another aspect. A man that could spend a huge portion of his life living a lie, cheating and manipulating others, would surely have made more than one enemy. Enemies have been known to kill. In over fifty years of lying and deception, is it really believable that JM Fetters had only *one* enemy? As the English side of the St. John-Brown family would say, *not bloody likely*."

There were smiles within the jury. Alan looked to his man in the gallery to see if the man thought things were well, he saw that he was.

"You will have available for you in the Jury room, along with other documents, the journal that Brian Blacksmith kept while dutifully following what he thought were his parents' wishes. I am going to read some excerpts to you and discuss them." Alan picked up the journal, placed his reading glasses on and kept the jury spellbound. He read,

"March 10 1957, The task that I face is a little intimidating, as I am not supposed to use myown financial resources.

March 10 1957 The man I was to meet behind a wharf shed was three hundred pounds at least. He stood expectantly at the wharf gates. As I approached him, he proffered a piece of paper. "If you are the man who wants to work your passage to Africa, you can be a steward." he said. "Sign this and get your gear on board. We're due to cast off." Then I saw the ship, well, not exactly a ship. It was a three thousand-ton, rust-ridden steel hull dented from one end to the other. It was a dirty, scary, small, very small, tramp steamer called the SS *Flowergate*." "

"Ladies and gentlemen, here we have a very wealthy individual, who is used to the best things in life, who has just recovered from incredible injuries, whose parents have died, and this is thrust upon him. You can tell from the tone so far, that he is not happy. Let me go on,

March 11 When I told him that I was led to believe we were going to Africa, he replied, "We might just be going there one day."These shipping companies had no concerns about ordinary seamen.

Now he is being told that he is just an '*ordinary*' seaman. Brian Blacksmith has never been an ordinary anything.

The *Flowergate* looks like it is closer to the bottom of the barrel. The crew cabins smelled not of the last sweaty, unkempt booze-sodden poor soul, but of every sailor of the same ilk who had preceded him. This was disgusting, but it was to be my home for however long it took to get to Africa. God! I hope we get there sooner than later.

Can you imagine the frame of mind that my client must have been in, seeing his world getting worse and worse by the hour? I digress,

I can see plainly this is going to be rough. There is total crew of twenty-seven men. Only five of us are white, and the captain is an unwashed, smelly man, over-weight by at least 150 pounds. There is a chief engineer who seems barely capable of riding a bicycle and yet he is an engineer. Another steward is an inveterate Scottish drunk, who relishes his desire to break my wee bonny nose with just one blow. Thankfully, he seems to like me and as he kept up his drinking, he soon lost his desire to maim me for life. The chief steward is nothing better than a washed-up bully. He certainly isn't washed. His cabin stinks to high hell. The rest of the crew is made up of Africans, Somalis, Laskas, wherever they come from, and other forgotten nationalities.

I want you to take note here. There is no differing attitude toward anyone on the ship, be they black, white or whatever.

March 29. There are rumors that we are going to the West African Coast.

April 5. I was woken up during the night by the sound of the anchor cable clattering up the hawser. At first it was thought we were going in. No such luck. At dawn the Canaries were nowhere to be seen. We were going due south again. I don't know how the crew can live with such uncertainty.

April 8. Four days and still none knows or will tell…After what passes for lunch Roddy tells me he overheard the captain talking about Capetown, South Africa. Roddy rekons that's another two days away. We are close to the equator and it is getting very hot. The deck is hot to walk on. We have gone right past Nigeria. I guess that's not a good sign for me

April 10. Around midnight we dropped anchor off shore. The word is out, we are at Luanda in Portuguese West Africa.

April 11. No one is allowed ashore. The decks are swarming with the local natives trying to sell us things, including their sister, or if you want it, their brother. It's disgusting. By the evening watch, some supplies have been brought aboard, the locals pushed ashore and we are leaving. I have been told that half our cargo of shoes was offloaded. Nothing came on except a plethora of bananas and some supplies. Ollie, the cook, will have one hell of a time serving those up for long. But it was good to taste fresh fruit

April 12. The captain announced this morning that we are going to Accra in Ghana where we will offload the balance of our cargo of shoes and we then are going Las Palmas. I don't know whether to be happy or angry. I am starting to wonder if I will ever get off this ship

Almost two weeks on a dilapidated hulk of a filthy ship and with no hint of being any closer to his destination. I don't know about any of you, but I would be getting pretty pissed off. Excuse my language. Back to the journal,

April 23. What a night I had last night. It was too rough for me to journal. I thought crossing the Bay of Biscay was scary when we were loaded. Going back across empty is enough to scare the strongest individual. We were tossed around like a shuttlecock. Move forward, bang, stop, lurch forward again, bang lurch stop. It was endless. The horrendous bang sounded like steel on steel. I was so sure we were going to sink. It sounded like the ship was breaking in half, or least chunks of deck were being ripped off. I went to my cabin and pulled the stinky blankets over my head and hoped for the best. Thank god it's over. I thought it would never end. I can't wait to get off this…this..

May 2. . At last, some activity. The chief steward told me that our instructions were to proceed alongside Lagos and await further instructions. "Is that far enough inland for you my boy?" Not knowing any better I decided to go along with it. At long bloody last, I might be getting closer.

After weeks chugging along on the *Flowergate*, being fed in accordance with maritime rules, I needed a change. (Incidentally, they tell me that maritime rules were written in the early 1800s for the sailing ships of the day and not for the 1950s. So, eight ounces of meat a week, a piece of fruit daily, lots of bread, and weevil-ridden biscuits were well out of touch with reality. Shit, this was ridiculous.)

After I worked up some courage, I boarded one of the primitive dugouts to be taken to the Lagos side of the mighty river. It felt like I was taking my life into my own hands. Visions of being beaten and robbed fueled my imagination. But this was the only way to leave the pitch black of Apapa's cargo-laden dockside, which I imagined to be lurking with huge black Maasai or Zulu warriors, waiting to do unimaginable things to me.

I felt I needed to be as low-key as possible, or at least appear that way. But maybe I was afraid to show my fear and weakness Great ditches lay open beside the roads with huge sewage pipes yet to be connected. Excrement oozed out unconnected seams. Apparantly the British had left projects unfinished and the locals never got round to completing them. I hurried back to my cramped, paint-peeling cabin on the rust bucket that offered me the only form of refuge I could find.

These black people were nothing like those in America. It was as if the warrior these people has in them, has been knocked out of their American counterparts. As I write this, I must wonder what in this experience did my parents hope I would gain?

Notice the description of the local people, not negative, almost reverent, Masai warriors. The Masai are strong fearless fighters, hardly anything someone would look down upon. This hardly sounds negative towards the black warriors.

May 7. All I had ever read about the wild creatures that live in Africa had not prepared me for this experience. Quickly, the ocean was was behind us and the wide river mouth narrowed at an alarming pace. Distant riverbanks now became muddy groves of tangled tree roots, so close one could almost touch them. As bad a cook as Ollie is, what he made was fit for a king compared to the culinary activities on the ship's deck. The self-appointed Nigerian helpers invited local natives onboard where the decapitated snake bodies and the plumper of the monkeys are being prepared for cooking.

The next part I am going to read is important,

With all the logs chained and ready to go, I had been assigned to stand the evening watch at the ship's portside bow. The evening watch suited me, as it lasted from four o'clock until six. There was still daylight left when I was joined by the Sapele harbormaster, who spoke with the most perfect English accent. His enunciation and grammar were spellbinding.

Notice my client's acceptance, respect and admiration of the man he is talking to.

Listening to him talk reminded me of JM Fetters, plumb in the mouth style of speech. The man opened up and told me his life story without any prompting. The situation could not have been better. I think JM will like this one. The man's name was Leslie Garunds Amabollo.

Leslie appears sad that the education he received was not available to his boys, as his English connection, he says is invisible to the English, in the eyes of the law. When I asked him if he minded if I made a record of his story for a project I was working on, he was proud, willing, and happy to sign it.

The ship's four-bells signaled the end of second watch, eighteen hundred hours rang out. While the watch change took place, everyone else started to gather at the bow, pointing at a large, black, bloated body, its leg grotesquely snagged in the anchor cable. It is as if the body has been inflated to stay afloat. The spectacle did not seem to have any importance to the local populace who are busy at their own appointed routines.

A well-kept motor launch with official insignia emblazoned on the colorfully painted superstructure sped to the *Flowergate*'s bow, where the huge anchor cable links disappear beneath the murky water. The bow wave created by the boat made the dead body a dam-like obstacle, but this was quickly fixed by the man standing erect on the launch's bow. He used a long boat hook to untangle the body, generating a huge roar of approval from the natives that have are travelling with us. The body, quickly, gained speed on its way downriver, toward the sea.

"Why did they do that?" I asked Leslie. "I would have thought they would have pulled the body out."

"No reason to. He is dead. Probably deserved to end up that way. Some pretty bad people upriver from here. Nobody is going to tell the police anything. I took the opportunity to ask Leslie if he would send my journal and photographs to America for me. Leslie agreed and took the details, refusing any form of payment. He promised to have the film developed and sign the pictures before sending them. I don't believe I am taking any chances, as Leslie comes across as a very dependable man.

"Leslie Amobollo came across as a very dependable man." Alan set the journal down, put his hands in his pockets and appeared as if he was searching for his next comment. "I see nothing that would support the prosecution's claim that Mr. Brian Blacksmith is a racist. I agree, he didn't use that word, but he did go all around and over it. I found that quite objectionable. In fact, I found Brian *Ojukwae*

Blacksmith's brief relationship with Amobollo quite endearing. I am pointed in emphasizing *Ojukwae is* Mr. Blacksmith's middle name. Mr. Blacksmith's great grandfather, Judd Cane, adopted an orphaned child of a black slave in America and took him to England in the 1800's, for a better life. So fiercely proud was the family of Judd Cane's actions, that the child's name '*Ojukwae' was given to Mr. Blacksmith's as a mark of respect. I sense a degree of pride in this family towards their black connections, rather than the type of hate the prosecution has offered you.*"

"Another interesting point is that no discussion has come up about the journal of Miss Lillian Blacksmith. The so-called despicable brother went to great lengths to protect his sister's privacy and dignity. Well, you may ask why? Not fearing the outcome of this trial, Mr. Blacksmith's promised his sister that he would protect her, shall we say, private life. Suffice it to say, that Miss Lillian..." He stopped for moment, turned to Lillian and said, "Forgive me, Miss Lillian, but I feel this is important. He continued, "Miss Lillian being a beautiful, attractive woman, had garnered endless compliments from the male population. Suffice it to say, she has availed herself of those attentions. In the face of a murder trial, her brother put her dignity above all else. That doesn't sound like a man full of anger. Anger is an overwhelming force that usually robs a person of rational."

"The prosecutions theories of greed and black hatred just do not fit. Just do not fit. There is so much doubt flying all over this case that it would not be reasonable to find my clients guilty. Reasonable doubt is all you need to acquit them." Alan detailed Fetter's connections with the family and the meeting of the defendant's mother, Angela Rose Blacksmith, formerly Angela Rose St-John. Brown. At the time, she was a wealthy young married woman, away from her husband and family, in America. It is quite probable that at this time, she had been seduced by Fetters." He pictured for the jury, a time line of Julian Fetter's career and involvement with Angela Rose that was pungent with innuendos and suggestions of paternity of the defendants. He stopped to allow this statement to hang in the air.

He slowly looked at each juror before carrying on, "Somebody fired two bullets into the chest of this despicable man. The prosecution has failed to prove it was either of the defendants, though God knows it could be understood why they might want to do it. It just has not been proved because there is no evidence that clearly points to my clients having committed this crime."

"No investigation looking for other fingerprints. No ownership trail for the murder weapon. A great deal of uncertainty about the office door being unlocked. The list goes on. I thank you so much for incredible patience with me." Alan Goldfard nodded toward the judge as he said, "Your Honor, it has been a tough day on the jury and I have quite a bit of ground left to cover."

The judge quickly picked up on the attorney's direction and called for an adjournment until the next morning.

***

The following morning Judge Haron quickly garnered the proceedings into action with, "Mr. Goldfarb, the floor is yours."

"Thank you, Your Honor." Turning to the jury Alan started, "Good morning ladies and gentlemen. I hope you are well rested. Take a look at my clients. You are here to decide their fate. That's just the way it is. I would like you to know something about them. Let's start with Miss Lillian. This lady was born into a wealthy family. She was well educated and many might say born with a silver spoon in her mouth. What would you expect a spoiled young person to do when the war broke out? What *she did do* when the Second World War broke out, she got her hands dirty and spent the entire war on the production line at Curtiss Wright putting airplanes together for our boys to defend us. She was so passionate about it, she even encouraged her mother to join her. Can you imagine, very wealthy people who have no need to work at all, coming home from work with greasy hands after building airplanes all day? I'm not even sure I would do that. You might be starting to get a different perspective on Lillian.

After the war she worked for small airlines, starting at the bottom, loading cargo, cleaning engines, answering the telephone. She did this at three different fledgling airline companies. Through sheer hard work and dedication, she eventually owned two of them. She went on to form six, yes, six, small regional airlines. She is an extremely wealthy, well-respected woman in the airline industry. She became a mature adult that anyone would be proud to call his or her daughter. I would."

"Now let's focus on Brian. Same wealthy privileged family, what did he do in the war? He volunteered to join the Navy. *Volunteered.* He did not use his wealth to run and hide in one of the family's many Caribbean hotels. He rose to the important position of ensuring that our ships were properly stocked and armed before they left America to defend our nation. He might not have faced hostilities, but he made damn sure our boys were prepared for anything that came their way."

"Since the war, he has amassed a formidable portfolio of patents. He has developed a world-class hotel in Tanganyika. He has developed properties in the Caribbean, creating many jobs for the local people, where there were none. He has amassed great wealth and his companies employ thousands of people both here and abroad and currently employ a great many black workers. Would a so-called greedy, racist person spend his efforts creating opportunities where there were none, particularly for black people? I think not."

"Looking at both brother and sister, neither of them is hurting financially. They don't need their parent's money. Why do I tell you this? A remarkable thing about the prosecution is not what they told you, it's what they didn't tell you. You will recall the documents entered into evidence." With dramatic flourishes, Alan held up each document as he referred to it. "The codicils; one for Mr. Brian Blacksmith's and one for Miss Lillian Blacksmith's" Slapping these onto the defense table, he held up the Will. Flipping through the pages of the voluminous document for effect, he continued, "The Will. Yes, the Will. It certainly is a great thick document. I suppose it has to be big, considering the immense wealth it pertains to. Why is this Will so important? After all, it appears that the prosecution thinks the codicils are more important. They spent a lot of time on them. The codicils are one page long, only one page long. Doesn't it seem odd that so much time has been spent on two one-page documents that are a part of what feels like a fifty-page, main document? I will tell you why the prosecution kept your attention away from the Will, here's why; the prosecution, myself, and JM Fetters are the only people who know the contents of the Will." He paused for effect and continued, "I see that most of you don't understand. Nor did I, until the defendants explained it to me."

"Why did the defendants not know what the Will contained? Because it never actually given to them. They were never given the chance to read it. *They never laid eyes on the contents.* Now, you may well ask, why? For a moment, let's take a careful look at this situation. I believe that each of you members of the jury have family. Suppose for one moment, your father asks you if you would witness a letter he has to sign. What's your reply? Sure dad. Your father hands it over to you and you take his pen, sign the document without reading it and give it back him. Not such an odd scenario any more. Let's go one step further, how many of you read everything you sign? Probably most of you could not even recall what was on the form you signed when you registered your car, got your driving license, signed for a package at the door. Those documents are one page. The Will is over fifty pages long. Now, add to this situation, Mr. JM Fetters was the family attorney before these defendants were even born. They have never known life without him in it. They have witnessed JM Fetters telling their parents things and their parents accepting his word, not once, not twice, but continually. They both have been using him as their own personal attorney for many years since growing up and leaving the family nest, as it were. So, it is fully understandable that they would accept his rendition of what the Will said."\

"Why is it important that you understand that they did not know the full contents of the Will? It is important because it reduces the prosecution's arguments to a sheer flight of fantasy. I would like you to watch them as I read the Will, you can draw your own conclusions."

"Objection, Your Honor," Mr Chantwell called out. "The jury can read the will for themselves."

Judge Haron looked across at the prosecutor and saw him realize the mistake of interrupting the defense. She just put her finger to her lips and went "sssssh."

Alan walked over to his table and made a production of drinking his glass of water and refilling his glass. He gestured to the bailiff for more water. The air in the courtroom was pungent with expectation. The sounds of people shifting in their seats added to the tension. Alan cleared his throat and started reading loudly and clearly. "I am reading the last Will and Testament of Mrs. Angela Rose Blacksmith, as she survived her husband by one hour and therefore her assignments take precedence. The court was listening intently when Alan said, "All my worldly assets and property are hereby bequeathed to..." as he read out the name of the benefactor; the court erupted into tumultuous cacophony of noise. Judge S. Haron banged her gavel repeatedly in an attempt to regain control. Reporters tumbled over each other in an attempt to be the first to carry the news out of court. Outside the building, television and radio reporters were caught unprepared for what was happening, each trying to get information from the exiting crowd.

Chapter 45

AUGUST 15th 1957 The Buffalo Courier-Express and The Buffalo Evening News headline banners blared out the court's decision. The verdict of the lengthy trial took up the entire front page. Both newspapers, as well as radio and television coverage, were the topic of conversation and covered the proceedings in depth.

Sitting quietly in their family home, Lillian and Brian studied the reports in great detail. Nothing about them displayed their emotions. The silence was periodically punctuated with sighs and gasps.

BLACKSMITH'S
NOT GUILTY
Attorney JM Fetters death ruled homicide by unknown hands

THE WILL DETAILS TURN CASE ON IT'S HEAD

Yesterday saw Brian and Lillian Blacksmith walk out of State Court free of all charges against them for the murder of local attorney, JM Fetters, or was it, Surtees? The jury witnessed, first hand, the surprise of the Desmond and Angela Rose Blacksmith as the will was read aloud. It apparently became evident that neither defendant was aware of its true contents.

Follow the twist in this trial if you can. There was the Will of the late Desmond and Angela Rose Blacksmith. There appeared to be two codicils to that Will. There were two journals, one belonging to each of the defendants. Finally, there was the Will of JM Fetters, the dead attorney who was the focus of this saga. All these documents became intertwined to create a confusing dilemma.

THE PROSECUTION

The trial was a case of bungled evidence on the part of the investigating officers. It was theorized by the prosecution that the defendants had knowingly entered the offices of the late JM Fetters with intent to kill. They speculated that the defendants were fueled by racial hatred and greed.

The Will is estimated to be in excess of four hundred million dollars. The value of the estate was also purported to be motivation. The prosecution did little with the Will other than to refer to its value. They focused on the codicils at great length.

These codicils to be carried out before the defendants inherit under the Will. In its efforts to demonstrate racism, the prosecution produced a witness from Nigeria and a frail aged secretary.

In the codicls, Brian Ojukwae Blacksmith, note the middle name, was required to go to Africa. He was charged with photographing local sights, in the tiny up-river village of Sappele, with a local inhabitant in the picture. Then, he was to have that person photograph Brian himself in the same location. He was to conduct an interview with the local person and produce a record of it for approval by attorney, JM Fetters. He was at no time to use his own funds to carry out the task. Brian Blacksmith completed his tasks to the fullest.

Lillian Jane Blacksmith was similarly charged with going to Uluru in the Australian outback to perform similar activities. Her meeting and spending time with an aboriginal named Ben Franklin changed her perspective on life and she failed to complete the task. (You, the reader cannot be blamed for thinking this is turning into a fantasy.)

The implication that started to take place is the stuff romance novelist's dream of. When one considers the background of JM Fetters, the so-called victim, a pattern is starting to emerge. It turns out that JM Fetters, was in fact a Julian Surtees, and was born in England in the 1880's. A law school graduate, both Julian Surtees' parents were employees of the defendant's grandparents, Michael and Penelope St. John-Brown. The Surtees ethnic back-grounds go back to black slavery in Morocco and Spanish peasants. Fetters carried that black blood in his veins, which was slightly perceptible in his coloring. The Surtees, Fetters' parents, met an untimely death on the RMS Titanic, which appears to have become the turning point at which Julian Surtees decided to become JM Fetters.

The prosecution made attempts to tie race along with greed as a motive. This brings us to the gun used to carry out the killing. They were unable to prove which of the two gunshot wounds killed Fetters. The defendants led the police to the gun, without prompting. With a lack of evidence to support the defendant's claim of a third party having fired the shots, the prosecution tried to hang the blame on the only known persons present, Brian and Lillian Blacksmith. With flimsy evidence being presented as to who fired the murder weapon that was found in a stairwell of the lawyer's office, it appeared the prosecution was floundering.

In calling the deceased's private secretary as a witness, the prosecution attempted to cast some light on the possible bloodlines of Fetters being passed down to the defendants. Suggesting infidelity on the part of the defendant's mother appeared to be a last-ditch effort to bring race into the equation on the prosecutions side.

THE DEFENSE

Defense attorney, Alan Goldfarb, claimed that an unknown assailant had fired the gun from behind his clients, who were unable to identify that assailant. Under cross examination, the investigating Police Officer revealed it to be unlikely that the defendants knew anything about other documents that were found underneath the deceased's body. What was found was, two Wills, both were registered at the

County Courthouse. There were two codicils, neither of which had been registered at the courthouse. There were two agreements, signed by the defendants, to complete the codicil's requirements. They were attached to journals documenting the completion of the requirements. None these documents had been registered or even signed by the defendant's deceased parents or by the defendants. Only the agreements to undertake the codicils' terms were signed by the defendants. They were therefor determined to be invalid, unenforceable documents. The codicils required the defendants to carry out tasks as a condition for their inheritance. The convoluted tasks appeared to have been designed with failure in mind. Attorney for the defense, Alan Goldfarb, suggested that the tasks were the work of vengeance filled attorney's attempt to make the defendants aware of the possibility of their black heritage.

The late Desmond Blacksmith and his wife Angela-Rose, parents of the defendants, had left their estate, to be administered by JM Fetters to charity and causes for the betterment of the community. Goldfarb stated the prosecution failed in their attempt to use the Will as proof of motive.

Attorney Alan Goldfarb's summation was a one and one half day journey that detailed Fetter's connections with the family. He outlined the meeting with the defendant's mother, Angela Rose Blacksmith formerly Angela Rose St-John. Brown. At the time, she was a wealthy young married woman, away from her husband and family in America. It appears that at this time, he claims, she had been seduced by Fetters. He pictured for the jury, a time line of Julian Fetter's career and involvement with Angela Rose that was pungent with innuendos and suggestions of paternity of the defendants. By the time he finished with the closing phrase, "Somebody fired two bullets into the chest of this despicable man. The prosecution has failed to prove it was either of the defendants. He went on to say, "though God knows it could be understood that they might want to do it, that does not change the facts. It just has not been proved beyond a reasonable doubt that they did do it, because there is no evidence. The only things that bears' any resemblance to reasonable doubt in this trial is the prosecutions hope that you will swallow his fabrication. I think there is more than a reasonable doubt that you would do that." sic.

THE JUDGE

The trial of the Blacksmiths had the makings of a primetime soap opera. Judge S. Haron, presiding over the murder trial, stated that the death of Mr. Fetters by a person or persons unknown, had no bearing on the late Desmond and Angela Rose Blacksmith's Will. There was no disputing the Will of the Blacksmith's parents, had left everything to JM Fetters in his life expectancy for the betterment of the community. There have been suggestions that the dubious parentage of the Blacksmiths could place them in line for the estate of Fetters. Judge Haron pointed out if that was to be the case and the Blacksmiths had been found guilty of Fetters murder, they would have been ineligible to inherit from his estate if found guilty, which they were not.

The judge went on to point out that since the Blacksmiths were found not guilty, they could stand to inherit if indeed the estate had been left to them, which it wasn't. The judge further said the matter of paternity has no bearing on the Will of Fetters or any other Will. It turns out that the Original Will of Desmond and Angela Rose Blacksmith was an enforceable legal Will and stands. The codicils, which had never been witnessed or filed with Erie County authorities, were determined to be false and therefor unenforceable. The will and testament upon the life and estate of JM Fetters now comes into force. The irony was the estate of the parents, Desmond & Angela Rose Backsmith, was therefore a legal and binding that the inheritance now fell under the control of JM Fetters, who had left his own Will, which dealt with the dispersal of the estate. That having been said, Judge S, Haron stated the jury found the defendants not guilty. The judge, with a parting comment said aloud, "There may be grounds to contest the Fetter's will if the bloodlines can be proven, but what's the point it can be argued that the Fetter's will appears to be in accordance with the spirit of the Blacksmith original wishes and did not leave anything to the defendants."

This reporter recalls that someone once said, "He who laughs last, laughs longest." We are not sure who is laughing at this riveting saga has left us all with a true mystery, an unsolved murder and a very wealthy negro scholarship fund.

The headlines of the next daily newspaper read.

"LET HIS '*WILL*' BE DONE." WHO'S '*WILL*',
THERE WERE TWO OF THEM?
OJUKWAE MIELAM NEGRO COLLEGE FUND
ENDS UP WITH A JACKPOT OF A
$400,000,000 ENDOWMENT

('Vinnie.') M. Vizine staff reporter

The End.

Acknowledgements

Harrison Demchick, you encouraged me to keep going and I glad that you did. Your review of the fledgling manuscript, intimidated, informed and gave me boundless motivation. I don't know if I have done you proud but I certainly hope so. This story owes its life and vigor to you. I owe my boundless enthusiasm to your professional manner and creative insight.

To my wife Jan, a woman who everyone that meets, says she has earned a place in heaven for putting up with me. Four long years with this project and you have supported me all the way. You never waivered

At the completion of the final book of the trilogy my appreciation to Amy Moebius de Brahe and Karen DeGarmo, is still as strong as ever. Their never-ending support and encouragement and insisting that I write this story has never faltered. Without them I know that I wouldn't have started, and here we are finding ourselves at the completion the story.

My appreciation to Jean Maslen, my tireless English friend, who has allowed me to bend her Lugs(ears) every Sunday morning since the writing of this book began, four years ago. She has been a staunch supporter. We both have the small English countryside village of Shepperton to thank for our connection. Jean, I even mentioned the second World War. I Bet you never saw that coming.

To Seema Maheshawari, your kindness and patience with my questions and seeking of your opinions is really appreciated. In your own quiet way, you have given me much food for thought

Special thanks to Mo, Maureen Aderman who came along at the last moment and gave a fresh perspective on the story.

Thanks, and bless all of you.

www.ingramcontent.com/pod-product-compliance
Lightning Source LLC
Chambersburg PA
CBHW070711100726
47907CB00001B/137